W9-CXN-012

First Year

First Year

A NOVEL BY
J.O. Salls

Birch Grove Publishing

Teaching

They make paper airplanes out of
Test announcements.
Across the yard, two boys shout.
One screams, "I'm sick of it!",
Misses the other with a roundhouse right.
Small boys, huge hurts.

The dog days of teaching
Seem to trot in earlier each year.
To my left, it seems
They're always noisy now,
Hands on, mouths wide as
Giant frogs catching flies,
Slippery tongues dripping
Bad language and attitude, man.

You couldn't give me an apple sweet enough . . .
You couldn't buy me an orchard big enough . . .

But
I read Richelle's passionate poem aloud
To my classes today.
They leaned forward into all of her words.
Their eyes gave her poem a standing ovation.

First Year: A novel by J.O. Salls

This is a work of fiction. Any similarity to places, events or people living or dead is purely coincidental.

Copyright © 2010 Birch Grove Publishing. All rights reserved. No part of this publication may be used or reproduced in any manner whatsoever without written permission except in the case of brief quotations embodied in critical articles or reviews. For information, write to Birch Grove Publishing, PO Box 131327, Roseville, MN 55113 USA.

Publisher: Paul Nockleby
Editor: Judith Stone
Cover Art: Liz Rackl

august

Robert Baker

"You're still making up your mind," Alan Anderson, Blue Lake School District's new Superintendent of Schools, said with more interest than impatience. He slid a pad of paper with a key on top of it across his desk to the young man he'd just finished interviewing. "Visit the room. See if it feels like home. Write down your yeas and nays on that pad. That's a test I always give myself before I make up my mind about a job."

Robert Baker picked up the pad and key. "That sounds good to me," he said to the administrator, who had been his father's college roommate years ago.

The superintendent smiled. "Robert, there are very few outstanding teacher candidates available in August. You're unique, and I'm blessed. Your credentials are impeccable. I hope you'll choose to join our faculty. I don't want to pressure you, but I'll sure like it if you say yes to our offer. Oh, and don't let the room number throw you," he laughed.

Robert left the office and ascended the flight of stairs that led to the room. He was impressed by the gleam of the hall floors and the lockers lining them. This massive school building was old, but it was cared for with a respect bordering on reverence. The empty hallway echoed his footsteps as he strode toward the classroom that would be his if he accepted the position he'd just been offered. He liked the feel of ownership that evoked. Room 313 was his for the taking. It was up to him.

As Robert inserted the key he noticed a slight trembling in his hand. It was a sign of nervousness as well as a by-product of the six hundred miles he'd just driven. Well, why wouldn't he be nervous? This was a big deal. For months he'd been preparing himself for his first year of graduate school. Now he had minutes, not hours or days, to decide if this would be his first year of teaching instead.

He withdrew the key, turned the silver knob, and opened the door. The room, like the hallways and stairwells, gleamed. It smelled as fresh and clean as a northern breeze. The student desks were arranged into six perfectly straight rows. He walked to the nearest row and ran his hand across the remarkably smooth and unmarred surfaces of several desk tops. The gray metal teacher's desk in the front of the room looked newly painted as did the cushioned office chair behind it. The lectern next to the desk had been sanded and shellacked to a fine finish. Even the metal filing cabinet showed little wear. The custodial staff must be superb.

He strolled across the room, laid t
he notepad on a student desk, and proceeded to the bank of windows

that overlooked the manicured green lawn four floors below. People took care of this place, inside and out. Education mattered in Blue Lake.

What he was seeing intrigued him as much as what he'd been told about this teaching job. In many ways it was a perfect fit. He'd be teaching American Literature, which he loved, to six eleventh grade classes, meaning he'd have one preparation. He'd had three as a student teacher at the Merymin College Lab School.

Still he'd felt compelled to tell the superintendent, "I was ninety percent sure I'd be attending graduate school. My folks and I agreed that unless something special came along, I'd pursue college teaching. This looked special to us. It's the timing that's caught me off guard."

He shifted his focus beyond the rooftops of houses to the street that led from the school to downtown Blue Lake. Three blocks down the road was the apartment that could be his home. It had been the last stop on the tour of the town Alan Anderson had given him. "I know this little apartment isn't much," the superintendent had apologized. "The first floor used to be a mom-and-pop grocery. The boarded-up storefront sure lacks curb appeal, but as you can see, this apartment is fully furnished. I can assure you the rent is reasonable. It's close to school. And it's available. Housing is at a premium in college towns by mid-August."

Raised in the similar community of Forest City, Robert knew that was true. "It would be fine. Well . . . adequate," he'd added with a grin.

Had he and Nancy Morgan married after graduation as planned, that apartment would be far too tiny. However, Nancy hadn't been thrilled when talk of graduate school became intertwined with thoughts of marriage. She'd informed him that though she loved him, she had no intention of putting her own dreams on hold while he pursued his. Instead she'd made the decision to pursue her goal of becoming a registered nurse. So Nancy was not a factor in this decision. That seemed pretty ironic at this moment.

Enough of that. It was time to sort this thing out.

He retrieved the note pad, took a pen out of his coat pocket and settled into the third student desk in the window row. He wrote, "I've been a student all my life."

That was the truth. His parents had prepared him to be a student from birth. They were reading to him long before he could toss his favorite rattle over the crib rail. Besides books, the presents he was given, from Tinker Toys to unassembled bikes, were designed to challenge his hands, head, and determination. His parents assisted him when asked, but the longer that request was in coming, the greater the praise he received. They'd prepared him perfectly for school. Reading was the basis for everything. When you faced challenges such as he did in subjects like algebra, geometry, and the sciences, or participated in extra-curricular activities, determination was an invaluable asset.

His traits and training earned him an academic scholarship at nearby Merymin College, where his father was the business manager. Robert worked in the student union, as a teacher assistant, and as a dorm counselor so that he could live on campus. His years there were capped with an excellent student teaching experience at the Merymin Lab School and admission to graduate school at the U.

That was part of the problem. He'd lived his entire life within his comfort zone. Attending graduate school full-time would offer more of the same. Did that make sense? There were alternatives. Alan Anderson had concluded part of his pitch by saying, "So how's this for a clincher, Robert? You can earn your Master's Degree here at Blue Lake State. It isn't a huge university, but it is a great and growing school."

"So, why should I take this job?" he wrote, then added "My Parents? Those Kids? That Trio of Teachers?"

He knew his parents would be thrilled if he was hired by the Blue Lake School District. Relieved, too. The extended economic burden graduate school would inflict on them, as well as him, would be eliminated. 'Merymin College Business Manager' was an impressive title on the office door, but its prestige wasn't mirrored in his father's paychecks. His dad was undoubtedly emphasizing that fact when he left the monthly bank statement on the kitchen table the morning Robert drove off to Blue Lake.

Robert slid out of the desk, ambled to the lectern, and stood behind it.

Then there were the kids. The first reason that he might want to say yes to teaching was the experience he'd had with those eager eighth, tenth, and eleventh grade students he'd taught at Merymin Lab School. He filled the desks in front of him with the faces and forms of those students, their eyes eager, their hands shooting into the air almost before you finished a question. Every day with them had been exhilarating. No wonder people went into teaching if it made you feel that good!

The "trio" were the three high school English teachers who initially sparked his interest in becoming a teacher. His sophomore instructor, Mrs. Vam, might stand behind the lectern where he stood now, but only to take attendance. She conducted her classes sitting in a student chair placed as close to her students as she could get. She was all about caring, encouraging, and honoring ideas. Mrs. Macauley would stand behind the lectern beaming and clapping her hands with glee after opening her textbook to yet another selection she loved. The mercurial Mr. Prizinski would use the lectern as a prop for his dramatic lectures, a leaning post for listening, or a launching pad that sent him zooming around the classroom. The trio's personalities and techniques were wildly different, but they shared an intense love for what they were teaching and those they taught. If he could inspire students the way those teachers did . . .

"Times up," Robert Baker announced to himself. He picked up the pad, pocketed the pen, and left the room.

"Still undecided?" Alan Anderson asked as Robert reentered the office.

"No, sir," the young man said. "I accept your offer."

"Terrific!" the superintendent enthused. "I'm delighted. I must tell you that the Blue Lake School District is considered a prime plum to pick in this state's education orchard. So we've achieved the perfect union. Great applicant. Great system." He patted the contract lying on his desk and handed it to Robert. "I had Mrs. Mosmund prepare this in case I got lucky. Look it over and see if it's satisfactory."

He watched Robert scan and sign the document. "I think you'll be very happy with your decision, Robert. I know I was elated to sign on here." He rose, reached across the desk and firmly grasped his new hire's hand. "I believe we rookies both have a truly enjoyable year ahead of us," he said.

septemBeR

Patty Light

Patty Light was late for class. She hated that. The fight with her mother caused it. She wasn't sure why they'd fought this morning. She'd just come from the bathroom into the kitchen after doing her makeup and hair. A last glance in the mirror had told her she looked fine. Pretty, even.

Her mother wasn't though. She sat at the kitchen table staring out the window. Her gray-brown hair was frizzled, and her lean face was pale and tight. Her lips looked thin as pencil lead. Just as gray and lifeless, too.

But they sprang back to life as soon as she saw Patty. Why was Patty so slow? Was the bathroom a mess as usual? Why did she get up so late?

"It's only seven o'clock," Patty protested softly.

Her mother's eyes glared red and angry. She'd been losing weight again and her green bathrobe hung as loose on her body as though it was her husband's robe—if she had a husband, that is. The room around her was unlit, dark and formless like the bathrobe, like her mother's personality had become.

Her mother barked on. Patty tried to avoid listening, knowing she'd hear nothing new. That never helped, but she always tried. The words, the voice, the tone, like a fork being dragged back and forth, back and forth across the face of a plate. She wanted to explode, but if she did, she was sure her words would gush out in vicious spurts that would taste like blood in her mouth. She'd rage and scream and nothing would be changed anyway except her teeth would all be pointed and red saliva would pour out of each corner of her mouth. She no longer felt pretty. She didn't say anything, just choked down a piece of toast with cheap margarine on it. "I gotta go," she flung over her shoulder as she hurried into the front room, grabbed her windbreaker and ran out of the house, her mother's voice trailing her. "Sure. Gotta go. Gotta go. Can't wait to get out of here. Hey, pick up your dishes . . . "

God! Oh God!

She realized she was standing alone in front of her locker staring into it. The hall was empty. The bell had rung. She had heard it but not heard it. She'd heard, but not heard, the kids clicking their lockers shut and shuffling away down the hall, their voices fading. It was like only her home was real, and school—and the rest of her life—was a dream. Or home was the nightmare you couldn't awaken from and escape.

Anyway, she was late again. This had been going on for several years. But for her first class on the first day of school! She hated that. Her mother had screamed at her for nothing! Nothing! Nothing! When Patty arrived at school, she had had to scurry into the first girls' rest room she saw to wash away the stains of mascara from her face, for if she had learned not to talk, she hadn't been able to harden herself enough not to cry.

Gotta stop this, she scolded herself, or I'll start again. She willed her mother out of her mind and headed for her first class, Creative Writing. As she hurried down the hall, she again realized how much she loved this place. The halls were shiny and clean. The classrooms would smell of chalk and books. School was her haven, her sanctuary. Her mood swing moistened her eyes. She reminded herself that she was late to leaven her happiness so that a new set of tears, this time of joy, wouldn't streak her cheeks.

She glanced at her watch. 8:18. "God!" she muttered. She was relieved to see that the door to room 212 was open. As she slipped in, she looked at Mr. Hunter standing in front of the room, his eyes cast down at the lectern.

She slipped into an empty seat near the front of the room, thankful he still hadn't looked up. When he called her name in his deep voice, she raised her hand. When he repeated her name, she heard his irritation. He looked up and his hazel eyes swept the room. The little knot of fear that always lurked in her chest unraveled and spread and her heart quickened. But his eyes softened a little when she tried to explain her lack of oral response and softened still further, almost to sadness, as he tried to explain his bad mood. Her fear reduced into that small, eternal knot.

Kyle Hunter

"Patty Light . . . "

For sixteen years this gnawing nervousness had bitten into Kyle Hunter's stomach and perspired his hands. He disliked the first day of school—the first week even. He ought to be over that by now. But he wasn't. He sighed, glowered and growled, "Patty Light . . . "

"My hand was up, Mr. Hunter. I'm sorry. I got here late. I didn't know we were supposed to answer you out loud."

He glanced up. Beautiful eyes, he noted. Windows of the soul. Been crying though. Wind blown hair. "You are," he said, "both late and correct." He shook his head, scolding himself for sounding so impatient. He saw embarrassment and hurt in those eyes and felt instantly guilty. "I'm sorry Patty. I'm always like this on the first day. Ask anyone. It can't help but get better, right?" Her answering smile was tentative but genuine. Her brown eyes danced self-consciously. "I'm sorry. I'm not always going to be a jerk. Really."

"Get 'em in line or they'll get you" was a truism he'd heard from a veteran teacher the first year of his teaching. He'd tried to follow it and thought he'd done pretty well. But there was always a tinge of doubt. This girl, for instance. She wasn't being a smart aleck or even unpleasant. He felt the touch of guilt he often felt when disciplining students. They all had their stories, their lives, and their reasons for who and how they were.

"Mr. Hunter," a short boy with glasses and eager eyes said, "aren't you going to call any more names?"

"I'm sorry, son. It's opening day," he answered, as though that was supposed to explain everything. "Frank Martin . . . er . . . Marin."

"Yup," came the answer, deep and flat as though muffled by water. Kyle spotted the source seated in the last desk in the fifth row. The boy looked like a refugee from some "Happy Days" reunion except there was nothing happy in his demeanor. His hair had so much spray on it, it looked like a helmet; he wore a leather jacket like bikers do with the back of the collar half flipped up. He was sprawled in the desk, his left leg extended into the aisle. The rapid drumming of his right knee betrayed his tension. The late James Dean, Kyle thought. Or with that black hair, more accurately the late Elvis Presley.

He continued to take roll, the vague irritations of opening day like fingernails scraping the inside of his skin. Thirty-two students were assigned to his elective Creative Writing class. Dumped, in a few cases. Thirty-two and he knew there'd be a few more added from the list of juniors and seniors who were enrolling in Blue Lake High School for the first time today. They'd hear about his plans for the class and read his syllabus, but they wouldn't believe it could possibly be that tough until the first serious assignment was given. Some would realize they really didn't want to work that hard. Then would come the drop slips accompanied by accusing eyes or red-faced apologies, and he'd end up with thirty or so students. That was too many, but writing classes offered so many surprises and unexpected delights that he always ended up stopping himself on the way to the counselors' office and never insisted they trim his roster.

"Okay," he said when he'd finished, "if I have to take roll every day, it'll shoot half the period. Alphabetical order folks. It's faster and easier for yours truly." Students always groaned and muttered after that announcement. Some things never changed. "So you'll get to hear me say your name one more time. Aren't you thrilled?"

"Aw, geez, Mr. Hunter, can't we sit with our friends?"

"I get sick when I don't sit near a window. Ask my mother."

"That means I'll have to sit behind him in every class . . . "

In spite of himself, Kyle had to smile.

Frank Marin

Frank Marin sat in the back seat in the fourth row. He always took the back seat when he could. No one bothered him there. Sometimes he wished they would, but he was glad they didn't. Occasionally he pondered that paradox, but he couldn't come up with anything.

The dark brown jacket, almost the same color as his wet-slick hair, was too hot. It was totally uncomfortable, but he couldn't bring himself to take it off. Its upturned collar rubbed against the back of his neck. That was irritating, so he dropped his head forward. He thought he must look like a turtle sticking its head out of its shell now. So he lifted his head a little and glared out under his dark, prominent eyebrows.

In truth he knew the jacket was a shell. Frank Marin was not unintelligent. He knew the jacket covered and protected him and projected an image. He thought he looked good in it. It fit with his heavy hair, his eyebrows, and his prominent lips. It got him a little attention without his having to make any effort. The attention was silent and distant and had been ever since his family moved into town the previous April. But it was there.

Frank had bought the jacket a week before the move. He'd put it on the same day he fell into the unsmiling silence he still maintained. His burly, balding father often told his straight-laced, graying and quiet mother that two things were true of Frank these days: he never talked, and he always wore his jacket. He knew his father couldn't stand either of these truths.

His father wouldn't be too hot about a third truth either. If he wasn't so thick, he'd know.

When Hunter called his name, Frank surfaced from his thoughts like a diver deprived of air. "Yup," he forced out of his throat. He felt soaked on the outside, dry on the inside. Weird.

He felt a familiar wash of self-consciousness, as though people were shining bright flashlights at him. He dropped his eyes and stared rigidly at the desktop. He felt Hunter's hard gaze on the top of his head like it was a laser burning a hole through his hair. Weird. Man, that's a weird idea, he thought. He'd noticed he had a lot of weird ideas. People would think he was nuts. Maybe this Creative Writing class was the right place to be. Almost everyone here was a nut in one way or another, and he'd heard from someone sometime during the summer that Hunter would go crazy over the nuttiest pieces of writing! Maybe he'd fit in here a little bit.

Still his head burned. It felt like his face was about to go up in flames, and his mind's eye could visualize smoke rolling off his wet hair, not to mention his damp forehead and hands. He was caught between the desire to laugh at the pictures in his head and the feeling he was being pinned to the wall by his staring classmates. The mix resulted in the irritation that seemed to be his most comfortable emotion. Go on, Hunter, call the next name. The teacher did, but that did not stop the perspiration rolling down Frank's sides from his armpits. He needed to leave, but the thought of all those flashlight eyes trained on him again and the thought of Hunter shouting his name if he did, nailed him to his chair. God, what he needed was a joint to settle him down a little bit. Then it wouldn't matter for a while and his damned head would shut up.

Gail Hunter

Gail Hunter wheeled the old Volvo out of the dirt driveway onto the highway. She loved this countryside. The sweet damp pine smell rode the western breeze in through the open driver's side window. She felt exhilarated by the fragrant coolness of the early autumn day.

She headed the car down the tar road toward town. She'd planned to take Kyle to school earlier, but he'd wanted to ride his bicycle the five miles because, he'd said, "It might settle my first-day nerves, at least a little."

"Sixteen years and you've still got first-day nerves. How can you stand it?"

"I can't. It's parts of the other 189 days that make up for it."

She'd accompanied him outside into the chill of the very early morning, loving the sight of the four tall pines that shielded their house from the highway, but wondering how he'd avoid freezing wearing only his light blue windbreaker.

"No sweat . . . for sure!" he'd smiled. He'd given her his usual brief kiss and mounted his ten-speed LeTour. She'd watched him pedal down the driveway. Near the end of it, he'd half turned to wave and wobbled his beloved bike so precariously she thought he was going butt over teakettle for sure. But he'd regained his balance quickly. She heard him shout something about "a new trick I learned," as he glided down the road.

It made her smile. Mostly she loved the man. But there were things she had to do for herself to assure the continuance of that emotion. Now. Before it was too late instead of just late, before she was too afraid, too set, too rusted over.

She glanced in the rear view mirror. Her blonde hair was a bit loose. She brushed a strand from her forehead. "Well, it looks carefree," she told herself, "and it makes me look younger." She'd have to fix it before the interview. Right now the wind felt good in her hair, and on her face.

The thought of the interview sent a spasm of nervousness through her. "You're smart. You're a hard worker. You'll be fine," she told herself, speaking aloud as she'd become accustomed to doing in her empty house during the day. It seemed to create an instant companion for her and saved her the trouble of running around the countryside seeking a social life. "They'll love you," she said, and lapsed into silence as she approached the city limits of Blue Lake. Conversing with yourself on the open road is one thing. Tooling through town yakking away with no one beside you can earn you a reputation. Pretty soon all the pretty young things around town would be pitying Kyle for being married to a loony and would resume talk about those "poet's eyes," whatever that meant, and how they had "just loved his classes" when they were in school.

She glanced at her watch. Nine-thirty. The interview with Kerns Clothing was at ten-thirty. She decided to drive past the school. She liked the connection with Kyle's separate life that doing that gave her. He was likely to bring his job home with him in the form of reams of papers and piles of journals and the books, but he wasn't likely to talk much about any of it. So this pause seemed important.

She eased the accelerator as she passed the yellow school zone sign with its two stick children on it, one wearing square little black pants and one wearing a triangular little black skirt. Actually those two little connivers were skipping school, sneaking off to his place for a little stick love. She smiled. Kyle wasn't the only one who could create instant short stories out of nothing.

She pulled to the curb and shut off the car. She gazed at the old building with its scrolled entrances. A palace once, really. A centerpiece for this town. Now it was overcrowded and aging despite the care given it, and the new addition was only a pile of paper dreams. Kyle's room was 212, squarely in the middle of the second floor of the building.

The green grounds were empty except for a single student, a tallish boy in a leather jacket who had left the sidewalk in front of the school and was striding across the grass toward the main thoroughfare. His head was down and his elbows back like wings since his hands were thrust into his jacket pockets. He can't even feel the breeze in that hot jacket, Gail thought. Must be hot as a firecracker in there. Too bad. Beautiful autumn day like this. There must be something wrong with him. Maybe he's not just skipping, maybe he's sick.

"I love this day!" she said softly, but passionately, dismissing the boy from her thoughts. This blue-sky, white cloud, west-wind day thrilled her. She started the car and headed toward downtown for the interview.

Doubt creased her happiness for a moment. If she got this job, it would involve travel to other towns and to the Cities. It would involve some training, two weeks in the Cities at least, and meetings and shows thereafter. But her part-time minimum wage job at Warrum's Drug Store was neither financially nor emotionally rewarding. She and Kyle would never get to do what they wanted – okay, mostly what she wanted—until she made some real money.

She should have talked this whole thing over with Kyle. But she hadn't because she knew he might try to stop her. He'd even discouraged her from working part time, encouraging her to concentrate on her photography instead. But that well had gone dry, and her present job was dust. She needed something new in her life. She almost threw the word "someone" in there for the daring of it, but stopped herself. It didn't feel funny or entertaining. It felt scary. It was a little too close to how she sometimes thought while knocking around the house. She needed a challenge, a real job, not a man, to fill the empty spaces in her life and psyche.

Spotting a parking space near Kerns' Store, she allowed herself one more oral statement. "They," she muttered into her shoulder as she parallel parked the car, "will love me. I am as beautiful as this day." She loved the feeling the words sifted through her. She felt young and like it was the first day of spring, not autumn.

Sam Strand

Sam Strand had been principal at Blue Lake High School for twenty-two years. Every March for the last six, his friend Stuts Bergman had approached him about selling insurance. "Sam, you know every family in town," Stuts said, "or at least you did until this crazy growth spurt hit. Still, you'd make President's Club in two years. Beat heck out of that chicken scratch they pay you. If you stay in this racket too long, you're gonna start tippin' the balance in favor of your enemies. Folks don't respect teachers like they used to, you know."

Sure, but Sam would miss this day. He'd miss these opening day assemblies, those smiles in the halls. He'd even miss the hassles in the office because every now and then a kid would find himself during or after one of those teeth gnashing conversations with him, and that was rewarding. Sam was positive dollar bills couldn't replace that feeling. Or the satisfaction when some kid came back after a few years in the world and sat in the same straight-back chair kids always had to sit in and said, "Thanks for being firm, Mr. Strand," or "Glad you made me see how I was and what would happen if I didn't change," or, "You were right, sir." Or the former students who just came in to say hello and show him pictures of the wedding or the new baby or talk about college or the new job. All of that fulfilled his life. Why give up fulfillment for sales pitches and a few trips to Florida?

Well, there was one reason now. Still, Sam wasn't ready.

He uncurled his lanky frame from the folding metal chair behind the lectern. Most of the school board members were sitting behind him. So was Superintendent Allan Anderson, the man twenty years his junior whom the board had hired to fire him. Well, maybe "fire" was too strong a word. Let's just say, "Encourage to retire."

Shaking his head, Sam returned his thoughts to the students packed into the auditorium in front of him. Fifty-thousand school assemblies all over the country, pretty much all the same. I do it every year, and I love it. He glanced at Anderson who nodded coolly. Boy Wonder makes good. But why spoil my mood?

Sam shuffled to the microphone. His green sweater felt as comfortable as the whole scene in front of him did. He had about fifteen sweaters and eleven were some shade of green. They were famous in Blue Lake. The lights were dimmed in the auditorium so he saw the faces dimly, but he could feel the mix of respect and restlessness, energy and boredom that characterized every student crowd. Nevertheless the vibrations today were mostly positive.

He raised his right hand, palm forward and hung it in the air until the noise in the room abated. "I suppose you're wondering why I invited you all to my party today," Sam began. Trite as heck. He loved that line as much as he loved his green sweaters, his slightly scuffed brown loafers, and the thousands of students who had preceded this bunch in front of his eyes today. He felt a wash of love for what he was, who he was and what he was doing, and love for those he could not see who could see him. He loved the friendly derisive laughter and groans that followed his old joke. The sounds settled pleasantly in his ears as he raised his hand again for silence.

At moments like this it did not bother him that a board member had informed him that before Superintendent Anderson was hired, one of the topics raised in his interview had been how he would go about easing older educators, like Sam Strand, on to pastures the color of his sweaters so that younger, less expensive men and women could take their places.

Robert Baker

Robert Baker stood in the back of the auditorium. He was trying to decide what he felt. Excited? Nervous? Scared? Confused? All four emotions seemed to fit. This was his first day of working with kids in his first year of teaching.

Robert Baker was twenty-three years old and looked younger. His sandy brown hair sloped above his blue eyes. He was of average height and had a wiry, slender build. The school secretary had mistaken him for a new student when he walked into the main office for his August interview even though he'd remained in college an extra year to complete his education credits and student teach. He'd loved college. His student teaching experience had helped him determine his final choice. But his stomach was churning as he stood at the back of the auditorium observing the opening assembly.

Thirty-four students had appeared for his third period American Literature class preceding the assembly. The computer printout roster had listed only twenty-seven. Since there were only thirty desks, four of the junior boys had perched on the windowsills. Somehow they had managed to push open all the windows while he tried to figure out the best way to take attendance.

The breeze wasn't unpleasant, but it blew the computer sheet off the lectern while he was writing his name on the blackboard. That brought laughter from the class. "That's a dumb thing to laugh at," he blurted. The chuckles subsided, replaced by a silence that felt hostile. He was sorry he'd been so churlish. He wanted to say, "I'm just really nervous right now," but he didn't.

The classroom was silent. His stomach clenched. He glanced at the names on the roster, feeling the need to rescue himself from the sudden hostility. "Looks to me like we need more desks in this room. Would someone like to volunteer to go to the office to find out where we can get some chairs?" No hands leapt into the air. He couldn't understand how one remark could charge the atmosphere like this. "Please," he added, trying not to sound like he was pleading.

Finally one of the boys seated on the windowsill said, "I'll go if my buddies can go with me." Robert hesitated. The idea felt like a red flag flapping in the breeze blowing through those opened windows. Still, you needed to show trust for your students, didn't you? He'd heard that in more than one education class.

"Them chairs are awkward to carry, sir," the boy added. "We could each carry one."

The boy had logic on his side. "I guess that makes sense," Robert answered. "Okay, go." He wasn't comforted by the smirks that slid across the four faces, but he couldn't figure out what else to do. The boys sauntered out of the room. The rest of the students watched them, many with similar smirks on their lips. Then they turned back to Robert.

"I'm going to have to call roll since I don't know you." He called Angela Claire's name, but there was no response. He repeated the name, but no one answered. Must be absent. Must actually be thirty-five in this class. But Alan Barbarie didn't respond, nor did Dwight Conger. Could be the boys who went to get the chairs. But when Beverly Dwayne and Sy Fairmont also didn't answer, he stopped.

Only one student seemed apart from the unspoken revolt that had taken place. She looked straight at him, her deep brown eyes moist. She saw his notice of her raised hand. "Is it okay if we answer you orally when you call our names?" she asked.

He'd sensed no sarcasm in the question. He had not, in fact, given them directions to do so. He should have apologized for that, but instead said, "Yes, please say 'here' when I call your name." The students finally did that, or at least provided their own variations of the word. When he was finished with the roster and the slips he'd found on his desk, the only unchecked names were the four boys who had gone in search of furniture.

They had probably been gone ten minutes. Glancing at the bell schedule on the wall, he noticed that the bell was about to ring, the boys were still gone, and an attractive young lady was walking into the room with a slip of paper in her hand. She smiled prettily as she handed it to him. She smiled at the silent class, and then threw a seductive grin and wink over her shoulder at him as she exited the room. He glanced at the paper and saw that it was an add slip with the name "Frank Marin" on it. He willed himself to say, "Frank Marin. Is Frank Marin here? Frank Marin." No answer. He was either one of the four boys or simply not present.

Just before the bell rang, a custodian appeared with the four chairs on a rolling rack. He pushed it inside the door against the wall to get it out of the way of the students. "Here's your chairs, Mr. Gerney," the man growled.

"I'm not . . . the boys . . . " Robert began.

The man either didn't recognize his misnaming of the instructor or ignored its importance. "Oh, they said you told 'em they could head for the assembly since the bell was about to ring."

"Oh, I, well, the . . . " Robert stammered as the janitor went out the door. A gust of wind burst into the room through the open windows and sent the roster sheet twirling into the air again. It descended rather artfully and skidded to a stop midway down the aisle between the third and fourth row of chairs.

No one picked it up. They sat and stared at Robert Baker. Why are they so hostile? The bell jangled and the class stood up and exited. At least they stepped around the roster instead of on it.

When the room had emptied, he had looked down at his hands clutching the edges of the lectern. His knuckles were white.

He stood in the darkest corner of the auditorium. He hadn't heard a word Principal Strand said so far. Reliving the third period had filled every corner of his mind.

"Mr. Baker? Mr. Baker? Oh, I see him there in the back of the auditorium," he heard Sam Strand's voice say. "Mr. Baker is our new English teacher. He'll be teaching juniors. Let's give him a hand."

Robert stepped forward and raised his hand tentatively. The applause was polite. He heard a short girl in the back row just in front of him exclaim to her friend next to her, "He's cute!" But he couldn't shake the tingling sensation that coursed through his body. It was as though he'd just awakened from a bad dream. Maybe that was what it was, just a dream, an aberration that he was blowing out of proportion. He forced a smile in the direction of the short girl, who was still looking at him, her face wreathed by his response.

Ed Warrum

Ed Warrum shuffled out of the assembly with Shellie Chaine dangling on his arm as always. She was so often with him he scarcely seemed to notice her presence. Listening to Principal Strand was, for him, like listening to the way he wished his father was – firm, but also warm and understanding. He could be tough like his father, but he had a sense of humor. Listening to

Principal Strand was like standing in a warm shower, not the shower of words his father endlessly poured that either scalded you or rained icy chunks all over your nerves. Nope. The feeling you had after listening to Strand was like you felt after a hard football practice when the shower sent a steady stream of relaxation over you in the steamy room filled with your fellow survivors of the football wars.

Football. Yes. That was the crux of the matter. Football. He could get sick of the sound of the word even if he loved the texture of the game so much: the body-rich feel of a strong tackle; the exhilaration of heaving a perfect spiral down the field into the waiting arms of Billy Cloud or Clyde Conners; the togetherness after the game in the locker room.

That was the good stuff. The bad stuff was the unrelenting pressure his father applied. An old-fashioned butt kicking is what it was. The jerk. Well, that's what he was. His face reminded Ed of a clenched fist when the family—himself, his younger sister Jenny and his mother—were seated at the dining room table by his father's fiat, he and his father at opposite ends of the table reviewing the whole game, every game, just about every damn play of every damn game.

They'd started doing this when Ed was in Pop Warner football in sixth grade. Then it had been fun. He could visualize the precipitous downhill slope the conversations had ridden since then. Increasingly his father focused on his faults and Coach Howard's stupidity. Ed Warren, superstar, super shlub. Every move analyzed. The end of football as a team sport.

When he tried to inject his own opinions of the game or defend his coach, his father listened impatiently or cut him off, scowling and drumming his fingers on the table.

"Ah, heck, he means well," Ed muttered, not realizing he was speaking aloud.

"Talking to me?" Kyle Hunter asked as Ed and Shellie passed him just outside the auditorium doors.

"Oh . . . um . . . ah . . . no," the boy responded, embarrassed. Mr. Hunter probably thinks I'm nuts, he thought.

"Nice game last Friday," the teacher added. Blue Lake had drubbed Hudson 37-6. Ed had thrown three touchdown passes and punted for a thirty-seven yard average. His father – businessman, sports genius, and now school board president – Pete Warrum, had informed him during the table "discussion" that his passing was fair, and that Howard had pulled him to the bench too early. Third quarter! How was he going to build the statistics college recruiters love so much sitting on the bench?! College scouts come to see you because of statistics, not because your coach is a nice guy.

"Thanks," Ed answered, forcing a smile. He liked Mr. Hunter. He was like Mr. Gerney had been, a good guy who liked and was liked by kids, but foursquare about what he expected.

The fact was Ed Warrum liked Mr. Hunter, Mr. Gerney, Coach Howard, his girl friend Shellie . . . He liked just about everyone.

Maybe that was why he felt so guilty about hating his father.

Billy Cloud

Billy Cloud sat in the last seat in the middle row of Robert Baker's seventh period American Literature class. Given a choice, he always sat in the last seat in the middle row. He liked to observe people, and this seat offered the perfect vantage point.

Billy Cloud knew the assumptions many teachers made about him. About "his people . . . his kind." They assumed from his skin color, his raven hair, and his handsome, high cheek-boned features that he was an "Indian." That prompted the further assumption that he sat in the back seat because he was shy, taciturn, turned off to school, or maybe hung over. Depended on which myth the instructor preferred. In some ways it was an advantage. When they discovered he was bright, articulate, and funny, they were far too pleased and overly enthused. After all, he knew plenty of Indians who shared those qualities with him. There were plenty of success-ful Indian attorneys, authors, athletes, business persons. Native Americans supplied the Armed Forces with a higher proportion of warriors than any other group.

Billy and his friend Sally Long Arrow were two of the three dozen or so obviously Indian students who walked the halls of Blue Lake High School. Billy guessed there were a larger number of people living in or near this northern city whose blood included more than a few drops that were Native American.

He liked being Indian. His father, an artist, teacher, peaceful activist, and mostly Lakota, and his mother, a potter, weaver, mathematics profes-sor at Blue Lake State College, and mostly Anishinaabe, had seen to that.

They had moved to Blue Lake for the same reason they had moved to other cities and towns—to experience it. They liked its setting of pines and birch trees and rolling hills to the east, its clean, wide streets, busy down-town shopping area, and the college that nestled near the shores of Blue Lake before expansion pulled much of it away from the water. His father's paintings and carvings and his mother's profession enabled them to live pretty much where they chose. As his mother said, not ironically, "We like to bring the Indian mystique to as many places as possible."

Billy Cloud wasn't smiling now. Hostility was an uncomfortable emo-tion to observe, and it was all there was to observe in Mr. Baker's seventh hour class. Billy believed that most students were good people, but you'd never know it by this. The noise in the room had been overwhelming. The current silence was deafening, and had been since the teacher snapped at the class. You could cut the hostility in the air with a knife, and if you did, you'd hear it flopping like a fish on the floor.

New to the school, he was only beginning to understand the genesis of the problem. It had something to do with a Mr. Gerney who had taught in Blue Lake High School last year. It might also have something to do with Robert Baker's youthful appearance and the uncertainty that danced in his eyes.

There were two things Billy Cloud knew for sure by the time the bell rang. For whatever reason, this class had made a mass decision to rebel against the instructor. And Mr. Baker didn't quite know what to do about it.

Greg Schwarz

Red Howard lifted the whistle around his neck as he seated himself at his desk in the coaches' office. He held it in his hand for a moment. Its tarnished metal coolness pleased him. He opened his palm to talk to it. "You," he said aloud to the whistle, "are an historical icon. You are thirty years old today!"

His assistant coach, history teacher Greg Schwarz, ambled into the office and pushed the door shut behind him. He seated himself in the battered wood office chair that contrasted with Red's ancient leather one. He stretched his muscular legs full length in front of him and ran his long, thick fingers through his short black hair. "Good practice. That Billy Cloud's getting to be a better receiver every day. He and Ed have a real rapport going on with those down-and-outers."

"Yeah, looks good," Howard answered absently. He wheeled his chair around and stared at the flaked green paint on the office wall. "Pete Warrum's driving me crazy, Greg."

"Yup," the other man said. "It was bad enough to hear him at the games. Now he's sitting in the bleachers at half the practices."

Howard scratched his bushy gray-red hair, then folded his arms across his chest. "I've been coaching thirty years here, Greg. Thirty years. I've coached winning teams and teams that couldn't beat their grandmothers. I've coached kids with crew cuts and kids with hair down to their shoulders. I've listened to fathers whining, because their sons weren't playing enough. I've seen kids so buzzed on marijuana they hardly knew I was kicking 'em off the team." The coach straightened and wheeled his chair toward his partner. "But I've never been as sick of a human being as I am of Pete Warrum."

"Yeah," Greg agreed, "a real jerk."

"Greg, we've got a good football team. We've got a chance to go unbeaten. Yet he's trying to mobilize the boys at the coffee shop to get me canned the minute we lose a game. We beat a good Hudson team by thirty-one points, and he has his buddies hollering and booing when I pull the starters." Howard shook his head. "Makes you wonder what keeps you in this racket."

Howard wheeled his chair back to the desk and stared through the big office window into the locker room. "Look at that kid," he said. Ed Warrum was slumped on the bench in front of his locker, his shoulders sagged, twisting a towel in his hands. "That kid may be the best quarterback in this state, and he's miserable. No matter what he does, it isn't enough." Howard whacked his hand on the desktop. "Is it worth it, Greg? I've coached thirty years. I've laughed and cried with thousands of kids. I love these boys, Greg. I love this game." He pushed away from the desk and stood up. He leaned his stocky frame against the filing cabinet. "I love this stuff, and I'm thinking of resigning, Greg."

"Pete Warrum isn't . . ."

"Pete Warrum is. He's the worst, but far from the only. I've seen kids get sick before games from the pressure their parents applied. I've seen 'em punch their lockers even when we won because they'd screwed up a few times and knew they'd hear about it. But I've never seen a kid hung out to dry like Ed is." He rose. "I'm gonna talk to the kid," he said, opening the office door.

Kyle Hunter

Dinner was done. Kyle Hunter leaned back in his chair and stared at his wife. He liked the way her jeans molded to her hips. He also liked the fact that she was home from the two-week training session in the Cities.

He'd even left the stack of papers he had to correct on his cluttered desk at school. He was glad she was home. He'd missed her.

He pushed back from the table and locked his hands behind his head. "I'll wash the dishes," he said.

She turned and smiled. He liked that smile, the full, natural lips, the straight whiteness of her teeth. "You are a pretty, sexy woman," he said, moving to her and circling her wrists with his hands. "I missed you. More than I knew I would." He kissed her lightly on the forehead, released her wrists and plunged his hands into the soapy dishwater. "I'll wash. It's actually because I hate wiping dishes."

"Me, too," Gail answered, pouring herself a cup of coffee. "That's why I leave them in the drainer to dry. I suppose you're too busy to notice."

That stung. It was a sore subject, one of the weapons she had pulled out and pointed at him when she announced her interview, its success, and her new job.

❖   ❖   ❖

She'd been ecstatic at first. He thought the whole house was glowing when he came home, but it was the brilliance of her smile and the light dancing in her eyes that truly shined. The smile had faded when instead of congratulating her, he'd said, "I wish you'd talked to me about it."

First she'd answered, "I wasn't sure I'd make it. I didn't want to say anything until I'd been through the interview."

He'd sighed and sat down next to the stack of papers he'd brought home, the introductory essays that would tell him who those people were who were sitting in his classroom staring at him. "What's it involve?" he asked.

She told him she'd be a buyer for four of the clothing lines sold at Kerns Stores in Blue Lake and four other Kerns Stores in the northern part of the state. She'd be specializing in dresses, jeans, and "intimate apparel." She smirked when she said that. He usually liked a bit of innuendo. His only response was a frown as he thumbed through the papers. "I didn't know this town had so many clothing stores."

"It doesn't," she said. "I just told you I'd be a buyer for Kerns Stores in this part of the state. I'll be doing some traveling."

"Overnighters?"

"A few. Sometimes."

"So you'll be doing some one-nighters," he unwisely added, thinking he would sound salaciously funny.

She ignored the wit in his remark. "Fine!" she said, her hands flying to her hips, her blood boiling to her face. "Fine! Yes, and two-nighters and three-nighters, and even weekers. I'll be making trips to the Cities to attend workshops and fashion shows. I might even go to Chicago. Or New York!"

Kyle tried to cut his losses. "I like it when you're home at night," he said, setting the papers beside him on the couch. "I don't want you to keep the job. Working at Warrum's store part time is enough."

"It isn't enough for me!" she exploded. "It pays minimum wage. I can't stand Pete Warrum and his rat mouth, and I could get laid off at any time." The mirthless smile on her face stretched almost to ugliness. "As opposed to 'laid,' according to you!" Her fingers curled into fists on her hips. "It isn't what I want to be doing tomorrow, much less the rest of my life. I didn't try to major in merchandising in college for that! It's not what I want to do!"

"Apparently neither is being a wife," he shot back before he could stop himself, "who would tell her husband what she's thinking about before the decision's made!"

She stamped her feet. Her middle finger flew into the air. "Is the husband you're talking about the one who dives into his endless stack of papers and journals every night and couldn't hear a firecracker explode in his ear when he's reading! The husband who's always taking college courses that require reading, reading, reading and ten page papers! The husband who can hardly manage to say hello when he struggles home from school at six p.m. because he'd rather coach or correct than come home! The husband who brings home a hundred journals to entertain himself over vacations! The husband who does the p.a. for games so he won't have to stay home on Friday nights! The one who advises the school paper so he has an excuse to go to the school on weekends!"

Both of them could have stopped, but neither one did. He knew he should have congratulated her in the first place. Instead he'd whined like a child coming home to a house that was empty because his mother was working.

But his blood was shooting through his veins even though there was truth in everything she said. It didn't matter. "I'm a teacher," he shouted, "a damn good one! I work at my profession!" And again he charged over the line, knowing even as he said it that there was as much fiction as fact in the statements he was spitting at her. "I do the extra crap for you! We need the money!" He knew how idiotic the statement sounded and how it fed her fire.

"Yes," she spat back, the heat of her rage carrying her until she loomed directly over his crossed knees, "you're a damn good teacher and a damn poor husband! You don't even talk to me anymore. You're so busy with your damn job and your damn preparations you don't even hear me when I talk to you! You know your students far better than you know me. And you don't even care!" Her anger had burst into tears then, and she'd turned and raged out of the room.

He'd sat on the sofa stunned to numbness by the argument. I'm really out of touch with her, he had admitted to himself. I know Patty Light as well as I know Gail Hunter, and I've just barely met her.

"Silence again?" Gail's voice floated through his thoughts and into his ears. He'd absently finished all of the dishes except for the potato kettle.

"Sorry," he replied. "Thinking."

"About school?"

He let it go. "No. About us."

"And."

He dried his soapy hands on the dishtowel, forgetting that was one of the little things he did that irritated her. Did she want a fight? He didn't. "How was the seminar?"

"It was good. I learned a lot. Oh, lots of stuff reminded me of college, except more current. I have a computer seminar next month for three days in the Cities." Her softened voice acknowledged the sadness in his eyes and the slump in his shoulders.

He leaned against the sink, feeling a little lost and afraid.

"In the Cities?"

"Yes," she retorted, the edge creeping back into her tone.

"Listen," he pleaded, "I'm sorry about the way I've been. It was the change. It scares me." The house felt cold and dusty. He saw the papers he'd left sprawled around the sofa. "School changes all the time. I didn't want that to happen at home too. But I'd do it differently. I'll try to do it differently now. I'll even try to pick up after myself." He smiled warily.

"You'll kiss my lips instead of my cheek when I leave, or you leave?"

"No. I will drag you by your hair under a pine tree and give you the most ferocious goodbye you ever had," he tried.

She laughed. The tension broke, and she was relieved. She didn't want to be forever angry with this man or to distance herself from him further. Distance had been their problem. Her unhappiness and feelings of confinement for the two years they'd lived in the farming community of Samstown in the western part of the state was where it had started. Actually it was a pretty and friendly place. She'd found that out the year they left. It seemed she was always finding out after it was too late. She'd found out how much she wanted children after her first miscarriage. Up until that merciless day, she hadn't been sure at all. She'd just been endlessly sick.

"I wanted them," she said out of her thoughts.

"What . . . " he asked, confused by her drift.

"The babies. Both of them. I wanted the first one as soon as I lost it, Kyle. I wanted the second one every moment of those three months until it was gone." She leaned into him.

"I know," he replied, knowing that the depth of loss that had hit him had been filled by his busyness. Knowing that wasn't true for her, but determined to let her say it for a change, ready to hear it for a change, here and now in this moment that could heal a breach or widen it. His arms encircled her.

"I'm always looking back, always regretting the time I waste being miserable," she said into his shoulder, tracing the tips of her fingers along it. "Poor Kyle. I must be awful to live with. I'm so sorry." She fell silent, stepping back and rubbing the backs of his hands that now rested lightly on her shoulders.

"Anyway . . . it wasn't that way for the second baby. I was so ready. Every day I thought of names. I could see her face. I remember it rained and rained that autumn. The pine needles sparkled. I was so sure. Oh, Kyle, I lost the baby."

He pulled her close again and her cheek rested against his shoulder. She just let the tears flow, let them flow and flow.

Finally she continued. "So . . . I took all that emptiness inside me, and I wanted you to fill it up. Every day."

"And I didn't do it at all. I didn't even recognize it."

Gail shook her head. "No, don't. You couldn't do it. I just kept wanting you to. I didn't want to feel empty and resentful. I just did. I couldn't figure out what to do about it."

The trouble, Kyle realized, is that I didn't even notice.

Gail lifted her head off his shoulder and slid out of his arms. He felt warm-cold like the wind on a late August evening was wrapping itself around his skin. She wiped her tears with the back of her hands.

"Kyle, I didn't really, really know this until I took this job, until after we had that fight, and I was in the Cities."

He could think of nothing to say, so he said, "Yes." Changes were inevitable, and he could learn to live with them or not. Those were his only choices.

OCTOBER

Frank Marin

Dear Mr. Journal,

The stars are like fireflies tonight. Hey their moving. Wow, it's my head. Excuuuse me!

Hey, did you see the old farmer down by the old barn west of town? Naw, you never did. That old barn is near where I used to live. No, no, I mean it's near our farm near that town where I used to live. Whatever. Anyway I had a friend there named Shmitty. He had some bad habits that I learned not to avoid.

Anyway Shmitty and me used to talk to that old farmer. Shmitty was a smart ass so the old guy really didn't like him much. Shmitty would say things to him like, "Hey your old barn is rotten as your teeth" and he'd think that was really really funny. Things like that all the time. The old guy liked me though. I was real quiet even when I didn't want to be. I liked to study the lines in his face. They were real deep. Like furrows. Like you could run a real real real real tiny little fleet of trucks through them and it would be like going through tan mountains.

But what if you drove off the edge of his chin? I mean you'd fall down down, down down past his checkered shirt, past his bib overalls, past those buttons on his fly, past his baggy pants legs. Maybe if you were lucky you'd get caught in the rolled up cuffs of his pants legs. But man you'd be screamin and screamin all the way down once you left the edge of that old round chin. And you'd be thinkin "old man I really loved them wrinkles. They was so safe."

And I did you know. I loved that old man. Last person I ever loved. When Shmitty would leave – - God, I prayed when I prayed, I prayed Shmitty would leave so those tears of anger in the old man's eyes wouldn't leave the edges where he had them tucked cuz then Shmitty would have razzed him, called him an old woman. Sometimes I hated Shmitty. Rhymes with shitty you know. Anyway prayin worked back then and Shmitty would always leave because he'd get bored and mad because nobody'd laugh much at his smart ass jokes so he'd leave. Then the old guy and me would talk. He was real lonely. But a nice old guy. We'd feed the chickens. Pet the dog. Hey I just reread what I just wrote. Know what, I never thought I could write this good.

Hey I just thought this thought. What if when you fell off the old guy's round chin you missed his pants cuffs and crashed to the ground? But the ground was real kinda soft because it had just rained. Or maybe it was soft because it was where the old mans tears finally fell every day after I left and he thought of all the hurting stuff Shmitty said to him. Anyway you crashed and you got kinda wrecked but you was still alive. Know what? If that happened that old man would get down in the mud on his hands and knees and he'd take them big gnarled hands of his and he slide them s-l-o-w-l-y under you. He'd pick you up r-e-a-l s-l-o-w and he'd get up real

real c-a-r-e-f-u-l and he cradle you in that old log of a hand and he take you into that old faded red house of his. And he'd set you down real c-a-r-e-f-u-l. He'd build you the most beautiful tiny little house you ever saw. And he'd put it somewhere where you could feel the sun and wind if you wanted. But where the birds couldn't getcha.

Gotcha?!?

Is the man real?

Tell ya one thing. Last person I ever loved.

Frank Marin tipped the sturdy white farm chair he'd insisted on bringing with him when his parents moved to Blue Lake. He was sitting on its back two legs and rereading what he'd just written. It was good, so good that he felt like crying. So good that he willed himself not to rip it out of his composition notebook, crumple it, and throw it away like he'd done with all the other writings he'd tried. Some of those were probably pretty good too, he mused sadly.

Robert Baker

Robert Baker pushed himself up to his elbows and stared at the tan shades tinged with predawn light. Then he pushed the covers off and sat on the edge of his bed.

Finally he rose to his feet and shuffled to the bathroom. He stared at himself in the cabinet mirror. His aqua eyes were clouded with weariness. His stubble seemed to have turned gray. He felt sad looking at himself. "Who are you?" he asked the mirror. "Well, whoever you are, we have to go to work. But let's look at the bright side. We still have work to go to."

He dropped his rumpled pajama bottoms and stepped into the shower. He wanted the shower to wake him up, so he turned the balance spool toward cold. He also wanted to discover he had wandered into someone else's bad dream, and that if only he could keep his eyelids apart long enough, he could walk out of it and into a pool of sunshine that would move with him all day long.

❖ ❖ ❖

The trouble had begun in his third period class when the silences that had greeted his efforts to promote discussion in the past month, save for Patty Light and a few others, gave way. He supposed he should have been grateful to hear other voices for a change. But it sure hadn't been pleasant.

The smallish kid who occupied the third desk of the window row, Allan Barberie, was sitting sideways scanning the room as Robert took attendance. Apparently he received a signal of support from someone, for as soon as Robert closed his attendance book, Allan turned his head toward him and raised his hand. Without waiting to be recognized, he said, "A lot of us have been talking, and what we want to know is what happened to Mr. Gerney? We were all looking forward to having Mr. Gerney be our teacher."

Approving murmurs supported the boy's comments, and a smile spread across his face. "He was the best teacher in the school," the boy added. At least he hadn't added, "And you're the worst."

Kathy Poulin, sitting in the row next to the long cork bulletin board that lined the inside wall of the classroom, was waving her hand.

"Yes," Robert said, pointing to the girl without answering the first question.

"What's your first name?" she asked, her dimpled face beaming.

The question was too ridiculous to acknowledge. He ignored it and turned his attention to the literature book in front of him. He heard the scraping of desk legs against the floor and glanced up. "Dincha hear my question?" Kathy prodded, her eyes sweeping the room and then staring at him. "Or doncha have a first name? Is your first name Mister?"

"Nah," interjected the class clown, Jerry Jons, who sat in front of her. "His first name is Baker. His name is Baker Baker," Jerry giggled into his hand.

"No," Kathy screamed, her red face shining. "It's Butcher! Butcher Baker! Butcher Baker, the candlestick maker!" The whole class seemed to suck in its breath. She knew she had them, and she knew she'd rendered him speechless with surprise at the way this thing had fallen out of control, so she screamed, "If you're a candlestick, I just might blow you out!" Exhalation came with shrieks of laughter.

That did it. Those who weren't already riding the bandwagon leapt on. The room screamed with voices and laughter.

Robert Baker couldn't believe it. Nothing he'd heard in his education classes had prepared him for this, for what was happening to his classes, for the derisive shouts he heard walking home from school, for the hang-up phone calls or the calls consisting only of heavy breathing . . . He felt like screaming, too. Wouldn't that have been great in front of thirty-four students!

Fortunately or not, a girl entered through the open classroom door, a white message slip held between her thumb and forefinger. It wasn't difficult for her to notice the ambiance in the room and even easier to join it. She put an extra twitch in her hips as she walked to the lectern. She extended the note toward him and cooed, "Got a little message for you, honey." Then she winked and twitched out of the room sending little wave greetings to her gleeful acquaintances as she exited.

The note inquired as to whether Frank Marin was present. His eyes swept the packed room. He couldn't remember if Frank Marin was in this class or not. His mind could hardly focus on the question.

He was about to say, "Please quiet down," but the fire drill bell rang, and the students rose rapidly sending a desk toppling to the floor as they funneled out the door.

No one bothered to pick up the desk. When he looked down, his hands were again clutching the edge of the lectern so fiercely that his knuckles were white. He glanced toward the door and saw Patty Light standing just inside it. Her brown eyes were full of anguish.

"I'm sorry that happened, Mr. Baker," she said softly. "I hated it. Most of us aren't really like that. You'll see." She blushed. "Gotta go outside. So do you." She left quickly.

Robert was grateful for the young lady's thoughtfulness, but embarrassed to be in need of it. He exited the room, closing the door behind him, and walked down the empty hall. He doubted he'd be able to find his class outside, actually hoped he wouldn't and that the period ending bell would ring soon after they returned to the room.

The only good thing that had happened that whole day was that the students from all classes were summoned for an emergency assembly in the auditorium. There Principal Strand told them in that their reaction to the alarm had been atrociously slow and unruly. The principal roared the rules for fire drills and ordered his teachers to repeat the rules each day at the beginning of homeroom until all their students could recite them from memory. By the time the Mr. Strand finished, the passing bell was ringing.

Apparently his third period students had used the fire drill break to pass on news of their successful harassment to students in the classes that followed. The salvos were less virulent, but they were definitely variations on the theme and intent. Chance Edwards began the fourth period with, "How come we never do anything fun in here? Mr. Gerney's classes were fun." His classmates were only too happy to furnish examples even though most had never had the man as a teacher. "We heard," was their explanation. Chelsa Jonas' opening fifth period question was, "How come you gave us a lit book that's so boring? I looked through the whole book and there's not one thing that's interesting." Radley Billings' sixth period contribution was to ask why Robert always wore a suit and tie and if the reason was to hide the fact that his shirts were always wrinkled.

He responded that he'd heard enough foolishness for one day, that he was tired of wasting time listening to idiotic questions instead of discussing the assignment, that he believed in giving students freedom of expression, but this was ridiculous.

"Mr. Gerney never said anything like that to his classes," Dana Rey told him. "I know because I was in two of his plays."

"I'm not Mr. Gerney," he said.

"That's for sure," Dana shot back.

That was when he lost it. "Enough!" he shouted, pounding the lectern with the side of his fist. "I've heard enough! I've got a curriculum I have to teach, and by golly I'm going to teach it! From now on, we're going to focus on what we're here for! I'm going to do whatever it takes to make that happen! The assignment's on the board. Copy it down, open your books and get to work!"

They did, but not happily.

The icy silence of the seventh period was, for once, a relief. He pointed at the assignment on the board and said, "Get to work." Most at least opened their books. Perhaps they had no friends in the previous classes.

The period and day finally ended with the ringing of the last bell. Or so he thought. No sooner had the students slouched out than Jojo Hansen, the English Department chairperson, hurried into the room. "Can I talk to you for a few — well, quite a few — minutes, Robert?" she asked, her Nordic face tight with worry.

He was sure someone important had heard about the day's happenings in his classes, and she'd been sent to comfort him, chastise him, or fire him.

He was wrong.

"I'm really sorry to be the bearer of unpleasant tidings, Robert."

They were going to fire him! Because he wasn't Gerney!

"I need to give you a little background about the request I'm about to make. May I sit down in this student desk?"

"Sure," he answered, slipping into the desk next to the one she'd chosen. He'd been receiving bad news all day standing up. He'd better sit down this time.

"Last night all department heads and Principal Strand met with the school board to request additional teachers, books, and desks. We're short of all three. Miss Winters has already resorted to having a number of her juniors share their American Lit books. The school board told us that all additional hiring and purchasing had been frozen as of September first due to budget constraints. That decision must have been passed in one of their famous executive sessions. They said we'd just have to go to the storeroom, make use of the old textbooks there and shuffle kids to classrooms that aren't full. Mr. Strand fought long and hard to get them to change their minds. No soap.

"After that meeting I couldn't sleep, of course, so I spent the entire night trying to figure out what to do. I'm sorry to say the best I could come up with is terribly unfair to you.

"Since we have no desks to spare, we have to create a new freshman study hall first period. You're one of the few teachers free that period, and the only one who has no extra-curricular duties. We can place only newly enrolled freshmen in the study hall, so you and they would have that in common. We hope we can limit the number to twenty. You'll be robbed of your preparation period, which makes me feel awful, but first period study halls are often the easiest to supervise, so maybe you can do some preparation then. In exchange you'll be removed from the list for supervisory duties. It's not an equitable trade, but it's something."

"Well, sure, I can handle that," he responded. This wasn't great, but it was a heck of a lot better than getting fired.

"Wait. There's one more thing. Remember, I mentioned books. How we're already short. The only alternative is to make use of old sets in our storeroom. We have forty old American Literature books. Quite a few selections are the same as the newer ones, but far from all. Miss Winters already has three preps. If you're willing to take on a second prep, you'd need to collect the newer books from one class and give them the older ones. That might make that class feel they're being picked on, of course.

"I went over these ideas with Mr. Strand during my department chair period. By the way, just to let you know we aren't picking on you because you're new, I'm giving up that d.c. period to take a sophomore study hall we need to create. Mr. Strand said he hated that we even have to think about these changes, that maybe he should take over a class or study hall himself. But he's already overwhelmed. He'll go along with these ideas, but only if you'll agree to them."

"I can use the old books with my seventh period. They're not exactly wearing out the new ones."

"Why thank you, Robert," Jojo said, her worry lines melting into a relieved smile. "Mr. Warrum was right last night when he called you Anderson's Wonder Boy."

"Reality. That is the rub," he spoke to the shower stall walls, the cold water stinging his body alive. He pushed the spool in and stepped from the stall. He shaved, willing his mind to unwind.

Everything in his background said that you solved your own problems, and you didn't quit until the problems were solved. You didn't give up. You did not quit.

He pulled on a pair of cords and a white shirt. If I don't wear a tie, he pondered, maybe that will help. But you were expected to wear a tie at Blue Lake High School as far as he could tell. He'd seen exceptions, but most of the men wore coats and ties. So he clipped on his tie.

I'm probably making too big a deal out of everything, he thought. Today is the first day of the rest of my life. Live while you live. Nothing is as bad as it seems. He continued to string clichés together as he donned his brown blazer and walked to the door. Every dawn is a new beginning, he finished firmly.

He opened the door and walked down the stairs from his apartment into the brisk and blue October morning. Students were streaming down sidewalks on both sides of the street towards school and driving by in their cars. As he joined the flow, he heard his name shouted out the open windows of some vehicles, but he refused to show a response. This was going to be a better day. Nothing could ruin it. No matter what.

It was a matter of drowning or not drowning. If you fall in the water and do nothing, eventually you'll sink like a stone and that will be it. Or you can flail against the inevitable and if you gain control of the flailing, it will look and feel like swimming, and you can struggle your way to shore.

That was it. Get control. Don't give in. Or give out.

He greeted the freshmen who filed into his newly born study hall with a fixed frown. Nobody could say he didn't learn from experience. This group was about to find that out.

As soon as the final bell stopped ringing, he pointed at the desks and ordered, "Take a seat in each of the five rows beginning from the window row. I want no more than four in a row so I can keep an eye on each of you. For now you can sit where you choose. As soon as a roster from the office arrives, you'll be put in alphabetical order. Move into those desks now."

The students were caught between the obvious urgency of getting into a desk quickly and being hollered at if they ran. Most chose to walk as rapidly as they could. When Robert saw the first desks in each row were empty, he growled, "Get into those front desks!"

The freshmen sat wide-eyed and wordless in front of Robert Baker. The size of those eyes and the rigidity of their bodies told him that he'd managed to move in the direction of terrifying these kids. Theirs was not the silence of defiance. These kids were nervous, scared, and trying at least as hard as he was to figure out how they were going to make it in this school.

Robert pivoted, pick up a piece of chalk from the chalk tray and wrote his name on the board. Then he turned toward the students. "Let's start all over," he said. "My name is Mr. Baker. I'm a little like you. I'm new to Blue Lake High School. I'm a freshman, too, except you have to add that word 'teacher' to the description."

Patty Light

Dear Dreams,

I walked along the shore of Blue Lake for miles and miles today. The lake was a shimmering blue. The wind was soft and feathery and lovely to feel on my skin. I wanted to take most my clothes off and let the wind wrap around me, but, of course, I didn't. I wanted the wind to take me and carry me away. I dream in the wind. The wind is my everlasting friend.

I went to the grove of pines. It is in the county park and must be at least five miles from this town. There was no one there, and the grove is located far from the road, far from the lake. Thank God! So I walked into the grove and found a place that was almost all shadow and shade except for a few places where the sun filtered through and lay in little pools of light. (That reminds me of the video we saw in Mr. Baker's class about Thoreau. I wish the kids would . . . . Another time.)

I wasn't thinking about that or anything in the pine grove. I just felt and listened and looked. Do you know that the sound of wind in pines is like the sound of a waterfall? It is, but it's also unique and special. It reaches deep into my heart, in a way that is lonely but as soothing as water washing over me. It moves my heart even writing about it.

As I am writing this in my room now, I think of the sound. It is a sound full of peace and sadness and . . . It's a quiet smile and a sliding tear . . . Oh, I don't know! I can't capture it. Words can't. I need the wind to write itself. I need wind words to write wind sounds. I need to live forever in a grove of pines.

Oh, just go listen to it yourself sometime. If you haven't. But I'm sure you have.

Now my mood's gone. I let life intrude and it blew away the woods and left me here in this room. Or maybe it's because I couldn't "write the wind." Isn't that silly? Or maybe it's this room. My poster tells me to listen silently, tells me that the truth is beauty and beauty is truth . . . .

I want to write a short story for you. It's about a girl whose "gift of truth" was a house of screams and silences. Whenever she was away from that house, it looked cold and gray and dingy in her thoughts. The sunlight would hit the windows and slide down the windowpane like dusty yellow rain. It never spilled into her room or any room in the house. She never saw a shaft of sunlight with sun dust dancing in it inside her home. The sun stopped dead at the windows. Sometimes all that light piled up so thick she couldn't see through it to the grass and trees and house next door, and she was afraid that if she went outside, there would be so much light that her eyes couldn't handle it and she'd go stark raving blind.

So she would turn away from the window and look at the darkness that was her house, which was what her soul was becoming as well. Sometimes she felt like she could kill in the darkness. Or she could scream like the frightened child she really was and run and run and run to . . . Her closet. And curl there in the deepest, darkest corner. And wait and wait until the walls absorbed her and sifted her up through the roof where she would lie on its rough and slanted shingles like dew until the sun entered her and took her with it into the sky to join with a million other drops of dew to become rain for the rivers and lakes and oceans . . .

*Or to become part of a cloud and drift in the whisper of the wind. "Free at last,"
she would sing with Martin Luther King, "Thank God almighty I'm free at last."*

Wouldn't that be . . .

I enjoyed my walk.

P.L.

Sam Strand

Sam Strand leaned back into the soft leather principal's chair. He hadn't ordered this piece of furniture. It had appeared in his office prior to the opening day of school. He figured it was an early going away present, one they'd normally give him at a school-wide assembly to honor his "retirement." Ah well, maybe this forced finale was for the best. There were far too many students for him to handle as the sole disciplinary authority in the school. True, the counselors had been given small stipends when they agreed to deal with minor discipline problems in their own way. It saved the District money and took a small portion of the burden off Sam. When he retired, they'd save more money since he was at the top of the salary schedule. Likely they'd use their savings to hire a young principal and, hopefully, an assistant principal since enrollment had now risen to 992 students. So maybe his exit would be the best thing for them, the faculty, and the school. Real educators think like this, Sam mused. The public doesn't give us nearly enough credit for our altruism.

"This chair looks out of place behind this massive old desk, doesn't it, Kyle?" the principal asked. "No answer needed. It's a rhetorical question and an opinion expressed from the boss to one of his underlings. I'd like to lean back and put my big brogans on top of that pocked surface, but I suppose it would be an inappropriate posture from which to discipline or expel students. What do you think? No answer needed, of course."

The younger man seated across from him in the plastic student chair smiled. "This is why you asked me to stop by, Sam? To listen to you reassert your waning authority?" He feigned rising.

"Well, no, Kyle. I asked you to drop by because it gets lonely near the top, and a man gets to thinking thoughts too young for his age if he talks to teenagers all day. Just the other day, this kid, Matt Morgan, walks in with these purple streaks in his curly locks, and he's all dressed in black, so I use three decades' worth of teenage expressions to tell him how striking he looks."

Kyle smiled. There was no man in the world he liked better than Sam Strand. It was like having a second father who was your boss and one of your best friends.

Sam leaned forward and relaxed his elbows on his desk, which, of course, he loved. Maybe they'd give him the chair and the desk as well! He folded his hands. "The real reason I asked you to come in is to gossip," Sam continued. "I want you to tell me about some people. I don't give a hang what's on your mind."

The two men laughed. "Shoot 'em to me," Kyle said. "All I need is name, rank, and grade-point average."

"Robert Baker. You know he came to us highly recommended. I was on vacation, but Alan Anderson —you may have heard of him, he's the new superintendent and a favorite of mine — hired him. He told me Robert has one of the best academic records he's ever seen, and it's true. His G.P.A. is 3.87. No easy courses either. Top recommendations from his professors and his supervising teachers where he student taught. Bright. Intelligent. Personable. Held many positions of some importance in various student organizations."

"He's a perplexed and unhappy man, Sam. I've been in the English

Department meetings a few times with him. He isn't talking much. If I ask him there or when I drop by his room how things are going, he answers 'okay' or 'fine,' but won't go beyond that. It's not true. He's as wired as a terrier, and his eyes hurt to look at."

"Here's the problem, Kyle. One anyway. The man is bright, and he's always been an achiever. He grew up in the town where he went to college and benefited from placement in advanced classes throughout high school. So he was cocooned by his own drive for academic success. He decided late in his college career that he wanted to teach. They should have placed him in a more challenging school, preferably away from the city, for student teaching, but instead they awarded his excellence by placing him in the college Lab School. It's a perfect teaching situation—small classes, bright kids—but not very realistic. There's some relationship between Anderson and Baker's father, so he got the chance to interview Robert — and here he is. He's bright and he loves his subject, but he's naive about kids."

"He's replacing one of the most popular teachers to ever teach in this school who decided to leave the profession very late in the summer, and the kids thought he'd be their teacher," Kyle said.

"Yup. Ted Gerney was a brilliant teacher, but he did no favors for his replacement by leaving when he did. So here's the problem. Robert Baker comes out of that atmosphere, moves hundreds of miles from his roots, steps into the oversized shoes of this icon and wham! He's idealistic, naive, and vulnerable. The kids spot his Achilles heels. They resent his being here. He can't be a buddy or boyfriend. And their reaction to him has put him in shock."

"I'll tell you, Sam, I love kids, but when they get a herd mentality going, they can be pretty damaging. Their brains can fly right out the window. And most of our classes are so darn big now, managing the size becomes a major challenge, let alone teaching them anything."

Sam sighed. "I've got a gut feeling the boy could become an excellent teacher given a chance. But I also believe this could be a dangerous year for him. Teaching is getting harder all the time, especially since that worthless national report came out years ago. I cheered the thing at first. I figured they were actually going to use it to improve schools. Then I found out it was government commissioned and actually the first step in a persistent effort to undermine public education. Lord knows why. Maybe they've got a plan I can't see."

The principal leaned back. "Kyle, teaching's never been easy. Way back in the sixties, it was known that teachers were at high risk for nervous breakdowns. Making it in this profession is a mighty struggle and not many come into it as prepared for battle as they need to be. When the Ted Gerneys leave teaching and the Robert Bakers are victimized for entering it, we're in trouble. And, I think it's going to get worse."

"You're telling me all this because . . . "

"I'd like you to give Robert Baker as much support as you can. I hang around his door now and then and observe him that way. His classes are sullen and unresponsive. I don't have time to sit in his room and observe every day, and if I did, I'd kill whatever confidence the man has left. I can't walk in and threaten the kids because they aren't really doing anything 'bad.' Anyway, I've got to maintain a reasonable tone for the job I do in this office or this whole school will turn into a burning bush. You've got over 160 students and papers piled to the ceiling, but if you can find time for him now and then, maybe you can help him work a little miracle."

"Sure, Sam, I'll give it a shot."

"Thanks," the big man said. "I'd like to see Robert succeed even if he is Anderson's fair-haired boy."

Kyle heard the tone of Sam's voice when he uttered the superintendent's name. "You and Anderson don't get along?" Kyle was surprised. He'd been impressed by the administrator's attitude and his smooth firmness at the few teachers' meetings he'd attended.

"You could say we see eye to butt. His eye. My butt."

Kyle was puzzled. The statement was pretty un-Samlike. "What do you mean?"

"I thought it was common knowledge. Common only to me I guess. You don't know one of the agreements Anderson made when he got his job was to ease me into retirement? The school board thinks it's the fiscally responsible thing to do, and that I'm too much of a geezer to do this job, anyway."

The teacher was shocked. The whole faculty would be. Sam was Blue Lake High School. He'd been an excellent man to work for and with for decades. "I can't believe it."

"It's true. I'm old enough to go. But I resent it. The decision should be mine. I've earned it. And I resent Anderson agreeing to that condition. But I don't want to talk about that any more. I want to ask you about a couple of our students."

"Sure, fine," Kyle agreed.

"Patty Light."

Kyle's eyes widened with surprise. "Patty Light? I love the girl. I'll tell you, the work she does for me is prime stuff well beyond her years. She's bright. She works her head off." Kyle hesitated. "You're not going to tell me she's pregnant, are you!"

"No, no, quite the contrary. But is she always 'with you' in class?"

"It sure seems that way to me."

"Notice anything unusual about her?"

"You are trying to tell me she's pregnant."

"No. Not."

"Well, she doesn't smile a lot. But I take that as being serious and dedicated. If she dreams or drifts in class, it isn't apparent to me. If she isn't pregnant," Kyle asked, "why are we talking about her?"

"The girl caught my eye two years ago when she came in as a freshman. Quiet kids aren't that easy to spot, but there's something a bit odd about her. Am I wrong or does she not have any close girl friends? When I see her in the halls, she's alone. Does she have a boy friend?"

For some reason Kyle needed to defend the girl. "Geez, Sam, this social stuff is way overemphasized. There are lots of high school girls without boyfriends and vice versa."

"But how often to you see a kid her age lacking both? Whom does she relate to in your class?"

"Probably me," Kyle admitted. He still couldn't bring himself to find anything wrong with the girl. He thought she was great. "What's your point?"

"I think she has home problems. I went through her papers with Leann. Her mother's a single parent. In Patty's two years here I've never seen her at the school. There's no reference to the father. From all appearances this young lady is achieving at a first class rate. The focus of her entire life is this school."

"I can see why you're concerned."

"And since what I'm about to say may be the misplaced agonizing of an old man, I want it to stay right here and between us."

"Well, sure, of course."

"My concern is this. You just told me that Patty relates mostly to you. I think most of her teachers would say the same. But this worries me a little. More than once when I've wandered by Robert Baker's room after school, she's in the room talking with him. She's the only student who is. So I'm just going to ask you to be a alert to that situation, too, even if it was presented to you by a muling old has-been."

Kyle lifted his briefcase into his lap. "I'll do as you say, Captain. I'll be all eyes and ears."

The two men rose. "Say," Sam said, "I hear your wife is working for Kerns Company. How's she like it?"

"She likes it. How about you, Kyle, you were about to ask. I'm learning to. See ya, Sam," Kyle concluded, turning and leaving the office.

It was nearly six 'o clock, Sam noted. Maybe miracles do happen. Teachers like Kyle and him were still married despite keeping these atrocious hours and then bringing their jobs home with them anyway. Of course his wife was a saint. Gail Hunter must be, too.

Billy Cloud

Seventh period American Literature was dead in the ice, so Billy Cloud, at the urging of Mr. Baker, transferred to the third period class, picking up a teacher's aide noncredit assignment with the Physical Education Department to do so. The unabated silent hostility in the seventh period had become too hard to endure. He'd made his last attempt to help Mr. Baker promote discussion in that class. Baker had given up, too. On that last day he and Billy dialogued about "Sinners in the Hands of An Angry God" amidst the deafening silence of the other thirty-one students. Baker shrugged his shoulders, gave Monday's assignment, and retreated behind his desk. All books except Billy's remained closed, and the students stared at the teacher or out the window. It was the most aggressive silence Billy had ever heard. Turning a page of his lit book resounded loud as a rifle shot.

After class Mr. Baker crooked a finger and summoned him to his desk. "I hate to lose you from this class, Billy," the teacher said, "but I could hold class in a cemetery. The pressure on you not to perform must be tremendous. So take this note to the counselor and see if you can get transferred. Third period would be the best bet. It's noisy, but there are a few who care in there." The smile on his lips was stretched tight.

"Thanks, Mr. Baker. I'll take noise any day. These guys are driving me nuts!"

"Me too. Me, too."

Billy saw something leap and fall in Baker's eyes, which he replaced with a blink and then a stunning neutrality. "Gotta do these essays, Billy. By the way, you play football, right?"

The teenager thought most of the teachers went to games and assumed the question was rhetorical. "Right."

"Know Ed Warrum very well?"

"Well, yeah, sure."

"The guy's got an attitude problem." Billy watched anger replace opaqueness in the man's eyes, but he was surprised Ed Warrum was the reason.

"Sullen. Unresponsive. He's in the third period class. Maybe you can talk to him?"

"Sure," Billy agreed. About an attitude he'd never seen? Well, maybe he would. "Gotta go, Mr. Baker. Thanks for the transfer."

The process took a couple of days since it required rearrangement of Billy's schedule. Counselor Barnes seemed irritated to be dealing with it, eyeing the boy and saying he'd have to verify with Baker. Billy followed the man to Mr. Baker's room. Once the teacher affirmed his approval, the counselor asked Billy to step outside. From there he could hear what sounded like Mr. Barnes lecturing Mr. Baker. He didn't hear Baker's voice.

When Billy left the seventh period class, it was like someone had opened a freezer door and released him into the sun. Like today's, he noted gratefully as he walked the miles home from school after football practice. He was alone and liked it like that. This way he could inhale the aroma of

Indian Summer and observe the descent of the sun amidst the feathery western clouds. He could listen to the leaves skittering across the roads and sidewalks. It was late and the sun was resting on the tips of the trees. The day was gentle as a caress.

He liked walking alone. It gave him time to feel and think. He'd done enough thinking for one day, he decided. He'd save thoughts of the football game until tomorrow, thoughts of school until tomorrow. For the rest of this walk and this day he'd get as close as he could to wind and weather and himself in it. He'd never been taught this attitude toward existence. It had been modeled for him ever since he'd been old enough to know what he was seeing. He was aware on this autumn day how fortunate he was that that was true.

Kyle Hunter

As usual the teacher's lounge was abuzz with teachers by the time Kyle arrived at 7:15 a.m. after his bike ride to town. When he strolled in, Patty Green was already regaling Gen Daws with details of a late evening phone call. Red Howard and Greg Schwarz were huddled in two corner chairs talking about the Big Game coming up against St. Andrews on Friday. Art Close was staring out the open window, a copy of the morning paper folded under his arm. Nelson Jack and Shirley Dee were nestled on the old brown sofa Sam Strand had donated to the place. Kyle knew Nelson and Shirley would be sitting there. They always were these days. He smiled as he stopped in front of them. "Well, kids," he inquired, "planning education, recreation, or procreation?"

"What's Dee question?" Nelson smirked. "Shirley, you jest?"

"Actually we are talking about procreation," Shirley interjected. "Nelson needs a few pointers on it so he can effectively present it to the boys' health classes this week."

"At least that's what I told her," Nelson leered. They both giggled.

"See ya, kids. I need coffee and actual adult conversation."

"Ain't no adults here, Kyle. Just us teachers."

Kyle left the two chortling on the sofa. He snatched his coffee mug from the rack of mugs above the small sink, poured himself a cup of the brew he knew would be strong enough to hold a spoon upright, and slid into a metal folding chair across the table from the two coaches.

Kyle liked the lounge at this time of year. Despite nagging problems, teachers were mostly optimistic and enthusiastic people, especially on sunny, brisk mornings in October. Since there were few other compelling reasons to remain in the profession, he was aware that the bond that brought them together was the love of what and whom they taught. They, like him, were teachers because they couldn't ignore its persistent call, and the persistent possibilities inherent in that calling. Of course it was much easier to see that now than it would be in January.

Kyle was sure the two men across from him would agree with those sentiments if he vocalized them. Instead he said, "Morning, Coach H. and Coach S. How's tomorrow look?"

"Looks tough, Kyle," Howard responded. He never said anything else to the public and never said that to his players. "Just about as tough as the old stomach feels this morning. Guess I'm as nervous as usual. You'd think I'd get over that, wouldn't you? Anyway, St. Andrews has a fullback that weighs 220 pounds and a line that averages ten pounds per man more."

"But," Greg Schwarz noted, "they're slower than animal crackers, so Warrum and Cloud will zip by 'em like fleas."

"Great similes, Greg," Kyle said.

"It's a pretty accurate size comparison though," Red groaned, kneading his sore stomach.

Greg leaned toward Kyle, his muscular arms on the table, and lowered his voice. "Seriously, Kyle, I hear you got a problem in your Department. Robert Baker? Kids say he's an alien life form. Say they never see him in the cafeteria because he's always out to lunch anyway."

"Sometimes, Greg, you're even less funny than I think you are. Robert Baker is not a topic for your adolescent humor. He's a first year teacher who's struggling some and that, as you may remember from your own experience, is not fun." Sometimes the big guy irritated him. His boundaries of good taste could be broad as a football field. "All he'd need is to hear a crack like that from one of his peers."

Greg leaned back in his chair and folded his arms across his chest. Hurt by Kyle's reaction, he defended his comments. "Hey, I'm sorry, man. But you know it's true in school just like anywhere else. All I'm saying is some are winners and some are losers. What I hear is that Baker's a loser."

Red Howard's elbow crashed solidly into his assistant's ribcage. Robert Baker had entered the emptying room just in time to have heard the last sentences. He paused uncertainly at the adjacent table, his face flushed. He reminded Kyle of those cartoons where the lines shoot out from all sides of the character's face interspersed with large drops of sweat. Just as Kyle started to say, "Good morning," the young teacher wheeled and left the room.

"Geez, I'm sorry, Kyle. Sometimes I think I oughta cut out my tongue."

"Not a bad idea, Greg," Kyle said as he rose from his chair. "The world would certainly be a quieter and better place if you did."

As he headed out the door, guilt whipped through him. Greg talked too often without thinking, but the man's body was mostly comprised of heart. He should have been a little gentler with him. Then, too, Sam had asked him to speak with Baker a week ago, and he hadn't done it yet. The old

saying 'All the world avoids a loser' flipped through his mind. He threw the
thought away. He'd talk to Baker soon. But right now he had to get to his
homeroom. The bell was jangling, twanging his nerves like a tuning fork.
"Zero for two," he muttered.

Frank Marin

Frank Marin wished he hadn't arrived at school on time, but his parents
insisted on giving him a ride this morning. Maybe they were just trying to
spend a little more time with their son.

Whatever. When he swung open the door of their aging Ford and slid
out of the vehicle, the walkways and steps were full of kids. He slammed
the door shut and strolled up the sidewalk without looking back or to either
side. He shoved his hands into his jacket pockets, but kept his elbows close
to his sides as he maneuvered around the groups of friends gathered in
conversation. He heard snatches of some of it as he passed, mostly about
tomorrow night's football game with St. Andrew. Since he wasn't living in
a bubble, he was aware of the game, but it irritated him that everyone was
so interested. He hoped Blue Lake would lose so these snobs, this school,
and their team weren't as hot as they thought they were.

Maybe if he was back home, he'd care. Maybe he'd have even gone out
for the team this year. Coach Haynes had approached him several times
to rejoin the squad he'd quit after his freshman year. That was when he
started hanging out with Shmitty, and the stuff Shmitty liked didn't go very
well with football. He could still see the hurt in his father's eyes when football season rolled around, and, without saying anything, Frank didn't go
to practice. Instead he hung out with Shmitty, who did all the talking and
convinced Frank to grow his hair longer. He was thinking of returning to
the sport his junior year because he was getting pretty sick of listening to
Shmitty, and Shmitty started wanting him to buy the stuff he'd hooked him
on by giving it to him. So he'd decided he'd rather listen to the Old Man
Corgan talk, and he was really thinking about playing football and avoiding Shmitty when his folks announced they were all moving to Blue Lake.
Then it became moot. He'd never make the Blue Lake team even though he
was six feet tall and pretty strong from the farm work. Nobody ever asked
him anyway.

In fact after the first few days, nobody noticed him in the oversized
classes he was stuffed into. It was easier that way. He wouldn't have known
what to say if they had tried to talk to him except that he wished he still
lived where he used to.

Maybe if someone had asked him about playing football, things would
have been different. Nobody did. So he met a few guys in August after he
came back from working on Corgan's farm for two months. He'd hung out

with Shmitty a few times back there and done a little stuff with him. The guys he met reminded him of Shmitty. They knew people who sold stuff more serious than Shmitty ever had. They shared a little of it with him. He liked the way the marijuana sent him drifting, so he started building a stash for when he needed to relax. That need came on pretty fast. That might not have happened if someone had noticed him. Their fault.

He built a stash, but he didn't like the guys much. Too much like Shmitty, dominating him all the time and not really liking anyone, not even each other. When he decided he'd developed a sufficient supply, he simply avoided them.

Armed with these thoughts, he arrived at his locker. He whirled the combination lock through its clicks and opened it. He thought of shedding his jacket since it was a pretty nice October day, but couldn't bring himself to do it. He stood in front of his locker, looking into it for a long time as though there was something there he wanted. There were books and a notebook. He didn't crack them open except in class when the teachers looked at him. He stood in front of his locker, his hand atop its door as student noise washed around him. He turned his wrist enough to see that the bell would be ringing soon and finally grabbed the notebooks and books.

As he ambled down the hall, Mr. Hunter passed him. "Morning, Frank," the teacher said. Frank knew that thing he wrote about Mr. Corgan was good and that he'd probably write more good stuff if he tried. But Mr. Hunter was one of those guys who'd stand there and look at you and ask you questions about yourself. He didn't want that. So he'd quit handing stuff in.

The other guy who seemed to notice him was Baker. The difference was Baker would give you these quick looks, sometimes confused, sometimes curious, but usually angry. But he was probably paranoid about the way the kids talked about him.

As he entered his first period class, Frank scanned the room. No one in the room looked like him with his anachronistic leather jacket and long, dark hair. If he didn't want attention, he wondered why he looked like he did? Then he slid into his desk, glad that it was at the back of the row. For a second there he'd felt that bright light beating on him even though he couldn't remember anyone looking at him.

In the third period Frank nearly achieved self-inflicted whiplash. Despite his best efforts, he showed the fear he always felt when he heard a sudden shout. He was sitting in the back seat in the fourth row and had skidded the desk back so he could extend his legs instead of bumping them on the underside of the desk. He had his head tilted down and was drawing little tomadic swirls on the inside of his notebook. Suddenly Mr. Baker's voice roared through his ears on its way to Ed Warrum seated two rows to his right. Frank snapped his head up so fast it nearly sailed off his neck. That caught the teacher's attention and he drilled a hard look into Frank before dancing it over to Ed.

Unfortunately neither he nor Mr. Baker nor Ed Warrum knew that each of the three had found the most effective way to cover fear was to almost involuntarily whip on a mask that looked to all the world like anger.

Ed Warrum

Ed Warrum sat slumped in his desk. He glared at the little swirls of writing on its top without really seeing them. He was distracted. It seemed like his gut and heart and brain were all jammed together. Images of explosions formed in his head. His headache played them, displaced them, played them again.

He flipped open his literature book, seeing no words. Last night had been worse than any night he could remember, and it was driving him crazy. It had been bad enough when his father attended games, and they held those post-mortem reviews. Now he was taking time off from the store to watch at least part of most practices. "Crap!" Ed mumbled, the words lost in the general classroom noise. "Dammit, dammit, dammit." The scene ran through his head like a video repeating itself over and over.

He had pushed himself away from the dining room table, his spine aching from the high-backed straightness of the chair, his head spinning with frustration. "I gotta go study, Dad," he'd pleaded, pushing up from the chair.

"That's fine," his father had answered. He pointed at the chair, "But I want a response before you go. I want to know who the best coach on that football field is."

"It's Mr. Howard, Dad. I told you that. I like Coach. We're unbeaten. What do you want!?"

"Howard's over the hill," Pete Warrum said as though Ed hadn't spoken. It didn't matter what Ed said. So why ask! "He's a figurehead. Oh, maybe he could coach ten, twenty years ago, but he's lost it. Schwarz is the real coach. He isn't afraid to kick butts. Howard is."

"You call pacing the sidelines and hollering 'kicking butt'? Schwarz is a good coach, but Howard makes the decisions. He wins the games." Ed rarely talked back to his father. His voice quivered with the effort of it. His face and hands felt cold and wet. But he didn't quit. "Half the guys on the team would probably quit if Schwarz was head coach." He knew that wasn't true, crazy really, but he had an overwhelming need to fight off his father's opinion.

"See!" his father shouted, slamming his fist on the table, causing everyone seated there to flinch. "See, Ellie! That's how it is these days. We've got a bunch of milkweed crybabies on that field, and we wonder why they can't play football!" His face was fixed in a vicious smirk, his round chin jutting toward his son.

Ed shot out of his chair, his own palms slamming on the table. "What in hell are you talking about?" The words strangled out of his throat. "What do you want? We're unbeaten! Nobody's come close. You're so crazy you can't even see! Nothing's good enough for you!"

Pete Warrum leapt out of his chair. He bounded around the table, his water glass in his right hand. Ed froze, his eyes wide and unblinking as his father threw the water in his face, then hurled the glass against the wall where it shattered. He could not move as his father's open hands flew through the air and slammed into his chest, the sound crackling in the strident silence of the house, the force sending him reeling against the wall, his father's ham hands clutching his shirt just below his chin.

"Don't you ever talk to me like that again, you punk!" his father boomed, whacking his son's back against the wall. "Don't you ever swear at me!" He slammed the boy against the wall again. "Don't you ever talk back to me!"

If only he could have released the fear. If only he could have been angry instead of shocked. If only he had doubled his own fists and slammed them into the man's paunchy gut, his ugly flushed face! Should have spit in it! Should have spit right in that ugly mug!

❖   ❖   ❖

"Ed Warrum. Earth calling Ed Warrum. Mr. Warrum?" The voice came out of the distance. Disoriented, caught in the space between the whirling memory and reality, Ed could not respond. He raised his gaze and looked toward the sound, heard the nervous laughter that sprinkled the room. "Hey . . . you . . . . Ed Warrum!" The voice thudded in his ears.

"Uh . . . yes . . . uh . . . Mr. Baker . . . "

"Care to join us?" The red-faced teacher roared, his hand sweeping the air to indicate the rest of the class. The room was silent. Shellie Chaine, sitting in the first row had her head so low she'd catch her nose in her book if she closed it.

"Big game tonight, Mr. Warrum?" Ed hated that. He hated being called that. The teacher's voice was raspy, his knuckles white as always as he clutched the lectern.

"Yes, sir," the boy answered.

"Well, I know that," the teacher retorted. "I read the papers. Do you read, Mr. Warrum?"

"I haven't seen today's paper," Ed answered. I wish I knew what we're talking about, he thought desperately.

"Your book!" The teacher's voice cracked as his anger increased. Someone in the room emitted a shriek of laughter. Then silence. "Do you read your book?"

"Yes, sir," Ed replied.

"Then would you care to answer my question?"

"I'd like to, sir, but I didn't hear it." He was looking at the teacher's face now, and he saw anger and despair mixed in its features. It was just how he felt last night. Now he only felt lost, and everything was out of control.

"Did you read today's assignment?"

"No, sir. I was going to, but something came up . . . " came down, went sideways, turned upside down . . . his mind continued. Ed had never been more miserable.

"Some stars do read," the teacher spat out at him.

It was a mess. Ed could think of nothing to say except "sorry," which he mumbled as he lowered his eyes to the book. Mr. Baker had become a bull-dog all of a sudden. If he quit struggling, maybe the man would let go.

"What did you say?" the teacher hammered.

"Mr. Baker," Patty Light's voice floated over the silence. "Mr. Baker, can I answer the question?"

"Yes," the teacher replied, his voice sounding defeated and sad.

Ed stared at his book, his eyes blurred. Damn, he thought, damn! I don't know what's going on anymore.

Kyle Hunter

Kyle Hunter felt good as he emerged from the locker room into the cool autumn twilight. His "red shirts" eighth grade footballers had downed the "green shirts" 14-6, thus securing the totally unofficial junior high intra-school football championship. The kids acted like they'd won the Super Bowl. "Big potatoes," Kyle murmured happily. Vince Lombardi was wrong about winning being the only thing, but winning sure felt good.

His mood diminished when he saw Robert Baker emerge through one of the rear doors of the school. He remembered the comments of both Greg Schwarz and Sam Strand. The slender man's posture was slightly slumped, his head down. It had been weeks since Sam talked to Kyle and almost two months since school began, and he hadn't done a single thing to help the guy out. Too busy, he excused himself. "Oh, sure!" he muttered.

He headed for the bike rack, unlocked his Schwinn, and pedaled in the direction Robert Baker was walking. "Hey, Robert," he shouted, "hold up a minute."

The startled teacher jerked his head around, a reflexive reaction that told Kyle this wasn't the first time the teacher had heard his name unexpectedly shouted. Robert was obviously relieved when he saw Kyle peddling up the parking lot.

Kyle braked his bike and planted his foot against the curbing. "Heading home?"

"Yeah," Robert answered and dropped into an awkward silence.

Kyle said, "Say, my wife's in the Cities at a computer workshop or something. I haven't had much of a chance to talk to you, so I thought maybe you'd like to go out to the Duck Blind – it's a supper club – eat some food, drink a few beers."

"Uh . . . sure," Robert answered.

"I don't think we'd fit on this bike. You got a car? I've never seen you driving to school, come to think of it."

"Uh, it's a clunker. Old Dodge. Can't afford anything else right now. If you don't mind riding in it . . . "

"Tell you what. I live straight out Highway 2 about five miles out of town. Left side of the road. Little red house. It's hard to see from the road because of the big pines in the front yard. But they're easy to see. Look for them. Hey, I'd better get this bike home before dark. No lights. Give me forty-five minutes. I'll stand in front of the pines. They're close to the road."

"Okay. Sure."

"See you in a few minutes," Kyle finished, waving his way down the road.

❖ ❖ ❖

"That was good," Kyle stated, admiring the slick bones of what been the primest of ribs.

"Excellent," Robert agreed. "So's the view," he added, nodding at the moon-sparkled waters beyond the window.

"So's the waitress. May." Kyle motioned to the only waitress there, who was also the owner's wife. An excellent halo of curly blonde hair framed her flushed Nordic face. She smiled fondly at Kyle. "Got two beers for the road?"

"Sure do," she nodded, moving toward the small bar in the corner of the dining area where her husband was dispensing drinks to the only other customer still in the place, a man with gray sideburns and business suit.

"Eddie's the last of the living hippies," Kyle said, indicating the bartender with a flip of his hand. "For years he was the only man within five hundred miles who still wore a pony tail. In fact, he was a kid in California. Says he left when the place lost its ambiance. Says this is the only place he's been since that has ambiance. That's why he and May stay."

"Doesn't that put people off . . . the hippie look . . . around here? Isn't Blue Lake pretty conservative?" Robert asked.

"Some, sure. Eddie says some people find their way here walk in, take one look at his hair, sniff the air figuring the scent of marijuana must be in it, and scurry out the door. But anyone who stays and has a meal is hooked for life. I'd guess the guy sitting at the bar is a salesman from the Cities. From the way he's jawing with Eddie, you can tell he's been here before. I bet every time he's in this territory, he stops for food and conversation."

"Kyle and Gail come here at least twice a month," May said as she set the beer in front of the men. "I hear him telling you how wonderful we are, which is true, but he hasn't told me who you are, which is rude."

"Jeez, I'm sorry, May. Robert Baker—May Swanson."

"Pleased to meet you," May said. "New in town? Or just visiting our friend."

"New in town. I . . . Some say I teach." He paused, embarrassed. "Your meal was excellent. I . . . "

"Why thank you, Robert. Come see us again." She smiled, then cocked her head toward Kyle. "Bring Gail too. I suppose she's home ironing your underwear."

"Actually she's in the Cities ironing out computer programs. She's a liberated working girl."

"Oh, so you finally took the shackles off her ankles. Good for you. That clanking when you two walked in was getting on our other customers' nerves. Well, boys, I'm not quite so liberated, so I have to get after those dishes in the kitchen. I'll take these along if you're done licking your plate, Kyle." The men watched her walk to the kitchen, her hips flowing in her unconsciously sensuous way, a final bonus to a meal at the Duck Blind.

"Pretty lady," Robert said.

"At least." Kyle sipped his beer, then fixed his gaze on the other man. "Your response to her question wouldn't exactly take the NEA Convention by storm."

"No, I suppose it wouldn't." Robert's face looked thinner, more tightly adhered to his bones than Kyle had noticed before. His eyes took on the hooded look.

"Look. Take it easy. I'd like to take advantage of this opportunity to get to know you. Especially since we share the same department and some of the same kids."

"I'm sorry," the other man said, directing his eyes out the window. "It was . . . it was an honest response. I don't feel much like a teacher."

"How's that?"

Robert took a long drink of his beer. Maybe it would loosen him up. He looked like he needed to talk. He set the glass down and curled his fingers around it. Then he said, "I've always had an image of what a teacher is."

"Which is . . . "

"Someone who stands straight and tall in front of the classroom and has an... an aura. The students are hungry for what he or she has to offer because what the teacher knows is so interesting."

"All your teachers been like that? Mine? Quite a few were, but not all."

Robert's smile flickered. "No. But the ones I remember. I suppose Gerney was like that."

"Gerney was an excellent teacher, Robert. He knew how to ask the right questions. He was an excellent lecturer. He was a presence. The kids liked him a lot. But he wasn't perfect. He had an ego, and sometimes he pandered to them to insure their love. He was creative, but sometimes his games and activities were more entertaining than informative." Kyle was being a little rough on his former colleague. He was well aware that stepping into Gerney's shoes presented a major challenge. "But he was good. No doubt. A natural teacher who's no longer teaching. The profession shouldn't lose people like him."

"Or replace him with people like me," Robert muttered.

Kyle leaned forward. "Listen, Robert, I feel for you. Those are big shoes. Anybody would have trouble stepping into them."

"Sure, I know, but this much?" Robert shook his head. "I had no idea kids could act like they do. I suppose it happened when I was in high school, but I didn't pay any attention. I was busy and interested." He wanted Kyle to understand him, Kyle or anyone. He took another swallow of his beer and plunged ahead. "I guess where I lived everybody I knew pretty much respected the value of getting educated."

"Teachers were paid well?"

"I guess. Not many left anyway."

"So it was pretty ideal."

"Yes. So was the Lab School. I could hardly get the questions out before a dozen hands were waving in the air. I couldn't read their essays fast enough for them. They were eager with a capital E."

"Must have been fun."

"It was great. Unreal, too, I've found out. I'm like some kind of alien who's suddenly dropped into the real world without instruction about how to deal with it."

"Your education classes didn't deal with it?"

"Education classes? Great theories. But my professors must not have been in a real school in twenty years. I've tried about half the stuff they talked about. None of it has worked very well for me so far." He wrenched his gaze back to the window, his brow knit.

"That bad?" Kyle asked. He'd seen teachers suffer before. His own experience contained bad moments, though he doubted teaching had ever brought him this low.

"That bad," the other said.

"I'm sorry to hear that."

"I guess I see through a glass darkly," the teacher said, sloshing the remains of his beer around and around in his glass. "But maybe you had to be there."

"I talked . . . Sam talked to me."

Irritation shot into Robert's face. "What right has he!"

"Easy," Kyle urged, raising his palms. "Easy. Look. Sam cares. About you. About the school. He wants what's best for you. He said he's seen kids do what they're doing to you before. It's mob psychology."

"Why hasn't he talked to me?"

"He should. He will. The man's overburdened. He's the only real disciplinary authority in the school. There should be an assistant principal but there isn't. So he hands the ball off to people he trusts sometimes, and we fumble it because we're busy too."

Robert reached into the jacket draped over the back of his chair, and fished folded pieces of paper out of one of its pockets. He unfolded one, a slight tremor in his hand, and handed it to Kyle. "Seen anything like this before. It was in my P.O. box in the office this morning."

The note was scrawled in barely legible handwriting. It read: *"Dear Bobby boy. We don't like you. We'd like to roll your car into a lake with you locked in it. But we won't. Instead we will stay like we are and drive you back to the loony bin you come from."*

Kyle's was shocked. In his years he'd seen and heard some nasty stuff, but nothing more vitriolic than this. "Look, I'm sorry. Does anybody know about this? You've got to turn it over to Sam."

"Think he's got time to look at it? Or will he ask you to look into it for him? I did ask the secretaries if they'd seen any kids around the P.O. boxes. They said they hadn't noticed anyone in particular, but they were with kids who came in tardy. Everyone's busy."

At a loss, Kyle pursued a thought he'd heard early in his career and dragged it into his mind. "This note? Try to remember it's one kid who wrote this."

"With about thirty cheering every word."

"Maybe, but I hate to believe it. I think it's one kid. Oh, maybe he showed it to a few others who thought it was some kind of a weird joke."

"Twenty or thirty could have written it. I've got ten more like this, maybe worse. Believe me, they don't like me, Kyle. I'm not Gerney and that's it as far as they're concerned. Listen, I love my subject. I thought I wanted to teach." He dropped his palms on top of the table without strength. "From the moment they walked into my room, they haven't given me a chance. Every mistake I make lasts forever in their minds. They don't even know that I'm a human being."

Kyle was stunned by the man's despair. Blue Lake didn't have much of a turnover of teachers, none in the English Department for six years until Gerney left. In the lounge or after faculty meetings, he and his peers sometimes acknowledged the road they traveled was slanting downhill, but accepted that and pressed on. Perhaps this young teacher was revealing how far things had fallen when he wasn't noticing.

Nevertheless Kyle tried to offer something positive. "I think many of those kids may not know what they're doing or why. They're just caught in that herd mentality. Listen, Robert. None of us reaches everybody, no matter what. Try to think about the ones who are responding to you." He waited a moment, then continued. "There are some you know," he emphasized.

"Who are they? I think right now it's important to think about them."

"Uh . . . yes . . . yeah. I suppose it is," Robert agreed. It was tough to crawl out of the hole he was in, but he tried. "Billy Cloud. Yeah, there's a kid who cares. I had him transfer to my so-called best class. Nils Larson doesn't say anything, but he works hard. So does Rebecca Buckanaga. Jerry Burger. Lance Hayward. Ann Nolen. Sally Long Arrow. Teresa Hazlitt. Patty Light. The freshman study hall so far. Yes, there are a few."

"Try to center your thoughts on them," Kyle urged. "Aim your teaching at them. Some of the others will follow in time." It was too obvious how thoroughly the young man's self-image was shaken. But Kyle knew what he was saying was true. He'd experienced it. "Does that sound logical to you? Like a good idea?"

Robert inhaled deeply and exhaled slowly, trying to release the tension that gripped him despite the beer and despite evidence that maybe he wasn't hopeless after all. He tried a smile. "Yes. Sure. I'll give it a shot."

"And keep talking to me, will you?" Kyle pleaded. He pointed to the note on the table. "Can I turn this over to Sam? I'll tell him to have the office secretaries keep an eye on the P.O. boxes. I'd guess you're not the only one getting crank notes like this one."

"Selfishly I hope I'm not. But I'd just as soon you didn't show Mr. Strand the note. It's embarrassing to me. Maybe I deserved it a little bit."

"No one deserves it." But he handed the note back when Robert extended his hand. "You're sure? I'm not positive it's best to let kids get away with stuff like this."

"I'm not either. Heck, I'm not sure of anything right now, including all the times I've said 'sure' to you in the last few minutes. But maybe the kids will decide I'm a good sport or something, that I can take it without running to the principal. Maybe it will help if I can just let it go." He paused. He might as well put one last subject on the table. "I have to admit I heard what the football coach — Greg something or other — said about me that morning. When your peers . . . "

Kyle interrupted. "Greg Schwarz has no peers. In most ways he's a fine fellow, but he occasionally has no sense. His problem is that sometimes his mouth goes to work before his brain does. And that, my friend, is the truth." He glanced toward the bar. Mr. Gray Person had exited. "This place is pretty empty. I expect we should empty it of ourselves too." He glanced out the window. "Lord, that moon on that water is beautiful."

As the men shrugged into their jackets, May emerged from the kitchen. "Hey, May," Kyle called, "how about accompanying us down to the lake. That full moon on the water is too good to pass up, but we need a woman to make the experience complete. Eddie, lock this place and lead the way. We are two lonely men in need of nature's respite and conversation with real adults."

"Sure boys," the blonde answered, tossing her apron on the bar. "But does Eddie have to go? Shoot. Oh well, Eddie, grab a few bottles of beer. We need to try to shine a little light into these lonely lives."

Kyle's impulse turned into a good decision. The quartet settled around the picnic table the couple had placed near the shore for times when they "needed their own space," as Eddie put it. Prompted by a few questions from Kyle, the two were soon talking about places and faces they'd experienced. The wind blew warm out of the southwest. The moonlight danced on the moving waters. The world had things to offer beyond kids and classrooms. Sometimes teachers needed to be reminded of that.

Greg Schwarz

The faculty of Blue Lake High School often expressed mixed feelings about the hype surrounding athletics, but Greg Schwarz had no doubts about how he felt. It had been his experience ever since grade school that the Big Games welded whole schools, whole communities together. If a few people stood at the fringes or walked away in disgust at the way athletics outstripped academics in importance, so be it. For most, Big Games were a unifying factor. Conversations had a starting focus. Excitable souls had a contagious outlet.

As Greg stood in the packed gymnasium listening to the chants and cheers while waiting to speak, he closed his eyes and immersed in the crisp unity of the student body's response to the cheerleaders. He let it soak into his big frame, heard it thumping inside his rib cage. His chest expanded to hold the thrill of the moment.

Red Howard usually let his assistant coach speak at these rallies. "You pump 'em up, I make 'em weep. Generally, pump is preferable." Red might have "made 'em weep" on this day of the seniors' last home football game, but that stomach of his still wasn't right. You'd think after thirty years, a guy might get over that anticipation, but maybe that's what kept Red in it. Caring that much. Whatever the case, Greg was glad to be speaking. He had no doubt the pump would be primed.

"And now," pretty, redheaded cheerleader Nancy Wane was sing-songing, "Here's our great assistant coach, Mr. Schwarz, to say a few words."

They don't cheer like that when I enter the classroom, the coach admitted as he neared the microphone. "Hey, look at you guys. You're standing. I feel like a rock star!" he roared as he grabbed the mike.

Greg loved these moments in front of the students, microphone in hand. It was as close to glory as a grown man could get and still not make much of a living. He reveled in these upcoming minutes in which he would play the assemblage for all he could squeeze out of them.

"Hey, what's everyone so excited about?"

Friendly laughter scattered through the crowd.

"Something going on in Blue Lake today I haven't heard about?"

Then, as planned, brunette cheerleader Shellie Chaine raced to the microphone and shouted into it, "Gee, Mr. Schwarz, didn't anyone tell you?"

Shrieks of laughter rose from the freshman section, which hadn't seen Greg work a crowd.

"Tell me . . . what?" Schwarz asked, displaying that wide-eyed bear and beehive look that always got them roaring.

"Gee, Mr. Schwarz, didn't ANYBODY tell you there's a FOOTBALL GAME TONIGHT!" The expected cheers and laughter engulfed the speakers.

"Sure . . . uh . . . uh . . . omigosh, what's your name?"

"Shellie! Shell. E.! My goodness," the cheerleader stage whispered, placing her hands on her hips in a wonderful portrayal of a pout.

Raucous laughter awarded the skit. This was a new wrinkle from the master spirit booster.

"Oh, yeah. Ha, ha. Sure, Miss E., there's always a game on Friday nights. I know because I always go."

Good natured, predictably derisive groans greeted that response.

"MISTER SCHWARZ, didn't ANYBODY tell you what's so SPECIAL about this game?"

"Gee, I don't know. I don't think so. Golly, Shell, what IS so special about this game?"

"Well, actually, Mr. Schwarz," Shellie answered into the microphone, hands still on hips, foot tapping in a great imitation of impatience, "nothing. I mean nothing if playing the game that could send us into the STATE PLAYOFFS is nothing."

The gymnasium erupted into the wild cheers the students had been breathlessly withholding. "Didn't ANYBODY tell you that, Mr. Schwarz?" Shellie concluded in a high-toned voice that was a grand impersonation of someone who pities you while reveling in her own superiority.

"Good work, young lady. You oughta get an Oscar," the coach whispered as the audience cascaded groans and shouts down on them. Then he hooked the microphone back in its stand and assumed a wide stance behind it. "Well, yes, I guess Coach Howard did mention something about that during the week. I guess that's why we were working so hard in practice."

Light laughter anticipated the coming crescendo.

That's the entertainment, kids. Now here comes the inspiration! "Seriously, folks, YOU know that I know this is a pretty big game tonight. My history students know it for sure. Our lesson for today was brainstorming ideas on how to beat St. Andrews."

Loud cheers and catcalls were aimed at the sophomore section of the bleachers.

"Because we want to start a whole NEW history of doing that!"

Roars of approval rewarded Greg's turning of the phrase.

"And we figured it out. We're going to beat them because Blue Lake has the BEST HEAD COACH in the state. Wait," he ordered, holding up his palms. "We're going to beat them because we may not have the greatest athletes in the state, but no team — NO TEAM ANYWHERE — WORKS as hard, PLAYS as hard or wants to WIN as much as the BLUE LAKE LAKERS! Wait. We're going to win because no team—NO TEAM—gets the support from its cheerleaders that our team gets."

Cheers from all and whistles from the boys elevated the upbeat tone.

"We're going to win because we have the BEST BUNCH of SENIORS we've EVER had as far as spirit and desire are concerned. Stand up, you guys; show 'em who you are. Wait," he again ordered and the crowd paused in hearty anticipation. "And we've got the BEST SPIRIT in our underclassmen that I've seen since I've been coaching here. You guys stand up now. All right. C'mon, everybody. Let them know you appreciate them."

Bleacher-shaking, foot-stomping cheers filled the big room from floor to roof.

"Hey, Joe and Jerry, you guys stand up, too. How are the girls gonna know what a coupla hunks you are if you don't let 'em see you?"

Laughter and cheers awarded the comment, proving that Greg had this audience in the palms of his hands.

He lowered his voice. "You know, I want to tell you it's a privilege for me to coach at this school and to coach these guys." He paused and let his eyes sweep the crowd. "And it's even more of a privilege for these guys to be coached by me."

Laughter and groans and the friendliest boos ever stretched the coach's face into the broadest of grins.

"Okay, okay," he smiled, holding up his hands again. "Let's see you all at the game tonight. With all of us working together, we ARE going to BEAT ST. ANDREWS!!" he finished, his fists shooting into the air, provoking the wildest applause yet.

As Greg left the stage, he spotted Ed Warrum slouched on the bleacher seats in the middle of the group of football players. The boy's face was expressionless as he stared down at his shoes. Greg shook his head. If Ed couldn't get his act together, Blue Lake was going to lose tonight by thirty points.

❖   ❖   ❖

It was like living in a nightmare. His. Red's. Ed and Pete Warrum's. Greg could have claimed the gift of prophecy.

It sure hadn't helped Red Howard's sour stomach when he found Pete Warrum standing on the sidelines as tonight's Blue Lake Booster Club's volunteer on the down box. Greg could see the dismay in his friend's strained face. Or maybe it was some sort of virus the coach had caught. Certainly he'd been involved in big games too many times in his thirty years to get this upset about one game or one person. And as much as Pete Warrum irritated him, Red Howard had swallowed a whole lot of bad apples over the years without getting food poisoning. So Greg decided it had to be a virus. What he didn't know was that the pain Red had been feeling for several days was now climbing towards his chest.

If Red and Greg were bothered by Warrum's presence on the sideline stripe, his son was blown away by it. Midway through the second quarter, Red turned to Greg and said, "I've got to pull Ed out of the game." There was no choice. The youngster was as tight as a bowstring. His hands were boards. He'd fumbled three snaps from center deep in Blue Lake's own territory, thrown an interception, and tossed a wild pitch into his own end zone, which St. Andrews had recovered for a touchdown. When he tossed three straight passes well beyond the racing reach of Billy Cloud and Cory Conners, Red made his decision.

Greg knew it was the last thing Coach Howard wanted to do. He'd watched his potential all-stater slide a little in each of the last five games. Fortunately, the opposition hadn't been that strong, so he'd been able to stick with his quarterback; he'd been able to wait for the young man to forget himself long enough to make the plays that had earned him a reputation as a brilliant college prospect over these last three years. To an extent that strategy had worked. But not tonight. The coach had to do something. Hollering at the kid wasn't the answer. Pete Warrum was proving that. Both Greg and Red knew that an arm around the shoulder and quiet encouragement held more potential.

The score was already 20-0. Blue Lake hadn't moved the ball at all. The usually boisterous fans in the stands had grown silent and restless. Greg was sure he'd heard a few scattered boos amidst the groans and isolated shouts as Ed overthrew yet another receiver or turned the wrong way for a hand off. He hated that. No high school kid should ever hear that. And for sure it would do Blue Lake's brooding star no good at all.

So Red called timeout following a St. Andrews punt and gathered the team around him on the sidelines. "Phil Darrin, we're going to start making use of your running skills. Fred Flanders, you're in at quarterback." He saw the sophomore's Adams apple bobbing like a cork in wavy water. The boy had heard the booing, too. "You'll do fine, Fred. We need a new strategy. Just run 45 and 37 dives." The substitute rubbed his hands on his thighs and nodded. "Easy, son. You've had playing time all season. You'll be just fine." Red clapped his hands. "Let's go, boys. We're not out of this."

Greg gathered the team around him and bellowed, "Let's get those daubers up. Let's go! Let's go!" His enthusiasm worked into the group. As it dispersed clapping and hollering, Red turned and looked for Ed Warrum. He found him huddled among the substitutes lining the bench as though hiding; his shoulder pads raised high, a warm-up jacket draped over his helmeted head.

"Call the plays, Greg," Red instructed his assistant. Then as Phil Darrin bolted over right guard for a first down, he made his way through the irregular line of substitutes who'd leapt off the bench at the sight of an actual gaining of yardage, and sat down by Ed Warrum, who remained slumped on the bench, his hands curled around the face guard of his helmet as though he wanted to twist it until his head unscrewed and fell off.

The coach waited until the cheers of the crowd told him Phil Darrin was making another decent gain. He eased the jacket off and slid his arm over the boy's shoulder, the bill of his cap touching the quarterback's helmet. He said into the boy's ear hole, "You're going back in real soon. For cripe's sake, forget about your old man and have some fun out there."

As Phil sprinted down the sidelines for another long gainer, Greg saw that the down box was prone on the grass just outside the chalk line. He whirled around, but, screened by the excited reserves, could not see Pete Warrum racing toward Red Howard nor the shove that drove Red's chin into Ed Warrum's shoulder pads. The coach nearly toppled backwards off the bench but grabbed Ed's jersey and caught himself. He jerked his head around. Pete Warrum's face jutted tight against it. The raging man's hands clutched the coach's jacket. "What the hell are you doing!?" Greg heard Pete scream. "Why the hell is my son out of the game!" The athletes on the sideline were frozen in place as Greg pushed through them.

He caught a glimpse of Red wrenching the man's hands from his jacket and shoving him back. "Get out of here," he rasped, the words tearing the breath out of his lungs. "Get out of here." The words boiled out of him before a spasm of coughing ended them.

Pete Warrum was about to lunge at Howard again when Greg bear-hugged the man and danced him away and the coach suddenly sank to his knees. Red Howard could barely breathe. His vision began to blur, but he saw, as in slow motion, Greg Schwarz dragging Pete Warrum backwards. He watched someone in a blue coat racing toward the two. He recognized the blanched face and unblinking eyes of Ed Warrum peering into his, the choked voice pleading repeatedly, "Coach! Coach! You okay? You okay? Coach!" He felt a giant fist inside his chest squeezing the breath out of him. He saw Greg Schwarz pushing players aside. He felt an oxygen mask clamp over his nose offering slight, but blessed, relief.

Then the world whirled into a kind of gray echo and became distant. Pain roared in his chest, but he could hear voices and silences until he slipped into unconsciousness as he was being carried to the ambulance, his cold hand clamped to Greg's.

Robert Baker

Robert Baker's first visit to a Blue Lake High School football game was disappointing, shocking, exhilarating, shocking and even a sliver hopeful.

Everyone in school had been talking about the St. Andrews game even if they weren't talking about it to him. You had to be deaf to miss the conversations it provoked before and after class and in the halls.

Robert had not gone to the three previous home games because he didn't need another opportunity to be rejected. But that awful October day had had its benefits. The following day, he'd welcomed the new freshman study hall to his room, and they looked as lost, scared, and needy as he sometimes felt. They actually studied in study hall and sometimes brought their neediness to him.

"Enough" had become his mantra in periods two through six, and he'd informed all his classes he had a curriculum they had to get through and if they didn't want to discuss, he was going to lecture and they were going to write. They hadn't liked that, and they hadn't liked it when he shouted down the noise levels and told them if they wanted to pass, they'd better get to work. Nor did the seventh period like it when the book exchange occurred, but all they did was turn their thermostats down to frigid. He'd taken control of his classes even if it wasn't the way he wanted to teach.

So he'd decided to attend the St. Andrews game. In the first place he loved the game of football. In the second, you'd have had to be a mummy not to get excited by Greg Schwarz's pepfest performance. The guy had a big mouth, but he sure knew how to move a crowd and he sure was popular. Quite ironically, it was Greg Schwarz who cinched Robert Baker's decision to go to the St. Andrews game.

Still wary, he timed it so that the game began before he arrived. Unfortunately someone spotted him buying a ticket at the ticket booth. Unfortunately, too, the section of the bleachers where most students sat was closest to the entrance. A group of boys in the top row turned toward him as he walked by and slowly drew their middle fingers under their noses.

That behavior was an unsurprising disappointment. What was surprising was the putrid play of the Blue Lake Lakers. They were awful and Ed Warrum was the worst. Robert had overheard the buzz about the boy's All-State ability. The only state that could be was the state of chaos. But when Coach Howard pulled the kid, the boos and shouts aimed at both quarterback and coach by the adults around him were shockingly cruel.

Those shouts suddenly diminished in the midst of a second fine run by the Blue Lake halfback. That's when Robert noticed the down box on the ground and then everyone on the Laker sideline pivoting away from the playing field toward the bench. Then he saw Coach Howard crumpled on the ground and Schwarz dragging a man away from the coach. The crowd grew utterly silent as medics rushed onto the field. After quickly checking vital signs, they carried the coach on a stretcher to the ambulance at the far end of the field, Schwarz by its side, his hand on the coach.

Then he walked back, head down, and the team huddled around him. One man near Robert hollered loudly, "It's the championship for cripe's sake! Let 'em play!" Too quickly, isolated shouts of "Let 'em play" evolved into a chant throughout the crowd.

They got their wish. And play they did!

The second half was exhilarating to witness. Ed Warrum had been jolted awake. The quarterback's passes were sailed in perfect spirals and were totally on target. Billy Cloud and the other wide receiver made catch after catch and the halfback continued his excellent running. The offensive and defensive lines turned into walls of stone. The entire crowd from both towns was on its feet the entire fourth quarter, Robert included. The Blue Lake fans went absolutely nuts when Warrum zipped the winning touchdown pass to the leaping Billy Cloud.

That should have been the memory Robert carried home, kids who loved their fallen coach playing their hearts out for him. That obvious fact was not so obvious to a number of the fans around him as the crowd funneled out the gate. One exuberant adult voice shouted, "Ol' Pete sure knows how to make a coaching change, don't he!" Another added, "Guess that's the only way they could get Howard to retire!" A third chimed in with, "Now we know Schwarz is the real coach of that team." There were plenty of shouts of agreement.

Robert couldn't believe what he was hearing. He was about to speak up when a younger voice not far away hollered, "Hey, maybe he can convince his son to go after Baker the same way," followed by cackled comments from those around him.

One comment stood out from the others for Robert, however. A higher pitched voice screamed above the tumult, "Shut up, Jeffrey! What's wrong with you? Get away from me or just shut up!"

Well, Robert thought as he walked home in the dark, that last response was something. It was really something. That girl deserves a medal.

ΠΟΥΕΠΒΕR

Billy Cloud

It was good to be on Moon Ribbon Ridge surrounded by the woods and watching incredibly large snowflakes drift from the sky into the silence. Silence. That's what Billy Cloud appreciated most about this place. Silence so profound that the creaking of the trees in the breeze was the major sound.

He adjusted the canvas bow and arrow pack slung across his back, then walked along the spine of the ridge for the first time since the steamy August day he'd discovered this place. It wasn't steamy today. This bike ride had been accompanied by the platter-sized snowflakes twirling into his face on a northeasterly breeze. There were moments in the ride when he laughed aloud at the insanity of his choice of transportation. Mostly, however, he was invigorated. By the time he reached the base of Moon Ribbon Hill, he felt fully alive.

As he strolled the ridge, his mind drifted back to that steamy day of discovery. The memory stretched a wide smile across his face.

It was shortly after he and his parents moved to Blue Lake. He'd mounted his bike that day to explore the terrain along the tarred county road that ran past his new home, the Cloud House Art Gallery.

He'd been lucky to notice the possibility of the path that led to this ridge. Its entrance was camouflaged by tall grass, twined brush and overarching trees. He later decided destiny, curiosity, and keen eyesight deserved equal credit for this discovery. Curiosity had compelled him to yank his bike through the tangled foliage. Within it he'd found the overgrown ruts of what must have been a logging road in the distant past. He'd pedaled his bike up the faintly discernible dirt path that remained until he arrived at the foot of a sharp rise. The lure of further discovery sent him scrabbling up it until he stood on what he later named Moon Ribbon Ridge. Luck and effort had enabled him to find his own private sanctuary. He'd seen no "No Trespassing" signs, spied no discarded cans or bags of trash along the path, and found no blackened fire rings or other evidence of recent use on the ridge.

Walking west along its spine, he saw the beginnings of the wooded terrain's slope toward prairie. Walking east, he noted with satisfaction the unbroken forest rising on waves of hills as far as he could see. He knew there was nothing but woods from here to the county road. That was also true to the north except for the meadow just below where he stood on the ridge.

He descended to the meadow, drawn by its verdant grass, the asters, primrose, black-eyed Susan, and columbine that populated it, and its meandering stream.

The ridge blunted the faint breeze, rendering the meadow as flower fragrant, humid, and still as a hothouse. Perspiration rained his body, and the stream became irresistible. Reaching it, he paused, looking and listening for other two-legged or four-legged interlopers. Hearing only bird songs and his own breathing, he doffed his clothes and slipped into the chest deep water to cool in its quiet current. Sufficiently relieved of the heat, he ascended the bank and stretched out in the tall green grass to dry.

He was more exhausted and at peace than he realized. He promptly fell asleep. Much later, he wrenched awake to escape an increasingly uncomfortable dream featuring himself seated in the middle seat in the middle row of a school classroom filling with unfamiliar faces. All eyes were focused intently on him since he was both new and nude.

Mosquitoes and horseflies also contributed to his wide-awake as they swarmed his unadorned form. He leapt to his feet, flailing at the horde, snatched his clothes and shoes and flashed up to the ridge where the early evening breeze diminished the siege of the twilight bugs.

He hurried into his clothes and was about to slide down the incline to retrieve his bike when he noticed the huge yellow half moon topping the treetops to the east. He was already late for supper, so he decided to remain on the ridge until the moon's light turned white. A line from the poem "The Highwayman" danced into his head, and he named the rise Moon Ribbon Ridge.

An hour later he strolled into the kitchen of the Cloud House and immediately asked, "You and Dad wanna go for a ride? I've gotta show you Moon Ribbon Ridge."

His mother glanced up from the book she was reading in the breakfast nook. "That's a good start, Billy, very poetic, but you've missed the best meal I've ever cooked unless you come up with a truly wonderful story about where you've been."

Apparently he'd met the challenge. The beef roast dinner was as tasty as its cook claimed. When he was done eating, the family hopped into their car to check out Billy's claim, parking at a turnout down the road from the entrance at Billy's insistence.

Soon they were wandering the moon-washed ridge, only night birds and the breeze rippling the silence. Finally, his father put his arm around Billy's shoulder. "It's no wonder you had a hard time leaving. This is a worthy place. Perhaps we should reclaim it for our people. It feels as sacred as anywhere I've been. It would have been an excellent place for a vision quest when this was still Indian land. Which it is again for the moment," he added with a tight smile.

His father then sat down on the ridge, Billy next to him. His mother stood behind his father, gently kneading his shoulders. "Sometimes I wish I'd lived in a time before land became a reason for war," his father said.

"Before night became a thing to fear. It would have been a pure way to live. On the other hand, we're fortunate to be living in a time when the history and culture of our peoples have finally begun to matter to those who recognize the importance of who and what we were and are. What breaks my heart are all those years in between and the suffering endured. Think of the perseverance it took to keep the cultures breathing and hearts beating when it could have all died." He'd bowed his head a little. "When someone gains, someone else loses. I don't know why it has to be that way. But treasure this place while you can."

❖   ❖   ❖

Billy had seated himself on the edge of the ridge in the midst of his remembering. The wind and accumulating snow were beginning to chill him. "Anishinaabe snowman," he muttered, pushing to his feet and brushing the snow from his orange hunting jacket. It was a good day and a good place for remembering, but shelter would make that activity more comfortable. He moved toward the small grove of pine trees clinging to the western slope and inserted himself within its canopy of branches. He slid his back against the trunk of the largest, scanned the immediate area for animal life, and let his mind drift again.

In two weeks the regular deer hunting season opened. He would participate. That kind of hunting had its own scents and textures—the feel of the smooth wood stock of a rifle, the cool gleam of the barrel, the gunpowder odor of the fired weapon. But he preferred the more solitary art of bow hunting. It seemed fairer.

He let his mind continue to drift where it wanted. Eventually it settled on the football games.

❖   ❖   ❖

He couldn't remember many facts of the last half of the St. Andrews game. He could remember the emotions of it, though. The shock of the stretcher bearing Coach Howard disappearing into the maw of the ambulance; the stark silence in the stadium as the ambulance left the field, its red lights pulsing. The immense sadness flowing from Coach Schwarz as he gathered the team in the end zone, pointing toward the disappearing lights and saying softly, "We can call this game, or we can play the rest of it. There's no wrong answer. It's your choice. Either way, I'll understand." Then he shoved his hands deep in his pockets, dropped his head, and left the huddled team in the corner of the end zone.

"We're going to play, we're going to win," Ed Warrum stated, tears streaming his agonized face.

That was how Billy remembered the game—a river of tears, a roaring current of emotions. Bodies flying all over the football field. St. Andrews overwhelmed. Ed's passes stunningly accurate. Phil Darrin trying to ignite the team before the clash, unstoppable after it. Himself levitating high above the defender to snatch Ed's last pass with his outstretched hands; the final score of 28-21. The team refusing to celebrate.

The following Friday they'd traveled halfway to the Cities to play Echowood, an outer suburban school, in the state semifinals. Coach Howard's absence gave the event an unnatural feel. The quiet and caring head coach wasn't there walking among the boys and engaging them in small talk that generally had little to do with the upcoming game. If he'd been there, he'd have encouraged the boys to "give their best," because that's all he ever asked and that's all that truly mattered.

He remembered sitting next to Ed Warrum just before Schwarz called the team together. The quarterback's demeanor was wired with intensity. Ed turned toward him, his face fixed and fierce. "This one's for Coach, too. That's the only thing I'm thinking. This one's for Coach Howard."

Schwarz delivered the same message Coach would have in the same tone, but you could see by the shine in the big guy's eye he really wanted to win this one for Coach Howard. That may have been the only game where winning mattered as much to Billy as the pure pleasure of competition.

But winning hadn't happened. Echowood had its own adrenaline, superior size and a considerably shorter bus ride. It had been a beautiful game to be a part of though, and a brilliant game for Ed Warrum. His passes were crisp and zipped into the numbers nearly every time. Billy would never forget the seventy-two yard touchdown he and the quarterback engineered. He'd flared to the right and then shot straight down the field. Ed's spiral dropped into his outstretched hands as soft as a down pillow. Billy caught it in full stride, sailed over the outstretched body of the only defender and sprinted to the end zone. That had been pure pleasure, and it had broken a seven-seven tie at the time. The two had hooked up seven more times during the contest. But by the middle of the fourth quarter, the Lakers were physically and emotionally exhausted, and Echowood pummeled its way to a game-winning field goal with seconds on the clock. 24-21.

Billy blinked the current scene back into his vision. The sun had broken through and was filtering light through the evergreen branches. Broad blue patches dotted the western sky.

Patty Light would love this, he thought, even though he'd yet to talk to her face to face. His certainty came from observing her and listening to her in Mr. Baker's class. There was ample opportunity for that pleasure. The third period English class raised friendly noise with one another from the time they entered the room until the day's lesson began. Then the friendliness slumped to silence. Inevitably, Patty Light owned the hand that danced the air when discussion was desired. A few others eventually joined her. He was one of those.

He heard crackling in trees below and caught the velvet glimpse of two sleek brown deer tiptoeing into the meadow. They froze for a moment, their noses and ears trained in his direction. "Go in peace, my brothers," he called to them. "Find Patty Light and tell her about the handsome Indian you saw sitting on the ridge today." Their long ears flicked forward as if to capture his words before they bounded away into the woods.

Billy laughed and settled back against the stump. Laughter felt good. Being a little crazy felt good. The climbing wind felt good. Thinking of Patty Light felt good.

The leafless birch and oak and maple trees below him creaked and groaned in the rising westerly. He listened to the waterfall wash of it through the pine boughs. His heart was full. He sat in silence, stilled his mind and came as close to becoming the day as he could.

Sam Strand

"Greg Schwarz did a terrific job with those boys, don't you agree, Sam?" Superintendent Alan Anderson said, leaning back in his leather office chair, his fingertips thrumming its arms.

"Well, sure, Alan," Sam answered seated in the middle of the three padded armchairs that faced the administrator's desk. "But you have to recognize that Red's heart attack – that whole scene – Greg would be the first to tell you that the emotions generated by that lifted the team right off the ground."

"Agreed. But it takes a first-rate coach to focus that emotion. You have to give Greg credit." The superintendent pursed his lips. He was a youthful looking man of forty-six. The brown hair waved and sprayed across his forehead was a nice touch. He was personable with teachers and outgoing with the public.

But Sam couldn't bring himself to like the man. He thought him to be single-mindedly ambitious and willing to sacrifice others for his own advancement. Sam realized his judgment was overflowing with bias, given his own situation, but he didn't care. He just didn't like this guy.

"That really was quite the comeback against St. Andrew, wasn't it," Anderson said. "Twenty-one to zip. Twenty-eight to twenty-one. Warrum, Darrin, and that Cloud kid were brilliant."

"Yes," Sam answered, "very exciting." There's something coming up soon I'm not going to like, Sam surmised.

"That was an ugly scene when Pete Warrum charged Howard."

"Yes, it was. Trouble is, even if we'd had all the security in the world working, it wouldn't have stopped Pete since the Booster Club let him roam the sidelines. Not model behavior for a school board chairman."

"True. Sam, I'm genuinely sorry about Red's heart attack," Anderson continued. "I'm glad that it turned out to be fairly moderate."

"So am I. But is there a point to you calling me in on a Saturday for this conversation? Seems like we could have held it in the halls anytime over the past two weeks."

The younger administrator dropped his left hand on his desk and leaned forward. "There's a body of opinion in this town — which I neither like, nor agree with — that believes if it had to happen, it was a good thing for our football team that it happened at the time it did."

"You mean because it fired them up?"

"Well, that. But beyond that, I'm sorry to say, there's a strong belief that Red Howard was not the real coach of that team. Greg Schwarz was. I've had calls and conversations suggesting the team was better off with Greg running it. Quite a few, especially members of the Booster Club, told me they thought Schwarz should take over for good."

"That's crazy!" Sam exploded.

"They don't think it is. Howard pulled Ed Warrum out of the game. Schwarz put him back in. We won. That's their reasoning."

"Red was talking to the boy!" Sam could barely believe what he was hearing.

"The way the Booster Club likes to tell it, Red was chewing out the kid cap to helmet. That, they say, is why Pete Warrum went after the coach."

"And you believe that!" Sam snorted. He was ready to leap to his feet and exit this charade.

"Not for a minute. In my conversations with Red and from attending the games, I think the thought is absurd. But I'll tell you the Club has its ducks lined up, and they're quacking in unison."

"You expressed your opinion?"

"I did. But it doesn't matter what I say at this point. There are a significant number of people in town who've chosen to believe the B.C. They cite Red's health problems or his age, and they use those factors as two more reasons for Red to step aside."

Sam rose and paced to the window overlooking the school's brown front lawn and sighed. "I think you still haven't made your point," he said. He needed to be at the window. The room felt claustrophobic.

"This is the point, which I don't expect you to like. I'm not too crazy about it myself. Given the state of Red's health and what I've just told you, it's probable that his ability to coach effectively would be impaired. So I've recommended to him that he consider stepping aside and that he recommend Schwarz be named to replace him. Red is old enough to retire from teaching, much less coaching. I know the teachers here have excellent retirement benefits."

Sam pivoted from the window. "You said those things to Red? Right after he got out of the hospital?" He threw his arms in the air. "Are you nuts?"

"Listen, Sam, I don't mind your disagreement . . ."

"Of course you do," Sam interrupted.

"Probably," the superintendent acknowledged. The one positive Sam could give Anderson right now is that he knew how to maintain his cool. "But maybe you'll agree that it's likely Howard won't want to coach again anyway. If that's the case, we'll need a head coach. After the playoff game, I received numerous calls from suburban schools inquiring into Schwarz' availability. And not as an assistant. I need to start filling teaching lines and coaching positions in January. If I don't secure Schwarz, he may go for those greener pastures. They pay much better than we do, you know. And there's one more factor that you also won't like to hear. The college athletic director called me. With another manufacturing plant opening next summer, he believes our school having a young, dynamic coach like Greg will encourage parents of good athletes to locate in this town, and that will also benefit them."

Sam wished he was amazed. Instead he felt rumpled and old. Something had been happening to this town and to the teaching profession for a number of years, an erosion so subtle that you didn't know the ground was disappearing until you looked up and found yourself in a chasm. "Did you tell Red all of this?" he asked.

"Only some of it. I'm not a total ass."

"That's debatable. When did you call him?"

"I called him Friday afternoon."

"At his house. While he's recuperating." Sam slumped into the chair he'd previously occupied.

"I thought it would be better to hear it from me than some other way. Listen, Sam, I'm trying to be fair. I offered him the chance to step down on his own terms. He's thinking it over."

"You're a great man, Alan. Let me get this straight. You're pushing Red Howard to quit coaching because a few influential people think you should. But you're also encouraging Red to retire to save the district bucks."

"That's sounds more cynical than I like to think I am. But I admit money matters. The state wouldn't have written the retirement laws the way it did if money was no factor. They sure weren't just being nice to teachers. I didn't need to talk to you, but did, Sam. Board members have come to me. The majority agrees with the Booster Club. They've even prepared a statement honoring Red's service and his wonderful career."

"The majority is the Booster Club. This whole thing makes me sick," Sam groaned. "Not only does this undermine the man, it dishonors him."

The superintendent put up his hands. "The proposal to accept Red's resignation as coach and name Schwarz as his replacement has been written. If Red ascents, it will be presented at the school board meeting this month. If not, it will be presented in revised form at another meeting. That train is roaring down the tracks, and I don't think I can stop it. So I'd prefer a united front. But you're free to say anything you want to the board."

"Do you suppose they'll like me disagreeing with them," Sam retorted. He rose from his chair. "Listen, Alan." He slapped his hands down on the desk. "I talk to Red Howard two, three times a week. He was thinking of quitting. He would have, I think. You didn't need to do anything with Red Howard. You did. In the long run, you'll suffer for doing things like this. You're bright enough and you're charming, but you're kissing too many butts. In the end that's going to make you stink. If that's how you administrate, you'll end up being seen as mouth unaccompanied by a working brain. The board will dump you when you're no longer useful to them, and I won't be sorry."

The superintendent pushed himself out of his chair. "That sounds like a threat."

"No threat," Sam said. "Fact." He turned to leave.

Anderson moved around his desk. "Wait. Listen, Sam, we have to work together for the rest of this year . . . "

"There you have it folks," Sam muttered to no one. He opened the door, then turned. Alan Anderson stood in front of his desk, his hands shoved loosely into his pockets. Sam felt sad. "You know, Alan, part of the problem with this whole thing is that it feels like a rehearsal for another meeting you and I will have later this year. These agreements and understandings are hell, aren't they."

"Yes, they are," the superintendent said. Sam nodded and left the room.

Alan Anderson remained seated on the edge of his desk. Then he walked to the window. Looking down, he watched Sam's lanky frame emerge on the front steps. He watched him descend the steps and walk down the sidewalk, his tan trench coat flapping in the breeze.

Anderson returned to his chair and sat there for a long time, his fingers drumming its leather arms.

Patty Light

It was in November that Patty Light began to inhabit Robert Baker's classroom daily after school. She'd gone to Mr. Barnes, her counselor, and requested that she become Mr. Baker's student assistant. Barnes pointed out that she had no free periods. Patty told him she was willing to do the work after school and that the experience would look good on her college applications. Barnes raised his right eyebrow and studied the girl's clear eyes and guileless face and agreed to her request. There was little doubt that Baker like any teacher, especially a first year teacher, could use the help.

Patty was attracted to Robert Baker's intellectual depth and sensitivity. She was also attracted by his underdog status with the students. She was convinced that the man needed someone to help him and hungered for someone to talk to who cared about what he was trying to do. And she needed to work for and talk to someone who was observant and caring and shared her love of the power of words and the beauty of nature.

She'd watched Robert Baker struggle through the chronological approach to American Literature for two months and watched her classmates react with negativity, boredom and unwillingness to attempt to comprehend Edwards, Franklin, Emerson, Thoreau, Hawthorne, Longfellow... She'd felt a thrill of recognition when she read and reread Emerson's "Self Reliance." Thoreau's writing validated her solitary journeys to her favored pine grove. Whittier's "Snowbound" made her cry when the class read it aloud. Even the flatness of the students' readings didn't dissipate the sense of family so pervasive in the poem, so lacking in her life. She'd cried in her quiet room the night before when she'd read it and almost cried in class the next day. Robert Baker had recognized the emotion on her face and after class asked her if she wanted to stop by to talk when she had time. When she had time was now, officially, every day.

When she stepped into his room, he'd stopped correcting papers and was staring out the window watching the November day gray to twilight.

"Mr. Baker?" she said as she hesitated by the door.

"Come on in, Patty," he said, swiveling himself in her direction and indicating a student desk near his with his hand. She sat down, and he looked at her across the expanse of his cluttered metal teacher's desk, his eyes a little sad. "I was just wondering why you were so emotional in class, and if there's anything I can do to help?"

She answered, "It was the poem. I loved the poem. I guess I get a little too emotional."

Then she became lost in the sadness in the teacher's eyes and interpreted his willingness not to hide it as an unspoken compliment to her. As she surfaced from her reverie, Mr. Baker was saying, " . . . a pleasure to have someone in class who responds to poetry and ideas."

"Who's that?" Patty asked in embarrassment.

"You, of course," Baker smiled. It was good to see him smile. He seldom did.

"Oh . . . me? Oh my!" she exclaimed and that struck both as quaint and funny and they laughed. He seemed to laugh easily. That this was the first time she'd heard him do so sent a rush of warmth through her.

When the laughter subsided, Robert Baker explained, "What I said was I'm really grateful for you, and a few others, of course. I'm glad you're in my class." The man's face was faintly red. "I don't know what I'd do without people like you." He rustled the papers in front of him. "Why did that poem move you so much?" he asked. "Do you want to talk about it?"

Patty decided to hazard a mostly honest response. "It was the feeling of family. I don't have brothers or sisters." She did not add 'living with me.' Instead she said, "My family isn't close, but whose is?"

"Not many, I suppose. My family was pretty close. I'm embarrassed to admit this is as far from them as I've ever been. At least for this length of time." He reddened a bit more. It made him look young. He smiled. "The first day of class all I could think was 'I want my mommy.'"

The self-deprecation worked. He flashed a wry smile with only a hint of hurt. This second smile sent another wash of warmth through his listener.

"I like 'Thanatopsis', too," she said. "It's so peaceful. If death is like that, it must be wonderful to die."

Robert's alarm at the statement sent the smile fleeing from his face. "It can be wonderful to be alive, too, Patty," he said. He shuffled through the papers on his desk. "Speaking of . . . here's your essay on the poem. It thrilled me to find this much depth in a student essay. It's overflowing with feelings and thoughts, Patty. I don't see a tenth of that in most of these things." He swept of his hand over the essays, then locked his hands behind his head and looked out the window.

"You don't like it here much, do you?"

"Not very often. Not so far," Robert admitted. "But I'm going to give it my best shot. By the way," he said looking back at her, "I never did thank you for stopping after class when we had that . . . trouble. I needed that."

"That's okay," she smiled. For a moment their eyes locked, then he dipped his a little, bouncing his gaze off the papers in front of him.

"Going to leave pretty soon, Mister Baker?" The drawling voice startled them. Robert whipped his head toward the door. "Gotta clean up. Don't want to rush you though."

Patty glanced at the clock above the blackboard. "Five thirty!" she said. "Goodness, I didn't know it was that late! I'm sorry."

The custodian grinned. "Isn't a problem for me, Miss. Just wondering when the room might be empty." His face wrinkled into a smile.

"I'm glad you did. My mother will be worrying if I don't get home soon." She rose and gathered her books in her arms. "Thanks, Mr. Baker, for talking to me." She started toward the door. "Oh," she said, stopping and putting her books on a student desk and extracting the white sheet sticking out of her literature book. "I forgot to give you this, Mr. Baker." She hurried to his desk, the form giving permission for her to be his student aid extended toward him. She waited while he eyed the form, then fought the smile that threatened to break across his face. "If it's all right with you," she said.

"It certainly is," Robert said. "Thank you, Patty."

"Thank you," she said and waited. "You need to sign that."

"Oh. Oh, yeah. Sure. Where? Here? I should have known that. Guess I'm the new kid in town." He signed the form and handed it to her. She thanked him and inserted it in her book. The custodian stepped inside the room, pulling his broom toward him as she breezed by.

"Pretty thing, isn't she," she heard the janitor say as she hurried down the empty hall.

She was immensely glad for this day. She pushed open the heavy steel outside door and entered the brisk November post-twilight. Her feet danced down the broad cement steps. She liked Mr. Baker, she loved poetry, and her new duty would give her a reason to delay going home. She felt good for a change at 5:30 p.m. Usually by this time she'd discovered whether her mother was raging or mute, a tornado or a lump. Today that wasn't the case. She'd hold the feeling as long as she could. Who knows? Maybe not even the acid drool of the house could eat it all away. Who knows? Maybe when she got home, her mother would be happy too.

Kyle Hunter

Kyle Hunter snatched the letter opener and slashed open the envelope. He withdrew the neatly folded, scented letter and began reading it with apprehension.

Dear Kyle,

I know I should have called, and I know how frustrated you will be by the time you read these words. But I also knew if I called, we'd argue, and I knew there wasn't any use arguing since the decision has been made, and I can't change it unless I want to lose my job. And I don't. (At least I don't think so. At least not right now.)

Really, the news I have for you is kind of awful in a way, and I'm putting it off. You know, like when I stick my toe in the water to see how cold it is and then slowly get my whole foot wet (like fifteen minutes later). And by the time I've inched my way into the deeper water, everyone else has toweled off and is ready to leave.

Well, eventually I do end up getting wet and wondering why I made such torture out of it. Why couldn't I plunge in like you do?

I'll bet you're getting irritated at me. So I'd better plunge in.

Kyle, they like me. They like the work I do. They said my buying record is one of the best they've ever seen from a new hire. They say I've laid such a solid foundation that with just a little bit of intense "on the job training" I can be spectacular! (Their word, not mine!)

Oh, this is so hard, Kyle. Plunge, Gail, plunge! Kyle, since I am already in the Cities for the three-day buyers' seminar and the Sunday through Tuesday convention presentation, they . . . they . . . (oh!!!!!!) All right. I'm just going to write it. Right now. They want me to stay through the remainder of the week and work with Sally Lass as she makes her rounds of the stores in this area. Especially since the day after Thanksgiving is such an important day in our business. They'll pay my room and board and my mileage. Everything! Kyle, I know that takes me right through Thanksgiving weekend. But what can I do? I either work with Sally Lass or risk losing what I've gained. That's what they say would probably happen. (See, I did discuss it with them.) They said success on this job takes commitment and sometimes even sacrifice, and either I have it or I don't. I asked if you could come down so we could spend Thanksgiving together. But they said we'd be meeting most of that day to work on Christmas and Spring (!) advertising and promotion and would be celebrating a corporate Thanksgiving lunch before "hitting the sack early" so we could be "up and roaring" early Friday morning.

Ohhhhh, I feel so awful. I feel sick to my stomach that I am writing these words and that I am going to do it exactly the way they say I must. I feel sick and selfish for being willing to set you aside. It just breaks my heart. But I have to do this. For me. And it will only be once. I promise. They promised. Just this one time.

Now the good news (if you haven't crumpled this letter and thrown it into the trash). They want to meet you. By Saturday night we'll be done and there will be a big dinner—a late Thanksgiving—for us and for our spouses, boyfriends, or girlfriends who have "put up with the inconvenience." A Thanksgiving for "their understanding and support."

Please come down to the Cities for the dinner, Kyle. Please. I know how angry and hurt you must feel right now. But this is important to me, and it's important to me that you support me. And it is one time only.

Please call me as soon as you've read this (and calmed down), so that I can tell them you'll be here so they can complete the reservations.

And read this! You might be too mad to believe this right now, but I love you!!! Now. Please call 1-838-666-1234. Please call right away.

I love you!
Hugs and kisses,
Gail

He crumpled the letter like a sophomore boy might have. Then he laid it on the coffee table and smoothed it as best he could. He folded it over the crumples and shoved it back into the envelope. He picked that up between his thumb and forefinger and sailed it across the room. It thwacked against the wall and fell to the floor. He glared at the fallen missive, waiting for the churning to subside. Then he crossed the room, picked up the battered envelope, extracted the crumpled letter, smoothed it again, snatched up the phone, dialed the number Gail had written, and waited for an answer.

There was an echo in the long distance transmission, so he literally heard his disembodied voice say, "Sure, Gail, I'll be there. What time is good for you?"

Frank Marin

It was the rarest of November days. The morning dawned blue, bright, and warm. Frank re-awoke to the Tuesday sun at ten that morning. He'd decided not to go to school the night before in the middle of a buzz. The hard part was faking like he was going to go in the morning. That ruse required him to get at least half-dressed so he could join his parents at breakfast before they both set off for work. He shook out about a fourth of a bowl of corn flakes because he wasn't hungry. He was in the bathroom "getting ready" when they left. He set his clock for ten because he knew from previous experience that when the school found his name among the missing, they always called shortly after ten. He'd answer the phone and scruff up his voice so he sounded older. He'd inform the caller that Frank suffered from asthma and was having a bad day. He'd figured out that the school was pretty overwhelmed with busyness so they wouldn't follow up because he kept forging notes by signing his father's name. They had few clues as to what his father sounded like or wrote like so there was no worry. Heck, they didn't know what Frank sounded like. He hardly talked when he was straight.

This decision had become more easy for him over the past month. Part of that had to do with his new friends from college. He'd been walking downtown one afternoon and these guys had walked by him. This one guy had said, "Hey, Elvis. C'mere!" The kid was crew cut and muscular. Frank had felt the familiar flash of fear that leapt through him whenever someone he didn't know noticed him. The two guys stopped him. "Elvis," the slender one with the sunglasses said, "got a joint?"

"Sure," he's answered, "I got some stuff. Not great, good enough."

Good enough for sure. They got into the muscular kid's rattletrap Ford convertible and drove somewhere and got wasted. The two had laughed and told him what a great guy he was. He'd liked hearing that. He'd told them his name and number, so they knew where to call when party time came a few days later.

Darned if he didn't fit right in. No problem. He looked older than he was. He had a little money because of a small inheritance from his grandmother, never spending any of it except for drugs or booze. He never had to talk much unless he was half blitzed, and then no one gave a crap what he said. Everyone laughed real easy at those parties, so sometimes he'd trot out a joke or say something that seemed clever. Everyone laughed and laughed, and he felt funny and good.

He jerked upright when the phone rang. "Cripes, it's Pa," he muttered. But the clock said 10:20, and Pa never called until the noon break at the plant. His mother worked there, too, but she never called. Scared of him, he figured. He felt bad about the way he sometimes snapped at her and shut her off, but her questions lit lights in his head. Like she knew the answers but wanted him to say them. Now she just looked at him with those sad gray eyes and clipped her mouth shut.

"The phone, the phone," he told himself. "Get the phone." He rolled out of bed and trundled down the hall. He didn't feel too good. He snatched the phone off the hook just before its noise burrowed straight through his skull.

"Hey, figured you'd be home on this beautiful summer day." It was Brian. "Got your butt out of bed, right?"

"Yeah. Kinda sick."

"Got a cure for you, my man. Me and Brick are lookin' out the dorm window and we cannot believe our eyes. I push open the windows, and I feel that warm sun lickin' all over me like a beautiful woman."

"Already juicin' huh," Frank stated.

"You know it, my man. And I feel so good I'm gonna throw me a party out in the forest. And you, my fortunate friend, are invited."

Party. That would take care of the headache and the cramp in his stomach. He'd relax real quick.

"When?" he asked, feeling eager. But his voice sounded flat in his ears. Brian's too. "Hey, man, don't you wanna go?"

"Sure do!" Frank answered, pushing as much excitement into his voice as he could.

"Oh, yeah, I forgot. Got Sleeping Beauty out of bed," Brian said. "Anyway, since you didn't ask, party starts at high noon." He paused. "Got some stash, right?"

"Sure, always," Frank muttered into the mouthpiece. Why'd they have to ask that? Every time! He always had it. And he'd keep having it as long as the inheritance and the money from last summer's farm work held out. As long as his parents kept giving him guilt money to repay him for the fact they were working stiffs and not around their son as much as they should be.

"Good," Brian concluded. "That's more like it. Want us to pick you up?"

"Sure."

"Bring a few bucks for the keg and bottle fund."

"Sure." He had a few bucks.

"And the stash. You're sure you don't wanna go to school instead?"

"Pretty sure. Pretty darn sure."

"Be there in twenty."

"Good." Frank hung up the phone and hustled into the bathroom. He hurriedly showered and dressed. Despite the blue day he snatched his jacket out of the closet when he saw Brick's Ford pull into the driveway.

It was lucky he did. The day blew away at about 4:30 that afternoon.

The party had begun with the usual fifteen and, as usual, mushroomed to well over fifty as the hours passed. Frank was happiest with the fifteen. He got lost in crowds.

There was an urgency in him today. He wanted to get blown so far away that he wouldn't find himself for days. And when he did, he wanted to land on the farm listening to Corgan talk. So he wanted to combine vodka with his marijuana. He sought out Shannon, who always brought a case of booze with him and sold it at parties, and paid him ten bucks for a pint of vodka. He mixed it with soda and juice and just roared. The rush was exquisite.

Someone had brought a ghetto blaster and had it cranked. He danced with a girl named Betts. He felt loose, and he knew he looked good even with the bottle tucked into the inside pocket of his jacket so no one could steal it. He and Betts danced to a slow one real close, and he was a rock. She felt the bottle inside his jacket. "I could use some of that," she cooed into his ear, her hips against his jeans. "I want us to have a good time."

As far as Frank could tell, she was beautiful. They strolled off from the rest and slid down against a tree. She pulled his bottle from his jacket and the vodka from the bottle. They shared a joint. "I get passionate when I'm loaded," she promised, her blue eyes wide as an empty street.

"Me, too," Frank growled and handed her the bottle again. She took a long drink. "I'm on fire!" she squealed. "Feel how warm my tummy is," she suggested. He did and took a long drink from the bottle himself. "Let me lick it off your lips,' she purred.

"Yeah," he grunted.

They lay on the ground then, occasionally returning to the bottle. Frank was vaguely aware of the roar of the party and vaguely aware of the wind roaring in the treetops. He wasn't aware that it was getting colder. His body was too full of steam.

She fell asleep locked in his embrace. She felt good, her face red and warm against his cheek. He held her tight as he could, tilting his head once to drain the bottle. Then he snuggled against her and fell asleep.

Something wet hitting his face awoke him. At first he thought it was Bett's lips, but it was cold. He lay there for a moment, his head huge as a watermelon. Finally he rolled over and pushed up to his hands and knees.

Betts was gone and the ground around him was white, the only seeable thing in the blackness that had descended. He remained in that position until he was sure he wouldn't heave, then forced himself to his haunches, his hands on his thighs. He sat like that letting the world whirl around him. He felt sick. He clenched his teeth and sat there.

Eventually his teeth came unclenched and chattered like Corgan's false teeth. It was really cold. His legs were soaked with cold. He reached for the tree and hugged the trunk, slowly pulling himself up. His head whirled, and he leaned it against the rough bark until he felt better.

Finally he pushed away from the tree and stared into the dark. He didn't know where he was. Then he saw the red glow in the distance. "Fire," he mumbled. "Party." Oh, yeah. Better join the party. He shoved his numb hands into his jacket pockets and stumbled through the underbrush, waves of nausea washing behind his teeth. He kept walking and kept his eyes open even though snow was pelting his face. He fell once, breaking the fall with his shoulder because his hands wouldn't leave his jacket pockets. For a moment he couldn't bear the thought of getting up. Then he thought, I'll die here if I don't get up. His hands still wouldn't release their grip on his pockets, so he rolled over on his back. Then he lifted his legs and dropped them rapidly, pulling himself into a sitting position. Then he curled his legs under him and got to his knees. Finally he stood up. He turned in a circle until the red glow settled into his sight.

When he reached the low fire, he saw the body next to it, motionless. He nudged it with his foot. The guy was covered with a frosting of snow. He nudged him again. "Hey, man, wake up." There was no one else here, he noticed with a jolt. He nudged the body again. There was no reaction. Then he slid his foot under the guy, tightened his leg and flopped the body over. He could see blood trailing from the guy's mouth and nose.

"God, he's dead!" Frank groaned. "The guy's dead!" he repeated in a voice so tight and high he hardly recognized it as his own. "They'll think I killed him!" He wheeled and ran a few yards, then skidded to a halt in the wet snow. From the haze in his head emerged a single path of clear thinking. He returned to the fire and looked for the relatively wide trail that he, Brick, and Brian had followed in the afternoon. It was easy to spot because it was whiter than the tree-covered area that lined it. He walked with deliberate steps from the fire to the trail.

He had gone perhaps fifty feet when four figures loomed just a little further up the trail. Oh god, they'll think I killed him. He wanted to run, but could not move, fear rooting him to the spot.

The four approached him and stopped when they reached him. He didn't recognize the face that pushed into his. "Hey, anyone still back there..."

"Uh . . . " Frank couldn't talk. His grunt sounded like a mouse's squeak.

"Anyone still there?" the voice shouted. "Len is missing."

"Uh . . . yeah," Frank managed. He thought as fast as his brain would let him. "Yeah. Guy's back there. Hurt bad. I just woke up and found him."

Three of the figures scurried past him toward the fire embers. "Where were you going?" the face accused.

"Uh . . . for help. My . . . uh . . . hands are frozen. I . . . uh . . . tried to pick him up, but my hands are frozen." Frank wasn't sure he was lying. His hands felt like clubs. They'd think he killed that guy.

They didn't though. Frank and the face returned to the fire. The other three had lifted the body to its feet. Two were holding it, while a third forced the fellow's mouth open and poured something from a bottle into it. The body coughed violently. Thank God.

After a time the guy — Len — revived enough for the others to drag him down the trail. At the end of it a van waited with its motor running. Frank crawled in with the rest. The old vehicle rattled down the road.

"Freeze it off out there?" the face inquired amiably.

"Not quite," Frank replied. "What happened to Len?"

"Remember the fight, man?"

"Sorta," Frank lied. "I was pretty wasted," he continued giving his answer a fifty-fifty split.

"Betts was playin' up to Len, there, big time," the face said, nodding at the sleeping body, "and old Bennie got ticked. Remember? Say, wasn't she pullin' on yours, too? Seems to me I saw you and her go somewhere."

"Naw, not me," Frank lied in case these guys were Bennie's friends. Or Bett's. Or Len's.

"Anyway, that was one helluva fight, wasn't it? Half the guys there fightin' and they didn't even know why," the face remembered. "You get cold-cocked? Don't see no bruises. 'Course it's a little dark in here."

"Frank started to tell the truth. "I got real wasted and crazy so I . . ."

"Ran when the rest did when they thought they heard a cop siren," the other finished.

"Yeah. I hid behind some trees and darned if I didn't fall asleep."

"Eyup. Hey, some of us are goin' over to Betts'. Keep it goin'."

"Betts?" Frank said surprised.

"Eyup. Man, she told old Bennie to go soak in the lake. What a jerk that guy is! So we're celebrating. Her folks are in Florida. Wanna come?"

"Sure," Frank agreed. He felt greatly relieved. Life was pretty funny. Here he thought he was either gonna die in the woods, freeze to death, or get killed by the body's buddies, and now he's going to a party. What a life! What a great bunch of guys! How lucky can you get!

The party stormed and ebbed like the weather outside throughout the night and the next day and into the evening. Frank had no idea where he was except somewhere out in the country. But he shared his stash, and Betts warmed up to him again and drank her father's vodka with him.

Turned out that she wasn't a high school chick like he thought, but a freshman at Blue Lake State. Shoulda been a sophomore, but her parents had sent her away to Brown. She'd managed to party enough to fail all her classes and get her butt kicked out of there. So she was back home, and her parents weren't right now. So here he was, Frank Marin, Blue Lake High School's Invisible Man, running his hands all over a college girl.

Eventually he had to take a ride home with Brian on Wednesday night just past midnight. Betts' folks were scheduled to be home Thanksgiving afternoon. So those still there straightened up the place and left.

Brian dropped Frank a block from his house at his request. "Great party, huh!" he said as Frank got out.

"Yeah. Great," Frank agreed, but his voice had gone flat again, and Brian eyed him quizzically. "I mean it. I'm just tired, man."

He stood on the sidewalk and watched the car burrow into the darkness. He shuffled through the snow toward his house. He hadn't been home since Tuesday morning, but he'd called Wednesday afternoon from Bett's bedroom where it was quiet and said he'd gone grouse hunting with Brian and Brick, and the car had broken down at Pete's place in the country. The storm had knocked out the phones or he would have called on Tuesday or

Wednesday morning. "Good story!" Betts had exclaimed after the call.

That woman had the reddest lips and the whitest teeth!

Anyway, there'd be no problem at home.

The only problem he did have was that as soon as he'd shut the door of Brian's Ford, loneliness descended on him.

When he entered his house, the only sound he heard was his own breathing. He took off his shoes and padded down the hall to his room. He shut the door carefully, then walked to the backyard window and opened it to let the air lessen the odors of smoke and drink on his clothes.

Then he pulled the can of Pine Scent out of his closet and misted the room with its fragrance. The only trouble was he felt empty, sad and small. I need another, he thought, but instead collapsed on his bed and fell asleep.

Kyle Hunter

The storm began on Tuesday and lasted through Wednesday night. The roads were still open though travel wasn't recommended. Kyle hadn't planned to go to the Cities until Saturday morning anyway. There was no point in going earlier. Gail would be busy, and when she wasn't busy, she'd be tired.

School was cancelled on Wednesday. That provided Kyle an extra day to reduce the pile of papers awaiting his attention and to do some review reading for his English classes. He'd been teaching that course for five years, but he kept it fresh by seeking new ideas, images or inspirations. The house was quiet. The fierce and holy howling of the wind through the front-yard pines and around the corners of the house and the beating of the driven snow against the walls and windows provided a sound track for his endeavors.

Thursday was more problematic. He'd not spent a Thanksgiving alone since he was in college, and then only once. Since his marriage to Gail, they'd had his folks in from Blackmore and hers from town, or they'd traveled to Blackmore. Part of that pattern began unraveling five years ago when Kyle's father was discovered to have advanced colon cancer. The disease took him within five months. As if in sympathy with her departed husband, his mother contracted cancer a year later and was gone in eight months.

Gail's parents had moved to Arizona last year, tired of storms like this one. So he and Gail would have spent their first Thanksgiving alone. Together, of course.

Consequently Kyle felt restless and hollow in the quiet house. He punished himself for Gail's absence by eating a bowl of soup for lunch. Unable to achieve interest in the football games on TV, he shoveled a path to the old red garage, swung open its ancient doors and retrieved his cross country skis from the rafters where they'd snuggled next to Gail's since last March.

He took them to the utility room in the house, dug out the ski wax, and prepared the skis for the day. After donning thermal underwear, sweater, light jacket, and the same stocking cap he always wore on his winter wilderness expeditions, he laced up his ski boots and headed into the woods behind the house to create a trail.

The day turned partly sunny as he plowed through the fresh snow. The trees creaked against one another in the brisk breeze. Looking up, he saw clouds sailing the sky on its breath. The exercise invigorated the sludge his blood was turning into from too much sitting, paper correcting, and thinking. Still he couldn't escape sadness spiced by a generous sprinkling of anger. He and Gail had grown to treasure this quiet push and glide through the natural world. At least he had, and he thought she had, too. At this moment, he wasn't sure. There seemed to be a lot about life he wasn't sure about anymore. He fought the threat of descent into depression. The day was too alive and beautiful, the contrast of white birch trunks, green pines, untrammeled snow and bluing sky too striking to ignore.

That evening he tried to call Gail at her hotel room. Listening to the endless buzzing of the phone on the other end sent ribbons of red threading through his brain. By the time the desk told him there was no answer, and he'd left a message with the desk clerk informing Gail he'd try to get to the Cities by noon on Saturday, he was blazing. She hadn't even considered that he'd want — need — to talk to her!

His delicious rage turned sour about two in the morning when he was still rumbling around the house whistling crumpled messages he'd penned against the wall and into the wastebasket. About that time, the sound of freezing rain heralded a rise in temperatures outdoors and a chilling of his own. He went to bed, the sheets cold, his mood icy as the rain.

On Friday most of the state was a skating rink, the snow sculpted into crusted waves. The local radio announced another storm was rolling in behind the ice storm and would hit sometime after twilight tonight. Kyle turned the radio off and picked up the phone. The same desk clerk answered. This time Kyle left a message saying that if the weather forecast came true, there was no use battling it for 24 hours in the Cities.

Gail finally called Saturday noon. Since the Cities were being hammered like every place else, she did not dispute his decision. Kyle asked for a review of her activities, since he did not particularly want to talk and had little to report. He clenched his teeth to rein his resentment of the cheerfulness in her voice and her tardiness in returning his call. He did well, holding his responses to an occasional "uh-huh" and "that's interesting." Her failure to apologize, and the contrast of the fullness of her last three days with the near emptiness of his own had him at full seethe by the time she announced another special meeting had been called, and she had to go if she wasn't going to be late. He listened to her bluebird "Goodbye, I love you," said,

"Likewise," and waited for her phone to click before slamming down his.

In the middle of the night after hours of staring at the ceiling, Kyle admitted to himself he'd fallen in love with self-pity, and he would be wise to modify that ardor.

Greg Schwarz

Greg Schwarz eased his chair back from the dining room table. "Wonderful meal, Beth. Wonderful. Never had a better roast in my life, and as you can see, I've had plenty of roasts in my life." He stood up and cradled his plate in one of his hands and grabbed his glass with the other. "I'll do the dishes."

"At one time in my life I'd have said a loud yes and hallelujah to that offer, Greg. Apparently all you and the Redhead talk about is football. Otherwise you'd know we've gotten so rich that the big lug bought me a dishwasher in September. Figured his coaching check would cover the cost and the loss of listening to me sing my way through the washing while he did the drying. Anyway, you two have things to talk about, so you'd better do that before Red falls asleep in front of the television set." She nodded toward her husband who had moved from the table and settled himself in the green La-Z-Boy recliner in the front room.

"She thinks I've been crippled by this heart thing," Red said without irritation. "She's afraid if I fall asleep in front of the TV, I might start dreaming about those pretty young things I saw at school every day and decide not to wake up. Doesn't know I have eyes only for her."

Greg settled onto the sofa. Dusk was falling on Thanksgiving. Detroit had won their Thanksgiving game on their home turf again. The two men talked about the game for a few minutes before Greg raised the issue he'd avoided all day. "You're feeling okay, Red?"

"Sure. You need to get married so you'll have someone to take care of. You've been hovering all day. When you're not hovering, you're peeking side-eyed. If Beth wises up and can't stand me anymore, why maybe I'll marry you. Though I doubt you can cook water. And, finally, to answer your question, I get tired a little easily, but I'm doing pretty well. It wasn't a minor heart attack, as you know, but it wasn't fatal either. If Beth continues to wait on me hand and foot and trots me out for a walk now and then, I should be fine."

"Then let's get the school board to delay this coaching thing. I was shocked when you called and electrocuted when you said the board was ready to move on this deal. This has to be the most ridiculous crap I've ever heard."

"No, I'm not going to fight it, Greg," Red replied, folding his hands on his chest.

Greg shot straight to his feet, then afraid he'd alarmed his friend, bent down and rubbed the back of his calf. "Charley horse," he explained, then sat down and continued the ruse. "Truth is, Red, if you keep surprising me like this, I'll be the next heart attack victim. So why won't you fight it? You know, I thought Anderson was an okay guy, but now I see him as an opportunistic jerk. Doesn't he give a darn about you? Or me? Why in the world would he call you so soon after you got out of the hospital anyway?" Greg clamped his mouth shut. He was lathering his own emotions and working on Red's. Didn't he care about the man either?

"I'm tempted to agree with you about Anderson," the coach responded, "but I can't decide if I do. You know, he's a youngish guy who snatched a nice plum when he got this job. You also know that the money crunch has settled in on public education pretty heavily. And the other thing you know is that the nature of the school board has changed. Back when I started here, there was a mix of rural, professional, and business people who all had one goal in mind—provide the best education they could with the best teachers they could get." He studied the wrinkles on his knuckles for a moment. "Now everybody elected to the board is there because they have an agenda they're promoting. The last election's poster child is Pete Warrum. I digress. What I meant to say is the current board is all about image. Winning games. Championship football teams being led by a young, vigorous coach."

"I don't know, Red," Greg said, struggling to keep his roiling emotions in check. "I don't think any of that matters. You're a great coach who's produced many great teams and given this town many championships. Now because of Pete . . . "

"Warrum's just the lunatic fringe of what's been coming on for awhile," Red interrupted. "The worst thing about him is he's wrecking his son and this community's attitude. Whatever damage he inflicts on you or me is minor by comparison. His major victims are his family and himself. I guarantee you that when he has a heart attack like mine, that poor, pale wife of his will be cheering. And those kids will stay as far away as they can get.

"I told you earlier I was thinking about quitting. Heart or no heart, I'm fed up. I'm sick of watching kids pressured. I'm sick of the screwed up priorities."

"But the precedent," Greg protested.

"Is something you'll have to deal with, and for that I am sorry. I wish you luck. Not many state playoff teams sack their head coach, I'll give you that." He dropped his hands in his lap and glanced at his friend. "If you were less of a man, less of a coach, if you cared less about kids, I might try to hang in there, Greg. Probably not, but maybe," he smiled at the other.

"I'm thinking about resigning, Red. The whole thing makes me sick."

"I can't blame you for thinking about that. I'd hate to see you go and won't encourage it, but I also won't discourage you. But don't get too hasty."

"I don't know if I want to take thirty, forty years out of my life and then get crapped on."

Red lowered the footrest on his chair with its lever. He stood up and motioned with the back of his hand for Greg to slide over on the sofa, so he could sit down beside him. Then he said, "I don't see it that way, Greg. These years have definitely been worth it for me. I loved what I was doing just about every minute I was doing it. I got to coach my son, and he got to play on some very good teams. I cared for the kids right through the minute my heart attack hit. Still do. Downtown had never mattered, and for me, personally, it has begun to matter too much lately. I suppose I'm sentimental for the days when there was pride at having a team doing its best and your son and your daughter doing his or her best. Now days even winning isn't enough. Lombardi was wrong. The joy is out of it for me, Greg. Except for the kids. Maybe God pushed Pete Warrum into me, so I'd have this heart attack and find myself a new life. Anyway, I agree a little bit with the boys downtown. This team was very much a product of your work. You designed the defense and coached that awesome line."

"Just a darn minute here . . . "

Red put up his hands. "I'm not criticizing myself. A good head coach — and I'm a very good coach —recognizes talent and uses it. I made excellent use of your abilities and your heart, and we both made excellent use of the talent on our team. We gave it everything and the kids did, too. In truth, this is a great time to quit."

Greg had one argument left. "Just one more thing, Coach. By not putting up a fight, you're letting the Booster Club, the school board, and Anderson get away with it. The jerks win."

"Sometimes victory is in the eye of the beholder. Beth thinks my decision makes me the winner. Right, Beth?" Greg had not noticed the coach's wife standing behind them leaning against the door frame.

"One hundred percent, dear. Besides," she continued as she moved behind the couch and kneaded Red's neck, "the Redhead and I have a good time thinking about ways we could even things up if we wanted to."

"Yup, we have. Lotsa folks think Beth and I are talking about my health when we take our hand-holding walks. Actually we're devising fiendish plots."

"I thought you had a heart attack, not brain damage. What are you talking about?!"

"Our favorite so far is this one," Beth said. "Just as the Board is about to act on Red's resignation, Red requests that the board consider whether someone who is asked to quit coaching because of a heart attack should also be asked to quit teaching, a more important job."

"We enjoy making up ways to add fuel to the flame. Can't you see the headlines? 'Championship Coach Forced To Quit Team and Teaching.' I don't know that we'll do it, but it would be fun if we did."

Gail Hunter

By the time Gail Hunter returned to Blue Lake early Monday afternoon, her husband was in school teaching his fifth period class. She wasn't surprised by the depth of his ice when he arrived home about six that evening. She cooked a tasty chicken dinner that hit the table shortly after he hit the door, furnished the small talk during the meal, and sat quietly on the sofa watching TV while he read in his favored reupholstered rocker. She sent trial balloons of conversation into the air every half hour or so and was not surprised to see him prick each one with grunted responses that tumbled them airless to the floor.

Gail knew her inattention to her husband over the long week looked aggressive and was almost inexcusable. It was true the meetings had been long, as had the social hours that followed. It was true she was in a constant state of exhilaration about how well her venture into the business world was working. It was also true that she knew where she could find him if she'd lift her hotel room phone, that she'd find a message for her at the front desk if she checked, and that she'd purposely waited until Saturday to do so.

Guilt about being that way came and went during the few moments of free time she had during those days. But she was on a high and enjoying the ride immensely. She genuinely assumed that a call to or from Kyle would bring her down, maybe even tie a rock to her mood and sink it. She reasoned that she needed to be as up as she was for the workshops and meetings. Once immersed in them, she didn't think of Kyle at all.

It was only on Monday driving north on the freeway, the sun blinding bright on the glittering white of iced snow that lined the road, that she allowed the spurts of guilt to turn into a river and scolded herself for the unkindness of her assumptions. She was still quite sure she loved the man and quite unsure why she was treating him with contempt.

So the evenings of that week in Blue Lake were spent chipping at the ice quietly and patiently until the final melt on Friday night when they fell into each other's arms as though returning from a time at war and held each other tightly all night, the full moon's light moving around the house from window to window as the night slipped by.

ᗡECEᗰBEᖇ

Patty Light

Dear Nightmares,

I walk so slow you'd think I'd just finished walking around the world. Everywhere I look it's raining, raining, raining. I can see chunks of trouble spill out of the high hills all around. People are raining down in tumbling descent. War is everywhere. Children are starving everywhere. People are shooting each other everywhere.

Everything is gray and heavy and sad. Then red flows through the gray, a lava flow of violence and anger and sorrow. Faces melt into the flow, but sometimes I see isolated eyes, wide and terrified.

Oh, Mr. Hunter, what a world I see! Do adults care? Do teenagers care? Does anyone care?

Do I care? Oh, so much!!! So little!!! I could scream!!!

I move in slow motion along the edges of this horrible landscape, this world full of fires, the flames shooting bright and yellow, everyone walking by, not caring.

Do you care, Mr. Hunter? Do you hear the screams? You do. You do. I know you do. Otherwise I wouldn't write my nightmares for your eyes, your heart.

Are you afraid for me? Don't be. This is how I escape the gray, crawl out of the mud, use the fires to light the nights.

I don't do drugs, Mr. Hunter. I know that's what you're thinking as you read this. Is this quiet, intelligent girl doing drugs? I don't do drugs and I don't drink. It's just anger and a little craziness that brings me nightmares that sometimes seize every cell in my brain for a while. My pen spills them out on paper and they go away.

I trust you. Don't talk to me about these entries please. They say what they say. I'll say no more. I won't explain or defend.

I think of you reading these words, and imagine your reaction. I feel moistness at the edges of my eyes. You feel deeply. Thank you.

My ears have found words to hear. Words of sadness, gladness, beauty and power. Little laughs. Little dreams. Do you know what I am saying? If you do, don't judge it please. They are as precious as sunrise and sunset. I need them more than breath or touch.

Oh, hmmm. I suppose this isn't your average "It's December, My favorite Christmas Memories, Yes, Virginia, There is a Santa Claus" journal entry.

Mr. H., I do wish you a Merry Christmas. Maybe Christmas will chase away some of the sadness I see in your eyes lately.

Vacations look to me like a long road on a winter night when the moon is gone, and I'm on foot and the dogs keep running down their long gravel driveways to yowl and howl at me and snap at my calves. I am most glad when vacations have *gone, and I am safe and warm in the school halls and rooms and desks again.*

Last, Mr. Hunter, thank you for adding Advanced Creative Writing to the schedule so I can take it next semester. Writing is my lifeline, and knowing that you'll continue to read, care, and hold any secrets, if I tell any, fills me with all the joy I need right now.

Oh, please have a Merry Christmas, Mr. Hunter! And Merry Christmas to Mrs. Hunter, too!

Bon Noel,

P.L.

Robert Baker

It had become easier. If entering the classrooms with a stone-like visage was easier. It seemed to Robert Baker that calling this unsmiling demanding approach to teaching "easier" was damning it with faint praise. It was not the dream of teaching he'd brought with him to Blue Lake.

He had achieved the quieting of his classrooms, which gave at least the appearance that learning was occurring. That process had been helped by the low grades he'd had to place on the first quarter report cards.

The parent conferences that followed were surprisingly non-combative. Many parents apparently had heard too much whining from their children about their disappointment, even anger over the loss of Mr. Gerney.

One mother told him, "You know, Mr. Baker, it's like a divorce. One parent is gone and in the minds of the kids, he or she becomes the best parent that ever lived. It's even worse when no one has told them this was going to happen. The problem is you're dealing with a whole lot of kids who feel that way about their dear, disappeared Mr. Gerney, and they're remarkably adept at getting sympathy for their distress. We all love a shared emotion, don't we? I'm just sorry that they're taking such advantage of it and making life so hard for you as though you'd caused the situation. I want to apologize for my daughter's part in that."

In fact, quite a few parents had decided to give the young instructor some slack. They promised that the underachieving ended the moment they saw those grades. After all, they expected their sons and daughters to continue on to some kind of post-high school education. Robert earned a degree of their cooperation by acknowledging up front that he realized he'd replaced a very popular teacher and that he was aware of the students' disappointment. He also admitted that the size of his classes had made it difficult for him to know his students as individuals.

Kyle, who sat a table away, later told the first year teacher that his handling of the conferences was impressive and that it had taken him years to be as open and non-defensive as Robert had been.

Those grades and Robert's new persona combined to create quiet, but sullen, classrooms. The low grades forced students to open books left stubbornly closed the first nine weeks. The parents had let their sons and daughters know it was in their best interests to get with it. More than a few students found themselves grounded until proof of change was evident.

The by-product was that the students acquired additional reasons to maintain their resentment of Robert Baker's presence.

The trouble was that this new persona was as hard on Robert Baker as it was on his students. If he was the driver of his classes, tension was riding shotgun. That was the price Robert paid for the vigilance it took to keep his classes focused. And that required maintaining the new persona because learning was occurring. Never mind that discussions he still kept trying to promote rarely developed except in one class. Never mind the symbolism of books being opened as though their covers were made of granite. Never mind the groans that greeted the oral reading he forced the students to do so he could get a fix on their reading aptitudes. Learning was occurring. This new self was achieving what the real Robert Baker couldn't. It held even the most virulent of students at bay. They'd once had him cornered and nearly cowed. They'd achieved that without imagining that the outcome would be that he'd claw his way out of the corner and emerge scarred and changed in a number of ways.

He'd decided to ignore the fixed curriculum in an effort to make his assignments relevant to what was going on in the outside world or in their lives. So he'd assigned Jack London's classic short story "To Build a Fire" in early December, shortly after the Thanksgiving storm, then followed up with a video of the story he'd purchased in college.

Most of the meager student responses dismissed the main character as stupid, the story as boring, and the admittedly flawed film as fake. That was the end of it.

The third period had furnished the exception to those reactions. Even Frank and Ed had lifted their eyes to watch the video.

As soon as the film finished, Jerry Jons said loud enough for all to hear, "Talk about stupid and boring!"

Patty Light's hand waved in the air. "I don't think so," she said. "I think the man was arrogant for ignoring the warnings, but we all do foolish or dangerous things sometimes. People say, don't do this or that because you might get hurt or hurt someone else, and we go ahead and do it anyway. Besides, the main character was new to the Yukon, he had a dog with him, and friends not that far away. Maybe he overrated himself, but he thought he could make it."

Billy Cloud was next. "I don't think stories about trying to survive are ever boring. Surviving in a hostile environment was the story of America before it was America. Storms showed up. You didn't have a TV or radio to warn you. No snowmobiles to come and pick you up if you got in trouble. Surviving was hard. Still is for a lot of people. Heck, two people in the state died storm-related deaths last week."

The discussion continued for another half hour, finally winding up with normally silent Tad Danther asking with interest, "So that last scene in the movie where those three guys, including himself, trudge across the snow and look down at the guy . . . what the heck was that about?"

"It might have been a hallucination," Billy answered. "I've read or heard that people who are on their way to freezing to death, but get rescued, say that they had hallucinations before they were saved."

Patty added, "I think the man was holding on to hope. He tried everything he could think of to stay alive, and even though every single thing failed to work, he held on to the hope that somehow he would survive right up to the second he couldn't."

When Robert thought about that discussion, Patty's final thought stood out for him: "He held out hope that he would survive right up to the second he couldn't."

Then he'd think, thank God for Patty and the others who joined in, even for Jerry Jons, who had put the discussion in motion. Thank God he had one period where he could listen to voices other than his own. Thank God for those freshmen who never heard of Ted Gerney and gave him an hour a day to be the Robert Baker he really was and were pleased when he came to their desks or they to his desk to get the help they needed or share what was on their minds and hearts.

Thank God, too, that the Snow Ball and Christmas vacation were coming up soon. The students hadn't been as hostile the last few days. Most likely they didn't want to do anything that would get them suspended from going to the dance or anything that might cause their parents to rethink their Christmas lists. Maybe he could afford to dial down a little. Maybe the Season of Peace was bringing a little peace into his life too.

Sam Strand

"Your son's attendance is falling off badly," Sam Strand told the tense couple seated across from him, so close to his desk their knees were touching it. They sat ramrod straight. The desk must look an acre deep to them, Sam realized, and he must look like a judge seated in the plush leather chair behind it.

The portly, balding man wearing a blue work shirt and jeans was sweating profusely. He dabbed at the perspiration with the red handkerchief he wadded in his fists when he wasn't using it. The angular, slender woman at his side was pale and motionless. Only the way she worked her lips against her teeth conveyed her anxiety. "Mr. and Mrs. Marin, according to our records, Frank missed eight days of school and parts of five others in November. Prior to that he missed classes and days sporadically. I think he was only absent three full days in October, though he did ditch classes now and then. I know we're behind in reporting this to you, but there are reasons. One is that we've been getting signed excuse notes from you, Mr. Marin. The other is that our overburdened counselors and office staff simply cannot keep up with the paperwork, nor can our teachers. We have no attendance officer. Enough of my excuses. I called you in for a conversation, not my monologue. You received our letter?"

"Yes, we got the notice December first," Mike Marin answered, his voice low and shy. Sam could tell the man was cowed by him, by the office, by the desk. He had to physically close part of the gap that separated him from Frank Marin's parents.

"Excuse me," he said. He rose and moved a plastic chair usually reserved for students from the corner of the office and placed it adjacent to the couple. "Darn leather chairs are cold in winter," he said. "Now why don't you move your chairs around a bit, and we can get a little more informal here."

The two obeyed as Sam guessed they had obeyed parents, teachers, bankers, and bosses all of their lives. They were good people who were scared and confused. He glanced at the clock. 12:35. He knew Mr. and Mrs. Marin – Mike and Nancy – had taken an hour off work and that made them nervous. He'd better get cracking.

"Were you aware of the absences?"

"No," Mike answered. "Oh, twice I guess. I always call at noon just to make sure the house is empty."

"You wrote those excuses though?"

Mike Marin shook his head. "I only wrote two."

"Anyway, you had some suspicions about your son?" Sam tried to keep his tone conversational. He had no desire to offend or alienate these two people he had taken a liking to as soon as they entered the office.

"No . . . yes . . . I guess so. Frank's been prone to be sick the past few years now and then. Oh, maybe ten, twelve days a year. Nancy and me both went to work in the other town – Bethel Ridge – after we almost lost the farm." He swiped the perspiration that lingered between his nose and upper lip. "We had to save the farm."

"Can you tell me a little about that?" Sam asked. "The farm I mean."

"Well, sure," the man responded, tucking his work shirt self-consciously. "Me and Nancy started buying that farm way back. Five years before Frank. Just a small farm, 240 acres. Not real good crop land down there in Bethel Ridge, but we wanted to farm, and it was so darn pretty. Tried everything to make it go. But we took a beating. Bought used machinery, and it would wear out. New stuff is incredibly expensive.

"Anyway, when he was twelve, Frank went to work for Mr. Corgan up the road, worked for him in the summer doing chores to help us out, mostly so he'd have somethin' for himself. Pay his own way. That seemed pretty mature to Nancy and me, I s'pose," Marin said, glancing at his wife under his thick eyebrows. "That's bad, makin' a kid work that young."

"Frank liked Mr. Corgan," Nancy Marin said. She was a slender woman who looked at you when she spoke.

"Yes, he did," Mike Marin agreed. "I think he misses him. Anyway, he worked for Mr. Corgan, and I went to work at the car repair shop in town, but that still didn't do it. Bethel's a real small place. So Nancy went to work at the hardware store in Norman. That left Frank home alone a lot out there on the farm. He never said nothin' though. I mean he was 13, 14 years old. Never had many friends. Then he started hanging around with a kid named Shmitty at school. We didn't like him that much when we met him." Mike shrugged. "But what can you say when you leave your kid alone that much? 'Be grown up, take care of yourself, but we'll pick your friends?'"

Sam nodded. He was pleased by the openness of the man and aware of the emotional effort Mike Marin was expending. He wondered how well the couple could handle the hunches he had in mind. But he wanted Mike, who had fallen silent, to finish his story first.

"So you sold the farm?" Sam prompted.

"No. No, we didn't. Came darn close. The government pretty much wanted it. The sheriff was gettin' his hammer warmed up to post notices. No, we would have lost the land, but then this new fiberboard plant opened up here, and I'll tell you when we heard they were hiring, we drove up here two days early and camped right at the front of the line. We're good workers. Our references say so. So we both got work. We're making enough with our jobs and renting the farmland to the neighbor, so we can make the payments."

"If we lost the place, Mike would curl up and die," his wife interjected.

"So that brings us almost to the present. How did Frank feel about moving?"

"He wasn't happy, but he never says nothing," Mike reported. "I wasn't sorry we were moving him. Some things I didn't like in Bethel Ridge."

"Which were?"

"He was a good student until tenth grade. Then his grades started fallin'. Used to be an ambitious kid. But all of a sudden he never had homework."

"He got very moody," Nancy Marin added.

She has a hunch, too, Sam concluded, about what's going on.

Nancy Marin's angular face was expressionless, her long, slender fingers intertwined in her lap. "He started arguing with Mike for no good reason. Then he'd look so sorry that we couldn't bring ourselves to punish him."

Mike continued, "Even Mr. Corgan. Like I said, Frank loved that old fella, but one night Cory called me and said there wasn't any use Frank comin' around any more, because he wasn't doing much work, and Cory couldn't afford to pay him for doin' nothin'. Said Frank just sat around waiting to be told what to do next and didn't do it very well. Especially when the Schmitt kid was around. I guess that helped us decide to move. Thought the change might be good for Frank. Couldn't get a hell of a lot worse. Frank loved that old man. And then . . . " Mike stopped. "Sorry about the language. And my grammar. Never was much good in English." He mopped at his streaming forehead.

"No problem. And thank you for all the background information," Sam said. He admired Mike Marin's forthrightness.

"So what do we do? Nancy can't quit her job, and I can't quit mine. The kid just sits in his room with the window wide open." He glowered. "We're trying to keep heat costs down, and he has the da . . . the darn window wide open. Sometimes I feel my fingernails diggin' into my palms. But I can't hit my kid. Then I feel guilty because I feel like I want to. Then I can't say nothin'." He slumped in his chair, worn out from talking so much.

Sam decided to take the plunge. "Does Frank have any friends? He doesn't seem to make friends easily in this school."

"He has college friends," Nancy volunteered. "Mike and I hoped that was good when he told us."

"But we never see 'em," Mike said. "They drive up, he runs out, and that's it."

"Or he meets them downtown," Nancy added.

"I want to talk to you straight," Sam began. "We've had other students who followed patterns similar to your son's. Sudden changes in mood and behavior. Bad attendance. Falling grades. Sometimes those are adjustment problems. Sometimes home problems. But quite often it has to do with drugs or alcohol." He stopped to let his statements ride the air to the ears and minds of his listeners. Nancy Marin did not move. She sat straight and still in the plastic chair. Disgust crinkled Mike Marin's features. "Do you find possibilities in what I said?"

Nancy Marin answered, "Yes."

"I don't think that's fair, Mr. Strand," Mike murmured. He wasn't used to disagreeing with a principal. "I mean, drugs and alcohol, that's a pretty serious charge." As he spoke, Nancy Marin looked at her husband, sadness in her eyes.

"Just a moment, Mr. Marin," Sam said. "I want you to believe me when I say I'm not charging your son with anything. Even if he has a drug or alcohol problem, it wouldn't be a charge. We're interested in what's going to help Frank and help you."

"I still don't think you can . . . " Mike began but lapsed back into silence.

Sam leaned forward, his hands resting on his knees. "All I'd like you to do, Mr. and Mrs. Marin, is try to keep yourselves open to all possibilities. I also want you to believe that whatever the problem may be, help is available."

"Well, I really don't think . . . " Mike began, but his voice trailed off.

"You may be right. Probably you are," Sam soothed. "Anyway, I do have some pamphlets I could give you about the subjects I mentioned if you want them. Am I getting pushy?"

"I'd like to have them," Nancy Marin responded. "Even if Frank doesn't have any of those problems, there are lots of kids that do, and some people at the plant that do, and I'd like to know more about it."

Sam recognized what a diplomatic statement she'd made. Mike could not counter it. He slid his chair back and reached around the desk to its open upper drawer, retrieved a packet of literature and handed it to Nancy.

The parents sat in silence. They're waiting to be excused, Sam realized. He glanced at the clock. "It's one fifteen," he noted, genuinely surprised. "I'm sorry. I lost track." The couple stood up, she clutching her purse and the packet, he with his hands folded at his belt line. Sam stuck out his hand. Mike clutched it, his hand damp, his grip firm. Nancy's was equally firm.

As the pair left, Sam dropped his lanky frame into his leather chair and sighed as the chair also did in accepting his presence. Those two came in here scared to death of me, Sam mused. Maybe everything about education wasn't so perfect in the good old days after all.

Billy Cloud

Descending the front steps of his home, Billy Cloud inhaled the December morning, then exhaled a stream of winter breath white as the fresh-snow terrain. He'd decided to traverse the three miles to Blue Lake High School on foot rather than ride the school bus. He preferred meeting the day that way whenever possible. Besides, the exercise kept his body primed for whatever sport was in season, that currently being basketball. Jogging to town wearing boots would make him feel like he was flying when he donned tennis shoes later today.

He also wanted time to think. Last night as he'd sat in the breakfast nook reading "A Christmas Memory," the story Mr. Baker had asked his English class to preview for oral reading, a vision of Patty Light reading the same story slipped unbidden into his mind. She was sitting at a desk, a reading lamp haloing her book. She wasn't just reading the story, however, she was living it. He could tell that by the shifting expressions on her face. The idea of the two of them engaged in the same assignment at the same time spread a rush of warmth through him. That encouraged him to imagine how it would be if they were physically together here. She would be sitting across from him in the nook. Their feet would be almost touching as they read. She would glance up from her book to discover how intently he was studying her face as she read and tell him in her quiet song of a voice,

"I love this story, Billy. Do you think it's as wonderful as I do?" He could see in her soul-filled eyes that she was thinking, "Oh, I hope you do!" The vision was so intimate and real that he willed it to remain between his eyes and the book for a long time before ordering it to recede so he so he could resume reading. He'd finished the entire selection because he knew that's what she'd do. When he'd later crawled into bed and closed his eyes, her endlessly expressive face had been waiting there to lead him into dreams.

He tightened the straps of his backpack and walked down the snow-dusted driveway to the road. He noted that the house across it remained uninhabited. It was a decent place, but his Dad said he'd only seen one person showing interest in it. Maybe its proximity to the Cloud House was a factor. He quashed that thought as soon as it landed. He had better thoughts to think like how the Light family should rent that place. Patty would love living in a country house nestled in nature. He'd listened to her carry the discussions in Mr. Baker's class for three months. Hawthorne, Longfellow, Thoreau, Emerson, Dickinson... She revealed no details about her personal life in those discussions, but she revealed a whole lot about how important the natural world was to her.

He ran in place for a few moments so the warmth in his muscles could catch up with the warmth in his heart. Then he commenced an easy jog toward town. Patty Light, Patty Light, Patty Light. The emergence of her image last night and the way it stirred him still caught him a little off guard, but he was, after all, the same guy who'd called out her name to the deer in the meadow below Moon Ribbon Ridge. Truth to tell, he'd surprised himself then, too. He'd thought of her as interesting, admirable, and intelligent. That was the first time he realized he thought of her as more than that.

It hadn't taken long to notice Patty Light after he transferred into third period English. Mr. Baker had added a desk for him in the window row. It afforded a perfect vantage point for observing his new classmates. Most were as warm with one another as the seventh period were ice-encrusted. The hum of random conversations and activity within the room lasted until the bell rang. Students like Jerry Jons roamed the room talking, laughing, and gossiping. It was when class began that most students fell into silence.

Patty Light was different. She was remarkable for being so unremarkable, noticeable for making no effort to be noticed. She wore longish skirts, modest blouses, and sweaters as muted in color as the end of autumn. Her hair always looked a little wind-blown. She wore no jeans, jewelry, or makeup. She neither smiled nor did not smile. But there was an aura about her, a subtle glow, that he found increasingly intriguing. He wondered at its genesis and guessed at its sources. The easiest guess was that she, like him, usually walked from home to school and hers was the glow of the physically fit. Eventually he perceived it also had to do with how pleased she was to be in this class. When she entered room 313, she always walked slowly to her desk. He watched her scan the room, absorbing every detail and every person in it. She never spoke to anyone, but that didn't seem to matter. When she reached her desk, she'd slide into it, open her book like it was a treasure chest and become absorbed in it. Once class began, she morphed into this verbal student who carried every discussion Mr. Baker tried to promote and participated in every activity Mr. Baker devised. As the weeks passed, he realized that love was the source of her glow. She loved nature, books, and learning in all its forms. She loved thinking and sharing her thoughts. She loved school.

But these realizations were so subtle that he hadn't realized how much space Patty occupied in his subconscious until he heard himself call out her name to two deer in a woodland meadow.

"Getting a little carried away here?" Billy asked his ears. The intensity of his thinking was being matched by the rate of his pace. If he maintained it, he'd arrive at school an hour early and a sloshing sack of sweat.

'A sloshing sack'; that's what he remembered himself as being on his last day in Miss Lowell's second grade class, but then he'd been a sloshing sack of tears. Miss Lowell was his first and most enduring love. Her whole class loved her. She was the kind of teacher whose open heart embraced every child she taught. But on that day he was the last one remaining in the classroom, too sodden to move because he was sure he would never see his beloved Miss Lowell again. His parents had told him that the Clouds would soon be drifting on to another town. That's why he was sitting in his desk crying like a baby. Miss Lowell could have told him he'd have to leave before he flooded the room. Instead she slid into the little kids desk next to his and stroked his back as he choked out the tragic news. She listened, her eyes shiny. Then she said, "Billy, I'll never forget you. You have a beautiful heart." Then she said, "Billy, when I was a student, one of my very wise teachers told us this. He said one of the most important things we could know about life is that when a broken heart mends, it mends stronger than ever. I've always remembered that. I hope you will too."

He'd never forgotten her or those words. He patted his chest with his gloved right hand. "It's beating strong, Miss Lowell." It was not strange to him that thinking about Patty provoked memories of Miss Lowell. Caring was spelled with a capital C for both of them.

So it wasn't like he didn't know what love is. He'd had lots of little loves in addition to his big love for Miss Lowell. His seventh grade classmate Annie Lawrence was one of his favorites. Annie hadn't initially approached him with caring warmth. Hot under the collar was more like it. The strokes she'd given him were solid whacks to the shoulder because he'd ignored her playground pleas to toss her the football he was twirling in his hands. "So run out that way," he'd pointed with seventh grade boy disdain. She'd run like the wind, and he'd sent the pigskin sailing after her. She'd caught the thing over her shoulder! At full gallop! That was impressive! They became fast friends from that moment on. Theirs was a buddy love, so it survived when Annie developed a crush on a ninth grader who'd made the varsity football team. The love he and Annie shared was the kind that plastered a big smile on your face when you thought about it. The only time they touched in a loving way was when they shared a goodbye hug and quick kiss the day the Clouds sailed on to another new town.

Kiss. Caralee Croonquist could definitely do that. 'Warm' didn't quite describe that relationship either. 'Hot' did, but not under the collar. Last winter she'd raised his temperature considerably when she leapt on his lap at a friend's party and remained there the rest of the evening. For several months thereafter, it wasn't weather that sucked the moisture from his lips. His father eventually was moved to present him with a packet of Chapstick and comment that he hoped he shouldn't be handing him a packet with significantly different contents. "Hot fires burn fast, but the flames can leave a lot of scars," was all his mother said. When he and Coralee finally used their lips for talking, they discovered that other than ardor, they didn't have that much in common. Nevertheless, their farewell kiss the night before the Clouds blew along left a pleasant aftertaste.

Reaching the town's outskirts, Billy slowed to a walk, smiling, and checked his watch. He still had forty minutes before the school bell rang. He congratulated himself on the time he'd made and his wise use of it, then veered from the main drag and trotted down to the footpath that bordered Blue Lake. Fewer people. More thinking.

So. He might not have been around the block, strictly speaking, but he'd walked down quite a few sidewalks. He couldn't for the life of him picture Patty Light leaping onto his lap. He didn't know if she could catch a football. But the openness of her heart and her compassionate nature were obvious.

The iced-over areas of Blue Lake were gathering the gold from the sunrise sky as he attained the path. The open areas rippled in the light morning breeze. This was going to be a beautiful day. Wherever she was on her walk, Patty Light was loving watching it being born as much as he was.

His thoughts kept circling back to her. He was going to have to take this fascination to the next level. Like actually conversing with her as Billy Cloud, one person, to Patty Light, one person. No third persons, such as authors and poets and teachers allowed. On this beautiful day, it was finally time to get to know Patty Light better or find out the reason why not.

❖   ❖   ❖

Mr. Baker's decision to have the class read Capote's "A Christmas Memory" orally the last day the class met before Christmas vacation was inspired. It was an excellent story, and the kind of assignment the fabled Mr. Gerney would probably have given.

The class must have thought so. They read the story well. Given the option to decline to read, only Frank Marin exercised it. Even Ed Warrum read until his voice choked, and he shook his head. The hour was going so well, the teacher's only reaction was to ask Angela Adams to pick up where Ed left off.

The concluding paragraphs were Patty's to read. Her voice conveyed the narrator's yearning and heartbreak with such a depth that the entire class simply closed their books and sat in silence until the bell rang.

Whether it was coincidence or destiny, Billy found himself next to Patty Light in Mr. Baker's room at noon. He'd decided to ditch lunch and use the time to congratulate the teacher on the success of the assignment. The teacher deserved that. Patty was already there when Billy arrived. "Hey, Mr. Baker," he said as he joined the two, "I need to tell you that today's lesson was perfect. And planning it out so that Patty would be reading those final paragraphs was pure genius."

The teacher displayed a rare smile. "I'm afraid you'll have to chalk up pure genius to blind luck or the frog in Ed Warrum's throat. I love that story. I was scared to death the kids wouldn't, and I'd be left with egg on my face again. It went so much better than I dared to hope. You're right about Patty. No one else could have read those paragraphs with such compassion."

Patty reddened. "I came up to wish you a Merry Christmas, Mr. Baker, not to fish for compliments."

"You two and this class have already made it merry." The genuine joy on the man's face was a pleasure to see. He glanced at the round room clock. "But I don't want my celebration to cause you to be serving detention on the last day of school. Better get going to your classes."

The two left the room together and walked down to their lockers, savoring the visit in silence. Patty turned in front of her locker and said, "Thank you for doing that, Billy. It meant so much to him. And to me, too. I want to wish you a really Merry Christmas, too."

"And I want to take you to the Snow Ball," Billy blurted, surprising both. The girl's eyes instantly moistened. "Hey, I'm sorry if I waited too long to ask you."

"It's not that. It's just that I never ever expected to go to the Snow Ball, and I never ever expected to be asked. It makes me want to cry. I'm such a baby."

Billy was amazed. How had this girl with so much going for her eluded the interest of the Blue Lake boys?

She fumbled with her combination lock. "I don't know how to dance," she said, peering at the lock.

"I do. I'm quite good at powwows and not bad at sock hops either. I'd be happy to teach you. I've noticed you're quite teachable."

"I'll have to ask my mother," Patty responded, turning towards him. Her eyes told him that would be a difficult. "She might have to say no."

"If she does, then maybe we can walk around and around your block and talk instead. Because," Billy confessed, "I really want to know you better."

Ed Warrum

It was after basketball practice, walking home alone in the soft fall of December snow, walking past the brightly lighted Christmas windows of downtown Blue Lake, walking past Hansen's Sports and Hardware, stopping in front of the black and brown gleam, turning away, turning back, staring, staring at the gun's brown stock, the black gleaming barrel, feeling the chill coursing his spine, feeling the ice seize the inside of his forehead until his head throbbed. It was then, eight days before Christmas, one day before school let out, one day before he was taking Shellie Chaine to the Christmas dance, four days before he was to begin his vacation duties at the store, three days before the long string of Sundays at home continued. It was then that Ed Warrum decided what he wanted to buy for his father's Christmas present.

He pulled open the heavy door of the Sports and Hardware store, the chain of tinkling Christmas bells hung on it singing their little welcome as he entered. The bells continued to tinkle as the door closed. Ed shuffled around the store, feigning interest in toys, silverware, lamps, baseball gloves, basketballs before stopping in front of the glass case containing knives, compasses, and other hunting devices on both shelves and a small collection of pistols on the right-hand side right beneath where his gloved hands rested on the counter. He stared at the pistols before wrenching his gaze to the rifles. He wasn't here to buy. He was here to get information.

"Ed!" boomed the big voice of store owner August Hansen as he moved down the aisle toward the athlete. "How's the basketball team looking? As good as the football team?"

Ed could care less, but he couldn't sound that way. "Looks pretty good, Mr. Hansen," he answered.

"You sure?" the man asked as he moved behind the glass case, his big belly split above and below the case by it's wood trimming. "You don't exactly sound enthused."

"Tired," Ed answered, shoving his hands in his pockets, not thinking to remove the gloves. "Hard practice today."

"Well, I'm sure. By golly, it is almost six o'clock. That man trying to get us another championship team maybe?" The big man smiled, arcing his white mustache.

"Yeah, like Coach Howard did."

"And Schwarz, of course," Hansen added genially. That fired into Ed's gut like a swarm of hornets. Are you one of those, too, he wanted to ask.

Hansen cleared his throat. "Well, what can I do you for?"

Ed was standing in front of the gun case as a result of inspiration, not preparation. He should have gone home. Nope, couldn't think there, couldn't have one single thought of your own there. No, he should have gone for a long walk and gotten a story together before coming in.

"Son? Ed? You okay? You're looking a little pale."

"I think maybe I'm getting the flu," Ed lied, his stomach full of hornets. "I . . . uh . . . I just came in, because I saw that rifle in the window . . . "

"Sure is a beauty. I don't shoot guns but I wouldn't mind settin' that Winchester on a wall hanger above my fireplace. Darn thing looks good."

Hansen's response gave Ed time to think. "Well, you know my Uncle Ned, down in the Cities?" The store owner shook his head. "Sure you do. Mom's brother. You met him at church when he came up hunting a year ago. Tall skinny guy about my height? Curly brown hair?" The big man finally nodded. It helped Ed that everything he was saying was true at this point. "Well, you know he just took up hunting a few years ago, and he's using an old gun he bought at an auction. When I saw that . . . Winchester . . . I thought maybe it would be fun for me and Mom to surprise him at Christmas." Ed's hands were back atop the glass case right above the pistols as he talked. "How much would a gun like that cost?"

"Well, I don't rightly know. My brother Fred handles the sports end of this enterprise. There's a price list back in the office. Want me to check?"

"If it isn't too much trouble," Ed answered, trying to sound interested but casual. It probably didn't matter since his voice always seemed to emerge in monotone anyway unless he was ticked off. He watched the big man amble toward the office, then spread his hands apart so he could see if the pistols were priced. He saw tags hanging from the trigger guards. He didn't want to lean over to look, but thought he saw that one was priced at $125. He looked up as Mr. Hansen walked in his direction. "So?"

"That one's pricey. Around four hundred. Of course it's top of the line."

"I don't know anything about guns, Mr. Hansen," Ed said truthfully. "Uncle Ned's the only one I know of in our family who has a gun."

"I didn't think your old man was a hunter," Hansen boomed. "Probably a good thing with his temper. He mighta shot Coach Howard instead of just tackling him." Hansen found that funny. He was chortling.

Ed wanted to pick up a pile of hammers, hurl them through the plate glass windows and then at everything glass in this place. Instead he ground his teeth until they felt like stubs, keeping his eyes fixed on the rifles behind the weapons case. He exhaled the longest sigh of his life and regained his composure. "Well, maybe I should come back and talk to your brother about this gun stuff before Mom and I decide."

"Good idea. My expertise is hardware."

Ed nodded and exited the store. He didn't feel like Mr. Hansen was watching him leave, which meant he'd conned his way through this thing. As he swung open the door, its bells tinkling again, he glanced back, and Hansen was busy with another customer.

Ed did not buy a rifle. He did not buy a gun in Blue Lake at all. Instead, three days later he borrowed the car known as his 'mother's car' to escape another gray, fingernails-on-a-blackboard Sunday afternoon. He told his parents he was going to see Shellie. His father didn't like her. Girlfriends weren't good for athletes. Girls were if you knew how to use them. Anyway, he was watching an NFL game and not really paying attention.

Ed drove out of town and headed for the Dantana Rod and Rifle Outdoor Store situated twenty-eight miles northeast between the highway and woods and nothing else. The place was known for selling guns to anyone who'd buy, and it was open seven days a week.

He told the bearded, uninterested owner that his father wanted to take up target shooting, and he wanted to give him a live action pistol so he could escalate to offing rats at the dump, maybe teach Ed how to shoot. The man showed him a used gun and sold him a box of bullets with it. Ed didn't have to sign a thing. When he looked for registration numbers on the piece, there were none. The man placed the gun in a box with no words on it. Then he wrapped it up and handed it to the boy. "I think I'd carry that in my trunk until I got home if I were you," the bushy man growled. "That'll keep you outa trouble if you get caught speedin' or somethin'." He permitted himself a brief smile. "Also me. And I do care 'bout that. Hope your old man enjoys the piece," he finished.

"Yeah. I'm sure he will. He'll be real surprised," Ed answered. He left the store, and popped the pistol box in the covered wheel well in back. He'd retrieve it when his father was at the store and his mother was in the house and hide it in his closet. For a brief time on his drive back to town he felt something other than hopeless. But by the time he stopped by Shellie's home for a few minutes, the hornets were again at full fury in his gut.

Kyle Hunter

The winding down of the Christmas shopping season and the New Year's ordering brought Gail Hunter home from her round of regional stores two days before Christmas vacation. She was looking more vibrant than she had for some time. Her thirty-six year old figure was trim. She dressed more stylishly than she used to, having the pick of the clothes she chose for the stores. The red blazer outfit she was wearing "in honor of the season," was purely and simply smashing. Her blue eyes were electric with excitement.

Not caring to cook or be cooked for on this Thursday evening and knowing he'd agreed to chaperone the school dance Friday night, Kyle called the Duck Blind. By seven o'clock he and Gail were in the car. Neither said much, saving that for the intimacy of their favorite place.

By 7:45 Gail had hugged Mary and Eddie like the long lost friends they were for her, and the two had slid into their favorite booth by the window overlooking an icy lake sparkling under the winter moon.

"It's like we're having an affair," Gail smiled, her face alluring in the flicker of the seasonal candle on the table. "I love this place."

"It is a little like sneaking off with a lover," Kyle said.

"Don't, honey," Gail urged, stroking the veins on the backs of his hands. "I'm happy. I want to stay happy. Tell me about school."

"You want to stay happy. School won't help that right now."

"Then I'll talk about my travels," she said with insistent brightness. She did throughout Duckloaf Delight dinner.

There was a song in her being that Kyle had not known how much he missed. He wished he wasn't experiencing jabs of resentment. How come they could make her so much happier than he could? Following the meal, and sipping an after-dinner drink, he gave in to it. As Gail lifted her glass of wine, he admitted, "I'm jealous."

Gail held her glass just below her lips. "Jealous?" She set the glass down. "Kyle, I'm not . . . I wouldn't . . . I . . . "

"No, no, no," her husband said. "Not that. No, I'm jealous because you're so excited and happy about your work. I haven't seen you this up for a long time. So . . . I'm jealous."

She turned his hands over and placed her palms on his. "You don't need to be."

"I know," he answered, twining his fingers with hers, then smiling. "Do you know the only way I'll be able to drink this beer is to tip it with my tongue or topple it with my chin and lap it like a dog."

"I choose doggy style. Go for it," Gail laughed. Then she shifted into a different brightness. "Kyle, I have something to tell you."

"I thought you didn't do that," Kyle mocked.

"Listen!" she ordered. "Do you know what I did?"

"I thought you didn't."

"Kyle, you sex obsessed idiot, please shut up. What I did was, I took the articles you wrote for the *Blue Lake Chronicle* and the articles you wrote for the Association newsletters . . . "

"And made a dress of them?"

"Will you shut up? No. Listen. I made copies of them and gave them to Mr. Clyde Waters in Minneapolis."

"Clyde does what?"

"Kyle! Listen. Mr. Waters was impressed."

"No doubt Mr. Waters thought my words had a wonderful flow."

"You're impossible."

"That's possible. Who's Clyde Waters?"

"He's the head of our advertising division."

"Yours and mine. I didn't know we had one. Do we really need one?"

"I'd love to be furious with you, but I just can't be. It's so good to be sitting here with you and laughing."

"Yes," he agreed.

"Now . . . " she continued, straightening her shoulders, her blue eyes sparkling. "Mr. Waters would like you to apply for a position in our advertising department. He says if you're as sharp as your writing, you'd have a great future with the corporation."

"Whoops. Wow," Kyle whispered, surprised by her words. "I don't know what to say."

"That's a relief," she laughed. "Kyle, there's no hurry. He says you should take plenty of time to think it over. The rest of the school year. It's a big decision. We'd have to leave Blue Lake. It would be a big change."

Kyle couldn't identify his feelings. Sadness? A little pride maybe? Panic? He'd thought about leaving the teaching profession now and then, but not seriously and not with a serious prospect in front of him. "I'll think about it." he concluded.

Robert Baker

It was on the Thursday afternoon before vacation began that Robert Baker's seventh period class erupted. He wasn't at all sure how the chaos began. Perhaps it was because he was so wearied by the rigidity he'd been forced to adopt to control his classes and get them to produce. Perhaps it was the anger at his being there at all that this class, more than any other, had nursed and fed since the first day of school. Perhaps it had to do with the stunningly low grades he'd had to put on their first quarter report cards. Nearly a third had flunked, and no one had earned higher than a C.

Parents cared about grades. That had forced effort out of students in all his classes. But these students sure didn't like it. And they sure didn't like him. This person in front of them whose eyes portrayed nervousness, then fear, then anger, this intelligent, and desperate man was almost universally viewed as the enemy.

Because he was in the first year of his teaching and because it was outside his experience and because no one had warned him, Robert Baker didn't realize that many students become singeing wires when vacations are near. Because he finally had their attention and grudging compliance, because the curriculum told him he had a specific amount of material to cover, and because he thought a school should be a place where people learned, he ordered the class to open their textbook to read "A Christmas Memory," a perfectly appropriate piece for the season and the day. The other classes had done so. Even Ed Warrum's voice had choked with emotion when he read. He'd given them and his other classes the choice of reading the piece aloud or silently. Most had chosen silence, but they'd maintained it, too. The delicate story was quite irresistible.

But his seventh period class resisted. Groans greeted the assignment.

Then Barney Blair said, "Go to hell."

The unexpected reaction threw Robert off balance. The expletive lit a fuse in his brain that crackled and flared. He rushed the boy's desk and thrust his face within inches of the other's. "What did you say?" he shouted. "What did you say to me?"

He later wished he'd just sent Barney out of the room. But he hadn't. He'd exploded. It was a perfectly human reaction, but he was never given room to react in a human way. Barney knew he had a room full of allies poised and waiting in the electric silence for his response.

"I said go to hell. Get your ugly mug out of mine. Your breath stinks."

Robert could hear knees knocking against the bottoms of desks in the deadly silence as the class readied to rise. "Get out!" Robert rasped.

The boy sneered. "You can't tell me what to do. You ain't my father."

The room exploded. Robert shot bolt upright. He looked around for someone to send to the office to get the boy out of his room. But everyone was out of their seats. Somehow all of the windows had been thrust open and cold air was rushing in, steaming the heat in the excited bodies. He looked back at Barney, the only person in the room still seated, the ugly sneer fixed in wild triumph.

Robert had never felt so helpless. Students were racing around the room. He saw three boys and two girls fling their textbooks out the open windows. Then the five turned to eye him with menace. Two boys crashed into the blackboard, one trying to snatch the textbook from the other who was yelling, "Stop it, stop it! Leave me alone!" Something wet and solid hit his cheek and another hit his shoulder and popped over it. Something hard whacked the back of his calf. "Sit down!" he shouted against the din. "Please sit down!"

He whirled toward the door as Sam Strand rushed in. "Sit down!" the principal boomed, grabbing the shirts of two students near him into his big fists. "Sit down!" he boomed again, slamming the boys into the nearest desks. "Sit down," he boomed for a third time. "If you're not in your seats in five seconds, you're out of this school forever." Robert watched the students scramble for whatever desk was close. "Get in your assigned seats!" the administrator thundered, his face and neck red.

The room was suddenly silent, only the knocking of desks against one another breaking it as students scurried to reestablish the destroyed rows.

"What in the name of Beelzebub is going on here!" the principal shouted into the flushed faces, his own livid. "Who started this!?" There was a tense silence. "If you don't tell me, you're all out of this school." Well aware that Principal Strand was a man who kept his word, eight pointed toward Barney Blair. "You get out of here and get to my office. You'd better be praying when I get there. Hard." The boy hurried out of the room.

"This," the principal thundered pointing his index finger at Robert, "is a teacher new in this system." Robert stood rigid behind his lectern, scanning its surface as though the answer to his miseries was written on it, his face screwed into anguish and embarrassment. "And this is the way the Junior Class of Blue Lake High School treats its new teachers?" His hand swept across the suddenly straight rows of desks. "I'm ashamed that you are students in my school! I'm ashamed that I'm the principal of a school where something like this can happen!" His anger elevated. "We don't train animals here! We teach students! We teach ladies and gentlemen!"

"You're juniors and you act like you're in diapers!" he roared.

He leveled his tone to mere intensity. "We try to support our new teachers here. We've got too much to do to help them as much as we should. But I hang out by classroom doors sometimes. I'm too aware that since the first day you entered Mr. Baker's classroom, you haven't given him a chance. Because his name isn't Gerney, and he doesn't make every single moment of your time entertaining. Gerney elected to leave this school. Mr. Baker didn't tell him to leave.

"Don't shake your head at me!" he thundered. "Do you know how immature your reaction to this man has been? I hear you in the halls. You sound like three year olds. Every day that he comes to work, which has been every single day so far this year, Mr. Baker stands in front of you in the classroom. There are thirty-plus of you and one of him in all of his classes. Those are pretty long odds. But every day Mr. Baker takes on those odds and does his level best. You ought to treat him like a hero. All of my teachers are heroes. But instead of giving him cooperation, you give him crap! It makes me sick.

"I want to be proud of the students in my school. You have embarrassed yourself, your school, and your principal in front of a man whose only desire is to help you learn by being given a chance to teach. Mr. Baker, I apologize for these students, and I apologize for not stepping on them sooner. Please give me a class list, so I can have individual conversations with these people. Perhaps I can convince them to become more suitable for inhabiting a classroom."

Sam returned his attention to the class again. "If I perceive, suspect, or hear about any problems anywhere in this school involving any of you, I will do my best to see that you do not graduate from this school," he threatened. He turned to Robert. "I suspect that you'll have no more problems with this group. I'll be checking from time to time to make sure I'm right."

The silent room pulsed like an open wound for the rest of the period. The books still there were opened, but Robert was aware of the many eyes focusing as much accusation as they could muster in his direction.

Barney Blair had created this chaos. But it was obvious the seventh period students believed Mr. Strand's intervention was Robert Baker's fault.

Sam Strand

Sam Strand turned his white Ford Taurus left at the corner of Pine and Eighth Street. The blue winter sky and the pure white of overnight snowfall made for a beautiful Friday morning. Near the Living Waters Lutheran Church on Pine, Estelle stood waiting for him, stamping her feet and over-shivering inside her leopard print coat. When he eased the white car to a stop, the small, bright woman opened the door and jumped in.

"We've got to start meeting like this, Sam," she smiled, then mugged into a grimace. "You've got to be more prompt though. It's freezing. I must have been standing there for a good two minutes. Trouble is, this car looks so much like dirty snow I thought I was being attacked by a snowdrift."

"Kids at school have been looking for this car for years. I always park next to a snow bank in the winter. Perfect camouflage. In May I paint it green. Then it's good to go for the summer. If we have a drought, I have to add a brown tint. Autumn is the real challenge, though."

The friends laughed. He'd been in the AA program for twenty-six years, and she'd qualified six years later. She was currently more faithful about getting to meetings. He and Estelle called each other on a regular basis whether he was seated around the table all the time or not. As she told him, "You may be able to miss a meeting, but you aren't going to miss Estelle."

"So," she inquired, "we're going to see . . . whom? Sarah Light?"

"Well, no, Estelle. Actually I've been meaning to tell you that Sarah's my wife and her last name is Strand. She's the light of my life, however."

Estelle slipped her arm through his. "You are so sweet, Sam. Why don't you divorce Sarah and marry me? It will take a great burden off her, and I can use my manipulative powers to keep you in your place." She patted his forearm and returned her hands to her lap.

"Those meetings are doing you a lot of good. No, seriously, we're going to see if we can see Megan Light. Her daughter's name is Patty Light. Patty's turned in about five work, study and early college scholarship applications. Three are unsigned by her mother and the other two have an illegible name scrawled in the blank. This girl deserves as much help as she can get. She's one of our best and hardest working students. I've tried calling her mother during the day. No answer. I've tried after school. If anyone answers, it's Patty, and her mother can't come to the phone. Reason I called you, other than to hear your sexy voice, is because I have some hunches about what may be going on in the Light household. If my hunches are right, I wanted Mrs. Light to meet someone who has really been sick!"

Estelle slapped her hands on her cheeks. "Thank you, Sam! I don't know when I've felt so not complimented!"

"When you tell her your story, it will be living proof that progress, not perfection, is our goal. And she'll be so encouraged that one can make so little progress in twenty years and still stay sober. She'll realize that if there's hope for you, there has to be hope for anyone."

Estelle had become an instant favorite of Sam's the night she stepped in out of the cold for her first meeting. Her growth had actually been quite visible, and it had not taken long for her playful wit to surface. He enjoyed whatever time they found reasons to be in one another's company.

"So, my dear, this trip has been brought to you by intuition. You can tell that to Tad when you get home."

"Oh, he won't even ask. He knows you're trying to seduce me, and that my remarkably good taste in men will never let that happen."

While talking, he'd noted the house numbers. He eased the accelerator and pointed to a two-story house on the right side of the street. Gray and peeling, the place looked ignored. "It looks depressed," Estelle said.

"And closed," Sam added, easing his car to a halt in front of the house. "All the shades and drapes are drawn. I have a hunch this will only work, if at all, if you accompany me to the door."

The friends walked gingerly up the walkway. Someone had tried to keep the path open, but the snow had slicked to ice. Apparently most of the shoveling took place after dark. Estelle clutched Sam's arm to keep from falling. He left her standing at the bottom of the stoop while he ascended three of its four cracked concrete steps, then rapped lightly on the battered aluminum storm door. He waited for several moments, then rapped more firmly. His peripheral vision thought it saw a flipping of the drapes that covered the picture window. No one appeared at the door.

"Call her name," Estelle suggested, intently observing the house.

"Mrs. Light," Sam complied. "Mrs. Light, are you home?" He thought he heard the word "don't" from inside the home, but if he did, it had woven with the wind so well he wasn't sure. "Mrs. Light . . . " he repeated. But he didn't want to draw attention from the neighbors. Or frighten Patty's mother. That wouldn't do anybody any good. "Mrs. Light, I'm here to talk about Patty's early college scholarship and work-study applications."

The house maintained its mute response. "Guess we'll go," Sam decided and descended the stairs. He turned to look at the house. There was no movement he could discern. He shrugged his shoulders and placed his hand on Estelle's shoulder to signal it was time to depart.

The two settled into the Taurus. Sam let the motor idle for a moment, then eased away from the curb. He shook his head. "Am I crazy or did you see that drape move a little?"

"Yes, I did. As we pulled away, I saw a shade upstairs move as well. It was like the wind was breathing on it so a little sunshine could penetrate that place."

The principal headed his car straight down the street rather than retracing the route that had brought its riders to the Light house.

"Sam, it's finally happening!" Estelle exclaimed. "We're actually racing off to begin our long delayed mad, passionate affair!"

"Whoops, sorry, my dear," Sam grimaced. He performed an illegal U-turn at the next intersection and headed back up the street. "I got lost in thought. I think I'd better get to the meeting tonight, Estelle. I lost it yesterday in front of a class full of students."

"Meetings never hurt, but sometimes kids deserve what they get."

"They deserved it all right. But it took me all night to calm down. My anger was righteous and right. But I can't convince myself that it was that good for the teacher I was defending or for myself."

"All we can do, Sam," Estelle said, patting her friend's arm, "is try to do the best we can. I haven't a second's doubt that's what you did." She gave the arm a playful slap. "That's for you to decide. A meeting always helps me. In case you've forgotten, it starts at eight."

Frank Marin

God Mr. Hunter

Yes, God Mr. Hunter. That's who you think you are. You think you know my secrets? Nobody knows my secrets. My stupid parents are making me come to this stupid class, this stupid school, but they don't know my secrets. You stand up there with that phony serious look on your face and every time I look up at you, you're staring a hole through me. You think you got it made with your combed hair and your beady hazel eyes that all the little girls "just love". You make me itch. This whole school makes me itch. It's so damned cold in here. Why don't you turn up the heat? Nature boy. I heard you open the windows to watch the snowflakes swirl in. Idiot. You just do it because all the girls giggle and jiggle and pout and purr, and you just love that. You go for the young stuff you pervert. I saw you looking at Patty Light. Many times.

Know why I'm so angry? God, I wish these fifteen minutes were over. These fifteen minute writings suck. Just like you. It's so damned quiet in here. I can't stand it. All I hear is the scratching of pens on paper. Why did I come to school? Cuz my old man had me by the shirt after he talked to Strandy Dandy and he stands in my room every morning until I get dressed and shoves me in the car and watches me until I walk through the damned school door and then there stands Strand watching me, and he always has that grin on his face and he says, "Good morning, Frank." Watches me until I walk into the damned classroom. Why's everybody watching me!!!! I hate the guts of everyone in this school. Oh, yeah. Merry Christmas, Hunter Punter.

"Time," Mr. Hunter called. "As I said, I'll read these and let you keep your journals with you over Christmas so you can write in them." He waited while the mandatory protests passed around the room. "If it's real personal, put 'Don't Read' at the top and I won't read it."

"If we're going to put 'Don't Read,' why do you want us to pass it in?" Dan Jansen asked.

"Yeah!" Frank grunted. But his voice sounded loud as a cannon fired in a bathroom. He pulled his head into his raised jacket collar, waiting for Hunter to return the shot. The teacher either hadn't heard or chose to ignore the comment.

"Because, Dan," the instructor answered with the same reasons as always, "most of you won't put 'Don't Read' because you're so confident about your writing. Besides it's fifteen points whether you allow me into your lives or brains or weird thoughts or not. All I have to have is your name to prove you tried. Nothing' to lose, right?"

"I guess not," the boy replied, finishing the game.

"Pass 'em up," Hunter ordered.

As murmurs of conversations accompanied that activity, Frank crumpled the paper he'd written and passed in the paper that was blank except for his name as he had whenever he'd been in this class for the past two months.

When the teacher told the class they could talk quietly for the rest of the period, Frank sank into himself. God it was hot in this room. Why didn't Hunter turn down the thermostat! His armpits were soaked with perspiration under his jacket. Sweat was sliding out of his hair and down his cheeks. He swiped at the dribbling ooze with the backs of his hands.

Wouldn't even be here if it wasn't for Strand and his parents.

Wouldn't be with his college buddies either. They hadn't called since he told them he'd have to lay low for awhile since his parents were nosing around his room. He hadn't talked to Betts either. When he called last week, she answered. It wasn't easy for him to ask for anything, but he asked if they could meet somewhere. She said sure, she could drive into town and pick him up. She thought his stuff was really good. So she did, and they rode around for a while, ending up at the park. She kissed him hard a few times and mentioned how she could use a few tokes off a joint to help her relax and open up. When he told her about how his parents were all over him and how he'd had to secrete the stash for a while, her body froze. She patted his leg and said that her folks were on her case, too, and if she wasn't home getting supper ready for them and stuff like that, they might ask her to leave the house, and she didn't have a penny to her name. Then she drove him back and dropped him a block from his house and said, "Call me when things get better." He knew what she meant.

God, I need a joint, Frank thought, then watched the second hand on the round school clock above Hunter's desk inch around and around for the rest of the period. God he hated school!

Billy Cloud

Since he hadn't heard from Patty Light concerning his invitation to her to accompany him to the Christmas Snow Ball, Billy Cloud decided he wouldn't go either. It saved him the trouble of asking for use of the family car. It also made him feel a little lost and lonely. He'd had visions of himself fetching the young lady from her home, a pretty smile erasing the usual seriousness from her face. His vision showed the two riding down the quiet streets of Blue Lake, snowflakes twirling under the streetlights and in front of the car's headlights, neither of them talking much, the pleased flush on her cheeks radiating warmth across the car seat to him. He saw them floating the blue-lit dance floor, she shy and a little awkward, he with his hand gently touching her back to guide her, the palm of her hand resting on the skin of the palm of his hand, her eyes gazing around the room with wonder, then meeting his.

So much for that vision, Billy thought as he walked alone through the emptying Blue Lake business section. The dance would begin at eight, and it was just a little past seven-thirty according to the giant watch fob clock that ticked above the entrance to Joely's Jewelry. He watched cars of students glide by, some filled, others containing only a boy and his date, a number filled with only boys or only girls. Some drivers or their passengers recognized him and waved. The window of one car rolled down and a girl shouted, "I'll save a dance for you, Billy!" He smiled and waved and felt lonelier than he had. This is stupid, he mused. I could go to that dance and have a good time. Instead I am wandering down Main Street feeling extremely sorry for myself. I walk alone all the time and love it. Tonight I hate it. What's wrong with me! Maybe I will go to the dance. Darn it!

Instead he stopped under a streetlight, bit down on two of the gloved fingers of his right hand to pull the glove free, reached in his jacket pocket, and withdrew the paper containing Patty's address. If he couldn't see the girl, he could at least see her house. He'd located the area she lived in on the city map he kept in his desk drawer. All he had to do was read the street signs to follow the path he'd traced on the map.

Stalking deer and other game was an activity he'd engaged in for years with varying degrees of pleasure and guilt. Stalking girls had never been in his repertoire. Oh, he'd had dates and friends who were girls, but he'd been content to let stuff happen. He'd never forced the issue. That realization almost made him turn around and go home. Then he decided that he and Patty ending up at Mr. Baker's desk together was one of those things that was supposed to happen. Her lack of response to his invitation was countered by his memory of her words and the look in her eyes before fear of her mother's reaction competed for space. She would like to have gone. She's waiting for me to execute Plan B.

Snowflakes were twirling in the light of the street lamps as he strode the sidewalks. "That's a pretty chintzy return on my vision," he told them.

It wasn't a cold night, somewhere around thirty, and his brisk pace provided warmth. He'd like to take Patty cross-country skiing under a full moon sometime. It would feel like this, and it would be great following her jacket and jeans down the silent, blue-white trail, the wind soft and westerly... "Vision man," he muttered. He checked another street sign under a streetlight and discovered he was close to Patty's home.

There were houses with outside door lights on, so Billy was able to establish the pattern of the house numbers. He told himself the good spirits of the other world had seen to it that lights were lit so he could discern the path to his destination. But he had to concede that some lights were on because the teenage inhabitants of the homes were where he wasn't.

As he continued down the street, he counted the house numbers since the outside lights were fewer. The houses were older and leaner.

He reached what he was pretty sure was Patty's home, but continued down the block until he saw another house number. Then he turned around, counting backwards, and discovered he'd been right.

The house was tall and thin. It had two stories. Though it couldn't be later than eight o'clock, there were no lights on downstairs. Upstairs a single light, probably from the small desk lamp of a previous vision, cast enough light for it to crawl just over the lip of the windowsill. He had no doubt that lighted room was Patty's bedroom, and that she was sitting at the desk. Nor did he doubt that if he stood on the sidewalk where he was for awhile, she would look out the window and see him.

When she did, he would lift his hand and wave it broadly back and forth so the motion would catch her eyes. What would happen beyond that, he wasn't sure. Perhaps she'd call the police. Wouldn't that be great! Still, he stood on the sidewalk and waved at the window.

Patty's shadow disappeared. While he waited to see what, if anything, was going to happen, he wondered whether it was possible Ms. Light hadn't replied to his request because she lived in this house in this part of town. That seemed unlikely. Native Americans weren't exactly famed for fabulous mansions, complete with pale butlers, three greyhounds, and maids scurrying about. "Three greyhounds?" he muttered.

He saw movement and watched Patty emerge on the sidewalk and walk toward him. When she was next to him, she put her face close to his and whispered, "I knew you were coming here."

He whispered back, "Your vision apparatus is better than mine." Then he added, "Why are we whispering?"

"My mother's asleep, and the last thing I want in this entire world is for her to wake up." Though they were whispered, the words struck Billy's ears like needles of freezing rain. No wonder they weren't going to the dance.

"I've come to escort you around the block," he whispered, "about fifty times, I hope."

"It's a beautiful night," was her response. Then each slipped their hands into their own pockets, their elbows almost touching as they strolled down the street away from Patty Light's home. "Let's walk down this way for awhile," she said in a low voice. "Let's keep walking straight." He glanced at her. Her shadowed eyes seemed sad, or maybe it was the lack of light.

The two walked for a long time, walked as far as the road went and the town terminated, then returned on the same route. He never broke her silences. He let her do that when she was ready, and she was ready only for quiet comments on the beauty of the night and gratitude that he had come to share it with her.

Ed Warrum

Christmas vacation turned out to be not too bad at all for Ed Warrum.

He took Shellie to the Christmas Snow Ball because he'd promised he would. Though he didn't feel festive, he liked her. She shared no blame for what happened in his home and with his father. Those were topics that rarely entered their conversations. Even after Pete Warrum had made an ass out of himself, when he shoved Coach Howard at that football game, they spoke about the problem briefly. Ed said, "Sometimes my dad is an idiot." That was enough for both of them on that subject.

Shellie preferred the sunnier scenes in life, like Ed's brilliant play after the altercation. She balanced his moodiness with her eternal ebullience. She was an enthusiastic, cheerful cheerleader who never asked too many questions and filled his silences with her chatter. She accepted moodiness as a guy thing and pretty much ignored it. Maybe she didn't delve deep, but the only times he found reasons to smile were when he was with her.

When Ed picked her up for the Snow Ball, Shellie looked stunning in her red Christmas dress with white fake fur trimming and a scooped neckline. Gazing at her while making small talk with her parents, he realized one of the things he'd lose if he did something stupid with that gun would be Shellie Chaine and evenings like this.

The thought made the event sparkle for him. The decorations in the gymnasium were iridescent. The scent of Shelly's perfume brought images of his mother's flower garden to mind. Her fluid movements on fast tunes and the feel of her body moving with his on slow ones were incredibly sensual. By the end of the dance he was awash with love and desire and Shellie knew it.

But he took her straight to the Burger Shelf for a hamburger and shake afterwards and stared into her eyes whenever she wasn't chatting with her many friends as they passed by their booth. He invited one of the couples to sit with them while his ardor simmered. He wanted to do nothing that would spoil this evening.

He went to work at his father's store the next morning. Doing so filled him with nostalgia. He was only eight when he begged Pete Warrum to let him do something at the store. That had been during the Christmas rush, just as this day was. The store had glittered with decorations, been stuffed with toys, and was full of shoppers every day. His job had been to rearrange the toys after they'd been pawed and scattered by customers. He had worked hard at the job to please his dad and enjoyed it.

The practice of having him work during vacations, some weekends, and summers had continued, and the place became a sanctuary. Pete Warrum was increasingly busy schmoozing his cronies in the apartment above the store where Ed and his family had lived until he was four. Because it was the oldest and largest store of its kind in town, it hummed with activity. Even when Ed took over at the counter, his proximity to his father was no factor. The elder Warrum was too busy and self-involved to pay attention.

Then, too, the addition of Gail Hunter to the clerking staff six years ago had provided his first experience with love. He was eleven, and she was exceptionally beautiful. She treated him with the kind of affection that women without children of their own find for the children of others. She floated through his dreams, more exquisite than any princess in a Disney movie, and he never lost his awe of her. Even as his father's obsessive dreams for his son's athletic success and his arrogance over the success of his business increased and began to rub the nerves of his employees, Gail Hunter never altered her attitude toward Ed.

He worked mornings because basketball practice was held in the afternoons. Mornings were when Pete Warrum exited the store to spend an hour or so drinking coffee with his buddies at the Burger Shelf. Fortunately, too, basketball held only a little interest for Pete. He saw it as a way for Ed to stay in shape. His son's future lay in football, not round ball.

Ed was an excellent athlete. He had begun the season's practices as the starting forward. The turmoil of October and November had destroyed his focus and turned him listless. It didn't matter to him. Basketball practice kept him away from home for several hours, as did games. His father and mother showed up for home games. Pete occasionally questioned the wisdom of his son sitting on the bench, but Ed's lack of contributions muted further comments. Having achieved the upper hand in molding the sentiment of those who mattered, Pete was not about to blow his advantage over a sport unimportant to him and a son who obviously wasn't too hot about the game himself. For Ed, it was as though he had fashioned a strategy to pull the plug of the blinding spotlight football shined on him. He was content to have it remain that way.

Since their last fight about Coach Howard, the subject had not come up at home, nor was it apparent at the store. As Ed swept the floors, stocked the shelves, or waited on customers, he began to hope that controversy was not only dead in the house, but also in the community. Now that football was over, maybe his father realized what a fool he'd made of himself, how he'd changed from a parent who could show respect and affection to one who burned white hot with ambition for his kid and didn't care who got hurt in the process, even if it was Ed. Maybe he was capable of changing back.

Ed wasn't sure he believed that, but he allowed the Season of Hope to filter some optimism into his head. Maybe that gun, carefully boxed, wrapped, and bowed, could remain in the back of the right corner of his closet hidden by a pile of his shoes. Maybe some day in the early spring when the ice thawed on the lakes, he could take a lone walk along the shore and hurl it toward the deep water and never think about it again.

His hope for that outcome might have remained stronger had not Mrs. Hunter come into the store on the morning of December 30th to return some perfume her husband had bought her for Christmas. Ed was attending the counter and his father was out for coffee. When he looked up from the register and she was across the counter from him, he felt the full rush of years of affection. She was more beautiful than ever.

"Happy New Year," she greeted. "Oh, I know I'm early, but we're leaving town to go to the Cities, so I know I won't see you before it's already next year." She smiled, then patted his hand, which rested on the corner of the register. "One thing I miss about working here is watching you rush around during the Christmas season. You've always been my favorite."

Ed smiled as shyly as an eleven year old. He wanted to say, "You want to know how I've felt about you for the last six years?" Instead he said, "Gee, it's good to see you, Mrs. Hunter. The store isn't the same without you in it. How's your new job?"

"Well, I have to admit it's causing me to put a lot more miles on the car. But I also have to admit I love it."

"That's great," Eddie replied, meaning it. Then he noticed the small bag in her hand. "Is there something I can help you with?"

"I hope so," Gail answered, extracting a small bottle of perfume from the bag. "Kyle . . . excuse me, Mr. Student, I mean Mr. Hunter, bought this perfume for me for Christmas. I guess the poor dear forgot how allergic I am to it. I think I lost twenty pounds sneezing last time he bought it before we figured out what the problem was." Her light laugh sounded to him like wind chimes brushed by a breeze. "Ky . . . Mr. Hunter can remember every student he's taught, but not every perfume he's bought. Okay if I return this?"

"Sure, Mrs. Hunter. No problem. I suppose Mr. Hunter is pretty glad to get away from us for a while. Hope he's having a good vacation."

"Well, yes he is. We've done some cross-country skiing. He's even finished reading all the student papers he brought home for the holidays. He's been bothered about the next school board meeting though." She placed the perfume in his hand. "Don't drop it or your father will be very upset. I think it's pretty expensive."

Ed set the perfume down with mock carefulness, then bent down on his haunches to search for an exchange form. "You said Mr. Hunter was bothered by the school board meeting? How come?" He found the form and stood up. He slid it and a pen toward Mrs. Hunter. "Just sign where those check marks are and put the name of the perfume in the blank next to it."

As she wrote, Gail replied, "Truthfully, I'm not too sure. I've been gone a lot, and Ky . . . Mr. Hunter brings papers home from school, but not problems. He says when he leaves the castle, he leaves the keepers as well. I think it has something to do with one of your coaches," she concluded as she finished writing and slid the paper back to Ed. She was sorry she'd broached the subject since she'd heard Pete Warrum's name connected to it, and sorry that she'd made her husband look bad.

Ed had heard the rumors. But his father had been silent on the issue for a month. "Maybe they're going to give him some kind of award," Ed said, willing himself to believe that might be true. "I'll ring this up, Mrs. Hunter, and give you your money back." He did so, carefully counting it into her palm. "There you go. Say 'hey' to Mr. Hunter."

Gail put her hand lightly on Ed's arm. "It was really nice seeing you, Eddie. You take care of yourself." He watched her walk out of the store. Mr. Hunter is a lucky guy, he concluded.

Several more customers had collected at the counter. He shuffled mention of the board meeting into a far corner of his mind. This Christmas vacation had surprised him with its lack of conflict, had in fact presented him with moments that glittered and memories of better times in his family. A poem Mr. Baker had mentioned said, "Hope is a thing with feathers." Ed had allowed hope to enter his emotions, and it had taken flight. He wasn't going to let it fall back to earth easily.

Kyle Hunter

Christmas passed pleasantly enough. Gail had had to work two weeks straight servicing special orders, preparing inventories for the new year and running to the Cities to two special meetings dealing with product lines desiring to penetrate Kerns Stores.

The corporate Christmas party was actually held on New Year's Eve, the days around Christmas being far too active and important to set aside time for relaxation, much less celebration. The corporate party was open to any employee in the five state area who could get to the Cities to attend. Many had been to previous parties and opted out. Thus newer employees, residents of the Cities, and executives dominated the list.

The idea of corporate parties rang no bells for Kyle Hunter. He pictured the event as a roomful of men in pin-striped suits and women dressed to the nines and wearing too much makeup. The talk would be so oily that by evening's end the floor would be slicked.

Nevertheless, he accompanied Gail to the Cities. Kerns provided all out state employees with two-night reservations at the upscale Brentwood Hotel where the event was held. The Hunters spent New Year's Eve day within the place, since it contained everything they needed.

At the party, Gail, dressed in a soft blue party dress with a neckline exactly low enough, was a star. Everyone seemed to know her and like her. A few evinced light lust. The innuendo contained in several greetings and comments to his wife, even before the hors d'oeuvres were consumed and the drinking escalated, didn't please Kyle. One handsome, if florid, character went so far as to regard Gail's pert breasts and shapely legs. He leaned close to her ear and stage whispered, "Four to go is right!" He was not pleased when his wife responded with a brilliant smile, a light push on the Lothario's shoulder and an, "Oh, you." She retained that neon smile when she whispered in Kyle's ear, "He's a sexist flirt. He says things like that to all the girls." Kyle couldn't quite manage to believe that.

For a while Gail kept him on her arm. It was foolish, but he felt like he'd crashed this party where everyone else was at ease. Jokes were told, hugs exchanged, discussions of the status of seasonal sales occurred. Hands rested comfortably in the small of other people's backs during conversations, seemingly ready to slide downward at any moment. Gail finally loosed her arm from his, pointed at a smashing brunette woman standing near the cash bar, and said she had to talk to Rita, who was a regional buyer like her. Kyle was left in the center of the room. Dressed in his blue blazer, his dark blue clip-on tie, his white shirt, his navy blue slacks, his black loafers, he felt naked standing by himself, knowing no one and unable to bring himself to change that. Now he knew how Robert Baker felt in the faculty lounge. He really had to do more to help that guy out.

When Gail returned bearing glasses of punch, he smiled wanly at her. "You're right. I read too many journals. I'm starting to think like a journal."

"What?" she responded to the non sequitur, with a quizzical half-smile on her face making him think she thought he was a bit daft and she wasn't. It was the only expression her face developed that he couldn't stand.

"Nothing," he replied. "Why don't you go ahead and butterfly for awhile, and I'll find a corner in which to stand."

"What?" she said.

If he had to look at that look for ten more seconds… "Socialize for a while. I'm worn down from meeting so many people. I need a break. Go talk to your friends. And please don't say 'what' one more time."

"Kyle," she said gently, "do you want to go?"

"No." He shook his head, "I don't. Big boys don't cry. I'm okay." He was sure his comment hadn't made a lick of sense, but he'd opened his mouth and the words popped out. What could he do? How could he blame her if she looked at him like his marbles were scrambling for position?

As for Gail, she shrugged her creamy shoulders. "If vague and feather-brained," she laughed. "Okay. Go look out the windows, but please don't jump." Then she walked away toward one of her bosses, whose name, Kyle had learned, was Fred Waters, her hips swaying slightly. Waters was already engaged in entertaining several other women including Rita.

It was snowing outside. Kyle stood by one of the room's ceiling-to-floor windows and watched it. He was always uncomfortable for a while around people he didn't know. That was why the first days of school made him irritable and edgy. It was a character flaw of which he was aware. Unfortunately it served to develop a bit of wariness in his students. That aided his classroom management and would be overcome later because he loved what he was doing and cared about students. Still, at times like this, the flaw was a burden. He wished he could turn it on and off with a switch.

It was true, however, that people rarely know how to react to teachers. They either feared them, put them on a pedestal, loved them, resented them, or pitied them. It was hard to be normal with people who couldn't quite see you as human, an alien who worked with other aliens called students. And an English teacher! Once they got past dealing with the fact that you taught and were overworked, underpaid, and probably didn't do a lousy job, then they had to react to you as an "English teacher." They "just loved" English or "hated it." It was either their "favorite subject," or they "couldn't understand grammar at all." "Poetry killed it for me." "I loved poetry." He could write the dialogue ahead of time and hand out slips of paper, so the folks could just read them and not waste time thinking.

Aw, it wasn't that bad. He was emphasizing the negative again.

When he turned from the window, Fred Waters was standing next to him, a drink held in his right hand's thumb and forefinger and cradled in the palm of his left. "Lost in thought I see," the tall, dark-suited man commented, an easy smile on his face. "I'd bet a million dollars you were thinking about teaching. Most teachers I know think about it 24/7."

"You're right," Kyle acknowledged. "It's an occupational disease."

"I suppose it can be much the same in the business world. The difference is in the financial rewards obsession brings. I've read your writing. You're very, very good. That kind of persuasive writing can easily be converted into advertising for all the media."

He took a sip of his drink and glanced out the window. "Snow sure is beautiful, isn't it." Then he fixed his gaze on Kyle. "One thing I can assure you, Kyle, you'd make a lot more money working with us than you'll ever make as a teacher. We set a steady pace in our department and have a small group of dedicated people who share their ideas and are open and creative. Doesn't sound so different from teaching, does it? The difference is in the rewards."

Kyle nodded and continued to listen.

"As I said before, I have friends in your profession, and I have tremendous admiration for them. But I know from them that teaching is becoming more and more of a struggle. I don't think it's going to get any better. You're on the public rolls, and people are not going to let you know that you deserve to be rewarded. If they did, they'd have to pay you what you're worth. That would raise our taxes. And in case you haven't noticed, the folks in power aren't exactly raving about the job you're doing. They know how your bread is buttered. They know they're holding you hostage. They know if they point their fingers at you long enough, you'll weary of their negative attention and fall back into silence, so you can do your job.

"I suppose I have a vested interest in saying this. I hate to do so. My friends are stubbornly loyal and dedicated to what they're doing, but they're getting very tired. As far as I can see, you've no hope of things getting better in the future for teachers. Just more of the same. The opponents of public education have done their advertising well. They've undermined public confidence in every school and every teacher. Many swallow that whole except, of course, for the schools their kids attend and the teachers who teach their kids. With us, you'd join a company that's going to grow. You and your wife could realize some real fine times out of that. You could afford to enjoy some of the worlds your education's revealed to you. Please think about it. I wouldn't expect you to join us until the school year is over. I know how you folks are."

Waters placed his drink in his left hand and extended his right. "It's been good talking with you. I should say talking at you. When I start, I'm like a snowball rolling down a hill. Sorry." He grasped Kyle's hand firmly.

"I will. I'll think about it. And I actually don't mind being complimented," Kyle said. He genuinely liked the man and his enthusiasm. He could think of no arguments to counter the points Fred had made.

"Good," Waters said. "Now I'd better go kiss up to my boss. So that you'll see that no job is perfect. Not even in our company." He nodded, beaming, and walked away as Gail emerged from the crowd and headed his way, her hips swaying, her cleavage peeking above her scooped neckline. She looked stunning. How had he ever managed to take her for granted?

"I saw you talking to Fred," she said, no odor of alcohol on her breath.

"Actually you saw me listening to him," Kyle corrected and noticed the disappointment in her eyes. Why were his words so tinged with sarcasm these days? He added, "He's an enthusiastic guy. I think he offered me a job. Did you tell him to do that or send him to rescue me from myself?"

"No, Kyle," she insisted, disappointment still evident. "The only thing I did was show him your writing." She gave in. "So I suppose I did set it up. But I didn't tell him he had to like your writing. He decided. I didn't tell him to offer you a job. Gee whiz, who do you think I am?"

"The most beautiful saleswoman I've ever seen," Kyle said, placing his hands on her bare upper arms. "I am tremendously complimented by what you did and what he said. So I'm actually going to make an effort to enjoy myself for the rest of this evening."

And he did. He lifted himself out of his mental crouch and spent the rest of the evening thinking of himself as a prospective employee who should get to know his potential work mates.

When he and Gail returned to their room, she was exhilarated, and he relaxed into her glow. They undressed one another slowly, then made the most tumultuous love they'd made in years.

It was after they were done and Gail was asleep, her hair barely touching his arm, that a tremendous sadness coursed through him. He was thinking about quitting teaching, and the thought was breaking his heart.

Robert Baker

Robert Baker watched the heatless winter sun descend into the hills in front of him as he drove his new used Dodge sedan along the freeway. Swooping curves revealed woods and farms nestled in those hills and numerous neat little towns nestled in valleys along the way. He was returning from his Christmas trip home, a trip that looked so much like a disaster to his concerned parents that they'd cosigned a loan with him so he'd buy this newer car in hopes it would help lift his spirits.

He'd gone back east in hopes of escaping the rigidity that had altered his personality and the memory of the turmoil that had rocked his seventh period. That disaster had thrown him completely off balance, and his long drive home had given him ample opportunity to recall all of his other failures. It gave him plenty of time to build his anger over the fact that every time he seemed to be making progress something happened to convince him that he'd made no progress at all. It gave his anger plenty of time to burrow into his brain with the news that it was he who was to blame that this was so. He'd wanted to arrive home with stories to tell about his eager students, interesting colleagues and classroom triumphs. Instead he arrived with nothing much he wanted to share at all.

He'd always been "serious, intense, and driven to please and succeed," his father told his mother a few days after his return home. Teaching is hard work. He's just tired." That gave him an excuse to retreat into the small box of himself and to tape the lid from the inside so only he could decide when it was time to talk.

❖ ❖ ❖

Robert had visited Nancy Morgan the evening after Christmas at her parents' house. She'd come up from her nursing school for a three-day break.

They'd kissed each other on the cheek and watched television in the basement rec room with her parents.

"They haven't seen me since September," Nancy whispered to Robert when her parents trotted up the stairs to pop some popcorn for them. "They're determined to spend as much of the seventy-two hours I'm here with me as they can. But I think we can outlast them. Just like the old days. You do remember the old days, don't you?"

He did. They'd spent many a late night sitting on the sofa they sat on now talking of serious matters, but laughing a lot, too, before indulging in some serious necking with her parents asleep two floors above. "We're just plain wicked," Nancy would breathe into his ear. "Don't you just love it?"

He had. He did. Her natural ebullience and sense of play had helped him locate his own amidst his more reserved nature. Those qualities and her warmth and generous spirit were going to make her a great nurse someday. She'd certainly made the right decision for herself. "You must love your school," he said.

"I do. I love every minute of it. I love what I'm learning. I love that I'm already working with patients. Yes, I love my school. Do you love yours?"

"Not so much," he said. He might have said more, but Nancy's parents were coming down the stairs.

"Popcorn's ready, kids. Hope you're hungry. We popped two tons of it by mistake."

Since it was difficult to share his truths with Nancy's parents sitting there, Robert indulged their desire to focus on their only daughter's presence. Once the TV was off, they peppered her with questions about her experiences as though they hadn't already spent almost two days with her. They finally went up to bed just before midnight.

"I guess I forgot they were such night owls," Robert said.

"They weren't. I think they figured out what we were up to down here all those years and decided we needed some serious chaperoning," Nancy laughed.

"You haven't changed, have you?" Robert asked.

"I think I've grown up a little," she answered. "If I'd done that a little sooner, I'd have told you how important my dream of being a nurse is to me. Then my decision wouldn't have seemed like punishment for your decision to go to graduate school. Did it seem like that's what I was doing?" she asked, laying her hand on the top of the back of his.

"It did and it didn't. Waiting for me to make up my mind must have driven you nuts."

"No. I was miffed when you made that graduate school decision, then told me. Forgetting that I never told you a decision like that could get in the way of my dreams."

"Then I go and change the whole thing anyway."

"What bothers me right now, Bobby, is that I'm happy with the way things worked out, and you're not. If you'd never said a word, I could tell by your eyes."

He wanted to say, I wish I'd taken a teaching job sooner and we'd gotten married, but he didn't. She was happy and that was good. Instead he said, "Oh, teaching has its moments. My freshman study hall really likes me. I've got a few juniors who are outstanding. It could be worse. And sometimes is. End of story. Let's talk about you."

"No," she said as she curled her arms around his neck, "let's sit here and relive the old days for a few minutes instead. I want to know if it was as good as I thought it was."

It was. It was like finding an oasis in the middle of the desert, the water clear, cool, and unrippled by changing winds.

The next day Nancy needed to attend a reunion planned by other friends. She'd apologized and pleaded with him to meet her at the bus station the next morning so they could talk a little more and exchange a proper goodbye.

So he drove to the bus depot to watch her leave.

"It's really not going well for you, is it, Bobby," she said.

"No, not very," he admitted. He watched her bus slide into its slot outside the depot. He should tell her more, tell her all, but now there wasn't time. So he said, "It's a learning experience," to lighten her worry.

"Just remember, Bobby, you're smart and you're talented." He felt understood and vulnerable as he gazed at her sympathetic face.

He stood up and flipped up the collar of his coat. "Your bus is here."

She rose and put her hands on his cheeks. He wanted to lean into her hands, let go of everything else, hold her and be held by her. "Take care of yourself, Bobby. You are a good man." She kissed his lips and reached for her small suitcase, and took a few steps toward the passenger exit.

"Say," he said, "I could come down for New Year's."

"Oh. I'm working a shift and a half on both New Year's Eve and New Year's Day. That's how I got three days off to come here."

The bus rumbled beyond the doors. "I've got to go." She kissed him on the cheek and squeezed his hand. "Goodbye, Bobby."

He gave her a little wave, then dropped his hands in his coat pockets and watched her board the bus. She was fine. She'd always be fine. She was definitely a winner.

His father and mother had been a different matter. He'd tried now and then. He'd told them about the freshman study hall, too, and how they were all, like him, new kids on the block. He'd declined to tell them he no longer had a prep period. He'd said little else beyond small talk and polite pleasantries.

Robert spotted a motel advertisement for the next exit on one of those blue freeway signs. He decided to pull in for the night. He was as close to Blue Lake as he wanted to get right now.

Frank Marin

Frank Marin slid down in the back seat of his parents' old Ford. It was an embarrassing car to be seen in. The car's paint was fading, and its engine was louder than it ought to be because the muffler was the same one that came with the car 100,236 miles ago. He remained slumped almost below the window line until the family was well out of Blue Lake on its way to Bethel Ridge. It wasn't as though he was likely to see friends from school since he had none. His college buddies were long gone until January.

He'd noticed one thing in the bathroom mirror, though, while he was combing his long hair into its usual pompadour. His eyes weren't as milky as usual. In fact he could see his pupils clearly. His inability to get at his stash due to the close attention his dad and mother and the school were paying to him was responsible. He felt lousy, but he looked pretty good.

The Marin family was headed back to Bethel Ridge to check on the farm and do financial stuff at the bank. His parents were doing okay financially these days, so they were feeling good about this trip and walking into that bank with money in their pockets. He'd told his parents he wanted to stay in Blue Lake, but they had no ears for his words. He could understand that. He hadn't done anything to make them trust him. Besides, he wanted to go to Bethel Ridge. When he thought about the place, the hollow howl in his chest stilled for a while.

Halfway there, Frank admitted to himself that he liked the old Ford. He liked being slumped in its worn but clean back seat. He liked looking at the red, slightly wrinkled back of his father's thick neck and the regal way his mother occupied the passenger's side, arrow straight and alert. He felt like a little kid looking at them, and he allowed warm to roll around in his chest.

He had his portable player on and his earphones clapped to his ears playing that yowling hard rock stuff his college friends favored. He could hardly stand the way it knifed into his ears and made his brain buzz. He slid his earphones in front of his ears and dialed the volume way down. His dad was listening to the fifties and sixties oldies-but-goodies station he always tuned to after asking if it was okay. Frank objected because it was expected, but he liked those old songs. They had melodies you could sing and words you could hear. He wasn't about to tell his father that though, so he clapped the earphones over his ears snapped the player off, closed his eyes, let the music drift in from the front and fell asleep.

When he awoke, the car was rolling the hilly, sandy-soiled, rock infested farmland near Bethel Ridge. How could anybody think they could make a living farming here? Frank had asked his dad that when he was thir-teen and feeling smart. Cheap land and hard work was his father's reply. Remembering that, Frank felt sadness and pride for his old man. He tried to beat it away with his brain, but it wouldn't go. What was it about Bethel Ridge anyway? How could he feel so alive here and so dead in Blue Lake?

His dad eased the Ford into the Sunrise Motel parking lot at the edge of town. Frank wished they were staying at the farmhouse, but that was impossible. There wasn't a stick of furniture there, and everything was dis-connected. "Ain't nobody much stays here at this time of year, just enough to keep the place open. Chuck Wiggins is giving us a special deal on two rooms. I figured you'd be embarrassed to stay in the same room with your mother and me. But," his dad said, pointing a thick forefinger at him, "don't do anything to make us sorry."

Frank didn't answer, but he nodded. He stayed in the car while his par-ents signed in. Then they pulled the car in front of the two rooms, and Frank took his suitcase into his. It was small with a single bed, chintzy ply-wood walls, and an old TV. But he was as close as he could get to happy. He was back in Bethel Ridge.

The family ate at the Hurry Back Inn, the town's only restaurant. The food was excellent. Then his parents went to the bank while Frank strolled the two blocks of small stores and a gas station that comprised Main Street. In a town this size it was inevitable he'd run into Shmitty.

Frank's former friend came strolling out of the gas station as he walked past it. "Hey, Frankie-boy," he called, "long time no see." His voice retained the oral sneer that sometimes rubbed Frank's nerves down to the wood. There was a girl beside Shmitty wearing tight jeans below her short winter jacket. Even with her jacket on, it was easy to see she was well endowed. She reminded him of Betts. "Hey, you remember Bev, Bev Werner? Come on into the station. I gotta work 'til six. Talk about old times. Hey, how come you ain't drivin'?"

"Guess I never got around to taking the test."

The three sat in the station for half an hour, Shmitty doing most of the talking. Then Frank excused himself since he knew his folks' business at the bank would be winding up. Shmitty clapped him on the shoulder and said, "Hey, you know Bev here has a new friend named Annie who moved to town right after you left. How's about the four of us go for a little ride around eight o'clock or so?" Frank assented and left.

He and his parents took a drive out to the farm that afternoon. The fields were covered with snow. The gray, two-story farmhouse looked lonely. The driveway was snow packed so they made no attempt to trudge to the house.

As they headed back to town, his father eased the car to a stop in front of Corgan's farm place. "I got bad news about Mr. Corgan, Frank. He had a real bad stroke in November. They found him wanderin' down the road the next day, nothin' on but a tee shirt and bibbed overalls. He was limpin' bad and could only talk with half his mouth. He got pneumonia. They said he fought it hard and then got tired and went home to the Lord. December 26th." His eyes were on his son's face. Frank wanted to cry, but put his head down and turned his face to stone instead.

After supper at the Hurry Back, the Marins returned to the Sunrise Motel. Frank had been silent since hearing about Mr. Corgan. Frank said nothing about Shmitty because he hadn't had a thought about the boy since the news about Mr. Corgan.

As the alarm clock next to his bed flipped its numbers, he noticed it was 7:45. There was no phone, so he couldn't call to cancel the evening, and he sure as heck didn't want him coming to the motel where his folks would see him. They hated the guy. So Frank shrugged into the new lined leather jacket his folks had given him for Christmas. He thought about his dad telling him if he had to wear a leather jacket, he might as well be halfway warm.

He slipped out the door and walked toward town. When he spied a car roaring up the road, Frank began waving his arms. Sure enough, it was Shmitty, who executed a donut far too close to Frank for comfort. The car swerved to a halt as Frank scrambled into the ditch.

Shmitty jumped out of the car and ran in front of its headlights. He spied Frank and hollered, "Hey, Frankie-boy, didn't make you crap your pants, did I?" He put his hand over his eyebrows like he was saluting. Finally he slurred, "Hey, get outa da ditch and inna car."

Frank remembered how much he could dislike the guy, but he struggled out of the ditch and got in the car anyway. Bev was giggling wildly. She was on her way, too. She turned in her seat, sucked in her breath, and exhaled, "He's a maniac." And then, "Annie, this is Frankie. Frankie, Annie." She turned back and jacked up the volume of the radio.

Frank glanced at Annie as he slid in beside her. Though she was wearing a winter coat, he was sure she was as slender as Bev was voluptuous. Her face was winter pale, but kind of pretty if you could tell in this dim light. Her hands were in her coat pockets. Her voice was small when she said, "Hi."

"Hi," he grunted. The two sat in silence in the back seat as the car sped down the rural roads, the radio blaring and Bev giggling every time Shmitty touched her. The driver bent down almost against the steering wheel while going at least sixty. Bev whooped and screamed, but Shmitty sat up and backhanded a beer over the seat for Frank and another for Annie. Frank caught them and offered her one, but she shook her head.

Frank snapped the beer open. The first swallow gave him an unbelievable rush. By the time he finished the can, he was buzzed. "Great stuff," he told Annie. "You oughta try some."

"Not tonight," she answered in a near whisper.

Shmitty skidded his car to a halt when Frank was half done with the second beer. Frank knew they were in the country, but wasn't sure where in the dark. Since the car was stopped, and he was churning a bit and Shmitty and Bev were really smooching it up, he figured he should try a move on Annie. He quaffed a few more swallows of beer and was amazed at the heat coursing through him. He moved closer to Annie and draped his arm around her shoulders. She gave him a glance, then stared straight ahead. He felt embarrassed and removed his arm.

Shmitty glanced back. "Hey, buddy, go for it. Ain't nobody gonna bother us here. Old Corgan's dead." His right arm shot down past Bev's neck and his left was already somewhere else judging by Bev's squeals.

Frank felt sick. The car smelled steamy and close. Bev was hooting and hooting in the front seat. "I gotta go for a walk," he managed and slid toward the door.

"Hey, yeah," Shmitty howled, tossing Frank two more cans of beer. "Hey, Annie, take my friend Frankie-boy for a walk, will ya? Bev and me got a little business to take care of." His snarling guffaw grated like gravel on glass.

Frank was out the door, and Annie had no choice. He held the door for her until she got out, and then slammed it so hard the car rocked. They walked about ten steps. He turned to the girl. "God, we're in front of Corgan's place. Why did he have to park in front of Corgan's place?" They could hear yowling from the car. He wanted to race back and wrench the two out of the car and slam them against it. He wanted to scream, "Dammit, Mr. Corgan just died! This is Corgan's place!"

Annie was standing looking at Frank intently. "I'm sorry. I don't understand," she said.

"I knew Mr. Corgan. I worked for him. Come with me," he pleaded.

Having little choice, Annie nodded and they walked away from the car to the driveway of the farm. It was too dark to see the farmhouse. There was a wire and wood gate across the entrance. Frank shook his head and repeated, "Why did he have to park in front of Mr. Corgan's place? It's like humping on his grave!" The force of his words snapped Annie's head back. "I'm sorry," he said. "It makes me mad." He placed one of the beers on a fence post, and snapped it open. He saw Annie shake her head, but said, "I gotta talk to you about Mr. Corgan." How could she understand that or understand he hardly talked at all unless he was using or drinking? He couldn't tell her that. So he took a few swallows and plunged ahead. She was a captive audience. He leaned against the two-by-four topping the gate, stared into the dark farmyard, and talked more than he had talked forever.

He told her how he and his Dad had stopped at Corgan's from the time he was little. How he immediately liked the craggy-faced man who had no children of his own and took a liking to him as well. Even then Corgan lived alone. His wife had died in childbirth years before and the baby had too. Corgan seldom talked about that, but one day he and Frank were sitting on the hay wagon staring out at the harvested autumn fields and Corgan just started to talk. He told Frank that he figured his wife had married him, because her first name was Cora, and the two names sounded so good together. He'd married her because he was so much in love that everything he looked at sparkled. He said she was as strong as any man out in the fields, as good in the kitchen as any wife in the county, and soft and pretty and gentle when he sat beside her in church. When she got pregnant, some infection entered her body without either of them knowing. If she had pain, she never told him. One day he found her doubled over in the bedroom and rushed her to the hospital thirty-three miles away in Bentford. He drove there every night, and every night she was dying a little bit more and the baby was dying, too. He was holding her hand feeling her life flow away and cold replace it when she died. "When I looked at him, his face was all wet. He was crying all the time he told me the story, but he never made that sound." Frank wanted to tell more, but he was all welled up inside and had to stop before his chest exploded. He downed the last of the beer and reached into his other pocket.

All of the time he talked, Annie stood quietly looking at him, listening to him. She must be a saint. But when he fumbled his hand into his pocket, she said, "Please don't drink anymore right now." Though the urge drummed in his body and head, he honored her request. She'd listened to him. He could honor Corgan this way, too. So he said, "We'd better get back to the car. It's cold."

When they got to the car and opened the door, Shmitty was smoking and drinking another beer, his head tilted back on the headrest. Bev was clutching her coat to her chest. Neither one was talking. Shmitty slurred, "Hey, Annie, beer drive. I's be a bit drunk. And Frankie-boy here, he ain't old enough ta drive. Me 'n Bev'll sit back. We's gotta get a few things straightened out."

When Frank slid into the passenger's seat, his ankles clanged against the amazing pile of beer cans on the floor. He glanced at Annie who was looking at the cans. "I'm going to drive exactly the speed limit. If we get stopped with those in here, we'll be in jail for a million years," she said.

As she wheeled the car around, Shmitty ordered, "Turna radio up real loud, Frankie boy. We gonna talk 'bout stuff you don' wanna hear."

Frank obeyed the order and then put his head back against the headrest and closed his eyes. Corgan's face was behind his lids, and then Annie's after he'd opened his eyes and glanced at her features shadowed by the dashboard lights. Hope Bev's pregnant, Frank decided. Serve that jerk right.

Annie stopped at her house at the edge of town. Frank said, "I'm gonna get out here, too." Noticing her startled look, he added, "I'm gonna walk back to the motel. Gotta get rid of this beer smell." The couple in the back seat moved to the front wordlessly. He watched Annie walk in front of the headlights. She looked delicate and natural. He was sure she was going to walk or run right past him, so he said too loudly, "Thanks."

Annie stopped and the two watched Shmitty's car swerve down the road. She looked at him and took her hands out of her pockets. "You and Mr. Corgan have one thing in common. You both cry without making a sound. Although I don't think you knew you were." She brushed her right hand lightly his cheek and spread the wetness a little. "I have to go in. Please don't drink that last beer." Then she ran up the sidewalk and disappeared into her house.

Frank wished it was that easy. His brain was howling for more. It had lost its numbness and was filled with little bolts of lightning. Dammit. She'd listened to him. Mr. Corgan was dead. Didn't anything matter anymore except getting loaded? The lightning chiggered through his body. He fingered the can. Corgan peered down on him from the stars. Annie's touch brushed his cheek. This war was killing him. He snatched the can and lashed it across the ditch into the woods behind. "Dammit!" he shouted.

When he reached the motel, he entered his room quietly. The flapping clock read 12:02. He pushed up the window and hung a hanger with his jacket on it from the lever as the cold rushed in. He sat on the bed for a while. He needed some kind of story. He decided telling part of the truth would be his best strategy. He'd tell them that he'd gone for a walk. Shmitty had come driving along, recognized him, and convinced him to ride around. He'd apologize for giving in and drinking a couple beers to get Shmitty off his back. They'd be glad to blame Shmitty because they didn't like him. They'd be relieved he was being honest and that he hadn't been doing the drugs they suspected him of doing. And that would end it.

Why didn't I think of this earlier, he wondered. Then I coulda drunk that beer instead of throwing it away. He'd never find it now.

He undressed and crawled under the covers. He closed his eyes and saw himself racing down the dark road and plunging into the woods zigging and zagging among the trees trying to find that beer. Then Mr. Corgan slid under his lids and gave him that okay, thumbs-up gesture he used to whip out for him when he'd done something good. He was followed by Annie's dash-light face, and there was a pleased little curve to her lips Then Shmitty came leering in, sending beer after beer sailing over the seat into his waiting hands.

Frank huddled under the covers in the freezing room as the war raged on in his head, chest and stomach until it wore him out, and he finally fell asleep.

January

Sam Strand

Sam Strand turned his attention from the TV and looked at Sarah Strand over the rim of his half glasses. She was enjoying a "Cheers" rerun and did not notice him watching her. He admired her smile-creased eyes, her nose curved just like the one in the art school ads you used to find in newspapers, and her just-right lips.

Maybe because it was the New Year, a year that would very likely mark the end of his tenure as Blue Lake High School Principal, Sam was thinking about the past. He was thinking about how this cheerful woman had accompanied him to almost all the games, plays, concerts, and other activities at the high school all these years. It was his duty to attend many of those. It was her pleasure. You couldn't say all the Boyce years were.

Then he was thinking about those lean, hard years in Boyce when his pay was low, and he was idealistic, intense, insecure and a drunk.

Sarah had watched her husband's idealism drift into cynicism at the same speed that his affable social drinking drifted into alcoholism. His disease attained full flower shortly after he'd achieved his Master's Degree in Education. How ironic was that!

That year in the classroom was a perilous balancing act. He never missed a day of work because he didn't dare to; he feared his drinking habits would be discovered. They'd find out he practice drank every Thursday night and too much every weekend evening, nearly all of it at home where Sarah witnessed it. His energy was consumed in reigning in his churning emotions and devising a rigid mask to hide his turmoil. When the mask slipped, he covered the opening with sharp bursts of anger. His American History students became wary of becoming his targets. All were afraid of his final mask, the one that portrayed an endlessly angry man. The students thought they were mysteriously to blame for the way their teacher was, and they worked their tails off trying to please him.

Only Sarah knew the extent of his drinking. She took it for a while like nearly everyone did in those less informed years, but only for a while. She was as bright then as now, and she used her light to search out an Al-Anon meeting in a larger town twenty-two miles east. She went to her first meeting on the third Thursday in November and missed no meetings after that. Few weeks had passed since without Sarah attending a meeting.

Sam finally sought to allay her lack of interest in the many good reasons he had to drink, and his fear that she had become "one of them," by accompanying her on her trip one vibrant spring evening in May when his misery had become intolerable. He'd loved those breaking days of spring since he was a kid. But he no longer knew who or what he loved or hated and was unable to find pleasure in anything. He watched Sarah disappear into the Community Center building. Then he walked across the street to see that a little sign on the side of the Catholic Church contained the capitalized letters AA and an arrow pointed down the stairs. He followed the direction the arrow pointed and hadn't had a drink since.

"It's all your fault that I'm cranky and sober," he told her. "Your sunshine made my eyes hurt."

"It wasn't my sunshine that made your eyes hurt," she retorted.

He'd better try to call Mrs. Light again.

He picked up the phone and dialed. It rang three times, and someone lifted up the receiver. There was silence, only the hiss of air. "Hello," he said. No one replied. "Hello. This is Sam Strand, the principal at the high school." He heard a sound at the other end, like fingers tapping the mouthpiece.

"Hello, Mr. Strand," Patty Light finally answered, her voice soft and wary.

"How are you, young lady?" Sam asked.

"I'm just really fine."

"Is you mother there, Patty?"

Her voice hardened. "Yes. But she's not feeling well." Then he heard a tremor in it. "Am I in some kind of trouble, Mr. Strand?"

"Good heavens, no! You're one of our shining lights. No, you're certainly not in trouble. Actually, I have a need to talk with you and your mother, and I thought I'd seize the moment to do so."

"Well, I'm sorry, Mr. Strand, she's . . . not available right now." Patty offered no excuses or alibis. Maybe his hunch was wrong. When there's an abusive situation, those around it often find elaborate ways to cover it.

"Well, then, I'll talk to you, Patty. Just before vacation I was talking to Mr. Barnes. The college has notified us that they want to start a special program for advanced students in the Blue Lake area this summer. It allows you to earn a few college credits even before your senior year in high school. It has a cost."

"Well, Mr. Strand, thanks for thinking of me, but we couldn't possibly afford that."

"The fact is, Patty, there are work-study scholarships available on a need basis for students who have achieved exceptional results, but haven't accrued exceptional wealth. I can't speak to the latter, but I know you're one of our finest students, and that we have teachers who will be delighted to write recommendations for you."

"Oh," she answered. "Oh, my."

"I'd like you to come in to talk to Mr. Barnes and myself about this when school resumes. You'll find you're fully qualified for this opportunity."

"Oh, sure, Mr. Strand, I'd love to." Her delight made her voice sing.

"And, Patty, would you mind asking your mother if she'd give me a call about this. Parents should be involved. She can call me at school or at home. Or I can drop by for a visit."

"I'll tell her," the girl replied, the edge creeping back into her voice.

"Thank you. I'll look forward to talking to you in a few days. Happy New Year, Patty."

"Yes. Yes. Goodbye, Mr. Strand. Oh, and thank you. Goodbye. Oh, and Happy New Year to you, Mr. Strand. Goodbye." Her delight leapt into his ears. Sam returned the phone to its holder, smiling.

"You look mighty pleased with yourself, Mr. Strand," Mrs. Strand noted. "Have you been talking to that silly Estelle again?"

"No, my dear, I've been reminded that being an educator is worth it. I must say I feel pretty good about that. Get your coat. Let's go have a pizza and celebrate."

Patty Light

Patty Light returned the phone onto its cradle. "Patty Light, Patty Light, your life is fire, your life is ice," she whispered. Right now she felt like fire. Mr. Strand had talked about college classes! Mr. Strand had talked about a scholarship! He had told her she had a future. It was amazing! I could dance, her mind shouted, but her mouth remained locked in a small smile. Instead she slid her stockinged feet across the bare wood floor to the gray chair where she'd been reading her literature book. She reached for the switch on the gold floor lamp beside it and turned off the switch. Then she whirled and whirled and whirled until her skirt began to rise.

Almost all the lights in the house were turned off except the reading lamp on her desk that splashed a dim pool of light through her open bedroom door.

Her eyes adjusted to the dark. She tiptoed up the worn staircase. At the top, the door to her mother's bedroom was closed. In the silence Patty could hear her mother's ragged breathing. She pictured her sprawled on the bed, her skin sallow from winter and too few daylight expeditions out the door, the shades drawn to the sills. Little light ever found its way into that bedroom. That was the way her mother wanted it.

School Monday, she reminded herself. "Thank you, Lord," she whispered. School was where she was alive.

She opened her bedroom door, closed it, and sashayed to her desk, her ebullience moving her hips like a skater. She sat down, opened her journal and wrote.

Dear Dreams,

That greeting fits tonight. I've closed the door to my bedroom, but the door to my future has just been thrown wide open and there's so much light, why, I just gotta wear shades. Isn't that wonderful news! I'll spare the details, but I will tell you it is magical to me.

I even danced! Of course, I turned the lights off. I have a non-reputation to uphold. I'm even swaying in my chair right now. I'm so excited I can hardly hold this pen in my hand. The words I want to write seem stuck inside it because my brain is racing so fast.

It's dangerous for me to be this happy. Therefore I'm going to tell you a story that I think someone told me over and over. Or else I was very young and kept remembering it over and over.

Once upon a time there was a family of cats. (Yes, I must have been very young.) There was a momma cat, two boy cats, and a girl cat, who was the middle one. And a father cat. He was a tomcat. As tomcats go, he was more handsome than most. He had quite a lovely coat of cat fur, mottled into colors that seemed to attract all kinds of attention. It's true his fur was a bit scuffed from the battles he always seemed to find for himself, but when momma cat licked his wounds clean, he'd puff and preen and think he was the one who'd made himself beautiful. After awhile it seemed all momma cat did was lick those wounds clean, then step away and say, "Oh, my, how lucky I am."

The cat family seemed happy for a while. The first boy cat, Glower, was born, and a second boy cat, Phitt. They were cute little guys who inherited their father's beautiful coat and the memory of their mother's disappearing laughter as they raced and tumbled around the little home they lived in. When father cat, we'll just call him Tomcat, finally came home from some other cat house at night, Glower and Phitt would race to the portal to greet him, for he was their hero, and momma cat would sit on her haunches a little distance away and purr and thrum while the male cats played.

It was in between when momma and Tomcat's only feline offspring was born.

Momma sought to name her Snuggles, but for some reason Glower could not pronounce the name correctly, so he called her Struggles. Tomcat preferred to call her his Little Pussy Cat. When he was away, the kittens would play with great energy and were full of cat smiles and cat laughter all of the time. Struggles, Glower, and Phitt got along very well, and Momma was ever so pleased. Besides they provided her with company on the many nights when Tomcat was out riding fences or racing through dark alleys strewn with refuse and danger. At least that's the way he described it to his sons, and they fell asleep dreaming of such places. Struggles didn't, for she was sent off to help Momma clean the litter box and wash the crumbs out of the feeding dishes while the yarns were spun. By the time they were done, Phitt and Glower were so tangled in them they could give attention to nothing else the rest of the evening.

To shorten this becoming-too-long story, one night Tomcat came home, his back arched like an upside down U, shot right past the waiting trio and began to spit and yowl at Momma. Eventually the siblings slunk off to their box beds, but the yowling echoed all night and no one really got more than a catnap, if that.

Soon these nights were repeating themselves like the echoes repeated the yowls. One night Struggles slipped out of her box and crawled so low her belly dusted the floor until she could sneak a peek around the corner.

There her mother was frantically licking Tomcat's wounds, and there he was raining spit and venom all over her as he yowled and yowled and yowled. Suddenly Struggles felt the feathery cat weight of little cat paws on her shoulders. Bending back her neck, she found Phitt and Glower peeking around the corner with her. Then she saw them glance at each other, and she really didn't care for the evil that danced in their eyes.

They, of course, had decided that if yowling worked so well for Tomcat, maybe it would work for them, too. And it did. The more they yowled, the more licks, not lickings, they received. Soon that was all their lives were. They had neither time nor need to play with Struggles. Soon Mamma cat and Struggles were cleaning their litter boxes, too, in hopes of cutting down on the racket. So as time passed, Phitt and Glower became slick and fat and worth nothing in particular at all.

One night Tomcat came home already licked and preened. His handsomeness disappeared into the sneer on his face. He told Momma cat he'd had enough. His sons had become fat and spoiled and Momma's tongue had become so rough from all the licks she delivered that she was ruffling his coat instead of slicking it. He said he was taking Phitt and Glower with him, and he was going to turn them into real cats or know the reason why. He ordered Struggles to come to him. Struggles slunk out of her corner and rubbed against Tomcat's legs, then gave little licks of her own along one of them. Tomcat thrummed and purred, thrummed and purred and then whacked her away with the back of his paw, sending her tumbling and sprawling. Momma cat cowered. "I can raise my sons to become great Tomcats like myself. I have no idea what I'd do with Struggles. She can stay here with you, Momma cat, and you'll have some company. As for Glower, Phitt and myself we're off to California where the real fat cats prowl and momma cats with soft tongues abound."

So the three leapt off the portal and bounded down the street. Struggles settled her haunches on the portal and splashed tears on her fur as she watched them go. Twice Phitt turned around and meowed good-byes, and twice Tomcat's long clawed paw sent him somersaulting down the street and away, away, away. Struggles sat there long after the sun had set and darkness had descended. Then she went inside where it was dark also, but her sharp cat eyes could see Momma cat all curled around herself, her tail over her nose. Struggles went and lay beside her, and all night she could feel tremors moving from Momma cat's little white paws all the way through her haunches, her back, her cat shoulders, her flattened ears and she could feel the tremors transfer into her.

Sad story. Right, Mr. Hunter? It took Struggles a long time to dare to even imagine how happiness might feel.

P.L.

Sam Strand

Sam Strand could hardly believe his eyes. He was standing at the main entrance to Blue Lake High School greeting students with his gruff hellos when he saw a familiar face bobbing above the others. A crowd of students had gathered around the face vying for attention. It was Ted Gerney.

Sam was sorry that irritation buzzed in his brain at the sight of the popular former teacher. But it was Ted Gerney's late summer resignation that had initiated the circumstances that culminated in Sam Strand standing in front of a teacher's classroom roaring at its inhabitants. The sorry timing of his exit and the disappointment it provoked in the students placed the teacher who followed him in the crosshairs before he said a word.

Nevertheless this is America. A man or woman is free to do what he or she must, no matter who gets hurt. You couldn't throw this man under a bus or turn away in disgust because he wanted a different life for himself and his significant other.

Still, Sam was not sure what good Ted Gerney's visiting the scene of his many triumphs would do for the rest of the school, Robert Baker in particular. If the frazzled teacher was here watching students crowd around their returned hero, he might think about leaping out the third story window of his classroom.

"Get to your lockers. Class starts in five minutes," Sam boomed into the din. He achieved a satisfactory number of whines and gee whiz looks to know he'd been heard. The warning bell supported his message. As the students scattered, Sam extended his hand. "Ted. What brings you here? I thought you were busy making big bucks in advertising in the Cities."

Ted Gerney smiled that white-toothed killer smile that had caused more than one girl to rush to the ladies' room to regain composure. His blonde hair was perfectly combed. The man looked incredibly healthy. His grip was firm as he grasped Sam's hand. "Gosh, Sam, it's good to see you. One of the things I've missed is hanging around with you at the entrance, enjoying that special way you welcome students."

"Come on," Sam invited, "Walk down the halls with me while I make sure our roving bands have found their way home."

Ted, nearly as tall as Sam, matched his stride. "In answer to your question, Sam, the reason I'm here is because our company, having enjoyed an outstanding year, is rewarding its employees by sending groups of us skiing and chaleting in Aspen for a week and then tacking on four more days to unwind before our noses hit the stone again." As the duo walked, groups of students who'd spotted Mr. Gerney stood in the doors of their classrooms calling out greetings. Ted waved while encouraging them to get to their seats. It was a pity teaching had lost such a charismatic educator.

"So, I guess they call that a perk?"

"They do. And get this. They apologized for making us go during the holiday season. Said they had to do it that way since we were the new faces on the totem pole."

"Paid for everything, I suppose."

"Everything." Just then a girl darted out her room and threw her arms around Ted's midsection, squeezing him fiercely. Ted allowed himself to touch her shoulders lightly. "Katy. My most favorite student director ever. How are you?"

"I'm okay, Mr. Gerney," Katy responded, her smile quivering with excitement, her eyes dancing. "But we're only doing one play this year and no one-act. I'm really disappointed. If you were here . . . "

"It would be just the same," Ted interrupted, holding the girl's hands and running his thumbs along the back of them. "I'm going to be here for awhile. Let's do lunch in the cafeteria."

"Just like the old days," Jenny said as though last year was decades ago. "That'd be great, Mr. Gerney. I'll get the gang together." The bell ending homeroom rang and students spilled into the halls. Gerney shared hand-shakes, high fives, and hugs with a number of them before the halls re-emp-tied as the first period of the day commenced.

"The kids like you. Now that you've left, you're even more mythical."

"It makes me sad," Ted confessed. "You know what's crazy? When I began teaching, I was reluctant to get my hands within ten feet of a kid. Then we did "Oklahoma" in my third year and the kids were so great, I just had to hug everyone. After that it became commonplace for everyone to exchange hugs. Then one or two parents questioned the motivation, and I was told to be careful. Only pats on the back. I think it hurt the kids that people made something sexual out of celebration. I felt a little less human and a lot less me. Now I come back and because I'm not a teacher anymore, a kid like Jenny rushes out and throws her arms around me, and I'm free to show appropriate affection in return. It's kinda crazy."

"Education is," Sam agreed. "If you knew . . . " He wheeled around because two loud voices were blaring out of the home economics room. One was the teacher's. The other was Allan Barberie, a squirt of kid who tried to raise his height by blowing endless streams of hot air out of his mouth. The principal, student, and teacher arrived at the door at exactly the same time. "Allan, I heard you call my name. You must be dying to talk to me. I'm dying to talk to you. So let's go look out the window at the end of the hall and talk about your weather."

"Aw, geez," the boy whined, Sam's hand curled around his arm.

"I need to speak to my good friend, Allan, Mr. Gerney. Why don't you get a visitor's pass from the office and wander the school as you please? Try to avoid letting your worshipers crush each other trying to get to you."

"Sure thing, Mr. Strand. See you later."

It wasn't until later that Sam wished he'd requested that Ted Gerney, if possible, avoid going to Robert Baker's room even though it was once his.

But he wasn't sure that would have been the right thing to do. Sometimes letting life take its own course was the best decision. And sometimes it wasn't.

Kyle Hunter

When Kyle Hunter saw former compatriot Ted Gerney headed up the hall towards him at the beginning of the second period, the first word that popped into his mind was 'traitor.'

Ted arrived at room 212 and extended his hand. "Mr. Hunter." Many of the students entering the room smiled at him as they passed and whispered to each other as they went to their seats. "Does your frown mean you're having a bad day, or are you just not glad to see me?" Ted asked.

"Neither," Kyle said. "Sorry. How are you, Ted?"

"I'm good. But I have to say I've missed you guys."

"Likewise. The Drama Department's gone down the tubes in your absence."

"It would have gone down the tubes in my presence." Hurt played across the former teacher's features. He shook his head. "But that's another story I really want to tell you. When's your prep period?"

"Fifth. I'll be in the teacher's lounge banging my head against the wall."

"Good enough. I'll pick up some bandages from Nurse Beatrice."

"Can't. Nurse Beatrice is now Roving Nurse Beatrice. Cutbacks. She's doing the work of two or three. Every day she's at a different school."

"I know cutbacks," Ted grimaced. Then he smiled. "How's the beautiful Mrs. Hunter. I have no doubt I miss her a great deal more than I miss you."

"You haven't seen her in the Cities?"

Surprise replaced hurt on Ted's face. "The Cities! What are you talking about? You two aren't separated or something, are you?"

"No. She has a new job. Just like you." The bell rang. "Why don't you come in and say hello to these seniors. They're what you really miss."

Ted nodded. "Sometimes I miss the whole thing so much I cry myself to sleep, Kyle. Charlene has to keep my contract on the night stand, turn on the lights and point out my increased pay to me to get me to stop."

"Come on in the room. I'll take attendance, and you can take over."

Ted's smile was broad. The cries of, "Hi, Mr. Gerney," must have sounded like Tchaikovsky in his ears. He was in his element. "You girls and guys have to stop that, or you'll see a grown man cry."

"Tell them about the Cities. Tell them about the great plays and concerts you're seeing," he encouraged. He moved to the back of the room, leaned against the wall and listened as Gerney easily captured this crowd.

Ted moved Kyle's four-legged stool in front of the lectern and perched on it. "I suppose I could talk about the Cities. There's some great stuff going on there. The problem is I work with a bunch of old folks – you know, ancient like me – down there. They're fun and smart, but they aren't teenagers. I have to tell you, what I miss most about this school is you and all that you taught me in my eleven years here. So how's about you talking and me listening? You got questions, I'll try to answer them. But I really want to know what's on your minds these days."

The man's a natural, Kyle thought. Him not teaching is a tragedy.

Fifth period was the third-to-the-last period of the day. Only business teacher, Janis James, Greg Schwarz and Red Howard shared it with Kyle and only Greg came to the lounge often, but not in football season. The others had an office for sanctuary. This was his sanctuary. The coffee was here and the sofa. If he wanted to close his eyes a few moments, he could.

On this day he needed those moments to beat up the inside of his head. He had to work out this traitor image he'd treasured for the last five months. Watching Ted Gerney enchant his class for the whole period with his personality and his interest in them, Kyle realized that the latter reaction might have a lot more to do with him than it did with Ted.

The visitor's lanky frame popped through the lounge door a few minutes later. His eyes betrayed weariness. No doubt more than one of his former colleagues had succeeded in allowing him to take over their classes. "Whew. I knew teaching was hard work, but I'd forgotten how hard." He shuffled over to the sofa and plopped down. "I, my friend, am plum tuckered out. How did I ever do this job?"

"Coffee?" Kyle offered. Ted nodded so he extracted a visitor's Styrofoam cup out of the plastic bag atop the sink counter. "I'd give you one of these," he said, indicating the cups hanging above the counter sink, "but as you recall, they're all incredibly rank." He brought the cup and his own to the sofa, placed the white container in Ted's hands, and sighed down on the sofa. "Yup. It's hard work."

"The difference between teaching and most of the world of work is that teachers have to be on their toes all the time. In the office I work in, there's some down time and it's interspersed throughout the day. Not here, boy."

"You enjoyed yourself today?" Kyle asked, settling back in the sofa and sipping the strong brew.

"Mostly yes. It made me more than a little sad, too."

Kyle cut to the chase. "Then why did you leave? Last I saw you in June, I didn't have a clue. Then in August, boom, off you go. I know we get lost in our own worlds during the school year, but I figured we were friends."

He straightened and studied the muddy liquid in his cup. "This stuff is pretty awful, isn't it." The other nodded and waited. "Frankly, Ted, I felt deserted. We had a good thing going in our department."

Ted nodded again. "We did. But there was stuff going on beneath the surface that you don't know about."

"You're right. I knew nothing and still don't."

"Well, you're about to. If you want to, you can consider it a warning." Ted set the cup on the coffee table in front of the sofa.

"There are two central elements to this story. The last school board election was a disaster. Dr. Dansworth retired. Hobson, the lawyer, decided not to run because some of the guys who promised they'd look for him first didn't. So the choice came down to a group of people whose agenda included book banning, and another group whose primary interest was in promoting athletics. The first group was outspoken in what they hoped to do. The second was as slick as that Elvis look-alike's hair."

"Frank Marin."

Ted reached for his coffee, took a swallow, and grimaced. "Lord, this stuff is like flavored turpentine. Was it always that bad?"

"After the first five minutes."

"Huh. Anyway, you know who won. The second element was that Dr. Dansworth was retiring, and he wasn't about to crash through waves. He was worn out. The evil of two lessers emerged victorious. The two women who were running got swept away in the tide. These guys were organized."

"And?" Kyle interjected. "This period is only fifty-two minutes long."

"Would you edit Shakespeare? Okay. I never said a word I didn't love. I'll try. These guys were elected in November. By February I was receiving after-school visits from board members. Right at crunch time in the Contest Speech season. Questioning how many kids I had participating. Why those kids were mostly the best students. Man, that irritated me. They were good students partly because they were in speech. Amy Jackson was no Einstein. Neither was Brock Evans. They just worked their tails off because they wanted to be part of the team. Lots of kids did."

"You revealed this dark truth to the board?"

"I did. Forcefully, which I don't think they cared for. But I don't enjoy watching turkey vultures picking at carcasses either. So I blew them out the door one by one, and they stayed away for a while. Until May." Ted shook his head and glared. "You remember we did 'Midsummer Night's Dream'."

"Of course. It was great. Gail and I went twice."

"Then you remember our crowds weren't standing room only."

"True. But the ones there were as wrapped up in it as we were. Couldn't believe high school kids could crawl under the Bard's skin that deeply."

"That's what I figured. We did crap plays early on to establish the program. But once those years were done, I did plays that would teach the kids something worth learning and would educate the audience, too. For a long time I was left alone, and it was great. The kids in the plays and behind the scenes loved it, I loved it, our audiences loved it. These jerks get on the board and nothing matters except athletics and the bottom line."

"You weren't against athletics. You announced all the games I didn't."

"I think I am now. What happened was after the play was over near the end of May, three of these jerks show up at my house unannounced. Charlene is there, so that gives them another peg to hang their coats on if nothing else works. They don't bother with pleasantries because they don't like the way I react. They inform me of the necessity to cut programs. Especially extracurricular programs that aren't cost effective. They ask me if I know both of my plays barely took in enough money to cover the extra pay I get for spending about sixty nights a year in the auditorium working on those things." He grabbed the cup and crushed it.

"They tell me that they're going to introduce a new business item at the June board meeting that says no more than one play will be presented per year. The one act play will be cut because not enough students benefit from participation in it. The speech program will exist only if its coach works on a voluntary basis since travel expenses to the meets are so high. Did I mention the extra pay for directing would be cut by a third?

"When I try to tell them they're fooling with incredible learning experiences for the kids, that thirty or more kids are always involved in play production, that there's nearly universal praise for the quality of our productions, their answer is that they can trot over to the college to see the crap I do. That my plays are too advanced for high schoolers to handle.'

"By then, I'm losing it. I tell them I figure 'Sports Center' is the deepest thing they ever watch. I tell them they don't give a rip about kids. I tell them to get out. One of these weasels sneers and says, 'Your attitude is insubordinate, Mr. Gerney. That doesn't matter because we have the votes to pass these items anyway. And by the way, it would be better if you married Miss Antos instead of living with her.' I'd love to heave that jerk so far he'd sail through the picture window of the house across the street, but Charlene grabs my arm and says, 'He's not worth it, Ted.' And, 'By the way, I don't live here. I'm sure you didn't notice, but this is a duplex. I live upstairs. Do you want to sniff the sheets on my bed for evidence?'

"Everybody's boiling. So the jerk adds this. He's standing at the door with the screen door open. He turns and says, 'Oh, by the way, Miss Antos, perhaps you should reign in your boyfriend. We've received complaints about the hugging and touching that goes on during any project in which Mr. Gerney is involved. No one is accusing anybody of anything, but they're wondering if a good production is all he's after.' Can you believe it? I'll tell you that knocked it out of me. I knew I didn't want to teach here or anywhere else any more."

"Whew!" Kyle exhaled. "That scenario's both nightmarish and too believable, given the attitudes of our board members. But did you talk to Dansworth? Or Sam? If the teachers or kids had known . . ."

"We were enraged. And we were sorry we'd lost it. Charlene and I love this town. This school. So I went to Dansworth. He'd heard the story. Said he'd appreciated and supported everything I'd done. Said he'd support me one hundred percent at the school board meeting and that there was no chance they'd be able to fire me." Ted rose and walked to the big green waste bin and whipped the crushed cup into it. "That board is going to do everything it can to feature athletics. Anything that diverts attention is going to get squashed. Dansworth said it was incredibly stupid, and he'd fight it, but he was a lame duck. He suggested I take a leave. But I was fed up. Everything I'd accomplished counted for nothing. The whole thing sickened me. So I went looking for a job in the Cities, a friend got me an interview with this firm, and it's working out. I can't write like you, but I'm great at visualization and ideas. I fit. I no longer fit here, and I couldn't stand the thought of working under conditions like that. The money's double what I was making. There's nothing you or Dansworth or anyone else could have done. My bacon was burned. Maybe that's the way it's supposed to be."

"I doubt it," Kyle said, thinking of Red Howard and the upcoming board meeting. "But I'm afraid that's the way it is. I'm sorry, Ted."

The period was nearly over. Kyle rose and headed for the door, then turned. "What are you going to do now? I suppose you want to go to your old room, but I think you should wait until the end of the period. I don't think a visit from you would do your replacement any good. The guy is having a rough time because he's not you."

"I know," the other answered. "I was exposed to that unpleasant topic when I ate lunch with the kids. I tried hard to convince them Mr. Baker is not responsible for my leaving, and that they should give him the chance to be himself and succeed. You know how kids are. They think if they can drive the guy out, I'll magically return. I assured them that isn't the case. I'd undermine the whole system if I told them what I told you, but I tried to give enough hints to let them know why my leaving is irreversible, and that they ought to find out what this new fellow has to offer." He shrugged. "I tried. I don't know if many were convinced."

"I can't tell you how many times I've let that guy down," Kyle admitted. "This whole school has. We dropped him in the middle of the ocean and pretty much left him to swim to shore or drown. Even now, I don't know if I'm right about you going to his room. I'm sure the student wireless has alerted everyone that you're here. No class has been as asinine as period seven. Who knows, maybe a visit from you would help."

"What I'll do is stay here and see who comes in. If anybody needs me, I'll be sitting on this sofa trying to swallow some more of this awful coffee."

Robert Baker

Robert Baker had little doubt the topic would arise. Even though his seventh period class was still spooked by the image of Sam Strand bursting into the room and raining all over them, they weren't in any hurry to change their attitudes. If anything, they resented him more than ever. So he wasn't surprised when Taylor Antoine raised her hand.

"Mr. Baker, is it true that you told Mr. Gerney not to come to your classes?" Taylor accused, her round face fixed in a fierce frown.

"No, it isn't, Taylor. I haven't seen Mr. Gerney. I don't know what he looks like."

"He's a total fox," Jody Axton said. "Right, Taylor?" she added, poking the girl in front of her in the back.

"How come you didn't see him?" Taylor persisted. "He ate lunch in the cafeteria with a bunch of kids. Didn't you eat lunch?"

"As a matter of fact, Taylor, I didn't. I stayed in my room and read." As a matter of fact, Taylor, I don't have much of an appetite because I waste so much time in classes on conversations like this instead of teaching.

"You don't like Mr. Gerney, do you?" his inquisitor continued.

"I don't know. I've never met Mr. Gerney."

"He was a great teacher," Taylor stated.

"Were you a student of his?"

"No, I would have been, but you're my teacher instead," the girl answered, screwing her frown toward disgust. Her classmates were caught between gasps and giggles and stifled both. Robert could hear the oxygen funneling into their nostrils and mouths.

"He wouldn't have been here whether I am or not. He resigned and left Blue Lake. The job was vacant. That's how I got it."

Comfortable in her role as class spokesperson and enjoying the attention, Taylor folded her arms and continued. "So I suppose since you wouldn't let him come to the room, Mr. Gerney is gone and we won't get to see him." She willed a quiver into her voice in the last half of the sentence to emphasize the tragedy. Gerney would've been impressed.

"Taylor, if you'd been listening . . . " he began, but a knock on the door interrupted and carbon dioxide filled the room.

When Robert opened the door, a boy was standing outside it, a note in his hand. "Hello," he said. "What can I do for you?"

"Mr. Hunter sent me up here with this note. He said to tell you to do as you please. Whatever that means." He handed the note to Robert.

He watched the boy walk down the hall, then turned his attention to the note. It read: "Ted Gerney is in the teachers' lounge. If you would like him to come to your class, he's willing. If not, that's fine. K.H."

Since Gerney was going to be the topic of conversation anyway, the decision was easy. He might as well meet the man . "Taylor. Jody. Elvis has not left the building. Mr. Gerney is in the teachers' lounge. Why don't you two go down and get him and bring him here."

The girls leapt out of their seats, raced out the door, and giggled and danced down the hall. "Remember," one of his college professors had suggested during a lecture, "those students you'll be teaching are only children."

When Robert Baker watched the man enter room 313 behind his glowing escorts, he recognized part of Ted Gerney's mystique; he was handsome. Judging by the smile that wreathed his face and the confident way he surveyed the class in search of familiar faces, the man was pleased to have been invited. What former teacher, especially one whose legend grew daily, would not want to return to the scene of his triumphs?

Upon arrival the former teacher extended his hand. "I'm Ted Gerney."

"Robert Baker."

"I'm pleased to meet my successor," Ted said. "I hope you don't mind my interrupting your class. This is my old room. I miss it. For eleven years it was home."

"Sure, no problem," Robert replied, knowing that whether Ted Gerney had entered the room or not, this period was devoted to him. "Would you like to chat with the students? I have no doubt they'll enjoy that."

"I don't want to get in the way."

Too late to worry about that now. Robert took attendance while Gerney leaned against the wall and surveyed the room. Its thirty-two students sat breathlessly, their eyes rolling like marbles between the present and former teacher, silent as the circled wolves awaiting the battle between Buck and Spitz in *The Call of the Wild*, except this circle had chosen whom to root for. They were going to be disappointed. Robert had no intention of engaging Ted Gerney.

Once he'd finished his bookkeeping chores, he indicated the visitor with his hand and introduced him. "I think some of you know Mr. Gerney, and most of you wish you did. He's at the school on a surprise visit, and I know you'd like to spend part of this period visiting with him. Mr. Gerney." Robert moved to the back of the room and leaned against the wall next to the door.

Ted said, "Mr. Baker is right. I've been on a trip and had a few extra days, so I decided to pop up here. Truth is, I miss those of you whom I know, and I miss not having the chance to get to know the rest of you."

Angie Jensen raised her hand. "Then why did you leave?"

"It was time for me to go."

"We heard that you got fired so that Mr. Baker could get your job," the girl said.

Robert felt like he'd been kicked in the gut. It was all he could do to keep from doubling over. "Tell you what, Mr. Gerney. I'll go to the teacher's lounge for a cup of coffee so you and the class can talk freely." He slipped out the door before Ted could respond. He closed it and leaned against the wall. He felt sick.

Inside the room, Ted recovered from his shock at the nastiness of the statement and teacher's sudden exit.

"Angie," he asked, "how long have I known you?"

"Two years, Mr. Gerney," the girl said proudly. "I worked on plays for two years. And I was in Speech for two years."

"You're the girl I thought you were? Angie Jensen?"

Angie's lightly freckled face looked puzzled. "Why, yes, Mr. Gerney."

"The reason I'm asking is that the Angie I knew would never have believed such a ridiculous rumor in the first place. And, on the off chance that she did, the Angie I knew was too sensitive and smart to embarrass two people and herself by making a statement like that in front of a class. The Angie I knew would have come to me and said softly, 'Mr. Gerney, I heard this rumor, and I was just wondering whether or not it was true.'"

Tears coursed down Angie's cheeks.

"I love you, girl, so please, please don't have changed that much. And in response to what you meant to ask as a question rather than give as a statement, it's ridiculous. The truth is if this room was standing empty, I still wouldn't be here."

Outside the room, Robert Baker slumped against the wall. He felt like he'd turned to sand. Because he was unable to move, he heard bits and pieces of what Gerney said. Had he not felt so ill, he might have returned to the room, for he heard enough to gather that Gerney was supporting him. But he could not endure another body shot, not even the fear of one.

He headed down the hall. His footfalls echoed off the lockers, walls, and windows, it was so silent in the rooms he passed. He did not look, but imagined students were wondering who was making that racket. He wished he'd pass at least one room that hinted at the chaos he felt in his own. But by the time he reached the staircase that divided the two halves of the floor, he'd found none.

His coat was hanging in his room closet, his boots beneath. Nevertheless he hurried down the stairs and out the exit at the rear of the school near the janitor's storage room. He walked close to the building, flipping his suit coat collar up like a criminal avoiding detection. He ran across the open yard between the school and the road, wishing he was invisible. He strode rapidly across the street, and down the sidewalk toward the college. He would get lost there amidst the milling students until dark descended. Then he could walk home undetected.

He became aware of the cold knifing through his shoes. He almost laughed. He didn't know if he felt more like a criminal racing from the scene of a crime or an idiot who didn't know what cold was.

He realized what he was doing would be unacceptable to the administration.

It seemed crazy to him. But he could not bear to see even one more Blue Lake High School student today. He was afraid if he did, the encounter would drive him entirely over the edge.

He increased his pace down the sidewalk. His feet were freezing. He could feel the school lurking at his back, casting a gigantic shadow over him even on this gray and lightless afternoon.

Frank Marin

"Frank," Mr. Hunter said.

The boy looked up under his thick eyebrows and saw some girl, who was not in this class, leaving. He didn't know why he didn't leave. He hated Hunter's guts. Creative Writing! He'd gotten a D last quarter by pulling together a bunch of old stuff he'd written when he cared about anything and used it for a final project. Hunter had raised his stupid eyebrows at him when he handed it back. On the bottom, he'd scrawled, "You aren't a sophomore anymore, Frank. I'm giving you a break. You've got ability. Next quarter use it to write new stuff. Otherwise I'll give you an incomplete for the semester. D-." The jerk. Hunter saw right through him and still gave him a D-.

"Frank!" the teacher repeated.

"Yeah," he muttered, not looking up.

"You're wanted in the counselor's office."

Frank heard hints of laughter in the quiet classroom.

"Would you like to come and get this pass?"

"No," Frank grunted. But he couldn't stop the perspiration bursting out on his forehead. He stared hard at his clenched hands. If he moved, everyone would be looking at him. He couldn't stand that.

"Okay, the rest of you get started on the fifteen minute writing. Topic choices are on the board. Or choose your own. You can start," Hunter paused to glance at his watch, "in thirty seconds. Anyone who stops writing during the time flunks this assignment." He allowed a few seconds for the groans. "Go," the teacher said as sound subsided.

Frank waited. His knuckles were white, his fists red. His face felt wet.

He saw Hunter's gray pants next to his desk. The instructor slid a note under his hand. It said, "Outside! Now!" He could refuse. Could if his stomach didn't feel like it was full of rain.

Frank slid out of his desk. His boots banged like hammers on the floor.

"Write!" Hunter warned the rest. "Write!"

It seemed like the door was fifty miles away. Frank wanted to run but he'd sound like a herd of horses. So he walked. He finally reached the door. The coolness of the hall clamped on his wet skin. He kept walking.

"The pass?" Hunter said, his voice dripping. "I want to talk to you."

Frank could run, but what for? Hunter would shout, someone would come out of a room, and they'd call his parents. He backed against the wall, staring at his boots.

"This pass is about absences, Frank, and the way you're not working. I turned in a referral on you. Didn't you read any of the stuff I wrote on the few papers you handed in last quarter?"

"Yeah," he muttered. He'd read it. He'd seen the encouraging remarks early on and the questions and threats later.

"I've got thirty-two students in here, Frank," Hunter growled, his jaw jutting. "I can't baby-sit you. I would have talked to you before if you hadn't been absent for all the conferences I had with everyone else in the class. So maybe it's partly my fault. But it's also yours. You're seventeen. Old enough to take responsibility."

Frank glared at the scuffed toes of his boots. God he hated this.

"I've got to get back to the class. Here's the pass."

Frank remained leaning against the wall. His legs felt weak. He was very thirsty. It had been like standing in a white-hot spotlight. Finally he pushed off the wall and headed down the hall, his boots colliding with the floor. His throat was sandpaper dry. Maybe he'd be all right if he hadn't had those beers in Bethel Ridge. Sometimes he thought about standing with his hands draped over the gate at the old man's farm, and Annie standing silent in the dark listening to him. But mostly he thought about cans of beer with moisture sliding down the sides or the free float of a good buzz.

Frank stopped and stared at the pass. "Counselor Barnes." Thank God. He thought it would be Strand. Strand saw right through him.

He pulled a handkerchief out his rear pocket and wiped his face. Then he headed for the counselor's office.

Mr. Barnes looked up as the boy entered his crowded office. Folders were stacked on his desk and filing cabinet. "Yes?" the counselor queried, glancing over his reading glasses.

"Uh . . . I got this pass. You wanted to see me."

"Let me look at that." Frank handed him the pass. "Frank Marin." The counselor shuffled papers on his desk. "Sit down," he offered. "I'm sorry." He continued to shuffle papers. "Are you here on a referral?"

"Yeah," the boy replied.

"From . . . "

"Mr. Hunter."

Mr. Barnes pulled more slips from the stack. "Yeah. Matter of fact I have four referrals here for you. Hunter, Malone, Larson, and Charbonneau." He scanned one of the slips, then the other three. "Every one says the same thing." He looked at Frank and ran his hands through his thin hair. "You're the kid who transferred here last spring. I helped you make out a schedule."

"Yeah," Frank said.

"I got to apologize," Barnes said. "It's disgraceful that I don't know you better. Got five hundred and seventeen kids to keep track of. They talk about adding a counselor. But noooo. So now I don't get to know anybody very well." The counselor sighed. "It seems to me I've gotten other notes on you. In fact, I've sent a few out."

"I'm absent a lot," Frank admitted. He'd found out in Bethel Ridge in that morning-after talk with his parents that mixing in some honesty worked good. Parents, teachers, everybody wanted to believe the best. You just had to throw in a little truth and humility.

"Yeah? Yeah, that's what these all say. Why is that?"

Frank stared at the man, his mind working. Barnes' face was not unkind. He glanced at the man's eyes. There was no threat. Barnes' eyes just looked tired.

"Well, back in Bethel . . . "

"Yeah, you transferred from Bethel Ridge. I remember your mother came in with you. Nice lady."

"Yeah. Anyway back there we lived on a farm. Sometimes Dad had me stay home from school to do chores," Frank lied. Maybe once that happened. "He and Ma worked in town, so they couldn't do everything. When I had to miss school, Dad felt bad. I kinda liked it."

"Liked farm chores better than school?"

Better take this cool, Frank realized. "Well, school was pretty easy there. I got good grades," he added, the last part mostly true.

"And this school isn't so easy?"

Careful, Frankie. "Yeah, it's pretty hard. And it ain't... isn't . . . so easy to transfer when you're in high school."

"It isn't easy to transfer. I had to do that my senior year. Is that why you're skipping school so much?"

"Yeah, that's it." Then he remembered the notes he'd been forging. "And the asthma. It flares up sometimes."

Barnes leaned back in his chair.

"Look. I don't know if you know what the process is here. I'm a counselor, not a disciplinarian."

"Yes, sir," he said. Sir was a good touch. You gotta butter these guys up. Maybe he oughta try that with Hunter.

"Strand is the disciplinarian. We need a vice principal, too. Board keeps promising a vice principal. You go look for him!" Barnes snorted, waving his hand in the air. Startled, Frank started to rise. "No, no, no," Barnes continued, flattening his hand. "Sit down. The process is that you get referred to a counselor two, maybe three times. We try to work out the problem, help you understand what's going on with you. If there's no change," he raised his hands palms up, "then you get to talk to Mr. Strand. And he is not easy."

Frank was sure that was true. He had no desire to talk to Strand.

"So. Are you going to be able to change these patterns?"

"I think so, sir. I'll try."

"Better do more than try. This school is tough. We don't pass along and graduate people who don't pass their classes. Judging from these slips, you could be a junior for a long time."

There was a knock on the open door. A girl with curly red hair and freckles peeked in. "Excuse me, Mr. Barnes, aren't I supposed to be here now?"

The counselor grabbed the clipboard on his desk and thumbed through the slips on it. "What day is this?"

"January 10th."

"Yup," Barnes muttered. "Clarice Ammons, 9:30. College info. Yeah, Clarice, just a second. Wait in the outer office." He sighed again. "Too darn busy. So . . . "

"I'll try to . . . I'll get . . . "

Barnes stood up and turned to the window behind him, then turned around. "We try to help. You've got to try too." He scrawled the time on the pass and his initials.

"Thanks," Frank said, taking the slip. He left the office. What a piece of cake! He hardly had to say a word. Nice guy, that Barnes. Busy though.

Frank walked into the hall. He knew he'd have to put a little more into school. He didn't want to see Strand. Tomorrow he'd get at it.

Tonight he needed to celebrate his luck. Not to mention his skill. That sincere, humble, gee whiz stuff worked really well.

Greg Schwarz

"Now, Alan, let's get to the personnel business on the agenda." Board of Education temporary chairman Ed Arkin, the bank officer, began. He nodded toward the superintendent. "As you know, conversations and actions concerning personnel are executed in closed session in accordance with the Association contract." He addressed the *Lake View Chronicle* reporter, Sally Corday. "You'll have to leave, Miss Corday. This business needs to be taken care of in executive session."

Sally Corday was not popular with most board members. Born, raised, and educated in Blue Lake, her status as valedictorian had earned her a scholarship to a major School of Journalism. After graduation, she had surprised everyone by returning to Blue Lake to write for the paper her father owned. After the last election, she wrote an editorial, the message of which was, "This is what happens when the public is too apathetic or too afraid to fulfill its responsibilities to its children." The men on the board viewed her as obstinate, opinionated, and oppositional, but they grudgingly admitted her newspaper presented the facts of their meetings fairly.

Sally rose, but made no move to exit the library. Instead she aimed the rings of her spiral note pad at the chairman. "I object to being asked to leave. Red Howard, Kyle Hunter, Greg Schwarz and myself are the only observers here. I'm being asked to leave, but they aren't. Unless they're also asked to leave, I'll close my notebook, turn off my recorder, and stay."

Arkin sighed. "All of these men have reserved the right to testify concerning a pending personnel matter."

"Since your agenda stated only the words 'Personnel Matters,' I wonder how these men were able to decipher the specific matters when the general public wouldn't have a clue. Maybe it's a guy thing."

"Miss Corday, you know what I said is correct. Personnel matters are conducted in private to protect the party involved. That's in the contract."

"That assumes the party or parties need protection, doesn't it, Mr. Arkin? There is nothing in the contract, which I have read, that says the board must be protected. As elected officials, you're fair game for the press to observe and assail at will. So assuming one or more of those in attendance is the subject of these personnel matters, I will defer to their request that I leave, or to Principal Strand or Superintendent Anderson. Otherwise I will shut down the recorder, stuff my pen in my purse, and stay. I will report the outcome of this matter, just as I would if I weren't here. If the board forces me to leave, I'll file discrimination charges, Mr. Arkin."

"Alan, help me out," the chairman requested.

"If Miss Corday abides by her own rules, as recorded by my secretary, I see no harm in her staying," Anderson said.

"You're going to let her stay!" Pete Warrum, seated as an observer, roared.

"I don't believe you've asked to be recognized by the chair, Mr. Warrum," Anderson said. "If you have something to say, seek the recognition of the chair."

"Ed?" Warrum said, his scowl lasered on the administrator.

"Mr. Warrum, you have the floor."

Pete Warrum's red face displayed his anger. "I expect to have some things to say. I expect to say them to the board, not to the newspaper."

"You already have my word, Mr. Warrum. You won't be quoted. Everything said will be off the record."

"Right. You have no bias at all," Pete shot back. "Mr. Chairman, I demand that the board take a vote to remove Miss Corday from this room."

Randolph Roach shook his head, jowls quivering. "That's what you should have done in the first place, Ed. I have a business to run tomorrow."

Greg Schwarz predicted the outcome in his mind. Only Alice Kilvin, owner of the Reading Post Book Store and the lone holdover from the previous board, dissented. Roach, Arkin, Warrum, Payne, and Donald voted in the affirmative. The superintendent sat there in that cool to the point of being cruel way he approached everything.

"The vote has been taken, Miss Corday. Leave."

"Fine," the reporter replied. "Expect me to file suit."

"Make sure that recorder's off, Phil," Arkin ordered. "Then make sure the door's locked."

It's as though they're planning to execute someone, Greg groused. This is ridiculous. Red's not even putting up a fight.

"Mr. Strand, you'll speak first," Arkin continued. "Then Kyle, Greg, and Red. And Pete. Keep your remarks as brief as possible. It's late."

"I'll be brief and to the point," Sam Strand said, rising from his chair, his eyes fixed on the chairman. "I know Red Howard intends to resign as head football coach. That's Red's decision. I know the timing of this resignation was not inspired solely by Mr. Howard's health problem. I strongly object to the administrative and board pressure placed on him as soon as he exchanged his hospital pajamas for his clothes. I find that tasteless and inexcusable."

"We know Mr. Anderson telephoned Mr. Howard," Arkin interrupted. "We told him to. We'd spoken to board members. Consensus was reached and reported to Mr. Anderson."

"No, it wasn't, Ed!" Alice Kilvin said. "Not one of you said a word to me. Majority was reached, not consensus. I want the minutes to reflect that. I was never contacted and would never have assented.

"No one talked to me either," Jake Donald added, his face reflecting his hurt and anger. "Pete told me about this thing afterwards."

"We tried to reach you. You were out of town," Ed told him. "We'd achieved a majority."

"That's not consensus, is it, Mr. Arkin!" Alice said.

"Consensus was reached of those who mattered."

"That's good, Ed," Donald muttered, "those who mattered. Jee Zuz!"

"Consensus was reached. Continue, Mr. Strand."

"Sure, Ed. I want to repeat that the timing of the request was miserable. You cannot treat our teachers with this kind of arrogant disrespect. It's a dangerous precedent to exercise knee-jerk acquiescence to pressure groups or individuals. In my opinion, this situation promotes an atmosphere that will erode staff morale. The union rep will have no time to teach because she'll be defending one teacher after another. The Association Uniserv will have to rent a house in town, he'll be here so often. The losers will be everyone connected to this school including you," he finished.

"Your comments sound insubordinate," Arkin said.

"Only in a dictatorship, Mr. Chairman."

"Mr. Hunter. Perhaps you can spare the board the emotional rhetoric Mr. Strand has voiced."

"Perhaps not," Kyle said, rising to his feet. "I second everything Sam said. Red Howard's a class act. There wasn't a micrometer of class attached to the board's treatment of him.

"Among my many concerns is that this action has underlying agendas. I can't conceive of a board treating an employee this shabbily just for the heck of it. I believe part of your motivation is to save money. I'm aware program cuts have already occurred. You've lost more than one excellent teacher, and you're in danger of losing more. I suspect further thought-free reductions in programs and staff lie ahead and that offerings like my creative writing courses, which are successful and needed, will be gutted. Finally I'm outraged that public pressure by a vocal minority drove this situation."

Arkin turned toward the superintendent,. "Do you encourage insubordination as a requirement for employment, Mr. Anderson?"

"This is America. Can we continue?"

"Greg," the chairman said with relief, sure the tone of the meeting was about to shift since Greg Schwarz was the board's designated benefactor.

"Not Mr. Schwarz?" Greg said, rising. Arkin snapped straight in his chair. Donald shook his head, and Roach and Payne sighed in unison.

"I think you've made assumptions that aren't valid," Greg began. "You think I'm pleased to be in line for the head coaching job. Ordinarily I might be. But not like this. It's disgusting. You think I'll leap at this opportunity. I won't. If I take the job, it will be because Red Howard would like me to. I wonder what this board will do if we lose a few games next year. You'll hear voices barking in your ears again. Will you support me then? Some suburban schools are interested in me. I'm exploring that possibility. So don't go counting your coaching caps until you know there will be heads in them. Red Howard doesn't deserve what you're doing. I'm disgusted."

"We're going to save a lot in teachers' salaries next year," Roach said.

"Don't exacerbate the situation," Anderson ordered.

"Mr. Howard," Arkin sighed.

Red remained in his seat as he scanned the board and spoke. "Since you have no grounds for firing me, the board will be relieved to know Mr. Anderson has my resignation as head football coach in his hands as well as my resignation from teaching effective June 15.

"When I received Mr. Anderson's phone call, I was roaring mad, and I was hurt. I've given thirty years of my life to coaching and teaching at this school, and I've been darn good at both. Mrs. Howard reminded me how many times I'd said I might quit coaching lately, and that my comments had been particularly strong this fall. So you see, lady and gentlemen, this meeting wasn't needed, but the thoughts of my colleagues were. I love this school, I love my athletes, but I also love life. I think that's all I have to say except don't poison the well if you need to drink the water."

"Pete," the fully agitated board chairman barked.

"I'm too damned mad to talk. How do these people get off talking to the Blue Lake School Board like this!"

"This is America," Alan Anderson repeated.

"Do you have anything intelligent to say?"

"Well, yes, I believe I do," the superintendent replied. "First of all I apologize to Red Howard. I showed very poor judgment in making that call when I did. I'm going to give the board a slight excuse for the premature decision they made. We've been showered with phone calls and letters inquiring into Mr. Schwarz's availability. They feared if Mr. Howard's resignation came too late – or not at all – Mr. Schwarz might be gone. But the pressure applied was too much and much too soon."

"They could have asked me about that," Greg said.

"Yes, we –I— could have and should have."

That shifted the superintendent's attention to the teachers. "I had visions of coming here and being a forceful leader, academically and otherwise. I wanted this job, and I made tacit agreements with members of this board that I believed were in the best interests of the future of this school district. I am sometimes wrong."

He focused on the board. "I haven't heard these teachers say anything tonight that we shouldn't give serious consideration. However, this session was not needed, and we failed to discover that until today. I apologize to everyone for that fact."

"I think you're going to be looking for jobs in some very small towns next year, Mr. Anderson. After this matter is taken care of, this board is going to meet in executive session, and I'm sure we've got enough votes to require your resignation."

"Well, you see, there you have it. That's another meeting that doesn't need to be held. I shouldn't have to remind you that I signed an iron-clad three-year contract reviewed by your attorney and mine. The tacit agreements were verbal and, therefore, not binding. Now if you'll excuse me, you won't be needing me for the votes you feel the need to take." The superintendent rose and walked through the silence and out of the room.

Greg Schwarz took a measure of pleasure over the results of the meeting. But sadness watered it down. Red Howard loved this school even more than Greg. There was no reason for this dance to have ever been held.

Frank Marin

The old house was cold. Frank Marin was cold all the time these days. January was so cold here. Why couldn't he live in Hawaii? Loll on the beach. Stare at the bikinis worn by curvaceous coeds. Lay on the sand at sunset waiting for one to share a toke, sneak him a mai-tai, wrap herself around him. The sky blue, huge cumulus clouds catching the fiery sunset, the trade winds blowing . . .

So where was he? Scrunched into the corner of this frigid black vinyl sofa in this huge room waitin' to party. Partying was pretty much all he thought about anymore. Lately he'd wanted to get an early start. It was getting harder to catch a glow. A couple times he'd arrived at the summit just in time to watch everyone else vacate the mountain. The others had left in the cars and he didn't have one, so he'd walk home glowing in the dark, trying to hold on to that. Usually it descended into the anger that churned beneath the surface. By the time he reached home, it was all he could do not to trash the front door into splinters. Instead he'd take his boots off outside, no matter how cold it was, slowly turn the doorknob and slip like a ghost through the house to his room. He didn't want to have to handle the hangdog sorrow his father's face would show if he awoke and came out of his room, the way he'd stand there watching him. It hadn't happened, but that's how it would be. Or have his mother come out pale as ice, rigid as steel. There would be no words. Just that look.

So, ho, ho, ho, where's the glow? Brian and Brick were upstairs getting ready for the party. Brian had raised one eyebrow when Frank walked in hours early. "Put the beer in the fridge," he said. "Bring the smokes?"

"Sure," Frank replied.

"Good boy," Brian continued. "Gimme one. Brick and I will share it." He dug his elbow into Frank's stomach. "Head start, right?" He winked and took two.

That made Frank mad, but he held it. Those guys are good to me, he rationalized. They're my buddies. His anger settled into irritation that clung like tiny bats inside his body. He sucked the beer and tried to chase the image away. "Damn," he growled.

"What's going on?" Brick shouted from upstairs.

"Nothin'. I . . . uh . . . stubbed my toe on the sofa," Frank called back. What's wrong with me?

By eleven all the rooms were full. Frank was not drunk. Betts wasn't friendly. She was flirting with every fricking guy in the place while he sat and watched those red lips flash over those white teeth. He sat and felt his palms itch.

Brick and Brian were on Betts' list of flirtations. All night she glanced over at him while she talked and danced with one or the other. She knew the two were his only friends in this crowd. She knew he'd be fired with jealousy. She liked that. He sipped his beer and watched her and tried to divert himself by trying to count the number of beers he'd consumed. Then he watched Betts' hand rest on Brick's hip, and Brick twirl away from her toward the kitchen. Her hand hung where his hip had been, then dropped like it was weighted. Man, she looked really disappointed.

Then she straightened and came toward him. He was furious. He slugged down the remaining half can of brew and started toward the kitchen for another when she caught his arm.

"Hi, handsome person," she flirted.

"Sure," he shrugged. "What? My turn?"

"Are we mad?"

He hated when she talked to him like he was a little kid. "I'm gonna get a beer."

"Me, too," she said. "Wanna dance first?"

"After."

"Fine. I'm thirsty. Hungry too."

They headed for the refrigerator. He snatched two cans. His were gone. Somebody must be drinking his beer. He popped the tops and handed one to her. He heard the hiss of his and raised it to his lips. He watched her watch him, her milky eyes amused.

And then there it was! He finally hit it halfway through the can. He loved the beer, loved the can, loved the girl watching. Every inch of him swelled and glowed.

"Now we'll dance," he grunted. He reached out with his left hand and pulled her into him, cradling the beer against the small of her back. He felt the wet cold of her beer can against the back of his neck. He pulled her into him until her hipbones were tight against his.

He didn't know why he was walking in the snow. Last he remembered, he was holding Betts, angry and happy and hot.

So what was he doing walking in the snow and where was he? His feet were freezing. His teeth clanged like iron spikes. Why was he carrying his jacket on his arm instead of wearing it? Lucky he hadn't dropped it. He fought his way through the sleeves and grappled the zipper clumsily in his ham hands, thick and blocky as chunks of ice. He willed his fingers to tighten on the cold silver zipper and yanked it quickly up before his fingers could rebel. Then he shoved his hands in his pockets.

Where was he? In the distance he saw a streetlight and headed for it, his boots slipping on the hard packed snow. He walked as fast as his legs allowed.

Reaching the streetlight, he looked for a street sign. Where was he? Every street in Blue Lake had a sign. He peered down the road, saw a cluster of lights and hurried toward what must be the business district.

Eventually he stood in front of one of the store windows. 'Buford Drugs' the window read. Buford! What was he doing in Buford? Then he noticed headlights reflecting in the window. Hopefully it was a patrol car. The cold had knocked him sober so he waited until the car eased to the curb. The passenger door swung open, and Frank slid onto the sedan's bench seat.

"Cold," the lawman driving the car commented.

"Yeah," Frank mumbled. Think, he commanded his brain.

"Funny time to be window shopping."

"Yeah, ain't it."

"So?"

"Ah . . . my . . . ah . . . buddies and I were out riding. Uh . . . I had to take a leak about a mile out of town. So they stopped. I got out and went into the ditch." He warmed to his fiction, which could also be fact. "They'd been drinkin' a lot." He glanced at the man, who listened expressionless.

"I guess I'd better admit I had a couple too."

"No need to tell me that, son. I can smell it."

Oh-oh, Frank thought. He hurried on. "So anyway, they let me outa the car and took off. I couldn't believe it. Musta been two miles out of Buford. And they took off!"

"You don't need enemies when you're runnin' around with drunks."

Frank placed a crooked grin on his face. "And being one, I guess."

"Well, you don't seem too hammered to me, son." The heavyset man sat with his hands on the steering wheel. Occasionally the vehicle's motor sputtered, and he had to nurse the accelerator.

"Too cold to stay drunk," Frank said. He had the feeling the policeman was a little sympathetic. "Knocked the buzz right out of me."

"I bet," the other said, grinding the car into reverse. "I'm gonna take you down to our little jail house." He chuckled, listening to the clicking of the boy's bones as he jerked upright. "Don't worry, son, just gonna go there to call your folks. County pays for it that way. Take you to my house, have to pay for it myself."

Frank settled back in the seat. The mention of jail had shocked him. But this good ol' boy seemed to like him. He could call Frank's folks if he wished. Frank knew they were on night shift. There'd be no answer, and they'd never know about this night's adventures. He'd sleep in the cell. Then he'd catch a bus early in the morning and make up another story for his parents. They'd never know the truth.

"I said where you live, kid?"

"Uh . . . uh . . . Blue Lake."

"Your folks' names?"

"784-2646." For some reason he didn't want his parents named. It was like connecting him with them. Or them with him.

When the cop called, there was no answer. They'd unplugged the phone at night after a few of his friends had called really late and really drunk.

Lying on the stiff cot in the small jail cell later, he wondered what had happened to Betts. He'd been so angry for a while, he coulda killed. That thought chilled his chest and gut. He sat bolt upright on the cot. "I could have killed her," he mumbled in the empty jail. The chill escalated. "Nah," he told himself, "we were real friendly last I knew." The chill clung to all his corners. He wished he could remember what happened to Betts.

Kyle Hunter

Kyle Hunter sat in a student desk in Jojo Hansen's room waiting for the English Department meeting to begin. The department meetings were a way of touching base with one another. The meeting was held in Jojo's room because the revolving chair duty had whirled into her schedule this year. This practice had worked well at Blue Lake High School. The chairperson received light monetary compensation and a free period during which department duties would be accomplished. Six of the seven teachers in the department – Jojo, Fran Draper, Fred Weznerick, Nancy Dan, Holly Winters, and himself – had been employed by the school for years. Holly had taken on the reduced duties of the drama and speech programs following Gerney's departure. With the exception of Robert Baker, all were settled into their academic niches and allowed to remain in place so they could enhance their curriculums instead of continuously fitting into new ones. Sam Strand had devised this plan.

Because Robert Baker mostly maintained silence at the meetings, his colleagues shared indirect advice from their own experiences and bits of information with one another that they might otherwise assume the other members knew. Robert would jot down notes or nod his head. For whatever reason, he chose not ask many questions unless directly asked. Nor did he comment, complain, or ask for help concerning his own challenges.

Kyle and Jojo Hansen were the only ones who had spoken to Robert at length. Kyle's contribution was confined primarily to the dinner at the Duck Blind. He attributed his lack of further aid to his busyness, his quandary concerning the Kerns job offer, and his need to give attention to Gail. The result was that he was as guilty of offering neither enough ear nor encouragement to the young teacher as everyone else.

On the days he had sent himself on a mission to talk to Robert, either the room was dark, or Patty Light was there engaged in conversation or performing student assistant chores. It was easy for him to just move along.

While Kyle was sifting through thoughts and excuses, JoJo was attempting to begin the meeting. "Kyle. Kyle! Would you care to return from your other planet and join us?" she inquired in that perky voice that was almost as attractive as her perfect Nordic face and fit figure. He smiled vacantly. "This is going to be a short meeting. The National Honor Society meeting had to be rescheduled for four-thirty. I know. They're amazing kids. But you haven't heard howling until you've heard them lay into you for being late. I want to limit this to discussing problems you might have as this quarter winds down."

"Well, Jojo," Fred said, "I've been having trouble sleeping. I keep dreaming you ask me to marry you, and I keep refusing. It's a nightmare."

"I hope Alice slaps you silly," Jojo responded, "although she apparently already has. Anything of a serious nature? Grades for instance? Robert, this is new to you. Do you know you need to supply semester grades as well as quarter grades according to the school board's new policy? It's a way to help insure that our marginal students, especially if they happen to be athletes, don't flunk for the year just because they decide to take the second half of it off."

Robert, seated two chairs behind Kyle, nodded his head. Kyle wished he'd say something, but he didn't.

Jojo's gaze swept the group. "Are you sure there's nothing else. Anyone? Oh, by the way there's a marvelous tribute to Red Howard in the *Blue Lake Chronicle*. Makes me glad I decided to become a teacher. I suggest you clip it and put it on your bulletin boards."

Kyle wanted to drop into his Paul Harvey voice and say, "And here's the rest of the story," but he didn't. No use beating that dead dog.

"That's it then? Good enough. Straighten your chairs as you go, please. Thanks." Her apple cheeks glowed on her porcelain skin. Her smile revealed perfect teeth. Why in the world isn't she married? Kyle wondered.

As he turned to leave, he saw Robert Baker slipping out the door. He had to talk to the guy or he couldn't live with himself. He picked up his pace and caught the younger man as he began to ascend the stairs.

"How are things going?" Kyle asked.

"Pretty well," Robert replied.

"I've been wanting to talk to you. Don't do enough of that. Got a few minutes?"

"Sure. Come on up to the room." The two finished the flight in silence. Robert unlocked the door to his room, opened it and snapped on the bank of fluorescent lights closest to door, leaving his desk to the semidarkness of the late afternoon. He walked to it and settled into the chair behind it. "Oh, I'm sorry. Have a seat."

Kyle slipped into a student desk. "Any thoughts you'd like to share about Ted Gerney's visit?" That event was history to him, but Kyle doubted that was true for Robert. His disappearance from the school that day revealed how turbulent Gerney's visit was for him.

"Well," Robert responded, not looking at his questioner, "I was wondering how the door got locked."

"Custodian took care of it after he swept the floor."

"I was also wondering when I was going to hear from Mr. Strand." Robert fumbled with a button on his suit coat. He glanced at Kyle, then returned his attention to the button.

"I covered for you. Told the custodian you had an appointment and turned the class over to Ted instead of sending them to me. Sam never heard about it."

"It was a dumb thing to do, Kyle. I knew that as I was doing it. But I couldn't stand the thought of being here another second. I couldn't stand the thought of allowing one more student to verbally kick me."

Kyle stood up and seated himself on the window ledge. "I think you need to know Ted felt terrible about the way things turned out. He wanted to tell you. He apologized for showing up without giving thought to how that might affect anyone else. One of his faults is he's impulsive. That's one reason he isn't here anymore."

Robert rested his forearms on the papers scattered across his desk, his hands folded. "It did throw me. But everything does. At least I found out he's human. It was like he was some kind of god before. Now I know he's merely very gifted."

"He is," Kyle agreed. "But not quite the Zeus the kids mythologized. It was like Ted had suddenly died, here one minute and gone the next. You know how it is when people die. For quite awhile you only remember what angels or heroes they were."

"Anyway, thanks for covering me."

"Sure. But I don't want to have to do that again."

"I comprehend," Robert leaned back in his chair. "I do have one question."

"Shoot."

"I've overheard a rumor that Red Howard was fired."

Irritated, Kyle snapped, "Not true. Why would you believe that?"

"I didn't say I believed it."

Right, Kyle, ask this guy if you can talk to him and jump all over him when something he says bugs you. "Sorry. I know the real story."

"Can you share it?" Robert asked.

"In a shorthand way. I don't like the story. It was suggested to Red shortly after his heart attack that he resign as head football coach." Kyle resisted the urge to express further feelings. Robert Baker would feel completely walled in if he knew how politics were overwhelming education. "Some of us spoke our piece at the board meeting."

"He's been here a long time, hasn't he?"

"Yes, he has."

"And they treat him like crap. What hope is there for me? Except that I come cheap."

Before Kyle could answer, Patty Light walked in the door. She'd looked radiant ever since returning to school after vacation. He could hardly wait to read her journal. There must be something very good going on in her life.

"Hello, Patty," Robert said, brightening noticeably. "Mr. Hunter and I were just talking . . . "

"I can come back tomorrow," the girl suggested.

"No, that's okay, Patty," Kyle said. "I think Mr. Baker and I have discussed all the snowflakes we can for today. I've got to get home to the wife anyway." That was true. Gail was working in Blue Lake all week. "See you, Robert," he said as he headed for the door. "Got that journal all caught up, Patty? I have to collect them next week and count entries for the quarter grades."

"You know I do."

"Yes, I do. I'm just trying to prove that, contrary to popular opinion, I can walk and ask dumb questions at the same time. See you two."

Walking down the hall, he could hear Patty's voice excitedly exclaiming something to her teacher. Kyle loved that girl. She was a near to brilliant writer and had a heart like a rainbow. Obviously she opened up on a personal level with Robert Baker the way she rarely did with other teachers or her fellow students. Bright and needy. That was Patty Light. That was Robert Baker as well. Just like Sam Strand said. But fragile seemed like a better word. Fragile. Like his marriage.

𝓔𝓭 𝓦𝓪𝓻𝓻𝓾𝓶

Ed Warrum lay stretched out on his bed, his head sunk into his pillow. His eyes were on the ceiling, but he did not see the plaster curlicues that textured it. Instead he replayed the recent events of his days. He groaned and thrashed his head on the pillow, but the images wouldn't leave. He ached with tension.

"Okay, okay," he groaned and let the scenes play through his head like a series of bad dreams. Nothing had seemed real since he'd watched his father crumple Coach to the ground, and he'd heard Coach gasping for air. But everything mattered too much. He wasn't sure of anything at all except that these dreams were pervasive, black, and aching until they escalated into the red rage that felt as surreal and dangerous as a nightmare.

Like today. Why'd it have to happen? Maybe it was from working at the store too much during Christmas vacation, too close to his old man's thumb. He hadn't realized it then, but now those days seemed filled with him listening to his father spreading his b.s. about everything in general and sports in particular. Like he was the king of the world of sports and politics and education, but mainly sports because that's what his cronies from the quarterback-hoop-track-bat club knew anything about. Became king when Coach was deposed. Everyone knew who was behind that. If you were into power – and sports is power – then you admired the use of power and ignored its consequences. You elevated men like his father, who also happened to have a son who ought to be an all-stater, to an exalted status.

No one talked to Ed about that other than "nice game" or "way to go, kid." They talked to Ed's father about Ed because they knew who was responsible for making Ed who he was.

Which was crazy, maybe?

The kids in school who cared knew what had happened to Coach, but they didn't blame Ed. Kids are smart. They know you don't get to pick your parents. They know parents and children are separate people. They don't think about other people's parents much anyway. They take you for what you are or seem to be unless they get some kind of mass impression that carries around in whispers until everyone believes what they're hearing and ignores what they're seeing.

Ed didn't know whether or not they were hearing about him. That had become irrelevant. He had become an island because he didn't know what else to do. If the kids didn't understand that, they respected it and began to keep their distance until doing so became a habit. Even Shellie Chaine had found the need to step away. The ring on the chain she'd been wearing around her neck had begun to feel like an anchor, so she'd unhooked the chain, dropped the ring into her hand and placed it in his, tears tracing her cheeks as she turned to walk away.

So Ed was left alone, which he wanted to be, and felt as alone as he was. When he could feel, he felt sad about that. But not hurt.

The only thing that truly hurt him was when he saw Coach Schwarz. The big man would notice him, glower, and yank his gaze somewhere else. Ed tried to tell himself it wasn't personal, that when Schwarz saw him, the coach was reminded of his father's sins, that Schwarz wasn't angry at Ed. But it felt like he was, that he was welded to his father and deserved a piece of the blame for what was happening.

What was happening?

Maybe it was because his mother, looking pale and frail as an old photograph, had come to his bedroom and knocked softly as a cat rubbing its back on a sofa and told him his father wanted him to come downstairs and mingle with his cronies and an old coaching friend of his from the U. To avoid shouts, he did. The night was interminable. The coach was fat and tipsy. Retired, too, but Ed's father told him in a corner that the man had influence, so be nice to him. Nice was easy. Ed didn't have to say a word. Just listened to the old drunk belch out his stories of glory. Ed escaped back to his room around midnight, but his mother fetched him back, and he sat until one o'clock listening to his father talk about his teachers and coaches and former friends like they were trash suitable for burning.

Maybe all of that contributed to what happened today.

Ed supposed Coach Harkness called the Saturday practice as a disciplinary measure. The midsection of the season had turned soft as far as the Blue Lake Lakers were concerned. Their play had become erratic, and when they lost to a mediocre Crestwood team 57-51, the coach had had enough. He'd yanked Ed in the fourth quarter, telling him he looked like he was sleepwalking.

Sleepwalking, huh!

Maybe that was another excuse for his rage. For what happened. Everyone needs an excuse.

All he did at practice was bang the ball off the floor, the walls, and the backboard. Eventually his teammates clumped into groups and talked about him, except for Billy Cloud who ignored him and kept on shooting baskets and dribbling behind his back and flipping in reverse lay-ups.

Harkness noticed Ed. How could he not? "Come on, Warrum," he called twice. But what the heck, it was Saturday. Let the kid work out his snit about being pulled. Take it out on the ball and the wall. That's what Ed figured the coach was thinking.

Take it out on the ball and the wall. But Billy Cloud?

Why Billy Cloud?

"You guys, first and second string," the coach roared. "I want you to half-court scrimmage at this end. One team keeps the ball until they miss a basket or the other team takes it away. Couple changes. Dewlin, take first string right forward. Warrum, take second string right forward. Jones, jump in at center. Peterson and I are going to work at the other end of the court. Coach Saarinen had a wedding to go to this weekend so he isn't here. You guys police yourselves. Foul's a foul. Call it yourselves. Guy fouled gets three shots. He makes one, his team keeps the ball. I want you guys not to foul. I want you to play outstanding defense. Questions?"

There were none and he led his sophomore center down court. Being shifted to second team forward allowed Ed to escalate his anger. There was nothing unfair about the shift. He'd been playing lousy for two weeks. But he wanted rage. It was all he could feel except sadness and numbness, and it would be a disaster to feel those right now. So he seized the rage and wired his body with it.

The first team got the ball. "Rewards to the mighty," Ed grunted to Dale Dewlin, whom he was guarding.

"What?" the slender junior asked.

"Nothing," Ed grunted. "Play ball."

The first time Dewlin got the ball, Ed whacked him hard across the forearm. "Foul," Billy Cloud hollered. It was obvious. The slap had echoed off the gym walls.

"Hot dog!" Ed rasped. Dewlin tried to ignore him. He made two of his three free throws and went back to his position. There was fear in his eyes. The great quarterback was on his case.

The teams reset. Billy Cloud shot a no look pass toward Dewlin. Ed lunged for the ball and missed it, sprawling on the floor. Dewlin danced by his prone body and scored an easy lay-up.

"Five-zip," Billy Cloud chortled. "Nice drive, Dale."

Why was that so irritating? But what wasn't?

Dewlin continued to make Ed look silly. Everything he shot fell, and every fake or feint tied Ed in knots. He wanted to punch the kid in the face.

Finally the second stringers came up with a rebound.

"Seventeen-zip," Billy enthused. "Nice going, guys."

Up yours. Up yours. Aware that the thought was foolish, he nevertheless established a real target for his rage. Dale Dewlin was too easy.

The scene was as clear to him now as if he'd been sitting atop the rolled up bleachers watching it. Todd Flanders flipped a bounce pass to him. Dewlin was guarding him warily. Ed knew Dewlin would react to anything, he was so intimidated. He head faked toward his right. Then a quick step and behind the back dribble shot him past the frozen forward.

The rest came to him in slow motion. He hadn't really seen it then, but in his mind's eye now he saw Billy Cloud leave his man and head for the basket to cut off Ed's drive. He saw himself see Billy plant his body directly in his path. Plenty early. He coiled and fired the smoking rockets in his stomach and chest and head. The impact was vicious and sweet, his lowered shoulder crashing the other's body away from his charge, his own body following like a heat missile. The ball flew somewhere. He heard it bounce as he slammed atop the prone player. He twisted his shoulder for a second jolt, driving it into Billy's chest, and heard him gasp in pain.

"Jeez!" he heard someone shout as Billy's hands pushed him away. That should have been enough, but it wasn't. Ed rolled over and leapt to his feet. His hands were like rocks hanging on the ends of his arms. He grabbed Billy's tee shirt and wrenched him to his feet.

"Whatcha doin', man?" Billy gasped. "Foul on Warrum!" he shouted.

"Me!" Ed exploded. He saw his right fist fly toward the other's head, felt the awful crunch of flesh meeting flesh. He buried his other fist in the boy's midsection and saw him double over and fall forward with the blow.

"Jeez!" someone shouted again, and then a body flew into Ed's back and drove him hard against the black pad hanging on the wall behind the basket. Dewlin, Ed realized, stupidly surprised.

Ed heard Harkness screaming, "Stop it! Stop it!" Then the coach's huge hands turned him, whacked into his chest and drove him against the wall again. He was aware of Harkness' hands twisting his jersey, his knuckles rattling against Ed's clavicle. He felt himself lifted into the air and then his feet backpedaling, the man's legs beating like pistons. Then he was flying backwards before thudding against the hallway floor.

"Get out of here!" Harkness shouted. "Go shower and get out of this building." The man's face was blood red. Then the coach whirled, and Ed watched his gray shirt and sweatpants disappear into the gymnasium.

❖   ❖   ❖

"God," Ed groaned, sitting upright in his bed. Billy Cloud! The closest thing he had to a friend! Billy Cloud!

"I am going crazy!" he rasped.

He stared at the open closet. The gun was under the suitcase he'd laid atop a pile of clothes. It writhed like a snake in his mind. He wished it wasn't there. Why was it there? For his father? Or for himself?

"God!" he whispered. His tears were hot as boiled water on his cheeks. The gun was cold, living steel pressed against his brain.

Billy Cloud

When Billy Cloud emerged from the locker room, he headed for his hall locker. The left side of his face throbbed. Despite the ice Harkness had applied, the swelling atop his cheekbone partially closed his left eye.

He'd been dazed when Dewlin and Harkness rushed to his rescue. He'd watched Harkness wheel Ed through the open gymnasium doors and toss him like a rag doll. The memory gave no pleasure. The episode was totally confusing. That was the only conclusion he reached. He and Ed hadn't been close friends – as far as he knew, Ed had none – but they'd respected one another.

"Maybe it's my smart mouth, Coach," he hazarded, sitting on the training table as the big man applied pressure to the ice bag on his cheek.

"Encouraging your teammates is not smart mouthing," Harkness countered. "Ed's got somethin' in his craw right now. He's a miserable critter. I should have acted on what I was seeing a long time ago and kicked his butt out of here." The man was fuming.

"Gonna talk to him?" Billy inquired, wincing from the painful pressure the coach was applying to the ice bag.

"I suppose. I've never seen a kid change so much. Maybe it's drugs," he murmured.

"Dunno," the boy answered, then had to add, "I doubt it," not sure why he was defending Ed. Oh, to heck with it. It was a gut feeling. Whatever Ed was, it wasn't caused by drugs. He'd seen enough of kids on drugs in the Cities to believe his gut feeling. "Coach, if you press any harder with that ice, I'm gonna have to tell ya I'd rather have Ed punch my lights out."

Harkness laughed. "Sorry, Billy. I was thinking with my muscles. Which folks like Ed's father would say is how coaches usually think. Which may tell us something about Ed. Here," he said, seizing the boy's hand and sliding it over the ice bag. "Hold this for ten minutes or so. I'm gonna call your folks. If they can come and get you, I'll ask them to take you to the clinic. Far as I can tell, nothing's broken but . . . If they can't come, I'll take you." He walked toward the coaches' office and added, "I'll let you know," and disappeared into the office.

A few minutes later he pushed his face through the office door. "Your folks will be here in ten, fifteen minutes. Better get dressed. Put that ice bag on after."

As Billy walked to his locker, he was pleased to see Patty Light descending the stairway. He hoped she'd notice him as she headed to her locker. He cupped his palm and let his fingers hold the dampish ice bag against his cheek, sensing the added attraction of a wound might appeal to her empathetic nature.

It worked. She paused on the bottom step and advanced down the hall toward him. "What happened to you?" she called, continuing toward him. There was a subtle difference in her demeanor. A light inside the Light. "You're not going to tell me? Let me see."

Anytime! He lifted the ice bag from the swollen, discolored cheek. "Custer's revenge," he said.

"Oh, you. I know," she added, twirling toward her locker. "I know," she repeated, clicking her locker's combination and pulling open its metal door. "You got fresh with your girlfriend."

"I didn't know I had one. Who is she? I didn't recognize her fist."

"What did you recognize," Patty responded. This was definitely not the Patty Light that Billy Cloud had known, however distantly, but he wasn't disappointed. He'd not fashioned humor as part of the equation of getting to know her. Patty tried to turn serious. "No, really," she pressed, trying to set an expression of concern on her face, "what happened?"

"Someone wanted to see how deeply red a redskin's skin is red?"

"Oh . . . " she murmured, donning her coat. "If you don't want to tell me, don't."

"I'll tell you. Lord knows I want to tell you everything."

"Can I touch it?" she asked, surprising both of them.

Can you! Can you!! "Very lightly," he answered. "Very gently, please." There was no need for the caution he'd voiced to balance the shouting in his brain. Her touch was as brief and thrilling as the touch of butterfly wings. He was not sure why she wished to touch the swollen bruise. Fascination with the wounded? Red badge of courage? Stephen Crane was right? "I believe I'll go and have the other side of my face bruised now," Billy said, "if you'll wait right here." He took a few mock steps away and was pleased by the silvery tinsel of her laughter and surprised at how quickly her hand covered her mouth to cut it short.

"Billy…" she said.

"Okay," he said, the melting ice in the bag in his hand depositing a tiny pool on the floor. "Seriously, folk, what happened is this." He draped his hand over the top of her locker door and leaned forward. "As you may know, I just came from basketball practice. What happened is this. Someone mistook the side of my leathery face for a basketball and started dribbling it down the floor." He raised the hand atop the locker like a traffic cop to still the protest forming on Patty's lips. "And that, dear folk, is not that far from the truth." He loved those clear eyes of hers staring at him with amused consternation.

"One more thing, Ms. Light. I need to seize this moment of my personal agony and your touching interest. For at least four months I have been literally dying – no, no, I have been figuratively dying – to get to know you better. For," he plunged on, not only seizing the moment but wrapping it in a big bear hug, "I have eyed you from many angles, and I have listened to you speak with my ears wide open. I have seen no angles and heard no words that I don't admire. You know I'm rarely given to saying these many words in a row. Either you or the blow to my head has loosed my tongue as well as my marbles. Whichever pleases you is the one I'll credit."

Her eyes sparkled. Clearly she was enjoying the novelty of this experience. "I think your wounds have made you dizzy," she said.

"There is that chance," Billy conceded, dropping his arm from the door. "More's the pity it were so."

"Mr. Baker suggested Shakespeare to you, too?"

"More's the pity that is so." He looked at his watch. "Hey, 5:45. My folks are probably outside waiting for either me or my remains. Would you like a ride home?"

He saw moistness slip into her eyes at the mention of her destination.

"I . . . I . . . was going to . . . uh . . . my mother isn't feeling well . . . so I was . . . uh . . . going to walk home to let her have some . . . some . . . some peace and quiet." Her attention seemed far away now, her gaze drifting past him.

"Come on home with us for awhile then. You'll like my parents. I'd like to show you some of the stuff they do. Then your mother can rest." His smile was broad and inviting. "Then you won't have to worry about the hassle of meeting them after you fall madly in love with me." The frightened look on Patty's face made him drop his smile quickly. "I'm kidding. It's the wound. Please, let us give you a ride. I'd like that."

Her arms were wrapped around her books, clutching them close like a shield. Her eyes darted down the row of lockers, flicked across his face, found the books in her arms. "Do you know about my mother?"

"I know she has a daughter I want to get to know really well."

Patty kept her gaze averted. "You're sure you . . . your folks . . . my mother . . . I . . . I'll take a ride part way home."

He held out his free hand offering to relieve her of the books she clutched. She shook her head. "I think they're waiting," he said and indicated the doors at the end of the hallway with his hand.

As they passed the stairway, Patty glanced up. Mr. Baker was standing on the landing between the first and second floors. She lifted her hand from her books to give him a little wave. "Good night, Mr. Baker," she said.

"Good night, Patty. Billy," he added as an afterthought. He remained on the landing until the two students left the building.

Kyle Hunter

The day was white and brilliant blue. The two skiers established a smooth glide on the cross-country ski trail, the woman in front, the tail of her stocking cap swinging with the motions of her ski poles, the man trailing perhaps ten feet behind, watching the rhythmic sway of his wife's hips. It was Saturday afternoon.

Kyle Hunter had spent the morning reading end-of-the-quarter journal entries since he'd have to start dealing with quarter and semester grading next week. Gail had sat at the kitchen table working on her schedule for the following month. It involved travel almost every week. Both had been engrossed and worked in silence. Finally Kyle had risen from the sofa, stretched, yawned, and wandered to the window. "By golly, it's a beautiful day," he announced. "We can't waste another one inside, can we?"

The house was so silent the announcement sounded like a shout. Startled, Gail jerked her head up and stared at him. "What?" she said.

"I think we should eat a little lunch and go skiing," he said. "Like we promised we'd do in December. The only day we've been out on the trail was the day we made that pact."

Gail had laid her hands, clenched into fists, atop the schedule sheet. She'd said, "And you think it's all my fault. You think that since I got my job, it's all I think about and all I work on. You want to blame me and forget you're the one who's been bringing home all the work for years." Then she'd apologized. "I'm sorry. You're right. I'm stressing out over all the stuff I've got to do." She'd folded and unfolded her schedule and said, "I'll change into looser jeans."

"I'll go out to the garage and wax the skis."

So here they were skimming down the trail that ran through the woods behind their house and connected to two other lakes and a river. He generally let her ski ahead of him. Sometimes when he led, he set too brisk a pace. She never complained about that; she just maintained her steady rhythm and waited for him to discover he'd zoomed away. Eventually he'd stop, wait and say, "Maybe I'll see something if I slow down. You lead." After that had happened countless times in their early years of cross country skiing, they'd mutually decided to let her lead.

He enjoyed following her. The birches were intensely white, the evergreens deep green beneath the blue sky and above the white earth. Gail was wearing a short jacket over her ski sweater that just touched her jeans, and Kyle found the rhythm of her hips to be terrifically seductive. His wife was a beautiful woman and getting more beautiful all the time.

She wasn't a slow skier. For him it had been a matter of machismo, being ready to challenge the fastest when they joined faculty friends on the trail. For her, skiing was all about coordinated rhythm, about experiencing the blend of speed, ease, and grace the activity offered. That is what skiing behind her had finally taught him. There were enough hills on the trails to offer the exhilaration of speed. What her pace afforded was a sense of peace and a chance to observe the scenery.

Because of her, they'd acquired the habit of listening to the skim and shush of their skis, the rustle, creak and sigh of the wind in the under-brush, birches and pines, the cawing of raven and crows. Skiing was good for them. Today was no exception.

The activity vanquished thoughts of journals and grades. Instead he contemplated its aftermath. He saw the two of them walking toward the house, warmed by the exercise despite the chill of the day. Feeling over-heated in the house, they would shed their jackets. Then he'd help Gail pull her sweater over her head and would allow his hands to glide down her sides to grasp the white insulated shirt she wore underneath. She'd raise her arms in invitation. After that she'd unbutton his wool shirt and slide it down his arms. Eventually he'd turn on the shower to warm the water and they'd step in it together. They hadn't done that for a long time.

"Woof!" Kyle exhaled, the sound blending into the wind as his wife dis-appeared down the hill in front of him, and he prepared for the exhilaration of following her down the long slope.

Gail Hunter

Gail Hunter was aware of the effect she was having on her husband. She was also aware he had chosen the perfect wax for the trail conditions, allowing her to establish the perfect rhythm of poles, skis and body that entranced them both. She could feel his eyes on her, knew he was luxuri-ating in watching her graceful glide. Her senses were totally alive to the wind, the clean and crackling cold, the white and green and blue day sur-rounding her and her husband. When she came to the crest of the steep hill, she paused to glance back at Kyle bearing down on her before she planted her poles, thrust over the crest, and zoomed down the incline. The wind streamed off her in almost visible lines. Exhilaration swirled through her. If she lifted her skis, she could fly.

Kyle Hunter

As the Hunters neared their pine-hidden home, they could hear the ringing of the telephone from the ringer attachment Kyle had rigged in the garage. Gail kicked off her skis and ran to the house to answer it. Surprised by her haste, Kyle released the clips on his own skis, picked up both pairs and toted them to the garage. He leaned out the open door to hear if his name was being called. Since it wasn't and Gail hadn't reappeared, he assumed that she was on the phone and straightened up the garage before going inside, romance still on his mind.

He found that Gail was not on the phone, but in the shower. He smiled and discarded his boots and jacket by the door. He had his sweater off and was pulling up the top half of his insulated underwear when the splash of water ceased. Disappointed, he dropped onto the sofa. Gail emerged from the bathroom wrapped in a navy blue towel, another lighter blue towel wrapped around her head. She looked terrific. "I was getting so chilled," she explained, her teeth white inside her smile. "I had to tell him I'd call him back." She was oblivious to what he was sure was a stricken look on his face as she turned and sprinted to the bedroom.

Him, he thought. He whacked the arm of the sofa with his left hand. Who is "him"? Then he noticed a crackling chill on his own skin. He rose and moved toward the bathroom, removed his remaining clothes, stepped over the rim of the porcelain tub and pulled the shower knob. The water was still warm from Gail's shower. Oh, well, he thought, showering together wasn't actually that great. The water soaked one person while the other was two-thirds dry. One got red and wrinkly while the other got a second chance to chill. When you traded places, it was worse. The soaked soul half dried while the other soaked. Still the vision of water cascading off Gail's face and shoulders over her smooth skin was invigorating. He almost called out to her, but that would be stupid. She was dressed by now and on the phone.

Kyle pushed in the knob and stepped out of the shower. He was dismayed to hear Gail's laughter filter through the door. He thought about stepping into the room naked. But what if she wasn't on the phone? What if someone had been driving by and decided to drop in? Robert Baker? Highly unlikely. Greg Schwarz, maybe. Baker wouldn't be provoking the mirth he was hearing, but Schwarz might. Wouldn't Kyle feel stupid going out there to find Schwarz sitting at the kitchen table. The big guy would fall off his chair howling in laughter, producing a gigantic dent in the wood floor. The images made Kyle smile. Well, he'd chance it. If Schwarz was out there, the scene would give him fodder for a hundred teachers' lounge innuendoes in the coming months.

He grabbed the towel for emergency cover, opened the door, and stepped into the room.

Gail's back was to him. She was talking on the telephone and took no note of his presence. Instead she remained facing the picture window that framed the pines, the phone in her right hand. "Oh, you, you shouldn't," Gail scolded. Who is this guy anyway? Pinpricks of jealousy or disappointment – he wasn't sure which – bounced around in his chest. He wrapped the towel around his waist and went into the bedroom. He pulled on a pair of jeans, dropped a sweater over his head, pulled sweat socks on his feet, and reemerged into the room. Gail was still on the phone.

Kyle sighed and headed for the sofa and the pile of journals that awaited.

He thought he'd be unable to concentrate on the student writings, but Patty Light's was the first journal he took from the stack. Her writing always drew him in. Soon his wife's voice and her silences while she listened were in the distance as he became absorbed in his reading.

There were elements in the cat family story that caused him to reread it several times. It ended without Patty's usual disclaimers about dreams and symbols, but that was probably due to her belief that he understood that she wanted no interpretations of her psyche or emotional landscape, that he was privileged to be invited in, and that she'd close it off if he voiced questions about the content. He didn't want that reaction, and she needed these pages to release her angels and demons, her beautiful and frightening worlds.

Maybe he could think of a way to share his apprehension about Patty's story with Gail without revealing too much of it and nothing about the source. However, she was still on the phone, sprinkling the silence with bursts of laughter, which were more irritating than musical. So he set Patty's journal aside and opened Raymond Stevens.

Like a number of his students, Raymond had an intensely weird imagination. Undoubtedly he'd read too many comic books at too young an age. But the warping of his mind did enable him to produce some pretty intriguing creations. The current story had to do with a deranged snowmobiler who had lost control of his hands. His head loved to putt-putt slowly through the forest, but his hands desired speed, and since his hands controlled the throttle, speed always triumphed. The driver's head had no doubt disaster would occur, and it did. One night the hands were completely out of touch with the head and the speed was blinding. But not so blinding that the head didn't see the wire fence at the end of the snowmobile trail. The hands neatly zoomed under the wire along with the rest of the body, but the head wasn't so fortunate. The hands, body, and machine rammed into a tree, fiercely and futilely attempting to climb it, hands frozen on the throttle, snowmobile engine roaring. The head was roaring, too, screaming at the hands, "I told you this would happen, but did you listen. Noooo. You don't have ears! Now see what you've done. Oh, but you can't, can you. You've lost your head." The head continued screaming and the snowmobile roaring until both ran out of gas.

Kyle had just finished writing "effective, but I'm glad I haven't eaten yet" when he noticed Gail's thighs just beyond the journal.

Gail Hunter

"You can't hear a thing when you're reading those journals, can you?" Gail complained, hands on hips. "I've said your name at least five times."

"You were on the phone," Kyle defended.

"I've been off the phone for at least five minutes."

"Who knew? I thought it was welded to your ear."

"I don't appreciate that, Kyle. It was a business call."

"Folks at Kerns must be pretty cheerful, judging from the giggling."

"You didn't hear anything. You read those journals and it's like you're on another planet."

"And while you were on the phone, you were alert to my every move."

"Of course, I . . . uh . . . " she fumbled.

"I'll tell you what Gail, I'll sit here and sink my soul into a journal. You leave the room. Come back in without a stitch on and see if I notice you."

Her hands flew back to her hips. "What are you talking about?"

"I . . . you . . . oh, the heck with it." He dropped his hands to reopen the journal in his lap. Then he glanced up at her. "Who was that guy you were talking to anyway?"

Gail's face reddened. "Who said it was a guy?"

"You did. Nor do you blush when you've been talking to Phyllis."

"I'm not blushing. Oh, all right, it was Wayne Mars," she admitted, throwing her hands in the air, turning, and walking back to the table. "So?"

"Wayne Mars. He's the guy at the party who was looking so far down your dress that he knew the color of your panties, right? The guy who made those lewd comments about your cleavage if I'm not mistaken."

"You're jealous," Gail said in mock amazement.

"So what did Mr. Mars desire? Except perhaps you."

"It was a company call," Gail said too quickly. "He called to inform me of the new shows scheduled to introduce the spring fashion lines. If you must know."

"I think I should. It says on the certificate that I'm your husband."

Gail knew she was being a bit unfair. Wayne's call had contained considerably more than the information she was sharing with Kyle. And even if enjoying his aggressive attention made her feel a bit guilty and brought a blush to her face, it also informed her that on several levels she was a valuable asset to the company. It had been years since she'd felt this good about herself. Kyle wasn't going to spoil that. Nor was he going to like the next piece of information.

"There's a new manufacturer showing his line next week. It's a sudden schedule change, but he wants to get a jump on the others. The show is on Thursday, but Wayne wants us to come in Tuesday so we can meet their people and introduce them to our managers on Wednesday." Kyle's face turned to stone. "So I need to call the managers in this area tonight to tell them they'll be needed in the Cities on Wednesday." She shrugged her shoulders. "I'm sorry."

"I thought that was Phyllis' job," Kyle replied too quietly. She could feel him seething underneath. His students must be terrified when he speaks like that.

"She's out of town. That's why Wayne called me."

"I'm sure."

She changed the subject. "I'm not hungry, but if you want to go into town and get pizza ... "

Kyle stood up. "I don't think so. But maybe," he said, reaching into the closet by the door and retrieving his jacket. "Maybe I will." Since his ski shoes were by the door, he slipped his feet into them.

Gail needed to regain the upper hand. "I don't think you're being fair," she accused as he bent over to lace the shoes. "I've sat here for sixteen years watching you live in your own little world."

Kyle jerked erect. "It's my job! We've plowed this ground until there's nothing left but sand. Enjoy your calls." He stormed out into the night.

Kyle Hunter

Kyle Hunter had neither plan nor car keys. The full moon was hurling its blue-white light earthward. He had ski shoes on. He hadn't gone night skiing in years.

In the garage he re-waxed his skis, then set out on the trail he'd created. Without Gail to set the pace and because he was furious with the way the day had turned around, he pounded his poles into the snow and blazed down the trail in the same direction they'd skied a few hours ago. His arms and legs beat like pistons.

It wasn't until he hurtled off the trail and into the snow that he remembered how much moonlight alters the terrain. The snow was phosphorescent. The branches of the deciduous trees were clearly defined against it; the evergreens cast solid shadows across it. The light leveled all except the deepest dips in the trail. He wanted speed, but he didn't want to break an ankle traversing this surreal landscape. He wanted to exhaust the anger, jealousy, disappointment and fear he was feeling and leave it somewhere on the trail.

His rate of movement brought him to the crest of the hill before he realized where he was. By the time he jolted to awareness, he'd bolted over its lip. He could not even see the bottom of the hill, yet his skis were gathering speed. There was nothing to do but drag his poles and hope the skis would follow the trail's grooves. The wind speed created whipped against his face. It felt like his breath was being blown out of his body.

He was down the hill in seconds, but each second stretched into a yawning yowl. He was halfway up the next hill before his speed diminished, and he attained the top of it before gliding to a halt. He fought to recover his breath. He hadn't been that afraid for a long time. At least not of anything physical.

He stood in a pool of moonlight for a few moments. He had to get moving. He wasn't properly dressed for this expedition. If he stood any longer, his bones would be coated with ice. There was no way he could fight his way back up that killer hill. He'd have to take the same series of loops they'd taken in the afternoon to rejoin the main trail. This trip would last for several more hours.

Gail Hunter

Gail Hunter made her calls. When she was done, she realized she didn't know whether or not Kyle had taken the car to town. She peeked out the window, saw no light spilling from the garage and assumed he had.

She was enormously hungry. Perhaps she'd been hungry earlier and was too stubborn to admit it. Or realize it. In her own way, she was as oblivious as Kyle was when she was doing her work. She strode to the refrigerator and opened the door. Since Kyle was doing the shopping most of the time these days, its contents were reduced to bare essentials. He ate hot lunch at school and didn't need much here. She pulled the meat drawer out and found a package of turkey breast.

Kyle was right. Wayne Mars did find her interesting. Her mind, too, she believed.

She pulled a slice of the meat and placed it on the wheat bread she'd laid on a plate. She slapped margarine and mustard on another piece and took the food to the table. She sat by the phone as though expecting another call from Mr. Mars.

"Gail!" she scolded herself. "What are you thinking?"

What she was thinking was that she liked the attention. She liked her new job. She liked being Gail Hunter instead of Mrs. Kyle Hunter. She'd been that for years. Not a mother, not anything really except Mrs. Hunter, wife of the hardworking Kyle Hunter who was devoted to his students and seemed to have eyes and ears for every one of them, but not enough left over for her. Oh, that wasn't all true. It was more that she'd been too dependent on him to provide her with an image of who she was. Working part-time in the drugstore hadn't helped. She was nothing more than Mrs. Hunter there, too, with no kids to talk about. With this job, that wasn't true. Most of her colleagues had no idea who Kyle Hunter was. Those who did knew because she'd taken his articles and his hand and led him to them.

Poor dear. I've turned our worlds upside down.

As she finished her sandwich and downed the milk she'd poured, she eyed the journals sprawled across the sofa. Maybe if he'd share some of those magical pages with her, she'd feel more a part of his life and their lives too. Maybe she should pick one up and read it. Maybe that would stop the unraveling of the ties that bound – or separated – the couple.

She started to get up, then sat down. She shouldn't do that and wouldn't. That would fracture the trust between Kyle and his students and between

Kyle and her. After so many years, why in the world do that now? Besides, those pages undoubtedly contained thoughts and deeply held secrets that had to be shared with someone, but only some One. How would those writers feel if she ripped open those journals and stole those secrets for her self-satisfaction? Probably as violated as she'd feel if someone ripped open her brain and traced the confusion of thoughts and images dancing through it that she shared with no one.

It was nearly midnight and Kyle wasn't back. Gail chose to believe that he'd gone to town, maybe run into that lonely Robert – what was his name – Barker? Or Greg Schwarz – who ought to find himself a wife – and was having a few drinks at Dink's Tavern. Dink. Now there was a name.

It wasn't until she'd curled herself into bed under the heavy covers that she missed having Kyle snuggled against her to heat away the chill. It wasn't until then that her mind returned to the afternoon and she remembered the exhilaration she'd felt because of the smooth glide of the skis along the trail and because she knew Kyle was skiing behind her and wanting her terribly. A tremble drifted through her. Together they'd managed to throw the day away. That acknowledgment filled her with a sadness that washed on into her sleep.

Kyle Hunter

It was past two a.m. when Kyle finally leaned his skis against the garage and entered the dark house. He wanted to shower again, but definitely did not want to wake Gail. So he filled the sink with water, doffed his clothes and gave himself a sponge bath. Then he walked naked into the dining room and stood there for a moment. She wouldn't see him now either, of course. But who knows. If he'd been sunk into those journals the way he often was, if he'd been doing his job like she was doing her job, who's to say that he'd have noticed her if she walked into the room au natural.

The one thing he knew for sure was that this day had somersaulted. Blame it on the moon, he thought. Blame it on me. Blame it on us. I don't know. He still didn't want to wake his wife, so he headed for the spare bedroom, thinking he'd sleep on the pullout couch without pulling it out. Then he realized doing that would assure that both of them would wake up cold and alone in the morning.

He'd already been chilled three times today. Frost's poem, "Fire and Ice," flitted through his mind. This day had been fire and ice, several forms of fire, several kinds of ice. He decided he didn't want to add to the latter.

So he slowly opened the door to the bedroom to minimize its squeaking. He lifted the covers on his side of the bed and slid underneath them. The sheets had chilled in his absence. He lay with his back to his wife and pulled the quilt around his shoulders.

Gail Hunter

Gail awoke from her dreams as Kyle entered the room, but feigned sleep. The bed dipped slightly as he entered it. She remained lying on her side facing the window waiting for the overwhelming odor of alcohol to drift from him to her, but there was none. She was surprised, but she continued to pretend she was asleep and did not ask him where he'd been.

Sam Strand

Sam Strand got hold of Mrs. Meg Light after weeks of trying. He'd talked to Patty Light twice more at night. He'd told Patty twice he'd like her mother to come in to talk about the work-study scholarship. Patty had promised to ask her mother to do so, but her mother hadn't appeared. Sam was sure the young lady would recoil if he continued to call when she was home, so he'd confined further attempts to contact her mother to daytime hours. Thank the Lord he'd connected with Mrs. Light yesterday afternoon.

He backed his car out of his parking stall behind the school and headed for Elm Street. The mountain wasn't coming to MoSammed, so MoSammed was going the mountain. Kyle would appreciate that tortured pun.

Once again he stopped to pick up Estelle. Whatever else was true Mrs. Light's elusiveness gave him a hunch that if he approached her home solo, she would either be frightened into hiding or enraged. Having Estelle along would make his visit less threatening.

Estelle pranced down the steps of the brownstone house where she and her husband lived. Sam pushed the door open. She jumped in, shivering.

"It's January," Sam said.

"Certainly is. Classic January. The sun on the snow is almost blinding. But look at that blue sky!"

"Like I told you on the phone, Estelle, I got hold of Mrs. Light yesterday. She was very polite. A little distant, maybe. But in control of herself."

"You thought she'd be drunk? How often did you answer the phone when you were drunk?"

"Good point. But I've rarely felt so vague about a twelfth step call."

Estelle pulled her plaid scarf off her head and draped it around her coat collar. "I don't know if that matters, Sam. You tell me you've been observing Patty Light for over a year. You'd be remiss if you did nothing to check out your questions. Besides, you need to get Mrs. Light to sign those papers. If Patty lost her chance for that scholarship because you and I were afraid to approach someone who wasn't falling into their own vomit every night, that would be a tragedy."

"Thank you. You're as right as you always think you are," Sam replied, squinting into the mid- afternoon sun. "Of course those patterns could have everything to do with being a member of a broken family. Especially since Patty's an only child. That might have resulted in making both mother and daughter feel distinctly different."

"Just as she would if someone in her family were abusing alcohol, drugs or her." Estelle touched her friend's arm. "I think we all make these calls with a little apprehension, Sam. But if we care enough to take the risk, we might end up helping someone."

Sam smiled. "I knew . . . the Lord did anyway . . . that it was a marvelous idea to bring you along on this venture. Even if it ends up to be another misadventure. Here's where we turn."

As Sam closed in on the Light house, his impression was that the whole area was neglected. Even the road contained more and deeper potholes.

"Well, here we are, ready or not," Sam said, easing to a stop in front of the weathered house.

An aging Chevrolet was parked at the entrance of the mostly unshoveled garage-less driveway. Someone had tried to keep a path shoveled from the steps to the sidewalk, but patches of ice remained.

"Walk carefully, my dear," Sam suggested, opening his door and stepping into the late January chill. His arm supported her up the path to the steps. Curved slopes of iced snow packed the back of each step. Reaching the storm door, Sam rapped his glove on its bent frame.

"Just a moment," a voice called. Sam heard the snapping of the dead bolt lock and the turning of a key. Then the door opened and Mrs. Light's eyes peered at him from the interior gloom. "Come in," she said softly.

Sam motioned Estelle inside. "Hello," she said, "I'm Estelle."

Sam followed her in as Mrs. Light responded, "Um . . . I'm Meg Light."

"And I'm Sam Strand," the principal said, offering his hand.

Meg Light touched his fingers briefly before withdrawing her hand. "Won't you sit down?"

Sam's initial impression of the darkness within the house had been a bit harsh. It wasn't Versailles, but the drapes had been parted enough to allow a narrow funnel of light into the room. The small lamp beside the easy chair into which Sam settled and the vase lamp on the end table by the sofa where Estelle sat were turned on.

Meg Light seemed to balance on her toes. Like the furniture, she had a remembered prettiness, but was a bit too thin to give the impression of healthiness. Her brown hair was carefully combed. Like her daughter, her brown eyes communicated shyness and a bit of fear. "Can I offer you coffee?" she asked. "I'm sorry it took me so long to open the door. It isn't tight and when it's so cold, we lock it to keep the draft from freezing our feet." Her long fingers picked at the pleats of her print dress.

"No problem," Sam responded.

Meg Light waited uncertainly. "Coffee would be wonderful," Estelle said. "It is so cold outside, I feel like an ice carving." She smiled warmly. "Can I help you?"

"No, it's in the kitchen. Well, of course," she added self-consciously. "Where else would it be?" Estelle supported her with an easy laugh. "Um . . . yes . . . I'll get it." She ran her hand across her forehead to brush a loose strand of hair. "I'll be right back."

"Thank you," Sam said. As she left, he scanned the room. Everything was in perfect order. The freshly polished coffee table gleamed as did the wood on the sofa and the chair in which he sat and the cabinet-style stereo under the picture window. Thin gauze curtains hung from rust-flecked rods over the side window across from him, the shade was drawn three-quarters down. The living room smelled of the pleasing scent of polish. That mixed with the antiseptic aroma that emanated from the kitchen. Meg Light had gone to a great deal of trouble for her visitors.

He heard the tinkling of the cups on the silver tray Mrs. Light carried into the room. He watched her set the tray carefully on the coffee table, her knees bent, her back a bit too straight. "I need to . . . I'll get the coffee now," she explained and hurried back to the kitchen.

Bleach, Sam decided. That's what I smell. The odor dominated, an almost too clean smell. Proving what?

"I'll pour," Estelle volunteered when Meg returned with the silver coffee pot. "Please let me do that. Otherwise I'll feel useless and pampered."

"Um . . . that would be nice of you. I'll get the cookies." She disappeared and returned with a plate of homemade chocolate chip cookies.

"Why don't you sit down and take a rest," Sam suggested. "I think you're spoiling us. Those cookies look delicious." Meg thrust the plate toward him. He took two and accepted the cup of coffee Estelle extended to him. "Now, please have a seat. I think I am fully served."

"Mmmm . . . Yes. All right," Mrs. Light answered. She backed toward the straight-backed dining room chair at the far end of the sofa. She sat down, her back straight, her hands smoothing her skirt before she folded them on her lap. "Is . . . is Patty in trouble? I can't imagine it, but . . . I know you said something about scholarships, but isn't it unusual for . . . "

"For an administrator to visit a student's home?" Sam interjected. "Not really. I don't do it as often as I'd like, but I've been visiting parents for twenty some years. I like to get to know the parents." He smiled at the intimidated woman. "By the way, these cookies are delicious. That's one of the reasons I like to visit homes."

"I . . . thank you . . . I know I haven't been to any parent conferences," Meg Light said. Her eyes fell to her hands. "I . . . Patty . . . Patty's always had good grades, so I . . . thought there was no need." Her eyes darted from Estelle to Sam and back.

"Do you work?" Estelle asked.

"No . . . yes . . . I . . . . It's just that Patty's no trouble. Are you sure she isn't in trouble at school? Oh, my, she couldn't be pregnant!" Her hands folded and unfolded in her lap.

"No, no," Sam assured her. "She's a fine young lady. Let me explain. It's our policy to try to involve parents in the planning of their sons' and daughters' futures. I'm encouraging Patty to enter a program we've worked out with the college that would allow her to earn college credits this summer and during her senior year and would also provide employment at the school during the summer. I suppose she's talked to you about this?"

"Yes . . . She spends most of her time at home studying in her room. I . . . she's very mature. But she was so excited about this program. I've never seen her so excited."

"One reason I needed to talk to you," Sam resumed, "is that the applications for work aid and the scholarship are a little intrusive. These days it's mandatory for parents to file rather complete financial information with these applications. So we need your help to help her. Perhaps your husband . . . "

"My ex-husband provides nothing," she said. "He does nothing for us. He has no idea. Patty thinks it's her fault. It isn't." The pain of this testimony crimsoned her face. "We're on welfare, Mr. Strand. We've been on welfare for many years. Since I could no longer work."

"Divorces are never easy, are they?" Estelle affirmed.

"Mine wasn't," the woman said. "I haven't seen my sons . . . " Then she clamped her mouth shut.

Sam realized he was staring intently at the woman. He tried to hide his surprise at discovering Patty had siblings. To relieve the tension that had entered the room, he extended his cup toward Estelle, and she refilled it for him. He took another cookie. "If I keep eating these, I'm going to have to skip lunch at school.' Then he addressed Mrs. Light. "Patty has great potential. Will you fill out whatever information you can?"

Meg Light looked at Estelle. "The divorce was hard on Patty. Her father deserted her . . . us. He said he had no desire to raise girls." Her face was shiny with perspiration. It was easy to tell she didn't talk about this subject much. "I don't want to bore you with our troubles. Are you a teacher?"

"No," Estelle answered as easily as if she'd been asked the time of day. "Oh, I've worked on some school committees and did some chaperoning while my boys were in school. But, no, I'm just a friend of Sam . . . Mr. Strand's. We both attend a self-help group meeting. Sam sometimes asks me to come along with him when he visits parents, especially female parents. The gossip in this town can be terrible. These days one can't be too careful. There are people who would love to pin something on my friend or other teachers. So I'm here to help that not happen.

"Yes, well, I know how they gossip. Would you like more coffee?" Estelle asked and poured a cup for herself. She offered to do likewise for

Mrs. Light, but the slender woman declined. "I'm already too nervous."

"I'd better pass," Sam said. He reached into his briefcase and extracted a folder. "But I will have to get back to school soon. Our counselors don't really like doing my job as well as their own. Not all of our students are as diligent as your daughter." He laid the folder on the table. "The forms you'll need to fill out are all in there. I'm sorry, but . . . "

"I appreciate the interest you're showing in Patty," Patty's mother said as she rose from her chair. "She's very excited about this opportunity. I'm sure she'll help me fill out the forms."

Sam and Estelle rose as well. "I included a card with my office and home numbers on it and Estelle's, too. She's done financial aid forms for her boys in the past. So if you can't get hold of me . . . "

Estelle added, "So if you need help or want to talk . . . "

"Thank you," Mrs. Light answered curtly. "It was nice to meet you, Estelle, and you, Mr. Strand."

Estelle smiled. "Perhaps we'll see each other again."

Sam put on his topcoat. "Thanks for your time, Mrs. Light," he said as he opened the door and followed Estelle out. As he descended the steps, he heard the sound of the key in the lock.

Back in the car, Sam ventured, "She was sure ready for us to go."

"If you're implying she needed a drink or a pill, you may be right," Estelle said. "On the other hand, you have to admit that woman must love her daughter. This visit was hard for her. That house sparkled. It was not easy for her to talk with us, but she did. She told us more than she wanted to. The poor thing may just be worn out."

"How long do you suppose she's been divorced?"

"For her it was yesterday. Some people get hurt so badly the pain never leaves. They get so used to it they're afraid they'll be an empty shell without it. Others find the pain a useful excuse for doing what they do."

"Like an alcoholic and his drink. Were my suspicions bogus?"

"I don't know, Sam. I do know if there was evidence, she covered it well. Unfortunately, perhaps. Meanwhile, you can rest assured that in her heart of hearts, she loves her daughter. That makes your visit worthwhile."

"True," Sam replied. Nevertheless, he couldn't dismiss his uneasiness. Whatever else was true, he was aware that Patty Light's life was no easy ride. The potholes in her path made the ones jiggling his car seem like mere scratches on the road's surface.

Greg Schwarz

Rage and cynicism were foreign to Greg Schwarz' personality. So was the thundering silence he carried into his classrooms. He was normally a gregarious man. He loved teaching partly because the profession allowed him to be who he was – enthusiastic, funny, and even a little silly when appropriate.

He brought those same qualities to coaching. His virtues were enhanced because he worked with Red Howard, whose reserved, confident personality balanced Greg's extroversion perfectly. In his six years in Blue Lake, Greg had come to revere his mentor. The two had collaborated on a string of winning seasons. Greg hadn't envisioned any of that ending.

Red's heart attack had shocked him, but the actions of the school board and superintendent were equally shocking. That whole scenario caused him to question his decision to become a teacher and coach. If what happened to Red and what was happening to Sam Strand were indications, he'd be an idiot not to seek another place to teach or another way of making a living. He'd resented the manner of Ted Gerney's departure, but he'd begun to comprehend it. Loyalty meant nothing. It made him sick.

Greg's anger was eating him alive and eating at those around him. His sullenness was driving students away from the room where they used to enjoy spending time.

Ed Warrum had sought sanctuary in that room. However, the last time he'd stuck his head in the door was a few days after the school board meeting. When he walked in, Greg didn't see Ed Warrum, he saw Pete Warrum's son and couldn't hide the disdain that shot from his eyes at his immobilized target, who stood transfixed by the burning gaze, then pivoted and exited the classroom.

Greg battled his reaction every time he saw the teenager. He was aware of its injustice. So he began turning in another direction whenever he spotted Ed, at least until he heard about Ed attacking Billy Cloud. That incident justified his outrage. Like father, like son. Anyone gets in your way, beat 'em into the ground.

Thus it was Greg found himself standing in the hallway after school on a January day hurling thunderbolts at the boy walking by with lowered head. That was when he felt an arm snake through his.

"Come to my office," Red Howard ordered.

Red wasn't scheduled to resume teaching duties until February first. "What are you doing here?" Greg asked.

"Come on. I'll explain in my office."

The coaches' office was dark and empty when the two entered the locker room. Red switched on the lights. "My chair," he said to the ancient La-Z-Boy recliner that dominated the room. He nestled into it while Greg took the chair where he always sat.

"So . . . " Greg said.

"So I'm here under doctor's orders," Red explained. "Said I'm going to drive Beth to drink if I don't get out of the house. Said I should start coming to school at the end of the day, start getting into the routine, and find out if I want to do this."

"And?"

"I do. I love this place."

"Geez, it's good to see you sitting in that chair. Makes me want to cry. Truthfully."

"Truthfully, there's one other reason I'm here. My undercover sources here have been giving me reports I don't like hearing."

"About the kids subbing for you?"

"No, Greg. They're about you."

"Me!" Greg thundered.

Red ignored his tone. "You. My sources tell me the real Greg Schwarz left town after the board meeting, and his body has been taken over by a glowering monster."

"That's not fair. I can hardly stand this place."

"It shows. I saw it for myself today. It's ugly, Greg."

"Red, I've been so darn mad, I can hardly stand it. Or myself."

"That's the point. You think I can't afford to be angry, so you've decided to be mad enough for both of us."

"The whole thing makes me want to puke."

"Me, too. But it isn't worth staying sick forever. May I remind you for the hundredth time that I was thinking of quitting anyway." He raised his hands to forestall Greg's retort. "No one's suffering over this thing like you are. I'm not. Beth is delighted that I'm quitting. But it's turning you inside out. I watched you glaring at Ed Warrum a few minutes ago. Pure rage. If I were that kid, I'd dive so deep under the nearest rock I'd have to speak Chinese when I came out the other side."

"Every time I see him, I see his father. I don't suppose you heard what he did to Billy Cloud?"

"I did. My sources are thorough."

"And you think that's okay?"

"No, I think it's awful. But that's no more Ed Warrum than you're Greg Schwarz these days." Red gazed at the coach he loved like he loved his own sons. "You and Ed are two of the most fragile people I know right now. You both have your reasons. But he's just a kid, Greg."

"And I'm not."

"I don't want to belittle you. You're such an optimist, such a believer, that the stuff that's gone down has thrown you hard. It goes against everything you believe ought to be true. You're a hundred percent right. But," Red cautioned, the fingertips of his hands touching one another, "being right serves no purpose if it's killing who you are in the process."

"It is."

"Well, as they say, 'get over it'. There are too many kids who want to come to your room and feel happy and safe again, especially the boys."

"I could use a girl or two in there, you know. I get pretty darn tired of the guys." Greg had to smile. He felt like he used to when his father came home, and the two sat and talked. Or maybe it was just knowing Red was okay, that he was back, that softened his anger.

"If you keep looking as angry as you did in the hallway a few minutes ago, you'll have a long wait for that to happen. Anyway, Beth wants you to know what you need is not a giggling gaggle of girls around you. You need a wife."

"She said that, didn't she?"

"Those were her exact words after she watched you flirting with those cheerleaders during that pepfest."

The laughter sounded so good and felt so rich Greg found it hard to stop.

Kyle Hunter

Toward the end of January, the edge entered the faculty lounge. If you'd been teaching for a while, as the majority of the Blue Lake High School faculty had, you'd know the edge was predictable. It was a seasonal and cyclical circumstance just as other moods, modes, and activities among teachers and students were. Nevertheless the edge always felt freshly minted. And nowadays, the opportunities for students to lose focus or screw up their lives were more numerous, the glittery distractions more spangled.

So the edge inhabited the lounge and the classrooms as well. January was harsh anyway. The days seemed either overcast and gloomy or bright and bitterly cold. You arrived at school with the breaking of dawn and left for home as daylight was dying or dead. You looked around and reaffirmed your classes were, indeed, too large. You discovered that a few students had begun to quietly drift weeks ago when you'd been too busy to notice. Checking your grade book for the upcoming quarterly and midyear report cards, you were distressed to notice how many unsubmitted assignments there were. Sprinkled through the daily routine, these seemed to be no real problem. One or two unprepared students a day, a few absences for which work was not made up, a flunked test or two.

Now you looked at the blank squares in the grade book and wondered from where they'd come. How could you have been so inattentive? Insignificant within the slew of students who paraded through your room each day, they felt like gaping holes now. So you had to decide whether to give the recalcitrants one last chance to compensate, the absentees one last chance to turn in what they knew was due two days after their return, the space cadets one last chance to drop in from the ozone. A minority, those drifters, dreamers, cons, and skippers, but in your mind they loomed large. You struggled to stop feeling like you'd failed again, struggled to stop feeling like you'd been sleep walking when you'd thought you were wide awake and working.

Those were Kyle Hunter's thoughts as he listened to the lunchtime hub-bub in the faculty lounge. Grades were a strain. Only the purely objective had serenity about grading, and even they were sometimes thrown off balance by the blank square syndrome.

"School," said math teacher Barb Peterson, "would be a great place to work if it weren't for grades." Someone saying that was a requirement of the semester ending ritual.

"Right, Barb," Kyle said, pushing his lunch tray away.

"I just counted up and found out Cessy Roland has missed eight classes this quarter. I knew she was missing some. But that little vixen never missed more than one a week until this week. I was shocked! And she's missing four assignments. Tomorrow she and six other students will walk in and say, 'Can I hand in this makeup work? Geez, it was in my locker for forty days, and I just found it under the forty day old tuna sandwich my mother made me take to school. Geez, she knows I hate tuna. So I stuck it in my locker and forgot about it. Darned if I didn't put it on top of my makeup work.'"

"Yeah," interjected history teacher Melanie Malone, "and at least six students will tell me that they did too hand in those assignments, though my records clearly show they didn't. Three will have parents who are totally convinced their darlings would never lie. At least one will come storming into my room."

"I thought you said there'd be six," Kyle noted.

"I did. I'll find number six's tucked in a book because it was handed in late or mixed in with another class' papers. Then I'll think maybe the rest aren't fibbing, and I'll be here until ten searching every nook and cranny. In the end, four of the five will bring in the assignment the next day, having 'found it in the bottom of my backpack' or 'golly, giggle, giggle, there it was lying under my bed in my room.'"

"Already happened to me," Clyde Ron, the shop teacher added. He leaned forward, drumming the long table with his fingers. "Course what's new? Every quarter, every semester, every year for eight years. Still," he said, tugging the hair on the sides of his head in mock agony, "yet, still crazy, I listen. I'll tell ya, it's dangerous how some can lie straight faced while they cry. And that's just the boys."

"Or act so angry!" Barb exclaimed. "Knowing full well I'm right. It's Academy Award acting."

"This new kid," Melanie said, "well, he isn't new, but he's here so seldom in class any more he seems new . . . Frank Marin? There's something seriously wrong with him. He came up to the desk yesterday. Well, I asked him to, of course. He's missing twelve assignments. He stands there wearing that black jacket he always wears, staring at my chest. I tell him he's missing twelve assignments, and he stands there with that blank look on his face. I say, 'Didn't your parents get the mid quarter warning slip? Didn't they talk to you? Didn't I hand you a copy of it after class five weeks ago when you were missing five assignments?' He shoves his hands in his jeans pockets, and I can see his fists bulging his pockets. Finally I say, 'Frank, can you hear me?' Nothing. 'Frank!' And I'm screaming almost. He finally tears his eyes away from my chest, and he looks at me like I'm a burglar breaking into his house. He looked so invaded. Then he says, 'What?' I picture my little fingers grabbing that jacket collar and . . . Then after I repeat he's missing twelve assignments and has twelve absences since January 4th, he says, 'That's your problem' and walks out!"

"Some parents, too," Clyde muttered. "We're baby-sitters, cops, hall monitors, bathroom monitors, paper shufflers. Give them a hundred and whatever a day. See how they feel."

"Well," Kyle said, "not every kid is a Frank Marin. He's an extreme, isn't he, Melanie?"

"You're right, Kyle," Melanie agreed. "Most kids aren't wolverines."

"Dare I say," asked Dale Dorness, Blue Lake School's speech therapist seated at the end of the table, "that most kids are pretty good?"

"You dare say that in two weeks, Dale," Jan replied. "During this week the blanket is thrown over them all and I'm Witch Hazel. We will all resume human form next week. Until then, keep your sympathetic liberal tongue still and your understanding liberal lips sealed."

"Can I at least pucker them?"

"Only if you're preparing to kiss my butt." The conversers exploded in laughter.

"The bell never rings when you need it," Kyle said. Then it did. "I'm sorry I mentioned it. Sorry, kids, sorry."

"Back to the cave," Clyde stated.

"The salt mines?" Dale offered.

"Too late, Dale. You'll never be one of us," Jan said.

"What I can't figure out," Melanie admitted to Kyle as they headed for the door, "is why when the kids screw up, I feel guilty."

"Welcome to education," Kyle said as they melted into the stream of people in the hall.

february

Billy Cloud

"Your parents are very talented. And generous," Patty Light told Billy Cloud as she watched him secure the clamps of his mother's cross-country skis. "It was nice of your mother to let me borrow her equipment."

"She's a nice lady. By the way, you must have big feet," Billy said, tilting his head back to catch her prettiness. "Dad always says it would take a big pair of feet to fill Mom's shoes. These shoes fit you perfectly."

Patty wobbled on the skis. To steady herself, she pushed her poles into the soft snow on either side of the double tracked trail.

"Just think of the skis as extensions of those big feet," Billy suggested.

"Oh you," she said. "I haven't been on skis since I was little," she explained. "My grandparents gave my brothers and me these tiny skis. We ran right outside and put them on. I bet we fell five hundred times in ten minutes. Makes me wonder why I want to do this."

"It's because you love this winter world, and you want to be out in it. You shoulda let yourself fall just now, Then you'd remember all that falling didn't hurt. Like they say, if you ain't fallen, you ain't skied."

His own skis waited beside the trail, which began in the woods behind the Cloud House and intersected with the state trail a mile away. As he stepped off the trail to get them, his feet sank into the fresh snow. He stepped gingerly onto each ski and slid his boots into position. "This is how you can close those bindings yourself," he instructed her. He inserted the metallic tips of his poles into each clamp's hole and pressured it until it caught.

"That looks so . . . " Patty began.

"Sexual?" Billy blurted, the word leaping from his lips before he'd even thought it.

"I was going to say easy," she grimaced, her eyes more full of wondering than wonder.

What an idiot! Billy scolded himself. "Sorry about that. Darn tongue goes on automatic pilot sometimes. I guess I thought you were one of the boys." Oh, that was lame. He rarely talked like that to the boys or anyone else. If she knew how to spring those clamps, he was sure she'd whack those skis right into his shins. He pressed his lips tight to prevent inflicting further offense.

But Patty slipped the hook out of his mouth. "Are you going to give me a few tips? About how to ski, that is?"

"This book I read says, tell beginners 'if you can walk, you can cross-country ski,'" he responded gratefully. "It's a basic truth." Then his trickster tongue betrayed him again. "And I know how well you walk."

"Well, I know how much you talk," Patty rejoined, eyes sparking in a way that could mean either defiance or enjoyment of this exchange, "and you talk very, very much." Then she surprised him further. She stuck out her tongue at him like a child would.

"It's not snowing," Billy said, relieved by that response. "So you can reel that tongue back in your mouth. I'll let you know if it starts snowing. Here's a clue. The flakes are white and no two look alike."

"Well, I would say it takes a flake to know one," she declared, her gloved hand pointing at him and then flying to her mouth as if to stuff a burst of laughter.

Billy hoped it was the latter. Laughter was the only quality he'd found in short supply in Patty's arsenal of virtues. He'd be pleased to provoke her to laughter.

"Are we going to ski or not?" she asked.

"Of course," he countered. "Did you have doubt?"

"Well, yes, and thank you," Patty replied as she tried to move down the trail, legs and arms stiff, ski poles plowing the snow that lined the trail. "Darn it," she muttered. "This is hard."

"Bend your knees a little and lean a little forward," Billy instructed. "Push off with one foot and glide with the other. It is like walking, only better. Let me go ahead of you. Watch what I do and imitate it. I'm pretty good at this," he finished, flashing the grin she could never help but return with a brief smile of her own.

Exaggerating his movements for her benefit, Billy achieved a rhythmic glide. He was sure he'd messed up a few minutes ago, but this day was close to perfect otherwise. His persistence in convincing her to visit the Cloud House was paying off. Whenever their schedules had coincided after her assistant duties and his basketball practice, he'd taken to walking her part way to her home, though no closer than a half dozen blocks. When they stopped at the invisible line that marked her private territory, he always repeated his invitation. Her reply had remained the same. "Thank you. I'd like that. But my mother . . . Goodbye. I have to go." Then she'd hurry down the sidewalk without looking back. Last Wednesday, she'd said, "Yes. Is Saturday okay? I'll meet you here."

Her visit had gone terrifically well. Patty had marveled at the delicate and detailed miniatures of ducks, grouse, pheasants, deer, fox and eagles his father fashioned from wood. Her eyes conveyed her deep appreciation for the pictures of modern and traditional Indian motifs and portraits he painted as well as the intricate woven baskets and beautifully turned pottery his mother produced.

Eventually Billy's mother had pointed at the skis resting against the garage and asked Patty if she wanted to try skiing on this white and blue February day.

Billy became lost in his thoughts and adrenalized by them. When he finally thought to glance over his shoulder, Patty was a distant miniature on the trail. Not good. If he were her, he'd be boiling. He snowplowed to a stop and side-stepped off the trail.

He watched her approach. She was a quick study. "I think I'm exactly imitating you," she called, "but I'm not going anywhere."

"My fault," he said as she neared. "I was in such a hurry to get you going, I forgot to check the wax on those skis." As Patty pulled alongside, he added, "I always carry wax in my pocket. Let me release the clamps, and I'll re-wax your skis."

She stopped him in mid bend. "No, I'll do it." She inserted the pole tips, released the clamps, and stepped off the skis. "No comments needed, please."

He knew it was perverse, but he liked this fresh feistiness. "Imitate this," he said and made an exaggerated motion of zipping his lips. Then he cradled a ski against his shoulder, applied blue klister, and produced a cork from his pocket to rub the wax smooth.

As he reached for the other ski, Patty said, "Let me." He shrugged and handed her the tube and cork and rose to watch her work. She replicated his procedure perfectly. She returned the wax and cork, reinserted her feet in the skis, and secured the bindings. Admiration was only the first feeling this little scene provoked. "You are definitely getting the hang of this," he told her. "You lead for awhile. Now that you're decently waxed, I ain't sure I'll be able to keep up."

"You're so full of it," she said, then resumed the trail.

He watched her slide by, then eased behind her and studied her determined struggle to find the rhythmic glide he'd exhibited. "Relax," he ordered. "Enjoy yourself." He watched the bobbing of her head, her brown hair framing her stocking cap, her red jacket rippling in the breeze, her faded jeans clasping her hips and legs, her effort beginning to ease. The pulse in his wrists and chest beat in rhythm with her movements.

Within minutes, he was watching her glide, her skis skimming the tracks. He shouted, "Way to go!"

"Watch what I do and imitate me," she sang over her shoulder as she replayed Billy's exaggerated motions. Then she settled back into her own rhythm. "It's like flying," she cried into the wind. If she was flying, he was soaring. Every inch of him delighted in her delight, delighted in the great good fortune of her being in his life, delighted in this perfect winter day. "It's wonderful!" he heard her sing, and he wanted to zoom next to her, whirl his arms around her, hug her vibrancy, and lose himself in her loveliness.

Suddenly she accelerated and disappeared from sight. "Omigosh, the hill!" he shouted. He'd forgotten all about the hill, an easy enough slope for an experienced skier, but a precipice to someone new to skiing. "Tuck!" he shouted frantically. "Snowplow," he cried, forgetting the words were meaningless to the novice.

"Oomph," he heard her cry as he approached the incline. She missed the curve in the trail at the bottom and whooshed off it into the fresh snow. Her poles sailed from her hands, and her skis crossed as she toppled face first into the unmarked white.

Billy raced down the hill, kicked out of his skis and thrust his arms under her armpits. He lifted her awkwardly out of the snow as his boots sank into it, her skis still crossed beneath her. She trembled in his embrace. "You okay?"

"Just scared," she whispered. "My arms kept sinking in the snow. I couldn't push my face out of the snow." She was clutching his jacket to balance herself on her crossed skis. "I suppose no one ever drowned in snow." She tried and failed a smile. "I'm such a klutz."

"No, no, it's my fault. I get so stupid around you. I forgot all about the hill." She lost her balance and fell against him. He wished he wasn't feeling so much warmth where her body was touching his. "My skis," she murmured.

"Here, put your hands on my shoulders and I'll unsnap the clamps." She obeyed, and he bent down to push the release with his hands. She stepped carefully off the ski, uncrossing her legs, brushing his arms as she did so, her hands lightly weighted on his shoulder for balance. He shuffled to reach the release on the other ski and felt the heat of her hands penetrating his jacket. He released the remaining binding and straightened, his hands rising to her elbows, her hands still on his shoulders. "You're sure you're not hurt?" he repeated, his voice thick in his throat.

"Just embarrassed. I feel really inept," she said and did not remove her hands.

"You ain't skied if you ain't fallen," he reminded her, his hands still on her elbows.

"Well, then, I've skied, haven't I?" she said, her fluttering hands telling him she'd achieved balance.

"Yes, you have," Billy answered, his eyes riveted on the flushed glow of her face, her deep brown eyes, her unpainted lips. "You sure are pretty," he heard himself saying, his hands moving of their own volition down the sides of her jacket to her hips.

He felt the tremor generated by his electrified hands race through her body. She stumbled backward, nearly falling, pleading almost inaudibly, "Don't. Please don't."

He stared at her, withdrawing the offending hands. He stepped back as well, sinking into the soft snow.

"I'm sorry," she whispered, her arms crisscrossing her chest, her lips trembling, her eyes full of anguish.

"I'm the one who needs to apologize. I'm an idiot. My stupid mouth. Stupid hands. I oughta slap myself silly."

"It isn't you. It's me," she insisted.

His gloved hands felt Mickey-Mouse huge hanging at his sides. He shoved them into his windbreaker pockets. He searched for words to ease the scene, came up empty and gave up. Just as well. His mouth had betrayed him all day. So instead he said, "We'd better get back to the house. It'll be dark pretty soon."

"I think so, too," she said. Then she offered him a bridge beyond the moment. "Billy, I hope you're going to show me how to climb this hill with skis on. So we can get to your house before dawn." It was a needed, vulnerable plea, and it reached deep within him.

"Yes," he said. "Yes, you're right. You're a quick learner. Just watch me and do what I do." He turned too quickly to retrieve his skis, tripped over the buried tips of hers, and sprawled head first into the snow.

It was worth it. As he lay prone, the snow icy on his forehead, nose and chin, he heard her sing, "I already know how to do that!" Then her melodic laughter chimed the silence. He pushed his face fully into the snow and raised it to her, his snowy grin provoking another round of release from his mystifying friend.

Patty Light

Dear Wonderful, Worrisome World

I can't begin to tell you! I'll write these words, commit these days to paper. Days never in my dreams. I thought all my days would remain the same until I grasped the tassel between my thumb and forefinger and shifted it to the other side. I am surprised, delighted, and afraid.

She asked me to help her fill out the papers. She sat beside me, sad and anxious. She scattered our circumstances across the top of the form and asked me to make sense of what I was seeing, asked me to find the right blanks for the right numbers, watched me patiently, carefully. It felt like love. Right here. I know it hurt her to lay out our lives, in numbers for other eyes to see. It took hours to decipher with her sitting beside me as still as if she would shatter if she moved. The numbers finally flowed through pen to forms. When we were done, she wrote her name in legible letters. She sat for a time with her eyes on the forms before she rose and walked upstairs, glancing briefly at me, love swirling in the air until it misted into my heart. I heard her door close with a soft series of squeaks. I did not hear the clicking of the key in the lock.

I delivered those papers two days ago and I'd learned that life can rise.

I want to tell you about a place I visited, Mr. Hunter. You should visit, too. It's a big older house a few miles beyond the edge of town that's been partially converted into the "Cloud House Gallery." It took my breath away. There are miniature woodcarvings of birds and animals so delicate and detailed. There are bold, larger pieces – eagles, hawks, bears. And people. All are Native Americans. That's true of the paintings, too. The artists all have Native American blood pumping through their veins.

Mr. Cloud is a carver and painter and teacher of art. Mrs. Cloud is a weaver and potter and teacher of mathematics at the college. Their son is a student, an athlete, and a writer, too. He should be in your writing class. He showed me this poem and gave me a copy.

THE WOLF IS CALLING
Weaving my way through the city streets,
Trying to find a space where the air smells sweet,
I was living inside a bad dream,
But very soon I'd be awakening.
Here are the changes that I see.
The wolf is calling me wild and free.
Everything I really wanted was somewhere else,
Waiting and waiting and waiting for myself.
The pine trees hold last night's snow.
The sky is crystal and so is the cold.
There are so many things I need to know,
So touch me and teach me and free my soul.
The night is stars and a lonely field.
I hear no sound of automobiles.
The wolf is calling with a wild thrill,
Waiting and waiting and waiting for me still."

I love this poem. I love that place. It made me feel peaceful, but it also made me feel alive and less alone. It had laughter and music and the aromas of art and artists.

That isn't all, Mr. Hunter. I went cross-country skiing. I've wanted to do that for a thousand years. I started out awkward and self-conscious, but my friend said if you can walk, you can ski, and, lord knows, I can walk. My friend was right.

It was cool and quiet and blue and beautiful in the woods where we were, but the exertion of my effort wrapped me in warmth. It was like walking, only freer, like running, only easier. Then I was gliding, and it felt like flying. Eventually I lifted my eyes from the tips of the skis to the pine boughs and birch trees drifting by. Then I tilted my head way back so I could see the sky, as deep and blue as I've ever seen it.

So, of course, all of a sudden I was whizzing down a hill. I saw the curve and missed it and ended up with a face full of snow. I fell but it hardly mattered at all.

I want to answer your question, Mr. Hunter. My stories are stories. Mr. Baker says that many stories reveal many things about their authors. I suppose that might be true for me. But I don't know that. My stories just fly out of my mind onto paper. If I ever know more than this, I'll let you know.

I have a question, too. Sometimes when you're through immersing yourself in your art, which is teaching us, and we're working and you're wandering about, I watch you watching us. There are times when your eyes seem as sad and lonely as Mr. Baker's, and sometimes as hurt and angry as Mr. Schwarz' have been lately. I wonder why. But maybe you don't know the answer to that any more than I know the answer to yours.

Oh. Speaking of. I saw Mr. Schwarz in the hall today. He smiled and said hello. I was so relieved! For the longest time he looked so full of thunder that I slid along the lockers across the hall so he wouldn't notice me though I don't know why he would anyway. I guess we all have our secrets and sorrows, and furies. Right, Mr. Hunter? But it's nice to see a person can get over them. Don't you agree?

P.L.

Robert Baker

"If I could, I'd teach all the poets and writers grouping them thematically to show how timeless and universal their hopes, dreams, thoughts and themes are. How great ideas and writings live forever. Emerson, Thoreau, Hawthorne, Hemingway, Steinbeck, Harper Lee . . . "

Why am I telling Patty Light this, Robert Baker wondered. How could it possibly mean anything to her? Oh, well, it meant plenty to him to see her brown eyes sparkle with comprehension. He expected them to glaze over at any moment, but then he always expected that, and it never happened. She was amazing, and he was amazed. This young lady made him feel alive and intelligent and like teaching was worth it. What a gift she was giving him! She was enabling him to survive this year! "But the curriculum guide says march them forward in lock step from the beginning. I love all the literature, but it must seem disconnected and dry as a bone when it's isolated like that."

She was sitting on the end of the radiator box away from the vents and near his desk. She used to always sit in a student desk a few feet from his desk. Lately she'd taken to sitting on the radiator box. Maybe it was just because economics dictated that school thermostats be kept at 65 degrees and she was cold. Maybe it was because what was happening in her life was causing her to move more freely through it. Right now she was sitting on the radiator box after finishing her task of correcting quizzes, her long gray skirt falling over her knees to the calves of her slightly parted legs. Her red Nordic sweater looked soft. Its fabric must feel pleasant on her skin.

In some ways he knew he should haul himself out of Patty Light's life. He felt foolish in the silence of the room when his thoughts swam towards her like she was a rock and clinging to that rock was the only way to keep him from sinking. The trick was not to want or need to cling too closely or too long. That was the danger as well.

He would never have put himself – or her – in this position where admiration, gratitude, even a kind of love for who she was whirled through his head and heart. He would never have wanted to be this needy, this self-centered.

"Mr. Baker?"

"Sorry, Patty, I drifted somewhere in space for a moment, didn't I? You were saying?"

"Nothing. That look on your face touched me. You looked so emotional."

"Drifting can do that to me."

She adjusted her skirt a little. "Emerson and Thoreau mean a lot to me," she said, sliding off the radiator and settling into 'her desk.' "I'm glad we studied them. I find so much hope in their words. They make me believe. When I read their words, I want to sing. And Hawthorne . . . ."

Lord, he loved that verbal paragraph. He loved the moistness in her eyes. He loved the depth of feeling that spun those words to her lips. His efforts had a worthy recipient.

"Hi, Billy," Patty suddenly said, smiling radiantly.

"Hi. Hello, Mr. Baker," Billy said.

Robert leaned back in his teacher chair. "Billy. How was practice?"

"Not bad," the boy replied. "I think we're going to be pretty good when everyone gets back on the same page."

"Yeah, I heard about the trouble with Ed Warrum," he said with some satisfaction. Ed's sullen face slid easily into his mind's eye.

"Uh huh," Billy said. "Well, that's all over. Dewey's playing terrific. Ed isn't unhappy about coming off the bench. His dad's not too thrilled."

"Guess he jumped you because Harkness is too big," Robert persisted. "Jumping people must run in the family."

"Yeah," Billy replied in a puzzled voice. "Well . . . "

Out of the corner of his eye, Robert watched Patty rise and walk across the room. There was more grace in her movements now, the lightness of being loved. Billy Cloud was certainly good for her. Billy could lift her up in the same way that he might drag her down. Billy Cloud could make her smile the same way he might cause her tears.

"Have a nice evening," Billy said to the teacher.

"Night, Mr. Baker," Patty added.

"What, night's better than evening or what?" Billy kidded. "Have a nice night, Mr. Baker."

Robert watched them leave. He straightened the papers on his desk. Dammit, I like Billy, he told himself.

"Well, stupid, she's still coming in anyway. You thought she wouldn't." he mumbled aloud, his teeth clenched. "Jerk! You jerk!" He slapped a textbook on top of the papers. "All you need is to be a jerk!"

He walked to the door, snapped off the lights, and leaned against the wall. I should tell her I'm too dependent on her, so the visiting will have to stop. Correct papers and that's it. Would that hurt her? If she had better things to do, wouldn't she? Would she understand that at all? He knew she knew he was a teacher, and she was a student. He suspected that truth was evident to her, but more weighted for him right now. He knew it was up to him to change. It wasn't her responsibility. Nor was it his wish to sully anyone's purity of purpose, hers or his. He stepped into the empty hall, and then pulled the door shut harder than he needed to.

Ed Warrum

God, I have to talk to someone. Ed Warrum pushed himself up on his elbows. The red digital numbers on his bedroom clock radio read 3 a.m.! Every night it's three, four, five. Can't sleep, can't think straight, can't talk.

He pushed the heavy covers off and sat up in bed staring at the closet. The gun was in his mind almost all the time. He could feel its weight in his brain, see its snub-nosed silver anonymity. It looked like a cap gun, but it wasn't. It was real. He'd read the thing about the kid in Wyoming. God he'd identified. His dad hadn't been that physical, but mentally, emotionally, he was a bulldozer, strewing wreckage in his wake. And physically he was getting worse. Not hitting much, at least until tonight, but threatening, doubling his ham fists, banging those fists on the table during those interminable post game "discussions" he'd restarted when he discovered his son had been demoted to the second string. He didn't give a rip about basketball, but he was the King of Sports in Blue Lake, and it sure as heck didn't look good that his son had been demoted.

Tonight Ed had broken his silence. He'd heard more than he could stand. He'd shot back.

Shot back. The gun, always the gun. After that his father had doused him with an entire pitcher of water! Now there was an escalation! Water glass to water pitcher! What next! Fill the bathtub and push his son's head under? Or maybe he'd just shove it in the toilet!

Anyway, after his father threw the pitcher of water in his face, that had almost done it. The scene played over and over in Ed's mind.

It had happened after tonight's game. His dad already knew why Ed was in trouble. Harkness had come over the night after the incident with Billy. God, you should have seen the Old Man cover that one. He kissed up to Harkness like he was some college recruiter or something. "Yes, Sir. No, Sir. I'll have a talk with the boy, Sir. Thank you for caring, Sir."

Bigger'n he is. That's the story. Six foot five, two hundred and fifty pounds. Old man can't push him around. He thinks basketball doesn't matter anyway. It's the ego thing. I'm good, but I'm too small to play basketball at a major school and there's no way I'm not going to a major university. No Blue Lake College for Daddy's boy! So basketball doesn't matter that much.

Only attitude. "Recruiters might talk to Harkness, and he'd tell 'em you got a horse crap attitude!" his dad screamed once the coach was gone. "That idiot's dumb enough to say something like that." Ed twisted out of bed and padded across the cold wood floor to the window. The moonlight was bouncing off the snow, turning the world blue-white. He leaned against the dresser and stared at the bare oak tree beyond his window. Tonight took the cake. Tonight slathered the cake with sour frosting. Tonight was it. Especially after that other night.

His father had circled the subject ever since Harkness' visit. Now he said it. With that damn smirk on his face. After Blue Lake High School had won its third straight game with Ed substituting off the bench. "At least you plugged that Injun kid. He's a hot dog. He's a bum. They're all a bunch of bums."

"What are you talking about?" Ed asked incredulously.

"That Injun kid, Cloud," his father roared. "Oh, sure he's a pretty good ballplayer. Five years down the road, he'll be under a tree suckin' 'em up like the rest of 'em."

"What are you talking about? I had no right to hit him. He's a great guy."

"You don't talk back to me! Embarrass me in front of Harkness! Idiot comes to my house because my kid cracks an Injun kid like I'm to blame. Get out of my face!"

Ed wheeled out of the dining room like he was on skates. He'd known all along who he really wanted to hit.

There was that. Tonight there was the water pitcher.

Ed hadn't played until the fourth quarter. Heck, Dewey had played terrific. Fifteen points, four rebounds. He'd taken the pressure of replacing Ed Warrum, who had started as a sophomore, and he was playing really, really well. Blue Lake had won 78-64. Ed got into the game when Dewlin collected his fourth foul early in the fourth period. Billy Cloud fed him some beautiful passes including one on a fast break, two on two, when he'd drawn the defenders to him and then flipped the ball behind his back to Ed, who took one dribble under the basket and banked a reverse lay-up off the board. That had brought the crowd to its feet.

"Hot dog play," his father declared as the family sat around the table for the post game review and analysis as presented by Mr. Business, Mr. Sports, Mr. Coach, Mr. I-know-Everything. "The Injun plays to the crowd all the time. Nothin' but a hot dog."

"I got ten points," Ed responded, his insides heaving. "I got ten points because Billy threw me good passes." He didn't want to fight. How many ridiculous comments did he have to hear?

Ed stared out the window. He couldn't say his father got angry then.

His father was always angry. He couldn't say his father's face scrunched up. It was always scrunched up around this house. His Dad's buddies really ought to see him here. Then they'd wonder how the heck he could be leading them around by the nose.

"That's another thing," his father bellowed. "Ten points in one quarter. Edwards had ten the whole game."

"Edwards shot five for eight," Ed retorted. "He played terrific defense."

His father had never bothered to criticize Harkness or the basketball team before. Basketball never mattered. Why now? Basketball had been like a vacation for Ed. It had been like being on a playground after school. He wanted to get out of this room. Or lash back.

For once in his life lash back. End it. Why did he have the father who was the lunatic!

"Dad," his mother said. Had her voice always been so full of nerves, so quiet you could hardly hear it? "Let's go to bed," she finished, rushing her words. "It's late."

"You shut up!!! We'll go to bed when I'm finished. You always take the kids' side!" Ed's sister slid out of her chair. "You sit down! This is a family meeting!"

Ed couldn't stop himself. He slammed his fists on the table. The water pitcher in front of his father jumped from the impact. The glass next to it rolled off the table. "Oh my," his mother whispered.

Ed thumped his fists again. He choked out the words. "This is not a family meeting! This is not a family!" His fists banged the table again. "Leave them alone! Leave her alone! Leave me alone!" he screamed. Tears streamed down his cheeks.

Then the full pitcher of water splashed into his face.

"You little jerk!" his father roared, hurling the pitcher toward the front room. "You don't talk to me like that. You make me sick!" Then he ripped his fist into Ed's stomach. He watched his son crumple to the floor. "Everybody get the hell out of here!" he ordered.

Ed heard his sobbing sister scurrying across the carpet and up the stairs. He pushed himself up to his arms and knees. Doubled over in pain, he stared at his father's shoes and watched the right one being withdrawn from his view.

"Pete! Oh my lord! Don't!" his mother screamed.

Then he saw the other shoe disappear. He remained staring at the carpet listening to the pad of feet and did not move until he heard doors closing upstairs.

❖   ❖   ❖

Ed stood in front of his bedroom window. He wanted to take his fists and shatter the glass into a thousand shards, grasp the shards in his bloody hands and rip his skin until blood fountained from it. Take a shard of glass in one hand and the gun in the other and race to his father's bedroom and . . .

"Oh, God!" he groaned. "Oh God!"

He had to get out of this house. Now.

He dressed quickly and quietly. He pulled on his letterman's jacket, moved the shoes and clothes and picked up the shoebox in which he'd hidden the gun. He extracted the gun from the box. He grabbed his duffel bag and shoved in two pair of pants, a couple sweaters and shirts, some socks, some underwear. The bullets for the gun were in the shoebox. He took them out, dropped two bullets from the box into his hand, put the rest back into the shoebox and shoved it into his bag. He slid two bullets into the chamber of the gun. Then he picked up his tennis shoes, slid the gun inside one and stuffed both into the bag. He pulled on his sweat socks and shoved his shoes under his left arm. He'd put them on outside. He didn't want to wake up anyone. He withdrew his billfold from the top drawer of his bureau and checked to make sure the money his father had paid him for working during the holidays was still there. It was.

He didn't want anyone to wake up. The gun was in the bag. If his mother did awake and came out of the spare bedroom where she now slept, he'd simply run. He was sure she wouldn't utter a word, just motion for him to run, run, run!

If his father came out of his bedroom, he'd shoot him.

Ed exited his room and slipped down the carpeted hall and stairs. He slid his feet across the bare wood of the front room. The white linoleum of the kitchen glowed blue in the moonlight. He eased open the kitchen door and stepped out onto the concrete back steps where he put his shoes on. Then he walked past the garage to the street. He had no plan. He hadn't grabbed his mother's car keys. That was out. It'd wake everyone.

He did know that there was a five a.m. bus that went through St. Michael to the Cities. It must be getting close to 4:30 by now. He'd buy a ticket to St. Michael; tell the bus folks at the cafe he was going to visit his cousin, who actually was a teacher in the high school there. When he got to St. Michael, he'd buy another ticket to the Cities.

He didn't know what he'd do there. Just get out of here and disappear.

He was relieved that a college kid was manning the bus ticket counter. The kid had no idea who he was. So Ed bought a ticket to the Cities. He boarded the mostly empty bus and took a window seat toward the back. A few moments later the bus pulled out of the parking lot. Exhausted, Ed leaned his head against the window. He couldn't close his eyes for a long time; he could hardly blink. It wasn't until the bus had rolled through Buford, thirty miles southeast of Blue Lake, that he found sleep.

Luckily Ed Warrum's billfold contained all the money he'd gotten when he cashed the Christmas work check. His first day in the Cities, he checked into the Holiday Inn near the bus depot and the downtown area because it was nice and because it was close. He felt free and light and had the first good night's sleep he'd had in months or would have for days to come.

The next morning he checked out at eleven, knowing he'd soon be broke if he didn't. The trap would snap shut in a hurry if he insisted on the luxury of a Holiday Inn. So he grabbed his duffel bag and headed away from down-town. He knew from previous trips with his father to games and state tour-naments at the U that the cheap hotels were not far from where he was.

He opted to stay at the first one he entered, the Concord, a four-story walk-up. He knew it would be cheap when he walked in and saw the sag-ging sofa in the cluttered lobby. The two men seated on it were staring at nothing. Their faded jackets and loose pants had obviously been worn for days. This place he could afford. It wouldn't be pleasant, but staying here would buy him time to come up with a plan.

But planning didn't occupy much of his mind as he lay in the middle of his bowed bed that night. Instead he pondered how his parents were react-ing to his absence. The embarrassment would drive his father even crazier. His defeated mother wouldn't say anything and neither would his sister Jenny, whom he'd left there alone.

His father would make up some lie. Maybe he'd say Ed had been sick, which was the cause of his recent misbehavior, and they'd taken him to Mayo for a checkup. More likely, he'd claim Ed had been invited by recruit-ers to get an early look at a couple of colleges, and since he wasn't play-ing much on the basketball team, his dad decided he might as well go this week. Yeah, that would be his father's fabrication. He'd puff and strut and repeat that one so often, he'd grow to believe it was true.

The second night at the Concord Hotel was exceptionally noisy. Drunks night out – and in. There were only men at the hotel, most of whom ignored him or peered at him furtively ducked their heads and looked away when he returned their gaze. This night the halls echoed their shouting voices. When he heard the thud and grunt of punches being thrown not far from his room, he tried to pretend it was his father puffing and groaning with the pain of receiving the blows, but the thought provided neither pleasure nor release. He was glad when he heard someone shout, "Stop it, you guys stop it, or I'm gonna call the cops!" followed by scuffling feet. The rest of the night was punctuated by other short, profane arguments inside the hotel, and bursts of words from the street below as well as the roar of hot-rodders blowing carbon on the drunks as they sped by.

Each night Ed lay in his bed with his hand resting atop the duffel bag that housed the gun.

This morning he'd had enough, and his billfold was thinning. He threw his dirty shirt, jeans, socks, and underwear into the bag and dressed in the only change of clothes he'd brought along, a heavy flannel shirt and another pair of jeans. He pulled on his shoes and jacket, left the dank room and hurried down the stairs.

A sallow faced man tugged at his jacket sleeve as he strode through the lobby. "Got a quarter, kid," he asked. "I only need a quarter, kid. I'm starving to death." He looked it. His face was a folded series of drooping wrinkles. His watery eyes were frightened and sly. His hand trembled on the boy's sleeve.

"Sure," Ed answered. His slid his hand into his pocket and fished out the two quarters in it. 'Don't ever give those bums anything,' he heard his father say in his mind, a scene from some other trip, probably to a U football game. He and his father walking down a street somewhere near here toward the stadium. Some guy who looked like this one wandering up to them asking for money. His father yanking him away from the stranger. 'You give 'em a quarter, they want a dollar. They'll beat you up and turn you upside down to see if you got any more money.'

Ed sensed then and now that wasn't bad advice. "Look, Mister," he said, "this is almost all the money I got," as he dropped the quarters in the man's hand, "or I wouldn't be staying here."

"Fer shure, fer shure," the old man replied in a pleasant slur. Then he shuffled to the sofa and the men who'd been there the day Ed arrived, his back curved as a turtle's shell. "Got a quarter? I need a quarter, fellas," Ed heard the man pleading as he walked out.

The city cold smacked him as soon as he emerged from the building. He clicked the snaps of his letterman's jacket, wishing it had a collar to turn up, and headed away from the wind down the street, not sure where he was going. He thought about the old man. His eyes. Someone at school had eyes like that. Who was it? His mind saw a black leather jacket, upturned collar, and hair like Elvis use to have. A kid in Baker's class. Yeah, that was it. That kid who always wore his jacket. What was his name? Martin? Oh, yeah, Marin. Frank Marin. The only kid in school who looked as miserable as Ed Warrum felt.

"Nice butt!" he heard a voice say close to his ear. He realized he'd stopped at a corner for the red traffic light without knowing it, and a group of shoppers had clustered there waiting for the light to change.

"Huh?" he grunted, half-hearing the words, not even sure they were directed at him.

"I said 'ni-i-i-ce butt,'" the female voice sing-songed into his ear. He felt a gloved hand gliding his jeans.

"I . . . " he said, but the light changed, and then there was no one around him, just the group of shoppers charging across the ice pocked street. Well, he hoped it was the one whose blonde hair curled out from under her stocking cap, its tassel bobbing with the bounce of her walk, who'd been so familiar with him.

For a moment he felt buoyant and aggressive. Then he realized the encounter was as impersonal as you could get. But mainly how odd it was that someone would do that, then just walk away and giggle about it with her friends as they skipped down the street. 'Bet I made that hick's day,' she was probably saying.

Suddenly he realized with a shock that what she really was doing was picking his pocket. He frantically felt his right back pocket. No, the bill-fold was still there, thank God. Nevertheless he shifted it to his right front pocket. The girl in the stocking cap was nowhere in sight. The city was like that. He felt small and simple. It didn't matter to anyone that he was here.

It might matter if they knew he had a gun in his duffel bag.

He walked several more blocks. He looked down the street and stopped. At the end of the block, a group of five men or boys, all dressed in the same black jackets Marin wore were standing and staring at him. One pointed and the five began to advance in his direction. He hoisted the duffel bag up under his left arm and unzipped it a little. Then he turned and walked with long strides into the wind. He had a gun, but there were five of them. Maybe they had guns too.

At every corner, he searched in each direction for a building he could duck into. Occasionally he checked over his shoulder to discover the five were keeping pace with him, maybe even catching up. He saw a swagger in their gaits that was absent from his own.

Finally he spied a 7-11 a block to his left. Numerous pedestrians were headed in its direction. Whatever intentions the five stalkers had, they'd be less likely to follow through in such a public place. He hoped. He did not want to display fear by running, but he did increase the length of his strides as he headed for the store.

As he pulled open the door to the 7-11, he saw that his tormentors had closed the gap between him and them. He also noted with gratitude that the place was full of people. Scanning the store, he spied a space where a bank of three phones had once hung on the back wall and headed there. One pay phone remained. He wished he hadn't given the old drunk his last two quarters. Otherwise he could call 911. However, his pursuers didn't know that any more than they knew he had a gun. So he walked toward the phones to play out his bluff or to protect his back if the bluff failed.

Ed stood staring at the phone in front of him. It hung naked on the wall above the metal platform from which a phone book would have dangled had not someone ripped it out of its chain holder. He felt the nudge of a shoulder just beneath his own shoulder blade. He set his duffel bag on the platform, then faced his aggressors.

The boy who gazed up at him was perhaps six inches shorter than he was. His black hair was swept straight back from his forehead. His clear face seemed to be one round smirk, but his voice was mild when he said,

"Thought we was after you, eh, fella." The boy's eyes glittered with amusement, probably because the odds favored a triumphant outcome to their pursuit. Ed wasn't sure what message he was receiving.

"My pace give me away?" Ed asked without interest in the answer.

"Could see you sweat a block away," the boy said. "Could hear the crackle of sweat drops freezing before they hit the ground."

"I don't think so," Ed answered, leveling his eyes into the boy's. He should feel fear, but all that was apparent to him was a focused anger. "I didn't care for the numbers, but that's it." Besides he had a gun. Why would he sweat anything but the sentence he'd receive if he used it? "You guys hang out waiting for a guy walking alone so five of you can handle him?"

The boy shoved his hands in his pockets. He showed no fear either, but his dark eyes evidenced pain at the implications in Ed's question. "Nah, man, you got it wrong. We was just following you for fun. Saw your jacket, thought maybe you was from the suburbs, thought maybe we could make you wet your pants a little. Saw the name Lakers on the back. Don't know no Lakers around here. Only L.A. But we were just having a little fun with you. Kept looking over your shoulder, you know. Us, we're pretty peaceful. Wouldn't hassle no punk, get in trouble for the heck of it."

"That's nice to know," Ed said. He guessed the kid was eighteen. He was fully facing him now, leaning hard against his duffel bag, his hands loose in his pockets. He let his gaze sweep the crowded convenience store. The boy's five friends were scattered along the aisles, each glancing at him as he noted their presence. "Lotta people in here," Ed observed.

"That, too," the boy half smiled, then said with more seriousness, "Thought maybe you was holding in that big bag of yours. Lotta guys come down to this neighborhood are selling. We don't like that. But your eyes are too clear. You're nervous, but not the right kind of nervous. If you had money, wouldn't be in this neighborhood unless you was selling."

"So . . . " Ed said.

"So on behalf of my boys, I'd like to wish you a nice day and suggest that you return from whence you came, as Mr. Shakespeare would say. Would also like to say that if I might be wrong and we find you dealing in our neighborhood, we will beat the living crap out of you."

"Two things," Ed rejoined, bending a little into the boy's steady gaze. "One is you won't catch me dealing. Two is, it will take more than five of you to beat the crap out of me." It was a foolish thing to say, but he felt no remorse. His anger was rippling his muscular arms. A fight might feel good.

"Whoa," the boy said, smirk still in place. "That was a dumb thing to say, that last one, but if the first is true, we'll never have to test that theory. Good thing."

"Yeah, it probably was dumb, but I'm a little angry and uncomfortable. Comprehend?"

"Right, man. You're probably here because your old man beats on you. I comprehend. Jacket too light. Wrong shoes for this weather. Left in a hurry." He extended his hand. "Regular shake. No gang stuff. You ain't no gangbanger." Ed took the hand. Its grip was firm and the release quick. "Hasta," the boy said and turned on his heel. Ed watched him slowly gather his group and leave.

When he was sure they were gone, he turned to the phone. He stared at it and relived the scene he'd just experienced. He'd been wary but had not been afraid. He had been angry, but not paralyzed with anger.

It was only his father who could do that to him.

He needed to call somebody. But not his father, nor would he place his mother in the middle by calling her. His isolation had narrowed the list of those with whom he could speak to, well, no one. Except Shellie Chaine. He'd iced her, but he knew that beyond her unwillingness to dive into the depths with him without knowing why she should, she retained an interest in him. He could see it in her sad glances in the hallways and in class. She knew there was an answer to the mystery he had become and would remain at the edge of the crowd to find out what it was. If he could talk to anyone, it would be Shellie Chaine. But not in this place. It was too noisy in here, and if he spoke loudly, his reward could well be a jail cell. He had the gun.

He walked out of the 7-11 into the biting wind. He looked both ways, but his potential adversaries were nowhere in sight. The cold slapped his face. It shot up from the bare concrete sidewalk right through his "wrong shoes" into his calves. The wind whirled around the corners of buildings, snapping at him as he returned to the Concord Hotel where he'd noticed a phone booth tucked in the far corner of the lobby. The near euphoria he'd felt over the confrontation ebbed. He figured he was more lucky than smart. That kid had a brain and probably a sense of decency. Another group might have a different kind of leader and more aggressive intentions.

He reentered the hotel's ragged lobby, glad to be out of the weather and faintly relieved by the familiarity of the place. The old man was still circulating. He'd had some success. His gait was looser and sloppier than it had been earlier. His watery eyes were redder, and the palpable reek of alcohol rode his words when he leaned toward Ed and repeated his only question "Hey, kid, got a couple quarters. Sure could use a cup a coffee."

Ed fished his billfold out of his pocket. His thawing fingers stung. He knew it wasn't smart to expose money to this man or the others scattered around the room. But he wanted to be done with him. He grasped two dollar bills with his fingers, extracted them, and thrust them at the drunk. "Here. Now leave me alone."

The old man burst into tears. He accepted the bills and cradled them in his trembling hands. He glanced at Ed and whispered, "Why, God love you, son. God love and protect you forever." Then he shuffled out the door.

Ed was surprised at how much the man's words touched him. He was near to tears. God, he must be crazy or crazy lonely. He had to talk to someone.

He crossed the lobby and stood at the registration desk until the thin man with the darting eyes who had taken the money for his room noticed him. "I need some change," Ed said. The man eyed him. "For a phone call."

"Give me a dollar. I'll give you four quarters. That's it. You'll have to tell your mommy you love her real fast or call collect."

What do you know! Ed's mind shouted. He wanted to grab the jerk by his coat lapels and shake him until his teeth fell on the counter. He wanted to whip out the gun and shove it under the man's stupid nose. God! He said, "I'll call collect," and handed over the bill. The desk clerk spun the quarters on the counter and walked away.

The phone booth was an open booth with a wooden partition on one side and the dingy green hotel wall on the other. Ed leaned into it as much as he could and deposited a quarter. Putting the phone to his ear, he pushed the "0" button and listened to it buzz five times before the operator said, "Can I help you?"

"Uh, yes. I'd like to place a . . . uh . . . collect call to Shellie Chaine in Blue Lake." He stopped. He felt foolish calling collect.

"Whom shall I say is calling?"

"A friend."

"Is this a prank call?" the operator accused. "If so, please hang up."

"No!" Ed answered desperately. "I'm Ed Warrum."

"I have no listing for Shellie Chaine in Blue Lake."

"Her dad's name is Aaron," Ed added quickly.

Unsnapping his letterman's jacket, he listened to the burring of the phone, hoping no one was home. No. He had to talk to someone. He was as isolated as a mummy.

"Hello," said a voice in Blue Lake.

"Long distance calling collect for Shellie Chaine. The caller has identified himself as Ed Warrum," the operator intoned. "Will you accept the charges?"

"Long . . . collect . . . Ed?" he heard Shellie's mother's voice stutter on the other end of the line, then, "Shellie. Ed's on the phone. Long distance. Collect," muffled through Mrs. Chaine's hand. Ed thought he heard a response from an uncertain distance, then, "Yes, we will. We're already being charged for it."

There were a few seconds of silence. Then Shellie was talking, her voice flat with anger. "What do you want?"

"Uh . . . I'm in the Cities, Shellie."

"Is that far enough away so you can stand to talk to me? If I pay for the privilege?"

"Listen, Shellie, it's not your fault." His voice was thick in his throat.

"I know that!" she broke in heatedly.

He moved closer to the phone, squaring off the people in the lobby. "Shellie, don't. I'm half-crazy."

"Obviously. What's her name? How did you find a city girl? Did she dump you? You want to cry on my shoulder!" She sounded ready to slam down the receiver.

"Don't hang up, Shellie. Please. I have to talk."

"All right," she said. The wires hummed with silence.

"Listen, Shellie, can you come down here?"

"You are crazy. What? You want to introduce me to your girl friend?"

"There's no girl. There's nothing,"

"What? I can't hear you," Shellie rasped.

"Shellie, I ran away."

"From home? That's third grade stuff, Ed. Got another story?"

What's the use? But why shouldn't she be angry? He'd turned to ice around her.

"This is costing my parents money, not you," Shellie shot through the line. "Are you going to talk?"

"Yes. God, yes!" He looked down the lobby. No one was paying attention to him.

"Shellie, I've got a gun." He felt the dead shock at both ends of the line.

"Oh God, Eddie," she finally breathed. "What's wrong with you?"

"I'm half-crazy," he reiterated. The image of the gun, silver and snout nosed, beat in the center of his brain again. It waved in the air, sometimes sweeping an unseen audience, sometimes pointing directly at his own head.

"What are you going to do?" Shellie whispered, afraid to finish her thought.

"I don't know. That's what scares me."

"Talk to me, Eddie," Shellie pleaded. Her sudden softness was jarring. He felt exposed as though his secret was being shouted around the lobby by the old derelicts.

"I'm in a hotel lobby. I can't say much. There are people all around."

"Don't do that Eddie! Don't push your silence on me again! I don't deserve that!"

He felt himself sink back into ice. It was too hard to talk. It was easier to sink without explanation, without revelation. He wanted to hang up. He should never have called. It wasn't fair to her.

"Eddie, tell me where you are," Shellie demanded. "Talk to me. You are not going to freeze me out again! It's too miserable! You called me!"

Ed's guts were whirling. Who was he protecting? Why should he be standing in the lobby of this sleazy hotel? What had he done? He'd called Shellie to save his own life. Who in heck was he protecting?

"Where are you? Talk, dammit!"

"I'm standing in the lobby of the Concord Hotel in the Cities. It's a flop-house for drunks and druggies. I'm almost broke." He pulled the phone tight against his mouth. "I'm here because if I weren't, I'd use the gun."

He heard the catch in Shellie's throat. She was trying desperately to contain herself.

"Eddie," she said. Then she tried to fill the silence. "Mother said your dad is telling everybody you're not in school this week because recruiters at the U and private colleges invited you down. He said it was unusual for a junior in high school to get this much attention. He told her your phone had been ringing off the hook ever since those playoff games. She said he was much too eager to tell that story, and he never looked her in the eye once."

I must care, Eddie thought. He's still breathing.

Shellie lifted the silence. "Where's the Concord?"

"Near downtown," he answered. "Near the river. It isn't a nice area. You shouldn't come here."

"Near the university?" Shellie asked, her voice thin with tension.

"Yeah, eighth and something. But I gave up my room. I don't know where I'll be tonight. Why? You gonna call the cops?" He hated himself for the question. Why had it whirled out of his mouth?

Shellie ignored it. "Mother used to go to the University for summer school. Can I ask her? Maybe she knows a place to stay."

"No," Ed started to answer foolishly, but he could already hear Shellie's mother say, "Ask me what?" in the background. "Shellie," he said into the receiver, but she wasn't listening to him. He couldn't make out her words, but he could hear her tension, and Mrs. Chaine's voice in the background. "Shellie," he repeated, but he did need a place to stay. He couldn't spend another night here.

Shellie's voice reappeared in his ear. "Mother says to take a bus to the University. There's a Lutheran Student Center there where they might put you up, especially since it's a weekend. What?" she said, her voice muffled by her hand, then, "She says they won't charge you because you're Lutheran, but it would be nice if you'd put a few dollars in the basket by the door when you go."

"All right," Ed said. He had no alternatives. Everything looked crushingly gray or dangerously red to him right now.

"She says to take the bus that says 'University' and ask the driver to tell you when you're near the Lutheran Student Center," Shellie continued. "She says they're real friendly, and they all know where it is."

"All right," Ed replied.

"She doesn't remember the address, but she says, 'just ask'." Shellie paused. "Eddie, call me collect tomorrow morning from the Student Center if they'll let you."

"Okay," He paused. "Shellie, I'm sorry."

"I'm glad you called." Then she continued in a voice that was too light to hide her heartbreak, "Eddie, don't do anything silly."

Ed had always liked the atmosphere around the University. He had liked it best when he was young in better days when he and his father had journeyed to fall football games at the Stadium and to the state basketball tournaments. For as long as he'd known what a ball was, his heroes had been the athletes who wore the University colors. But it the whole atmosphere captured him: the unique stores near the U, the intense variety of people who crowded the sidewalks, the brassiness of the fraternity and sorority houses . . . Well, the whole thing.

Right now he felt a little better.

"Here we are kid," the bus driver called over his shoulder as he shooshed his bus to a stop. "Walk two blocks straight north – that way," he pointed as Ed rose and moved toward him. "Look to your right. Big white house. Used to be the Brandon Mansion. 'Course there's a few white houses 'round here. But this one's BIG!"

Ed nodded and turned to descend the steps. "Oh, yeah, one other clue. There's a sign in the front yard that says 'Lutheran Student Center.' That should help." The bus driver chuckled. "Good luck."

"Thanks," Ed managed as he exited the big vehicle.

Dusk was climbing the eastern sky. Ed quickened his steps along the gray sidewalk, feeling an urgency to get to the Center. They might have some idea of a decent place he could stay. Another night in the Concord would be as bad as being at home.

The sign was easy to see, a big white banner planted by the sidewalk that led to the door of the house.

Not knowing whether to knock or not, he did. He wished he could just turn the knob and walk in. Or turn and leave. He rapped his gloved hand against the big wooden door a second time. He thought he'd seen a light through the curtained windows as he walked up. Maybe it was just a night-light left on when no one was there. He was about to leave when the door opened and a stocky, ruddy-faced young man stood grinning at him. "Hi," the fellow said.

"Uh . . . hello," Ed responded.

"Come on in," the other encouraged, sweeping his arm in a welcoming motion. Ed stepped inside, grateful to be out of the cold. It seemed he'd been cold for days.

"Welcome to my cottage. Sorry we were so slow to answer the door, but hardly anybody ever knocks. They just walk in. Rude. So we thought maybe it was just some atheist throwing snowballs at the house. Then we figured, hey, it's too cold to make a snowball." The young man smiled.

His cheerful blue eyes sparkled. "I talk a lot. I'm Don Bradley. You're . . . ?"

"Ed. Ed Warrum."

"Come on into the dining room. Pastor Dan's in there. You go to school here?"

"No . . . I . . ."

"Come on in. Pastor's a nice guy. Visiting campus?"

"Uh . . . yeah . . . I." Ed fumbled, following Don into the square, high-ceilinged dining room. An oblong oak table, refurbished and shined, dominated the center of the room. Seated at it was a youngish looking, blond-haired man. He wore a sweater over a white collared shirt, looking very much like a student.

"Pastor, this is Ed . . . "

"Warrum."

"Have a seat," the minister said, indicating a chair around the curve of the table. He rose and extended his hand. The cleric's handshake was firm and confident, not like the dishrag Ed offered him.

The three males eased into chairs.

"What brings you here?" the minister queried.

"Uh . . . I'm a high school senior . . . and I came down to look at the University and attend a game. Coach Franklin . . . uh . . . wrote and said . . . uh . . . he'd like to talk to me so I came down to . . . to do that."

"You drink coffee?" the minister asked.

"Not much. But when it's cold like this . . . uh . . . once in awhile." The big house felt drafty and Ed shivered.

"Don, want to make us a pot of coffee?" the pastor asked. "Sure you do. Your eagerness is obvious." Turning to Ed, he added, "Don is the unofficial resident in this place. He's lived here for three years."

"I plan to stay here right through to my doctorate, my post doctorate dissertation, and my stints in the theology and law schools," Don said. "And then to raise my family. Okay, Captain, I'll make a pot of my famous egg coffee." He pushed out of his chair. Rising, he added, "Ask Pastor to explain the relationship between Darwinian Theology, Einstein's Theory of Relativity, and Jacksonian Democracy, Ed."

"I . . . uh . . . don't know anything . . . "

"Neither does Pastor Dan, but he'll talk for hours anyway," Don laughed. "Right, Pastor?"

"Get hence, miserable one," the minister said. "Ponder what I told you yesterday about the disconnect concerning intelligence and your brain." The two had an easy rapport. Ed had an easy rapport with no one.

As Don pushed the swinging door that opened into the kitchen, Pastor Dan leaned his elbows on the table and fixed his gaze on Ed. "He's a good guy," he said.

"Seems real nice."

"Why don't you take your duffel bag off your lap and put it on the floor, Ed. Take off your jacket if you want. Might as well be comfortable."

Ed slid the bag to the floor. He unbuttoned his jacket, but didn't remove it even though he'd instantly liked this minister whose clear gaze rested on him without threat.

"You're from out of town?"

"Uh . . . yeah . . . Centerville," Ed lied. His gaze fell from the minister's face. He stared hard at the shiny brown surface of the table.

"Don," Pastor Dan called. "Come here."

"Yes, oh yes, my Captain calls," Don mocked as he pushed through the kitchen door.

"I'm hungry. Aren't you?" Don nodded. "You hungry, Ed?"

"Uh . . . sure . . . " Ed answered. And he was. Ravenously hungry. He hadn't eaten or thought about eating all day.

"I know you don't do dinner, Don," the minister continued, "but you do pickups. Right?"

"Girls? Not very often, sad to say."

"How about pizza?"

"Yes, sir. I do that considerably better than I do girls."

The minster fished in his pocket, producing a set of keys and some bills. "You want to drive the Mustang?"

"Henry Ford couldn't drive that Mustang, Pastor Dan. It only moves by the power of prayer. You buy. I drive my car. How's that?"

"Fine. Here." He handed Don the money. "There's no hurry. Get the Chicago Special."

"Terrific," Don replied, taking the money. "Can I also get Kate on the way? We were going to study together at her place, but this would better. You're paying for the pizza. Besides, she's in love with you. She'll think she's gone to heaven when she gets to peruse your handsome mug while chowing down on Chicago pizza."

"She has admirable taste. Fine."

Don left the room, and Pastor Dan turned his attention to Ed. "You're a basketball player?"

"Well, yeah. Better in football, I guess," Ed said, shifting in his chair.

"Then you must be terrific in football if Coach Franklin wants to talk to you about playing basketball." Ed went white. He felt like he'd walked out of a sweaty locker room into a frigid January twilight. "Let's go in the front room. Don's built a fire in the fireplace. Sofas are old but comfortable," he finished, rising to his feet. "Leave your bag here if you wish.'

But Ed picked the bag up before following the minister into the capacious living room.

The heat from the fireplace felt good, but Ed felt miserable. He was a lousy liar. No practice. Too late now. He sank into a gray sofa and stared at the fire, his duffel bag between his feet. The minister sat in a stuffed arm-chair across from him with his back to the fire.

"Let's start over," the minister said. "I know you're not being straight with me. But you could say the same about me. I'm not proud of how I approached you. So I'll tell you that as soon as I heard your name, I remembered who you are. I'm a huge football fan, and I never miss watching state high school playoff games anywhere in the area if I can help it. You're an excellent football player. That Billy Cloud is too." He stared at the flames licking the piled logs in the fireplace. "Why the lies?"

The word hurt. Ed was not a liar. "I don't know."

"Mrs. Chaine called. She said she hoped you'd be coming here. I should have told you that, too."

"She what?!"

"She called and said she hoped you'd be coming here," the Pastor repeated, his gaze constant on Ed's face. "She said her daughter Shellie is a friend of yours."

"I gotta go," Ed said, pushing up from the sofa.

The minister extended his palms in a calming gesture. "She said you needed to talk to someone. 'Desperately' is the adverb she used. I'm some-one. I listen. Don't go."

Ed felt like he could explode into a million slivers. "God!" Tears slid down his cheeks. "God!" he shouted.

The Pastor rose and placed his hands on the boy's shaking shoulders. He left them there until Ed sank to the sofa, crying soundlessly, seeming not even to breathe.

The minister pulled a hassock from in front of nearby armchair and sat on it, close, but not too close, to the boy. "You're a powder keg, and you're ready to explode," he stated, his hands folded into one another. "I think you have to talk to save yourself from that."

Ed's head hung so heavy he didn't know if he could lift it to meet the minister's eyes. His body felt encased in concrete. He'd never been so tired. "I'm here because I wanted to kill my father."

The pastor gazed steadily at Ed.

"I hate his guts."

"Talk about it," Pastor Dan encouraged.

"I got to. I'm going crazy."

The phone near the room's other sofa rang. "That's Don," Dan said. "He's aware I hoped to talk to you. When I don't answer on the fourth ring, he'll know I want him to take a little longer with either Kate or the pizza. Hopefully, he'll choose Kate. It's the arrangement Don and I always have," the minister said. He smiled briefly, but Ed was unable to respond to it.

"He knows?"

"Only that your friend Shellie's mother called. He answers the phone

here. Screens the calls so I don't have to say unchristian things to the tele-
marketers."

The ringing phone seemed to seal Ed up. His eyes went dry. His lips
were a tight, thin line.

"Let me tell you a little more about myself. I'm an ordained Lutheran
minister, but I've given hardly any sermons. I got into youth work at my
first church in South Dakota. Six years ago I was given the chance to serve
as chaplain on this campus, and I've been here ever since. I don't live here,
but I spend most of my time at this house. Mostly I talk to students. I've
heard a lot of true stories, many happy, some sad, some tragic. So that's
me." He paused and eyed Ed. "I can see you withdrawing. I hope you
won't do that."

"That's what Shellie said," Ed muttered. "I don't know why she talked
to me." He glared at the minister. "I don't know why you would either."

"You're hurting. Shellie and her mother think you're worthy. I'm scared
for you. I'm scared for your family. That's why I want to talk to you. Reasons enough?"

"What I said . . ."

"You aren't the first son who's ever wanted to blow away his father.
Cain was. But," he added leaning a little forward, "you didn't do it. You
said you're here because you wanted to kill your father. You're also here
because you didn't want to. Do you know that?"

"I dunno. I dunno." Ed's hands were clenched tightly. "In my duffel bag
. . . I have a gun."

"How long have you had it?"

"I bought it before Christmas. I told the guy it was for my father. Well,
it was."

"You never made a move to use it though?"

"I laid awake nights thinking about how I'd do it."

"Why did you want to kill your father?"

"Because he's killing me!" Ed burst. "Because he's killing my whole
family. Because he's killing himself."

"How?"

The boy's anger strung taut wires through his entire frame. The minister
could hear him ticking.

"How?" Dan persisted. "Does he beat you? Don't clam up now."

"He's hit me a few times this year. Never did before. God!" He looked
hard at the minister. "God, he used to be a nice guy. When I was little. God,
he took me to games. We were always playing catch. I thought he loved me.
I didn't know he had plans for me!"

"What happened?"

"He's nuts! He's gone nuts!"

"How? Why?"

"He won't let me be anything but the greatest football player in the history of the state. So he can claim credit. He can't think of anything else. He can't leave it alone."

"Obsessed. Living his life through you."

Ed rose and paced the room, leaving the duffel bag on the floor in front of the sofa. "Look, I'm good. Give him credit. I'm good. Just not good enough for him. Gotta think like him. Be like him. No one's good enough for him. He attacked my football coach, you know that?"

"Verbally?"

"Heck no. That wasn't enough for him. He tackled him on the sidelines during a game. Gave him a heart attack. No coach is good enough. Nobody in the world is good enough for him!" Ed returned to the sofa and perched on the edge of the cushion. "Look. After every game we go through the whole thing play by play. The whole family has to sit and listen. I hear his sick version of every mistake I made, every mistake the coach made."

"He never sees anything good about you?"

"Sure. He blows me up like a balloon. Then he throws rocks at me." The boy slammed his fist into the palm of his hand. "Then this year he starts coming to practice, and I listen to him bellering all the way through practice. At games I can hear him above the whole crowd. Then . . . God! Coach takes me out because I'm playing like crap. He's talking to me, trying to get my head screwed on right . . . and my father . . . " he drove his fist deep into his palm, "my father runs at my coach and starts pushing him around. If I wasn't in shock, I would have strangled him right there! My father could have killed Coach!" He dropped his hands to his knees.

"You have a right to be angry."

"Coach quit his job because of that. He's a great guy and a great coach, and my dad makes him quit his job!"

"Well, you did say he had a heart attack?"

"Whose fault is that?" Ed exploded.

"Your dad contributed to that heart attack," Dan replied. "He didn't do it all, but he contributed." He paused, letting the boy feel his emotions. "Did your father change after that?"

"Sure. He got worse. He and his fricking friends were proud of getting Coach to quit! They decided Schwarz, he's the assistant coach, is their guy. They were proud!"

"Your father's pretty extreme the way it sounds, but he's not the first father to go off his nut because of his dreams for his kid. But it sounds to me like your father needs a lot of help."

"Me, too. I hate myself as much as I hate him."

"Hate does that, Ed. It turns around and attacks us. That's why we've got to talk it out, work it out, find some way to get rid of it. It shrivels our own souls."

"So what do I do?" Ed moaned. "Everything's crap. I don't talk to anyone. My grades suck. I've alienated my friends."

"But mostly you're hurting yourself, Ed. Can you sit down?" The boy nodded and sank back into the sofa. "It's worse since you got the gun, isn't it," Dan stated.

"That's true. I hadn't thought of that, but . . . yeah."

"You and your father tangle pretty often?"

"Every time he opens his mouth."

"Every time he gets into you, you know you have the gun and you think about using it. On him . . . or yourself."

"Yeah. Him. Myself. The guys that followed me down the street this morning. The hotel clerk . . . "

"So, in effect, you're killing him or yourself or someone else over and over in your head. That's hard to deal with." He paused. "Ed, can you give up the gun?"

"I . . . I don't know. I . . . I like the . . . I don't know."

"You're here because you didn't really want to shoot your father. You ran rather than do that. And I think you're here because you don't really want to kill anyone. Including yourself. And you're afraid you might. So?"

"So?" Ed repeated, raising his hands imploringly, then dropping them to his knees again.

"Look, Ed," the minister said, "I'm not going to tell you that giving up that gun will change your father at all. But it will change a lot of things for you. You won't have to think about using it every time life gets hard in your house. You won't have to run those scenarios in your brain anymore. You won't have to carry the guilt about what you're thinking anymore. If you get rid of the gun, the possibility is gone. You won't accidentally use it and ruin your life and your family's lives."

Ed could not speak. His insides were chopped and fragmented. He'd thought about the gun so much for so long it seemed as much a part of him as his hands. "That's sick!" he muttered.

"What?"

"Just a dumb thought. About the gun. My hands."

"Can you give up the gun?"

"I think I have to. You're making too much sense. But I don't know if I can stop hating my father." He did not add, "So I think I'll keep the gun," but he thought it.

"I'm not going to tell you to do that. Do you want to give it – the gun – to me? Or . . . we're not very far from the river and it's open. Is the gun registered?"

"No," Ed admitted. "All the writing was rubbed off."

"It might be best to drop it off the bridge and let the river turn it to rust."

Ed nodded. The two rose and slipped on their coats and walked into the chill of the February night. Ed saw snowflakes twirling in the streetlights. They reminded him of stars, and he realized he'd not seen stars for a long time. His breath curled into the cold air. He hadn't even noticed that for a long time. He'd been like a dead man. Yeah, this was the right thing to do. He suddenly felt so buoyant he was almost giddy. He felt the heat of tears at the edge of his eyes. He wiped at them with the hand that wasn't holding the duffel bag.

The minister and Ed walked until they came to the middle of the bridge. Ed placed the duffel bag on the ground and unzipped it. He thrust his hand in until he felt the cold metal at the bottom. He gripped the gun and extracted it.

Pastor Dan leaned on the railing and watched intently as Ed extended his arm over it and released the weapon. Ed could not see the thing fall. The sounds of passing cars obscured any splash he might have heard.

The two stood silent on the bridge within the wetness of the snowfall.

"Pizza time?" Dan asked.

"Yeah," Ed breathed.

"Tomorrow morning we can talk some more if you wish. I'll make a few calls that might be helpful. Then we can see if the Blue Lake Express runs in both directions."

"Anything else you want to say about my future life?" Ed asked.

"I never give the final score until the game's over."

The two left the bridge and headed for the Lutheran Student Center. Don, his study partner, and the pizza were awaiting them when they reached the house. Ed did not know if he was more hungry or tired. The food was delicious, but he could manage only a few slices. The minister recognized his weariness and led him to the "guest bunk room," a small room at the far end of the third floor of the huge house.

Ed sank into a deep, but not dreamless, sleep. The dream was this. He and Dan were standing on the bridge. Ed extended his arm over the railing and dropped the gun. As soon as he did, he felt an overpowering emptiness and then panic that the gun was gone. Looking down he was startled to see the weapon whirling amidst the falling flakes of snow just out of his reach. He draped himself over the railing and stretched his arms as far as he could. The gun whirled and glittered just beyond his grasping hands. He willed his arms to lengthen and they did, but always the gun descended just beyond his reach. The void in him filled with a great sorrow, and he determined that he would leap into the air after the thing. Just as he lunged, Dan's power- ful arms encircled his waist and leveraged against his fall. Bracing his feet against the bottom of the railing, the minister yanked the boy fiercely from his doom, but as he did, Ed saw with clarity that the gun had finally hurtled downward. And into the waiting hand of his father who was now aiming the gleaming weapon straight at him, his face a rigid mask of hate.

His father's face and form widened, became deep, became the river. The gun was large as a barge. If he could break the grip of the minister, who was speaking into both of his ears at once, he would dive over the edge of the bridge directly into the black tunnel of the muzzle of the gun and jam its blast so that all of its fragments would explode into his tormentor. But the pastor held him fast until the river washed away all trace of his father's form, and the gun sank beneath its surface.

Robert Baker

Robert Baker admitted to himself that he was disappointed to find Ed Warrum's name on the absence list both Thursday and Friday. He'd become obsessed with the attitude of the all-star athlete. It was, perhaps, a bit unjustified. Ed Warrum was hardly the worst behaved student in his classes. As a matter of fact, there was hardly any behavior at all. Ed Warrum was a lump, a log, a stone that rolled in and out of class. In some ways that's what could drive you crazy. The shouters, spitwad throwers and smartasses you could harangue outside the classroom door or after class. Those who didn't bother to hand in their work would find their retribution on their report cards.

Ah, retribution, he mused, staring into the gray outside his apartment window. Retribution. Grading could become a process of getting even. He could learn to enjoy penning the angry red F.

He'd never thought this is how it could get for him. He'd never dreamed that teaching would be like that.

He moved to the apartment-sized refrigerator in his apartment-sized kitchen, snatched open the door, seized a bottle of beer from the shelf, and flipped the door shut. He worried that he was drinking too much these days. But what was too much? He rarely had more than two. Just enough to wash down his tension a little. He twisted off the cap, lifted the brew and took several swallows. He didn't like the taste of beer, but he did like the feeling it created in his stomach, then his chest and finally his head. He drank it to relax, he told himself. Just to relax.

He sighed again, moved to the window and leaned against its frame. The street below was mostly empty. He could see snow caught in the pools of the streetlights. It was a gentle scene he'd loved since childhood.

The few cars that passed seemed caught in the ambiance of the evening, gliding slowly up or down the street. For a moment he felt peaceful. Uncomfortable and strange, this feeling. Too long gone. The prickly tension that accompanied most of his waking and sleeping hours had come to feel normal. Its absence created empty spaces that hungered to be filled, causing him to replace moments of peace with a variety of emotions.

"Ed Warrum," he said aloud, refocusing on the student who dominated his thoughts almost as much as Patty Light. He walked back to the table by the kitchen window and shuffled through the papers on it. He snatched Ed's Poe report from the pile. There it was. A couple pages that could have been paraphrased from an encyclopedia or one of those brief biographies that killed long dead authors one more time with their blandness.

Oh, in truth, it was about average. The words were spelled right. The punctuation was in the right places. The paragraphing was correct. So technically it was maybe a little above average. But it had no personality, no originality. In that way it was worse than some of the less proficient pieces that at least showed a real person was doing the writing. All-star athletes should either be very good or very bad. This report showed nothing at all except the task's lack of importance, the lack of importance of Robert Baker's class, the lack of importance of Robert Baker! He could take that from some, but . . .

The knock at the door startled him. He hadn't heard any one ascending the stairs to his second floor habitat. He jerked his head so fast he nearly gave himself whiplash. Feeling oddly guilty as though he'd been thinking illicit thoughts or planning illicit plots, he pushed his chair back and headed for the door, half expecting to find Ed Warrum, or maybe his father, standing on the other side, face fierce with accusation.

Instead he found Kyle Hunter.

For a moment Robert was annoyed. He'd grown used to being alone with his thoughts. He'd found a furrow he'd wanted to keep plowing, and now he was interrupted, caught red-faced with his guilty thoughts and a beer on the table. It took effort to push those impediments aside so he could greet the only colleague he had at school who showed much interest in him.

"Hi," Kyle said into the silence. "Wife's out of town, so I thought I'd come up and see if pizza interested you."

"Sure. Come on in," Robert replied. He realized he'd failed to eat and that he was on his second beer. He felt slightly drunk and embarrassed to be found in this condition. "Have a seat," he offered, indicating the chair next to the table.

"You've eaten?" Kyle asked, seating himself and unzipping his coat. "I know it's kind of late. I was watching basketball practice, and I realized I'd forgotten to go home. Then I started talking to Jake, the custodian, and we got into this political discussion about education. The guy's pretty bright." He smiled at his own pleasantries. "Anyway, as I walked into the lack of February thaw we call weather here, I started thinking about my dark house with the thermostat set at 58 degrees, and I thought who needs that? Then I said to myself, 'Self, do you suppose Robert Baker has a date tonight, it being Friday and all?' Then I said, 'Having heard no rumors, I doubt it.' So here I am."

"I'm glad," Robert said. In a way he was. Kyle Hunter was one of the few who took time to talk to him and the only one who sought him out. "Care for a beer?" he inquired.

"I'll pass. It would knock me on my can."

"I know what you mean," Robert responded, indicating his half empty bottle. "I forgot to eat and had that much, and I'm about one-fourth buzzed."

"So what do you think about pizza?"

"Sounds fine." Robert was pretty sure he'd already answered that question. "Where they got good pizza?"

"Ronald's."

"Give me a minute to . . . uh . . . wash up."

"Sure. Why don't I call Ronald's and order? Then they'll be ready for us when we arrive. Have you eaten there? House Special's terrific."

"Fine. I'll be back in a minute."

Robert went into his apartment-sized bathroom. Mostly he needed to brush his teeth. It wouldn't be good to appear in public smelling like a brewery, especially if they ran into any kids. Why supply nails for the cross?

Robert had not visited Ronald's before. In fact he rarely ate out. Avoiding unstructured contact with his students – or worse, students who'd heard about him without knowing him at all – had become his modus operandi. Then he realized Kyle Hunter would buffer any negative attitudes towards him. He'd be safe enough in Kyle's company.

Entering Ronald's, Robert immediately liked the place. It had a north woods ambiance with its heavy beams and wood that was rough-hewn and slivery-looking. The place smelled of pizza and wood, good smells. "This place new?" he asked Kyle.

"Just remodeled," the other answered. "Usually much busier," he added, indicating the empty booths and tables. "Want to sit over there toward the back?"

Robert had sought to expel his nervousness as they'd strolled the six blocks from the apartment. He'd been betrayed when he involuntarily flinched as a car eased by them. Kyle had to notice that, and he had to notice how Robert stopped dead in his tracks when the car paused at the stoplight, its occupants rolling down windows, popping heads out, and hurling indistinct words before the heads disappeared.

As they moved toward the booth, Robert noted that the two waitresses leaning on the counter near the kitchen, Sarah Fine and Gracie Jens, were students of his. He saw Sarah's arm move as though she was elbowing the other. Sarah cupped her mouth with her hand and whispered into Gracie's ear. The latter responded by hiding her mouth with her hand as the low tinkle of the girls' giggles reached Robert's ears.

He tried to kid himself, as he slid across the cushion to the far corner of the booth, that Sarah had whispered something like, 'Don't look now, Gracie, but someones handsome just came in.' But he was quite sure Sarah had whispered something so derisive to Gracie that she could hardly hide her shock and delight.

" . . . wrong," he heard Kyle finish.

"What?"

"Something wrong?"

"Uh . . . no."

"You were looking pretty submerged."

"Sorry. Thinking about kids, I guess."

"February blues," Kyle stated. "We all get 'em."

"Even after all those years?" Robert asked, glad to escape further questioning.

"Yeah, even us old guys. Once that pattern sets in, it's set in concrete. Just like opening day jitters, Thanksgiving Irritation, Christmas Cantankerousness, May Days Doldrums. Not to mention Spirit Week Wackiness. It's almost too predictable. Like the bend-you-double agony of quarter and semester grading week is."

"You don't make teaching sound too great."

"Ah, but it has its moments. Sometimes when I think . . . ." Kyle began, but stopped. "It has its bright and shining moments."

"Somehow that's escaped me. I take that back. A few bright and shining moments have occurred as a result of me losing my prep period. I guess I must be a really good study hall supervisor."

"Listen. The first year is the worst. Just like in marriage. Nothing they taught you in those education classes could have prepared you for the situation you're in."

"For sure!"

"Hello," Sarah said. Robert hadn't noticed her approaching the booth and jerked his head toward her voice. He wondered if he'd said something she shouldn't have overheard.

"Mr. Hunter, you want your usual coke."

"Sure, Sarah."

She took a few steps away, then returned. It looked like a planned insult, her addressing Robert as an afterthought.

"Mr. Baker?"

"Yes, Sarah?" he said sharply. She looked startled.

"Um... ah . . . what would you like to drink?"

"Coke's fine."

"Your pizza will be ready in a minute, Mr. Hunter."

Robert was irritated at both the girl and his own reaction to the perceived slight. He gave these kids a hundred ways to push his buttons.

The girl returned with the sodas, followed by Gracie with the pizza. "Your pizza, Mr. Hunter," the latter said, sliding the platter onto the table. Sarah set the two glasses down without smiling, and the two walked away.

Robert stared after them and felt Kyle's gaze on him.

"Relax," the older man suggested. "Enjoy the pizza. It's great."

"Yeah," Robert sighed. He wished he could relax.

The two men talked of small matters as they polished off the pizza. Aided by the tasty repast, Robert curbed his irritation at the earlier snubs.

"One thing I've noticed since Gail took that job of hers," Kyle was saying as he eyed the last piece of pizza on the platter, "is that left to my own company, I think too much. Want that last piece?"

"Isn't it supposed to be bad luck to eat the last piece? I don't know that I want bad luck."

"Bad manners. In either case, I'll chance it if you won't." Kyle pointed at the piece, and snatched it.

"You were right. It was good," Robert said resting against the back of the booth. The girls were in front talking to the only other people who'd come into the place, a group of college boys seated at the round table by the front window. The talk was boisterous, but not obnoxious.

"So how's it going? Classroom I mean?"

"Oh, you know, a little better, I guess."

"It's like anything else," Kyle said. "There are many tricks to our trade. Trouble is a trick that worked beautifully in one class can sink in the next."

"Sort of like walking through a swamp."

"Something like that. It takes a lot of experience, a lot of trial and error to discover what works. Trouble is although we were once kids, you can't quite think like a kid unless you are a kid."

"I'm not all that far from being one, you know. When I went in the office the first day of workshops, the secretary thought I was a new senior."

Kyle laughed. "Looking young won't be so tragic in a few years."

Robert realized his face must have portrayed the incident as serious. He laughed with his peer.

"I'm going to get some coffee. Want some?" Kyle slid out of the booth. "Sure."

He watched the slender, confident man ease over to the counter. He watched Kyle wave his hand dismissively. "No, no, girls, I'll get it. You go ahead with your flirting." A chorus of approval bellowed from the front. Robert envied the easy rapport the man had with a variety of kids and adults. No effort, no self-consciousness. It must be beautiful.

Kyle brought back two white mugs of steaming brew. "Fresh and hot," he noted, setting one in front of Robert and following the other into the booth. "Cream, sir?" he asked, flipping two containers out of his pocket.

"Were you always so comfortable with kids? You relate so easily."

"Only after a good meal," the teacher laughed. "After a good meal I love everybody. Kids are really grateful the cafeteria serves great lunches. Anticipation keeps me happy." Robert had to join in Kyle's laughter. "Seriously, yes, I like kids. Sometimes I can't stand them, but in general I like them a lot."

"I tend to feel just the reverse. I don't want to, but I do."

"Makes it hard to teach what with all the other drawbacks, doesn't it?"

"I'd say. Did you feel that when you . . . "

"When I was young?" Kyle finished. "The first year was hard. First few years. Teaching's a new way of relating to people. I'm a student at heart."

"Me, too."

"That isn't bad, you know. It can be turned into a real asset. A true student is really interested in what others are thinking and saying."

"I got too busy defending and protecting myself. They've stayed after me since the first day."

"Listen. What's going on has nothing to do with you. The kids are reacting to a situation."

"Yeah, I know, Gerney was god. Is that my fault?"

"No."

"It feels like it's my fault. I can't measure up."

"Listen. What's happened is that you've been caught in a perfect storm. A perfectly awful storm that is. You replace this popular guy who has quit his job very late in the summer. The town is experiencing an amazing population spurt that a failed bond issue has left the school ill-equipped to handle. Your classes are all oversized so it's really hard to even get the names straight, much less who they are and what makes them tick. The school board freezes all hiring and purchasing of supplies to 'encourage' the public into passing their revised bond issue. So there's no relief available, and not enough administrators to check up on things. Then you're robbed of a prep period to make things work. You should give yourself tremendous credit. Many would have raced out the door and never come back. You show up every day and give it your best. Try to ease up on yourself a little."

Robert wished he could. It was amazing how fast he could become a maze of taut wires. "Yeah. My head knows. But my stomach forgets. Then my chest forgets. Then my head becomes convinced it was wrong."

"Tell you what. Whenever you need it, ask me to remind you. I should be talking to you more. My fault. Anyway, if your head needs to hear that you're doing well in a very tough situation, I'll talk to your head. You'll have to take care of the stomach yourself though." The two laughed again. Robert was startled each time he did. It felt disloyal to the feelings that dominated his days.

"Thanks. I got a question. Is it going to get easier?"

"Sure . . ."

"No. I mean this year. Are the kids going to forgive me this year?"

Kyle hesitated at the edge of the question and then dived in. "I can only tell you what happened to me and what I've seen. Some kids are like some older people. Once they get an idea, it's like cutting concrete with a butter knife to get them to change it. They'll hang on to it long beyond the point of reason. They can change, but it takes a group consensus to do it. But some do swim against the flow. I survived my first year. At some point – - maybe then, maybe later – I learned to accept that it pays to be satisfied to reach a few. Someone in that heaving horde of hormones has to be getting what I'm trying to do, has to be benefitting, and that makes it all worthwhile. Sure, I want 'em all. Truth is if you get a few, eventually others will follow. Now, you can't tell me that there aren't a few you know you're reaching."

"You're right. I can't."

"Good. Well," Kyle finished, glancing at his watch, "I should get home and throw a wrist on the thermostat."

"Yeah. Me too. Got the usual pile of papers to read. Kyle, I really appreciate this."

"No problem," his fellow teacher said as he pulled on his coat.

As the men walked out the door, Sarah called out, "Good night, Mr. Hunter." Because she didn't add Baker's name, Kyle did not respond.

"Why do they have to be like that?" Robert muttered.

"Sometimes they're thoughtless and self-centered." Kyle answered angrily. "Try not to worry about it too much," he urged.

Later Robert sat at the table in his apartment, staring again at the stack of papers awaiting attention. He liked Kyle and realized his advice was valid, even essential. Make your mind emphasize the Patty Lights and Billy Clouds and Sally Long Arrows you're reaching. Forget the Ed Warrums. Forget the Sarahs and Gracies who treat you like you aren't there and wished you weren't. Maybe he could do that. For now all he could do was endure the frustrations facing him daily and find eventual release.

Patty Light

Dear Journal,

She doesn't trust it. She wants to. She wants to believe miracles are dancing all around her. She wants to frolic with the dancers. Instead she settles back on her haunches and watches the joy with suspicion.

She is full of yearning to comfort and be comforted. But she's afraid. That's why we find her curling into yet another corner, protected by two walls from pain or bliss. Her eyes are as wide and unblinking as a painting of her would be. Her eyes memorize every movement in any scene before her. But her kitten instincts keep her still. She sees the potential of disappointment.

She's even afraid of the leaping, laughing, somersaulting someone. When he even leans her way she leans away. She is afraid she will awake from her kitten nap into another dream, old and awful, that he will morph from her kittenish comrade into the tiger hiding in her memory.

Seems like a potential catastrophe to me, Mr. Hunter. Wouldn't you say so?

As for the other, she does and doesn't know what has happened. Her unclipped claws dig deep into the pads of her feet. With a single outward flick they can puncture skin and draw blood from the wounds she leaves even if she doesn't want to. Sometimes gentleness emerges, only to disappear. Then she ministers to her own worn coat in preparation for the dark and the alleys littered with caved-in garbage cans, crumpled butcher paper and scraps of old meat.

But!! Have you ever read Emily Dickinson's poetry, Mr. Hunter? The line that springs to my mind is, "Hope is a thing with feathers." It makes me think of a baby bird, maybe a robin, whose fluff has turned to form. Forced from the nest by its mother, it chatters from the ground. Its parent passes by singing encouragement. The time has come when the baby bird must fly to survive. It finally flutters its wings and lifts itself into the air and trills with delight. It attains the lowest branch on a nearby tree, and sings as though it could already see the whole world below its wings. That would be my wish.

Here is a poem I wrote not long ago.

"February Thaw".

Splashing through pools that were ice,
The footing is slick underneath.
Smelling spring in the breeze,
Knowing it waits far from me,
February thaw.
The house I enter is cold,
A note two sentences long,
"I'm sorry" the first sentence reads.
"I love you" the second goes on.
February thaw.

These may be the most hopeful words I've ever written, Mr. Hunter. Please treasure them.

PL

Billy Cloud

"Holy cripes, I'm stuck," Ed Warrum moaned. He looked ridiculous bent over like that, part of his perspiration-soaked sweatshirt pulled over his head, the rest matted to his chest, back and shoulders, its sleeves binding his extended arms. "Help! I'm stuck! I've got claustrophobia!"

Billy Cloud stifled a laugh as he walked over and tugged the shirt over Ed's head.

Ed straightened. "Thanks," he breathed, the shirt still hanging from his hands. "Claustrophobia. Even my hands have claustrophobia," he wheezed, shaking his hands frantically to free them. "From now on I play on the skins team, or I'll just have to bunch it."

Billy laughed and seated himself on the long brown bench that fronted the locker room lockers. "'About Friday last week Coach was ready to bunch it for you."

"He missed me then," Ed said. Then he added, "Sort of like a farm boy misses the smell of manure."

Zip your lip, Billy cautioned himself. This guy has a wicked right cross.

Ed sat next to the lithe guard. "You agree that my behavior has been crappy?"

Billy checked Ed's face. The grin remained though it looked more strained, like it was caught on his cheekbones. "Well, no. Aggressive maybe? Unpredictable maybe? Crappy? Well, maybe that's accurate after all." He paused for effect, elbowed Ed lightly in the ribs, and slid away feigning fear. "Is white boy building slowly toward another right to the eyeball?" Holy cripes, he thought, am I crazy?

The smile dropped from Ed's face, but it wasn't anger that replaced it. It was sadness. "I'm sorry about that."

"I know. You told me on the phone."

"Yeah, but this time my old man and Coach aren't choking it out of me."

"Am I to infer that there was a slight lack of sincerity in your initial offering?"

"No." The crooked grin returned. "A total lack."

"Actually I guessed your heart wasn't in it by the sound of your teeth grinding. Do you know how irritating the sound of teeth grinding is when it's right next to your ear?"

"Equal to the irritation of knuckles next to your eye?"

"So you were attending a comparative irritants seminar while you were gone! What a good use of your free time!"

The smile faded. Why can't I lay off? Billy wondered.

"No. But I did use the time pretty well."

"I can tell. You seem to have lost a little weight, the sweatshirt not with-standing."

"About ten ounces, actually. But it was a big ten ounces." Ed rose and peeled off his practice trunks. "You folks shower, don't you? I'm starting to get chilled."

"Yes, but usually we wait until you folks are done 'cuz you get so jealous of our beautiful bodies. It's hard for us to deal with the inadequacy you feel."

"Come on. I'll be brave and take the chance."

"I've been brave all my life."

Ed groaned and disappeared into the shower room. The rest of the team had finished showering and were dressing, some eyeing the former combatants with wary interest. The shower room was still steamed and the water hot. It felt good. Billy's muscles had begun to stiffen after the hard practice. "You looked pretty good out there today," he told Ed.

"Not bad for a second stringer," Ed burbled, his face turned into the water.

"Tournament time brings out the best in the truly great."

"That's what Dad told me last night. You feed him his lines? Or does he feed you yours?"

Billy saw the angry face of Pete Warrum in his mind. "Neither, I hope," he blurted, then added, "Just kidding."

Ed turned and let the water wash over his shoulders. "Don't apologize. I can hardly stand him myself. That's why I've been such an ass."

"Kind of figured that. That's why I didn't punch you back that day. I said to myself, 'Self, this guy has anger in him that can't possibly be caused by someone as wonderful as me. Therefore I won't engage in fisticuffs with him.' But I have also discerned that your dad might be a tad hard to get along with."

"The only person I ever wanted to hit was my father."

"You ever talk to anyone about it?"

"As a matter of fact I did. Want to hear about it?"

"Yes, but not in here. My body is wrinkling."

"You must think I'm some kind of weird idiot," Ed said following Billy out of the shower. The locker room was empty. Even the coach was gone.

Grabbing a towel, Billy nodded. "Yeah. Well, sure. But I figure, hey, he's a great quarterback. It goes with the territory. Give a quarterback a great arm and a pushy old man. Zap! Instant weird idiot." Billy studied the other's face, noted his confused eyes and the smile placed to mask confusion. "It is about your father, isn't it?"

"Yep," Ed answered, tying a towel around his waist. He slumped on the bench. "Yeah. Is that an excuse?"

"A reason maybe," Billy answered, leaning against a locker. "My old man – who would tattoo this Indian if he heard me call him that – isn't like that, but he's been around. The black eye – by the way getting that black eye wasn't all bad, I'll tell you, but that's another story. Anyway, I told him about it. He said straight out, 'It had nothing' to do with you, Billy, even if you are a smart mouthed jerk sometimes. Nope,' he says, 'Ed's father is driving him crazy. He'd drive anyone crazy.'" Billy watched anger shadow Ed's face. "I don't want to hurt your feelings. Maybe Dad and I are wrong."

"No, you aren't. I'll tell you, Billy," he said, almost pleading, "he wasn't always that bad. He was pushy, sure. I'll bet my first rattle was shaped like a football." He snorted a tense laugh. "Half my memories when I was a kid are playing catch with him. See, he had this dream that I was going to be special. Worked good for a long time. He was always encouraging me, patting me on the back." He leaned against the green wall, his head tipped back. "But something happened. Seventh or eighth grade. I was a big kid then . . ."

"You're a big kid now."

" . . . And good. In those days we played other schools all the time. Dad loved that. He didn't miss a game. I could run, pass, tackle – you name it. Even then it was okay. But somehow, it started getting real important. Eighth grade," he said, sliding into a sitting position on the floor. "He started talking about the University. About me playing quarterback for the U. Heck, that was my dream, too. But all of a sudden I was hearing his voice at games above everybody else's. Then we started having these stupid after game sessions we've had ever since. Wasn't so bad then. Mostly praise. Like I said, I was big . . ."

"And good. Don't forget good."

"Yeah." Ed had to smile. "Yeah. I didn't. Neither did he. But I scored on a lot of long runs and threw what he called 'terrific' passes that kids dropped most of the time. He'd gripe about that a little. Did you know I started for Blue Lake High School varsity as a freshman?"

"I heard that," Billy said, seating himself. "That was because you were big and good."

"Young, too. We weren't much good that year. I was young, but Dad was thrilled I was starting." The veins popped out again. "But that's when it really started getting bad. He memorized every play I played. Had mother keeping stats. You ever seen my mother?"

"I don't know."

"She's gray, man. Everything. Hair. Face. Soul. She wants to disappear. That was the year she started getting quiet. She's scared senseless of my old man." Ed's anger was raw on his face. "Seen my sister?"

"Yeah. Jenny. Pretty. What's she, a freshman?"

"Yeah. She's scared senseless, too. She hasn't said four words in the last two years in our house. Ever notice how white she is? She wants to be a ghost. She's smart and athletic, but she never got five minutes of attention from Dad in her whole life. We all sit around the damn table after every game, almost every practice. You shouldn't have to hear all this. But Pastor Dan said I had to start talking about what's going on. Keep the pressure down." The grin reappeared. "So now you know why I was wailing on you." The grin fell away. "This next is scary. Can you handle it?"

Billy nodded.

"I bought a gun before Christmas. In case I had to kill my father."

"E-yeah," Billy exhaled.

"Pastor Dan said I would have killed myself first. Or some innocent person who accidentally lit my fuse."

"The gun?"

"Gone. Pastor talked me into throwing it in the river."

"Good move!" Billy breathed. "Who is this guy?"

"When I was in the Cities . . . when I ran . . . I called Shellie when I got really depressed and crazy. She and her Mom maneuvered me to go to the Lutheran Student Center at the U. It's a long story. He's a good guy. Anyway, I talked to him, and he talked me out of . . . "

"Yeah."

"I call him once a week. He said I could call more if I need to. But he said I had to have people up here to talk to. You're the first except for Shellie. I haven't told her too much. She's scared of me. Or for me."

"Well," Billy said as he pushed himself to his feet, "I'm honored. Going to talk to anyone else? Someone older and, unlikely as it may seem, wiser?"

Ed laughed. It looked good on him, but you could tell he hadn't laughed in a long time. Still, seeing his mask crack a little was a small pleasure, even if his laughter conveyed less mirth than pain. "I thought maybe Mr. Schwarz. Or Pastor Dan said the Lutheran minister, Barker, is a good guy to talk to."

"Of course he'd say that," Billy joked as he grabbed his shirt from his locker. "Those guys stick together. Actually Pastor Phil is a good guy. We church-hop fairly often into his church. Although he's leaving to be a missionary in Africa."

"So." Ed pulled open his locker, its tin clatter echoing in the empty locker room.

"So is it better now?"

"A little. Pastor said I need to work on praying for my father. Said it would give me something to think about instead of gettin' caught up in his ranting. It helps a little. Dad talks. I try to pray right through it. But I still feel like punching his lights out most of the time."

The two boys finished dressing in silence. As he buttoned his shirt, Ed said, "Thanks, Billy."

They headed for the locker room's double doors. "I'll get the lights," Billy said, snapping them off.

Patty Light was by the exit doors, staring into the darkness that had descended. "There's one Light you wouldn't want to turn off," Ed said in a low voice.

"For sure. Come along. We'll walk you downtown."

Frank Marin

Since his conversation with Mr. Barnes and his night in the Buford jail cell, Frank Marin had tried to get a grip on his drinking, his drugging, his academics, and his attendance at school. His goal was simple. He'd be under unbearable pressure in his yearlong classes if he didn't pass the first semester. Everyone would notice, especially his parents. Their sorrowful silence would burst into anger, and they'd make rules he'd have to defy to keep himself sane, driving them insane in the process. So he cut his drinking to next to nothing.

That wasn't so hard. His college buddies had told him they'd have to cool it to get their second semester started right so they could skate later. That was a good thing. It saved Frank a bunch of money and stash. Betts was trying to maintain peace with her parents so she could stay put in their house. So she'd told Frank they'd have to ice it for a while. Having a vacation from the stormy emotions he experienced around her wasn't all bad. It gave him more energy to focus on passing his classes

He did. All except Hunter's. But Hunter had to pass him for the semester because Frank had nailed that D the first quarter. He'd managed to pierce through the hate he had for the man to turn in a few reworked pieces written in years past. If he'd done nothing, Hunter had him. But he did exactly enough to foil the teacher's preference. He got his D and he was done with big deal Mr. Hunter.

The second semester landed him in a cooking class because there was nowhere else to put him. He figured he could get interested. The teacher, Ms. Foy, was young and easy to look at. Yeah, he'd get by. The absence of booze had cleared his eyes again. He liked his eyes not looking like milky pools. He'd begun to think of himself as pure ugliness. He now knew he wasn't that bad.

There were only about three things wrong in his life. One would begin to rectify in a week or so once he'd earned a little good will in the new semester. Teachers like the student who suddenly comes to life.

Another thing wrong was that he was darn lonely in Blue Lake. He didn't look it. He looked angry, bored, or blank. But he felt it. Since he and his family moved in, he hadn't acquired one friend. No one showed the slightest interest in him in this school, not even those whose habits matched his. Their tight user groups eyed him with suspicion or distaste.

The only ones who seemed to really notice him were the teachers.

And that was his third problem. In Mr. Hunter he'd found the perfect host for the emotions that buzzed his brain. Hunter saw right through him into his habits, his loneliness, and his fear. Everyone seemed to like Hunter. Not Frank Marin. He wished he'd never handed in that writing about Mr. Corgan. Ever since, Hunter had put the pressure on him. Frank hated that.

The trouble was that Hunter was no longer a factor. Frank Marin had to find a new target. And did. He'd been there all along, but Frank had not thought of him until now. Best of all, Mr. Baker would be available for the rest of the year.

There was no way he could hate the man. Feigned disdain would be a better building block anyway. There were plenty of students who displayed disdain for Mr. Baker. Even when his room was quiet, as it generally was these days, it felt nasty. Baker would be a less dangerous target than Hunter. He couldn't hate Baker, but he could cause him problems, and that would enable him to have an in with his classmates.

Frank forced a smile to his face as he sat in the back of Baker's class. He wanted to shout to announce his new attitude toward the teacher. He glanced up and was surprised to find Mr. Baker mirroring the tense smile he'd placed on his own face. He was surprised to see hints of the fear and loneliness in Mr. Baker's eyes that he felt in himself. He was surprised at his rising regret about the choice he'd made and tried to extinguish it before it burned away his plans.

The bell rang and Frank exited the room. He'd wanted to feel a sense of triumph. Instead Robert Baker's eyes followed him out of the room and down the hall and stared at him from the window at the end of it.

Greg Schwarz

The Greg Schwarz sitting behind the elevated study hall desk in the long, rectangular study hall room was not the enthused and jovial Mr. Schwarz the fifty study hall students had become used to seeing again. This Mr. Schwarz was silent as lightning, and the way he was whacking his pencil against the edge of the desk was making them very nervous.

These students were well aware of his absence from school on Monday and well aware of the difficult day they'd given his substitute. They knew that he rarely missed school, but frequently warned them that if he ever did, his replacement should be able to report that his students shined like stars and behaved like saints.

Greg Schwarz sat ramrod straight in the chair behind the metal desk and scowled. He'd soon be expressing about half the rage and disillusionment he felt to this group. The rest would remain inside his head and chest. For that they should be grateful.

❖ ❖ ❖

Greg Schwarz hadn't been sick. He'd spent Monday in the Cities because he'd received an unsolicited call from the superintendent of a suburban school begging him to come down to interview for the head football coaching position at his school.

It was one of the area's more affluent school districts. Most of the houses were mini-mansions, which both enticed him and put him off. He'd grown up in a northern mining town where only upper management owned places as nice. His father had attained the level of foreman after decades of service to his company while a steady stream of outsiders were awarded the positions those houses symbolized. Nevertheless, his father had remained loyal to the company, and unwavering in his appreciation of his work.

"We sought you out because our Booster Club members were mighty impressed with the job you did at Blue Lake last fall. Your ability to step in and bring that team to the state semifinals is exactly what we're looking for here," the superintendent had told him.

"Red Howard deserves the credit."

"One of the qualities emphasized in the articles we read was your sense of loyalty. We admire that. We did some checking with sources in your community, however. The consensus was that you were very much responsible for the team's success. Mr. Howard supported that impression when we called him. He speaks highly of you."

"He would," Greg said. "He's a great friend."

The administrator tilted forward in his executive office chair, his hands folded on his desk. "This is an up-and-coming community, Mr. Schwarz. Most of its residents are upper middle class white-collar workers. These people are winners. School is important to them. Winning is important as well. We've assembled an excellent staff to take care of the academics. Unfortunately we've been unable to find a football coach who has satisfied the community's athletic expectations. That's why we called you."

"And you'll be happy if I win some football games."

"The community will. Since I work for the community, I'll be happy too."

"Not so different than Blue Lake. I wonder why I'd want to make this change if it's no change at all."

The superintendent remained unruffled. Alan Anderson could take smooth lessons from him. "For one thing, although our parents are passionate about sports, you won't be physically attacked," he said. "For another, we pay better."

The interview ended shortly thereafter. Although he wasn't at all sure he wanted to join a community bereft of hardscrabble residents, he agreed to consider the offer.

Driving north to Blue Lake, he became increasingly uncomfortable. His recruitment was the result of Red Howard's misfortune. He felt disloyal for having even interviewed for the job. Loyalty was a shining virtue in his family. He was uncomfortable with the thought of leaving the school that had given him his first teaching job and the opportunity to work with Red. He'd enjoyed every year he'd taught there. He'd loved the challenge of motivating average students like himself to achieve success through effort and determination. He'd be guilty of abandoning those students and athletes, who consistently rewarded his effort with theirs. He doubted that his father had ever considered leaving the mining company. He felt like a traitor to be thinking about leaving Blue Lake.

On the other hand, much was changing in Blue Lake. Red Howard and

Sam Strand would be gone at the end of the school year. Most teachers were too overwhelmed by their workloads and oversized classes to maintain the camaraderie that had characterized the faculty until recently. The current school board sucked.

The novelty of the fresh and tender meat tossed in front of them had been too tempting to too many of Greg Schwarz' students in all his classes. The young-looking man who awaited his first period physical education class in the locker room with a whistle dangling around his neck looked saturated with nervous vulnerability.

He was a Blue Lake State Graduate School English major who was augmenting the income from his work in the college union by taking substitute teaching jobs. A few students had begun the deterioration of the day by telling the lad Schwarz had excused them from class participation because they'd had the flu. Then they'd gone to the corner of the gym, taken out a deck of cards, and played poker. The remaining boys noticed, but played a little listless basketball before originating an impromptu game of dodge ball near the period's end, ignoring the substitute's request that they stop.

The second period crew took cues from the first. They convinced the substitute to ignore Mr. Schwarz' instructions that they review the rules of gym hockey in preparation for the test that would allow those who passed to play the sport for the next two weeks. Instead they said they'd show him they already knew the rules if he'd let them play. The gym hockey quickly descended into wrestling matches unaffected by whistle blasts and pleas to cease. The period ended with the boys streaming out of the locker room five minutes before the bell rang.

News of sub's inexperience preceded him into the third period study hall. He was already aware he was going down to defeat as he pushed through the noise. He pleaded for quiet and then sat slumped in the chair behind the desk while the students roamed the room.

For the rest of the day, he presented Greg's lesson plans to his social studies classes, asked for cooperation, and sat behind Greg's desk staring at the spiral note pad he'd brought along on which he'd jotted thoughts and topics related to Greg's plan. Occasionally he repeated his ignored pleas that the students do the work, and ended each period staring desperately at the round clock in the back of the room.

Greg had a seventh hour preparation period. The substitute teacher was seen fleeing out the front door by a student who shouted, "Hey, going back to the college to change your major?" as though he and his compatriots had won something. This morning Greg had read the substitute teacher's scrawled summary of his day. The last sentence said, "I don't think I'm cut out to be a teacher," and set Greg's anger and disillusionment ablaze.

Forgetting that he'd see most of them more than once, the students in his physical education classes were surprised when he uttered only clipped references to yesterday's debacle. In the first period he'd simply said, "Since some of you took the class into your own hands yesterday, and the rest of you went along with that. I guess you need a reminder of who's running this show." Then he ordered them to run laps around the gym and up and down the bleachers until they collapsed in sweaty clumps against the gym walls. In the second period he sat the students down and handed out the rules test. His only statements were, "Until you pass this test, you are flunking this class," and, "Don't even twitch until the bell stops ringing."

Now he sat in front of fifty students in this elongated room. The only sounds were the humming of the florescent lights and the rapid tapping of Greg's pencil. A few students eased into the quiet conversations the teacher normally tolerated as he strolled the room to help them with academics.

Greg's fist thudded against the desktop, breaking the pencil in half. "Shut up!" he shouted, bolting to his feet and around the desk. "How you dare even move your lips I have no idea! Just shut up!" He stood on the raised desk platform, towering disappointment raging his beet-red face. "You think I was sick yesterday? I'm never sick! But I'm sick today! I'm sick because I read the note my substitute wrote at the end of sixth period yesterday!" He leapt off the platform and stormed down the middle aisle. All eyes followed him to the back of the room where he whirled and threw his arms in the air. "What were you thinking? Don't answer that! You weren't thinking! You were too busy being jerks!"

Greg lapsed into a muscular silence and roamed up and down each aisle before returning to the desk and slamming it again with his fist. "I ought to throttle every one of you! I ought to send every one of you to Mr. Strand's office and ask him to suspend every one of you who made it happen, and every one of you who let it happen here and in every class I teach! And that's every one of you!

"Did you think Mr. Happy Guy was kidding when he told you if he's gone, whoever is in front of you is to be treated like a king or a queen? No problems, I told you! I'm gone one day and this man who wants to be a teacher walks into my classes and gets bushwhacked! Every single period!"

He slammed the desk with both fists. "This young man wanted to be a teacher! You didn't even treat him like a human being! You wrecked his day and thought it was fun! But you did more than that! You wrecked his dreams for his the future! Listen! Listen to this! Look at me! Heads up, eyes open, look at me! What you did embarrasses yourselves, your school, and me! You don't give a crap, but I do! Mark my words," Greg seethed, "you'd better not have kids. There won't be anyone to teach them. There won't be anyone who will want this lousy job anymore!

"Get out your pen and a piece of paper. Every one of you is going to write a letter of apology to Mr. Herndon. It better be thorough and from the heart. You will give it to me by the end of this period. If you don't, I'll put you on detention for a week, and if you're in one of my classes, I'll suspend you from it."

The study hall remained morgue silent for the rest of the period. Greg waited by the door and collected the apologies as the students filed out at the end of it, then followed them into the hall. As he emerged from the room, Robert Baker walked by silent as a shadow on the opposite wall and slipped into the men's faculty rest room.

Guilt lanced Greg Schwarz. He'd screamed at his students for mistreating a young man he didn't even know, and he'd done exactly the same thing to Robert Baker when he labeled him a loser in the faculty lounge. His students weren't the only jerks walking these halls.

Despite being dogged by that realization, Greg forced the needless abuse of another young man to the forefront and maintained his anger. He repeated his message to each class, requiring every student to write a letter of apology. They dove into the assignment, grateful to avoid the total rage that had flattened the study hall.

By the end of the day, Greg was drained. Long after the halls emptied, he remained at his desk struggling to escape the downward spiral of his thoughts and emotions

Then Sam Strand wandered into the room. "You're working late," Sam said as he slid into the student desk that fronted Greg's.

"But not hard except in my head. I'm thinking evil thoughts about my students, my profession, and myself. Did you get the sub's report I sent up?"

"Yes, I did. Disheartening isn't it. I wish Mr. Herndon had called the office, but the poor guy was undoubtedly in shock. It's a good thing I had the report, however. A parent called to complain about you calling his kid a jerk."

"I called them all jerks. But if the shoe fits . . . "

"That's what I told the man. If the shoe fits, have your son wear it. If it doesn't, why is he worrying about shoes? He's still wondering what I was talking about. You look tired and sad, my friend."

"Strange thing happened, Sam." Greg rose and walked to the window. "I got angry and told the students so. I mean really angry. Justified too. So how come my anger is taking bites out of me? Why do I feel so lousy?"

"How was the interview?" Sam inquired. Greg's head snapped around. "Red told me. Now we'll see whether or not three men can keep a secret. One and two couldn't."

"It was disappointing. I didn't just say no. Or yes. The place is probably full of classier Pete Warrums. What's that got to do with anything?"

"A lot. Given the scant evidence you're providing together with what happened yesterday, not to mention October and January, my guess is that a very sad thing is going on inside you. Truth to tell, I hate to see it happen."

"It being?"

"A loss of innocence. I think you're mourning your loss of innocence. Your highly desirable naiveté has taken a pummeling this year."

"I sure as heck don't like it."

Sam draped his arm around the shoulder of the young coach. "Don't worry too much about it. Nobody took Red's deal harder than you, but I've watched you recover your energy and optimism. You're resilient. I suspect you'll resurface again, a little changed maybe, but still intact."

Sam dropped his hands to the chill of the windowsill. "I called the college and offered the Dean of Education an apology for our students' behavior. I assured him it had everything to do with the herd instinct and nothing to do with the teacher being substituted for. We're going to try to set up a meeting with the young fellow to see if we can restore his desire to teach."

"Maybe he's better off if you can't," Greg grimaced. He returned to his desk, and pointed at the stacks of paper apologies. "These are written regrets. I'll look them over and put them in your box before I leave. Maybe that will help us all."

"It can't hurt. I also want to interview a cross section of eight students from each of your classes. I don't want these sophomores thinking only you is offended."

"That's a lot of kids, Sam."

"Yes, but I'll see some I rarely meet in my job. It might be refreshing." The principal turned to leave, then stopped. "Maybe they're right about me being too old. I clean forgot the other reason I dropped by. I have good news. In addition to ratting on you, Red informed me that his doctor has cleared him to return to work the first week in March. There must be something special about what we do."

Greg was glad to hear this news even if at this moment he could not begin to understand why Red would want to come back. Nor could he fathom what it would take for Robert Baker to keep showing up day after day. All he could do was shake his head and wonder at the mysterious magic that made you want to keep teaching even when it was driving you crazy or breaking your heart.

march

Frank Marin

Towards the end of the second quarter, Frank Marin and his parents made a deal. If he passed most of his quarter classes and all his semester classes, he could look for a job. If he got one, he could keep it as long as he was passing his classes, even with a D. They took his desire to work as a hopeful sign. He saw it as a necessary evil.

It wasn't that he couldn't work. Mr. Corgan thought he was a wonderful worker, and he was until other interests overtook him, the interests that now dominated his life. If he didn't get some money, they'd be hard to sustain. The inheritance from his grandmother, which his folks should have withheld until he graduated, wasn't going to last forever.

So he needed a job, one where he wasn't in the public eye because he couldn't stand the glare. He needed one not a lot of people wanted so the employer would take a chance on him. Not everyone wanted to hire Elvis.

He found a job unloading trucks for the town's largest grocery store. The trucks started arriving by five a.m. That suited him fine since he wasn't using or drinking. When he wasn't using, he couldn't sleep. Too wired. So trucking down to unload trucks at five a.m. was no problem. When he resumed his favored life, he could just drift from party to platform. It was the perfect job. Perfect for his employer too. He was paid a dollar an hour less than the others since he was still in high school.

The two guys that worked with him were straight-laced college dudes with clipped hair and bulging arms who'd come in off the farm to work their way through school. Eddie and Albert. Nice guys. They didn't treat him like an inferior like some college guys did. As long as he lifted his share of the load, that was all they cared about. He identified with the hard farm history the two talked about, even added a word or two now and then though he didn't talk a lot. He liked listening to them. And not once did they call him Elvis.

He was, for a change, in a win-win situation. Doing physical labor reminded him of the Marin and Corgan farms when life had been better. The first week of work drained him because he was out of shape, but by the second week the potato sacks and fruit and vegetable crates weren't so heavy. His arms and legs hardened and he liked that. He got his first paycheck on the Friday of the second week. He liked that. He put it in a shoebox in his closet since he was determined to last a month before using again. It wouldn't be pleasant to be slogging around drunk in the March snow anyway. Springtime would be the time to fly.

He tried to occupy his mind by developing little schemes he could hatch in Baker's class. He hadn't much luck. By the time school started, he was worn out from working. By the time Baker's class rolled around, he was zapped. All he could do was yawn. By accident he discovered a vocalized yawn could stop a teacher's voice in its tracks and earn a few wicked smirks from the in-crowd. The first time he apologized in his low rumble of a voice, some kids laughed. After that he planned the yawns, doing the bit once every few days and always saying, "Sorry," afterwards.

When Baker finally did get irritated enough to call him to the desk to talk to him, that was okay. Frank told him about his job. That totally disarmed the teacher.

Frank didn't want to get too obnoxious in the class though. He admired Patty Light. She and the Cloud kid carried the class. It took guts to stick out like that. She didn't wear makeup and her clothes didn't match the stuff most the girls wore. Her hair wasn't carefully combed. But there was something about her, maybe that she was different and he was different, too. One thing for sure, thinking about her made it harder for him to act out against Baker. She liked the guy a lot. Frank was sure she'd protect and defend him against anyone. Like if they were doing it to Baker, they were doing it to Patty Light as well.

Ah, heck where was Hunter when you needed him! But if he'd acted out against that guy, his little fans would have crawled all over him. In Baker's class, they'd applaud.

One morning in mid-March when Frank arrived at work, Eddie and Albert were leaning against the wall of the grocery store, arms folded, talking about the weather. It was a beautiful morning. The wind blowing through the dark from the southeast felt fresh and clean on his face. The temperature gauge on the back of the building read 48 degrees.

"Storms coming," Albert was assuring Eddie. "Even if I hadn't heard it on the radio, I'd know. Way too warm. Pretty soon that wind will be a pure easterly and that storm will be ducking its head and plowing in underneath. Wait and see." Eddie nodded. "Morning, Frank," Albert said. "Good thing the truck's coming today. Won't be anything moving but snow drifts tomorrow."

"Beware the Ides of March," Eddie said. "Albert's never wrong about the weather." Geez he liked these guys. They had fun, but they didn't have to play games with other people's heads to enjoy life. They were comfortable in their own skin and at ease with each other and even with him. The only price he paid for being around them was doing his share of the work. He envied them and wished he had turned out like that.

Once the semi was unloaded and he was shuffling towards the school, he noted that the wind had, indeed, shifted to the east and increased its speed. He flipped up the collar of his jacket and dug his gloves out. Albert said a storm was coming, and he was never wrong.

Thinking about the coming storm reminded him of Thanksgiving. That storm. The college crew. How Betts went after him. Burrowing into his stash or cash. It was worth something to flap your wings and fly. Worth something, too, to have your hands sailing all over Bett's body. That storm had been the zenith of everything.

Thinking about that brought a thirst he hadn't felt for awhile. It opened the hollow place inside him. His mouth went bone dry. The end of the month looked as far away as the stars.

"Damn," he muttered aloud. "Damn." He wished he wasn't thinking about parties, drinking, and using. When he'd looked in the mirror this morning, the pupils of his eyes were brilliant. Their whites were eggshell white. On the way to work he'd noticed the sky and its stars. He liked Albert and Eddie, and they didn't seem to mind him at all.

"Damn," he muttered again. He wished he wasn't suddenly so thirsty.

Kyle Hunter

"My impression of Greg Schwarz," Red Howard stage-whispered to Kyle Hunter, "is that he is one of the world's great eaters. Look at that tray. That mound of mashed potatoes looks like the snowdrifts we'll see after our annual mid-March blizzard hits. A full third of a turkey swimming through the gravy. Three of Mrs. S's famous dinner rolls. Two slices of her famous homemade pumpkin pie. Cranberry. A dollop of sweet potato. Two cartons of milk. Good heavens, haven't you eaten since I left?"

Greg's face spread into a pleased grin. "Yes, Mrs. S. is a genius. Never has a budget so small produced such wonderful results. Excuse me, Skim Milk Red, while I dig into this luscious repast."

"Someday, we'll have to roll you down the halls and oil you to jam you through doors."

"Your envy does not flatter you. Or me for that matter," Greg countered between forkfuls. "To be as well fed as I am and yet as desirable is a combination reserved for elevated mortals."

"Only a deranged mind could produce so much self-delusion in so few words," Kyle observed. "Red, what say we slide away from this carnivore and indulge in intelligent conversation."

"Pure envy," Greg said.

"How's the week gone, Red?"

"Doc said the first week back, I'd be surprised by how tired I am. That's why these first two weeks are three hours a day. Heck, I argued with him and Sam both. Been walking one, two miles a day. I'm fit as the proverbial fiddle." His thinned face showed weariness. "Doc and Sam were right. Gawd, Kyle, I don't know how you teachers do it. This is hard work."

"Windy in here," Greg said, his fork spearing the second slice of pie.

"Don't worry," Kyle said, "you've too much ballast to blow away."

"Don't worry at all, Greg," Ginny Float chimed from the next table. "You're putting it all behind you."

"There's a storm of envy swirling this room. Storm coming outside, too."

"Storm?" Ginny responded. "So that's it."

"Heard it on the radio this morning. Major March blizzard heading this way. Whole state actually. It shouldn't hit until afternoon or early evening."

"That's why the kids are flying around like darts. I swear they feel a weather change from their toes to their souls."

"Better not arrive until I'm out of here," Red said. "You teachers will trample me trying to beat the kids out the door."

"Teachers are just tall kids anyway, so I've heard," Greg noted, finishing his pie.

"How do you do that? Inhale that stuff?" Kyle asked.

"Red," Greg said, dropping his hand on the older man's shoulder, "did you ever notice how an English teacher never uses more than twenty words to say what would take anyone else at least five?"

"Almost anyone else, Greg," Red laughed. "And now, as Shakespeare would say, I must get me hence." He slid his chair away from the table. "In all sincerity, lady, gentleman, and Greg, it feels doggone good to be back."

"In all sincerity, it's doggone good to have you back. This isn't home without you," Kyle responded.

"I concur," Greg nodded. "Fully," he added.

"You know what I thought about sitting around all these months?"

"Me, of course."

"The kids. Those doggone squirrelly, unpredictable, drive-you-nuts, God-love-'em kids. See you folks," Red said as he pulled on his coat. "Keeping them in line will be like trying to drown ping-pong balls. Enjoy."

"At best," Kyle agreed. "Tell you the truth, though, I like a good storm. I get as excited as the kids."

"Like I said earlier," Greg noted as he dumped the refuse on his tray into the wastebasket.

"Yes, Plato, but I'm a bit worried about this one. Gail's supposed to drive home today."

"She's a big girl. She can take care of herself. Want coffee?"

"Sure. Due to the anti-stimulation of your conversation, I'm nearly asleep."

"We always mock what we can't understand," Greg stated as he headed for the row of cups hanging on hooks above the counter. "Yours is the one with the lipstick?"

Sam Strand

"This," Sam Strand told Alan Anderson as the two stood at the big window in the superintendent's office and watched the snow swirl, "may be the hardest part of a superintendent's job. When should he call off school and send the kids home? He's listened to the forecast. But the calls he'll get will make him wonder if anybody else did. If he sends them home when the storm is in its infancy, he'll be accused of not giving a rap about education. If he waits until the storm is roaring, they'll tell him he doesn't give a rat's rear about kids."

"This is true," Alan Anderson replied as the two watched students stream out to the line of yellow buses. He'd waited until 2:45 to close the schools. If the storm progressed faster than predicted, some buses could end up in ditches.

"The second hardest part is when to reopen. If you decide not to reopen and the sun comes out, knives will be unsheathed all over town, all aimed at your back."

"True again. I found that out the day before Thanksgiving. The clouds parted for three seconds and I got four calls. I think I prayed for snow, sleet, and thunderstorms just to show 'em who was right."

"And got most of that. You're a powerful man, Mr. Superintendent."

"It's difficult for me to believe you've come to my office just to praise me, Mr. Principal. I sense something else is on your mind."

"See what I mean. You have marvelous insight."

"Shall we sit? I think most of the students are bussed, driven, or booted out of here. Most teachers, too, I notice.

"It's in the contract, sir. Health and safety."

Anderson moved to the leather office chair behind his desk, and Sam seated himself in the comfortable vinyl chair on the opposite side. "I love this chair," Anderson said. "You ought to be sitting here by right of tenure and talent. Didn't you want this job?"

"No, I never did. It's too far from kids and teachers. Too business. Too ivory tower."

"I suppose we should get to the heart of whatever has kept you here, Sam. The superintendent does not want to find himself in a ditch, either."

"All right. You were informed about the rotten day our college student substitute teacher had here recently? You read his report? And my report?"

Anderson nodded three times.

"What's your status concerning next year?" The question was a non sequitur, but Anderson answered anyway. Sam rarely asked pointless questions.

"I want this job, Sam. Blue Lake is a growing town with a growing college and a pool of teacher prospects close at hand. There's a good chance of passing the building bond issue if I work at it the way my predecessor didn't."

"That's unfair, Alan. The man gave himself to this school and community for decades."

"You're right, and I apologize. What I really wanted to say is, yes, I want this job, but I hope I didn't sell myself out to get it and keep it. I'm puzzled as to why you're asking."

"To get to the heart of the matter, one reason I'm here is to ask you to demand that the school board hire an assistant principal as soon as possible. We could use two, but at least one. We need someone now."

"I understand that."

"Our board doesn't. The majority will sacrifice anything to achieve their own goals. You're going to have to fight for what you want educationally, and you're going to have to fight to run a good school. I'd just as soon you start that fight now."

"Red's situation was hard on you."

"That's an understatement. Situations like that are going to crop up more and more as the school grows, the classes become more overcrowded, and teachers have less hope for relief. This job would kill me if I stayed with it the way it is. But it will kill or chase off anyone who replaces me as well. I can't get out of my office. There's a steady stream of kids waiting at my door. I could stop problems before they happened if I was out in the halls and in classrooms. The last classroom I was in was Baker's in December. My counselors have to act like vice principals. That's not their job."

"I hear you."

"It's going to take more than hearing, Alan. I found out about the substitute's horrors at the end of the day. Consequently a young man who had a heart for teaching no longer does. That's a tragedy. If schools continue their present course, it will become a repeated tragedy."

Alan nodded. He was staring at his shoes the way he always did when he was listening and processing. That habit drove Sam crazy. He wanted to reach across the desk, grab the man's chin and yank it up. Instead he said, "You've really got to stop that, Alan. You're shoes aren't that pretty, and most folks will think you're uninterested in anything but leather. It's a bad habit. It makes you look weak! Look them in the eye, Alan! Look people in the eye, pound your fist on the desk like this, and fight."

The administrator sat with his hands folded, his gaze trained on his subordinate's face. "I'll work on it. I have discovered that you're often right, if not tactful."

Sam's wrinkled face broke into a smile. "That pose looks a little too pensive, but at least it's an improvement. One last thing. At the beginning of the year, I couldn't stand you. But you showed me something at Red's hearing. I've come over to your side. You're young and smart, and you've got guts.

That matters. You've got the energy of youth. This school needs you worse than you need it. Keep that in mind because it's going to be a fight to keep this thing going.

"Here's a last bit of advice. I think the only time I see you in our halls or offices is when you're squiring some VIP around. I know this district's growing fast, and you have other buildings to attend to. But become less aloof. You're not going to know how things work unless you watch things working. You're going to be a lot more effective if you do. There will come a time when this district will be so big, you won't be in the halls. As they say, 'seize the day.'"

"Points well taken."

"Oh," Sam added, "You should meet with the man we've wrecked. Maybe you can rebuild him."

Alan nodded.

"Go home so you'll miss those phone calls," Sam suggested over his shoulder as he left the room.

Once the principal was gone, the superintendent pushed back his chair, extended his legs and stared at his shoes. He rather liked this posture. It conveyed humility and careful contemplation. But maybe Sam was right. Sam was right about a lot of stuff.

Alan walked to the window and watched Sam Strand exit the school through the main doors. He saw the principal turn and look.

"I do like my shoes, Sam," he mouthed, pointing vigorously downward.

Robert Baker

Ah, he'd become nothin' but a mole burrowing between banks of snow lining the sidewalks from his apartment building to the school in the early morning dark when not much moved except for the those delivering morning newspapers. All day he was popping his head above the lectern or book or papers piled on his desk to monitor whatever activity was occurring. Then he'd stay in his room with one bank of fluorescent lights humming, working and waiting for dark so he could scurry in anonymity back to his apartment.

He'd begun training for moledom last fall when a trip to the grocery store on the night of a football game had shown him that almost no one was there at that time. Another foray, when he'd discovered later at night that he was out of milk, revealed that teenagers aren't prone to hang out at grocery stores after eight p.m. Since then he'd confined his shopping to those times.

Oh, it wasn't that bad, was it? Or was it?

Robert shoved as many of the stacked papers as he could into his briefcase. Sometimes he felt like he'd rather toss 'em out the window.

"Hey, students," he'd say, "most of your papers are on the ground three floors below. To get them back, walk down three flights of stairs and into the cold to remind yourselves why I tossed 'em. Darn things were so rote and light of thought, I figured they'd fly up and away in the breeze above the trees, but darned if the dull weight didn't tumble them like rocks."

But no. He'd read every last one. That was the trouble. Too many to read. He could never catch up.

He shook his head again and wandered to the window. He watched two figures emerge from the main doors and duck their heads against the gathering wind and falling snow. He knew one was Patty Light. She'd shine in utter darkness. Therefore the other was Billy Cloud. The two advanced to the sidewalk fronting the school. Billy turned and waved. Robert thought they'd noticed him peering down and had begun a wave back when he noticed a third figure shuffling toward them. He knew it was Ed Warrum by the way his head hung down even when he joined the other two. The three progressed to the corner. What were those two doing with that jerk?

"None of your business," he told himself. But it felt as though two of his only friends were consorting with the enemy. Warrum's influence could lead them down the same way it had so many other juniors. "Be fair," he scolded himself. Warrum has been a little more . . . what . . . alert? Awake? Showing some semblance of life. At least his eyes, the few times he looked up, weren't entirely vacant, his face didn't always portray the mask he had mastered much of the year. Someone was home even if he wasn't answering the door.

Why did he waste so much time thinking about that guy?

But at this moment he knew why. He'd just watched Patty Light, Billy Cloud, and Ed Warrum walking down the street together. Ed had powers of persuasion you didn't have to hear to recognize. He was the king of the silent defiant, the majority in all in his classes. He was a master of doing just enough to get by without giving you a single excuse to get on his case, the role model whose technique so many mirrored. And now he'd gained the attention of Patty and Billy. If he could lead others down, how could they befriend him and avoid being swept into the current? The question filled him with a fear not so far from panic. If they sank, how could the rest of those swimming against the current hope to stay afloat?

As he pushed away from the window ledge, he noticed a tingling in both of his arms as if they'd fallen asleep. Odd. He must have been standing there longer than he thought and at an awkward angle to boot. He shook his arms until the tingle lessened, then stuffed his hands in his pockets and sat down behind his desk.

Well, he told himself, Patty Light, wasn't gone yet. She still worked in his room. Even stayed longer than usual on nights when Billy Cloud and his teammates practiced late. She was as bright a beacon as ever even if her aching need for someone to understand her head and heart and celebrate the gifts of her mind had diminished. The balance had tipped. Basketball season was over. Billy Cloud's excuse for coming to the room could be gone. Patty offered her presence more for his needs than hers. How long would it be until she climbed off this teeter-totter, and he thumped to earth alone.

"Well at least until spring," he muttered. "Who teeter-totters in March?" That struck him as funny, and he couldn't help but smile. "Count your blessings," he told himself. "Today is today."

He wandered to the closet to retrieve the sheepskin jacket his parents had given him for Christmas. He loved that jacket almost as much as Frank Marin must love his. Heck, get himself some hobnailed boots, they'd be twins. Tough on the outside, jelly on the inside. His eyes had found Frank's recently. The kid's eyeballs had danced like marbles in an earthquake, and he'd turned beat red. Oddly, that had put a lump in Robert's throat, and he'd aimed a smile of reassurance the kid's way, but by then Frank was staring hard at his desktop. Robert understood that kind of self-consciousness.

He grabbed his briefcase, snapped off the lights, eased out his door and shut it slowly and softly. A mole avoiding notice. He felt too hot in his sheepskin jacket as he walked down the empty halls and wondered how the heck Frank could wear his all the time.

He continued down the stairways and finally into the fast falling snow. No car headlights beat into the gathering storm. That meant there would be no cars rolling by, faces pressed against the windows displaying a variety of crazed expressions, no cars with half rolled down windows and extended hands with upraised middle fingers, no one shouting his name and connecting obscenities with it. No fear of his freshmen seeing and hearing those things. He was determined to protect their innocence as long as he could. It was too beautiful and valuable to lose any sooner than they had to.

"Silent snow, secret snow, you should know I'm so grateful," he murmured. The swirling flakes and powerful wind isolated him. He burrowed into the storm, becoming white as his own ghost, his bones clattering in the cold.

Ed Warrum

There was no heartbreak for Ed Warrum when the basketball team lost in the District semifinals to Providence by the score of 74-67. The Prowlers were talented and big. The two forwards were 6'6" and the center was 6'8". Pushing his 6'2" frame in among those trees in his role as number three forward had been hard, pleasurable work. It also served to hide him in a forest of bodies far from the howls of his father.

The loud Prowler crowd mitigated those howls anyway as did the hopeful Blue Lake fans. It was a close game until Billy Cloud fouled out with two minutes left. After that it was a parade to the foul line for Providence as Blue Lake tried to stay close. Both teams played well. Ed was satisfied. He'd played well, too. Besides that, he knew he could have been dropped from the team for missing a week. He could be sitting in a jail cell for carrying an unlicensed weapon. He could be facing a trial for shooting his father. Or someone else.

The downside of the season-ending defeat was that it removed a shield of time between himself and his dad. It also raised the possibility that without the bonding brought about by sports, his friendship with Billy Cloud, the only person with whom he'd shared any of his truths except for Pastors Dan and Phil and Shellie Chaine, might sputter or terminate.

Ed was exploring this mix of thoughts as he emerged from the school and ducked his head into the wind. Then he heard Billy's voice calling, "Hey," and glanced up to see Billy and Patty waving to him.

Now the three sat sipping cocoas at the Burger Shelf. Ed hadn't been in the noisy teen hangout since December. It was good to be back and good to be sitting across from Billy Cloud and Patty Light.

"You were magnificent last night," Ed told the slender guard.

"Yes, I was. It was magnificent the way I drove the lane time after time right at those three Sequoias planted there. Smart, too. And wasn't it courageous to keep doing that as blocked shot after blocked shot came zinging past my ears?"

"Twenty-four points ain't that bad, fella."

"But off seventy-four shots?"

"Seventy-three. I looked it up in the charts." Ed was delighted. He could hardly believe he was sitting here and joking with Billy. He'd made this scenario impossible a few months ago.

"Billy made ten out of eighteen shots. I read that in the morning paper," Patty protested.

"Well, Patty," Billy said, "they didn't count those fifty-six blocked shots as shots. The ball has to fly at least ten inches from the hand."

"This false modesty, Billy, is it to impress Patty? If that's what attracts someone like her to someone like you, I need to learn the technique."

"Aw, come on, I've seen Shellie draped on your arm."

"Lately?"

"Well, no. Want me to talk to her? I could tell her how much better a person you've become since you started hanging with us."

"Which is your subtle way of telling me without you two I'd be nothing."

"Yes. I love to state the obvious to the oblivious."

"Seriously, Shellie doesn't quite trust me anymore."

"The city trip?"

"No, my trip began long before I hopped that bus. I got completely wrapped up in myself. Left her out there by herself."

"But you must have . . . "

"I didn't tell her a thing, Billy. Couldn't," Ed said, staring out the window at the wind-blown snow. "I couldn't figure out how to say it."

"Maybe," Patty interrupted, "it – whatever it is because nobody's told me – maybe it's because she felt left out and untrusted, and took it personally. Sort of like I feel right now."

"Easy, my friend. You know why she's so upset, Ed?"

"Well, I . . . "

"She's an animal lover, and we got her goat."

Patty crossed her arms, and turned her face blank.

Ed could tell she was upset. "Billy hasn't said anything to you about it?" Patty shook her head.

"Not my place. Yours. I'm too busy impressing her with my intellect and wit to deal with trivial matters like life and death."

"Besides which, Patty," Ed implored, "I told Billy some pretty personal stuff. He was honoring my trust in him even more than I thought he would. You gotta admit that's an admirable quality."

Patty unfolded her arms. "You're right.'"

"Had to tie my tongue in a square knot every day to keep silent."

"But you have a friend who needs to know about it. You agree?"

"That's your call. But I sure don't dare disagree."

Ed's story was far too emotional to fully expose in this public place, but for fifteen minutes he offered bits and pieces of it to Patty.

When Ed was done, Billy asked, "Your father doesn't drink, does he?"

"No, not a whole lot," Ed said, shaking his head and noticing the flush that raced across Patty's face. "Why?"

"When I was a kid . . . way back then . . . "

"Last Wednesday?" Patty said, recovering herself.

"Monday. Anyway, when I was a kid, we had an uncle living with us for a while. He drank quite a bit. I was sitting in the kitchen one day munching a cookie, and Mom says, 'Frankly, Dad, he's driving me crazy. I'm going to an Al-Anon meeting. So are you. And you, Billy, are going to an Alateen meeting.' 'He isn't driving me crazy,' I said, 'in fact I think he's pretty funny.' To make a short story shorter, she went, Dad went, and I went. Quit going after my uncle went home. But I learned some stuff while I went. Too bad your Dad doesn't drink."

"So?"

"So maybe I'll give you some pamphlets I've got. Can't hurt. Stuff about detachment. Not taking responsibility for how other people are."

"Billy," Patty said." Would you like to meet my mother sometime?"

"Of course."

"Pretty soon," she said firmly.

Ed glanced out the window. Huge snowflakes danced in front of it. "Looks like its time to leave. It's really getting white out there. What time is it?"

"You might try looking at your watch," Billy advised.

"Uh . . . cripes, it's almost five. My dad . . . " He caught himself. "Who gives a darn."

"Well, you for one," Billy suggested, sliding out of the booth. "Come on, we'll walk you to the gallows. Dry your tears. Hold your hand. Whatever it takes."

His fear, defiance, and anger wanted to surge. He followed his friends out the door, repeating the "Serenity Prayer" Pastor Barker had given him in his mind: "God grant me the serenity to accept the things I cannot change, courage to change the things I can, wisdom to know the difference."

The raw wind slapped the storm against them. Patty impulsively reached to pull the boys closer to shield her. Then as though awakening from a dream, she released her hold and pushed her hands into her coat pockets.

Billy Cloud

Billy Cloud was mightily surprised when Patty Light hooked her arms through his and Ed's. Of course, the wind was whipping itself toward a frenzy and drilling the cascading snow into them. But being physically close for any reason was not her preference. "It's cold," he said to encourage her to maintain her hold.

"Yes," she said as she withdrew her arms and plunged her hands into her pockets.

Patty was shivering noticeably. "Want to come in to warm up?" Ed asked.

"Just for a second," she replied, shivering. Ed opened the door and the three hurried into Warrum's store.

They stood staring out the display window at the gathered storm. "Maybe I could borrow Dad's car and give you a ride home," Ed said without conviction. "Better chance of that if we'd won last night, of course."

"Nah, that's all right," Billy replied. "I love a good storm. Makes me feel alive."

Patty said, "I'd better get home. My mother will worry if I don't get home soon." She tried a smile. "She doesn't like me to be out after dark on school nights. In storms, I mean." The smile waned, and she returned to staring out the window.

"I'm going to walk her home," Billy said. "By the time I reach my house, I'll be so alive, I'll be sprouting wings. See ya." He held the door and followed Patty into the wind, hoping she'd allow his arm around her shoulders so he could shield her, keep her a little warm, a little safe.

Instead she wound her brown woolen scarf around her neck, and pushed her hands back into her pockets.

The two walked in silence for a few blocks. Finally Patty edged closer. "Ed seems very nice. And very sad."

"Yes, he is. Throw in a few shovelfuls of anger, and he's got quite the recipe cooking in his oven."

"I know he didn't tell me everything, but I appreciated being included."

"Glad to include you." Fearing he sounded flippant, he added, "Really."

The wind was forming pure white drifts across the sidewalks. Patty's bunny boots sank beneath the surface now and then as the two trudged on.

"Did you see Mr. Baker?" she asked after a time.

"Sure. Though it wasn't easy over that stack of papers on his desk."

"No. I mean when we left school. When we turned around and waved at Ed, he was standing at the window in his room. I'm sure he was watching us. He thought we were waving at him. His arm went up, and then he pulled it down quickly. I waved, but he'd already turned his back."

"He's in love with you, you know."

The statement rushed an angry flush to Patty's face. "No. No. I don't know that. I don't want to know that." She stared straight ahead. Billy fixed his gaze on her face, stumbling through a drift in the process. Being her friend wasn't easy all the time. But then she said, "I'm sorry. It just seems to spoil it. We like to talk, that's all. He's very deep, you know. He's very lonely." That thought brushed her shoulder against his. He could feel her trembling through the coats, but she did not move away.

The two walked the remaining blocks without words. Billy pondered how amazing it was that her shoulder barely brushing his could feel so intimate. Maybe it was best that she wouldn't allow him to be her shelter. When the two walked right past their parting place, Billy didn't point that out, and Patty said nothing about it. They continued down the drifting sidewalks, their shoulders whispering to one another.

As they neared Patty's house, she stopped dead in the beating storm. "The car's gone!" she gasped. "Billy, the car's gone!"

"Groceries maybe? Stocking up for the storm?" He saw how wide with fear her eyes were. He stared at her, not sure why she was so upset or what to do about it.

Patty raced up the sidewalk and disappeared into the house. By the time Billy followed her in, she stood transfixed at the top of the stairs, melting snow dripping from her coat and boots. "Of course she's not here," her voice floated down the staircase to him. "The car's gone. I'm so stupid." She released the small plastic bottle she was holding in her hand and watched it bounce once on the landing then roll down the steep steps. "I don't know what I was thinking."

"It's kind of dark in here. Can I turn on a light?'" Billy asked. He'd be happy to leave the lights off and encircle her in his arms until her fear and sadness were gone, but he didn't see that as an option.

"Oh, yes. I'm sorry. I'm so self-centered. There's a switch on the wall behind you."

Billy pushed the top button of the antiquated switch igniting the naked ceiling light at the top of the stairs. Patty shed her coat and boots and left them lying on the landing. She descended the stairs, then bent to retrieve the vial at the bottom. Even in the dim light, Billy could see her cheeks were damp.

"Do you want to tell me anything?" he asked.

"Oh, I do. I so desperately do. But I don't know how."

"You can say everything or nothing or anything in between. Whatever you do is okay," Billy told her. His friend was always intense, but when tension tightened the skin on her face against her skull like it did now, he was afraid for her.

"Why don't we go in the living room?" Patty said. She walked past him and switched on the lamp atop the end table. "Do you want to take off your coat? You can sit on the sofa, and I'll sit here in this chair."

He hung his coat on the banister ball and moved to the sofa without removing his eyes from her. The two sat listening to the snow whip the walls of the house. "It's so stormy. I should encourage you to go home," she offered, her hands clenched so tightly she looked to be in prayer. "But I can't. I don't want you to go right now."

"As I told Ed, I love storms. I have the homing instincts of Lassie. I'm fine. Are you?"

"No. I'm not. I'm like a little girl," she said. "I think my mother is supposed to be home unless I know she isn't going to be."

I don't think so, Billy thought. If there's a little girl in this house, it isn't you. The few times he'd suggested walking Patty to her house, her reasons for rejecting the offer were that her mother would be resting or wasn't well. But he said nothing about that. Instead he asked, "Do you think her getting groceries is a possibility?"

Patty nodded in weak agreement. "It's possible. We've been caught short before when there was a storm. Maybe she remembered that." She nodded again, struggling to convince herself this fiction could be fact.

"Do you want to call the police?"

"Oh, no. She'd be so embarrassed. They'd think I was crazy, a teenager complaining that her mother wasn't home." She forced a nervous laugh. "Anyway, doesn't someone have to be gone twenty-four hours before you can report them missing?"

Billy admitted he shared that impression. He looked around the room seeking clues as to why her mother's absence was so upsetting. The furniture was old but clean, the wallpaper faded, but not peeling, the floor uncluttered.

The house smelled antiseptically clean. If there was a problem awaiting his discovery, it had nothing to do with cleanliness. It might have to do with that small plastic bottle though.

"Are you looking for something?" Patty asked.

"Just letting my eyes sweep the room." He smiled. "Say, wouldn't it be great if eyes could actually sweep a room. Save a lot of work." He hoped his joke would be diverting. The vagueness of her smile told him it wasn't. "I'll stay here as long as you want me to," he told her. Confusion clouded her eyes. He wished he could withdraw the statement even if its intent was to comfort.

"Oh, I . . . oh, she . . . " Patty's hands were clenched so tightly her knuckles were bloodless. Finally she finished, "I guess you better not." She continued, "You should call your parents. It's dark. They'll be worried."

"That's true. Phone?"

"It's on the table in the hall," she informed him, unloosening her fingers and pointing to the narrow hallway. "There's a small table with a lamp you can turn on so you can see." She re-clenched her hands and pushed them into her lap. She did look like a little girl then. It hurt Billy's heart to see her like that.

He walked down the hallway and spied the dim definition of phone, lamp, and table. When he reached his hand down to switch on the lamp, it collided with something metallic and sharp. Whatever it was tumbled to the floor. Lighting the lamp, he discovered the object was one of those old pincushions he sometimes saw in homes of the elderly. This one was larger than most and laden with an array of large stickpins. He retrieved it, set it on the table, and dialed the phone.

"Suppose you noticed there's a flake or two of snow in the air," his father said. "We were getting worried. Teenagers in love don't always display good judgment."

Billy explained where he was and gave as much explanation as he could as to why.

"Think I'll come get you with the old snowmobile," Billy's father said. "It's really drifting out there." Billy wished he could say, 'that's okay, I'll just stay here', but that wasn't an option. "Mom could ride the new one over if Patty wants to come to our place." Billy loved the offer but rejected it. No way would Patty leave her home until her mother reappeared. So he gave directions to the house and cradled the receiver.

While Billy returned to the living room, Patty was in the kitchen heating a kettle of water on the stove. He paused at its portal to explain that his father would soon be on his way on their snowmobile and resumed his place on the sofa. She emerged from the kitchen with two mugs of cocoa. She handed him one, then surprised him by sitting at the other end of the sofa. She curled one leg under the other, as he'd done.

"You're lucky to have the parents you have," Patty said, holding the mug close. "You are so fortunate."

Billy nodded and sipped the hot brew.

"Remember the poem 'Snowbound'?" she asked.

"Mr. Baker's class. The deadly silence yet again."

"Why are the kids like that? That poem is so warm and beautiful. It's how a family should be. It's perfect. I'll bet it's what it would be like in your house."

"Well, not quite, I'm afraid. Darn TV works."

Patty ignored his comment and continued her vision. "I wish we were snowbound right now. I wish it would snow for days and days, and we could sit here and talk."

She stopped. "I'll tell you why that couldn't happen here, Billy. Because if my mother came home and saw us sitting here like this, she'd throw a horrible fit." Anger rushed in to displace her melancholy. "Do you know why she'd have a fit, Billy? It's because she'd think I'm just like her!"

There was suddenly such a gush of tears Billy had no choice but to slide down the sofa to her. He extended his hand and lightly touched her back. It was like his fingertips were touching bands of steel. All he could do was wonder at the story that overwhelmed his friend and left her defenseless. But she could share no more words, so the two sat like that, his hand lightly stroking her back, her arms drawn tightly against her chest as she cried until they heard the roar of a snowmobile engine within the sound of the whooshing wind and snow.

Patty moved away from Billy's soft touch and dabbed at her face with her sweater sleeve. When they heard the roar no more, she rose, walked to the door, opened it, and said, "Hi, Mr. Cloud. Would you like a cup of cocoa," traces of tears still on her face, her voice quiet, but not tremulous.

Gail Hunter

Gail Hunter slipped the aging Volvo out of the parking ramp into the Neon Avenue traffic, which was four o'clock heavy. What was she doing here anyway mired in this bumper-to-bumper mess? What was all this about? Just what was it she had set out to prove back in September? Was this the way to prove whatever it was? This traffic puffing carbon monoxide, its collective stench hanging under the leaden gray mid-March sky?

This man in the passenger seat?

"Ridiculous, isn't it," Wayne Mars said. "You're lucky. Most of us have to put up with this every day. For you it's a few days a couple times a month." The Vice President in Charge of Wholesale and Retail Operations began to slide his hand inside his winter coat toward the inner pocket of the dark blue suit coat underneath. "Mind if I smoke?"

"No. No, why should I mind. Just crack the window and add its stink to the general stink all around us."

"You're sure? If it bothers you, I won't."

"I'm sorry, Wayne. It's the traffic. I could bite a nail in half."

"You didn't say 'male,' did you?" the Vice President in Charge asked, a smile spread across his features to assure Gail that was a joke.

"That too." Gail didn't want to smile, but she did. Everything the man said took on innuendo. But people put up with it from him. Another man would get slapped silly or be left standing with his bare face hanging out for saying things this dark-haired, fine-featured executive said. It was that grin that never quite leered that eased him over the hump. Or into it. That and those just-that-side-of-innocent eyes.

"It'll take longer to get to the next stoplight than to drive to Blue Lake," Gail groused. "You're sure you don't want me to take you to the airport?"

"And cost the company a couple hundred bucks it doesn't have to spend? Well, ordinarily yes, but as long as I have the companionship of a beautiful woman, I think I'll pretend I'm a company man." Wayne dragged on his cigarette, the smoke curling over the edge of the window he'd rolled slightly down out of consideration for his driver's sensitivities. Not to mention her request.

Gail pressed the car's accelerator, beating the amber stoplight's shift to red. She berated herself for liking the compliment. "Easy," he cautioned as she approached the trunk of the Ford in front of her. "Bring 'em back alive," he breathed as she stomped on the brake.

"That was a long, long meeting today," she said to cover her confused thoughts. "It must be nice to have the executive privilege of walking out whenever you want."

"Well, my dear, since I planned the thing and talked to consultants more times than I can count, those strolls were sleep stoppers, not pulling rank."

"And what's to keep the rest of us awake except watching you sidle out the door?"

"Waiting to see when I'd get back in the sidle again, I imagine. Though if I'd known you were watching, I'd have sidled up a storm. Speaking of which, on one of my walks I flipped on the TV to catch the weather."

"And?" Gail asked, glancing at her passenger.

"Storm heading this way," Wayne answered as he snuffed his cigarette in the ashtray before flipping it out the window. "Not to worry though. They said it won't hit here as hard as it will hit further north." He quickly added, "Shouldn't get where we're going until tonight. You'll be home by then."

The traffic inched along. Gail's whole body felt flushed. She couldn't tell if it was embarrassment, excitement, or apprehension.

❖   ❖   ❖

Wayne Mars had noticed Gail at the employee introductory meeting the first week in October. She denied the importance of his instant attention by telling herself she was new, and an alert executive should notice a new face. Wayne was alert. Friendly and comfortable to converse with as well. Even when he slipped those sly innuendoes into short conversations between workshops or in coffee shops or at personnel dinners when he paused at her table – not to mention the after Christmas party – she assured herself it was just the way Wayne was. Watching him with others confirmed that impression. He was friendly, outgoing, self-assured, and handsome.

Wayne Mars had approached Gail about giving him a ride to Blue Lake on Monday just after the second workshop of the day. "The Prez says we've been neglectful of our northern friends," he'd explained in that hopelessly charming way of his. "Don't get me wrong. He knows and I knows and you knows," that sidesaddle grin creating a dimple in his right cheek, "things are going very well in our retail stores up there since you climbed aboard. They write telling us how delighted they are with you," he added, curling his long fingers around a can of soda he'd fetched from his suit coat pocket and handing it to Gail. "But if they don't see management now and then, they feel… I want to say hurt, but that's not what they feel. They're ticked off. Everybody needs to know they matter." The length of his eyelashes was extraordinary. His eyes were hooded as a hawk's, but comfortable as the family dog's. "You know how the northern area feels about the Cities. They believe we don't care if they exist. We like to prove to them that we do." Gail listened and sipped the too-sweet drink although she wasn't thirsty.

Wayne had gone on to explain how he'd save the company money by riding with her before renting a car in Blue Lake. He'd have to rent a car anyway if he flew. And those little planes they flew to small markets sometimes made him sick.

She'd said she'd think about his proposal and did all through the next workshop, for which he'd made her late.

She'd acquiesced. Maybe going to Blue Lake would give Wayne a chance to really meet Kyle. The two men had said hello at the Christmas party. Of course, Wayne had had to slip in those anatomical references. Anyway, parties were no place to get to know anybody. It would be good for Kyle to spend a little time with one of her company's people. It would help him feel less left out of her life. It might even help him make up his mind to leave his beloved students behind and take a job that actually offered a future.

Besides that, Wayne Mars was also married. She'd met his wife Alieta, and Alieta was strikingly attractive. Even Kyle would think so.

❖   ❖   ❖

The Volvo's two occupants exchanged occasional observations about city drivers and city traffic until the density of vehicles began to thin beyond the outer suburbs as dusk approached, hastened by heavy gray clouds sailing in from the west. Noting the overcast, Gail asked, "How's Alieta?"

"How's Alieta?" Wayne repeated, pausing to light another cigarette, its initial perfumed odor filling the car. "Alieta was fine last time I saw her."

"Last time you saw her?"

"She's on a trip," Wayne explained. "New York. She loves New York." He exhaled a smoke-filled sigh. "She was born with a silver spoon right there on the delivery table. She tries to hide that, but if you look, you'll find tiny tattoos of that spoon all over her personality."

"What's the English translation for that sentence," Gail snapped.

Wayne noticed the edge in her voice, but took no offense. "I'm really too cute, aren't I? Alieta is a beautiful, spoiled young lady. Who can blame her? She has it all."

"I thought she was very nice."

"She is. Really. She's spoiled, but not at all rotten. She just decides what she wants and gets it." Wayne eyed his driver. "I suppose this sounds like a line to you."

That was exactly what she was thinking. "Is it?" She switched on the car's headlights. Darkness was descending with extraordinary speed.

Wayne smiled. "Given the fact that you're lovely, I suppose it could be. I'm not quite sure. But," he added, straightening in the seat, "I don't think so. I think I'm telling you the truth." He slipped his cigarette out the window and reached for another.

"You smoke a lot."

"When I'm nervous. I've made myself nervous. Honest stories make me nervous. Lines don't. I'm telling you what I believe to be an honest story. You'll have to decide whether or not it's a line in disguise."

Gail sat at the small round table in the motel lounge. Wayne was gone to the men's room. "Beer goes right through me," he'd grinned, his dimple deep. "I'm really a lousy drinker."

So was she. The vodka and orange juice mix was in her head and the rest of her body as well. But she needed it. Driving those last eighteen miles through the wind-swirled snow had been terrifying. Even Wayne had lapsed into a tense silence, leaning forward in his seat and confining himself to murmured compliments about her driving ability. Had she not known the road so well, she doubted she'd have been able to stay on it. As it was, the barely visible letters of the Holiday Inn sign brought joy, but she ached from tension as she pulled into what seemed to be a parking place. Even registering for two separate rooms hadn't eased that.

The drink helped though. So she had another.

"So we're here," she said when Wayne returned and slid into his chair, "while Alieta heals her wounds in New York, and Kyle develops some in Blue Lake." The words sounded awful in her ears as she heard herself say them. It was like listening to someone at the next table. The words sounded suggestive and seductive. They sounded like something Wayne would say.

He let it pass. Was that his charm? How he knew when to let things pass? Maybe he was handsome, charming and harmless. A spaniel in collie's clothing. She felt drunk and silly and warm and wanted to laugh at the image in her mind. Wayne was saying, "Yes. She's not much for fights, but she recovers from them in style. It's not always New York though. San Francisco, L.A., Buenos Aires, London." The locales slid off his tongue like someone who had been to those places and many more. She felt small town, sheltered, and dull. Warm and lovely too. "Does Kyle fight well?"

"He fights quietly. Our fights are short, but our memories are long. We're both way too sensitive."

Gail could feel Wayne's well conditioned body though his clothing and hers as they danced. There were a few other couples scattered about the lounge tables. Judging by how they isolated themselves, they probably weren't married either. To each other. There were also a few salesmen sitting lonely and frustrated at the bar. Watching them dance. Getting hot watching them dance. Or maybe they were ministers. Just trying to tithe one on. She laughed lightly.

"What's funny?" Wayne breathed in her ear. "My dancing? It's not supposed to be funny. It's supposed to be sexy."

"I'll let you guess which one it is," Gail said. She felt his hand slide down her back. "Better not or everyone will know we're not married."

"To each other," he reminded her, pressing her into him. His legs were lean and muscular.

"Oh," she said, "Oh, yes. That."

"You know," he said, sitting on her bed in her room sipping the beer he'd brought along from the lounge, "you're innocence is very attractive."

"Translation," she demanded, seated in the desk chair, her hand stirring the drink she'd brought. "How'd I get to be this old and stay so naive?" She crossed her legs at the knee.

"No, no, no," he insisted, waving his bottle, his words beer-slurred.

"Yes, yes, yes. I am. I'm small-town born, small-town bred, still small town when I hit the bed. Live in a small house near a small town, and I raised a small family not at all," she insisted, her thumb and forefinger forming a zero. "Small, small, small. That's me. In your nutshell."

"Per-haps," he hiccupped. His dimple drooped with the effects of the many beers he'd consumed between dances, trips to the rest room, and intense attention to her. They'd left the lounge at one a.m., one more drink for each in hand. He hadn't mentioned his room or hers. He'd just followed her into hers.

She wanted to think, why am I here. But she knew why. This experience tuned every fiber in her. It felt exciting and dangerous. She'd never been anywhere or done anything remotely like this. Even in his present state – and maybe because of hers – the man looked incredible.

"I," Wayne announced, "am going to have one more swallow of this beer . . . because that's all that's left in the bottle." His face fell to alert and serious for a moment, startling Gail almost as much as the thrill she felt when his hand fell onto her knee. "I want you to know and believe that I ordinarily don't do these things or behave this way. I wouldn't want to offend you for anything."

He waved the beer bottle with his other hand. "And I am incredibly drunk. So," he held the bottle in front of his chest, "I must warn you that as soon as I swallow the last drop of this wunnerful brew, I," he thumped his chest with his pointer finger, "am going to take off every stitch of clothing I have. You may wish if you watch." She giggled again like a schoolgirl. "And I would so much wish that you would do likewise." His grin was full of lust, but there was no leer.

So she watched him take off his tie and shirt. He was as hard and muscular as he'd felt on the dance floor. "I have to visit the rest room," she said. His countenance sagged into an exaggerated pout. She couldn't tell if that look was genuine, but it sure wasn't alluring. "No, really, I do," she assured him. His face relaxed into its previous pose.

Calling it a need for privacy rather than time, she pulled the bathroom door shut. Then she peered at her face in the bathroom mirror. Her cheeks were flushed from the alcohol consumption, but it was her blue eyes she needed to see. She had to find out what she was thinking, what she was doing here, what she'd be doing to her life if this evening progressed.

She undid one button on the white cotton blouse she'd changed to when they'd arrived, and then another, watching her eyes for signs of doubt. But how could her mind deliver the message to her eyes as clouded by alcohol as it was? Her fingers rested on the third button, then re-buttoned the second. If there was a whatever, it wouldn't begin with her singing solo. Won't Wayne be disappointed! She smiled at the image of his crestfallen face.

Wayne had given in to the sleep that all that beer he'd drunk demanded. He lay sprawled on the bed, legs hanging over the end, having progressed only to unbuttoning his pants before the drinks did him in. She told herself she knew this is the way this night would end when she allowed him into her room. But she couldn't prevent an annoying feeling of disappointment. She would have preferred to make her own decision.

She re-seated herself in the desk chair and allowed her eyes to run the length of Wayne's body. Then she rose from the chair, fumbled in his pants pocket for his room card, grabbed her suitcase and headed for the door. If she was going to wreck her marriage, it wouldn't be by riding down the tracks with a drunken engineer.

Whether she'd lingered just long enough or a moment too long was a question that demanded no answer. Just as she opened the door, he snorted and then moaned, "Gail, Gail, Gail." Then he passed gas, made clicking sounds with his lips, and lapsed into deeper slumber.

❖   ❖   ❖

The snow departed late the next afternoon, but the cold winds creating the huge drifts persisted into the evening. Gail called Kyle around noon, telling herself she should have called the night before. She was relieved when he told her the storm had crunched into Blue Lake at about the same time she'd pulled into the motel parking lot. He furnished an excuse for her when he said he'd heard on the radio that quite a few lines in the area had been disabled by the wintry blast.

Gail had little desire for drinking in the motel lounge that night. Wayne's thirst was also more measured. It had apparently taken something out of him when he awoke alone and figured out he'd fallen asleep with Gail watching him last night. He didn't bring up the previous evening and neither did she. She was sure his ego was bruised. His demeanor suggested she'd won and he'd lost. Gail was uncertain of that. She was certain that she had come away with small secrets to savor and had been saved from the guilt that could have accompanied them.

Patty Light

Mr. Hunter,

As is not often the case, the lights are on all over this house. There is a ceiling light on in the kitchen. The end table lamp in the front room is lit. The lamp that sits on the night stand on the right side of the double bed in the other bedroom is on so you can see its light through the back window if you are stumbling around our backyard on a stormy night and want to be guided to our back door. You wouldn't be able to open it though. The doorknob is broken, and the door is double bolted. You would have to smash the door down to enter. I wouldn't recommend it anyway because each of the three wooden steps leading up to it is weak and you could easily fall through and break your ankle. The little desk lamp in my bedroom is on, but it always is when I'm in here and awake, so I can read or sit at this desk and write.

The house is quiet. The house is almost always quiet. You won't hear music in this house or the blaring of a TV set. We don't have a TV set. I have a small portable radio with earphones that my mother gave me some years ago, but it's never on unless I'm using the earphones. So you won't hear music unless I'm wearing the earphones and you put your ear right next to mine, so you can hear the tiny little spill-over of sound that I'm not using up. But nobody gets that close to me. So you won't hear music in this house. I rarely listen to it anyway. I'd rather hear the birds in summer or the wind in winter, the skittering leaves in autumn or the rain washing the roof and walls and lawns and sidewalks and world clean in the spring.

So this house is quiet. Quiet as a tomb.

The house is even quieter tonight except for the storms raging outside and within. It wasn't as quiet earlier. A friend was here who would fill the house with laughter if I would let him. I want to let him, but I can't. I never have friends over. But a friend was here tonight and I had to let him be as close as I could stand because, even though I wasn't wearing earphones and the radio wasn't on, I couldn't stop him from hearing how sad and jarring my music is and my friend couldn't stand to just sit and watch my heart breaking.

I know I've told you many times that what I write is what I write. I don't want to explain it, I don't want to be asked about it, I don't want you to share it with anyone else, and I don't want you to read anything into it. After all that, I wonder how you can stand to read it at all.

I know you think I'm good at it because your little notes tell me so, and because it's in your eyes when we have conferences. You think that I'm a poet, an artist with words. So do I. I like to be thought of that way and to think of myself that way. It lifts me above the life I live and the loneliness of living it. You and Mr. Baker and the other teachers reward my rising and being the best me I can be.

When I write, I never know what my pen is going to put on paper, and I think that's exciting, sailing into the unknown, my pen tugging me along like a child clinging to a kite string in April winds. I do know it takes me places I would not know how to go to otherwise. But sometimes it scares me.

I'm glad I wrote the cat story. But that family was a scary one to visit. When I left them, I felt sad and afraid and angry. I didn't know why then and I still don't. Then I didn't want to know. But now I do. Because there's something terribly wrong with me.

I want to quit writing about that. I want to write about how a snowflake must feel being whipped by a howling wind like the one tonight. But I can't do that right now. Even if I mask myself as a snowflake shredding into a drift, I'll leave you guessing what I'm really writing about and I'll become cold as that wind.

So instead I'll tell you that Ms. Amy Lowell was not wrong about patterns. I will tell you that my life has had many patterns within which it has been lived. The first ended when my father and brothers left with all of the threads unraveled and that pattern ripped to pieces. The second involved cycles of holidays and summers at my grandparents' farm in the southwestern part of the state. That one was buried at two funerals within a year. The third one is the one I'm living now. It is interwoven with long silences, brief but bitter storms, and being alone. Only the patterns of school have made life bearable.

Then Mr. Strand came by one day and offered a whole new design to lay atop all those patterns. The design looks so beautiful. I see it as pure white overlaying a background as deep and rich as the night sky. The new design lifted everyone. Everyone was so positive that the new design would work if we worked for it. I always had, and suddenly she seemed to be too. I saw hope in her eyes and relief that our lives weren't ruined after all.

But now another pattern has been ripped to shreds. I could sense it all the way home. I wanted to pretend the cold was the wind, but it wasn't. I knew as soon as I saw that the driveway contained only snow. I knew when I noticed my grandmother's pincushion with all of those ugly stickpins puncturing it. I knew it when I ran upstairs and found the empty plastic bottle.

I knew it, and I shouted out a truth about her I never wanted to tell to my friend or anyone. Or to even think it.

That's why I couldn't stop crying.

Mr. Hunter, the world is full of lonely people. I don't think I'm special in that regard. I watch people and I listen to them and even the ones who clump together clump together to escape loneliness. Some are nasty and cold and resentful to Mr. Baker because they agreed to be like that, and then they don't think they're lonely because they all think and feel the same thing. So if somebody has to be lonely and the target of scorn so they won't be, why, it might as well be Mr. Baker.

Right now the wind is blowing a million miles an hour and the house is creaking and groaning like it would like to fall over and I am the only one in it. When the pattern was in place, I was used to days like this and I learned not to be bothered, to think about other things, to do other things. But that pattern is ripped apart and I'm sitting here pretty much half-crazy. I want to hug and be hugged and I can't. I want to love and feel loved, but I hardly know how love feels. I have worked so hard and so long trying to be someone's savior, or at least someone's reason for going on. And now that has blown away in this wicked wind. Now I know I can't save anyone. Now I know I have to worry about saving myself.

Mr. Hunter, I am afraid. I am terribly lonely. I am struggling not to tear this paper out of my journal and crumple it up so you won't know who I am and won't have to carry the burden I'm placing on you. I hope I don't. I do not want to disappear. I want to survive.

I need help, Mr. Hunter. I need you to know all of this so you can help me find the help I need. I do not want to live like this anymore. It's too lonely and I'm too cold.

P.L.

Kyle Hunter

Kyle Hunter drove his truck home as soon as school let out. Someday when Gail made them rich and famous, they really would have to upgrade. Not that they'd get rid of the car. Heavens! Never! It would become his car. She could get whatever she wanted. The truck could sit beside the garage and admire the other vehicles and haul an occasional load of wood or some future purchase. Right now the lightness of the truck bed was making it fishtail all over the road. It wasn't so much going in the ditch that Kyle feared. There was plenty of snow to cushion a slide. It was the thought of shoveling out or walking home that gave him pause.

Nevertheless the truck, faithful and under-appreciated as an old dog, slipped and slid its way into the driveway of their country house. Kyle parked it on the side of the garage less likely to receive the brunt of the wind, leaving the garage for Gail if she made it this far. That was doubtful. But sure as shootin' if he put the truck in the garage, she would.

He made himself a hamburger and bean dinner, after which he settled on the sofa with the few papers he'd brought home to correct. The phone rested on the kitchen table. He expected Gail to call at any time to let him know he wouldn't see her until tomorrow.

She didn't though. Eventually he switched on the radio to discover the storm had downed scattered power and telephone lines in both the central and northern parts of the state. That explained the phone's silence.

He needed to do some reading anyway. He seldom read anything these days except student papers and assignment-related materials. If he did, he and his wife would never talk. He chose a book of poetry by Edna St. Vincent Millay. If he was going to tell the kids to read poetry, he should do more of that himself. Later he picked up *Black Elk Speaks* simply because he loved reading it. He reread the vision quest chapter, the howling wind forming an appropriate sound track.

Then he picked up a pen and opened the journal in which he never wrote as much as he should and sat at the kitchen table. He turned on the light next to the phone and tried writing a bit of poetry of his own. Nothing came for a while as he stared at the phone. Then he muttered aloud as he was apt to do when he was home alone, "Since I can't take my eyes off you, I might as well write about you, little fella."

Little phone.
Big power.
I long to hear her voice
Singing my name across the miles,
But all you offer is silence.
This time, too,
It must be true,
The lines are iced and down.

Kyle was not displeased with the product. It said what he had to say. He put the pen down and moved to the picture window. The night was dark, but the snow was phosphorescent as it slanted across his field of vision. The wind vibrated the windows and doors. Its howl sent a thrill through him.

He stood at the window for a long time, then stretched and headed for the bathroom to brush his teeth. Gail wasn't going to be here tonight. Her side of the bed would remain cold.

The storm had not abated by morning. The snow was lessening, but the wind was fierce. They wouldn't be working on phone lines in this weather.

Kyle knew it was a fool thing to do, but he decided to go cross-country skiing. He was drawn to wind, no matter what its texture, and he loved the purity a snowstorm furnishes and the drifts and eddies the wind sculpts. It was an edgy thing to do, cross-country skiing alone in a storm, but anticipation defeated common sense. He pulled on his thermal underwear, sweater and jeans. His ski boots awaited by the door. He wound a wool scarf around his neck, pulled his stocking cap low over his forehead, and headed out into the back yard, which was more protected from the wind.

Nevertheless, the drifts there were still formidable. He had to hop and plow to get to the garage where he kept the skis. The wooden doors of the aged structure were pretty well blocked. Kyle scooped and kicked enough away so that he was able to pry the left door far enough to slide inside.

The garage had windows, so it was light enough for him to see. His skis and Gail's leaned against the shelves that ran the length of the front. He seized the green klister tube and waxed his skis and hers. Maybe she'd want to go tomorrow or this weekend. He carried his skis out to the protected side of the garage and snapped the toe clips with his poles. Then he headed toward the woods where years ago he'd hacked a trail that started at the edge of the yard.

The beginning of the trail was obliterated, but he'd skied it a million times so he had no trouble spotting it. Getting there was another matter. Some of the snow had packed hard. Some was soft as a pile of feathers, and he sank deep into the white. By the time he reached the trees, the wind had painted the left side of his body white, and he'd worked up a sweat. Perhaps this idea was crazy. But once he entered the woods, he was more protected. He did not expect to ski far. He was out here to experience the storm.

It turned out to be a good idea. The wind was moving everything. The pine groves were laden with snow pluming constantly from their wind-danced branches. The naked birch trees creaked and groaned in the force of the wind. Far above the skier, trees, and blowing snow, the clouds raced across the sky. The world was alive and in motion. There was no time when he wasn't touched by the wind, and there was no time when he managed anything like a glide. But he was invigorated by his effort as his senses absorbed the day.

By the time he was leaning his skis against the work shelves, it was noon and he was worn, but happy.

The house felt incredibly warm when he reentered it. He doffed his clothes in the bathroom, showered, pulled on jeans and a sweatshirt, and wandered into the main room. The answering machine's red bulb was steady as Red Howard's personality. Either the lines were down . . . well, of course the lines were down. Who in the world would be out killing themselves in this wind just so Kyle Hunter could say hey to his wife?

Gail interrupted his lunch of canned soup, crackers, and two slices of wheat bread when she called. She affirmed that the storm had hit much of the state, which had resulted in a stay at the Holiday Inn near St. Anne that would need to be extended one more night. She apologized for not calling sooner, but Kyle told her he'd heard about downed lines and guessed the rest of her story. When the brief call terminated, he sat at the kitchen table by the window, sipped his soup, and watched the snow blow by in the fading light.

He opened his journal, picked up his pen, and wrote.

Winter Storm
The temperature's diving, the wind's raging cold.
We've sailed down this trail many times before.
The gliding is easy, but the hills become steep;
Soon only the gale is gathering speed.
We knew it was coming, we watched the clouds form;
Still we've gone looking for the teeth of the storm.
We see how the snow is slanted by wind;
It falls just like that in the deep woods we're in.
Looking ahead, it's a white world we see;
Looking back is looking at a deep mystery.
So once again it is you, it is I,
The clouds and the snow and the wind in the pines.
Is it thrilling or chilling to be where we are?
Will we go on half-blind until we've gone too far?
Will we tumble in the tide of the wintery sea?
Will we rise to the surface, just you and just me?
Will we sink to a stop at the lip of a ledge
To stand in the storm quite close to the edge;
Or ride on the wind past brinks of the rims
And follow the snow into the abyss . . .

Robert Baker

It was on the first evening of the storm that Robert Baker's emotions began to get away from him.

Living the life of the mole was fine – well, tolerable – as long as it was a choice. The afternoon of the storm was tolerable also. For a long time he watched from his window as the wind drove waves of white, and drifts clogged the streets. For a while he'd reveled in the storm. As darkness grew, his sense of isolation did too.

It was towards dark when he thought about Nancy. How good it would be if she was with him right now, how womb-like, safe and intimate these three rooms would be, how intensely they would hold one another! They'd stand at the window, she leaning back against him sipping wine, he setting his glass on the sill so he could wrap his arms around her and feel and smell her closeness. Eventually they'd return to the table and talk of happenings in each other's lives, the wine warming them, cocooned in compassion for one another. After a time, they'd retire to the bedroom and complement the wild event beyond the walls.

Yes, he missed Nancy. He should have married her right after finishing college. They'd talked about that, but agreed that it would be best to experience their own dreams for a while before merging them. Who knew his would turn out badly? Would that have been the case if she were with him? Would his disillusionment have been diluted if she'd been here to listen and support him through the nightmares?

He wanted to pick up the phone and talk to her. He had the phone in his hand before he realized he had no idea what her phone number was. He'd never asked! Or given her his! He could call her parents, but that idea seemed embarrassing. He imagined himself saying, 'Hello, I'm Robert Baker. I was at your house quite a few times over the years necking on the couch with your daughter while we watched TV in the rec room. But, hey, that's not why I'm calling. I'm calling because I was such a morose drag when I last saw her at Christmas that we never even exchanged phone numbers or addresses. I didn't supply many details about my life to her at that time, but I sure would like to now. No, no, no, it wasn't that. It was because I felt like such a failure. So I mostly sat in your rec room with my arms wrapped around myself even though she would have listened to every word I said. But I sure wouldn't do that now. I've got this pile of words tumbling all over my brain. I sure would like to share them with her now. Just a second, Sir, or is it Ma'am, please give me Nancy's phone number. I know she still cares for me. I could tell by the way we kissed when we were necking on your sofa the day after Christmas. It was like the old days, maybe even better because it had been so long."

Nope. Bad idea, that one.

Then he thought about calling his parents. That notion produced a burst of laughter. Call his parents? His mother could have been Browning's Pippa in a former life. If the poet were alive now, the poem's title would be "Rita Runs By" instead of "Pippa Passes". And his father could have been the poet himself. He'd felt that 'all is right with the world' way every day of his life. His ascent to his present status in the community had been steady, easy, and pain free as far as Robert could tell. He and his mother were the only two people he knew who lived truly untroubled lives. Well, Robert had, too, until his father helped him fly from their nest into this thicket of thorns. Their problem was they had no concept of how to deal with people who had problems. No wonder they were so happy. The best they would do is to assure him that nothing is that bad and everything will be all right.

So he put down the phone and returned to the window to watch the snow drift under the streetlights, and wondered why he'd decided to give up on drinking. Oh, yeah, it was because it never made him feel better for more than eight minutes and seemed to lengthen his worst moods toward endless, leaving nothing changed, his breath bad, and his stomach churning.

It occurred to him that he could call Kyle Hunter, but he remembered Kyle telling him his wife was scheduled to return from the Cities. In the best-case scenario, she'd arrived before the storm, and they were living the scene he'd imagined. In the worst, Kyle was waiting by the phone for her call or talking to her long distance. If none of that was occurring, Kyle probably had little desire to pick up his phone and find out it was Robert Baker whining in his ear, not Mrs. Hunter cooing.

❖   ❖   ❖

On the second night of the storm Robert Baker went stir crazy.

He'd spent the entire day reading the pile of papers he'd carried home in his oversized brief case yesterday. By five o'clock, he couldn't bring himself to read one more. By seven o'clock he'd eaten his wieners and beans dinner, reread the next two assignments in the newer lit book, and was back to staring out the window.

Robert couldn't stand the silence any longer. He couldn't stand the thought of watching his tiny TV by himself. He couldn't stand this apartment two minutes more. His head and chest and arms and legs were tingling, almost dancing, with nervous energy. So he wrenched his sheepskin jacket out of the closet, pulled a stocking cap over his head, stuffed a scarf around his neck, slipped on his boots and clattered downstairs into the night.

The wind was hurling the snow. But it was a silent night if you were referring to people and cars. No snowplow had ventured forth.

He walked three blocks to the corner under the bank sign and turned directly into the wind. It cut through every inch of his body, but, strangely, he stopped shivering. The snow on the sidewalk was thigh high, but he was exhilarated as he plowed through it. There's no understanding me, he thought. This is stupid. I feel great.

He trudged three more blocks past the blackened windows of stores at the lower end of the business district. Each hard-won step marched him further from the high school. Maybe if he pushed far enough, he'd finally exceed the length of its shadow. In fact if he took a left turn at the next corner, the shadow would be falling in one direction, and he'd be headed in another. He'd outfox the monster for once.

He did so and encountered an enormous drift climbing the brick wall of a building at a forty-five degree angle. He imagined himself placing his gloved hands together and diving into the deepest part, burrowing to the bottom, and awaiting the dreamy release said to accompany freezing to death. Later when their snow blowers struck the frozen substance of his once was, and they saw the peace he'd finally achieved, then they'd be sorry.

Sorry to see they'd always miss what they'd missed. Or. They'd take the frozen chunk blocking their progress, toss it into the back of the garbage truck and head for the landfill. Most likely.

"That is crazy! I am crazy!" he shouted into the wind. Then the quaking returned with such force his teeth beat against each other. The accumulated cold that had wreathed and waited for him clamped onto every inch of his skin. He turned and scurried back around the corner. The wind was so strong it sent him careening up the quickly filling path he'd created minutes ago. His exhilaration disappeared.

A block from his apartment, Robert spied the only other person he saw on his ridiculous journey. Whoever it was had been walking on the same side of the street as he, but was now crossing in an obvious attempt to avoid contact. It was hard to tell from the distance and in his frame of mind, but the figure appeared to be dressed in black. But then everything appeared to be black or white on this stormy March night.

Frank Marin

Frank Marin was wired. If he'd stayed at home until his parents arrived from work, a verbal brawl would have ensued. He never thought he'd hit his father or his father him, but Frank hadn't been this agitated in a long time. If he and his father did get physical, it had to be for a better reason than this.

So here he was racing through the raging storm, the wind and snow shredding whatever warmth the black jacket had in it. He wished he'd never thought of partying. He wished he'd never thought about drinking and using. He wished he'd never thought about Betts.

The snow was thigh deep on all roads and sidewalks. Why did he think Brady's would be open tonight? Why did he think someone would be waiting inside the alley door to let underage drinkers slip in for a quick exchange of bucks for booze? Who would be crazy enough to chase down a bottle or six pack on a night like this?

Frank Marin, for one.

Brady's was several blocks beyond the main business district, situated in a group of old brick buildings that contained cheap apartments on the second floors, an adult business, a pawn shop, and Brady's on the ground floors. He hadn't been to Brady's, but he'd heard that they sell to underage drinkers.

He plowed through the drifts in the alley. The side door was reachable, so he tried the handle, but the door was locked. The anxiety that had driven him here seized his mind. He hadn't risked being frozen to death to end this journey empty-handed. What did they care? There'd be no cops cruising, and they'd make a few bucks off him. So he entered through the front door.

The place smelled of stale booze and cigarettes. He stood just inside the door shaking off snow and looking around the room. Two men were seated at a table in the corner. Three more eyed him from a table in the middle of the room. Two more were sitting at separate tables fingering the bottles in front of them. The only woman in the place sat with a man in front of the street window. No one was at the bar except the bartender behind it, who called out, "Hey, kid, hey you, yeah, you by the door, come here."

Frank obeyed, patting the back pocket of his jeans to make sure his billfold was there. He sensed the glare in every eye.

"What do you want?" the bartender growled. His pinned nameplate said 'Jake'. "Lookin' for your old man?"

"Uh, no, sir, I just got off work at the grocery store and was supposed to . . . ah . . . meet my buddies from the dorm here."

"I don't think so," Jake said, his hands flat on the bar.

"It's . . . uh . . . true. But they ain't here. So I guess I'd like to buy a bottle of vodka and go."

"I don't think so," Jake responded, his mouth a thick line on his square, lightly bearded face. "I'd ask for your I.D., but there ain't no way you'd pass. If you're gonna pull this crap, practice in front of a mirror. You look like a deer seeing his first headlights."

"But I thought . . . " Frank began.

"We're under new management, kid. Mine. Old Man Brady's had one too many court appearances. Sell or it's the slammer. So he sold. To me. I locked the back door."

"But I thought . . . "

"I want you to get out of here, kid. I could get away with you pourin' booze down your gullet. Ain't no cops checkin' tonight. But with my luck, you'd get crap-faced and end up curled in some snow bank." Jake's heavy gaze nailed Frank in place.

"You ain't no college kid. You look old enough, maybe, but you're scared crapless. Thirsty too. On your way out, look around this room. Only people as thirsty as you. Now get out of here."

"Yeah, get out of here," called a man from the middle table. "I hear yer mommy calling."

"Long as Jake here won't take yer money, why we'd be glad to," offered another. "We'll just grab you by the ankles, turn you upside down and shake it out of you, won't we boys?"

"Ah, come on, boys," said the woman. "Leave him alone. He's cute. He can sit between my knees anytime."

"Get out of here, kid," Jake snarled. "Go home."

Frank wheeled and faced the blotched faces. He wanted to throw twin birds at his tormentors, but instead shoved his hands in his jacket pockets and pulled out his gloves. Then he sauntered to the door. "Hey, little boy thinks he's a big man. Let's screw his head into a snow bank," one of the trio said. Frank yanked the door open, and a gust of wind whooshed snow through it. "Shut the damn door," the same voice shouted. "Damn kids. They're all the same." Frank yanked the door shut behind him.

The wind tore through his jacket and shirt onto his perspiration-laden skin. If he didn't get home in a hurry, he'd be a chunk of ice standing frozen to death in front of this bar. That and the fact that he thought he heard the door creak sent him racing down the sidewalk as fast as the drifts allowed.

He plowed through the main business district shifting from sidewalk to street to sidewalk to find the least resistant paths. He was surprised that the effort felt good, the wind hurling its knives through his clothing felt good, the snow pelting his face felt good. He slowed when he lost his breath, but even the heaving of his chest was pleasurable. By the time he reached his darkened home, he was nearly ecstatic. His blood was pouring through his pounding heart. His skin tingled with life.

He brushed off as much snow as he could outside the house door and doffed his boots and jacket just inside it. A chill rippled his body, and he rushed to the bathroom to shower it away. As he undressed, a glimpse of his face in the cabinet mirror drilled a thrill through him. As he jumped in the shower, he knew Jake the Brake had done him a big favor. He also knew the chill would take its toll.

He was already sick by the time he crawled into bed.

Billy Cloud

Billy Cloud bounced between dreams and hazy wakefulness all night. In either state, his mind overflowed with images of Patty Light, her eyes full of stories he yearned to hear, and she needed to tell. The pill bottle rolling out of her hands. Her tears. The surprise in her eyes when his father produced bags filled with rolls, frozen meat, and canned goods his parents had packed into the duffel bag his dad hauled with him on the snowmobile. Her lonely wave as she watched him and his father leave the yard.

The driven snow was still rat-a-tat-tatting the walls as Billy arose, descended the stairs and wandered into the kitchen. His mother was seated in the breakfast nook thumbing through a book on Native American crafts. His father stood at the stove stirring a pot of oatmeal. The kitchen was warm and homey unlike the Light house.

His mother looked up from her book. "Good morning. Sleep well?"

"Not particularly." He glanced at the clock. "Okay if I use the phone?"

"The President might be calling, but I suppose."

Billy knew Patty would be near the phone unless her mother was home.

"Hello?" she answered.

"It's just me, Billy. Your mother's not home?"

"No, she isn't."

"Call?"

Her voice hardened. "She doesn't when she goes away. She just reappears as though she's been down the street visiting a neighbor."

"Maybe you should call the police now?"

"I don't think so. She's usually gone for three days when she's gone. I wouldn't know where to tell them to look anyway."

"You okay?"

"I'm fine. You know now this isn't the first time. It's just different."

"I could come over . . . or we could."

"Please don't, Billy. It's a blizzard. Then I'd have to worry about you."

"You're sure?"

"Positive. Thank your parents for the groceries. I don't know if I did."

"I will. I want to call you later," Billy stated as he stared out the kitchen window at the white-out the storm was creating, "I want you to call me, too. Even just to tell me you're okay."

"Yes. And yes." The phone fell toward silence, but she retrieved it. "Thank you, Billy. I don't deserve it."

"Yes, you do," he insisted.

She made an effort towards optimism. "I suppose we'd better end this. Who knows? Maybe my mother is trying to call. If she does, it will be the second miracle in two days. I can't explain now. But please believe you helped the first one happen. I'll call, Billy. Goodbye."

He had not hidden the content of his end of the conversation from his parents. He slid onto the breakfast nook bench across from his mother. His father set a bowl of oatmeal in front of him. "You're riding a roller coaster in a snowstorm," he said.

"Accurate observation."

"And will be for awhile, I think."

Billy watched him bring a bottle of milk from the refrigerator. "Your father and I like your friend," his mother assured him as her husband sat beside her. She pushed the bowls of brown sugar and raisins toward him. "She was so grateful when you brought her here. So polite and wide-eyed. She touched my heart. So much joy. So much sadness underneath it."

Billy added the raisins and milk and stirred the cereal. "Any advice?"

"You're sure you want it? You might not like what we say."

"Desperately."

"All right then. Dad, why don't you start?"

"We could be wrong," his father cautioned. "I might have had too much snow on my goggles last night. But it seemed obvious your friend had been crying." Billy nodded. "I'm assuming you were the comforter, not the cause." His son nodded again. "Then I'll press on. Your friend didn't try to hide she'd been crying. To me, that's a compliment to you. But it implies she's literally crying for help. She doesn't have the words yet. But it takes a lot of hurt and a lot of trust to show that much vulnerability."

"The way Dad described her, it seemed plain to me that your friend needs a friend, not a lover right now. That's a hard role to play and an easy one to violate. Think you're up to it?"

"I sure hope so."

"It can be hard to stay by the side of troubled people. If you can't handle that, let her know right away."

"I can handle it."

"I hope so, too. Your friend makes me want to root for her. To hug her."

"Same here. But hugging isn't such a hot idea. That's something else I have to talk to you guys about."

"Hugging?"

"Hugging her. Not even that. Touching her. I mean barely touching her arm or shoulder or back, not that other stuff. Any touch makes her tremble."

"Couldn't be your ethnicity, could it?" his father asked. "Some folks find us exotic and frightening simultaneously. You'll say she's not like that."

"Yes, I will."

"I don't know her well, but I'm inclined to agree," his mother said. "What you described gives me the sense that there are deep and painful issues in that young lady's life. I have an idea about what may be involved, but I'm not going to fill your head with my guesses. I have no right without more knowledge. I do warn you that you're going to have your hands and heart full. You're overflowing already. You'll need to accept that your friend needs help that you can encourage, but you can't supply by yourself."

Billy had that figured out. Helplessness wasn't fun. He spooned the oatmeal into his mouth. "Cereal's cold."

"That's what love does," his father said, scooping up the bowl. "Whoever invented the microwave was in love and darn tired of cold food."

For the duration of the storm Billy and Patty maintained a flow of phone calls. Because she'd had no other communication, the two traded assurances that downed lines might account for the silence.

School resumed Friday at 10 a.m., but only for town kids. The Clouds qualified for country bus service but there was none. Nevertheless, Billy trudged the miles to the school, the after-breath of the storm and his eagerness to see Patty Light invigorating the long trek.

He was waiting at her locker when she arrived shortly before ten. "Hi," she said. Her walk had rouged her face. Her eyes had diamonds he'd not previously seen. "Thank you for calling. I'd have been crazy without that."

"Likewise."

She hung her coat on the hook in her locker and draped her book bag on her shoulder. "I've been writing a lot, so I'm going to give my journal to Mr. Hunter to read." she said, her sparkling eyes delivering the message that more than extra credit was at stake.

"Mind if I walk you to his room?"

"No, but I'd hate to make you late for class."

"Not to worry. When I walked by Mr. Strand, he was telling a teacher not to take attendance until eleven."

"Gosh, I wish they'd do that all the time. It seems like I'm late every morning. Rush, rush, rush. That's me racing down the hall," Patty gushed as the two headed up the stairs. "I'm really glad to be here, Billy. I'm really glad you are too."

"Likewise," he repeated, pleasantly puzzled. For a change, Patty was out-talking him.

When they arrived at Mr. Hunter's room, Billy leaned against the wall inside the door and watched Patty approach the teacher's desk, extract her journal from her book bag and slide it across the desk. The teacher started to shake his head, but she pointed at a paper she'd taped to the journal's cover. She turned and walked the middle aisle to a desk in the back of the room, sat down, looked at Billy, formed an 'O' with the thumb and forefinger of her hand, then offered a small wave.

He returned the wave and strolled toward the science room past the scattered clumps of students in the hall.

After school he rejoined her at her locker. "Mr. Hunter's going to read my journal," she announced. Fear, determination, and relief took turns in her eyes. There was something mighty important written in that journal. He wished she could tell him what it was.

She realized that. "I'd tell you about it, but I can't. I'm afraid if I breathe one word, it won't come true. And I desperately want it to come true."

Patty phoned him Friday evening to tell him her mother called. "She said her car broke down. She tried to call, but the phone lines broke down, too, like we said. She didn't say where she is, but she said they're working on her car, and she'll get home as soon as she can."

Thus extending her daughter's isolation, Billy thought. But he said, "I'm glad she called."

Ed Warrum

Ed Warrum had lived the first four years of his life in a two-bedroom apartment above Pete Warrum's store while Pete "got his feet on the ground". When his wife became pregnant with Ed, Pete dismissed her from clerking in the store with the directive that Ed's early years were her responsibility. He'd take over later. Few who knew the Warrums thought about the sacrifices Ellen Warrum made after Ed's birth. Those who did observed how quiet mother and son were. Pete's friends kidded him that a rough piece of work like him didn't deserve such an obedient family. He'd laugh and explain they were what they were because they knew the consequences if they weren't.

By the time Ed's sister arrived, the store was doing well. Two years later, Pete bought a home in a tonier section of Blue Lake. Some said success and the house that made it visible went straight to Pete's head, but most admired the determination that had enabled him to work the long hours that made the house possible.

Pete didn't rent out the apartment. He didn't need the money, and it gave him a convenient place to take a break and host card games and meetings. As the years passed, he sometimes stayed at the apartment rather than coming home, especially after playing poker or after hosting the town's movers and shakers. It was there he met with those he recruited to run for the school board with him and developed the strategy that culminated in their election. Their strategy was to oppose the bond issue that would have added a classroom building to the high school. Their claim was that too much money would be spent for too little benefit. Their truth was that the bond issue contained nothing devoted to athletic facilities. Endless repetition and advertisements emphasizing the first reason convinced the majority of voters they were right. The bond issue lost, assuring Pete Warrum's status as a man of influence.

❖ ❖ ❖

So it was that as the great March blizzard streamed into the Blue Lake area, Pete sent his son home with the message that the store would be open late to "service the idiots who don't know enough to stock up until snow is up to their waist," and that he would ride out the storm in the apartment.

Ed readily agreed. Despite the counseling session Ed had had with Pastor Barker before the minister left for Nigeria, being around his father still made Ed's teeth clang. He was happy to escape the store even though he had to plow through thigh-high drifts; he was thrilled that the snow whirling through the pines, birches and elms and filling the roads and sidewalks would award his home at least one night's respite from his father's presence.

Ed's mother greeted the message with a thin smile. His sister ducked her head to hide her delight. Ed listened to her dance up the staircase to her room, probably to pray that the forecast of an extended storm was accurate. For this night for sure, Pete Warrum wouldn't be bellowing through the house, only haunting it.

Ed left his mother to her dinner preparations and wandered up the stairs to his room. He stood at the window watching the storm, his heart loving its power to bring peace. Supper was always served at six-thirty. Despite his father's absence, Ed had no doubt that would remain true. His mother was well trained. He was surprised when he heard a persistent knock at his door, and his sister's voice singing, "Dinner is ready." A glance at his alarm clock confirmed that it was only 6:00.

Pete Warrum always dominated the dinner table. Without his presence, Ed's mother was liberated to say that she was "startled at how loud the sound of breathing is." The three diners burst into a raucous laughter Ed could not remember ever hearing in this house. No one could stop until tears were streaming the faces of mother and daughter. Ed impulsively reached for his sister's hand, and it was warm in his own. She stared wide-eyed into his heart, crying, but laughing too, "I love this so much," her voice sang to his ears. She was able to say no more until her emotions ebbed, and she could add, "Mother has something important to tell you."

"Food first," their mother ordered. "Oh, my," she said, "your father's not here so right away I start telling you what to do! It's kind of fun!" That provoked another outburst. "Oh, my," she cried. When the tumult subsided, she said, "We really must eat. This meal will be the most succulent you've eaten in years. When I heard your father wasn't coming home, I poured all my joy into this meal."

Ed stared at his mother. When had he last heard her string together even a short paragraph of words? When had he ever heard a negative word about his father from her? How sick had his father become that his family could be so different, so happy, so free without him?

He set those questions aside so he could fully enjoy this atmosphere and this meal. The three ate like diners at a gourmet restaurant, savoring each bite. His mother was right. The hamburger exceeded the finest steak. The brushed but unpeeled potatoes, the gravy, swimming with mushrooms and sweet onions, the carrots and peas, the freshly baked bread were delicious. All except the bread would have made his father howl in disgust. The main meal consumed, Ed and Jenny's mother brought forth a freshly baked pumpkin pie. This was a Thanksgiving meal celebrated on the Ides of March by a family wombed and made safe by the howling blizzard.

The feast completed, Jenny Warrum suggested softly, "Now, Mother?"

"I think it's a good time," Ellen Warrum agreed, her voice not thin and reedy as it always was in Pete Warrum's presence. She gazed at her children, her eyes sad, but not averted. "Ed," she said, "Do you remember those quiet years we spent in the apartment?" He nodded. "What you probably can't remember is that all those years when everyone thought I was just a mousey little wife, I was also the bookkeeper and business manager for our store. Pete worked hard, but I worked hard, too. The difference was nobody knew that. Whenever you were down for a nap and often long past midnight, I worked on the books, placed the orders, and read the product information. I never talked about that, and it would never cross Pete's mind to mention it.

"As you've grown to know, Pete likes the spotlight and the glory, and taking more credit than he deserves. He could no more do what I did than he could throw a football like you. Because he is what he is, he has nearly wrecked our marriage. He is desperately close to wrecking his son, and his daughter is so far under his radar, she hardly feels like she exists. The situation for all of us is unlivable and unbearable." She paused. Jenny's gaze was fixed on Ed. She had already heard what was being revealed.

"I continued to be the bookkeeper for years after we moved into this house." Her voice was level. "Pete is obsessive. He was obsessed with developing a thriving business, and we succeeded. Since then, Pete – I cannot call him Dad or Father because he is neither to either of you right now – Pete has turned to new obsessions. He bulldozes anything and anyone in his way. He started out with good intentions, but he has become a bad man! I feel awful saying that and awful for helping him become that." The brutal truths made Ed want to recoil, even to defend the man. Right, defend the man I bought a gun to defend myself against. I am crazy. He sat silent waiting for the remainder of his mother's story.

The strain of breaking her silence temporarily drained his mother. So the family listened to the wind roar and watched the snow cascade past the dining room window. "We're going to be snowed in," Ed said. "He won't be coming home tonight, Ma. It's like we're the family in the poem 'Snowbound' Baker had us read. Except they were happy that their father was with them, and we're happy that ours isn't."

His mother resumed, years of imprisoned ideas and emotions finding freedom. "Ed, Jenny, I believe that Pete started out loving us. Then he got it all twisted up. You've seen enough of me shuddering and shaking and saying nothing. You need to know that years ago, I developed a plan I hoped I never had to execute. Pete never paid me for my work, so I paid myself. I opened my own bank account and picked up my statements rather than having them sent to me. Pete never guessed this was going on because he never looked at the books. He knew I was good at it, and he knew our business was thriving. If he had looked, he wouldn't have figured it out. It isn't his talent. When he decided to replace me with Dale Maddail, Dale worked with me. I told him the truth.

"I never spent a penny because I feared I was going to need it someday. Last fall when I saw what was happening, I took action. I found a partially furnished place just beyond the city limits – right across from the Cloud House – that we could rent. Long before you ran away, Ed, I signed the rent-with-option-to-buy agreement and have been making payments ever since."

"I don't know," Ed responded, shocked by his reluctance to consider this change, shocked by how much it felt like betrayal. "Maybe Dad will . . . "

"Maybe Dad won't," Jenny interrupted resolutely.

"I know you're surprised by all of this, Ed. Jenny isn't. Jenny and I have agreed we won't do anything until all of us are sure we want to. But I will tell you this, Ed. This family is imploding, and we are going to become even more damaged than we are. And that includes Pete." She looked hard at Ed. "Living this way is not worth the consequences, and nothing is going to change if everything remains the same."

Still Ed could only manage to say, "I'll have to think about this." He expected more disappointment than he read in either Jenny or Ellen Warrum's faces. Perhaps they knew his father would do or say something that would settle Ed's mind for him.

Pete Warrum sealed the deal almost immediately after his return home Friday evening.

The family was seated around the dining room table, the atmosphere the antithesis of the lightness and freedom of the preceding days.

The meal was eaten in silence. Everything Ed ate had the texture and taste of cardboard. He was sliding his chair back from the table when his father ordered, "Just a second. I want to talk to you."

Ed paused in mid-slide. He couldn't help thinking this is it! This is it! Dad can't ever leave well enough alone! This is it! His hands clenched and unclenched on his knees. His body felt as though it had been plugged into an electrical socket.

Pete Warrum came through in spades.

"I don't like the people you're hanging out with, Ed. When you came into the store with that Injun kid and that Light slut, I almost came down the aisle after you."

This is it, this is it, this is it! his mind shouted. He was amazed at the calmness in his voice when he responded. "I know you don't care for Billy Cloud. I do. But what in the world have you got against Patty Light?"

"That pill head!" his father exploded.

The statement was ludicrous. Ed's words tumbled out of his mouth. "I think you must have mistaken her for someone else. She's one of the best students in school. How would you know anyway? Does she buy pills from your store?"

"Listen, you little smart ass, you know I'm talking about her mother!"

"How would I know that?" Ed's glare flamed toward his father's face. "What about her mother?"

"I just told you! She's a pill head. And a whore. Everyone in town knows that. She's been buying pills from my store for six years."

"That makes her a whore? What does that make you, a pimp?" Ed knew neither could take much more, but he wouldn't let go. "Doctor's prescription, I assume?"

"Yes!" his father shouted, rising from his chair. He pointed a shaking finger at Ed. "But that's none of your damn business! Girl's going to turn out just like her mother! Girls always turn out like their mothers. I don't want you hanging around her! Only white whores hang out with Injuns!"

he finished, thumping his fist on the table, dishes leaping and silverware jangling from the force of the blow.

Ed wanted to pick up his chair and hurl it so hard the force would carry his father through the huge window behind him, glass flying everywhere as he flew through the gaping hole into the frozen wind and snowdrifts beyond.

Instead he focused on his impending freedom. This is it! This is it! He said, "Patty Light is a great girl. Billy Cloud's a great guy. May I go?"

"Get the hell out of my sight!"

Ed whirled out of his chair. But in mid-stride he stopped and whirled around. "Dad, it isn't Injun. It's In-di-an. Better yet, Chippewa or Ojibwa or Anishinaabe or Sioux or Lakota or Dakota . . . "

"Get out!" his father thundered, fingers clenched into fists, face and neck so red Ed thought he might have a heart attack right then and there, his mother disappearing into the kitchen, his sister long since disappeared to her room, her door closed, her silent celebration roaring.

Ed took the stairs two at a time, his mind singing. This is it! This is it! Knowing Jenny's mind and his mother's mind were singing the same song, knowing the wind was singing as it lifted plumes of snow off the drifts it had created and was now reconfiguring beneath the bright and burning stars.

Kyle Hunter

It was Friday morning by the time the storm blew itself away so that school, without bus service, resumed.

It was Friday morning when Patty Light brought her journal to Kyle Hunter's desk and laid it in front of him. He was about to tell her that journals weren't due yet, but the note taped to its cover stopped him from saying anything but, "Sure," and, "Thank you."

It was early Friday evening when Gail Hunter drove solo into the driveway that Kyle had shoveled from road to shed. He'd also hollowed a pathway to the house. When she stepped inside, Kyle was on the phone engaged in an earnest conversation. He gave her a small wave and raised eyebrow, placing his hand over the mouthpiece to say, "Just a minute," and then continued to talk on the phone.

She'd removed her boots and hung her coat in the closet before he finished. "Sorry," he said.

"Student problem?" Gail guessed, sitting down in the on the sofa.

"Yes."

"Which you can't talk about with me."

"I'm afraid that's true. I'm sorry. I missed you." She hoped he wasn't trolling the icy waters in search of a reciprocal statement. "I worried about you."

"I was all right. I wasn't alone," Gail admitted. "Someone from the central office rode with me. I was glad. The roads are bad." A quick blush sped across her face and disappeared.

The face of the party lech flashed into Kyle's mind, but he made no comment. Instead he said, "I am sorry I was on the phone. But the school was too public. So I had to make the call here. I'm sorry. I'm glad you're home."

"I'm just tired and a little crazy, I guess," Gail answered, her eyes sparkled. "I'm glad I'm home too."

Frank Marin

Looking back on it, Frank Marin was impressed with himself. He'd made it through March without a sip of alcohol or a single weed. He hadn't tried to contact his college buddies except for Betts. Betts was trying to make it through the month too, so, surprisingly, they'd talked on the phone lately, encouraging each other to hang in there and promising a pot of gold at the end of the snowbow. It helped that he was aware of his need to keep his job. It helped that Eddie and Albert knew his drinking buddies and spoke of them without respect. It helped that he liked these guys a lot better than them. They accepted him and had no intention of ripping him off.

Then there was that crazy night when he was really thirsty, and he couldn't get what he thought he had to have. He could thank or blame the storm for the episode, but mostly he could thank or blame Jake the Brake.

Frank had returned to work Monday. Eddie and Albert had greeted him warmly and inquired about his health. That felt good. Those guys he hung with could care less. They only cared about his stuff and his bucks.

Betts used to be like that too. But he and Betts had made it all the way through March without drinking or using and had become friends in the process. They'd learned they could make the choice whether to drink or not, use or not. They could take it or leave it. Tonight they were going to take it. They deserved it. Tonight it was time to celebrate.

april

Robert Baker

One night in early April Robert Baker dreamed of Nancy, whose presence might have saved him. He dreamed of how it would be if Nancy was with him now. It was morning in his dream. She was lying in bed and staring at him with the sleepy knowledge that something was very wrong with him, an awareness so alarming that she could not help but express her compassion.

In his dream Nancy sat up in bed and said, "Robert, you don't look well. Why don't you call school and tell them you can't make it today?" He dreamed of Nancy clutching the covers over her chest, pleading, "You're pushing yourself too much, Robert." She threw off the covers. "Let me call the school. You stay in bed, and I'll hold you while you sleep."

Lord, that sounded inviting, just curl up under the covers and continue to dream of Nancy holding him, close and warm and caring, striving to understand. Except even asleep he knew she was all in his head, everything was all in his head, his head and his chest and his stomach and his legs, all tingling now, craving a dance his body would not give them.

"Look, I'm okay," he mumbled in his dream as he headed for the kitchenette of the tiny apartment, too small for two people – too small for one – to live in. "If I'm not man enough to teach, I'll be the first to admit it. Or the last. I just want to get it over with."

He turned in his dream and Nancy was there. He came to her, and they circled their arms around one another. He felt great comfort and then great sorrow because she was not there, and there was no comfort.

His alarm jangled him awake and alone. He seized it and hurled it to the floor. He did not want the dream to end this way. He willed himself back to sleep, willed the return of the dream. In it he left the apartment and was standing on the sidewalk below looking up and waving to her, and she was in the window waving back, empathetic tears gliding down her cheeks, one hand brushing back her long brown hair, her eyes shining with admiration as he continued to battle certain defeat.

Then Robert Baker awoke with a start and sat bolt upright in bed, knowing he'd overslept, knowing he'd pay the price for that. He felt smothered by his covers and flung them away. As he pushed out of bed, he had the sense that clouds were hanging heavy against all the windowpanes in his apartment.

When he reached the bathroom, he stared into the mirror. His reflection assured him that something was happening to him. The skin on his face was too tight against his bones. His eyes were too bright. The realization did not feel like panic to Robert. Just a sensation similar to the one he'd first felt looking out his classroom window the afternoon of the blizzard. It felt like ants, he thought, burrowing under the hairs on his arms and the hairs on his head. The muscles in his chest and stomach seemed to tighten, relax, tighten, relax, of their own volition.

He thought about calling in sick and crawling back in bed with Nancy. Except that Nancy was a dream. "Just a nervous stomach," he told the room. "The usual ailment of the first year teacher," he told the rumpled bed covers. "At least this one." He bent over to retrieve the alarm clock from the floor and saw that its face was a mass of cracks. Still it ticked. He placed it back on the bed stand. Then he went to the closet and grabbed his shirt and pants.

He wandered into the kitchenette as he finished buttoning the shirt. He had no appetite for breakfast. He noticed the shirt was slightly rumpled. He could iron the shirt, but he didn't. He shrugged into his suit coat but left his ties draped over a hook at the end of the closet.

He pulled on his unlined spring jacket, which was shorter than his suit coat, exited his apartment, descended the stairs, and walked out into the April morning. He glanced up at the apartment window, wishing his dream was real, wishing Nancy was standing there.

Robert shook his head and tried to focus on the realities of the morning. The sky was, in fact, an unclouded blue. The scent carried by the light breeze hinted at the advance of spring, but also the uncovering of autumn's decay. The latter brought reminders of the days when his life first flipped on its side. But the scene created by the blue sky, budding trees and white, steepled church down the street evoked images of more pleasant times. He felt tears spring into the edges of his eyes.

"Oh, God, this will never do," he muttered aloud. He brushed at his eyes with his ungloved hands. Having done so, he glanced about in fear that someone had observed this action, heard his words. It was one thing to hold solitary conversations with himself in his apartment and quite another to be standing on a public sidewalk babbling and at the brink of tears.

His gaze swept right, straight ahead, and left. A block away towards school stood a tall boy in blue jeans, his letterman's jacket buttoned to his Adam's apple, his head tilted to the right. It was a moment that felt like an hour. The boy dropped his hands into his jacket pockets, lowered his head, and shuffled toward the school.

Because of who it was, Robert Baker had no trouble convincing himself that he had sensed, if not seen, a sneer on Ed Warrum's face before the boy turned away, that the athlete's shoulders had been shaking with low laughter as he ambled toward the school. Though he'd not seen him talking to anyone other than Patty Light and Billy Cloud recently, he accepted the probability that Ed Warrum would delight in regaling his fellow students with descriptions of the scene he'd witnessed.

Robert stood stock still for several moments as though the concrete had swallowed his feet. Then, as if awakening from a reverie, he rediscovered that he was standing on the sidewalk staring hard, but vacantly, at groups of students descending from yellow school buses or emerging from cars, and that they were circling into small groups to talk about the man standing alone in the middle of the sidewalk on this April morning that had originally offered the false hope of spring.

Robert wanted to race back to his apartment. But that would do no good. It would be useless. Better just to face the music. Do the dance.

Anyway it was his fault. He'd shot down the earlier hours by refusing to leave a hopeless dream, blowing his pattern of walking to school under the cover of darkness and entering long before the students arrived.

There was no choice now. Just do it. Get it over with.

He coughed and walked toward the school. He walked past the intent faces gathered near the doors, his eyes straight ahead, his mind seeing a hundred faces screwed into attitudes of ridicule and disdain, his ears hearing the "He's nuts" and the "What a jerk" and the "that guy's a bastard'" whispers the students were blazing to one another. Listening to the taunts drove his heart into his stomach.

He wrenched one of the auditorium entrance doors open and entered the school, the students funneling in behind him like a horde of cats trailing a lone mouse.

They peeled back on the second floor as Robert Baker began his ascent up the third when Superintendent Anderson stepped out of his office and shouted, "What are you doing up here? You know you're not supposed to be up here until 7:50! Get back downstairs or go outside!"

I don't know how much more of this I can take, Robert thought as he reached into his jacket pocket for his room keys. The admittance bell rang and he could hear the school begin to fill on the floors below as he unlocked the door. He willed the ants to cease their scurrying as he crossed the room to open the curtains.

"Good morning, Mr. Baker," he heard a chorus of voices behind him sing. He turned and four of his freshmen were striding across the room to join him at the window. "Isn't it a beautiful day!" Alice enthused.

Patty Light

Dear Desired Help,

Desperation enabled me to turn all of my journals over to you.

Watching you – Miss Elaine Stafford, Social Services Psychologist – reading my journals makes me feel naked. It feels like this is a big mistake that I'm responsible for. That's why I asked your permission to seat myself by the window where I could search the trees for buds. I need to believe in spring right now.

This is the second of the twice-a-week sessions that you, Elaine – "please call me Elaine" – and I have agreed to in order for me to "immerse in my recovery." The first session was devoted to "developing trust." This second one focused on you rereading my journals because I developed a zipped lip after making what you called the "surprising admission" that I have almost no friends.

"I'm different," was my explanation.

"In what way?" you questioned. When you ask questions, your piercing green eyes laser on my face, your gaze never wavering.

"Because I am no one's friend," I answered, telling you nothing, wishing you would at least blink.

You said, "You're very bright; your teachers all wrote that. They all wrote that you're an excellent student, thinker, and writer. All of that excellence might set you apart, but there should be a core group you would bond with. Patty, my hunch is that this fact has nothing to do with school, and a lot to do with your life outside the school. So can we talk about your home?"

I managed a physical description of the house. I felt exactly like J. Alfred Prufrock wriggling on a wall, especially when you asked, "How about the people? Your parents?" My lips zipped.

You gave in to my silence. "Okay," you said, "this is a difficult subject. Since writing is so natural for you, I'm asking you to write about your home and the people in it before our next session."

I must have had a terrified look in my eyes as you told me many thoughts and images in my journal feel like revelations to you, but they are presented in masks and metaphors. You asked that I write straightforwardly as I can and avoid placing metaphors between us. Your green gaze felt like searchlights seeking my secrets. You said that doing this could be key to saving myself from years, maybe a lifetime, of sorrows, angers and regrets.

And now I am about to do what you have asked me to do, Miss Elaine Stafford. I am going to trust my pen to tell the truth and you to help me do something with it. I have been sitting still as a stone for twenty minutes since I wrote that last paragraph, staring at this blank page. I am terrified. But here goes. Everything!

Do you know how much this frightens me? I do. But my mind is screaming for help. How can you help me if I can't help myself!

I don't mean to mask my thoughts so that only the Mr. Hunters of this world find meanings I hardly realize I'm expressing. But he is why I am writing these words to you. He honored my trust and relayed my cry for help. He has enabled me to get to this point.

So. The only other person in my home is my Mother. So I must write about her. My Mother, my Mother, my Mother!

First things first. I must thank her for her crazy absence during the snowstorm. I must thank God for the storm that kept her out of our house, but not out of my mind. Those days made me realize our house is as silent and devoid of life when she isn't in it as when she is.

What I just wrote howls with hurt! To express her with these words feels like betrayal! Even though her being gone and my only friend being there forced me to express a thought more evil I didn't know I was thinking until it leapt from my mouth!

Nor could I believe how hard it was to accept the comfort my friend offered and I desperately needed!

And how I tremble every time – EVERY TIME – anyone touches me or even wants to touch me! Every fiber in me screams for me to pull away!

I have veered down a side road. I always seek side roads when I don't want to go where I have to go I must focus on MY MOTHER!

If she hadn't unexpectedly disappeared, and broken the pattern of her going aways and coming backs, would I have ever asked for help? Is her suffering the means of my salvation? Isn't that a terrible price to pay! Will I accept this chance? I pray to every angel that I do!

MY MOTHER! My Mother is terribly lonely. She never got over my father and brothers leaving us. Her life stopped the minute my father's car disappeared with my brothers trapped inside. She turned off all the lights and pulled the shades and that is the way we have lived ever since.

Do you know how much courage it took for her to talk to Mr. Strand? To make it possible for ME to find a the light she's lost? Do you know how hard she tried for a while to live the way people do in the real world so I'd recognize real life when I saw it? So I'd have HOPE!

Of course she became afraid and returned to hopelessness. But she showed me I didn't have to live there too.

My Mother. As I think of her now, I think of her racing into storms over and over and returning battered and bruised inside herself over and over.

That is the way her life and my life have been since my father and brothers left, and she began bringing home the little bottles that lead her life.

My mother. Most of the time she's silent. But sometimes she wakes up shouting in her room, shouting down the stairs, shouting in the kitchen. I can hardly stand that! Then I hate myself for being glad for the pills that take her back to bed. I hate myself because I love going to school where beauty and life and hope exist. Because I get to see the sun. Because it's not home.

I know that she's sick and miserable. Sometimes I think if I can love her enough, it might not be true. But I can't believe there's that much love left in my heart.

I'm going to stop writing. I feel like I've been driving a semi down a mountain road full of hairpin turns and the brakes are grinding and smoking. I have survived but I am so tired right now. I don't want to think about fulfilling the promise that next time you won't be just reading my journal, that I'll be reading it aloud to you so that my voice is delivering my words to both our ears. You said that is as important as it is difficult. I don't want to think about that. All I want to do is sleep. And I will. As soon as my heart stops pounding, the throbbing in my head goes away, my hands stop trembling.

P.L.

Sam Strand

"Look at me, son, when I'm talking to you," Sam Strand snapped, "not out the window!"

Frank Marin's gaze fell on every picture on the wall, every chip in the paint, every book in the bookcase before he glanced at Sam's face and settled on his chin.

Sam grasped the pile of colored slips on his desk in his right hand and thrust them where the boy was looking. "These are referrals. These came from the teachers through the counselors to my desk." He knew the boy was finally with him when Frank involuntarily flinched. The flinch made Sam sad. This boy was all show, but his show was driving everyone crazy.

"The counselors send copies of teacher referral slips to me. They send me three colors. The blue one informs me that a student is being referred too often. The yellow tells me the counselors are nearing the end of their rope. The red slip says the rope has broken.

"There are multiple slips from almost all of your teachers this semester. Every one reveals you're not turning in your work, you're failing quizzes and tests, and your behavior is detrimental to the classroom. I've talked to these teachers. Every one said that following a promising rally in March, you've fallen apart in April. Every one says you've added disrespect and bad language to the mix and become the class clown as well as the class dolt."

Sam Strand shook his head. He couldn't believe what he'd said to Frank Marin. He'd always believed his duty was to rescue, to resuscitate, to redirect. To help. Not to tear down. What was happening to him?

"I apologize for that image." Sam sighed. "What's your story?"

"My dad beats me," the boy said, a smirk playing his lips.

"Then I'm going to call Social Services," Sam reached for the phone. "Your father fooled me when I met with him and your mother. I thought both were good people." He lifted the receiver. Sweat beads littered the youth's forehead. "It's the law. If I hear about or suspect abuse, I must report it to Social Services, the police, or both."

"I was being funny," the boy mumbled.

"You're sure? We can have Social Services or the police investigate."

But Sam was sure he'd heard the truth. "Let's start over. To what do you attribute the change in behavior that has made you a detriment to every classroom you occupy?" The boy stared at him blankly. "Let me rephrase. Why have you shifted from being an improving student to being an obnoxious jerk?" Good Lord, Sam thought, I've never, ever . . .

"Kids like it."

"Maybe a few bottom feeders do," Sam suddenly felt tired and sick of his job. He'd never used terms like these to describe students in his entire educational life. This year was grinding him to a nub. "I doubt the majority think highly of it," he amended.

"Check it out," the boy said, an insolent grin snaking his face. "Everyone's laughing."

"Did it cross your mind they're laughing at you, not with you?" Sam pressed. The question sent a flash of hurt into the boy's eyes. "Often when we see a student underachieving or showing sudden shifts in behavior, we discover that the student or someone in the family is involved with alcohol, drugs or both. Is that part of your problem, son?"

"Kids say they're making you quit at the end of this year," Frank sneered.

Even though Sam knew – knew! – this attack was a diversion, he couldn't stop himself. "In your dreams. I'd advise you to drop that line."

"Didn't say I said it. Said the kids did."

"Let's get back to you," Sam ordered. "I'm going to tell you that there is help available if drugs and alcohol are a problem for you or your family, and that I'll help you get that help. So I'm going to ask you point blank, are you involved with the use of drugs and alcohol?"

"Against the law."

"Then why are you giving your teachers grief and disrupting so many classrooms?"

"They suck." Frank's eyes refocused on Sam's chin. "You want to hit me, doncha?"

Sam slapped his hands against the top of his desk. The boy winced and leaned back in his chair. "I never hit a student in my life," Sam exploded, "and I sure as heck wouldn't waste a punch on you." Hooked again! He couldn't think of any way to get through to Frank.

"I think you want me to kick you out of school. Why is that, Frank?"

"Not son?" the teenager retorted. "I'm disappointed."

The principal sat back in his chair. "Do you know what, son?" Sam said. "Before I grant your wish, I'm going to gift you with a few observations." The boy dropped his head.

"I think you're disappointed in yourself. I've been to the place you inhabit these days. That was a scary place for me because there was no telling how far I'd go to get what I wanted. That's why I think you need help, and that's why I'm offering to participate. It will be better for everyone, especially yourself, if you accept."

"You don't know nothin'."

Sam sighed. "I do. One thing I know for sure, Frank, is that you've given me no choice. I'm suspending you for four days. I'm hoping you'll use that time to think about where you're headed. I know if you come back with the same attitude, you'll be out of here again. That suspension could end your school year. I don't want to have to go that far, and I hope you don't either.

But I'm not going to have you here wreaking havoc."

Good lord, Sam thought, that sneer is frozen. "Go to you locker, get what you need, and leave the premises. Your assignments will be mailed to you today. If you linger in or around the school, the police will be called, and you will be arrested for trespassing and loitering."

"You . . . " Frank started, but Sam stopped him.

"I've heard too much already. Get out of here."

Frank Marin tried saunter as he exited the office. When he reached the door, he wrenched it open. He was going to slam it shut. Sam Strand barked, "Don't even think about it!" Frank's hand leapt from the handle as though it was electrified.

Sam picked up the phone on his desk and rang the Marin's number to inform the parents of their son's suspension. A brief recording invited him to leave a message, which he did. He hung up and jotted a reminder to continue contact by phone and mail until he was sure they'd been notified.

The encounter left Sam drained. He was bone tired and dispirited. He'd let his AA meetings go. He needed a meeting for awhile, but had put that need on the back burner. He thought he'd adjusted the heat properly, but he was boiling dry. That could make a guy thirsty.

First things first, however. The final bell was about to ring, and Sam had to get downstairs to oversee an orderly exodus. As he donned his suit coat, Alan Anderson entered his office.

"To what do I owe this favor?" Sam asked.

"Is something bothering you or are you just not glad to see me?"

"Let's call that a toss-up. If you want to talk, you'll have to come downstairs with me. Be good for you anyway. Show you we do have students who need a bit of supervision." He pointed to the open doorway.

"That's one reason I wanted to see you," the administrator replied, keeping pace with Sam's long legged strides. "To tell you I again requested the hiring of a vice principal, and the board again voted me down."

"Was your request perfunctory or passionate."

"Passionate, I'd say. I saw tears in the eyes of our only supporter."

"Got to beat that bell," Sam said as he accelerated down the final flight. "Man could get trampled if he's not in the right place at the right time. Too bad you want your job so badly. Otherwise, you could cut loose."

"As you feel the need to tell me every time we talk." They'd reached the first floor, and the bell hadn't rung. "You're in marvelous shape. If I wasn't so much younger than you, I'd be winded."

"Destination achieved," Sam said, indicating the steps that led to the exit's double doors. "How come you can't convince board members to switch? You're quite the charmer. You charm me right out of my socks."

"Warrum's lackeys are lacking sense. He'll eventually hang himself."

"Already has, but the rope keeps breaking."

"When he succeeds, I'll get what I want, which is the freedom to have the people we need. I'm sorry to tell you that isn't going to happen in time to be of help to you." Sam half-expected Anderson to grasp him by the elbows, and plead, "You've got to believe me!"

He didn't. Instead the head administrator concluded, "So I am going to do penance for my original lack of integrity by spending more time prowling the halls here. I know you'll approve since it was your idea. I'll even offer to deal with students now and then to reduce your burden."

"I had one for you today."

"I think I passed him in the hall. Darting eyes, leather jacket. I was thinking more in terms of the newspaper staff and the Student Council."

The bell rang and the jangling Blue Lake youth tumbled out of their classrooms into the halls. Sam smiled. He loved these kids, no matter what.

Billy Cloud

Achieving the crest of Moon Ribbon Ridge, Billy Cloud dismounted his ten-speed LeTour. His thighs burned and perspiration rained down his face. He'd taken on the hill full bore and actually accelerated near the top. He loved that bike. He slid it under the branches of a nearby pine, loving the sound of the wind sighing through pine boughs. He loved the pounding of his blood through his veins after the ten-mile ride and the arduous ascent. Loved the crystalline freshness of the morning that spoke of spring even though patches of snow still lived within the woods.

He would have loved to have Patty Light with him right now to share her wide-eyed wonder at the beauties of this day. He wished she was beside him slipping her hand into his as she surveyed this remarkable terrain. Instead she was trapped in some counselor's office in Blue Lake. Changing her life. And maybe his.

That unsought thought startled him as much as a bear leaping atop the ridge would. "Good grief!" he groaned. What kind of miserable critter was he? Why would he toss aside all that love of a minute ago to think it?

If he didn't figure out what that was about, he was going to wreck a perfectly fine day. And he wasn't going to be worth a rat's rear to Patty.

Think, he ordered himself. What was it his mother had warned him pretty pointedly? "That girl is going to need a friend, not a lover. Can you handle that?" He hadn't a second's doubt. No siree. Piece of cake. He was already her friend. He already loved her. But he could handle, Randall. You betcha. He'd told her so without a second's thought. It was now obvious that what his mother suggested was more difficult than he imagined.

But why? His mind returned to the night he brought his parents to Moon Ribbon. Something his father said wanted to be remembered. He'd been talking Indian history, but what was his final thought?

Something about winning and losing. That was it. His father had said, "When someone gains, someone else loses. I don't know why. It doesn't have to be that way." Those were the words he needed to help him figure out why his brain was percolating like a crazy coffee-maker.

He descended to the meadow, and wandered toward the snowmelt-swollen stream. He sat on its bank and tilted his head back. A red tail hawk circled high in the sky, observing him. "Did Patty Light send you? Are you reading my mind?" he shouted to the bird. It floated away in apparent disgust, then folded its wings and plummeted like Billy's mood.

Someone gains. While he didn't know the details, Patty Light had everything to gain if whatever she'd written in her journal resulted in changes in the way she had to live her life.

Someone loses. Patty's mother might be one. That could be good, too. Maybe by losing her grip on her daughter's life, she'd get a grip on her own.

Some one could be also be Mr. Billy C. Cloud. He should slap himself silly for letting that idea cockroach his brain. It was blazingly selfish. But. But. It was the life Patty Light lived that she'd shaped into who she'd become. It was who she'd become that fascinated him. Why mess with a life that was working out so impressively? What's a few thousand tremors among friends? And, oh yeah, by the way, would she have need of him at all if the counseling was successful? "Aye, yi, yi, that is the rub," he muttered. Then, "Good grief!" He jumped to his feet and paced along the bank of the stream. "Where was I when I morphed into an s.o.b.?"

Why was he so worried? Change had been the story of his life. Moving from place to place was his parents' grand experiment. He'd been taught from rattlehood that change offered new places, people, experiences, and knowledge. Change was good. But not this change? "I," he hissed, "am ridiculous!"

He resisted an urge to leap into the icy stream to shock some sense into himself. Instead he dipped his hands into the churning flow, its chill stinging his fingers. He lifted the cupped water to his mouth, his tongue tasting the changing seasons in it. Change. Everything changes, for Pete's sake.

Ah, but maybe this twist in his thinking wasn't his fault. Maybe the reason for his trepidation was the nomadic lifestyle his parents had chosen without his permission. Proof? He'd had hundreds of acquaintances, but darn few friends. Why get too close when you know you'll be leaving them behind? That was why he was no good at this. If his family lived a normal life, getting close to someone wouldn't be so supercharged, and the fear of losing someone wouldn't be either.

"Good lord!" he sputtered. "I oughta throw myself on the ground, kick my legs in the air and suck my thumb until it wrinkles!"

He took a deep breath and tried to shift his mind out of passing gear into low. This was ridiculous. He'd started the day loving everything. Since then he'd dissed every aspect of his life. If he kept this up, he'd sure as heck know who the loser was.

He ascended to the ridge, plopped on its spine, and inhaled the spring-scented air. The sky was brilliantly blue. His mother was right. His father had added, "It doesn't have to be that way," as his concluding thought. The choice Billy had was to halt his emotional free-fall. It was time to count his blessings instead of being a creep. Time to dismount his high horse and send it out to pasture. After all, his life was actually good. So he'd better get over it and get with it. Like, being the friend Patty Light needed. Going to the Reservation with his parents when they asked instead of passing. Appreciating what he had.

He stood up and walked along the ridge to retrieve his bicycle. This session hardly qualified as a vision quest. Black Elk would laugh himself silly if he heard Billy call it that. Nevertheless, it had succeeded in reviving a view of his life that had gone missing shortly after his arrival. His thoughts were re-aimed in the right direction. Maybe that was part of what a real vision quest awarded. He stopped and performed a ritual of his ancestors. He raised his arms and thanked four directions for their many gifts.

He was riding unhurriedly back to town when he heard the car behind him. Something about the motor's faint howl grabbed his attention. When he glanced over his shoulder, the vehicle was toy-sized. He increased his pedal speed and glanced again. The teeth-like grill of the white car had already become distinguishable. The howl blended into the roar of excessive speed. Intuition told him the driver had no intention of veering out of his lane.

He jammed the bike's brakes and dove it into the deep ditch beside the road, his body sailing over the handlebars. He slammed into the opposite incline and somersaulted to a stop, the white blur of the vehicle so close its heat and stink gushed over him as its wind peppered the ditch with pebbles.

Billy lay gasping for several minutes before he could catch his breath. He was afraid he might have broken his ribs. And his bike. He flexed his fingers and toes to make sure they were working, then gingerly poked his rib cage. No intolerable pains shot through him. He was bruised, but not broken. His bike was sprawled in the tall grass on the inside bank. He was lucky to have cleared the handlebars. Both sleeves of his windbreaker were torn. He slipped it off to check his injuries and found a series of long, deep red scratches on his forearms and bruises on his elbows. His right shoulder throbbed. In fact most of his body throbbed.

"Could be worse," he mumbled. He felt a trickle of blood trailing down the right side of his head between his eye and ear. "Much worse." He removed his bike helmet and touched the small temple wound, then circled his arms around his knees and waited for pain and dizziness to ease.

Eventually he struggled to his feet and righted his bike. It was damaged but not debilitated. He wrestled it to the road and mounted. The front wheel scraped against the brake pads, but the bike was rideable.

As he wobbled homeward, Billy wondered whether that driver was crazy enough to want to take him out, if he hated Indians and saw his chance to maim one or if he didn't see him at all. Maybe he was wild with speed, drink, or drugs and he was totally zoned. Whatever. He was definitely a fricking idiot, and Billy would love to slap some sense into him.

Billy was halfway around the curve that brought The Cloud House into view when he braked so suddenly, he almost ejected over the handlebars again. That evil white car -or its twin – was parked across the road from his home. He couldn't believe it! He dragged his bike into the nearby trees and crouched at the edge of the woods. A man was standing near the vehicle, his back to the Cloud House, gesturing wildly. Billy heard him shouting, but could not make out the words. He saw his father crossing the road, pointing. The man whirled and thrust his arm upward as he rounded the car, wrenched open its door, repeated the obscene gesture, and got in. The engine's roar sounded all too familiar as the driver jammed the accelerator. The car hurtled down the road in Billy's direction as his eyes melded on the same silver tooth grill he'd seen earlier. As the car shot past, he glimpsed the glaring driver. He now knew who the fricking idiot was.

Billy retrieved his bike and wheeled it to the road. As he did, he saw a familiar looking figure walking with his father up the porch steps of The Cloud House. He remounted his bike and rattled down the road. As he approached, Ed Warrum and his father reemerged from the house. He heard Ed exclaim, "He's such a jerk!"

That confirmed it. That was Ed Warrum talking. Whether through malice or madness, it was Ed's father who had come close to killing him.

Ed Warrum

"What are you doing here? Don't you know this is Indian country?"

Ed Warrum and Billy's father had been too intent on Pete Warrum to notice Billy. Then they'd become engrossed with something Ed was holding in his hand as they stood on the porch. Now they finally noticed him.

"What are you doing," Billy called, "upgrading to a new father?"

"My gosh, what happened to you? You're a mess!" Mr. Cloud exclaimed as his son wobbled the bike to a stop, and he and Ed rushed down the porch steps.

Billy carefully laid the bike on the lawn and unstrapped his helmet. He squinted in pain as he removed it and scraped his head wound. "I thought I'd try ditch-diving once before I die. Or, should I say, so I wouldn't." Billy grimaced. "There was this guy who wanted to race me. Except he had this big car and I had this bike. We were only allowed to use one lane of the road. His rule. He won." He peeled off his jacket and extended his arms. Red fringes of dried blood trailed from the scratches on his arms. "I'm looking for your sympathy, people."

"We'd better clean those up," his father said. "That head wound too."

"I imagine. But first, Ed, what are you doing here?"

"Three Warrums are your new neighbors. Forget that. Your dad's right."

"That paper you're holding a peace treaty we're supposed to sign? Should we, Dad? Our winning percentage on those things ain't good."

"It's a restraining order on my father. He's not supposed to come within a mile of us. Mother left a copy on the table at the house. He came home at noon, found it, and he's already found us. Twice. Thinks he doesn't have to obey laws or court orders or have common decency. If your Dad hadn't threatened to call the sheriff, he'd still be here. I threatened the same thing, but he didn't move an inch." He pointed at Billy's arms. "I gotta help Jenny and Mom unpack. You'd better get those looked at."

"Our carefully planned escape from the house began exactly two weeks and three days after the blizzard. Every night after school, and in our rooms at night, Jenny and I each packed a suitcase and a box of our stuff. At nine a.m. every weekday after Dad left, Mom lugged our suitcases and boxes and hers and piled them into her station wagon. She hauled all that stuff here, and deposited it in each bedroom so we could repack.

"When we got close to done, Mom got hold of Joann Burst, who used to be the store's business lawyer before Dad fired her. Mom said he got rid of Mrs. Burst because he believed a male attorney projects a stronger image. Mrs. Burst can't stand Dad to this day. Anyway, Mom asked her to secure that restraining order I showed you because she knew Dad would hound us.

"We finished moving this morning. Dad made it easy by staying at the apartment above the store after playing poker with his buddies. When he does that, he stays downtown until noon and then comes home to harass whoever's handy. We were up before five and done before nine. Then they dropped me off two blocks from the store so I could work my Saturday morning shift. I got busy in the back room knocking down boxes and stocking shelves since he was nowhere in sight.

"Dad descended from on high a little after ten, but he didn't look too regal. His hair was half-combed, his eyes were bloodshot, and his shirt was wrinkled. He looked old and worn out. I thought, God, he's eating himself alive. I even thought that abandoning him was pretty cruel. I forgot how he did everything he could to drive us away. Man, I felt sorry for him.

"But then he sees me staring at him, so he walks right up to me and sticks his mug an inch from my face. 'What are you standing around for?'

he says. His breath smells like stale beer with a toothpaste chaser. 'These shelves should have been done an hour ago.'

"I just walked away."

"So that's the story," Ed Warrum concluded as he shoved the last of his shirts into the bottom drawer of the tall brown bureau in his bedroom. "Mom said she hadn't put our new address on the restraining order, but she knew he'd find us anyway." Ed sat down on the bed. Billy Cloud sat on the chair by the window, listening.

"Which he did," Billy finished for him.

"Yup. The first time he stopped, beat on the horn for a while and zoomed away. The second time you saw. He was a little upset."

"A tad," There was no need to tell Ed the rest of the story. Yet.

"But I'll tell you what's really stupid," Ed said as he rose from the bed. "I've still got this guilty feeling like we've done something wrong."

"I think I cannot quite understand that. Hey. My mother sent over some Indian tacos. We figure since you're new in our country, we should share our food with you by way of welcome. Then we'll teach you how to make your own. Then we'll teach you everything else you need to know. It's our historical duty."

Ed had to laugh.

On Sunday morning Pete Warrum's car again loomed like a white tank in front of his family's new home. He stood leaning against the passenger door, his arms folded like some cut-rate general. Upstairs, Ed stood beside Jenny as both stared out her bedroom window across the porch roof, their father fitting easily into the retinas of their eyes. Jenny did not wish to cry, but she was, tears tracing her nose and cheeks. She refused to leave the window. "I'm glad there's a restraining order that commands the Sheriff's Department to remove him from our sight. I'm glad Mom's making that call right now!" she told Ed.

Reassured that his sister would be all right, Ed descended the stairs. He listened to his mother reminding the sheriff of the restraining order, and telling him he or a deputy was needed now. Ed went outside and stood on the porch and mirrored his father's folded arms. He and his mother and sister were not in hiding. Pete had blocked the light from their lives long enough. If he came barreling up the walk, Ed would step off the porch and deck him.

That did not happen. The sheriff's car eased down the road and rolled to a stop behind his father's. An officer on the passenger's side emerged. He approached his father. Pete Warrum raise his arms, crooked at the elbows, palms upward, and roared, "What is this? A father can't see his own son!" The officer listened, hands on hips, as his father ranted. A second officer got out of the driver's side of the vehicle emblazoned with "Sheriff's Department" on its side and walked toward the two men, a copy of the restraining order in his hand. His father made a dismissive gesture with both hands, but moved around his car. He flamed one more glare toward the house as though its heat would set the place ablaze. Then he got into the car. Because the officers were watching him, he did not gun the accelerator or screech the tires as he left.

Ed stepped off the porch and called, "Thank you." The officers waved and drove off in the same direction his father had gone.

"We'll be all right," Ellen Warrum told her son when he went back in the house. "Pete doesn't want the attention of the law focused on him. It would hurt business if people heard the words 'Pete Warrum' and 'Sheriff' in the same sentence very often. I'm certain he won't be back."

"Ed, yesterday I called Pastor Raymond and made an appointment for you to talk to him. It's our church even if we don't go very often. Pastor Barker is gone, but you need to talk to someone outside the family. Take the car," she urged.

Ed chose not to. His father might have enough screws loose to invade the church office and try to wreck his meeting with the new pastor if he saw the car there. No, he'd walk instead. If his father was prowling around and spotted him, he was smart enough to know that a public shouting match wouldn't be good for business either.

"I was expecting to see more of you than I have over these past months," Pastor Raymond said. "I was disappointed to get your mother's call and discover that she, your sister and you have left your father's house." He leaned back in his black cushioned chair. "I would rather see the horse before I see the cart."

Ed sat across the desk in the metal folding chair provided for him. "Well," he fumbled, "I . . . I couldn't talk to him about coming here. He'd have thrown a fit. So it just didn't work out."

"Maybe it was embarrassing for you? Maybe you thought it was your father who needed the counseling, not you?" The questions sounded like accusations. Unlike Pastor Dan and Pastor Barker, this guy seemed to be making an instant judgment about him.

Heat surged into his chest, the same heat he felt around his father, and he tried to throw water on it. "Both of those may be facts, sir. It's embarrassing, maybe, but not just for . . . "

"To be this athlete who has everything going for him and is miserable anyway?" the minister interrupted, the fingertips of his forefingers and thumbs touching one another and the rest of his fingers intertwined as though he was reciting 'here is the church, here is the steeple' inside his head. His eyes were focused outside the office window rather than on the boy.

"That's not how I'd put it," Ed said, desperate to lower his thermostat.

"Which part? The athlete part, the everything part, the miserable part?"

Every question sounded like an insult. "All of it." Ed answered.

The pastor ignored his response, his face stern. "I know of your father more than I know him, but he's well regarded in this town. I'm told he started his business when the downtown was struggling, and the population was much less than it is now. His reputation is that he's a man who's worked hard for everything he's got. I do know that even though his attendance here isn't good, he's been generous in his tithing by mail."

Like Ed hadn't heard these stories a thousand times.

"He's built his store into a thriving business. It's one of my wife's favorite places to shop. He has such a nice variety of goods."

"Yes, sir," Ed said, the sun beginning to set on any hope of this conversation doing him any good.

"Running a business is hard work. Perhaps your father is tired." He glanced at Ed. "Well, don't you think that's possible?"

"Yes. But maybe if he wasn't also trying to run the town, the school, and every breath my mother, sister, and I take, he wouldn't be so worn out."

"You don't attend church very often. Not this one. Perhaps another?"

The shift in focus threw Ed for a loop. The question was irrelevant. "No. My father doesn't seem to believe in going to church much."

"Where is your mother in all this? I notice your father's store is open seven days a week, but I don't recall seeing your mother there. It's often the woman who gets the family to church. That was true in my family."

What's going on here? He's attacking me! He's attacking my mother! He's defending my father!

"If you were attending this church, perhaps any church, you would have learned the power of prayer. You would have prayed about this situation and taken care of it without the drama of moving out of your home and breaking your father's heart," the minister stated as firmly as if he was reciting the Ten Commandments.

"Could be." Ed was incredulous.

"Perhaps, too," Pastor Raymond continued relentlessly, his eyes again focused beyond the office window, "if your mother had taken responsibility for getting you – or herself – to my office before this crisis occurred, it could have been avoided. Those ounces of prevention are worth pounds of cure."

It was like the two were playing some weird card game, and the minister had ripped almost all the cards out of Ed's hands and kept throwing Kings and Queens on his desk, face up. But Ed still had an ace. "You heard talk about my dad going after Coach Howard at a football game, didn't you?" The cleric nodded. "What did you think when you heard about that?"

"I thought I was hearing about a man who loves his son and supports his son's athletic endeavors a bit too zealously. I thought about a man losing his temper out of concern for his son."

The Pastor turned his head toward the boy. The man's lips were curved as though the he'd trumped Ed's ace with the joker he'd flipped out of his own sleeve. Ed had no idea what was going on here or why. He needed to get out before he obeyed his impulse to leap across the desk and throttle the guy. Nevertheless, he sat as though filled with sand, not sure what he was waiting for except for this bad dream to end. Or to find out that the minister was playing devil's advocate, setting the situation up from the father's perspective so he could more confidently help the son.

Instead he heard this. "Our church rolls list two hundred families. Not all come to church regularly, but many do. My predecessor saw his role in the church as that of a counselor for everyday problems in everyday lives. He left behind a long list of adults, teenagers, and children who were making use of his, shall we say, talent. Including you. I see the role of a minister differently. I've tried to shift the focus of the church members off that kind of dependency. In the meantime I've listened to a variety of problems. Most are offering me a steady diet of small potatoes. I prefer not to be inundated with tiny potatoes," His face was wreathed by his cleverness. His inference was clear. But he wouldn't quit. "I, like your father, do have a wife and family who require my time and guidance too."

Ed shot up, clattering his chair to the floor. "Thank you for your precious time." He retrieved the chair, folded it and leaned it against the desk. "I'm sorry I took so much of it. I'll hurry home now to let my mother know that she and my sister and I are totally at fault for our problems. She's so dumb she doesn't realize that, and she needs to know it. We're so stupid we thought my dad had something to do with it." His head and chest were on fire. "Please let my father know you've granted him absolution!"

He wheeled around and wrenched the door open, poked his head into the empty hall, then whirled on his heel. "You'll be glad to know there are no potatoes of any size in sight." He left the door open and forced himself to walk slowly to the church door. He pushed it open and stepped outside.

He was surprised to find the sky not overcast, but deep blue, and the west wind was heavy with the scent of spring. Elation swept over him, maybe because he'd escaped, maybe because he'd heard what the man said, but accepted none of it, maybe because he'd discovered his father wasn't the only jerk in the world.

He became aware that he was standing on the sidewalk staring at the church. As he came back to himself, he glanced up and down the street to see if anyone was staring at him. Then he realized how similar he must look to how Mr. Baker had looked a few weeks ago. He and the teacher had that in common now. And if you saw Mr. Baker in unguarded moments like that one, you could see he knew about struggle, sadness, and desperation. Maybe he'd be the guy to talk to. Maybe he should seek the teacher out.

After all, Billy and Patty seemed to find him easy to talk to. He decided to check with them to see what they thought. He had nothing to lose. He'd scraped the bottom of the help barrel a few minutes ago.

Greg Schwarz

"Ladies and gentlemen," Greg Schwarz announced after downing the last morsel of the hot lunch Mrs. S. and her miracle workers had prepared, "I have been sitting here consuming . . . "

"And at a record clip," Kyle Hunter noted.

"As I was saying before the Duke of Rude broke my train of thought . . .

"Short train. Engine and caboose."

"Mostly caboose pretty soon," Red Howard added.

"Aw, come on, you guys. Here I am about to be profound in ways you can only envy, and you keep preventing that from happening."

"It's a public service," Kyle observed.

"Envy. That shade of green makes you look like you're on a chlorophyll diet. Don't you agree, Janis?"

"Yes, I do," business teacher, Janis James, replied from the end of the table. "But only because I'm in love with you, and I want to get on your good side while I can still find it."

"Janis, welcome to the KGH club," Kyle said. "It's Blue Lake High School's fastest growing organization."

"KGH? What does that stand for? Let me think."

"That should be novel for you," Greg said.

"I'll let you know if it hurts," Janis said, screwing her face into a portrait of pain. "Yes, it does. I don't think you should to try it, Greggie honey." She held her scrunch and screamed, "I've got it, I've got it, I've got it!"

"Good grief, that means I might get it, too," Greg groaned. "Janis, I'm afraid we won't be able to relate in that way any more. But while it lasted, it was good."

"Must've been a nice four or five seconds," Red said.

"You guys are absolutely awful," Janis scolded. "Here I am trying to play your little game, and there you are talking like eighth graders in the boys locker room. Disgusting. But I digress. 'KGH' stands for 'Kick Greg Hard!' Yea me. What's my prize?"

"The most wonderful four or five seconds of your life," Red suggested.

"That was a great try, Janis, so great that we'll adopt it as our own and dump our slogan. Yours is the action form of ours." Kyle said.

"Which is . . . ."

"I'm embarrassed to admit that the name we came up with is 'Keep Greg Humble'. But yours has teeth. Ours has no teeth. Ours is gummy."

"Does this mean that I, as a new member, have the privilege of unlimited Greg bashing?"

"Yes, and isn't it nice to have such a slow moving, ever broadening target upon which to release your pent-up aggression. I want you all to note to what lengths I went to not end that last sentence with a preposition."

"That's really impressive, Kyle. I once knew a guy whose last sentence to me ended with a proposition." Janis laughed.

"What happened?"

"I told him to go and find a kite with which to fly."

"Here's a question that I'd like all of you to answer," Greg said. "It's my own opinion that I am invaluable to this town, school, and faculty lounge. So my question is, would you folks miss me if I was gone?" He finished the question with a smile, but it looked forced, as though the muscles holding it were stretched to the limit. His eyes were suddenly wet at the corners.

"It would tear my lovesick heart out by its roots," Janis responded after she downed the last of her carton of milk. Then she noticed the sparkles at the edges of Greg's eyes. "Oh my gosh, you're serious aren't you!"

"It just sort of popped out of my mouth."

"No. You're serious. You've got losing coach's eyes."

The other men fell silent.

"Greg, are you leaving?"

"To tell you the truth, I don't know."

"I couldn't be more shocked!" Janis exclaimed.

"Aw, it's nothing. Just checking to see how much you all love me."

"Yes, it is," Janis insisted. "You're almost in tears."

Greg gave in. He was sorry he'd opened this box after keeping it shut all month. Only Red, Kyle, and Sam knew of his interviews and the offers. "Can't we just go back to kicking' Greg hard?" he pleaded.

"No. No, we can't," Janis persisted. "I know this is only my second year here, but you guys and Mr. Strand seemed like you'd been here forever and would be here forever. Like you guys were the pillars holding up this four story museum."

"Well, thank you, I think," Kyle said.

"No, no, I'm serious. I've been praying every night that someday I'll love this place as much as you all do. So will you please tell me what's going on, Greg? Or do I have to start rumors that you'll have to deny? Are you going to pull a Ted Gerney on us? Because I thought he loved this place, too, and he'd be here forever, too."

"To tell you the truth." His voice failed. "Ask Red."

"Red?"

"Greg's had offers. He's getting plenty from schools throughout the state. That's all I'm going to tell you. Except that I've told him to keep his options open."

"Why?"

"How's your class size? Have you tried to shoehorn any discipline problems into the line waiting to feel the weight of Sam's hammer because it's the only hammer in this school? Are you aware of the priorities of our school board? Nobody's been more loyal to this school or worked harder to make it better than Sam. But that doesn't matter. In the end they treat us like old gum they stepped on in the hallway. I'm miffed about that."

"Well, sure on the first one. I've got more students than machines, computers, or books. The second one, too. My classes are electives except for the students dumped in them now because other classes are overstuffed. I haven't paid much attention to the school board."

"It might be wise to do so."

"The fact is," Greg said, "their priority is about athletics and winning. That should make me happy. But they're willing to wreck everything else for that to happen. I don't believe in that, and I don't believe in killing off administrators and teachers to save a buck. I sure as heck don't believe in how they handled Red."

"You love our kids," Janis stated. Her eyes were unblinking. She stood, grabbed her lunch tray, and waited for Greg to agree.

"Yes, I love our kids."

"Well, you keep that in mind when you're thinking about abandoning us." She flounced to the waste basket, dumped her refuse, and turned. "If everyone runs away, who's going to change things?" She wheeled around and flourished out the door.

"Well, my friend," Red said, "you certainly changed the direction of the conversation, and you certainly got a passionate response to your question. I do believe I'm right when I say that passion is the root word. If I were you, I'd seek further counsel from that lady."

"I'll second that notion," Kyle said. "By the way, what was the great utterance you were going to grace us with before your train of thought derailed?"

"Oh, I was going to say that I just saw the tunnel at the end of the light. I kind of doubt that Janis would have liked it anyway."

Gail Hunter

Now it was a whole week. The Kerns Company decided it was inefficient to have out-state and interstate sales representatives traveling to the Cities separately for meetings and workshops. Why not bring them all in at the same time bimonthly for six days, give them all the same information, ideas, and style shows and give them more unbroken time to service their accounts? Barring special circumstances of course.

It made sense, but Gail wondered whether that contingency had been added with her in mind. "Boy, that's self-centered," she told the attractive image smiling back at her from the bathroom mirror. But she knew who was responsible for personnel development. It also seemed too convenient that all the representatives had been scheduled two to a room, and hers was the only one shared with someone unable to attend. Mr. Wayne Mars had informed her of that with a full display of his perfect teeth and flashing dimple. That was how Gail justified the thought this schedule had been designed with her in mind. "Well, it's not that obvious," she told herself.

It was Wednesday. Every element of the week had been charged with energy and excitement. Every meeting room glittered as if etched in crystal. It had been amazing. Perhaps part of that was because it was the middle of April, and the Cities were blooming. Stepping outside the hotel was like stepping into an arboretum. The scents of the season made her head swim and her heart sing. She hadn't been so in awe of the possibilities around and within her for a long time.

She finished her ablutions, stepped back to the bathroom doorway and let her robe slip off her shoulders. She looked good, her skin fair and mostly free of blemish, her blonde hair a little wild from the hair dryer, her body toned by the cross-country skiing.

Today was Wednesday – hump day. She was embarrassed by the quick smile she couldn't keep from her lips. She was like a teenager, full of blush and the rush of blood racing through her veins, her day, her life, and ripe for risk and adventure.

She left the magic mirror that reflected such a seductive image and glanced at the alarm clock between the two beds. It was only 6:30. She danced across the room and eased back the curtain of the fourteenth story hotel room window. She could see the roofs of the low-rise buildings that housed downtown department stores and specialty shops. Several blocks to their left were the theaters, restaurants, bars and the infamous strip clubs of Neon Avenue. Two blocks straight ahead, the next cluster of taller buildings rose into the morning sky. She knew the closest housed the corporate offices of Kerns Company on the fifteenth floor. She'd heard it contained a telescope because, "all the hip offices do." It was easy to imagine him training it on her hotel room in hopes of catching an early morning energizer.

"Oh, this is awful, I'm awful," she chided herself her as she struck a runway pose. "Your turn," she mouthed toward the office. Then she whipped the curtain closed. Spring ought to be banned, she thought with a wicked smile. She turned to get dressed and ready to go down to a day of meetings about subjects she enjoyed on a day full of unlimited possibilities.

Spring was irrelevant to the rest of Wednesday. The day was overloaded with meetings. Even lunch was a "working lunch." Dinner was a buffet served in a small ballroom followed by a too-long style show by manufacturers eager to place autumn collections. She'd awakened full of spring, and here she was thrust into fall.

There hadn't been a single break. She wished the day had begun with the sun blocked by gray. She wished she hadn't stood mostly undraped in front of the undraped window. It was a stupid thing to do. She resented Wayne Mars' failure to make an appearance. She wished she wasn't sitting on this plastic chair in this air-conditioned room feeling disappointed, hollow, and foolish.

You are stupid, her mind told her. You are crazy as a loon. Get a grip; get real. These browns and plaids, windbreakers and car coats, tweeds and jeans, skirts and dresses are your chance to write your own ticket for a change. Not trees in bloom. Or Mr. Mars strutting into the room.

By the time she returned to her room it was ten o'clock, and she was dog-tired. She wished the phone wasn't ringing, but it was. Kyle, she thought and doubted this would be a good time to talk. She'd been on an emotional escalator all day, its only direction down. Why add to that? She let the phone ring.

She groaned. Why was she so negative about Kyle? What had he ever done to her aside from being so dedicated to his job that she felt like an outsider? That and his failure to recognize the depth of her emotions. Or to deal with them. Instead of volunteering for everything, assisting with every activity, being totally absorbed in the lives of his students and totally oblivious that she didn't have one. Even now when she'd been gone part of almost every week servicing accounts, his work dominated the days and nights she was home.

The phone fell silent.

Why was she unrolling this scroll of his sins again? What was the satisfaction in doing that over and over? If she was looking in a mirror now, the face staring back at her would be angry and scrunched. Her blue eyes would be hard as marbles. Why was she doing this to herself?

The phone resumed ringing. All right, Kyle. Proceed at your own risk. She snatched the phone to her ear.

"Good timing, yeah," smoothed the voice on the other end. "Since I designed the day, I knew when it would end and where my exhausted minions would head. Though I thought you'd be back sooner."

"Are you calling us all?" Gail responded coolly.

"Only my favorites. How was your day?"

"Interesting but far too full. It looked like a beautiful April day outside, but you didn't leave time for a sniff of it. Keep the peasants at bay while the royalty play."

"Well, not quite, my dear." The man was like butter on the best piece of bread you ever ate. Right now that made her want to scream. But her fantasy morning wasn't his fault. She dreamed with her eyes open. "Gail," he continued, "I need to know from someone I trust what's working and what isn't. We're spending tomorrow putting together our next program. Your feedback will be helpful in giving us a jump-start. So speak."

She did. She concluded with her opinion that the day might have been brighter had the men and women from the office "descended for a visit to their lackeys' cells."

"Thank you for talking honestly, Gail," Wayne said with maddening calm. "I know it was a long day. We designed it that way. That's why they call Wednesday hump day, you know. It's all ride and glide afterwards."

"Oh, that's why. I always wondered. I'm so country."

"So tired, too, I think. I'm going to let you go so you can get ready to sleep." He paused. "I'm going to sit here for a few minutes and think about that. Then after a few more hours of work, I'll hit the hay. I'll see you in person on Friday." It was overkill, but his voice drained right through her. "Sleep well."

"Stupid, stupid, stupid," Gail growled as she slammed down the phone.

But behind her eyes as she flitted toward sleep were those eyes filtered through those incredible lashes, that one dimple smile, that night of the storm that took her right to the edge. "That gas," she said aloud and whooped with laughter and could not stop until her body gave up on her and fell asleep.

❖ ❖ ❖

Thursday was a relief. Gail awoke with no expectations beyond the day's schedule, which included seminars and time for buyers and sellers to wheel and deal. The fact that four fifteen-minute breaks had been inserted pleased her. He had listened. He hadn't merely wanted to keep his line humming.

Kyle called that evening. The call came at eight o'clock, warning her that it wouldn't be Wayne's honeyed voice, but Kyle's cautious one. In previous months he'd chosen not to call much, reasoning that he'd be bothering her if he got hold of her and fueling fantasies if he didn't. At least that was her interpretation.

The past month had been rife with silence. When she was home, he'd not said much below the surface. Neither had she. Oh, they'd gone skiing in the days after the storm, and she'd feigned interest while watching state tournament games with him on television. But mostly they'd danced around each other with perfunctory comments as they worked and watched winter wane. Careful was the watchword. She was sure he was relieved when he slid her suitcase into the car's trunk and closed it, then stood in the driveway with his hands in his jacket pockets, watching her back into the road and head for the Cities. She knew she was.

She picked up the phone and tried to put some perk into her voice. "Hello, Kyle."

"You knew it was me. That's very good."

"I don't get that many calls. Is everything all right?"

"I miss you."

She wanted to reply in kind, but couldn't. The only time she'd thought about him was Wednesday night. So she said, "Have you been busy?"

"Always am. That's one of our problems, isn't it?" His words were razor sharp inside her ear.

"If you called to fight, I'm hanging up," Gail snapped.

"I'm sorry. The house is empty. I'm tired. Life keeps changing, and I'm not handling it well. I just wanted to hear your voice."

"And check up on me?" Gail questioned and wished she hadn't. "I'm sorry, too," she covered, "and I'm tired, too. They're keeping us awfully busy. Anything new at school?" she asked to change the subject.

"Greg's looking around."

"For a wife?"

"No, he's too smart for that." Kyle sounded disgusted. "He's looking at other jobs. Getting offers. Winning is everything, I guess."

"Do you suppose you'd be getting letters if your students won a bunch of writing contests?" She knew her implication was that what he was doing might be valuable, but it wasn't valued. She let the question hang.

"It doesn't matter," Kyle answered, acknowledging the implication. "It was a beautiful day today. I rode my bike for the first time this spring. How's your weather?"

"Mostly air conditioned with a chance of fresh air seeping through an open door now and then," she said, happy to skip away from the controversy she'd created. "But I must tell you I'm responsible for us getting more break time today. I spoke up."

"You must have an in with the boss."

"You do and you don't seem to be getting many of your ideas put into practice. Maybe you should get a job where your employer listens to you."

"You've got a point there. Maybe it's because I can't . . . " He cut his sentence abruptly. "I just called to say I miss you. I've got papers to correct, and you've got things to do."

"Actually I don't. When our day is done, it's done."

"And the evening's just begun. I'm jealous. I gotta go. Have a nice night."

Silence hummed the line awaiting her reply, but something within muted her voice. Kyle added, "Goodbye," his voice as close to miserable as he let it get.

"Goodbye, Kyle," she answered. She couldn't bring herself to thank him for calling, but she held the phone to her ear until she heard his click, then the emptied line.

The rest of her evening emptied as well. She moved the desk chair to the window and watched the city lights until the phone rang again.

"Hi, Hon, I'm finally done," Wayne poured.

"I'm sorry," she said, "there's nobody here that answers to that name," and hung up.

She slipped into bed, but couldn't sleep. She was wondering why good days kept turning into bad and how much of that was her fault.

❖   ❖   ❖

On Friday the representatives had the option of remaining until Saturday morning or leaving for home once the evening buffet had been consumed and the rah-rah speeches given. Those who lived close by or far enough to fly opted to leave. Those who had created alliances, developed friendships, or wanted to party stayed to spend the night on the town.

Gail had made no effort to be included in any groups, but she had no desire to hurry back to Blue Lake either. She'd like to blame Kyle's call, but she'd made the decision to stay until Sunday before she ever left home.

She and Wayne Mars had little contact throughout Friday's events. Only at the employee breakfast when the backs of their fingers brushed as Wayne handed her a cup of coffee were they in proximity. He dropped in and out of the salesmanship workshops that comprised the day. Whenever he entered a room where she was, his eyes found her. He'd arch an eyebrow, offer a quick grin, and nod before exiting. It seemed too practiced.

Following the buffet and exhortations, she went back to her room. She'd have been better off with a roommate. Too much time to think had undercut a week she'd have thoroughly enjoyed without the undertows. The phone's message button wasn't flashing. No one wanted her. She couldn't blame them, only her confused and muddled self.

It didn't matter. She'd secured the room for the weekend on Wednesday morning. She'd paid for the extra night with her own non-refundable deposit. Being here was no more gloomy than returning to Blue Lake. Still, she could hardly remember that Wednesday morning dancer or the music that had moved her.

What moved her out of her room was the threat of thinking too much again. She now regretted her lack of alliances. It would be a distinct relief to relive the week with someone else and forget its gossamer wings. The latter had batted her against the windows and walls anyway. To escape more of the same, she descended to the hotel's bar and lounge. Hopefully she'd find noise and other people's stories to distract her.

The bar was crowded and raw with laughter. It was a dimly lit room except for the area around the shiny horseshoe bar. If there was anyone she knew, she'd have to work at spotting him or her. A couple suddenly deserted a small corner table. As she hurried towards it, the pair brushed by. Even in the dim, it was clear his hand was caressing her, and there was reason for their rush.

She plopped into a chair that faced the bar. The twilight ambiance rendered her barely visible. Observing and losing herself would suffice.

She was sipping the overly expensive rum and coke she'd ordered to justify being there when she felt a hand touch her shoulder. "It's best not to drink alone." Wayne smiled down at her. "Imbibery loves company. Why don't you join us? It's just the office crew celebrating a successful week."

She could think of no reason to refuse, so she took her drink and let him guide her, his hand touching the small of her back, to the far corner where two women and two men were seated around a larger table. "Sal, Frieda,

Jed, Rita," he said when they arrived at the table, alternating the names by sex or rhyme, "this is Gail Hunter, of whom you may have heard, but do not know. Gail is one of our rising stars." He offered her the chair he'd been using and dragged another from a nearby table. His voice hinted at the thickness drinking can cause.

The foursome shared Wayne's state of inebriation. "Hi," Rita responded on the group's behalf. "We're happy to meet a rising star."

"Not to mention someone who makes our stars rise," Sal joked. "That's why Rita's working for us."

Rita whacked him in the shoulder. "I'm the secretary," she leaned into Gail and confided. "Which means that I, along with Frieda, run this dog and pony show and let these dorks have the credit. Except for Wayne. He just grabs it and runs." She produced a pleasant leer. "Whatever it might be."

Gail had placed a smile on the way over and kept it there below her eyes.

Jed joined in. "Unfortunately Frieda and Rita don't give a it." The table-mates exploded in laughter. Gail forced herself to chime in. At some point maybe she'd even feel it like she felt Wayne's arm brushing hers as he rocked with laughter.

Frieda said to her. "We really aren't a bunch of drunks. We work hard. We're celebrating a great week. Did you think it was great?"

"All of the meetings were wonderful."

"We're also celebrating the best six months in company history," Sal informed her. "Business has never been better, especially in the northern part of the state."

"That's Gail territory," Wayne told the others. "Our field reps are the engines that make this company run, and hers is exceptionally well tuned."

"Wayne is just awful." Rita leaned into Gail again. "He makes every-thing sound sexual."

"Oh, really. I'll have to keep that in mind."

"Say," Sal said, "we'd better watch it. We're going to have Gail thinking that we're a childish, fun loving, party-going bunch who keep a telescope in the office so we can keep an eye on our representatives."

"They do, you know," Frieda said. "We can tell if the boys have seen anything when they don't stand up straight until they push their hands in their pockets."

Oh my gosh, Gail thought.

"I hate to say this, but I have to go," Wayne announced. "I have to get my wife to the airport. She's flying to see her folks for a week."

The preceding announcement was brought to you by Lech Incorporated, Gail told herself.

"Can I walk you to the elevator," Wayne asked as he rose.

"No, thanks," she said. "I want to visit with these nice people."

The four watched their boss leave. "Seriously, he's really a good guy," Rita told Gail.

"He'd give you the shirt off his back," Sal agreed.

"Or the pants off his butt," Frieda added and the quartet screeched so loudly that the remaining patrons turned their heads to check them out.

Gail knew Wayne knew she'd retained her room for the weekend. She also knew she'd see him on Saturday.

The knock on the door came early enough so that she might still be in bed. She wasn't. She knew who it was. His attraction to her was obvious. If this was a game, she wanted to see it to a conclusion. Had to even.

"It's a beautiful day," he greeted when she opened the door. She was dressed in jeans and a light blue sweatshirt. He wore the same outfit except the shirt was navy. "You aren't surprised to see me. You look great."

"No, I'm not and I'm going to keep these on," she announced. "I've been coming to the Cities all year, and I want to see them for a change. You're going to be my chauffeur." She slid a windbreaker from its hanger. He followed her out the door.

Wayne was a good guide. Raised in the Cities, he knew them well. He was good at zipping his Jaguar through traffic and wise in his choices of stopping places – the cathedrals, Zambro Park with its rolling hills and blooming flower gardens, the theaters and art complexes. He took her to an overlook above the river where they watched barges, tugboats, and early canoeists floating between the greening banks and trees. Everywhere, the perfumes of spring were intoxicating.

The downtown buildings gleamed in the blue day. He took her to lunch at a revolving restaurant atop the City Center building. From it she saw the Cities as islands of commerce amidst blue waters and verdant landscapes.

Their talk was airy, their subjects the places, people and objects that floated through their view. She offered no reaction when the back of his hand arched on the car's stick shift to brush the side of her thigh.

When he told her he had some fabulous houses to show her, she knew one would be his. She felt a protest rise toward her tongue, but quelled it. She told herself she wanted to discover how much disparity there was between his pursuit of a livelihood and the reality of the one with which she'd been living. There was enough truth in that for her to confine her words to appreciation for the large, graceful homes perched along the gentle rise to her right overlooking the lake to his left.

"There's mine," he said pointing to a large two story red brick residence with supremely white shutters perched deeper on the rise than its neighbors. Its expansive lawn featured two broad-branched Norway pines at either end of the house. He turned up the long, curved driveway and came to a stop between the rear entrance and the three-car garage built into the hill. "I assume you want to see the inside," he said, brushing her again as he shifted and shut off the engine. He opened his door and walked around the car to open hers.

She sat cinched by the seat belt. "Do you sneak all of us in through the rear entrance?"

"There is no all. I shouldn't have let you stay with those idiot friends of mine. They've warped your mind."

"Or you have." Gail unsnapped the belt. "Nice rear entrance though."

"Come on. Let me show you the place," he urged, opening the white screen door and the oak door behind it. "It's very nice. I'm proud of it."

It was more than nice. Extensive remodeling had converted small rooms into open areas of light. The wood floors gleamed. The furnishings were spare but rich. The place had obviously never been exposed to kids. "It's lovely," she told him. "You should be proud."

"So's the upstairs," he pointed and ascended the curved open staircase. He was halfway up before he turned. "It's safe."

She followed him, her mind a mix of red flags and relentless attraction.

He showed her the master bedroom with its king-sized bed, its walnut headboard, bureau and dressers, the walk-in closet where mostly Alieta's clothes hung, and the large bathroom off it with its gold-plated fixtures.

Down the hall were a guest bathroom and a bedroom that contained a regular-sized bed, a small desk with a computer on it, and a dresser. The rear window overlooked the garage. "Great view of the woods," he opined. "You ought to take a look." As she walked to the window and passed the open closet door, she saw shirts and suit coats hanging there. She continued toward the view anyway. The trees were a stunning mix of greens.

She sensed his approach. "Beautiful," he breathed.

She pivoted past him. "Your room?" she asked indicating the closet.

"I call it my office, but, yeah, sometimes."

She walked into the hall and stopped at the doorway to the bigger bedroom. "Do you prefer that?" he asked.

"I'm used to smaller rooms. Why isn't Alieta here?"

"She was here all week. She stays while I work late and leaves for awhile afterwards to get even."

Gail left the doorway and descended the stairs. She sat in one of the white leather easy chairs and listened to him padding into each room before coming down. The day had clouded over. Spits of rain spotted the huge picture window overlooking the lawn and the lake.

He sat on the sofa opposite her, his hands behind his head, a quizzical look on his face.

"Is it a requirement for continued employment?"

"Gail," he moaned, dropping his elbows to his knees and leaning towards her, "that is not a thing I do. It's not an initiation ritual. Why don't you believe that?"

"Lack of practice, maybe. Your beautiful wife so conveniently gone. Being brought in through the back door. You should have shown me your front lawn and the view of the lake," she finished, the rain washing the window and blurring the view. She pointed to the portrait of the two atop the fireplace mantel. "Is it because she has beautiful black hair and brown eyes and mine are blonde and blue, and you want a little of each?"

He shook his head, then pushed up from the sofa. "I think we'd better go. I think I've offended you severely."

She did not answer, but rose and walked through the kitchen and out the back door to the car. He locked the house, turned up his windbreaker collar and hunched against the increasing rain. His posture reminded her of the telescope story. She didn't suppress her laughter as he slid into the car.

"What?" he asked.

"I'll tell you later," she said, "but it isn't because I think I won."

The rain was pelting the roof of the car. "Mind if I wait until this lets up a little?" He looked miserable as a boy caught in his mother's purse.

She felt a stab of sadness for him, for Kyle, for herself. Visiting misery on others seemed to be a growing talent of hers. She could not help touching his arm. "No, it's all right. It's a beautiful house, Wayne."

"Alieta's father gave us the down payment," he said without having to do so. "For a wedding present. It was like a challenge. Could I support his daughter in style?" He looked at her, his cockiness dissipated. "I have. I've worked hard. Alieta doesn't like my hours, but she likes the life style."

"I imagine sometimes she feels lonely and left out of your life, and she's afraid you feel like a kept man," Gail guessed. "I don't know about the third, but I'm familiar with the other feelings. I should have shown you the house I live in. It's a one-story house with log siding. Kyle works the kind of hours you do. He could manage a little bigger payment, but if we saw a house within shouting distance of this one for sale, we'd shake our heads and drive by."

After the rain diminished, Wayne took her to dinner. Then he offered a movie and she accepted. It was a comedy about the complications of infidelity. They watched with their hands in their laps, neither one laughing.

When they returned to the hotel, Wayne checked the roster at the front desk to see how many workshop participants were still registered. Then she noticed him looking up and down the hallway as they exited the elevator and walked to her room. She unlocked the door and told him it would all right if he came in for a while. She went to the window and drew back the drapes. Below the wet streets sparkled with reflected light. "The Cities are pretty at night," she said. "Did you know what that movie was about?"

"Depending on your reaction, I'm either not that smart or that dumb.

One of the eight-balls in the office said something about it being good." He shrugged and showed his sidesaddle grin.

Gosh, and I thought there were only six, she wanted to say, but didn't. Don't water the tree if you don't want it to grow. Instead she said, "I have to get some sleep. I need to get an early start. Kyle has an imagination."

"So do I," he said as she guided him to the door, her hand on his back.

She turned him to her. "I have to figure out what I'm thinking, Wayne. Today I have too much empathy with Alieta." She let herself smile. "Timing is everything. You should have seen me Wednesday morning."

His grin burst into full bloom. "Maybe I did. That is a working telescope, you know."

Patty Light

"I want to try to talk today," Patty Light told Elaine Stafford. "I can write forever. But someday I have to be able to talk."

"You can talk. These forms from your teachers tell me you're quite verbal in most classes. One says you're the leader in his."

"That's Mr. Baker. That's different. I'll bet my other teachers didn't tell you that."

"As a matter of fact, they all score you above average in class participation. They say you're always prepared and always respond when asked."

"Maybe I can't stand silence."

"You mentioned Mr. Baker in particular. Can we talk about him?"

"I love American Literature."

"That was quick. And?"

"What do you want me to say?"

"It isn't what I want that matters. I'm wondering if there's more to it as far as Mr. Baker is concerned. He and Mr. Hunter are the only teachers you've referred to by name. I think we can dig a little deeper with them."

"I still don't know…"

"I'd like you to talk about Mr. Baker."

"I'm not in love with him if that's what you mean."

"That's quite a leap. Can you tell me about him? I don't know him."

"You do know he's my English teacher."

"Tell me more about him. What's he like?"

"Why is this so hard when writing about Mr. Baker would be so easy?'

"Well, Patty, it's risky. Once the words are said, you can't erase them, crumple them, or hide them. It's clear from your journal that you and your mother don't have normal conversations, just shouting matches once in awhile, with her doing most of the shouting. Or silence. Either extreme makes saying anything hardly worth the price. You're reluctant to burden her life with your problems anyway, though you burden your life with hers.

But I did notice in your journals Mr. Baker is one person you do talk with and that it was your choice to approach him. Can you tell me about that."

Patty took a deep breath. And let go. "I'd . . . He wasn't supposed to be our teacher. Mr. Gerney was. Everybody loved Mr. Gerney. He was this great teacher. The kids were expecting him to be their teacher. He wasn't, and they were really mad. Mr. Baker didn't have a chance."

"All the kids?"

"Just about."

"The infamous herd instinct. How did you . . . "

"I apologized for their behavior. He looked so shocked when they treated him like they did. Like he couldn't believe it was happening."

"Is there more to it than that?"

"He tries so hard. Almost everybody stomps on everything he tries to teach. Like he isn't even human. Like he doesn't have feelings."

"So you've decided to rescue him? Like you try to rescue your mother?"

"That isn't fair," Patty answered. "He loves what he's teaching. I can see in his eyes and hear in his voice how much he loves it. I love it, too. He's deep and full of thoughts and feelings and hardly anyone cares. I wanted him to know I care."

"That's why you became his student assistant?"

"It makes me feel good. I help him. We talk about stories and poems and ideas. There's nobody else I've done that with. I could fly when I leave his room."

"Do you have any idea how he feels?"

"He loves it," Patty said so boldly she shocked herself. "Oh, that's awful. Maybe I just think he loves it because I do. I'm so self-centered."

"That's one thing I think you're not. Quite the opposite." Elaine paused, and then plunged onward. "I think you need to know Mr. Baker wrote extensively about how important your presence has been to him. I know we're supposed to concentrate on you, but I can't help wondering how he's survived."

"He's changed the way he teaches. He's clamped down really hard. He's quit trying to smile. It's hard on him because that's not who he is. It makes me so angry," she said. "My class isn't quite as bad."

"Maybe because of you?"

"A little bit. But it really helped when Billy transferred in."

"Billy? I don't think I saw . . . "

"I told you I have a friend."

"No girl friends though?"

"There's no point in having friends at all. Billy just happened."

"Let's talk about him. I read about a friend in your journal. Was that Billy?

"Yes."

"Would you call him your boyfriend?"

"That would wreck it."

"Would he want to call you his girl friend?"

"Only if he wanted something. And if he did, he wouldn't be my friend."

"You like him though. As a friend."

"I like having a friend."

"Would you say you love him? As a friend."

"I'd never say it. It would be like lifting up my skirt."

"If he said it?"

"It would be like him lifting up my skirt."

"Do you think Mr. Baker loves you?"

"I hate that question! Billy said he does. It made me mad! It wrecks everything!"

"Is it okay for you to love someone?"

"If I don't say it. If I did, it would open doors I'm going to keep shut."

"The journal entries you asked Mr. Hunter to read, I read as well. The situation and feelings you described in it are what brought you here."

"Yes. But I think you don't want to see me again after what I've said."

"On the contrary, I'm so anxious to see you that I want to see you sooner than we'd scheduled. I want to see you on May 1st. I think we have lots of work to do, but you've done a ton today. I'm anxious for you to get that three thousand pound guerilla off your back and shrink that sucker to the size of a schnauzer.

"You did unlock doors today. A lot of memories and thoughts may rush through them. Keep your journal handy in case that happens and write whatever you need to write. Keep my card handy. Call me anytime you feel confused or overwhelmed, day or night. I want you to know we can meet before May 1st if need be."

She stood up. "In the meantime, I'd like to give you a thank you hug."

"I don't know. I'll try," Patty whispered. Every instinct told her to resist the request, but need leaned her into the arms of her counselor. She held on until her trembling eased and a moment of comfort wound through her defenses and hinted at how being at peace might feel.

Greg Schwarz

Clad only in his shorts, Greg Schwarz renewed the final phase of his Annual April Ritual. After track practice, he hauled a chair into the bathroom of his small apartment, set it sideways, stepped up on it, and looked at himself in the bathroom cabinet mirror. All he actually saw was the protrusion of his stomach over the elastic band of his shorts. "Disgusting," he growled.

He stepped down. If he gained much more weight, there wouldn't be room for him in his bathroom, and the chair would collapse under the stress.

He always delayed exhuming this ritual until several weeks after track practice began. Though he coached only the field events, he persisted in hoping wind sprints at the end of practice would reign in his girth so he could quit jogging. But for the fifth consecutive April, the mirror convinced him jogging would have to remain the major component of Greg's ritual.

Weight was no problem during football season. Laps, tackling dummies, blocking demonstrations and stress made sure of that. But the delicate balance of exercise and food significantly tilted over the winter while he concentrated completely on teaching.

I ought to join Kyle and Gail on the ski trails next year, he told himself. Or if George quits, I could assist Henry with the wrestling team. Now there was an interesting guy. Physics teacher and wrestling guru. No wonder his boys won trophies at State yearly.

But the wrestling program took too much time. Greg never felt like a natural teacher. He was, however, determined to be as good as he could be and that took the same focus he gave to coaching.

So . . . maybe skiing with Kyle and Gail. Or Kyle at least since Gail seemed to be off somewhere a lot these days. Thinking about that made him sad. To him, Kyle and Gail were the perfect couple, just like Red and Beth and Sam and Sarah.

He dug a sweatshirt out of the hamper. Three sweatshirts and they were all in the hamper. He endured the shirt's musty odor and itchy texture as he pulled it over his head. He really had to get himself to a laundromat!

He laced his sneakers and jogged into the April pre-twilight. The pervasive scent of spring, enhanced by a late afternoon shower, was unique to the North Country. He'd miss it if he wrenched up his roots.

He headed past the college to the lakeside running path. He preferred running towards twilight just as he preferred running streets and paths to circling the high school track. It was interesting to trot by the stately houses and manicured lawns, the college campus and its students, to the broad tarred path laid out between the lake and the houses. There were always joggers on the streets and path, most slimmer, who flashed smiles as they floated by him.

The older houses on the upper side of the path were mostly rentals. Not all of the occupants were students though. Some were untenured college teachers, some worked downtown, and some were teachers in the Blue Lake School System.

A short distance ahead of him, a runner bounced down the deck steps of one of those houses and jogged in place, long, slender legs glinting in the sun, brown pony tail bobbing. Nice, Greg thought, startling himself. He thought of women as sisters, like the three he had, and women thought of him as the brother they could kid with. When he noticed a woman as a woman, that was different and so was he. It made his stomach twirl the same way jogging did, thickened his tongue, and mushed his brain. Which was why it was unnerving when he heard himself repeat, "Nice."

The runner ahead began a slow jog toward the path as he neared. The two were going to intersect. He thought about slackening his pace, but that would look rude and be stupid. She'd sprint away like a deer anyway when she saw who he was and how much he looked like a postal box with legs.

The other runner resumed jogging in place. He was about to pass by when she joined him. "Coach," she said as she adjusted to his pace.

"Janis James?" He'd never seen her in shorts and ponytail. At school she wore business teacher suits or tailored slacks and blouses. But the voice and face belonged to Janis James. "What a coincidence," he remarked, his breathing becoming labored.

"Not exactly," she said.

"What?" He was perspiring profusely.

"You've been running by our place about this time every evening for a week. I've been waiting for you."

"How?" His rank sweatshirt clung to his rounded belly. His back roared with itch.

"I spotted you last week after I finished my run. Since then my friends and I have staked out the deck to watch for you. We thought we'd have to take shifts. But you're very predictable."

Gads, she was hardly breathing. He could collapse any second from oxygen deprivation. "Your friends?" he half-gasped.

"They think you're pretty cute."

That was too much. His lungs were so emptied of air he was fizzling like a balloon. He spotted the bench where he always stopped before turning back. "I have to sit down," he wheezed.

He expected her to offer a cheery farewell and whiz her merry in-shape way down the path. Instead she said, "Sure," shifted to idle, and seated herself next to him on the bench, her slender bottom grazing his hip.

Good grief! No wonder he couldn't catch his breath.

"Are you that out of shape or just excited to see me?"

Mostly the latter, he was shocked to be thinking. He recovered enough to answer, "I think it's my sweatshirt."

"Actually, since you've been rendered helpless and nearly voiceless by your sweatshirt, I'd like to resume that conversation from the teacher's lounge, Mr. Schwarz."

"You can breathe."

"Precisely. Besides, I've been trying to get your attention for two years. Now that I've sprung the trap, I want to keep your little paws in it. Who knows? If I wait until you get in shape, you might race away from me as fast as those football player legs of yours can carry you."

Like a boulder bounding away from a gazelle, he thought, trying to will his eyes off her tan gams.

His heart continued to thump at an alarming rate, but he recaptured his ability to inhale and exhale. "I'm ready to run again," he announced, mostly to avoid the topic she'd raised. Disappointment drew down the corners of her smile. Darned if that didn't touch his heart.

The two ran as far as the boat harbor that fronted downtown Blue Lake, Janis gliding gracefully, Greg's legs heavy as concrete. He could barely hear her easy breathing over his wheeze. They stopped at the pier, and she pointed at the orange glow of the sun on the lake while he bent over, clutching his shorts. Then she pointed back up the path. She established a much easier pace on the return run.

All the way back he worried about the right way to part when they reached her walkway. She solved the problem. "Come on up to the deck and rest for a minute. We've got iced tea in the fridge. I wouldn't want you passing out on your way home."

As he followed her up the sidewalk, squeals of delight emanated from within the house. "Must be watching a fun show," he said.

"They are," said Janis. "Have a seat on the porch swing. I'll be back in a sec." As she opened the screen door, she noticed him eying the swing and shaking his head. "Don't worry. It's been reinforced." Then she disappeared into a round of giggles.

By the time she returned with two tall glasses of tea, he'd gingerly seated himself on the swing and was swinging tentatively. He bent his knees and pushed his toes against the porch floor under the swing to halt its motion as she handed him a glass and sat next to him, brushing that exact same spot.

"I think you purposely cut our conversation short at your bench," Janis accused, but her voice was as sweet as fresh strawberry shortcake topped with a swirl of whipped cream. "So. Refresh my memory. Remind me of the reasons you're thinkin' of leavin' 'cuz it isn't pleasin' to me."

This whole scenario had evolved into something so pleasant, he had no desire to abandon it to reality.

"Are you all right? Are you still awake?" she asked into his hesitation.

"Yeah. I'm just trying to recover my ability to put a whole sentence together so you won't think I've had a stroke. What was the topic? Oh, yeah. Got it. The reasons I'm thinkin' unpleasin' thoughts of leavin'. Throats dry. Okay?" He took a delaying sip of the lemony tea, the outside of the glass moistened by the melting ice within. "Do we really have to talk about that? Can't we pretend I was just playin'? Know what I'm sayin'?"

"Yes. No. You weren't. Competitive rhyming won't distract my quest."

"Must I?" Either physically reacting to his reluctance or out of concern for the swing's stability, he pressured the toes of both his feet more forcefully against the deck.

"No, but I hope you will." She was studying his face with interest. Maybe that was reason enough to comply.

Then the extra distance he'd jogged and the multiple affects this lady was having on his psyche combined to create an excruciating charley horse along the entire length of his right calf. "Oomph," he grunted. The sudden shot of pain jerked his glass skyward. The tea leapt into his face as the glass squirted out of his hand and somersaulted to the deck. As he leaned forward to recapture it, his charley horse created a twin in his left calf. "Oomph!" he cried again as the glass rolled down the deck towards the steps. Janis leapt off the swing to rescue the vessel, upsetting its delicate balance. Greg pitched off it and belly flopped to the floor.

Janet heard the thud and whirled. "Oh my gosh! Greg, are you okay?"

"Charley horse!" he groaned. "Horses!" he amended.

She dropped to his side. "Where?"

"Calves, back, both," Greg moaned.

He felt her hands kneading the knotted muscles on his left leg, both his legs bent like a stop action photo of a broad jumper. He dropped his head on the arm that had saved him from a face flop as well. He heard the screen door creak, and Janis commanding, "Jane, Joan, Sally, wipe those stupid grins off your faces. Get over here and help me! He's got two horses!!" He heard the slap of bare feet pass his head and snorts of suppressed mirth. Then four pairs of hands were all over the massed muscles. "He'll do anything to keep from answering my questions," Janis stage-whispered to her roommates, broadening the snorts to tinkling amusement.

"Too bad the charley horses aren't in his thighs," one of his caretakers commented, sending gales of giggles swirling off the porch to the path, which caused several runners to pause in mid-stride to observe the activities.

Greg should have been embarrassed, but those hands felt so darn good, and his caretakers were so darn entertained that he could not stop the stupid grin that plastered his lips against his clenched teeth.

Ed Warrum

"It was something else," Ed Warrum summarized. "Worse than talking to my father. At least I know what to expect from him."

"Actually the pastor did you a favor. Prevented you from stereotyping," Billy Cloud said as the two left the locker room after track practice.

"Like stereotyping that all ministers care about people? Yeah, it would be awful if they were all like Pastor Dan and Pastor Barker. Anyway, for reasons too hard to explain, I got this thought that maybe Mr. Baker would be a good guy to talk to about this stuff."

Billy shot a surprised look at his neighbor. "Hmmm."

"I know you and Patty talk to him. I'm aware he has something against me, but . . . "

"Oomph!" Billy said as he banged his foot into the bottom of the first step. "Glad I'm wearing boots."

"That's what happens when you get lost in thought, my suddenly silent friend. Blinded by the Light?"

"Not exactly," Billy answered as they ascended the steps. "We decided to stay at the quiet end of the pool. Nope. I was thinking about something my Dad told me."

"Care to share?"

"Let's just say he believes that people can change. Sometimes even for the better. You for instance. Look how much better your life is since you changed your mind and decided I make a better friend than punching bag. Hey, I'll race you the rest of the way up. If I lose, I'll blame it on my broken toes." He was whipping up the steps before Ed could respond.

When they'd attained the top floor, Ed gasped, "Where we going?"

"To the quiet end of the pool."

Ed shrugged and followed Billy down the hall. He slowed as they neared Mr. Baker's room. "Hey, I don't know if I should just barge in there," he half whispered. "You didn't seem enthused about my idea."

"Not to worry. That's not why we're here, my friend. Patty asked if I'd mind walking her part way home."

"Maybe I should leave."

"No need. You're always invited."

Ed stopped as they neared room 313, shook his head, and pointed at the floor. The few encounters he'd had in that classroom with Mr. Baker hadn't been positive. No use pushing things too fast. It was possible the idea was as nutty as Billy's lack of reaction suggested.

He could hear Billy's voice and Mr. Baker's. He thought he heard his name and "oh" and "uh-uh" in response to it. Or was he just paranoid?

Then he heard Patty's voice. It always reminded him of quietly beautiful music. Good thing since she and Billy were still the ones in the class who did most of the talking. Ed was no better than the rest. No wonder Baker felt hostile towards the Big Deal Star Quarterback who sat and stared at his desk all period day after day. It had nothing to do with Baker, but how would he know that? And then there was that day in early April . . . .

By the time Patty and Billy emerged from the room, Ed was slumped against one of the lockers lining the hall.

"Oh, oh," Billy said, "you've been thinking again."

Ed straightened. "Hi, Patty." She smiled a greeting. Then the three descended the stairs in silence until they encountered Mr. Hunter headed upward.

"Students," he said.

"Teacher," Patty returned.

"Impressive recognition by both, don't you think?" Billy noted.

Once outside, Billy glanced at Patty, then upward toward Mr. Baker's room, then back to Patty with raised eyebrows. She shook her head and murmured, "Maybe later." The trio fell silent as they walked to the corner.

"It's a beautiful day," Ed said as they waited for the stoplight to change. "You two got time to go down to Lakeside Park and sit for awhile?" He wanted to talk about Mr. Baker, but he also wanted to avoid going anywhere near his father's store. His mother's and father's lawyers had arranged a meeting today. One of his father's requests was that during the period of separation his son would work at the drug store to keep the lines of communication open.

"Sure. It's Friday and it's the end of the month," Patty replied. Ed didn't understand her reason but was too pleased to question it.

Lakeside Park stretched from the road fronting the older section of the college campus to the lake a quarter mile away and featured playground equipment, picnic tables and a sandy beach that formed its boundaries. Only a few families picnicked near the playground. An exceptionally passionate couple were stretched into each other's bodies on the beach. The woman was blonde and wore tight shorts and a halter-top. She'd apparently oiled all the exposed areas of her body the way she glistened. The man lacked hair on his upper body and had acquired a wicked sunburn. Apparently numbed to pain, he poured liquor into two cups while the couple kissed.

"Whew, talented, that guy. Bet he can walk and belch at the same time." Billy fanned himself. "I think we'd best sit a ways away to avoid viewing the final meltdown."

"Yes," Patty agreed, shivering as she turned her back to the beach.

Once the three were seated at a picnic table, Ed asked if it was okay to talk about Mr. Baker. Patty assured him it was.

"While I was waiting for you guys outside the room," Ed began, "I was thinking about the reasons I should or shouldn't talk to Mr. Baker." Patty looked puzzled. "I don't know if Billy told you that I was thinking about it." She shook her head. "See, the deal is, I've been too much into my own crap to care about Mr. Baker, but I keep thinking about stuff he's taught us. Sometimes I even quote him to my mother and sister."

"You should tell him that," Patty encouraged.

"Do you know what's going on with him, Patty?" Billy asked.

"All I know is I'm worried about him. I haven't been in as much after school because of the counseling, but when I do get there, he's so grateful to see me. I correct papers and we talk about poems or stories or my writing or whatever, and he's so pleased. When I leave the room, I glance back and he's staring at me or out the window, and he looks so . . . so alone. I end up in tears, just like I am now." She dabbed at her eyes with the backs of her hands. "I can't hide these any more. I called my counselor about the way I cry so easily lately. She said, 'Cry. It's good for you.'"

The word "counselor" struck Ed. First of all because he needed one, but also because he had no idea Patty did. He asked, "You're in counseling?"

"Oh," she said, "I thought you knew since you and Billy are friends."

Billy shook his head. "Not my place to say. Yours. I'm glad you did."

"Why?"

Billy tipped his head toward Ed. "Not my place to say. His."

"I was talking to Billy about a bad counseling session I had with a pastor. Your counselor is good?"

"Yes."

"I thought I was the only one I knew who needed counseling. I thought you had it wired."

"You'd be surprised. But I'm surprised about you, too. Every boy in school wishes he was you. You know that day of the blizzard when we sat in the cafe and talked? That was the closest I've ever come to feeling like a normal human being. Later the same day I rediscovered how unnormal I am. So that's why I'm in counseling. But you wanted to talk to Mr. Baker?" she said to shift the focus from herself.

"Yeah, but I'm aware the man doesn't like me much."

Patty started to protest, but Billy stopped her. "No use telling you you're wrong. He's made a few comments, enough so that I talked to Dad about it. Dad guessed Mr. Baker needed a target for his frustrations. So he picked someone who might have been an ally, but wasn't. Sort of like you singling me out for that punch. I probably wasn't the worst guy you knew, but I was there when you needed me. Bad example maybe?"

"No, a good one. I haven't shown Mr. Baker much except the top of my head. I should've stepped up, but I didn't. So I was thinking about that and all the other reasons he isn't too anxious to talk to me, and I came up with the clincher. You got time to hear this story? Maybe it will help you two help him because I doubt if I can."

His listeners nodded.

"Beginning this month, I was walking to school. I saw him standing in the middle of the sidewalk across the street. Just standing there stock-still for a long time. I suppose I shouldn't have stopped and stared, but I did. I like to think I was concerned. So, anyway, while I was watching him, he did the same thing with his hands that you did, Patty, when you were tearing up. Then he saw me. I thought maybe he was embarrassed, so I turned away and went into the school through the unsupervised door.

"It was a real weird scene after that. I was in the hall looking at the trophy case, and I heard this noise coming from the direction of the doors. I looked, and there was Mr. Baker coming up the stairs with this gang of kids trailing him. I saw this one guy doing an imitation of way Mr. Baker walks in the halls. You know, like he's trying to be invisible. Everyone pointed at the guy and then at Mr. Baker and laughed and poked each other. It was ugly. Mr. Baker looked desperate. I felt bad for him, but I didn't do a thing about it. I turned my back and stared at the display case so I wouldn't have to watch. That's the problem. I never do anything." He shook his head. "You two do something."

"You've had a few problems of your own," Billy said.

"Maybe you can tell him about that sometime," Patty suggested. "It would be good for him to know."

"That's what I kind hoped you'd say since that's what I was thinking. Well, part of it."

Then Ed pointed at the empty swings. "You guys like swinging when you were young? I could use that feeling right now."

"I wouldn't mind swinging into spring myself," Billy said as he slid off the picnic table bench. "Or did I mean springing into swings?"

"It would be fun to have fun for a change," Patty agreed. "Mind if I join you?"

"Race you both," Ed challenged.

"Well, I don't know about her, but I'm mostly Native American," Billy replied, then zoomed off toward the playground.

"That's the second time today," Ed told Patty. "Some might say he cheats. Not me, of course."

Soon the three were arcing the air, Patty between the boys, her skirt tucked between her legs, not like high school students showing off, but like grade-schoolers, their toes pointing toward the shore where the lovers lay.

As they eventually eased to a halt, Patty noticed a figure slouched against a tree perhaps twenty feet away. "Doesn't he look familiar?"

Billy studied the form for a moment. "It's that Marin kid from our English class. I know the jacket."

"Yeah, yeah. Frank."

"He's drinking, isn't he," Patty said as they watched him extract a brown bag from between his legs and lift it toward his face.

"Might as well wear a sign saying 'I'm getting drunk' as to hide a bottle in a brown bag," Billy said.

"Looks like he's staring a hole through those two on the shore," Ed observed. "He probably doesn't even know we're sitting here."

"He probably doesn't even know he's sitting there."

"It's too sad for words," Patty said." She stood up. "Would you boys mind walking me toward home now?"

Frank Marin

It wasn't like he hadn't seen them. He'd seen them all right. He was sitting against the tree when they walked past him, not twenty feet away. That's why he stuffed the bottle between his legs and clamped them together. Last thing he needed was for someone to report to the school that he was drinking in the park.

Betts was laid out on the shore not thirty feet in front of him heating up the sand with Brick. One of Brick's buddies had seen Frank downtown and mentioned that Brick had been hustling Frank's chick, and he'd seen the two lovin' it up on the shore. That was why he was propped against this tree trunk now. It was pure chance that he'd seen Patty and her boys. He'd had to tear his eyes off Betts and Brick so he didn't explode across the grass and beat the crap out of somebody. And there the three of them were.

Ah, forget that. Forget them. His fish was frying on the beach. He reverted his eyes to those two. Friends. He sure knew how to pick 'em. His eyes threw flaming rivets at the tangled two. You'd think their hair would burst into flames. If Brick had any. But Frank was invisible. Just like he was invisible to the goody six shoes. Just like in school where nobody knew who he was until he started shooting off his mouth. Then they all thought he was pretty funny. Except for Strand, who didn't think he was funny at all.

Neither did Eddie and Albert. Since he'd been suspended, he'd come straight to work after partying by himself in his room. Couldn't sleep. Thinking, drinking, thinking. Didn't shower either. For two days the guys had just turned their backs. Finally yesterday, Eddie had said, "You know what, Frank, you stink. You've got to take a bath or something. I'm gagging." Then he and Albert worked as far from him as they could and turned him invisible there too. It made him sad. He liked those guys. The problem was they had no problems, so they couldn't understand why he did. But he'd heard what Eddie said, and he'd showered this morning.

He checked to see if anyone was looking, then took a tug off the bottle in the bag. He'd drunk three-fourths of this bottle and nothing was happening except it felt like someone had placed a boulder on his head.

Betts was glittering like a diamond in the sun. He was looking at her, and she didn't even know it.

He wanted to take another drink, but he was paranoid about his classmates. He jerked his head around to see if they were at the picnic table. They weren't. For some reason he felt abandoned. He jerked his head further and spied them. On the swings! Like little kids! She was sitting between her boys. Geez, he wished the wind would blow her skirt right up to her eyes. No, he didn't. He was disgusted for even thinking that. He admired Patty Light.

He'd been invisible in classes, too, until he decided he didn't want to be. Now he was Mr. Funny and Outrageous Guy who said the stuff everyone wanted to say but didn't. The only class he felt bad about doing that in was Baker's. Partly because Patty was in it and he didn't want her to think he was a jerk. Partly because he hadn't felt invisible in there. Baker wasn't his enemy at all. He was just the guy everyone wanted to get.

He took another glance at the swings, but the threesome was gone. So he turned his full attention to the sand bunnies. He could see himself exploding across the grass and giving Brick a kick with his boots he'd never forget. Could see him rolling in the sand gasping and pleading for mercy. Could see Betts' frightened eyes soften into admiration when she saw who had rescued her from that hairless piece of crap.

He couldn't see himself falling asleep though. He just did, just sort of slipped sideways off the trunk of the tree and sprawled next to it, his legs loosening their grip on the bagged bottle, his eyes floating back in his head.

He sat up with a start. It was dark. The bag was by his leg but the bottle was gone. Brick and Betts had stolen the bottle. The boulder had crushed through his skull while he slept, and his head was a throbbing mess. He needed a drink but his bottle was gone.

He wove his way home along the darkest streets he could find. He didn't want to feel afraid, but he did. Afraid someone would rush out of one of those strange houses and attack him. Afraid a dog with a lolling tongue and rolling white eyes would leap into the road and go for his throat. Afraid he was going to fall down and be unable to get up and get run over while he lay there helpless.

It took forever to get home. When he finally arrived, it was completely dark. His parents were working swing shift. Saving the farm and losing their son. His head was pulsing. His stomach was full of grease and nails. He stumbled to the bathroom and threw up. Then he stumbled to his bedroom and slammed its door shut.

He did not turn on the light to sit at the desk heaped with the spit wads he'd been making every night recently, the ones on the right regulars, the ones in the middle arrowed with small, sharp pins, the ones on the left packed with BB pellets. He did not picture himself putting his plan into action or the classroom roaring around him when he did. Instead he fell into bed and watched Brick and Betts writhing behind his eyes until he felt sick again and lurched to the bathroom, barely making it in time.

Patty Light

Dear Desired Help,

Tonight I write in my silent bedroom in my silent house after placing a call to you. I know tomorrow I will be sitting in your office shaking with fear, but oh so ready to remember what it is in the past that makes the present so difficult.

A week ago I came home from the Park where I saw and heard beauty, joy, lust, loneliness and sadness and felt it all. I had fun, too. Mindless as a child should be, swinging into the wind, feeling free. Flanked by boys, young men really. Feeling almost safe and almost free as we talked and played and walked. I loved that afternoon. I treasure it. But I ended up in my room not trusting its reality, not trusting my happiness, not trusting the friendship of my friends, not trusting my friends would remain my friends if they knew my darker heart.

That is why I called you. That is why I will be sitting in your office tomorrow waiting for you to finish listening to these words. For I want it to be real, I want to trust, I want days like today to happen again and again. I don't want them to become unattainable memories.

PL

Having finished reading to Elaine Stoddard, Patty Light sat staring out the window at her favored tree. Other trees had burst their buds. She'd watched the magic greening of trees, grass, and shrubs, seemingly within hours of one another. But this tree kept its buds tightly wound.

"Why doesn't it bloom?" she asked.

"Too much shade, too little sun."

Patty swung the office chair she was sitting in toward the counselor. "You're very clever. You're aware I identify with the tree."

"It doesn't take cleverness to recognize you ache to burst into bloom. I think you've progressed a considerable distance toward that goal."

"I didn't shake to pieces when I was swinging between Billy and Ed. That's progress."

"It is."

"Will it last?"

"Yes, I can confidently say it will because you're so willing to work for it."

"I am. Today could be a long day for you though."

"I have the whole day. It's yours."

"Oh, dear. It's beautiful out there, and you're going to be cooped up in this office. I feel selfish. Maybe we should postpone this."

"When we've made all the progress we can stand, we'll go somewhere. Shall we start?"

"Yes," Patty responded, not knowing whether it was anxiousness or anxiety she felt.

"I need to tell you I'll be pushing into places of pain."

"No pain, no gain. Right?"

"Right. Let's warm up by talking about last Friday. I've met Billy through you. Who's Ed?"

"He's Billy's friend. That's too easy. I don't go to games, but everyone says Ed is a great athlete. He plays quarterback on the football team. He plays basketball and track. He's tall and nice looking."

"And no shakes." Patty shook her head. "So other than his looks and athletic prowess, is there anything remarkable about Ed?"

"He's unhappy. Usually he looks like he's wearing a mask. Its message is, 'Leave me alone. Keep your distance.' But it's not what he wants."

"I wonder if anyone really wants that. You like him?"

"Yes, I do. He's honest. He's not happy with his life, but he blames himself. So he's like me. Who would ever think that?" She recalled Ed's request. "He needs someone to talk to. I told him I'd tell you that."

"That might be possible. Have him give me a call," Elaine said. "Anyone else at the park? I mean anyone you particularly noticed?"

"A boy named Frank who's in our class. He was sitting under a tree drinking. You could almost smell it from the way he looked. Even if you didn't see the bottle sticking out of the bag between his legs."

"How did you feel about him?"

"I've noticed him before. He wears his hair like Elvis Presley and wears a leather jacket and heavy boots all the time. I don't think he has any friends. He never used to talk." Patty paused. "Lately he's been making remarks to people around him in class. I can't hear his words, just the rumble of his voice. I've turned around when he's said something. He has this false grin on his face. Everyone is leaning away from him and giggling."

"So you don't like him?"

"I feel sorry for him."

"Anything else about Frank you want to say?"

"Well, it was obvious he was staring at a couple on the shore who were just about having sex on the sand in front of everybody." A tremor rippled her. She clenched her hands in her lap as though that would force it to cease. "Maybe she used to be Frank's girl."

"How did you feel about them, the couple?"

"I felt sorry for Frank," Patty answered. "Maybe that's why he was getting drunk." However, it was the couple that filled her mind, and her tremors persisted.

Elaine leaned forward. "That's interesting, Patty, but not an answer to my question. I can see you're trembling. You weren't before, so something about that couple triggered your reaction. If we're going to alleviate your pain, we have to talk about that and them. I need to ask my question again, and I need you to answer it as honestly as you can. How did you feel about the couple making out on the beach?"

"I thought they were drunk, too."

"That's what you thought. How did you feel?"

Patty gave in. "I felt disgusted! Revolted!" Her fingernails dug into her palms.

"I'm sorry, Patty," Elaine said, "but I have to pursue this, and you have to trust I know what I'm doing."

"I'll try," Patty forced through rigid lips.

"That couple is dominating your mind. What are you thinking about the woman?"

"I'm thinking she's stupid. No, not stupid. Pathetic. Sad and pathetic. He's using her, and she doesn't want to know it." Patty hissed the words.

"He poured liquor and kissed her at the same time!"

"Does she love the man?"

"She's desperate. She thinks if she lets him do whatever he wants, he'll keep her. He'll stay with her."

"He doesn't like her?"

"He doesn't care! She doesn't matter! He only cares about himself! If I walked by them wearing this skirt, he'd be thinking about reaching up it at the same time he was fondling her. He doesn't care about her at all! He'll say nasty things to her and about her after he's done."

"So how do you feel about him?"

"I hate him!"

"Do you know anyone like him?"

"My father," Patty whispered. "He's just like my father." Her hands flew to her cheeks, and she closed her eyes. "Oh," she gasped, and then, "Oh no." Then she sat immobilized and silenced.

Elaine Stafford placed a pack of Kleenex on the arm of her client's chair. "I think we're moving quickly, Patty. I'm going to let us rest a minute. I've got sodas in that little fridge over there. Want one?" Patty murmured a response, her face hidden by her hands. The counselor rolled her chair to the refrigerator, opened it, and took two sodas. She rolled back and extended one far enough from Patty so she had to reach for it. "I don't want you to go into hiding," Elaine explained, "because what's going to follow is really important. And really, really hard."

Patty reached for the drink. "I'm afraid," she said. "But determined."

"Yes. I think you want to get through this as much as I do. Can I ask you questions about your father?"

Patty remained immobile.

"You'll have to give me permission."

"I wish you wouldn't . . . I wish I didn't have to . . . This is hard. Okay. I mean it's okay. Not great. Just okay."

"Let's try starting with something easy. What did your father look like? Can you describe him for me?"

"I was only five when he left," Patty reminded her. "I think he was tall, but everyone's tall when you're five. He had light brown hair. Everywhere. Maybe he was handsome. My mother must have thought so."

"How did he dress?"

"One leg at a time?" Patty said to ease her tension. Elaine smiled, but made a circular motion with her index finger. "I don't know. I only watched him get dressed a few times," she continued, and then stopped in shock. She recoiled into her chair.

"Did you like him?" Elaine asked, her eyes searching the girl's face.

"I wanted him to like me and Mommy. He didn't. He liked my brothers. I was afraid of him."

"Why were you afraid?"

"Because of the way he treated Mommy. It was like he hated her."

"What made you feel like he hated her? Can you give an example of what he did?"

"I could tell you a hundred examples," Patty answered, her face rigid.

"Can you give me an example?"

Patty pushed a scene into her mind. "Sometimes at the supper table, he'd be sitting there, and Mommy would be cooking at the stove. He'd make us all sit there while Mommy made supper. He'd bang his hands so hard on the table the bottle by his plate would jump in the air, and I'd jump in the air, and he'd holler things like, 'Where's our food, you old hag!' and my older brother would laugh loud and repeat, 'Where's our food, you old hag!' Then my father would get this devil's smile on his face and say, 'Way to tell her, boy.' I'd look at my mother and her shoulders would be shaking. She never turned around until the food was done."

"Was your father ever nice to your mother?"

"Sometimes after something like that happened, I felt so sick and scared I couldn't eat. I'd go out in the front room and sit on the sofa. No one cared. My father and brothers would be in the kitchen talking really loud, saying bad things to my mother. When my brothers finally came running through the front room, I knew supper was over, and I wouldn't have to eat. Then I'd tiptoe to the kitchen, and my mother would be standing at the sink and he'd be standing behind her real close. I couldn't see his hands, but he'd be saying things like, 'You love it.' Somehow he'd know I was watching. He'd turn his head with that same devil grin on his face."

"Why do you suppose she let him do what he did?"

"She was desperate for him to love her. It mattered more than anything else. She'd do anything for him."

"Such as . . . "

"Anything. She washed and ironed and cooked and cleaned until the house sparkled. If he called her name, she ran to him. He could say whatever he wanted as loud as he wanted, and she never raised her voice. To him. Sometimes he'd come home late and sometimes not for days, and she never said a thing, just made him something to eat. I could smell him in my bedroom some nights, and I could hear them in theirs, and she never told him how much he stunk."

"I'm sorry I have to keep this going, but I believe I need to hear this, and you need to express it. I promise you it will remain between us. Can you tell me anything else your father did that upsets you?"

"He kept being mean. He didn't just touch her in the kitchen. He touched her anywhere and everywhere, and he didn't care if we were watching. He liked it. He'd reach up her dress or unbutton her blouse right in front of my brothers and me and say, 'This is the way you do it, boys.' And my mother would just take it, just stand there or sit on his lap or whatever he wanted and take it." She paused, shame and anger mixed on her face. "Sometimes he'd tell her she was too fat, and he'd push her off his lap. That's when she started taking her pills, I think, and he'd tell me to sit on his lap, and Mommy would get this horrible, helpless look on her face. He'd jiggle me and slide me and bounce me like I was two, and my older brother would laugh. Then he'd tell me to get off his lap, and he'd go upstairs, and Mommy would follow him and we could hear them."

"Your father was a sick man. You're lucky he left."

"It didn't feel lucky. It felt awful."

"Can you tell me about that – about when he left?"

"If I have to."

"I believe saying it out loud will begin to take away the power these experiences have over your life. That's why I'm asking you to try. If you can't, I'll understand."

"It's why I'm here," Patty said angrily. "To get away from him." She stared hard at her counselor and then at her clenched hands. She loosed the fingers from one another and gripped the arms of the office chair. "Here I go," she told herself in a voice close to a whisper.

"One day my mother came out of their bedroom and down the stairs and into the front room where my brothers and I were sitting watching cartoons. She was wearing a nightgown you could see right through in the sunlight. She pulled the drapes closed and walked by me and tapped me on the shoulder. 'Come with me,' she said. I followed her up the stairs. When we got to the landing, she said, 'your father wants to see you,' and she pushed me into the bedroom. I could see him lying on the bed, and I tried to stop, but my mother said, 'He wants to see you right now,' and she put both of her hands against my back and pushed me into the room." The words were flying out of Patty's mouth as though taking a breath would stop them forever. "He was lying on top of the covers without any clothes on. 'Come here,' he said. When I did, he said, 'Put your hands like this,' then, 'put them there.' My mother was in the doorway, and when I just stood there, she said in a voice that sounded like he had his hands around her throat and was strangling her, 'Do what he says, Patty,' then backed out the door. So I did and I looked at my father's face. He wasn't looking at me at all. He was looking at my mother. He had this awful, twisted look on his face. I did what he told me to do. I could hear my mother thump against the wall across from the door. I could hear her crying. Then my father pushed me away so hard I slid across the floor all the way to the wall. He jumped out of bed and pointed at me and shouted, 'You're disgusting! Your mother's disgusting. I'm outa here!' Then I got up and I ran to my room and shut the door. I could hear things slamming and him shouting and mother crying hard. He took my brothers and left that same day. I haven't seen him or my brothers since." She raised her eyes and looked hard into Elaine's. "It was awful," she finished. "It was all awful."

Elaine rolled forward in her chair and took Patty's hands in her own. "You're one of the most courageous persons I know," she said. Patty slumped back in her chair, spent.

"Now I need to tell you some things," Elaine said, holding her client's hands and searching her face. "The first is that none of this was your fault. Your father was a sick man and your mother became sick, too. Somehow you've had the inner strength to rise above them and create a positive life for yourself.

"But I also need to tell you what's evil about abuse. It keeps finding ways of reproducing itself unless its cycle is broken. You've bent it before and broken it today, and with further work I believe it will stay broken.

"And I want to tell you why I kept pushing you. When you wrote the cat family story in your journal, I believe you were calling for help. This story is in there. What we did today is remove its metaphors. You've found a way to fully free yourself of a significant, submerged event. I suspect you'll be experiencing a wild range of emotions for a while. The world may feel more beautiful and more painful than ever. That may seem like a high price to pay for freedom, but I guarantee from personal experience, it's worth it. For now, for my peace of mind, I need you to promise you'll call me every day to tell me how you are. And remember whenever the need arises, my door is open. Walk in without knocking.

"So. After you've rested, I'd like us to pick up a pizza. Then I'd love it if you'd take me to that favorite place of yours. We'll have a pizza picnic if you don't mind."

Patty nodded, then turned her attention to her tree. A smile touched her lips. "I was hoping it bloomed while I was talking," she said. "It didn't."

"Remember that tree, despite its circumstances, has continued to grow for years. Just like you. Give yourself and the tree enormous credit for that."

In mid-afternoon, the two exited the office, climbed into Elaine's Civic, and headed off to pick up the pizza. The route to Ronald's took them past the high school.

"I'm glad it's Saturday," Patty said. "This is one day I'm glad I didn't have to be there." Nevertheless, her eyes climbed the walls to the third floor to see if lights were on in Mr. Baker's room.

Her counselor turned left, a choice that resulted in her driving past the building Mr. Baker had pointed to months ago as being where he lived.

"That's funny. The door is open," Patty murmured.

"What?" Elaine asked.

"Mr. Baker's place. The door is open. I wonder if the wind blew it open. I don't think he'd leave it open on purpose." She noticed two boys with their backs to her wearing hooded sweatshirts entering a car parked around the corner. Her mind was too full. She closed her eyes. "I hope he's somewhere having a good time," she said. "He deserves to have fun for a change. So do I."

"That's certain. You really care for him, don't you."

Too tired to disagree, Patty murmured, "Mmmhmm."

She stayed awake long enough to direct Elaine to the small park four miles from town that bordered Blue Lake. She led her to the pine-populated ridge where she'd sought sanctuary many times over the years. She watched Elaine spread a brown blanket within the grove of trees, then managed to eat a few pieces of pizza before she gave in and stretched out on the blanket, protected by the trees and her counselor, and fell asleep.

She dreamt of herself swimming beneath the surface of Blue Lake, the glint of the sun hiding her from prying eyes. Like a dolphin, she could surface when she wished, so she felt no panic or need to breathe as she flowed with the current through the diffused light, trailing the bubbles that proved she was alive. When she decided to surface, she formed prayer hands and dolphined upward. She was just breaching the surface beneath the blue sky, the white clouds, and the sun when she awoke.

Kyle Hunter

Kyle Hunter knew he should stay home and watch his wife work on product sheets and order forms. He tried. He sat for several hours in the silent house and stared at the rapt face above the table, a stack of forms to her left, another in front and a third stack of finished forms piling to her right beside catalogues and fliers. This was a task she'd begun Friday afternoon. He knew she looked to him like he'd looked to her all the years he'd been teaching. No wonder she'd gone berserk.

The irony of this Saturday scene was that he had not one journal nor a single paper to read. The gods must be laughing so hard they were toppling off their thrones.

Whatever. Kyle couldn't take sitting here watching her face, her mind miles away, any longer. She might as well be in New York. He might as well be at the Blue Lake Municipal Golf Course.

"I'm going to call Greg," he said, "to see if he wants to go golfing."

"Mmmhmm," she responded.

"If you don't mind."

"Uh-uh."

"Maybe Robert Baker, too."

"Uh-huh."

Greg was happy to be asked. When Kyle tried Robert's number, a recorded message told him it was no longer in service. That was odd. Surely the teacher hadn't fled town between yesterday and today.

He decided to stop by the apartment.

"See you," he said as he opened the front door.

"Uh-huh," Gail murmured. As he closed it, he thought he heard her add, "Have fun."

He threw his clubs in the back of his pickup and headed for town. Greg would be meeting him at the clubhouse, so he'd have room for Robert if he wanted to go. On the way, Kyle revived his guilt about neglecting the young teacher. He had only vague impressions about how things had been going for Robert lately. The man still said little at department meetings, and his colleagues, Kyle included, didn't ask enough questions. He'd heard via the student wireless that Robert had clamped down, and his classes had become quiet and orderly. That was good news. Some teachers who had the reins yanked out of their hands never regained control. Conveniently satisfied, Kyle had immersed in his own classroom and omitted Robert Baker from his concerns.

He pulled to a stop in front of the building where Robert lived. The boarded store looked depressed. Robert's apartment above it was awfully small. It was a shame a beginning teacher couldn't afford better.

Kyle tried the entryway doorknob. It was loose, unlocked and barely caught the latch. He climbed the scuffed stairs, and knocked on the apartment door. Robert Baker called, "Just a minute," in an irritated voice.

"Oh." said Robert when he opened the door. "It's you. I thought it might be kids. A few have come calling. They sneak up the stairs, knock on my door, and then race down the stairs screeching obscenities. So I usually the lock the downstairs door and dead-bolt this one."

Oh, geez, Kyle thought. Why can't they leave this guy alone? But what he said was, "I tried to call. You didn't take your phone out, did you?"

"Want to come in?" Robert offered. "Nope. Unlisted number."

Oh, geez. "Kids have been calling, too?"

"With not pleasant things to say, I'm afraid."

"I'm sorry to hear that." Kyle paused, then continued. "The reason I came over is to ask if you're interested in playing a round of golf. Sounds like it would be a good idea for you to get away from here. You golf?"

"I have. Sure. Why not. Unless you're really good, I mean. I'm not that good. I don't have clubs either."

"Pro shop rents 'em out. Greg and I will treat."

He saw Robert blanch, undoubtedly remembering the crack Greg had made in the teachers' lounge. "You sure Greg won't mind. I don't think he respects me much."

"The only thing bigger than Greg's mouth is his heart. Problem is he shifts his brain into under-drive and his mouth into over-drive sometimes."

"Well, okay, sure. It might be good for me."

Better than holing up in this bandbox. That could drive a guy nuts.

Once they were in the truck, Robert asked, "How long does it take for a teacher to stop making stupid mistakes?"

"Oh, until the day after tomorrow. Reason is what works for one class looks like a mistake in the next. Why? I hear your classes are going well."

"From the outside maybe it looks that way. I have them quiet. I suppose that's half the battle. But it's like sitting on a volcano. They're seething, waiting for reasons to explode. I can't stand how grim I feel. It just gives them a different reason to despise me."

"Are you sure you're not being hard on yourself?"

"You didn't hear about that gang that trailed me from the entry doors halfway up to my room a few weeks ago? I thought it was the talk of the school."

"Not a word. But I've been isolating, trying to catch up on paperwork."

"I can understand that. Anyway, I don't know how many there were. I couldn't bear to turn and look until I reached my room. It felt like hundreds." He grimaced, reliving the scene. "I suppose it was twenty-five."

"Well, however many there were was too many. Did you report them?"

"Who would I pick? What would I say? Kids were walking up the stairs behind me?"

"Nobody noticed this going on?"

"Anderson did. I heard him shouting them off the second floor as I went up the stairs. It was too early for them upstairs. I think most of the classroom doors were closed. I decided if they hated me that much, and I was miserable, maybe they'd leave me alone if I loosened the clamps."

"Oh, oh."

"Yup. It started off as five minutes free talking time at the end of the period. I give them five minutes, they take ten and I end up shouting."

Kyle turned the truck onto the golf course road. The early afternoon was bright and blue. Maybe traipsing the course would ease the tension that had Robert rewired.

Greg was waiting when they entered the pro shop. Janis was leaning against the counter beside him. "Uh . . . hope you guys don't mind. Uh . . . Janis was thinking about golfing . . . "

"Actually, Kyle, I happened to call Greg this morning to find out if he was still a total gimp," Janis beamed. "Apparently not, though he's still walking gingerly."

"There's got to be a story here I haven't had the privilege of hearing."

"Oh, I'm so disappointed. I thought you boys told each other everything. He didn't tell you how my friends and I saved his legs? I can't believe it."

The rush of red to Greg's face made even Robert smile. "So anyway, I happened to tell Janis we were going golfing. And I asked her if she golfs."

"Like a pro," Janis acknowledged.

"That's what she said, and here she is. So if you guys don't mind, she'd like to join us."

"I've never seen my silver-tongued friend's tongue quite this de-sil-vered. I must say it's a treat to witness this. Mind? We'd be delighted."

Janis' tee shot proved she wasn't blowing smoke. Her drive sailed straight as a string for 180 yards and bounced for 20 more. Greg shook his head and smiled.

Then he nearly corkscrewed himself into the ground with a mighty swing that resulted in a topped ball dribbling ten yards beyond the tee. "Charley horse effect," he muttered.

"Greg has a Mighty Joe Young swing that produces Mickey Mouse results much of the time," Kyle informed Robert. "But the breezes he creates generally blow the ball further than that. There's someone here he's trying to impress, and it ain't us."

He was pleased to see another smile crease the younger man's face and equally pleased that Greg had reduced the pressure on Robert to perform well. Though his stiff swing betrayed self-consciousness, the young man managed to stroke the ball within fifteen feet of Janis's and enabled him to finally exhale.

The afternoon weather escalated to incredible. A warm breeze eased in from the southwest under the blue sky. Kyle, Greg, and Janis poked fun at one another and offered Robert encouragement. This round of golf was working out well. Kyle ought to thank Gail for making it possible.

Greg's game was as inconsistent as always. For every dribbled drive, another boomed off the driver, but rarely in a predictable direction. "Sometimes Mighty Joe gets his way," Kyle told Robert, "way left, way right, way short, and, very rarely, way to go."

"Robert," Greg quipped, "if I golfed like me, I'd quit."

The foursome achieved a relaxed rapport. While Robert remained reticent to risk the ribbing the others exchanged, he laughed out loud more than once at their jibes. That was progress.

When they'd completed eighteen holes, Greg announced, "My back hurts, my side hurts, my arms ache, my charley horses are having ponies. I'm having a great time! Everyone else ready to do early dinner at the Club? The food here is great. My treat."

"You heard all that from the expert on everything," Kyle told Robert.

Once in the clubhouse, Kyle phoned home. Response was slow, but at least the line wasn't busy. Still, he was about to hang up when Gail answered. "Hello, ma'am," he said, "my name is Kyle Hunter. My friends and I have completed eighteen holes of golf. Adding a fresh face to our mix might reinvigorate our cliché-ridden conversation. We took a vote, and you have been selected the lucky winner of a dinner at beautiful Blue Lake Country Club." He hadn't tried the light touch in a long time. Maybe that was one of their problems.

"Oh, Kyle, I'm sorry. I already ate. And I'm drowning in paper work."

Disappointed, Kyle replied, "I thought maybe a drowning person might appreciate being tossed a life preserver. I guess not."

"Please, Kyle, don't," she pleaded.

"I won't." He tried reversing the downward direction he'd chosen. "We're having a good time. Even Robert. And Greg's found a female friend," he added, hoping that bit of gossip might pique her interest.

It didn't work. "He's very fortunate. I suppose you'd like to find one too," she said, her voice too sad to be mocking him. "I'm very sorry, Kyle. I just have to get this work done today. They're calling later tonight."

"I'll bet they are."

"To check my progress. It's my job. You should understand that."

"It is and I should. You're right," Kyle agreed, struggling to wind up his call on a positive note. "It's okay. Like I said, we're having fun. Even Robert Baker has laughed a time or two."

"And you, too, I hope."

"Yup. Me too. Listen, I'll see you later after I take Robert home. Gotta go." He hung up the phone without either of them saying goodbye.

When he returned to the table, Greg was absent, but Janis and Robert were engaged in earnest conversation. That was a good thing.

"So what's the topic?" he inquired, sliding onto the vacant chair beside Robert.

"Teaching," Janis replied.

"Shocking."

"Comparing notes."

"Did you say nuts? Greg and who?"

"You. But I said notes. On the first year of teaching. We agreed it must be what purgatory's like."

"Or that other place," Robert added.

"Robert says his first year won't win any ribbons."

"But today will. Great weather. Great company. I'm truly grateful. I did admit to Janis that I'm envious of her. She's so up and enthusiastic."

"So I reminded him I'm in my second year, and that makes a big difference. My classes are mostly electives. And I didn't replace god."

"Good points all," Kyle said. "Besides, Robert, Janis is experiencing the exhilaration of snapping up the man she's pursued since she heard his first pep rally speech.'

"I gotta admit Greg's good at those things," Robert said. "Even I attended that league championship game. Never would have had it not been for that speech."

"I go to all the games," Janis proclaimed.

"No doubt to gain a better view of Greg's assets."

"You're awful, Kyle. I don't know why a sweetheart like Greg gives you the time of day. No, I go because it's fun. Also I see the kids in a different way."

"Another mistake I've made . . . " Robert said.

"I really didn't do that as much last year. I was overwhelmed by work. The first few games I went to, I ran into some students who gave me grief. So I stayed away for awhile."

"Exactly."

"Then I decided a few students were not going to determine my life and deprive me of things I like to do."

"I tend to think it's most of them. So maybe there's hope after all."

Greg returned in time to hear the last exchange. He placed his meaty hands on Robert's shoulders and kneaded them with surprising gentleness. "There's always hope, my friend. Teaching isn't easy, but it's almost always interesting." He patted the young man lightly on the back, and moved around the table to sit by Janis. "And once in awhile, you get a real nice surprise that just knocks you off your feet. That's what keeps me going." The others burst into laughter as the big man's face rushed to full blush. "Hey, you guys know that isn't what I meant," he protested.

"Today was a godsend," Robert Baker enthused as the teachers settled into Kyle's pickup. "I think there's hope for me."

"'Hope is a thing with feathers,'" Kyle quoted. "You know, I don't have the slightest idea what Emily Dickinson meant by that."

"Maybe she was writing about the angels in her life that gave her hope." Robert laughed. "Who'd think I'd include Greg Schwarz in that group? Say, since I'm feeling so good right now, I wonder if I could run a teaching idea I've been thinking about between my usual bouts of angst?"

"Sure."

"Well," he began, then stopped. Thinking about it now, the plan he devised seemed a little crazy. But he realized that one of this problems was that he hadn't asked enough questions this year. It was quite possible he might benefit from changing that. "Since I've had quite a few reminders that most of my students don't care for who Robert Baker is . . ."

Kyle glanced at his passenger. "Just a second. I need to remind you that the problem has been who you aren't, not who you are."

"I'm not the guy who's been riding herd on his classes, verbal whips at the ready either," Robert responded. "Anyway," he pressed on, "here's what I came up with. I had three terrific high school teachers. Mrs. Vam quietly conveyed how much she loved kids and how important their thoughts and feelings were to her. She was all eyes, ears and heart. Mrs. Macauley loved literature so much that she'd literally bend over double with delight or leap into the air with her glee to be teaching it. Prizinski was this dramatic guy who could make a grammar lesson as exciting as reading Shakespeare. One time he got so carried away he ended the period standing on his desk.

"My plan is to tell the kids a little of what I told you and tell them I'm going to try an experiment using those teaching techniques."

"Interesting. As long as you don't forget there's nothing wrong with being Robert Baker."

"I'm also going to try structuring my classes in a new way to do that. Here's how it goes. Monday will be 'Hear about it Monday'. Then, 'Read about it Tuesday'; 'Write about it Wednesday'; 'Share about it Thursday'; and 'Forget about it Friday', which really means free reading, library time or some activity I can dream up. So what do you think?"

"I think it sounds innovative and a bit risky. I also think if you keep in mind that you have an established fall back technique, it could work."

"We'll hope. You know, I really enjoyed sharing that idea with you, and I really appreciate your feedback. Maybe I ought to do this more often."

❖ ❖ ❖

The elevation of the man's mood made what they found at Robert's apartment building all the more devastating. The entry door was wide open. "Darn," Robert said, "did I forget to lock it?" He jumped out of the truck as soon as Kyle parked and hurried into the building. Kyle turned off the motor and followed him inside. This was no big deal, he was sure.

He was wrong. Each side of the stairwell walls had been sprayed with long, thick lines of red and yellow paint. Upstairs the words 'Bobby the Bastard,' 'Up yours,' and worse obscenities were splayed all over his apartment door and the walls beside it. Even the ceiling dripped splotches of paint. Robert Baker sank on the landing, his head in his hands. He could not prevent himself from crying.

"Damn it!" Kyle grated, "Damn it! I'm going to call the cops, Robert. We're going to get these vermin and they're going to pay!" Damn, damn, damn! his mind shouted. We were getting somewhere, you maggots! We were getting somewhere!

When Kyle returned, Robert was seated on the landing beating his doubled fists against his knees. Kyle sat beside him to await the police. Robert turned his strained face toward him. "They think they can make me quit. But they can't. I refuse to quit. I refuse. I refuse."

Sam Strand

All Sam Strand could do was shake his head as he sat with Kyle Hunter and Robert Baker in Robert's apartment. "It makes me want to punch holes in something!" Sam rumbled. "Grab the perpetrators by the collar and shake them until their teeth fall out! Why would anybody do this? They're sick little cowards."

"At best." Kyle eyed his colleague, who sat staring out the window.

"I know what I'd like to do in response," Sam said, "but I want to talk it over with you, Robert."

The teacher flinched. "Sorry. Lost in thought." He stared at the principal. "Sorry for ruining your Saturday, Mr. Strand."

"You've nothing to be sorry for. Whoever did this does. The question is what to do about it."

"The police dusted everything for fingerprints and took pictures of the footprints," Kyle said. "They'll find out who did this."

"I have no doubt this is the work of kids. What I'd like to do," Sam told the two, "is call an assembly and read the riot act to the entire junior class. This stuff doesn't happen in a vacuum. Read it to myself, too."

"Why?" Robert asked.

"Things like this happen partly because the administration has dropped the ball."

"I don't want you to call an assembly," Robert said.

"Why?"

"Nobody got beat up. Nobody died. Besides, they'll know why the assembly was called. I don't want the spotlight. I don't want them blaming me because they're being yelled at."

The three fell into silence. Robert was right. He would bear the brunt.

"How about making the annual May warning a little stronger?" Kyle suggested. "Every spring we deal with the same round of irritants, Robert — sunflower seeds, water pistols, spit balls, hormones in the halls, graffiti in rest room stalls. Every spring Sam puts out this announcement warning of consequences for these abuses. Maybe he could add more weight to it."

"I'd prefer that. It will be spotlight enough."

"You didn't do anything wrong," Sam reminded him. "What I've heard is that you've been doing a good job." He wished the young teacher believed him. "I'll honor your wishes. But I assure you that when these punks are caught, the consequences will be severe."

"Fair enough," Robert replied with a disturbing lack of passion.

Sam pledged to himself to be as attentive as possible to this teacher's needs over the next month. This invasion had pierced him deeply. He'd rather Robert was full of rage, even if that rage was directed at an administration that was no longer able to do its job.

Robert Baker

Robert Baker kept the ants at bay until Sam Strand and Kyle Hunter left early Saturday evening. Both offered to put him up at their houses until a dead bolt could be installed on the entry door. He declined. "I don't want them to think they've scared me out, even if they have," he told the two with a wan smile.

"Well, at least give me a call if you even imagine something might be going on around here," Kyle pleaded. "Or call 911."

"Sure," Robert said, knowing he'd do neither.

After Mr. Strand and Kyle were gone, he kept his TV and radio off and tried to read a few student papers. That was a mistake. He could not dismiss the image in his mind of students massed and ringed wherever he was, regarding him as an enemy who needed to be eliminated from their lives. Janis had assured him that wasn't so as had Kyle, as would Patty Light and Billy Cloud, as would his freshmen if they knew. But the image burned in his brain.

"That's nuts," he told himself, but he did not go to the window. He sat in the silence, amazed by all the pops, cracks, whirs and hisses emitted in this place. They beat through his ears into his brain until the ants reappeared.

Oh, he wasn't crazy enough to actually see them, nor to think they were real. But he could feel them funneling along underneath the hair on each of his arms, burrowing inward until they congregated in his chest and set his heart racing while his brain buzzed the news of their endless activity.

He roused from the table where he'd sat for hours and dropped fully clothed atop the covers on his bed. If the punks invaded again, they sure as hell weren't going to find him naked. They'd find him fully clothed and lethal. He wished he had a gun. But was glad he didn't. If he had a gun and they came again, he'd use it. That thought brought the ants to a dead halt where they chomped relentlessly at every nerve ending in his body.

He finally slept though he never knew he closed his eyes. Three times he heard doors slamming and raced to his own, hoping to catch and clutch the jacket of at least one invader and hurl him down the stairs. But he found no one, only the red and yellow words and the red and yellow stripes that glowed in the dark, pulsing messages of their disdain and his failures all night long.

may

Greg Schwarz

These had been great weeks for Greg Schwarz. There had been nothing to undercut his enjoyment of life, and Janice to enhance it. Life was good.

Then Sam Strand informed the faculty of the vandalism of Robert Baker's apartment building at the annual 7 a.m. Monday Morning May Warning Meeting. "I'm telling you because exaggerated stories will circulate among the students, and you need to know what's accurate and true." He supplied his dismayed listeners with the details he knew. "Kids talk," he concluded. "Keep your eyes and ears open. Robert believes calling an assembly will not be beneficial to him. I agree. Keep his name out of discussions of this announcement, but present its contents with a little extra passion. Impress upon your students that every word and warning is written in concrete. No exceptions."

"It's a shame," Janis told Greg as they exited the meeting. "Robert enjoyed himself Saturday. Then someone had to wreck it. It's not fair."

"It makes me want to vomit on someone. I've never had a year that gave me so many reasons to be ticked off."

The two entered the teachers' lounge and sat down with Kyle and Red.

"Kind of makes you wish for the old days," Red said. "Respect used to just be there," Red said. "You used to have to lose it. Now you're supposed to earn it. Hogwash. It's continually being eroded." He leaned forward in his chair, and folded his hands. "Did you ever see those polls that say a high percentage of people think public schools are lousy except for the ones their sons and daughters attend? The powers that be ignore the last half. Thus the growing disrespect. Thus the election of single agenda school boards. Thus the graffiti all over Robert Baker's entryway. It's sickening. Almost makes me glad I had the heart attack. Gives me an excuse to get out. And I'll tell you, I hate to feel that way. I've loved this job."

"Throw in thirty plus students in every class you teach," Kyle added. "Robert never had a chance. So this school, and maybe education period, is likely to lose two teachers forever. One was born to teach and the other, given a chance, could become a first rate instructor."

The warning bell jangled. "Guess what the kids will be talking about," Greg rumbled. "They'd better not be doing it where I can hear them."

Billy Cloud

"Baker, Baker, Baker . . . " It was like a sick chant. The whole Junior Class was talking about nothing except what had happened at Mr. Baker's apartment Saturday.

Billy Cloud hadn't heard about it until this morning. He'd spent most of Saturday making disturbing discoveries at Moon Ribbon Ridge and Sunday clerking at The Cloud House. He listened to the details of the story build as he walked the halls to his locker. By the time he got there, the tale had escalated from graffiti sprayed on walls and doors to the trashing of the entire apartment. The excitement of the storytellers boiled his blood.

He stood in front of his open locker staring at its contents, his ears filled to overflowing. How in heck could they enjoy that event, much less the endless re-tellings? Since he'd transferred to the third period class, he'd had the sense that Baker's troubles had lessened. Apparently that class was an oasis.

He boiled over. He retrieved his books and slammed his locker door. He turned to the teeming hall and shouted, "What's the matter with you!"

All within earshot fell silent. They'd never heard Billy raise his voice, let alone shout. He was known for his athletic prowess, intelligence, sense of humor. Not this.

"Leave it alone!" he blasted toward the stunned faces.

From somewhere within them, a voice whined, "Whatsa matter, Tonto!" Nervous laughter followed the remark, then silenced.

Billy dropped his books and headed toward the voice. "That, for one thing!" he seethed.

The crowd melted in front of his rage, leaving a tall, thick blonde boy standing alone by the lockers. Billy advanced, his hands flexing at his sides until he was close enough to see rivers of perspiration streaming the boy's face. He stopped inches from the other. "I assume you meant that as a compliment," he hissed in the boy's ear. "But Tonto's fictional. Try Little Crow. He's real. Crazy Horse. Bug-O-Nay-Ge-Shig. They're real. Better get to class now." He strode back to his books. The drenched, deserted boy wouldn't trouble him further.

The first morning warning bell rang. When he turned again the students had disappeared into their classrooms.

He calmed himself enough to realize that what he was hearing, Patty Light was also hearing. His emotions were churning. Hers would be off the charts. He slammed his books back in his locker, and headed down the hall to find her.

Ed Warrum

Over the past eight months, the students with lockers close to Ed Warrum's had learned to leave him alone. His morning visage was locked in a permanent scowl. His tense body language reinforced the message that it was best to stay away from him. Nearly all the time they did. He was satisfied with that. He had no words to explain what was going on in his life and no desire to share the details.

So why did his fellow juniors keep approaching him this morning with the opening line, "Did you hear what happened to Baker?" Maybe they thought it was a way to reconnect with him. Maybe they'd heard Mr. Baker didn't care for him. Or worse, maybe they thought he had a knife out for Baker like so many of them did. That thought made him sick. If they had that impression, how could Baker avoid it?

He listened, kept his mask in place, turned his back, and peered into his locker. The story kept changing, the tellers embellishing what they'd heard. It was like they were vomiting in his ears.

When Jerry Jons, the offensive football tackle, approached with his goofy grin and the same opening line, Ed shot out, "I've heard it, Jerry. It makes me sick. So why don't you shut up! You idiots think it's funny. I don't. Get out of my face and shut up!"

He pushed past the startled athlete and found himself ascending the stairs. He had no idea what he was going to say, but at least he could let Mr. Baker know some students besides Patty Light and Billy Cloud cared.

He was surprised to find Mr. Baker standing outside the door to his classroom. Students were staring at him as they passed. If he noticed, he didn't show it, his head unmoving, his eyes focused on the paper in his hand. If he were Baker, he'd grab one of those passersby and beat him until his brains rattled, or throw him face first against a wall. That was what he wished he'd done to Jerry Jons and every other fat mouth spewing in his direction this morning.

As he approached the teacher, he felt a sudden panic. What could he say? Doesn't matter, he told himself. I've got to let him know I care. Then he was standing in front of Mr. Baker, who lifted his gaze to the tall quarterback, his eyes pained. "I . . . uh . . . I just want to say I'm sorry for what happened at your apartment," Ed stammered. He stood there for a moment. The teacher did not respond, only stared at him, and then returned his focus to the paper.

Ed turned and walked down the hall. What did you say, his mind shouted, what did you say! 'I'm sorry for what happened at your apartment.' He threw his head back in dismay. Oh, god! It sounded like I was apologizing! Like I was the one who wrecked his apartment! He stopped in the middle of the hall. He wanted to pivot and go back to Baker's room, tell him he'd worked at his father's drug store all day Saturday as part of the mediation agreement, that he'd been nowhere near the apartment and would never dream of doing anything like that. But what was the use! His stupid mouth would just make it worse.

Patty Light

Dear Desired Help,

Why do TERRIBLE things happen to the people I love! Why did my father treat my mother like he did! Why is she destroying herself! Where are my brothers!

Why? Why? Why did those evil kids have to desecrate Mr. Baker's apartment! Is it somehow my fault? Is the mark of Cain on my forehead?

Oh God, I am so angry!

When I arrived at school Monday morning, I thought my life had turned toward the sun. I'd had that lovely time at the park with Billy and Ed. I'd had Saturday with you when I was finally freed of the anchor dragging down my life. I'd found the words I had to say. I'd shared the peace and beauty of a place I love with someone for the very first time.

And my mother had arrived home Sunday evening, not making me worry into Monday. Even though she looked worn and thin and hung over, she did not shout at me the way she usually does upon her return, just gave me a sad smile as though she sensed my life was changing and wished hers was, too.

I was finally a part of Spring.

My mother was in bed when I left Monday morning, and that was fine. I could have skipped down the sidewalk, but I didn't. I floated instead, floated beneath greening trees as dawn painted the eastern clouds red.

"Red sky at morning. Sailor take warning."

I didn't remember that then, only now. I wish I'd remembered it then. I wish I'd remembered it so that when I went to my locker, I wouldn't have been so shocked when everyone around me half turned their backs so they could talk about what happened to Mr. Baker. I wouldn't have been so shocked when his name whirled all around my ears from every side as they stole glances over their shoulders at me as though he was my lover instead of my teacher. I wouldn't have been so shocked at how they giggled as they repeated over and over and over the words someone had sprayed on his apartment door and walls, saying them just loud enough so they knew I could hear. I wouldn't have been so shocked and felt so much red rage building in me that they knew about this and some knew who did it, and no one said the names, just kept repeating the malicious words over and over and over.

I wanted to leap on the ones closest to me and clench my hands around their throats and scream, "He's a human being! He's a human being! He's a human being!" and sink my fingers into their soft, stupid flesh until they knew he is and I am, too!

Billy saved me, his face as raged as my heart, the words flying away as he pushed down the hall towards me, the people flying away from me as he threw his arm around my shoulders and made me walk down the hall and out the door. I knew he wanted to scream too and had to lock his lips tight against his teeth so he didn't.

We stood in silence for a long time listening to the tardy bells ring and I didn't care that I was late for class. We stood there until I could breathe again. We stood there with his arm around my shoulders. Then Billy said, "Let's check on Mr. Baker," and we reentered the building and climbed the stairs to Mr. Baker's room.

When I saw him standing outside his closed classroom door leaning against the wall, bent as though someone had punched him in the stomach, it broke my heart. I wanted to circle my arms around him until his hurt streamed away and he knew *some people in this place loved him and cared about him. "Not so good a morning, is it," he said to us, his eyes darting around mine as though it was he who had done wrong. He handed the slip of paper to me. The paper said, "Students. The administration and faculty remind you that you are expected to exhibit your best behavior on campus and in the community. Any incidents involving Blue Lake High School students will result in immediate suspension or expulsion for the rest of the year. There will be no exceptions. You have been informed and warned." It was signed, "Principal Strand."*

"All the teachers are reading this to their classes. Everyone will know it's caused by me," Mr. Baker said, his eyes dancing between Billy and me. "I don't care. Maybe it will save somebody else." He finally looked in my eyes and touched my hand with his hand, which was cold, yet wet, as he took back the note. "I'm okay," he said and forced a smile. "Look, nobody beat me up or took a shot at me. Cheer up." Then he said, "I need to talk to the kids inside. You'd better get to class." He put his hand on the doorknob. "Thanks for caring." He was still standing next to the open door of his silent classroom as we walked away.

When we reached Mr. Hunter's room, we stood by the door until he saw us and came outside. "I know why you're late," he said. "I know you don't want to come in, but I think it will be best if you do." After he wrote Billy a pass to go to his class, I entered Mr. Hunter's room, all of the students looking down, afraid they'd spy the mark of Cain on my forehead, afraid if they talked to me, their lives would go to hell, too. Then I sat down to write these words that you will be reading, my whole being racing between rage and heartbreak, rage and heartbreak.

Robert Baker

Robert Baker inhaled as deeply as he could, then exhaled as slowly as he could so that the ants would relax and go to sleep for awhile. He watched Patty and Billy shuffle slowly down the hall, then walked through the door to his classroom.

All the faces that had been staring rigidly at the front of the room turned toward him, their eyes a kaleidoscope of confusion, sadness and anger.

"Tell you what, let's take your desks and put them in a circle so we can talk," Robert said. "But count the desks in each row so we can put them back correctly. My other classes might get upset if their desks aren't where they expect them to be."

"You think?" Charlie Sanderson said as he and the rest of the freshmen rose to begin the task. "They must be the kids we heard in the halls."

The freshman arranged the circle silently leaving a space for Robert's desk, then waited for him to talk.

"The circle is sacred to the Indian tribes I know about," he began. "There are many reasons for that including that the earth is a circle and our lives are, too. For me there's something warm and friendly about a circle. A circle gives words room to breathe, and let's us see who's saying them without breaking our necks."

He scanned the faces. "I can see that many of you are upset. I hope if you have questions to ask and thoughts to share, you'll do that. So let's give it a go and see what we find out."

"I wish you were as cheerful as you sound," Alice Daniels said. "But I don't think you can be. We found out today what happened at your apartment on Saturday."

"Over and over and over and over," Charlie added.

"To be totally honest, I feel cheerful every day I watch you folks walk into this room. Today "cheered up" would be more accurate."

"Aren't you just furious?" Arnie Ament asked. He slapped his hands on the desktop. "I'd be so mad at that junior class I can't think straight."

"We don't know who the vandals are, so I don't know who to be mad at just yet. But, yes, Arnie, I have been furious and sad and hurt and scared for myself and for them."

Janice, sitting next to him, was sniffling softly. "Janice, do you have something you want to say?" he asked.

"Yes, but I don't think I can. I am so sad and mad that anyone would do anything like that to you. But the things I heard them saying in the halls made me even madder."

"Yeah," Barry Dwight agreed. "I grew up on a farm, but my dad drives truck, too, so we could keep the farm. Sometimes he takes me on his longer trips and we eat at truck stops. Some truckers talk pretty rough, but I never heard meaner talk than I heard today. It was as sickening as a dead rat in a toilet."

Red-faced, Randy Miklet growled, "I hate juniors! They're nothin' but a bunch of creeps!"

"I appreciate the feeling, Randy," Robert said. "I hope you'll think about that a little bit before you decide for sure. When I'm upset, I tend to throw the blanket over everybody, but everybody doesn't belong under the blanket. I teach juniors. Some are wonderful people."

"But I heard some of them saying they hate you," Cecily Quintero said tearfully. She was shaken. Hearing the word shook Robert too. "I couldn't believe it. How can they say that!"

"I think sometimes kids use words stronger than their actual feelings. I hope so. But the truth is, Cecily, that word really bothers me."

Robert glanced at the clock. The period was five minutes from being over. "I'm going to say one or two last things and then give you a chance to finish this discussion. One is that I haven't missed a day of school this year. You are twenty of the reasons that is true. Once in awhile I think about taking a day off, but then I think, if I miss school, I'll miss seeing my freshmen. That gets me to school every time."

"Your turn."

Alice raised her hand. "We talked a little while you were outside the room about what we wanted to say to you. It's really hard to know what to say, but we all agreed we should say this. We all really care for you and we know you really care about us. We think you're great and that's all that matters to us."

Those words flowed so deeply into Robert's heart he feared he couldn't speak. But he did. "When I was given this study hall, I had no idea it was going to turn out to be a blessing. I am lucky to know you. If I could hug you all, I would. Teachers aren't supposed to do that. But please consider yourselves hugged.

"Now, we'd better get these chairs back in place so the second period doesn't get upset. Of course, I am not saying that all of them would."

It was nice to have the period end on a note of lightness and laughter. It fortified Robert's resolve to endure the rest of this day.

Patty Light

Patty Light sat staring out the window at the maple tree as Elaine Stafford read the entry she'd written a few hours ago. The tree had leafed. The day behind it was milky blue and gloomy.

"I'm glad you called," Elaine said as she placed the journal on her desk and swiveled her chair towards the waiting girl. "How are you now?"

"I ache. It's too sad. They might as well have hit him. Then he could have fought back. They're such cowards!"

"Yes."

"So are the ones talking about it. They're just as bad."

"I agree."

Patty turned in her chair toward the counselor. "So . . . do you see the mark?"

"No. No mark."

"Then what's the answer?"

"We have found some of those answers. As for Mr. Baker . . ." Elaine stopped and considered her words carefully. "Teaching can be terribly difficult under the best circumstances, especially for young teachers. They come out of college full of idealism. Education courses generally fail to warn them that often their classes will be too large, that some students hate school as much as others love it, that student behavior is terribly important to their success. I have friends who went into teaching and left the profession disenchanted and heartbroken.

"I can imagine Mr. Baker's emotions right now. But I need to tell you that he's in a precarious circumstance. You're loyal and caring. Those are wonderful traits, and you've given him those gifts since you met him. No matter what happens, he will treasure that," Elaine said, aware her words were casting a shadow on the future. "Part of me wants to advise you to develop distance between you and your teacher to protect yourself."

"I wouldn't if I could," Patty said with disgust.

"I didn't think you would. But I needed to voice my concern. Your old wounds are barely beginning to heal. Are you sure you want to chance new ones?"

"Yes, I am sure of that. I've survived so far, haven't I," Patty said. "And you'll be here to help even if I disregard your suggestion because I can't follow it," Patty pleaded.

"Yes, I will," the counselor affirmed, her eyes expressing a mix of admiration and apprehension.

Frank Marin

Frank Marin lay on his bed staring at the patterns of plaster in his bedroom's ceiling thinking that he felt bad about what happened at Mr. Baker's apartment. After all he kind of liked the guy. But the plans he'd been working on for months were all but in place. What he heard a lot of kids say in the halls today confirmed what he already knew; Mr. Baker was his ticket to acceptance. He felt bad about it, but right now acceptance mattered more than anything or anyone else.

When he didn't drink or use, he didn't sleep either. Except in school. That was a mystery. How could you lie in bed all night staring at the ceiling, all the wires in your body yanked tight, and not get a millisecond of sleep, then in broad daylight with everyone watching, fall dead asleep at your desk?

Screwed up. That's what life was. Maybe that's what he was.

Aw, crap, why was he lying here staring into the dark so long it became light? He thrashed out of bed, turned on the desk light and bent the lamp head low so he could see the piles of spitballs on the desk. He swept the unarmed pile into the wastebasket, then unwrapped the others filled with pins and BBs and dropped their paper covers into the basket. He took out paper he'd torn into strips and began soaking and folding a new batch.

He thought he needed three piles. He was almost positive he knew the names of the guys who'd graffitied Baker's apartment, so he knew where to find the two allies he needed to divert attention from him when the day came. Both were in Baker's third period class. One was Jerry Jons. The buzz was that Giggly was the driver for the graffiti guys. The other was that noisy pipsqueak Alan Barbarie.

Heck, you'd think this whole thing must be part of God's plan. Though why God would have it in for Baker, he wasn't sure. It pained him when his mind showed him the surprised – or terrified – look in Baker's eyes when those wads with BBs in them exploded against the blackboard or ones with pins stuck in the suit coat he always wore.

God, it was too bad. It really was too bad.

Robert Baker

It wasn't even mid-May and the birches, maples, and oaks were in full bloom throughout the Blue Lake. The fragrance of lilacs was pervasive. Patty Light had resumed her duties in Robert Baker's room after school. Now more than ever, she felt the need to do so. Now more than ever, his gratitude was overflowing.

On this day, Patty Light's brown eyes were as sparkling as the day. Her long blue skirt was the kind that ripples in wind. Her white blouse was embroidered with a blue flower.

On this day, she mentioned Ed Warrum. "Ed was talking to Billy and I . . . " she began.

"I'm sorry, Patty, but please don't talk to me about Ed Warrum. I don't really care for Ed Warrum. Anything you have to say about him might be used against you." His smile was tight against his teeth. Her smile faded.

"But Ed . . . "

"What's this Ed bit?" Robert asked, opening a window through which the air flowed fresh, warm and scented. He turned to Patty, who sat in a student desk, her palms arched, her fingers lightly touching its surface. "Right now," her teacher said seating himself in a desk facing hers and looking at her, "I don't have much time to waste on Ed Warrum." He watched confusion cloud the shine in those eyes and felt compelled to explain. "I'm sorry but there are things about him that make my teeth grind. The top of his head, which is all I see every hour he's in the room. His silence mocking everything I try. I think he influences the others. I guess around here all you have to do is be an athlete."

Patty straightened in the desk. Confusion danced her countenance. She opened her lips to speak, but closed them and shook her head. Finally she said, "Nobody follows Ed. He has his own problems and thoughts, but he never tells anyone. Except sometimes Billy and me."

"And what does he say?" Robert asked, irritated. He did not want to talk about Ed Warrum with Patty Light. He wanted to talk about poetry and ideas and, he admitted only to himself, the desperation and sadness whirling within him with increasing intensity. But he did not. Instead he watched her face as she continued.

"Ed doesn't want to be the way he is. He has a lot of problems he's trying to deal with. He doesn't show it, but he's very sensitive. He thinks you're sensitive, too."

"Ed should know," Robert snapped, his mind flitting back to the two of them on separate sidewalks in early April, and the students Ed had undoubtedly encouraged to dog him as he tried to escape to his room. Then there was that comment a few days ago, Ed all but bragging that he was among those responsible for the obscenities on his door and walls.

"Don't let him fool you. He sees things and twists them to his advantage. Don't listen to him."

Patty Light's eyes were liquid now. "But he . . . "

Robert wondered at the look in her eyes. He feared that she totally disapproved of his attitude. Panic seized him as the words 'my greatest hope' burned in his brain. But his voice was so controlled, almost caressing, when he interrupted her that it seemed to be coming from someone else. "You're a wonderfully giving and open person, Patty. We don't have to agree about Ed. Who knows, maybe you're a hundred percent right, and I'm a hundred percent wrong. But can we not talk about Ed any more today?" Ah, but she looked so disappointed in him now, and so sad.

"Look," he said softly, "I don't need to tell you how tough this year has been. You know what's happened in most of my classes. A lot of kids hate me because of who I'm not. They refuse to see me as a human being with feelings, hopes, and dreams who is trying as hard as he can to get it right. So," he continued, "when they couldn't destroy me with their noise and chaos, they tried to do it with their defiance and indifference, then their taunts. They've invaded where I live. If this new teaching strategy fails . . ."

Patty stared at him, her eyes full of fear for him. She could not move or speak. He watched tears slide down her cheeks, and it broke his heart to see that. His head was whirling. He was sorry for every word he'd said. He had no right to burden her like this and no ability to stop the sorrow washing between them. All he could do was touch the back of her hand lightly and say, "I'm sorry. I shouldn't have said those things to you."

He heard the doorknob turn and then snap back. He glanced up quickly and thought he saw Ed Warrum's profile in the window for a moment before it disappeared. But that didn't matter. What mattered were the tears tracing the face of this girl who meant more to him than she'd ever know.

"Please," he pleaded, "forgive me. I didn't want to make you cry. I'd give everything I own if I could take back all those words I said."

His apology hung in the silence. He felt frantic with fear of losing her presence.

"Wh-what did you say?" Patty asked, wiping her tears with her hands.

"I said I'd give everything I own if I could take back my words."

"M-Mr. B-Baker," she sniffled, "e-everything you own?"

"Yes," he said, perplexed.

"Mr. B-Baker, th-that wouldn't be very much, would it."

And the two burst into laughter, rollicking laughter, laughter so deep and vibrant that joy and sorrow intertwined until they became the same, unable to stop, unwilling to stop, the laughter rolling in waves out the open window, spilling over the edge and down past the windows of the school until it fell distant but distinct into the ears of the lone student sitting on school's front steps.

Three floors above, the celebrants fell toward finale, snuffling and wiping better tears from their faces, bursts of laughter shaking loose like the little aftershocks. They looked out the windows at the cirrus clouds drifting the breeze beneath the blue sky before their eyes locked.

"Thanks. I needed that," Robert said. "Really. I needed that."

"Me too. But I'd better get going. They'll wonder where I am."

No, they won't, Robert thought, dismayed that disappointment bothered his chest; one of them was at the door just a few minutes ago at, of course, just the wrong time. He threw the thought toward the open window hoping it would be sucked up by the breeze and blown far from him forever. He eased out of the student desk and stood up. "I suppose that's so," he told her.

"I'm so glad I don't wear eye shadow and mascara," she smiled swiping at the last tear clinging to her chin with the palm of her hand. She stood up too, then crouched to retrieve her books from beneath the desk seat and pulled them against her. "I love these books," she told the teacher gazing at her. She straightened and placed the books on the desk. "Thank you for allowing me to be me," she said, her eyes shining again. She stepped around the desk and threw her arms around his shoulders. It was a hug as brief and deep as a haiku. When she stepped back, she showed no regret. "Thank you, Mr. Baker," she repeated as she picked up her books. "See you tomorrow," she tossed over her shoulder as she headed for the door.

"Thank you, Patty… for everything," was all he could think to respond. He stood rooted to spot where she'd embraced him, the spot where his hands had tentatively touched her shoulders in response. He watched her open the door. "You can leave it open," he said, and then listened to her footfalls echo down the hall.

Ed Warrum

Honoring Patty Light's request, Elaine Stafford had contacted Ed Warrum's home. Pete Warrum gruffly told her his son wasn't home and wouldn't be anytime soon. His anger had crackled in her ear. She'd subsequently contacted Mr. Barnes, who relayed her message to Ed. Mr. Barnes had told Ed, "She's very good," and a meeting was arranged.

After Ed arrived at the Social Services office, Miss Stafford informed him that she usually worked with teenagers whose parents had neither insurance nor the income to afford other counseling, as well as with teenagers in crisis. She knew of Pete Warrum's business, so she'd need a reason to justify dealing with a client not qualified under the guidelines.

That sounded reasonable – and cold – to Ed, not so different from his visit with the minister. He pushed his chair back and rose. Miss Stafford raised her hands and said, "Whoa. I said I need a reason, not privacy. Please sit down."

He did because he was desperate to talk to an adult not immersed in his situation. "What do I have to say?"

"Give me a reason. It doesn't have to be enormous."

"Would the fact that I bought a gun illegally so I could shoot my father qualify as a reason?"

"I believe it would," the counselor breathed. "It might even qualify as enormous." Miss Stafford whipped open her appointment book. "And the gun is where?"

"Rusting at the bottom of a river, thanks to Pastor Dan," Ed answered. It felt good to make that admission again.

"You're not saving your money for another?"

"Not at the moment. My work hours have been cut."

"At your Dad's store, I assume. Did you move out of your father's house? That would also qualify you."

"Yes. My mother, my sister Jenny, and I moved out. Jenny should get counseling, too," Ed told her. "Her problems are the same, but different."

They spent most of their meeting arranging times and dates for more. Just before the hour expired, Ed brought up the subject of Mr. Baker, and his desire to make things right with the man. He explained he'd failed the teacher all year and that a recent effort to rectify that had landed on the rocks. She suggested he keep trying.

He'd returned to school immediately after the meeting to do so.

He'd glimpsed Mr. Baker through the window. He'd only seen the back of the girl he was talking with, but he was sure it was Patty. As Ed turned room 313's doorknob, he thought he heard crying inside. He released the knob and hurried down the stairs and sat down on school's front steps. Almost immediately he heard distant laughter and traced the sound up the wall to Mr. Baker's room. He regretted not going into the room earlier. If it was crying he'd heard, he might have learned its cause. If it was a prelude to hilarity, he could have shared in it. Lord knows, he could use a laugh.

But if he'd gone in, his traitor tongue might have betrayed him again.

But. For the first time in awhile he had real friends. They were responsible for him finding a counselor who actually cares. This thing with Baker would work out, too. Something positive would happen. It might take a miracle. But hadn't he been sitting here listening to laughter tumbling out of Baker's window a few minutes ago. That, in itself, was a miracle.

Patty tapped him on the shoulder. "We're ready to go," she said. Billy was standing on the step above her.

"How long you been there?" he asked, rising.

"Awhile," Billy said. "We thought your Buddha-like meditation pose was awesome."

"No pose. How are you?" Ed asked Patty, scanning her face for clues.

"I'm great. Thank you for asking."

"I'm the one who needs to thank you. I had a meeting with Miss Stafford today. She's going to work with me and my sister, too."

"I guess it's a good day for gratitude," Patty said as the three descended the steps and progressed to the corner stoplights.

Billy said, "I'm grateful that I ran the 440 in 52.4. That's a blazing pace if you care."

"We don't," the others answered in unison.

As they waited for the light to change, a large older car with faded paint zipped through the amber. Its driver waved as he rounded the corner.

"Who's car is that?" Patty asked.

"Jerry Jons," Billy told her as the light changed and the three crossed the street. "You know him, the big blonde guy who sits by the door in third period. Plays tackle on the football team. Throws the shot in track."

"Never had an original idea," Ed added as they reached the opposite sidewalk. "Great follower. Which makes him a desirable teammate."

"You'd think he's a case of arrested development," Billy explained. "He's always giggling into his hand. We call him Mr. Giggles. He likes it."

"Why are you so interested in that car?" Ed asked.

"It looks familiar. I must think I saw it somewhere important."

Patty Light

Dear Desired Helpers,

Mr. Hunter: Without your intense interest in every word I write and your willingness to speak for me, what follows might never have been written. Over the past eight months more people have become special to me than in the preceding sixteen years of my life. Two are you, Mr. Hunter, because you treasure your students. And you, Miss Stafford, because your penetrating eyes and probing questions originate in your caring heart.

Which brings me to last Wednesday afternoon. I've read the phrase "an emotional roller coaster" a few times. It says much about what happened that day.

My primary purpose Wednesday was to try to create a bridge for Mr. Baker and Ed so they could meet halfway and realize they are more alike than different.

That didn't work. Instead my idea provoked Mr. Baker, which provoked tears because I wanted so badly for it to work. Which provoked a profuse apology from Mr. Baker. Which provoked such a hilarious (!) response from me (!) you'd have thought it came from Billy. Which provoked the most delicious, delirious laughter I've ever experienced. In both of us! It was so beautiful, so deep, and so free that I never wanted it to stop.

Of course, it did. But we had shared the one thing we never shared in all of our visits.

That day was emotional for both of us and to have it end sailing on the wings of laughter was so wonderful that I could not help but hug him. It was an impulse

I should have fought, but I was so moved and joyous, I had to express that beyond words.

It was a very brief and gentle hug. A touch really. I want you to know about this for several reasons. I'll never be sorry I did that for myself because both of us deserved that moment. But later it crossed my mind that if someone witnessed that hug, they might misinterpret it, so I want to say in my handwriting that Mr. Baker did nothing to cause it to happen and only responded with a butterfly brush of my shoulders.

The other reason I wanted to write about it, Miss Stafford, is that I neither shivered nor shook when it happened, or since then. Someday, Mr. Hunter, I or we will tell you why that matters. For now, please accept the truth that it does.

I think sharing this with the two of you is a good thing. I'm glad I've done it. It has not made the experience less treasurable. That's a good thing for me to know, don't you agree?

PL

Robert Baker

It took three days for the emotional valleys and peaks Robert Baker travelled with Patty Light Wednesday afternoon to transform into a long and slippery slope.

For one night and one day he simply treasured the day – his honesty, her compassionate response, his regret for her tears, the storms of laughter exploding from both after her terrifically funny comment, the swirl of surprise, confusion, gratitude, and affection that led to her sudden brief hug and his genuine, but even briefer, reciprocation.

On Thursday, Patty Light was as alert and forthcoming as always, but he sensed a relaxation of the tension that usually beat beneath the surface of her eager attentiveness. The roller coaster afternoon seemed to have left her pleased and relieved to have taken the ride. Her vitality nearly put his doubts to rest.

They might have remained at rest if Ed Warrum hadn't paused at his desk at the end of the period and said, "I stopped by your room yesterday. That must have been pretty fun. Wish I'd come in." Ed smiled at the teacher, who managed an attempt at his own as the boy walked away. But his thought was what did he mean by that? However, he willed aside his misgivings, even though Patty didn't appear after school.

❖ ❖ ❖

It was that night as he stared at the lesson plan notes strewn across his drop-leaf table that doubt resurfaced and began scrapping at his psyche. Reliving the afternoon, he had to admit he'd dominated it with his selfish obsessions, his anger, his needs. He'd almost coerced the comfort of the brief embrace. "That's not true," he told himself. "Not true," he kept repeating, each repetition failing to convince him that he had not taken advantage of Patty's compassion, that he had not crossed a line he shouldn't have when he returned the hug, however tentatively. But had he backed away or gently rejected her impulse, how would that have affected her?

"Only you, Robert Baker, would take a beautiful moment and think it into something bad," he told the bathroom mirror. Nearly satisfied with the truth of that, he struggled to concentrate on the pile of poems on his table, the best of which belonged, of course, to Patty Light and Billy Cloud. Although, he forced himself to acknowledge, Ed Warrum's wasn't that bad either.

But . . . But what? Why was he inviting doubt back into his brain? Why was he worrying about the possibility that Ed had noticed his hand touching Patty's? Worse yet, what if Ed had only ducked down the hall and then, intrigued by the laughter, returned to the door and witnessed the embrace? Was that what Ed meant when he said that stuff about something being "fun" and wishing he had "been there"?

Why was he so sure Ed wanted to harm him? The worst behavior the boy had ever shown was disinterest. Except there was that bit in the hallway a couple weeks ago. Like a perpetrator taunting his victim. Was that the intent of his comment today, too?

"Ridiculous," he angrily admonished himself. "Besides, Patty likes him." That mattered. He willed himself to return to reading the poems.

It was the comments of Dan Crannan, the custodian, the next day that did him in. The custodian intimidated him anyway. Custodians knew a lot about you even if you never talked to them. They had evidence of how well or poorly you ran your classes by the little signs students left behind – scribblings on desks, gum underneath them, crumpled papers on the floor or in the waste basket, the straightness of the rows, the chalked messages on the blackboards. Robert was paranoid without proof that the man held him in low esteem. If so, he couldn't blame the man. He'd been too worn and distracted to take care of things the way he should.

Patty Light came by on Friday to see if Robert had any quizzes that needed correcting. He did, and he let her do them. Glancing up from the modern poetry lessons he was preparing for next week's classes, he studied her at intervals to allay his doubts. When she was aware of his gaze, she shared unselfconscious smiles with him as full of poetry as any book.

Finished, she stood up and said, "I'll erase and wash the boards if you want me to." He nodded and watched her flow past him to the board and felt her presence behind him intermingling with the poetry in front of him.

When she was done with the boards, he said, "Thank you. The janitor will be grateful," just as Dan Crannan opened the door and trailed his broom into the room.

"He most surely is," Dan Crannan said, his face creased with a grin.

"Mr. Baker is lucky to have such an ambitious helper. If you'd like more work, Missy, we'd be glad to have you work for us. Board looks spiffy."

"Patty's my student assistant," Robert announced as though he needed to justify her being in the room.

"Why, of course she is," Crannan grinned. "I knew that. That's why she's here so often after school."

"Her schedule is full. It's the only time she can do it."

"Why, of course it is," Crannan smiled, resting against the side blackboard, his long fingers idly stroking the handle of his broom.

"I'd better be going," Patty said, bending to retrieve her books from the desk where she'd been sitting earlier. Crannan watched her with that permanent grin of his as Robert's gaze flitted between one and the other. "Good night, Mr. Baker," she said to the teacher, and then turned toward the door. "Good night, Mr . . . . "

"It's Crannan," the custodian told her, "but you can call me Dan. Most kids do. Dan, the man, that's my plan. I'm a poet and I know it, just like Mr. Baker. See, it says 'Dan' right on my shirt. Not like the teachers. You couldn't call Mr. Baker here Robert, now could you?"

"No, Mr. Crannan, I couldn't. Good night," she concluded as she left.

"Respect," Dan Crannan said as he peeked out the door at her walking down the hall. "It's nice to see a kid who has respect." He pushed his broom between rows of desks. "Pretty thing, ain't she. Natural."

When Robert did not respond, Crannan persisted. "Well, don't you think she is? I do."

It would be stupid to say he'd never noticed. "She's a very intelligent young lady," came out of his mouth. It sounded evasive and guilty.

"Why, I'm sure she is," Dan Crannan agreed, leaning on his broom. "Usually I try to wait until you and the young lady are done working before I clean your room. Hate to interrupt work. Besides I got all these other rooms to do so it isn't a problem. Thought I heard crying as I passed by the other day, figured I better let you work that out. But later it sounded like laughing. Guess my hearing's going or maybe I'm a little bughouse."

Dan Crannan rounded into the next aisle, pushing the desks with his broom to get at the occasional wads of paper and sunflower seeds the kids had dropped underneath them. Robert could find no words for the custodian's observation. A light line of perspiration formed on his forehead. He moved behind his desk and gathered the books and papers he was taking back to his apartment for the weekend.

Then he watched how the janitor left little piles of refuse at the end of each aisle to be herded together into his dustpan and dropped into the wheeled trash container in the hall. He wanted to leave, but he watched until Dan Crannan had swept everywhere, watched until the custodian paused again, and turned his wreathed face towards Robert.

"Got a little friendly advice for you if you don't mind, Robert. When you have such a pretty, sweet thing like that working in your room, it might be a good idea to leave your door open. Otherwise folks might get to thinking there's something going on in here. Which wouldn't be a good thing for people to be thinking, now would it," he finished. Then he dropped the grin.

"There are people in this world who love to make something out of nothing. I've seen it happen. I saw it happen to Gerney last year, and he's not here anymore. I always say never hand a can of a gasoline to pyromaniacs."

Dan Crannan had straightened and announced, "I see my work here is about done." He'd broomed the gathered trash out the door. Robert had listened to the refuse swish into the waste container and to the thrum of the wheels against the floor mingling with the janitor's whistling as he headed down the hall.

Robert spent Friday evening in his silent apartment trying to read through the poem interpretations his students wrote on Wednesday. Their words refused to penetrate his brain. It was already filled by Dan Crannan's.

Why couldn't he just be happy for a little while! Why couldn't he be free to treasure the few beautiful moments in his first year of teaching? Why were people like Dan Crannan and Ed Warrum able to create such havoc in his emotions? Why was he unable to stop his brain from lasering on the negative?

"Good Lord!" he rasped through clamped teeth.

But his brain maintained its relentless pace. Forget Ed Warrum. What if Dan Crannan was right? What if someone had seen Patty go in that room and was wondering why that door was closed, had been standing outside the door, their eyes converting an innocent student's gesture of empathy into an erotic act. What if someone was working to turn the whole situation into something wicked and forbidden. Wrecking the girl's reputation. Wrecking his.

He felt the ants awaken and begin to nibble at the nape of his neck.

"This is ridiculous!" Robert burst out in the building empty of everyone but himself. "There was no one out there, Robert! Nobody did anything wrong, Robert!" His words echoed off the walls. "This is nuts!" he growled. "This is crazy!"

Raindrops were streaming down the windowpanes, distorting the blinking yellow numbers on the bank clock blocks away. A single rumble of thunder followed a lightning flash. Someone honked a horn as a car zoomed past his building.

Robert sank onto the wooden chair by the table. He lapsed into sadness so suddenly it frightened him. The guilt he'd quelled rebuilt. Patty's actions and reactions were innocent all right. But were his? Had he allowed himself to nurture a kind of love for her to accompany his respect, admiration and dependence? Had he allowed the closed classroom door or at least appreciated that it was closed because it made the room feel more intimate when she was in it? Had he subconsciously led Wednesday afternoon's conversation to the point where he would end up as physically close to the girl as he felt emotionally?

"Ridiculous," he mouthed, but his voice carried only a little conviction to his ears.

What if others were harboring the ideas Crannan described? What if Patty exuberantly shared the story with someone she trusted who would race into Sam Strand's office full of outrage at the teacher? What if Anderson had to pick up his phone and tell his parents that their son had been fired for harassing a female student, that he was sorry, but there was nothing he could do? Gerney was gone, wasn't he? Crannan had implied that was one of the reasons. Questions and fears raced through his brain so profusely that he couldn't untangle one from another.

The ants scurried toward his stomach and chest. The room sped by his eyes. He felt himself falling into full descent. Perhaps this was it. Perhaps it had finally arrived. He gripped the seat of his chair and thrust his face toward the force of the fall, but felt nothing except his perspiration raining down. "Damn," he murmured. It would have been such a relief. The ants were invading the linings of his lungs and the arteries around his heart and his breath came in gasps. He felt dizzy and sick.

The descent ended with a loud thump that startled him upright in his chair. The room was still. The ants hurried to his darkest extremities to await their next dance. The sky seemed to be brightening He did not know if that was because it had stopped raining or if dawn was approaching. He did not know if he had slept or not. He did not know if he was dreaming or wide-awake.

His hands were as heavy as if anvils weighted them. He lifted them with exorbitant effort toward his drooping eyelids. He gave up and thumped his hands hard on the table and let his eyes clang shut.

He did not know if it was the soft collision of his head against the pile of papers on the table that alerted him to the sound of voices rising from the street. He did know it must be dawn because he could see how gray and cold the day looked and hear how heated the voices sounded, though he could not for the life of him decipher what was being said. He pressed his forehead against the wet window pane still streaked and stained by last night's rain and imperfectly saw four figures gathered near the corner on the sidewalk. He wanted to jerk his head out of sight but could not. Instead his aching eyes struggled to identify who was there. Finally he realized with sorrow that it was Ed Warrum, Billy Cloud, Patty Light, and Kyle Hunter who stood rooted to the concrete. What in the world were they doing outside his home on a Saturday morning he wondered, even though he knew the answer. He watched the boys holding each of Patty's hands protectively before releasing her to use their hands to engage Kyle in an animated explanation of something that could only be one thing. Patty Light's hands fled to her ears. Kyle's hands were extended palms outward to ward off the words flying towards him, and he was shaking his head to cast away the one's that got through. Robert watched him finally drop his hands into his pockets as he stared at the boys and then at Patty's face, his resistance washing away in her tears. Then all four turned toward the apartment.

Robert could stand it no longer. He snapped his head back from the window and closed his eyes against the voices until they faded from his hearing. Then his head thumped against the wet window, and his eyes flew open to find the sidewalk deserted as far as he could see.

His eyes, dry as desert sand, burned. The ants blazed through his body, then gathered in clumps at the nerve-endings of his hands and feet and stomach and chest and lungs and intestines to await their next release.

He experimentally closed his eyes. The world was blessedly black and blank behind his eyelids. He circled his arms on the table and allowed his head to descend into their cradle and fell into an exhausted sleep.

Greg Schwarz

Greg Schwarz rapped at the downstairs door to Robert Baker's apartment hard enough to send showers of paint slivers cascading to the sidewalk. He twisted the knob as he leaned against the door, but there was no give. Robert Baker was in his apartment, but he wasn't responding.

Greg shook his head as he turned to Janis. "I suppose if he did hear me knocking, he figured it was kids. Dead bolted door. Unlisted number. The only way he can be reached is if he makes first contact."

"Poor guy." Janis raised her eyes to the second floor windows. "He even has his shades drawn. It's like he's a prisoner in there." The teachers resumed their trek toward breakfast. "It's like solitary confinement,"

"Whoever broke into his apartment sealed that deal."

"It's a shame. You could tell he enjoyed golfing with us. I'll bet he would have enjoyed joining us today on such a beautiful morning. Don't you love this town after a rain? The air smells like pine and lilacs."

"Yeah," Greg agreed without enthusiasm. He inhaled the fragrances without appreciation. Ever since the vandalism, he'd been like that. "Can we skip breakfast?"

"Sure. But you'll be missing a meal. You're not okay are you?"

"I don't think I am. But it isn't my stomach. It's my head. Okay if we go sit by the lake?"

"Sure. I'd like to believe romance is causing you to choose lake over pancakes. Your face tells me that's not the case."

"I don't exactly feel like Don Juan right now."

She slipped her arm through his as a line of cars approached the intersection. Greg recognized the battered sedan in the lead. "Jerry. His parents should never have given him that car."

"You know them?" Janis inquired as the car eased past.

"Jerry Jons, the driver. Plays football. Pretty good, too." They watched the car slow near Baker's building. "I guess Robert's got his door bolted because of kids like that."

"He's a bad boy?"

"Jerry's as good or bad as who he's with. He's a nice kid, but desperate for approval. If someone tells a joke, he falls down laughing. If someone told him to walk off a cliff, he'd run. That's why football is good for him, and that car isn't."

The driver behind the boys honked, and the vehicle leapt forward.

"He didn't look happy," Greg said.

"I think I recognized his passenger. He's the kind Jerry shouldn't be with," Janis said. "They dumped him in my typing class. Frank Marin. That guy's got a mouth on him. Better have a talk with your boy."

They crossed the street and turned in the direction of the lake. Greg decided it was time to confess the sin most prominent in his mind. "Are you aware that you're keeping company with a jackass?"

"Of course I am, Greg. All your friends have told me that." She saw no hint of a smile. "I'm sorry. You're serious, aren't you?"

"Afraid so. I guess you never heard what I did to Robert in the teacher's lounge." She shook her head. "One morning I announced that Robert Baker was a real loser. I didn't even know the guy. Judged him from what kids said. While I was talking behind his back, he was standing behind mine. He hightailed it out of the room. Haven't seen him there since. There's a lot of wisdom in that room that might have helped him, and I made sure he didn't get that benefit. I'm as heartless as those punks that did his apartment." He shook his head angrily. "Sometimes I'd like to cut out my tongue."

Janis patted his hand. "The difference between you and them is they're congratulating themselves, and you're feeling awful about a few reckless words."

"Maybe."

"You're pretty tough on yourself, Mr. S." she comforted, entwining her fingers with his. "You're wrong about your heart. You wear it on your face. It's strong and healthy and cares about people. You just need to find a better use for that tongue of yours now and then."

Frank Marin

The short message —"I know what you did. I have nothing to lose by informing Mr. Strand. I suggest you call me" — that Frank Marin left on the

Jons' answering machine had been responded to immediately. He'd barely put down the phone when it rang. Frank had ordered Jerry to pick him up in front of Warrum's Store at 7:30 a.m.

It had taken one shot of vodka to settle Frank's nerves enough to make that call. It had taken one shot this morning to screw his confidence to the sticking point.

Frank heard the car rattling behind him as he feigned interest in Warrum's window display. He turned and there was Jerry Jons slumped behind the steering wheel, motioning frantically for Frank to get in the car. Knowing he held all the aces, Frank sauntered to the passenger's side, opened the door and slid in. "Good morning," he said. "Beautiful day, don't you think?"

"Geez," Jerry Jons groaned. His forehead was shiny. He shifted into reverse and backed the car from the curb. "Ed's inside the store."

Frank said, "No sweat, Jerry," as Jerry headed in the direction of the school. "Hey, it's fun ridin' with a friend of a jock hero."

"Geez," Jerry moaned.

"Hey, I got an idea. I hear he cut his girl loose. She's a fox. Since you're buddy-buddy with Ed, you must know his ex. Maybe you could introduce us."

"Geez. How do you know this stuff?"

"I got ears, man." Frank's tongue had turned silky smooth. "That's how I know about you. Half the kids in school know. They won't tell. I will."

The distracted driver nearly ran a stop sign. He slammed the brakes, skidding to a stop. "Know what?"

"Can we say vandalism? Can we say Baker?"

"Oh geez," Jerry moaned. "I didn't do nothin'."

"Drove the get-there car," Frank stated. "Drove the get-away car. You shouldn't brag. Say, I don't know where Baker lives. You do."

"Straight down the street," the tricked boy replied.

"I'd like to see it. Drive slow so I can get a good look."

Knowing he was trapped, Jerry offered no resistance.

"Aw no," Jerry groaned. "It's Mr. Schwarz." His voice was frantic.

Frank spotted the teacher down the street and the woman with him. "How's about I roll down the window and give 'em a holler?"

"Geez no," Jerry groaned, his foot pressing the accelerator.

"Hey, slow down," Frank ordered. "Hey, that's Miss James, ain't it? Take a gander at them legs, man." He laughed, the sound false and irritating even to his ears. "I said slow down! Where's Baker's place?"

"White building, boarded up window, second floor," Jerry mumbled.

"You know a lot for someone who didn't do nothin'."

"Oh, geez," Jerry groaned. "I just drove . . ." he started, and snapped his mouth shut. "What'd I ever do to you?" he said through clenched lips.

"Well, nothin'," Frank admitted. "It's just that I need to make points with Strand, or I need help with a project. Which one is your choice."

The driver of the car behind them blared his horn. Jerry jumped and pounded his foot on the accelerator, his car tires squealing. "Geez!" he hollered.

Frank cranked his head around and saw the teachers were watching. "You're a little too nervous, ain't you."

"If I get kicked off the track team, my folks'll kill me."

"The choice is yours. Ain't nobody gonna get hurt except you if you make the wrong one." He had Jerry Jons. "You ready to hear the plan? It'll just be a little entertainment for the boys and girls. So?"

"Ah, geez! Ah, geez! My folks will take this car away if I get kicked off the track team. I got no choice."

Billy Cloud

Long distance races were Billy Cloud's preference, but the track team was thin in middle distances. This Saturday morning, however, he was distance running. And for the first time since his parents had been there, he would have company on Moon Ribbon Ridge.

He rounded the first curve on the county road. No white cars in sight. The forest foliage displayed multiple shades of spring green. Aided by last night's storm, the air was sensationally fragrant. He stopped and pulled his tee shirt over his head to allow the west wind to envelope more skin. He loved this beautiful day.

Billy resumed his pace and bothered his mind about the beer cans, plastic ring holders, bottles, and cartons he'd found strewn along the ridge and its pine grove on his last visit. His sanctuary had been violated. That's why it was time to share it now.

Running against traffic, Billy noted a lone bicyclist topping a rise up the road. He angled toward the shoulder as the rider approached, a girl dressed in tee shirt and cutoffs, her legs motionless on the bike pedals as she coasted the gentle slope. She wore no helmet, so her blonde hair flowed in the breeze. As she neared, he recognized her as a Blue Lake High School cheerleader, Edna Something-or-other. A sophomore maybe? The girl squeezed her bike's brakes. "Billy," she called as she slowed to a stop.

"Edna," he said. "You live out this way?"

"Yup," she answered, planting her feet on the pavement. "Last house on the left, just like the movie. Except it isn't quite as creepy. I ride the same bus you would if you ever took the bus. Where's your bike? I've seen you zip past our house quite a few times," she continued, her lips stretched into a smile, her blue eyes star bright as she straddled the bar of her bike. "I know where you're going."

"Track," he evaded. "That's why I'm running. Headed for town?"

"Yup. Piano lessons. My piano books are in my backpack. Mom usually gives me a ride, but it's such a lovely day, don't you think?"

"Yes, I do. That's why I'm running, not dusting."

"I've seen the sign in front of your house. Can just anybody stop there?"

"Anyone smart enough to bike on a beautiful morning."

"Why thank you, Billy," Edna smiled, her perfect teeth glistening white. "I'm so glad I measured up."

Billy began to run in place. "Stiffening leg syndrome," he explained. "One thing though. You ought to wear a helmet. If you won't wear a helmet, don't ride a bike."

"It's in my backpack. I wanted to feel the wind in my hair. But if you insist on being a spoil sport." She clamped her legs tighter against the bar to balance the bike, unsnapped the straps, and swung the pack in front of her. "See. Right here," she said as she pulled out the helmet. She plopped it on her head. "Do you think I'm as pretty with it on?"

"Definitely," Billy said. Her question made him a tad nervous. Maybe he was vibing too much interest. But this break in his race to the Ridge was far from unpleasant.

Edna glanced at her wristwatch. "I'm going to be late for my lesson!" she exclaimed. She refastened the backpack, and placed her right foot on the upraised pedal. "Stop and say hi on your way to or from The Ridge sometime." She saw his startled expression. "I was in the yard when you whizzed by last week. I walked to the road and knew you were going to The Ridge. We found the trail years ago. It's beautiful up there. But we made our own trail from our house through the woods, hoping nobody else would discover the place. I don't mind that you did though," she finished. "Stop by later if you're still around this afternoon. We'll make you a glass of lemonade. My mom's an artist, too. Well, it was fun to ride into you. Bye," she finished as she remounted the bike. "Hey, you look really good with your shirt off," she tossed over her shoulder, trailing laughter after her.

Well, that was interesting, Billy acknowledged as he waved and resumed the incline more stiff legged than he desired. A nature-loving cheerleader. Guess they don't always need to be in front of a crowd.

That made him think that maybe he should reexamine his misgivings about Shellie Chaine being one of those joining him in a few hours.

❖   ❖   ❖

It was Patty Light he'd really wanted to share the ridge with, but he'd thought that was out of the question until she'd knocked that perception out of the park Thursday afternoon. Billy had mentioned that he was going to show Ed a favorite place of his because he needed to share it with somebody he liked."

"You don't like me anymore?" she'd teased.

"Heck. yes. I'd take you there in a Minnesota minute, but I figured you would . . . "

"I'd like to come along."

"Your mother isn't . . . "

"Not that I know of, but it doesn't matter. I've decided to parole myself for a day."

"Terrific. I'd planned to run out there in the morning when I thought . . . But Ed has to work half a day, then he's gonna drive out. Is it okay if he picks you up?"

"Yes. Of course. Tell him I'll meet him here. Thanks, Billy." She cradled her books. "I gotta go. I haven't paroled myself quite yet."

That night he trotted over to Warrum's to tell Ed he'd have a passenger. Catching a glimpse of Jenny seated behind her upstairs window reading, he decided to invite her, too. Jenny knowing Patty would be a good thing.

He'd mentioned Patty and suggested Jenny when Ed informed him apologetically, "I need to check with you about adding one more. It's ridiculous but Shellie stopped by my locker today. We haven't talked in months. Anyway, she said she feels bad about how we avoid one another. Like it's her fault." He shrugged. "One thing led to another and I suggested she could come along Saturday. If it's okay with you."

"Can we trust her to not tell everyone? Cheerleaders like attention."

"I can tell you she never told anyone about the gun."

"Ace, point and game."

❖   ❖   ❖

Billy did not slow down again until he surmounted the crest of Moon Ribbon Ridge. It was nearly noon so his friends should be arriving soon. He proceeded to the pine grove and ducked beneath the branches. A dozen beer cans and three empty whiskey bottles littered the needles underneath. Two used condoms lay like dead fish within the refuse. "Damn," he seethed. He'd have to bag those, too. There was no doubt that people of questionable character knew about this place now, and their numbers were growing. He tied the garbage bag and pushed it under the branches. He decided not to mention the finds to his friends.

Sun and wind had dried the ridge. The wet meadow and its swollen stream sparkled below. He plopped on the ridge and tried to dissipate his disappointment over his discoveries.

He heard a car slowing on the road. If it stopped, it would likely be the intruders. If it continued to the turnout up the road, it was Ed. He'd asked Ed to tell his passengers to make sure the road was clear before they ducked under the brush that hid the trail. His caution seemed fruitless now, but at least they wouldn't attract additional attention. He pulled on his sweaty shirt and trotted down the hill to meet them.

Minutes later, the five teenagers reached the ridge. "Whew," Ed huffed. "I suppose you're going to tell me you ran up this thing."

"Biked up it, too."

"You know, I've lived in Blue Lake all my life, and I didn't know this place existed. You move to town and find it within a few weeks."

"Indian, that's why."

"This would be a great place to meditate," Shellie said.

"Or to seek a vision quest. You know how we are."

"No, I don't," Shellie said, "but I'd like to learn."

"Let's just say it's like meditation only deeper. Good enough?"

"Good enough," the girl answered nervously. She shifted her attention to Jenny and Patty who stood on the far side of the ridge. "What's there?"

"Meadow, stream, many trees. Look for yourself."

"Here's your clothes," Ed said. He extracted Billy's rolled up shorts and a fresh tee shirt from his backpack. "Shellie made the sandwiches. They're in her backpack. Patty's got the water bottles, and Jenny has sodas. We thought we'd eat up here if that's okay."

"If it's edible and we clean up the mess. I'd rather walk the ridge first."

"Sure," Ed agreed, eyeing his friend quizzically as Billy stamped toward the corrupted privacy of the grove.

"It's beautiful," Patty told Billy upon his return. "It reminds me of 'Kindred Spirits'. I'm glad I'm here. I'm glad we're all here."

"I was hoping we could traipse around down there and in the woods," Billy griped. "Too wet for tourists."

The five teenagers traversed the ridge west and east. "I wanted to explore it all," Billy said as they returned to the plateau. "It's probably been thirty years since this place was abandoned. I wanted to show it to you before it was too late." He pointed at the backpacks. "Eat," he ordered.

The five sat in a loose semicircle. Jenny and Patty placed the sodas and water in the middle. Shellie pulled a large brown bag from her backpack and produced wrapped sandwiches. She handed one to each. Billy noticed her hand was trembling.

He felt Patty's eyes on him. "What?" he growled.

"I've never seen you act and look so unhappy."

Evidently hiding anger wasn't his talent. Making people tremble was.

"I'm sorry," he said. "Shellie, I need to apologize to you. When I get a good stereotype going, I make use of it at the worst possible times."

"Thank goodness. I thought you were wishing I wasn't here. It's a relief to know you were just treating me like your average empty headed cheerleader type. Or not."

"It has nothing to do with you actually. You were just a handy target. So, okay, before I manage to offend everyone equally, I'd better tell you what's eroded my jovial disposition. Last time I was here I found a bunch of beer cans on this ridge. Hauled 'em out. Today I found twice as many and other stuff you don't want to know about. It was stupid to think this was my personal place, but seeing it invaded by slobs has really ticked me off.

"I should have talked about this right away, but I was trying not to wreck the day and wrecking it in the process. The last thing I wanted to do is ruin everyone's appreciation for a place I love. Mr. Baker would call that ironic."

"He'd also call it heartbreaking," Patty said. "He'd understand why it breaks your heart to see something you love get messed up."

"I agree. I bet he'd like to be here today," Ed mused, "sitting here, looking around, talking with us. I actually thought someone should invite him. Not me though. My tongue turns into a hammer around him."

"I think Mr. Baker never had a chance," Shellie said. "Did any of you guys get to know Mr. Gerney?" Only Ed nodded. "Gosh, he was so beautiful, you know. He had this great voice. Even my mother was in love with him. He seemed to know everything. The girls would just about fall on the floor when he walked by. But everyone liked him, even the guys. I started working backstage on plays in eighth grade just to be around him.

"When we found out he'd left, wow, you should have seen the tears at cheerleading practice. Then someone started a rumor that the new superintendent fired Mr. Gerney so he could hire Mr. Baker. Isn't that dumb? You'd be amazed how many of us wanted to believe that so we could take it out on Mr. Baker. It was unbelievable the things that were said." She stopped. "I'm sorry. I talk way too much when I'm nervous, and I'm trying to show people I'm such a much." She shut her mouth.

"No, it's good." Billy said. "We discuss Mr. Baker a lot. I'll bet even Jenny has an impression of him."

"I do," Jenny agreed, pleased to be included. "Before I knew who he was, I heard people talk about him. Not nicely either. One day I saw him in the hall. I knew it was him by the way he walked close to the wall as though that would make him invisible. Just like me. But you know, the new freshman? They really like Mr. Baker."

"The difference between you guys and me," Shellie said, "is you cared. I listened to what everyone said and smiled and nodded like I agreed because I'm this privileged girl who has a really easy life, and that was really easy to do. I'm a real la-de-da girl. Sometimes it makes me sick. Little Miss If-You've-Got-a-Problem-Get-Away-From-Me. Just like when Ed . . . " She stopped and threw her arms around her drawn knees. "Shut up, Shellie," she muttered.

"It's okay to talk about Ed," Billy assured her. "We all talk about Ed. You're being kind of hard on yourself according to him."

"Ed? I didn't care about his troubles. I cared that he wasn't Mr. Happy Guy around me, and everyone saw it. I didn't even know he had a gun!"

"I didn't know he had a gun either. Until now. And I live with him," Jenny said, staring hard at her brother.

"I wasn't exactly forthcoming about that detail. Didn't know what to say or how. Didn't want to scare you, or for you to think I'd gone nuts. I'm sorry I didn't tell you, but more sorry I bought the thing in the first place."

"The devil's in the details," Billy offered.

"Sometimes the devil is the details," Patty said. "That's why they're so hard to figure out." She shook her head. "But I prefer to talk about everything except myself. I became an excellent student so I'd have plenty of everything else to talk about. That's a good substitute, don't you think?"

"Superior," Billy agreed.

"Superior is right. That's what I admire about you, Patty," Shellie said. "You don't seem to care what anyone thinks about you, but you care about everybody and everything. A lot of us admire you. You're so smart and out there. I wish I was like you."

"Why, thank you. But you wouldn't if I talked about me."

"You've certainly saved Mr. Baker, you and Billy."

"You had a hand in saving someone." Billy noted.

"You have the wrong girl."

"You didn't hang up when I called you from the Cities." Ed reminded her.

"But I accused you of . . . "

"You didn't hang up. Even when I said I had a gun."

"Yes, but . . . "

"You could have hung up. Could have thought I was lying to get sympathy. Or something else. Especially when I asked you to come to the Cities. 'Hey, I got this gun, Shellie, and, by the way, I got a room in this hotel, so why don't you race down here so I can show you my gun.' You had plenty of excuses to hang up."

"No, I couldn't have hung up. Well, I could have. In fact I almost did. But you sounded so desperate and I . . . Okay, I give up. I did it," she said, lifting her hands palms upward and shrugging her shoulders, "I saved his life, everybody. Well, actually I handed the phone to my mother and said, 'Hey, save this guy's life, will ya, I gotta do my nails. La-de-da."

"Turning to someone who can help is smart. And not that easy."

"I suppose that makes me smart then?" Ed offered.

"She wouldn't want to go that far," Billy said.

The group eased toward mirth and tension was vanquished.

Billy pushed to his feet. "You know a thing that would be intelligent would be to not jack our jaws this entire afternoon. Let's explore while we can. The sun is shining, the wind is winding, the meadow's blooming, the woods are lovely, dark, and damp."

The group followed him to the trail. He pointed towards the stream. "Personally I'd like to charge down to that stream and plunge right in."

"But . . . " Patty said, arching her eyebrow.

"I forgot to mention streams and swimming suits. But we could . . . "

"No. We couldn't."

"Your drunk intruder friends might not be able to handle," Ed noted.

"Please. That is not a pretty visual. I have an alternative in mind anyway. There's an old trail into the woods across the way I'd like to follow. You all might get a little wet. Unless, of course, we all . . . "

"Just turn and go," Patty ordered.

The sun was dipping west by the time the damp quintet cleared the entrance to Moon Ribbon Ridge. They were strolling up the road when they heard a car behind them. They turned and saw an older Mustang convertible, its torn top flapping. Three faces were visible. The driver pointed at them as he slowed the car and shifted lanes. The driver was the guy at the beach. Beach girl was in the back seat with a different guy.

"Hey, Tonto," the driver called, his sunburned face blotched by booze.

"That's twice in two weeks," Billy muttered to Ed. "Can't they think of anything new?"

The convertible eased next to them, its engine pinging. The driver exhibited a lopsided grin. The passenger had his elbow on the rear windowsill, a beer can clutched in his hand. His other hand was out of sight. The blonde next to him looked terribly unhappy.

"Hey, Tonto," the driver repeated.

Billy took a step forward, his fingers flexing. "Like I keep telling you white boys, Tonto was the brains of his outfit, but I tend to prefer Crazy Horse, seeing as how he was real." The passenger pulled his hand from wherever it had been and draped it over the girl's shoulder, swinging loosely across her halter-top. She flicked at it with the hand not holding her beer.

"Well, my most humble apologies, Mr. Horse. My friend Brian back there noticed you have three squaws and only two braves in your tribe, and we was wonderin' if we could borrow one or two for a little fun in the sun."

"I don't think so," Billy said. Ed stepped next to him.

"Hey there, girlies," Brian called from the back seat, his left hand cupped on the girl, who'd given up. Her milky eyes flitted between Billy and Ed. "Betts, she don't mind two guys, but it's kind of wearing her out."

Betts suddenly clawed at the offending hand, her fingernails trailing red stripes in their wake. "Cut it out!"

"Owww!" Brian yowled, wrenching up his hand and doubling it into a fist. "See what I mean. Betts is a little overwhelmed." He relaxed the fist and stroked her shoulder. "Ya see. That's a lot for Betts to handle. Brick here, he's thick and not just in the head. Me, I'm long and lean. Ask Betts. You little honeys look good and tight. Fresh. Bet you'd like to leap onto our laps for a change."

Patty surged forward, her face livid. "You go to hell!" she screamed. "You go straight to hell!"

"I was thinking these guys wouldn't be worth the trouble, but I've changed my mind," Ed growled, and the boys lunged toward the car. Brick jammed the accelerator and the car lurched away.

"That was fun," Billy fumed. "Cowards!" he shouted, shaking his fist at the disappearing vehicle, then staring after it, hands on hips.

"Those are the visitors you were concerned about."

"Most likely. Why did those creeps find this place?"

"Well, I don't know, but I'm pretty impressed with Patty," Jenny said.

"I lost it. They're pigs! And that poor girl . . . "

"Yes, but what impressed me most is that when you told them where to go, they took right off to look for it."

The group exploded into laughter.

"If they'd just waited a minute, I could have given them the address," Jenny added, provoking more.

"It seems to me," Shellie concluded, "that the mood of this group has greatly improved. Or am I just being way too la-de-da again?"

Sam Strand

Kyle Hunter had seated himself on the sofa in the teacher's lounge and balanced his cup of coffee on its worn arm when Sam and Greg walked in.

"Four more Mondays and we're done," Greg was saying, "unless some of our boys or girls make it to State.

"Anybody got a chance?" Sam asked.

"Sure. Billy Cloud in the 440, 880, and relays. Jerry Jons in the shot put and discus. Ed Warrum in both if he can focus. Relay teams for both the boys and girls. Sally Long Arrow is the best miler we've had since I arrived. Hannah Blakely could contend in the 880."

"Well, let's hope. It would be a nice way to end my career cheering on our kids. Besides," Sam added as he poured himself a cup of the thick black brew, "our school board would be so pleased."

"That last thought's almost enough to make a guy want to put tacks in the kids' shoes. So why are you here, Schwarz, instead of on the track?"

"Undermining the process. I gave the weight guys the day off." He sat down beside Kyle. "What a weekend!"

"So you stopped and smelled the posies, eh," Sam said as he seated himself by the table.

"She's a great girl, Sam. I'll never say never again."

"Do I hear a distant tinkling of bells?"

"I can think of worse sounds," Greg replied, surprising all three.

"I agree with that," Sam smiled. "When we were looking for a business teacher, one of the requirements was that she be a female who could stand Greg. What a challenge that was!"

He leaned forward in his chair. "Not to break the mood, boys, but how does it seem these days? Is our memorandum having an effect?"

"I'd say yes," Kyle said "It's been pretty mellow."

"I agree. But my opinion might be elevated."

"I've always thought of you as a happy guy, but this is the first time I've seen you giddy." Sam stood up. "Good. Mellow is the word."

The principal rinsed his cup, and hung it on its hook. His hand lingered a moment before he dropped it into his pocket. "You know, I'm going to miss this dungeon. I'm going to miss you guys. I hope the students go in peace, so I can also miss them as much as I want to." He did not look at the two as he walked to the door. He closed the door quietly as he exited.

Kyle Hunter

Gail was right. Kyle had no sense. The fresh stack of short stories and higher stacks of graded and ungraded research papers piled on his desk proved that. He should have assigned those earlier in the quarter so that by now they'd be graded and returned. He should be assigning haiku to the creative writing class and holding discussions out on the lawn with his English classes. But no.

It was an hour after the last bell rang. He could read ten research papers an hour if he graded without comments. But that would be a dereliction of duty. Doing justice to his students would keep him working late every night and all weekend. Good thing Gail was leaving tomorrow to visit her clients. She'd go nuts watching this happen yet again. He was hopeless.

Well, that was harsh, he defended himself against himself. He'd become smart enough to have the students research topics in which they were actually interested. That approach produced blank stares in ten percent, but the rest sported grateful smiles. "I'll be interested because you'll be interested. I'm doing myself a favor," he'd told his students.

There were, however, those blank stares. Some students remained in that state almost to the due date. Then they rushed to his desk pleading for help and extra time. He should quit caving, but those liquid eyes and shaky voices wouldn't let him. For some, a decent – or passing – grade hung in the balance. But he did inform each one, "If you're going to hand me a piece of crap, don't waste your time." Fortunately the papers that flew onto his desk on wings of gratitude were mostly worthwhile.

The last six students were in his room. They were required to write for an hour before asking for aid. Then they could approach solo or in pairs. Ten seconds after the expired time, Helen and Arnold stood in front of his desk, pencil, pen, paper and books cradled in their arms.

As Kyle shifted his gaze from reading to the two, a movement at the door caught his eye. Someone had poked a head in, and pulled it back.

All six recalcitrants were in the room. Was there a seventh he'd missed?

"Pull those desks up by mine," he ordered. "I'll be back in a minute." He hurried out and spied Robert Baker halfway down the hall.

"Mr. Baker," he called. The teacher stopped dead in the hall and slouched against the wall.

Kyle walked towards him. "You just stuck your head into my room?" he asked. Robert stared at him without answering. "You okay, Robert." The man looked totally drained. "Robert?"

"Oh, yes, yes, I just did that. Stuck my head in your room," he said, his eyes searching the hallway.

"You want something, want to talk or something?"

"Oh, yes," Robert replied, finally focusing on Kyle. "I stuck my head in your room because . . . because I thought Patty Light might be in there."

"That would be pleasant, but I haven't seen her. Was she supposed to correct papers for you or some filing?"

"No, no." He looked squarely at Kyle and seemed suddenly aware of his slouched demeanor. He straightened. "No," he repeated. "That's the problem. She came to the room to see if there was anything to do. I was pretty rude to her. I told her she could leave, except that I'm sure I used the word should instead of could. I didn't sleep well this weekend. Nerves. I was hoping she was in your room so I could apologize."

"She's pretty understanding. You sure you're okay?"

Robert pulled himself fully erect. If he did that once more, he'd be on his tiptoes. "I'm fine. If you see her, pass the message will you? I've got to get back to my room. Sorry to bother you."

"No bother." Kyle would have remained in the hall with Robert, but those six students were waiting in his room, the two seated by his desk probably perilously close to doodling on it. He'd check on Robert later.

❖   ❖   ❖

Robert Baker's room was dark when Kyle arrived. The door was locked and the drapes drawn. He tried one more twist of the doorknob before deciding Robert Baker had gone home much earlier than usual. Perhaps he'd read too much Shakespeare, but the phrase "signs and portents" popped into his brain. It was a foolish thing to think. He gave the door knob one more try before returning to his own room.

No matter how intently Kyle might have peered through the door's window, he would not have seen Robert Baker. The young teacher had pushed a student desk between the end of the blackboard and the inside wall of his room and scrunched himself into it. He was writing on the paper lying on the desk's pitted surface. He paused, pen suspended, when he heard the footsteps in the hall nearing, stopping, and fading. He sat there for a long time, writing and waiting for darkness so he could go home.

Frank Marin

Frank Marin could hardly believe his luck when Jerry Jons blurted out the name Al and confirmed what Frank already knew. Al was Allan Barberie and he was in Mr. Baker's third period English class.

Allan Barberie's desk was third from the front in the window row. He was a slender little guy with an eighth grade face and a mop of curly brown hair. The boy needed attention and was famous for exaggerating his misdeeds to anyone who'd listen.

Allan had sealed his fate as far as Frank was concerned. He'd gone into the boys' locker room to use the facilities the day after that thing at Baker's apartment. Allan had jumped on a bench to boast about his involvement and denied all the accusations that he was full of it.

Frank followed the boy outside after school. Allan was trying to talk to a group of boys as he exited the school, but the boys peeled away quickly. Allan was alone and looking it.

By the time Allan crossed the street, Frank had advanced within ten feet of him. He didn't want to confront the boy too close to the school, but had no idea where Allan lived either. This stuff was tricky and a lot of trouble.

About a block from the high school, Frank eased alongside the boy. Allan glanced up at the tall teenager, fear in his eyes. "I ain't gonna beat you up, Allan, if that's what you're thinking," Frank assured him in a low voice. The two continued down the sidewalk. "Just want to talk to you." He watched the boy's Adams apple bobbing like a cork in wavy water. "No, really, Allan, I just got a favor to ask of you. Can we stop and talk a minute?" The other reluctantly did, not raising his eyes above Frank's jacket collar. "I need a favor." Frank kept his pocketed hands doubled into fists for emphasis. "I hear you had fun at Baker's apartment."

Allan shook his head. "Not me. I didn't do nothin'."

Frank extracted his hand and put his index finger to his lips. "No need to shout, Allan," he said.

"I didn't do nothing," the boy whispered.

"No use lying. I got it all on my recorder," Frank lied.

"Recorder!" the boy hissed, his voice thin and cracked as October ice.

"I record all my classes," Frank lied. "Sometimes I record stuff that interests me like you bragging about trashing Baker's apartment."

"I didn't," the boy whispered. "I was just talking."

"Well, my little friend, I can't say you did or didn't, but Jerry says you did, the recorder says you did, and Mr. Strand will say you did when I give it to him."

"I don't hardly know Jerry."

"Ain't what Jerry says. But it doesn't matter to me. I could use a few points with Strand. I don't necessarily want to see him. What I do want is to have a little fun in Baker's class. You're with me or against me."

The boy's insides crumbled like old cookies. Frank had him. "Let's walk toward your place while I share my plan with you. It'll be fun. Kids'll think it's a scream," he assured the quaking kid. "Wednesday's the big day."

❖   ❖   ❖

Frank sat in his bedroom, his hollowed-out book compartmentalized into stacks of spit wads. Two piles were your regular slobbery spit wads cored with BB pellets for a noisy surprise. The middle pile held wads pierced with oversized pins. Under all three were thick rubber bands for propulsion.

He sipped the vodka he'd retrieved from the back of his closet. He had to save enough for a boomer in the morning before school. It would ease the guilt he felt about Baker.

He eyed the bulletin board above his desk. It was decorated with clusters of pinned spit wads. He grabbed a few from the stack and a rubber band from the book and backed to the wall. He laid the pin-pierced papers on the bed and slid the rubber band over the thumb and forefinger of his left hand. He snatched a wad onto his little slingshot, pulled, and released. The armed wad zinged right into the middle of the open space. He snatched and fired four more in quick succession. All clustered the first. The weeks of preparation were paying off. He winged a few of the BB wads. They crackled upon impact with the wood frame of the board. Practice makes perfect. His doubts disappeared. This was going to be good. The class would roar. Nobody was going to get hurt, just embarrassed a little. This was going to be fun.

Baker had told them on Monday that he'd made a few changes in this week's lesson plan. Tomorrow would still be "Write it Wednesday," but his latest teaching experiment would involve the blackboard and himself writing on it. That was perfect. Tomorrow was the big day. Tomorrow was actually today. And today was Wednesday.

Patty Light

Dear Desired Helpers,

It was a strange, mostly wonderful weekend. I found out many things on Saturday I don't know how to begin to tell you what they were. I discovered my friend isn't perfect, but he is invaluable. I found out people who radiate outwardly sometimes rain inwardly. I met someone who has suffered more silently than I, but found her voice and a smile. I saw and heard miserable people headed for hell and encouraged them on their journey. I saw how fear and sadness dominate more lives than mine.

I learned how healing laughter is. I learned how close we can come to one another if we remove our masks. I learned how inevitable it is that life will bring reasons to scream and how quickly compassion softens anger and fear. I learned that others value what I have done. I learned it is warm to be in a group of people who care for one another and share their sorrows and joys.

P.L.

Kyle Hunter

Wednesday morning dawned warm, blue and beautiful. As early as Kyle arose, Gail had gotten up an hour earlier. Part of him wished she wasn't so eager to hit the road. Part of him understood it didn't matter that she would be gone. For the next five days – to be honest, the next three weeks – he would be immersed in end-of-the-year duties and activities. It would all be like last night when their soup and salad lunch was followed by silent hours of him reading research papers. During a pause, he'd lifted his eyes to gaze at her sitting at the kitchen table awash in her own forms, plans, and duties. Her blue eyes were alive. She was oblivious to his stare, and not in need of his attention.

She'd already packed the trunk of the car with two suitcases of clothes, samples and brochures she'd be showing to store managers and shoved two briefcases of paperwork she'd completed or needed to work on in the back seat. She's very self-sufficient, Kyle realized and endured the threat that followed the thought. That's a good thing, he insisted to himself as he chomped his Cheerios and watched her get in the car and heard her start it. For a moment he thought she was leaving without a goodbye, but she was just repositioning the vehicle in front of their house.

He returned to the table and set the half finished bowl of cereal on it. She was wearing a new tan business suit that looked smashing on her. He was rather under-dressed, still wearing his blue and white striped bathrobe after showering. At least he'd smell good.

She popped through the door and eyed him, hands on hips, the hint of a smile on her lips. "You're kind of a mess with that hair sticking up all over the place and that face needing a shave. I'll be on my way so you can concentrate on getting ready."

"I'll step outside and wave goodbye," Kyle told her. "If you're lucky, maybe the wind will blow my robe open." She turned and let him guide her out the door. "You look great," he said as they dropped down the two steps. The grass was dewy under his bare feet. She walked in front of him, opened the car door, then turned.

"I know you're terribly busy. But in between stacks, could you think a little about the company's offer? They'll need to know your plans after the end of school."

"It's in the back of my mind all the time," Kyle said. That was no lie.

"Is school going all right? I should have asked."

"Maybe too calm to believe."

"I'd better go," she said, and left the open door to give him a quick kiss on the cheek. "Bristly," she noted. "But you smell fine. I hope your days remain the same," she said as she slid behind the steering wheel, the move-ment hiking her skirt above her knees.

He leaned in with one hand atop the open door and the other on the roof of the car. "Oh, baby," he said. He puffed his lips and returned a quick brush of his lips on her cheek. "Bristly," he explained. She keyed the car and lifted her left leg slightly to depress the clutch. "Oh, baby,'" he repeated, then closed her door. She shifted and eased to the end of the half-circle driveway. He watched, his thumbs hooked into the belt of his robe.

She rolled down her window. "Riding your bike?"

"Beautiful day. You bet I am."

"Wear a cap or bring a comb. Your hair looks awful."

"How does this look," he called, whipping his robe open and shut.

"Oh, baby," she imitated playfully. "But, shoot, I really do have to go," she called back, her laughter chiming over the lip of the window.

It had been the best parting they'd managed in months. He felt exhilarated this warm May morning. Maybe more days would start like this if he could give in, take a leave, and try the world of corporate advertising.

He reentered the house. Bathrobes and bristles weren't exactly suitable, and if he didn't get his rear in gear, he'd have to drive the truck.

Yes, he mused, as he donned his pants, buttoned his shirt, and combed his unruly mop, life might be simpler if he'd just say yes. But every single time he thought about leaving teaching, that ache in his heart emerged.

He walked to the garage and rolled out his bike. The morning was warming. It was a good thing he was leaving early and returning late. Perspiration peppered his forehead before he'd ridden a mile. He didn't know how hot it was, but it was plenty humid. That almost guaranteed a storm was gathering somewhere.

Robert Baker

Robert Baker's nerves were like wires constantly twanged and had been ever since Friday afternoon. His classes, which had been going relatively well, now seemed interminable. Every move he'd made to ease the tension doubled it. Today's was the latest experiment and might be the last. Today they were going to choose their own seating. Today he was going to try another in a two week string of experimental teaching techniques. But the success of this one in this class seemed terribly important.

He suspected he had a subconscious motive for the sit-where-you- wish tactic. It made attendance taking a time-consuming task. He knew the names and faces of his students, but locating them within the room was daunting. Completing the task would leave less time to agonize if this lesson failed. And it would be agonizing. He'd never wanted a lesson to reach his students as much as he did today.

This third period class was the closest thing he had to a "star class" and his greatest hope. But standing behind the lectern looking at them, he wondered if hope was a distant dream. In a monumental step toward his own self-destruction, he'd managed to offend the unoffendable Monday after school. Patty Light's head had snapped back as though she'd been slapped. He wished she'd been enraged by the tone of his rejection of her offer to help. He wished she'd stomped out of the room. Instead she'd stood there amazed, wonder and hurt in her eyes. Then she'd simply turned and left without a word, not pausing at the door.

He glanced at her now, his hands clutching the sides of the lectern, the fine film of perspiration lining his forehead generated by both humidity and nerves. She looked up from the book she was reading, flickered a worried smile, and returned to her reading, an island in a sea of noise. She was unbelievable. His heart leapt. Why subject her to the probability of twenty minutes of barely controlled chaos while he tried yet another teaching technique? She'd catch on to the method and message in ten seconds. Why not send her – and Billy, another island – to the library to do the research he should have requested of her on Monday?

He left the lectern and walked to her desk. "Would you mind getting Billy and both of you coming up to my desk?" he asked. "I need a favor." After Monday, why should she want to?

But she replied, "Sure."

"Could you bring your notebook up with you?"

"Sure," she said, her eyes scanning his face. She slipped out of her desk to fetch her friend.

He scrawled out the passes and handed one to each when they arrived. Patty flipped open her notebook and wrote as he talked. "What I'd like is for the two of you to do some research of critical commentary concerning the poetry of Edward Arlington Robinson, Edna St. Vincent Millay, and Wallace Stevens. Jot anything you can find related to "Domination of Black" by Stevens, "The Spring and the Fall" and "Renascence" by Millay, and "Richard Cory" by Robinson. If you can find the poems, have the library run about thirty-five copies of each. That would be helpful. Do that first and get as far with the rest as you can. Come back in 30 minutes. You can leave now. And thanks."

"No problem," Billy said. The two gathered up their books and left.

Robert stood behind the lectern and waited for the bell. He ordered his eyes to wander the milling room. Something about Allan Barberie, whose seating choice today was the first chair in the window row, caught his eye. The boy was even more fidgety and ill at ease than usual. He was fumbling for something in his pocket, his thin body full of taps and jerks, his middle school face replete with freshly bloomed pimples that looked like hives. The boy sensed Robert's attention and jerked his own out the window. There, Robert realized, was a kid who could identify with the result of the isolation and loneliness portrayed in the poem he'd be writing on the board.

The class's other famous fidgeter sat on the opposite side of the room. Robert turned his head and found Jerry Jons in the first seat of the hall row as always. However, the tousled boy with the goofy grin wasn't joking and giggling over everything. Jerry was seated and silent for a change, seemingly entranced by the pencil case lying on his desk.

Robert's gaze drifted to the back of the room. Ed Warrum shuffled through the door to the seat where he always sat, last desk, last row, hall wall. Robert had to admit Ed had shown signs of intelligent life lately, evidence of a heartbeat within his indifferent demeanor. Maybe the intimations that this athlete had problems were true. Or perhaps it was because Shellie Chaine had revived her interest in him. She was now sliding into the seat in front of his. She'd been another disappointment, relentlessly satisfied with her cheerleader status and her C average.

Frank Marin soon followed through the door. He heavy booted himself to the third chair of the middle row. The kid was impossible to miss, his leather jacket too familiar, his boots too clumpy. The boy's pompadour had flattened in the humidity and hung over his eyes. Or maybe John Lennon was his new dead hero. Frank sat down, extending his left leg far into the aisle. Robert pointed at the leg and motioned for the boy to move it. He was shocked when Frank responded. Not only that, Frank was the only student with a book resting atop of his desk. He was thumbing the cover as though eager to begin learning. Maybe there was hope after all.

The jangling bell jangled Robert's nerves. He jerked his head back as though he'd been hit. Keep that up and I'll end up with a sprained neck, he thought, not exactly an injury that would earn you a red badge of courage.

He scanned the attendance book, then the noisy room for thirty-three matching faces. Attendance and discipline mattered. Everything else was secondary. He was good at taking attendance. Maybe that was why they let him stay.

He finished, scrawled the names of two missing students, Angela Adams and Felecia Waine, on the slip, and closed his book. Immediately desks swiveled towards one another. Robert's heart fell with a thud. It felt like a mistake to have emptied the room of his two best students. But at least they wouldn't have to endure the emerging din. He headed for the door with the attendance slip.

Since only the window row remained relatively straight, its occupants staring at the day beyond the window, he chose it as his path to the door. Allan looked terrible, nearly sick, his face flushed. He stopped at the boy's desk and leaned over. "You feeling okay, Allan?"

The boy raised his liquid eyes up at the teacher and then down to his desk. "Yeah, yeah, I'm okay."

"You're sure?" Robert asked, not feeling the pin-bearing spit wad wing into the back of his suit coat.

"Yeah, yeah," Allan answered.

The journey to the door seemed endless. When Robert reached it, he hung the attendance slip on the clip outside and wished he didn't have to go back in. His plan for the period seemed senseless. He should be doing what he'd done with the rest of his classes, assigning the poems of Millay, and dividing the class into discussion groups who would report their conclusions tomorrow. Instead he'd battled with himself since Sunday as to whether to have his best class deal with "Domination of Black" or get rocked out of their complacency by "Richard Cory". Neither was in the book. He'd have to write either on the board. He'd settled on the latter. Its dramatic final lines would shock these kids into awareness of the awful price people pay who are isolated by fate or by others.

As he stood outside his door, he felt doomed to failure. But it was too late. What did it matter anyway? All you could do was try. He walked back into the noise, closed the door and watched legs withdrawing from the path he wound through the clumped groups of desks to the front of the room. He felt a pinprick in his shoulder blade and swiped in its direction, then forgot about it. He advanced to the chalkboard, ignoring little ripples of laughter that drifted to his ears from behind.

He grasped a long piece of chalk in his hand, and then stood immobile at the board. There was a name for this teaching technique he was about to use. He'd learned about its wonders in one of his education classes. It seemed terribly important to be able to tell the class later what the method was called, lest they think it was another loony notion of their loony teacher. He'd remembered it Sunday. But could he think of it now? He whacked his left hand into his right breaking the chalk in half. He had to remember the name of this technique so he could prove it had a name.

He did not know his immobility created a perfect target for two more pin-clad wads to arrow into his coat.

The Indirect Method! That was what it was called! The Indirect Method! You started to do something interesting without explanation, thereby Creating Interest instead of Demanding It! That was what he was doing, and "Richard Cory" was the perfect poem for it!

He threw a glance over his shoulder. Most of the class remained immersed in discussions about nothing. A few looked at him with smiles on their faces. Others had their hands over their mouths. Frank Marin was at the front of what had been a row, hunched over the open book, a blank paper ready for note taking. That was amazing!

He turned his back to the class. He was far too warm. The humidity in the room was atrocious. If his plan worked, he'd write the title, then first verse. Then he'd scuttle over so some could read that while he wrote the second. Then he'd scuttle once more, and write the rest in bold letters, each addition reducing the student's inattention as they were drawn first by curiosity and then by the poem's drama. The last two lines would be written in a triumph of silence. Gasps would escape the mouths of many as he stepped aside. He'd wait a moment, then turn and suggest, "Let's talk about Richard Cory," and their eagerness would be overwhelming.

He clutched the chalk in his hand and wrote the title, "Richard Cory." "Who's he?" someone said. "Are you putting him on detention," questioned another to sporadic chuckles. "I don't think he's in our class," spoke a third and light laughter lifted into the air. That was all right. Someone was looking. She'd caused someone else to pay attention. Then a third. His heart jumped a bit.

As he wrote, "Whenever Richard Cory went downtown . . . " the noise in the room grew. Someone must be telling jokes he couldn't hear, for the laughter seemed to be increasing. That was okay. That was okay. Their joviality would be jolted away by the devastating final lines. They didn't need to comment on every word. They were enjoying themselves. What was so bad about that?

He shifted to his right. As he did, he thought he saw something on the window side of the room splat against the board and tumble to the chalk tray. Probably a spit wad. Well, that was going to happen if his back was turned. He paused to see if this was an incident or a problem. When another didn't follow, he resumed writing. He finished the line, "He was always quietly arrayed," when someone near the front of the room said, "Air raid," as another papered pin plunked into his coat below his left shoulder. The burst of laughter surprised him. The joke wasn't that funny. But what did it matter? At least a few were following what he was doing. Others chortled at the braying tone of a honker's laugh. Another wad winged into the back of his coat. Robert thought about reacting to the joke. But they were talking. The method was working. Why spoil a good thing? A few were into it. They were setting things up perfectly. The last two lines would knock the smiles right off their faces. It would be tears instead of mirth. He wrote, "And still he fluttered pulses when he said good morning/ And he glittered when he walked," and someone, maybe Shellie, screamed, "He's writing about Mr. Gerney!"

He wrote more swiftly. He had to finish this before playfulness overwhelmed interest. He ignored the ping of something hitting the board to his right, ignored a voice filtering through the noise asking, "Hey what's going on?" and repeating his name several times until it was drowned by the crescendo of giggles rolling back and forth across the room. He increased his writing speed. He had to get this done before the class was gone. Those final lines had to appear soon, soon, soon. Just get it done. He wrote furiously, shifted once more, ignoring pinging sounds on both sides of him.

He'd finished "And Richard Cory one calm summer night" and bent over slightly to write the terrible and powerful final lines, bent just enough so his suit coat hiked to just below belt level, literally shaking with anticipation of the staggering effect of the last line when in quick succession something stung the hand that held the chalk and something burned into the nape of his neck. He stopped, in shock. A pinned wad winged into his exposed posterior just below his suit coat, hung there for a moment and jolted him upward as the class blared with laughter, blazed with laughter, stormed with laughter. He wrenched his head around and another missile tore a ragged line along his cheekbone just below his eye. He ducked his head back, bleeding, his right arm tightening, the chalk squealing a jagged streak upwards until his hand hit the top of the board, and the chalk shattered into shards and fell to the floor. He stood there with his arm like that, his back to the class, his head against the board as the laughter became a tangible, seeable thing, hot little people with hot red faces and brighter red cheeks filling all the air.

The sorrow began in his stomach and raced upward through his chest and into his throat. The anger began in his brain, burned through his forehead, dazzled his eyes, tightened his face into a rigid mask, his lips curled against his teeth. It raged into his throat where anger and sorrow choked him. He heard a desk crashing in the din.

"Damn you!" he screamed from the pit of his stomach upward through his strangled throat. "Damn you!" he screamed wheeling around, drawing his arm down, his fingers into fists, his torn cheek bleeding. "Damn you!" he screamed in the sudden silence of the whirling room, the red faces paling as they passed. "Damn you!" he screamed as his eyes found the fallen desk and the two boys sprawled on the floor one atop the other. He ripped his coat off and sent it whirling through the air, pinned wads sailing off before it fell to the floor. He charged the fighters as a boy streaked out of the room to look for help. He reached them and tore at the one on top as Patty Light and Billy Cloud raced into the room. He caught the boy's hair, jerked back his head with one hand and drew back the other, mustering all his strength to smash it into Ed Warrum's face as Patty Light screamed, "No! No! No!"

Her scream transfixed his fist in midair. He stared into the surprise in Ed Warrum's eyes. He dropped his arm and released his hold.

In the silence that enveloped the room, he slumped to his desk, his cheek dripping blood, his body crawling with ants. The silence, save for the sobbing of a few students, increased and became deep even as Billy Cloud moved to the front of the room and stood sentinel between the class and its teacher, even as Patty Light extracted a handkerchief from her purse with shaking fingers and pressed it against Robert Baker's wounded cheek, even as Mr. Hunter and Mr. Crannan, who clutched Jerry Jons by the arm, entered the room followed by Mr. Strand, even as Ed Warrum released his grip on Frank Marin and pushed away from him so Strand and Hunter could jerk him to his feet and Strand could march him out the door, even as Hunter approached Robert Baker's desk and stared into his opaque eyes and at the blood trickling beneath the handkerchief and down his cheek.

"You all follow Mr. Crannan to my room," he turned and told the class. "Don't say a word in the hall. Don't say a word going down the stairs. Don't say a word when you enter my room. Find a chair or sit on the floor. Don't say a word until I get back and ask you to. Billy, take the crying boy by the windows to the nurse's office. Ed, go to Mr. Strand's office. Patty, stay here with me. We'll wait a few minutes and then we'll walk downstairs with Mr. Baker."

Robert Baker sat silent in his chair. His eyes were empty as though his spirit had vacated his body and fled somewhere far, far away.

Ed Warrum

"It might seem ridiculous," Mr. Strand said, "for me to point out that fighting is prohibited in this school, and this is your second incident. Rules are rules or they're nothing at all."

"I was sorry about the first fight. I'm not this time," Ed Warrum said. "I'll take my punishment. I earned it the first time, not this time."

"I need to know what happened."

"I was sitting in back, last row. As soon as Mr. Baker was done taking attendance, everyone shifted chairs around. Mr. Baker started to write on the blackboard. The room was noisy. So Shellie and I started talking."

"To be like the rest of the class?"

"No. We were talking about stuff related to class."

"Such as?"

"Such as how Mr. Baker would have liked the place we went last Saturday. How we should write poems about what we did, what happened. We started to write one. Now and then we checked on how Mr. Baker was coming along. We noticed stuff hanging on his suit coat. Like wet Kleenex. Shellie said we should tell him. Kids were pointing and laughing. Anyway I called Mr. Baker's name, but he didn't turn around. So I gave up. Which was stupid. I should have gone up to talk to him. I didn't because he'd think I was trying to cause problems."

"Why would he think that? You're a troublemaker?"

"It's more like I'm a nothing. Which might be worse. I've had my problems. When I've tried talking to him, it hasn't worked. Not his fault. It just is."

"Go on."

"The longer Mr. Baker wrote, the more the kids were laughing. He didn't react except to try to write faster."

"I know the poem. He didn't get it finished."

"Then the laughing got really loud, so I stood up to see what the heck was going on. That stuff was hanging all over his coat. Mr. Baker was standing bolt upright. The class was roaring. That's when I headed towards the front. I saw Frank Marin had rubber bands wound around his fingers like slingshots. He was shooting pinned spit wads at Mr. Baker. I saw him pull back. I saw Mr. Baker flinch and duck his head. Everybody just roared. That's when I charged Frank. I knocked that sucker out of his desk. Mr. Baker thought I was the troublemaker. He was mad and bleeding and ready to swing at me. Patty stopped him. I kept Frank pinned until you and Mr. Hunter showed up. End of story."

"No one else tried to stop what was going on?"

"No. Patty and Billy weren't in the room. Most everyone thought it was hilarious. They only got quiet when they saw Mr. Baker was bleeding."

The administrator's intercom phone rang. He listened, hung up and told Ed, "The police are in the detention room. They were already here to talk to one of our students about the vandalizing of Mr. Baker's apartment. The other two have been apprehended and implicated the third. Judging by your story, you'll be happy to know that."

"Yes, I am."

"Go to the detention room and give the police your statement. If your fellow students corroborate your story, it will make some difference. Nevertheless I'm suspending you. It's best that a rule is a rule."

"Yes, sir, it is."

Sam Strand

Kyle Hunter ordered every student from Robert Baker's third period class to submit a written report of what had happened in room 313. Ed Crannan delivered the sheaf of papers to Sam Strand.

"Your job description keeps expanding," Sam said.

"No problem. Everybody is busy as a cranberry merchant. No reason I shouldn't be. Too bad about Mr. Baker. Hardest working teacher in the school, I'd say. Some nights I'll bet he heard the roosters crow on his way home, turned around and went back to school."

"The only good thing is his attacker was shooting pinned spit wads, not bullets."

"Hope it never comes to that!"

The students' reports made it obvious most knew what was going on, who was responsible, and who took action. Explanations for not intervening were variations of "we thought it was funny until . . . "

Sam groaned, picked up the phone and requested the presence of Frank Marin.

A few minutes later Frank shook off Fred Barnes' grip on his arm and shuffled through the principal's office door to the chair he'd occupied only weeks ago. "Frank have anything to say?" Sam asked the counselor.

"Whined about being treated unfairly. 'Why is Ed Warrum a hero? He beat me up. I didn't do nothin'," he mimicked. "If he was talking about school work, I'd believe him. I'm going back to interview more students."

The principal stared at the boy, then leafed through the reports. "You out of rubber bands and spit wads?"

"I don't know what you're talking about." Frank said as he slid down in the chair, head tilted toward the ceiling.

"Sit up straight!" Sam snapped. "I want to hear your version of what happened."

"Nothin' happened. Kids havin' fun. The usual."

"A teacher with blood dripping down his face is neither 'fun' nor 'the usual'."

"Didn't see that."

"You were flat on the floor when I arrived. How did that happen?"

"Ed Warrum attacked me."

"Why would Ed do that?"

A crooked grin crawled the boy's face. "Maybe because his girl is giving it to me."

Sam drummed his fingers on the pile of papers. This boy had more hooks than a fishing tournament. Ugly as they were, it was difficult to resist lunging for them. But he managed. "You were sitting in the front of the room?"

"Naw, I never sit in the front."

"You were in the front of the room when I arrived."

"He dragged me there."

"Your classmates disagree."

"Liars."

"Why would they lie?"

"They don't like me."

Sam tapped the papers with his index finger. "Looks like they do. Most thought what you did was cunning and funny. So funny they didn't stop you. You should be proud. Especially of those pins sticking in the suit coat." Frank did not reply. "Here, I'll show you." Sam spread the papers across his desk. "Read them. You'll like it."

"Bunch of lies."

"No, really," Sam pursued. "They were almost falling out of their chairs laughing. Baker was clueless. That was hilarious. This one and this one and this one...!" Sam repeated, pounding his finger on the reports. "They were roaring. And when Mr. Baker ducked his head as that last pin cut into his cheek! A riot!" Sam thundered.

"Wasn't supposed to . . . wasn't me."

"These papers name three students. Allan Barberie. Jerry Jons. Frank Marin."

"Why aren't you talking to the first two?"

"They're talking to the police. Jerry is in trouble. Allan is scared to death.

They have plenty to say."

"They're chicken crap."

"Why don't you admit it? You accomplished your goals. You got attention. Your classmates were entertained. The only person hurt was Mr. Baker."

"I'm sorry I . . . they . . . hurt him."

Sam Strand threw his hands in the air. "Why pick on Mr. Baker, for heaven's sake? He's the only teacher who's never written a referral on you!"

"I got nothin' against Mr. Baker. Kids don't like him. People pick on him because he's an easy target."

That was as close as Frank Marin was going to come to an admission. Sam picked up the phone. "Put Officer Burquet on, please." He cradled it with his shoulder and scooped together the papers. "Lance. What did Jerry and Allan have to say? Plenty?" He paused. "Come and get Frank Marin. You might have better luck with him than I." He hung up and stared at Frank. "The boys are singing like canaries, Frank. I'm going to do what I warned you I'd do. I'm suspending you for the remainder of the school year.

"I know that slippery slope you're zooming down. I know the signs. There is help available, and I am willing to help you find it, but my hands are tied beyond inviting you to an AA meeting. You, your parents, or the legal system have to take the first step. I'm praying that you see the light before you do something or have something done to you that's as tragic." Officer Burquet entered the office. "Go," Sam Strand ordered the boy.

❖ ❖ ❖

Sam stopped by Kyle Hunter's room. The teacher was angry. "Words and wildfires are the same thing in this school," Kyle seethed. "Some seniors came in laughing about what they'd heard. They shut up when they saw his students in my room. But I'm boiling."

"Thought I'd check on how it went with Robert. Should have been my job."

"It should have been an assistant principal's job, too, but we don't have one in this penny-ante prison."

Sam dropped his hand on Kyle's shoulder. "Robert?"

"Robert. He was bleeding. He never said a word. The ambulance showed up without sirens. But as it pulled away, I saw far too many student faces in the windows."

"I've already scheduled assemblies for tomorrow."

Frank Marin

It wasn't fun, but it wasn't hard either. Frank Marin had his story down pat. Strand hadn't believed it, and neither did they. But one cop said, he'd thrown a few spit wads in his day. His question was "Why add the pins?"

The question resonated. Why had he pushed it over the edge? He'd wanted to raise a little havoc, provoke a few laughs. For awhile the pin idea seemed inspired, those papers waving like little white flags all over the back of Baker's suit coat, the whole class pointing, giggling, roaring! That's what he wanted. Why did he have to zing that last one? He was riding the roar, and it carried him away. If that thing had bounced off the board, if Baker hadn't turned his head... It was funny. Then it wasn't. He'd never meant to bring Baker all the way down, but that was what he'd done.

"It will be up to Mr. Baker and the school if they want to press charges," the cop told Frank as he eased his patrol car to a stop in front of the Marin residence. Frank had his hand on the door handle, but the cop continued, "I'd keep my nose clean if I were you. Your name is in our records. We'll be watching for you."

"Thanks. I'll do that." The two shots of vodka he'd downed this morning were faint fumes in his brain. He was plenty sober enough to realize if he wanted to dig his own grave, everyone would hand him a shovel.

The cop wasn't leaving until Frank went into his house, so he turned up the walk, pulled open the front door, and shut it behind him. He wandered into the front room and saw the blinking light on the answering machine. He couldn't believe the school's stupidity. The reason his parents never reacted was they never got the messages. He erased them, just like he intercepted the mail to tear and toss the written communications.

He pushed the button on the phone to hear what they'd said. The voice in the answering machine announced two messages. The one from the school was to the point. The second was from Betts. Anger, jealousy, and longing filled him so full that he had to play the message twice to get beyond her voice to her words.

"Frankie, long time, no time. So sorry. I know you're mad at me. So are my parents. I'm mad at Brick and Brian. They treat me like crap, and I told them I was sick of it. You treated me good. Besides that, you feel good. You're more of a man than those two combined. Whew," the machine breathed, "it's hot today and thinking of you makes me hotter. Want to party? There's one this afternoon. New place you'd never find. If you want to go, give me a call, and I'll pick you up. Wear something tight. Whew," she finished.

"Whew," he mimicked. He suddenly believed this day was supposed to happen. After all, who knew Baker would spend the entire period with his back turned? Keep his suit coat on in this heat? If Baker hadn't turned his head and Warrum hadn't jumped him, the class would have ended with the room littered with spit wads and Baker wondering what happened. Instead Frank had been booted, and given the perfect excuse for flunking. And partying. That was the cake. Betts was the icing. Frank Marin was golden.

He decided to make Betts wait. Let her know you can't burn a guy, leave a mound of ashes and not get smudged. Besides he had to gather what money he had and steal the remainder from his parents. His mother left her purse in their bedroom. His parents chose to trust him. They gave him chance after chance, in this case the chance to rifle her purse as well as the money jar hidden at the back of the top kitchen cupboard shelf. He found fifty in the purse and fifty in the jar. They ought to bank their money or trade him in for a better son.

Betts sounded happy to hear his voice. Hers was slurry and purry. He gave her his address, and she zoomed up his driveway half an hour later, skidding to a stop a foot from the garage. He grabbed his jacket and hurried out the front door. Her window was rolled down, partly due to heat, partly to sober up enough to keep her car on the road. She wore a blue halter-top and tight tan shorts. Her hazed eyes were as inviting as a whisper in his ear. "You'd better drive, Frankie," she said, her voice low and lush. "I'm on my way to Saturday and it's only Wednesday afternoon. You got a license?"

"Of course," he lied. Truth was he'd never bothered. It would hardly be worth the pressure of the tests. "I'm a good driver."

"Got to stop at the liquor store," she told him. "If you got money, I'll buy beer and a couple bottles. If you don't, we may as well stay right here in the driveway because I'm broke, and they'll chase us away with sticks if we don't bring booze."

The familiar feeling of being used resurfaced. Betts had never done that. She'd drunk his booze and smoked his dope, but she'd never made furnishing them a condition.

They stopped at a liquor store at the edge of town. He gave her thirty dollars and sat in the car. Watching her walk provoked a low growl. But he wasn't the only one whose blood she rushed. When she reappeared, a crewcut man with big arms followed her, lugging the cases of beer. Frank watched in the rear view mirror as Betts opened the trunk. The man looked her right in the chest as she thanked him for his help. By the time she got back in the car, Frank was furious, and she knew it. "Don't be jealous, Frankie. I chose you to be with, didn't I?"

Betts directed him to the other end of town. Along the county road they followed, he saw a sign that read 'The Cloud House.' He knew what Billy thought of him now. Billy was tight with Patty Light, who was tight with Mr. Baker. He didn't care about Billy, but thinking about the rage Patty felt brought a hot flush to his face. He'd need a drink soon.

A mile or two beyond the last house on the left, he saw cars lining both sides of the road, tilted toward the ditches. Betts pointed and said, "There it is," and then "Pull in there." The rutted road he turned into was so full of cars that the trunk of Betts' car jutted into the road. "We'll get the stuff out of the trunk and then you can park this thing. I'll wait here for you," Betts smiled. After he'd unloaded the booze, she pulled two beers from a case, handed them to him, puckered her red lips and gave him a kiss.

He drove nearly two miles up the road before the parked cars petered out. Strolling back to the trail entrance, he popped a beer and drank it in a series of gulps. Then apprehension invaded his head. Betts had that piece of beef at the store tripping on his tongue. She could do the same with the college brats. He quickened to a lope, sweat swarming his face.

She was gone. So was the booze. He oughta take her car and leave her stranded. Park it in a tow zone downtown. Some threat. A ton of guys would be glad to ride her home. So he headed up the trail past herds of cars.

The ridge was rife with lightly clad bodies. Everyone was loud and laughing. Nobody noticed him. The meadow below was equally packed, its grass trampled flat. How would he find Betts in this mess? He needed a drink to shut up his brain. He popped the can and guzzled it. He finally spotted her standing at the edge of the stream talking to Brick. That made him sick. He lunged down the trail through the milling crowd. Then her hand was there holding another beer, and her red lips imprinted a kiss on his streaming cheek. She fingered his belt. "Some boys offered to carry the cases. I could hardly say no, could I? It saved you a lot of work." Her fingers curled his belt. He gulped several swallows of beer, beginning to get buzzed. Still he had to say, "I saw you talking to Brick."

"He was jus' 'pologizing," she slurred. "He wants to 'pologize to you, too. 'Cuz we saw you at the park, you know. But when I was kissin' him, I was wishin' I was kissin' you." She led him by the belt to the stream where she'd secreted a dozen beers under a towel. "This should be enough. The rest were our contribution."

Soon the sun was tilting toward six. Frank was so woozy he hardly noticed the hand that clasped his shoulder, barely heard the voice close to his ear shouting over the boom boxes. "Frankie. Long time, no time." He saw red. He brushed the hand off his shoulder and turned. Brick's sallow face awaited his gaze. "My man, why are we so testy?" Brick oozed. "We been missin' our buddy, Elvis."

"Been missing' my booze and buds," Frank snapped.

"Well, yeah, tha's true, too." Brick's face was far too close. His breath reeked cigarettes and booze. "But we missed you, too. We missed ya so much, we bought ya a presen', to remin' ya how much we love ya." He motioned to his friend. Brian fumbled in a duffel bag and produced a small box. He handed it to Brick. "Jus' a token of our 'steem and gradatude," Brick beamed. He extended the box, then jerked it back. "Presen' needs esplanation. I'll open it for ya." He tore off the top and turned the box over. He shook an object into his other hand. It was a pincushion loaded with pins.

"What the heck?"

"Acshually this is to remind' ya of Betts." He waved the object. Frank whipped his head around. Betts had backed away, her hands covering her mouth. He couldn't tell if she was crying or laughing. "This is to remin' ya of good ol' Betts 'cuz she's the bes' li'l pincushion in town, and nobody knows that better than Brian and me." He grabbed Frank's hand, flipped the pincushion over and ground the pins into his palm.

The pain was searing. Frank wrenched his punctured hand back as the pincushion fell to the ground. Rage tornadoed his body. He took a wild swing at Brick's chin. Brick stumbled back as Frank's hand flew by, the blow barely grazing him. He flopped backwards into the water, arms flailing. Then he sank.

Frank stood shocked and staring at the surface.

"He can't swim," Brian bellowed as he shot past Frank into the water.

Frank whirled away and plunged through the noise and bodies and up the trail to the ridge. He heard shouts, maybe screams above the blare. He bounded across the ridge and slid the incline. He raced past the flood of faces and reached the road, sure he heard his name shouted.

He reached into his pocket. Betts' keys were still there. He charged up the road to her car. Glancing back, he saw throngs of people staring in his direction. He leapt into the car, fired the engine and raced up the road.

Gotta think, gotta think, gotta think. He may have murdered Brian. He was driving a stolen car. He'd attacked a teacher. He scrambled the car south on the first gravel road he saw, clouds of dust trailing him. Gotta think. Gotta think. The only thought that surfaced was, go home. Go home to Bethel Ridge.

He skidded to a halt at a stop sign. The road was Highway 75. Darkness was descending. He forced himself to drive the speed limit as he skirted Blue Lake.

He did not stop until he reached the abandoned elevator outside the tiny town of Florence eight miles northeast of Bethel Ridge. He pulled into the empty parking lot and switched off the motor. There was undoubtedly an APB out for the vehicle and the thieving killer driving it. He tossed the keys into the glove box. Betts' vodka bottle lying on the seat, so he jammed it into his jacket pocket and got out of the car.

When he saw headlights up the road, he slid into the ditch and hunkered until the night was silent. He patted the bottle, but did not drink. If he did, he'd drink it all, they'd find him passed out in the ditch, and he'd wake up in jail.

Billy Cloud

Billy Cloud pounded the oval track. He wanted to run until his body was exhausted and his mind went blank. He veered off the track, waved at Coach Schwarz and pointed toward the street. He had nothing to offer the team. He needed to escape the school.

He ran to the corner stoplight and pumped his legs in place. His mind drilled back through the day. Baker had had a hunch things could fall apart. He'd sent Patty and him away to shield her from witnessing that. He remembered the panic in Patty's voice as they climbed the stairs and waves of noise washed down the stairwell. "That's Mr. Baker's room! I know it is!" He remembered Jerry Jons flying around the corner and down the stairs, moaning, "Oh, God, it's out of control," as he skidded by. That's when they'd bolted up the stairs two at a time as the noise morphed to lunatic laughter. Then it cut off as though severed by a knife, suddenly replaced by Mr. Baker's raging voice. They'd charged through the door and stopped dead in their tracks.

That scene was still surreal in his mind: Ed Warrum wrestling Frank Marin on the floor: Mr. Baker, furious and bleeding, yanking Ed's head back; Patty's scream stopping everything; the teacher slumped behind his desk; Patty pressing her handkerchief on his wound; himself between the class and the teacher; Mr. Hunter's stricken face; Mr. Strand's full of rage and sorrow...

He was loping without knowing it down the college campus sidewalk fronting the freshmen dorms. He jogged in place, awaiting a break in the traffic so he could cross to Lakeside Park. A convertible full of girls passed by whistling and waving silver cans. One screamed, "Hey, Tonto, wanta show me your tomahawk?"

He ripped across the road between cars, and through the park to the path along the lake. He was streaming sweat. The day was too hot and humid for the distance he was forcing on himself.

By the time he returned to the school, the track was deserted, the locker room blessedly bereft of boys although there was a light on in the coaches' office and muffled voices drifting through the door. He peeled his drenched shirt and shorts and took a long, cold shower.

He was buttoning his shirt when Mr. Schwarz and Ed emerged from the office. "I'm stopping by the hospital," the coach called. "Want to come along?"

"I need to go home first to get my head straight. Wouldn't mind a ride home though."

"I'll give him a ride to the hospital later," Ed said. "We live right across the road."

Billy recounted the trauma in Mr. Baker's room to his parents after supper as they sat on the porch sipping lemonade and watching the unceasing traffic. Billy said with certainty, "They're partying at my place. I knew that was going to happen." He paused. "I guess there were signs Mr. Baker might end up where he is now, too. What I'll never get is why it went this far."

"Getting a whole bunch of people to feel and think the way you do feels powerful," his father said. "So powerful you hate to let it go. So you convert more people to your way of thinking. That's easier when you create an enemy for focus. Mr. Baker was a convenient target. Who he was as a human being didn't matter. Neither did anything he did. An enemy can't do anything right."

"That doesn't make sense."

"Of course it doesn't. Sense doesn't matter. An enemy can't be human in your mind, so you dehumanize, even demonize, the enemy. You eliminate his or her human face and replace it with the universal face named The Enemy. After that, you're justified in everything you do. You recruit others. You declare war. You force your enemy to react in desperation and then use those reactions for more justification. You resist every change he tries to make; you ignore his attempts at resolution. You have overwhelming numbers on your side."

His father flicked at the moisture streaking the glass in front of him with his forefinger. "No matter how many deals you make – or treaties you sign – they don't want you to drop off their hook. So they keep inventing fresh reasons to keep you hanging there. They can't bear to let go of their delicious disdain and delusions of superiority. If they did, if they acknowledged that their enemy is human, too, they might wonder what in the world they'd been thinking, what in the world they'd been doing."

Patty Light

Dear Desired Help,

I tried to talk to you on the phone and learned you're out of town until Sunday. But I'd have to write this anyway. I was at the hospital today because Mr. Baker is. So were Billy Cloud, Ed Warrum, and Mr. Hunter. To reduce a maddening story to cold essence, he was attacked in class, wounded physically and emotionally, and has suffered a nervous breakdown. Visiting Mr. Baker isn't possible.

I asked Billy if he'd walk me home from the hospital. Tonight we were quiet. The road wasn't though. Car after car came racing by, brimming with people. We were sure where most were going. I knew that hurt Billy. But not one word crossed his lips, not even when some yelled things that made my hands clench into fists.

I knew my house would be stifling so I asked Billy to walk with me past it down the street to the outskirts of town. We reached the place where the road turns to gravel and sat on the lip of the ditch. The sky was deeper and darker than Mr. Frost's woods.

I told Billy I needed to talk. I told him about the mark of Cain and asked if I was partly to blame for what happened to Mr. Baker, if my spending time around him was part of the trouble. Billy said no. He said kids harassing Mr. Baker, refusing to cooperate, busting into his building, what happened today, those were the cause.

I wanted to close my eyes and breathe in the scent of woods and wildflowers. But every time I even blinked, I saw Mr. Baker's wounded face and felt his spirit leaving me for a faraway place.

I wrote a poem about Mr. Baker before I wrote this. I want to read it at the assembly. But I won't. I'm too different to speak for anyone else as far as Mr. Baker is concerned. So I called someone I hoped would be willing to read it for me. I almost dropped the phone when that person agreed to do it without hesitation.

Sitting here now in my room I am empty of everything but ache. The bloody handkerchief I used to soak up the blood on Mr. Baker's cheek lays like a crumpled rose on my desk. I want to sleep, but his face awaits. Maybe I'll close my eyes anyway and let sadness wash in and mix the ache into something bearable.

But before I put down my pen, I want to write this. After I was done talking, Billy said he wanted to share a quote he'd been told by his second grade teacher. She hoped he'd remember it, and he has. I think I should remember it for myself and for Mr. Baker, too.

"When a broken heart mends, it mends stronger than ever."
P.L.

Kyle Hunter

Shellie Chaine and Patty Light were standing at Kyle Hunter's desk when he looked up from the research paper he was forcing himself to read. "Yes?" he asked.

"I'd like permission to speak at the Junior Class Assembly," Shellie announced.

Kyle stared at the two girls. There stood Patty Light in a light brown blouse and long brown skirt and Shellie Chaine clad in her sky blue cheerleader outfit as though she hadn't guessed the Spring Sports Final Pepfest had been canceled. He'd half-expected Patty to seek permission. But Shellie Chaine? In that outfit? She could torpedo the whole thing. "I don't know," he started before he saw the resolve in his prize student's eyes.

"I've asked Shellie if she'd speak. I want to, but it wouldn't work. They'd drown me out whispering about how I love Mr. Baker." He was about to protest, but she shook her head. "Don't. I've already heard it."

"I'm like most of the rest of us," Shellie said. "Besides, Patty read me the poem she wrote last night that I'm going to read. So, in a sense, she'll be speaking through me without provoking all those annoying whispers."

Kyle found her remark too light by half, but Patty smiled. He was prone to give in as a favor to her. Still he didn't prevent himself from placing another hurdle. "The assembly's first period. That's not much time to figure out what else to say."

"I've been thinking about it ever since the incident," Shellie countered. "I fell asleep thinking about what I would say. When I woke up, I was still thinking about it. Doesn't matter anyway, Mr. Hunter. If all I did was read Patty's poem, that would be enough. I really want your permission to speak. I was in that classroom all year. That makes me partly responsible."

"I really want her to have your permission," Patty insisted. "It's the only way my words will get heard. I trust Shellie."

Kyle couldn't dismiss his misgivings. His only knowledge of Shellie was her role as cheerleader – an enthused, happy, sensuous cheerleader – and as the girlfriend of the all-star quarterback.

"Mr. Hunter?" Patty said, "The bell's going to ring."

"You have my permission," the teacher told the two. He just hoped Shellie wasn't seeing this as another opportunity to be the center of attention.

As Kyle Hunter watched Sam Strand advance to the auditorium podium, his concerns enlarged to include his friend. He saw how deep the furrowed lines on Sam's face had become and weariness in the man's bearing. The past nine months had worn him down. How could they not! A thousand kids stuffed into this ancient building; the school board refusing to approve additional educators at any level. That was nuts!

"This is hard for me," Sam began. "I usually enjoy talking to students. You know why you're here," he recovered. He pulled his tall frame straight. "I've demanded the attendance of this entire class because of the actions of a few. But actions rarely occur in a vacuum.

"There has been a mind-set that has dominated this entire class' relations with Mr. Baker from the first day of school. That mind-set has been aggressive, heartless and mindless and made what happened yesterday almost inevitable. That mind-set was accepted, encouraged, or permitted by the rest of us. It is so toxic it has infected students with no reason to think about Mr. Baker at all. Proof? One of those involved in invading Mr. Baker's building is a senior whose only connection to Mr. Baker is what he's heard from other students.

"I'll take my share of blame. I'm responsible for maintaining an atmosphere of respect in this school. I've failed. Nevertheless, this Junior Class had choices to make, and made one bad choice after another. The class witnessing yesterday's near tragedy made choices that were downright cruel. It watched a teacher humiliated and attacked and remained either hostile or amused the entire time! We are losing our ability to treat one another as human beings in this school! This has occurred on my watch. That will haunt me for a long time.

"The school year is almost over. I can think of only one consequence for this class. This is it. Any referrals involving any of you will result in immediate suspension. Your parents might fight that decision, but the school year will expire before it can be reversed. There is no reason I should have to carry out this edict, but if I have to, you have my solemn oath that I will."

Sam stood silent, his eyes finishing his address. Then he said, "Superintendent Anderson desires a few words with you."

"First of all," Superintendent Anderson said, "Principal Strand's decision concerning suspensions was made in agreement with me. Secondly, Mr. Strand is not at fault for the shortage of teachers and administrators in this school district. He's fought hard to change that.

"Now I want to talk about Mr. Baker. I read his grade transcripts and credentials. Those revealed Mr. Baker was an outstanding student, a two-sport athlete in college, a writer and editor for the college newspaper, and a first-rate practice teacher.

"I've learned that many of you fueled your behavior by passing around the false rumor that I fired Mr. Gerney so I could hire Mr. Baker. I never met Mr. Gerney. His resignation letter arrived on my desk in early August. I'm told that when he visited last January, he told many of you that you should treat Mr. Baker with decency and respect, and that his disappearance had nothing to do with Mr. Baker. Everything I've heard about Mr. Gerney says his word is golden with students. Why did you choose to ignore that and dishonor him as well as Mr. Baker?

"Finally, if you think you won a victory yesterday, think again. If you think you've put yourselves on vacation in your English class, think again. If you think you'll be taking advantage of a substitute teacher, think again. Mr. Strand, other teachers, and myself will be pulling the extra duty of teaching your classes. That will require extra work for us. And from you."

Kyle spoke next. "My name is Mr. Hunter. I teach Senior English. I'm speaking because Mr. Baker is a colleague, a friend, and a human being. I blame myself, all of us, and all of you who stood by and allowed attitudes and actions to escalate to the point they reached yesterday. I'm shocked that a teacher was attacked. I'm shocked by the reactions of too many of you.

"I visited the hospital last night. Mr. Baker's wound had been sutured. It and the wounds inflicted on his mind and heart will eventually heal, even though those wounds will leave scars. They'll leave scars inside you, and me as well.

"Mr. Baker has had to be exceptionally resilient to deal with what he was handed this year. Tough, too. Not like the cowards who invaded his building. The first thing he'll say when he begins to recover from what's happened is this. He'll say, 'It isn't that bad. Nobody got beat up. Nobody died.' That's what he said to Principal Strand and I after the vandalism.

"Mr. Baker tried everything he could think of to reach you. Why any human being should work as hard as he did and be rewarded so poorly is beyond me. Mr. Baker is a teacher and a human being, ladies and gentlemen. All your teachers and all your fellow students are human beings. That's it. When we human beings circle around to watch other human beings attack or demean one another, we are as guilty of the outcomes as perpetrators.

"A classmate of yours is waiting behind the curtains. She asked to speak to you. Give her your full attention."

Shellie Chaine emerged through the center stage's split curtains. A murmur of surprise washed through the audience. She stood at the podium clad in her cheerleader uniform. How could her classmates possibly take her seriously? Kyle watched her tilt the mike to her height, half expecting her to break into a cheer. 'Give us a B, give us an A . . . .'

Shellie spoke. "I asked to talk to you today because I'm one of the students who is responsible for yesterday. I'm one of the students who heard rumors and passed them on. I'm one of the students who listened to attitudes and pretended they were my own. I'm one of the students who nodded and said uh-huh and that's for sure and right on. I'm one of the students who did just enough to get by. I'm one of the students who gave permission for yesterday to happen in my class.

"What we did wasn't mindless. We knew what we were doing, and we really got into it. We totally ignored that we were doing it to another human being. Just like we ignored that those kids we picked on in elementary school and junior high school and now in high school are human beings. I wonder how many of them are walking around today with scars on their hearts and minds and bodies because of what we did?

"For myself, I want to apologize for my part in everything that was done to Mr. Baker and to those people. I hope I've learned a lesson I won't forget. I hope you feel the same.

"I have a poem a friend wrote. I asked if I could read it at this assembly because it says what I feel. I'm going to read it exactly as it's written.

"The Fall and the Spring
(Patterned on a poem by Edna St. Vincent Millay)
In the Fall of the Year, In the Fall of the year,
A young man came to teach us here,
A man with hopes and dreams and pride,
All of which would be denied.
The first day we walked into class,
His fate was sealed, the die was caste.
He was not the one we'd dreamed we'd see,
A willow where an oak should be.
We saw his face and whined and moaned
As though the fault was all his own.
From first to last it was too plain
He'd feel the wrath of our disdain.
He tried to teach us every day,
He tried a million different ways
To share the knowledge he had learned
And everything he tried was spurned.

But still he read each piece we wrote
And searched each one for seeds of hope.
We rewarded him with mindless hate
And venom worthy of a snake
In the Spring of this year, In the Spring of this Year
The price he's paid is much too dear.
The ways he paid will haunt our days.
We broke his heart a hundred ways."

Kyle stepped to the microphone as Shellie retreated. "Go to your classes," he ordered the audience. Then he turned to the cheerleader. "Well done."

"Thank you," she answered. "Mr. Hunter," she continued, her eyes pleading, "we went crazy this year. We're not awful people. Maybe we can prove that to you. And Mr. Baker, too," she added with youthful hope.

"That would be good," Kyle responded.

He joined Superintendent Anderson and Principal Strand as the auditorium emptied. "They were attentive. I think we, especially Shellie, reached some. Maybe they learned from this experience.".

"The school board didn't," Alan Anderson told him. "Pete Warrum phoned this morning. He's called a special board meeting to overturn Ed and Jerry's suspensions. The excuse is Ed is a hero, and Jerry ran for help. Forget about him driving that getaway car. Truth is, they're athletes who might make it to State. Alan Barberie's name was never mentioned. Or Frank Marin's."

Frank Marin

Dawn reddened the eastern sky by the time Frank Marin trudged into Bethel Ridge. He was glad it was early. He wouldn't run into Shmitty. As he neared the gravel road to his home, he paused, realizing he was passing Annie's house. Then he proceeded up the road to the community graveyard at the edge of town. Mr. Corgan and his family were buried there. He paused for a moment. He wanted to go into the cemetery, but he couldn't.

He left the cemetery and walked the road to the farm. The fields had been plowed and planted by the farmer renting the land. Most of the yard's trees had been harvested to make room for more crops.

Frank scuffed down the long, narrowed driveway to the house and entered through its unlocked front door. The interior was devoid of everything. He climbed the stairs to his old bedroom, shed his jacket, and rolled it into sort of a pillow.

He awoke exhausted and beaten. The house was torrid and airless. He grabbed his jacket and traipsed down the stairs and outside. The day burned. He was desperately thirsty, but the water was disconnected.

He pulled the vodka bottle from his pocket, lifted it and chugged. His stomach retracted and retched. He sank to the wooden steps and sat, his head between his knees, his injured hand throbbing. His stomach churned like roiling mud.

He had no hope. He rose, slogged to the barn, and slipped through its unhinged doors, looking for a length of rope to fasten to one of the cross beams. He found evidence of birds, bats, and mice but no rope.

He could not return to the dead house and felt such a terrific sense of loss that it nearly crumpled him to the ground. Finally, he turned away and headed toward Corgan's place.

He was leaning on the closed gate that delayed entrance to the Corgan farmstead when he heard a car in the distance. He could lift the looped barbwire draped over a fence post, slide inside and hide, but what was the point? So he stayed, arms draped over the gate, and listened to the car slow, stop, and silence.

He waited to hear his name called or to feel a viselike grip on his arms as they were wrenched back for cuffing. Instead he heard a quiet voice behind him say, "Frank." He looked over his shoulder to find Annie, her hands clasped at her waist, her clear eyes fixed on him.

"I thought you were the cops," he told her as he turned. A tall, slender man stood leaning against an old Plymouth sedan watching the girl and watching him. The man's arms were folded. He wore a faded Hawaiian shirt and jeans. "That's not the sheriff," Frank said.

"He's my father. Why would it be the sheriff?"

"I'm in trouble. How did you . . . ?"

"I saw you this morning. I thought you were coming to the house, but you didn't. I stepped outside and saw you stop by the cemetery. I was sure we'd find you here."

"Why would you want to?"

"Oh, I don't know. Maybe it's because I thought about you crying when you talked about Mr. Corgan."

"I'm surprised you remember that instead of what a jerk I was."

"Actually you were fairly considerate as drunks go."

"I threw away that beer like you wished I would. I regretted it afterwards, though."

"Do you want to throw away the bottle sticking out of your pocket?"

"Not really," he said, his stomach churning at the mention of it. He grasped it by the neck and extended it to her. "Maybe your dad would like a swallow," he said as her father straightened and walked towards them.

"We don't drink. We don't litter either." She turned and handed the bottle to her father as he approached.

"It's too hot to stand here," her father said. "If you want, we'll give you a ride to town."

"I'm staying at our old house," Frank tried lamely.

"Running water? Pump?" her father inquired.

"No."

"Then you'd better consider coming to town. I'll let you clean up at our house. If you don't, everything in the area is going to die from your fumes. I could smell you across the road. And you could die of heat stroke."

Frank had no answers. He followed father and daughter to the vehicle. The man turned toward him. "You'll have to put that jacket in the trunk. I'm tolerant, but I have my limits."

Frank shed the garment. The long-sleeved shirt under it was glued to his body by perspiration, but he felt naked. He thrust the jacket toward Annie's father, who declined it, palms up. "I'd only touch that with a pitch fork," he said as he opened the trunk.

Frank tossed the jacket in. Annie's father pointed at the back door, and Frank slid in behind him. "Roll down those windows," the man ordered. Only the wind through the windows broke the silence until they pulled into Annie's driveway.

"I think we'll talk on the porch," her father said. "I'll get us some water." Frank followed the two up the porch steps. He sank into the aluminum lawn chair Annie indicated before she sat at the far end of the porch swing. "Good thing the wind's blowing the other way. Dad's got a sensitive nose. I don't, but I still think it's a good thing the wind's blowing the other way."

Her father emerged with the glasses of water balanced on a tray and handed one to his daughter and one without ice to Frank before seating himself a ways away. "Sip that water," he said, "or you'll get sick."

"Why are you being nice to me?" Frank had to ask.

"It's his job. He's Pastor Richard Kaylen. I'm a minister's daughter. I just can't help myself."

Frank recoiled. He was sitting on the porch of a minister's home. He should be burning in flames. He set the glass on the deck and stood. "If you knew me, I don't think you'd want me here."

"You're already here," Pastor Kaylen pointed out. "We're short of saints. You have nowhere to go. You might as well sit down and tell us why we don't want you here. But I'm not a lawyer, doctor or priest, so I can't tell you what you say won't be used against you."

Frank sat back down. There was no point in running. There was no water, no rope, no gun, no knife, and no one. The cops would find him anyway.

He picked up the water and sipped. His stomach twirled. "Here's one reason. Do you listen to the news?" The minister nodded. "Did you hear about someone being killed near Blue Lake last night?" The minister shook his head. "Or drowning?"

Pastor Kaylen shook his head again. "There was a story about a booze party raid out in the country. A hundred kids, twenty underage. But no one died or drowned. That would have been the big story. You were there?"

Frank rubbed his wounded palm. "I took a swing at a guy. He insulted me and someone else. I barely touched him, but he fell in the water and sank. I ran."

"That's a long run from there to here," Annie said.

"I stole . . . I took my friend's car. I left it in Florence."

"Hmmm. Assault at least. Theft. Quite a rap sheet. Any other sins of commission?" the minister asked.

Frank had expected their shock to get him booted off the porch. "I got kicked out of school yesterday for attacking a teacher." That admission shook him more than the rest. He felt compelled to add, "I didn't mean for it to work out the way it did. I was trying to have some fun."

"A bad, busy day," the minister noted. He swung off the swing. "I'd like to discuss several things with you. But first I insist that you go up the stairs and take a shower. Drop your clothes outside the bathroom door so we can wash them. Your odor is bringing tears to my eyes. I'll leave an old bathrobe by the door for you to wear until the clothes are dry. Up. Follow me."

Too defeated to refuse, Frank followed around the house. The minister continued, "While you're in the shower, I want to call the police to find out if they're looking for you. I also want to call your parents. What's your last name?"

"Don't. It's not their fault," Frank resisted, and then gave in. His folks deserved to know where he and some of their money were. "Marin," he said and added the phone number. The minster motioned him inside. As Frank began to ascend the stairs, the minister said, "You're probably thinking about running. Keep in mind that the police will have little trouble spotting a boy racing around in a bathrobe. You might get thirsty, but Annie is pouring your vodka down the drain. I think it's in your best interest if we sit down after your shower, sip some more water and chat."

"We'll be good practice," Annie announced from the kitchen. "We're nice people."

Strand must have had a crystal ball hidden in his desk drawer yesterday. But even he would be amazed at how quickly his dire prediction had come true.

After toweling dry, Frank draped the towel around his middle and gazed at his wasted face in the cabinet mirror. Dark circles drooped under his eyes. His hair flew in all directions. His bloated stomach growled. What a loser, he thought. He saw an unopened toothbrush container on the sink and a tiny tube of toothpaste. Since his breath reeked, he used it.

Eventually he remembered the bathrobe. The heat was closing in on him, so he turned the knob and peeked out. The bathrobe was neatly folded atop a towel on the floor. She must have put it there. Bet she wanted to catch a glimpse of him. Bet she opened the door a crack so she could. Bet she was disappointed if she did.

He pulled on the frayed robe that reached below his knees. It had only a cloth belt to keep it closed. He felt naked. But he had to get out of this room.

It helped to step into the hall. The day remained hot, but cool by comparison. The floor creaked and he stood still. Where did he go from here?

Annie must have heard the floor creak. "Come down," she called. He wanted to think how hot she'd get seeing him this close to skin, but the sight of him was more likely to make her sick. Not knowing what else to do, he eased down the creaking stairs.

"I'm in the kitchen," she said when the creaking ceased. "I'm making poached eggs." He eyed the front door and imagined himself flying through it and down the dusty road. Sure. In this next to nothing blue bathrobe and bare feet. So he entered the kitchen and quickly slid onto a chair at the table.

"Dad had to go over to the church to talk to someone who's having troubles," Annie informed him. That gave him a rise. No wonder she'd wanted him to come downstairs. "He was reluctant to leave, but I told him you treated me almost like a gentleman before, even though you'd been drinking. Besides, we've got speed dial. All I have to do is punch one number and he'll be home in a heartbeat." The rise collapsed and he felt exposed. She placed a plate of eggs and buttered wheat toast in front of him. "Milk, juice, or water?" she asked. "We've been out of booze for the last ten years or so."

He opted for water and chugged. He was terribly thirsty. She recognized that, retrieved a pitcher of water from the refrigerator and placed it in front of him. "We ate," she answered before he asked. "Your clothes are drying. I should go check."

She exited the room, and he was sorry she was gone. He liked the way the room looked around her. He toyed with the eggs and forked some into his mouth. He was surprised how good they tasted, surprised his stomach didn't send them back up. A second forkful was sliding down his gullet when she returned.

"Still damp," she announced and sat in a chair across the table and to the right of his. "You smell much better." He could think of nothing to say and felt ugly and awkward sitting so close to her sunshine. Desperate to do something, he polished off the eggs without looking up, then fumbled for the glass.

"Dad called your parents. They weren't home. He left a message for them to call our number when they could."

"They're at work. They're always at work, that's why . . . " Frank started, then stopped. "They work a lot. They're afraid they'll lose their jobs if they miss work, and lose the farm if they lose their jobs."

"Dad also called the police. They said the county sheriff had alerted them about an abandoned car in Florence that he'd traced to Blue Lake. The police in Blue Lake told him a woman named Elizabeth something had reported that a guy she knew and her car were missing."

"That's Betts."

"Well, she didn't say stolen. Maybe you should call her and try to explain. Or call our police and tell them why the car's in Florence."

And that he'd driven it without a license. "Maybe," Frank answered. He fled the subject. "Your mother working late?" he asked to escape further discussion of or doing anything about anything.

"She might be. I don't know for sure."

"Well, you could call her," Frank said. "Where does she work? There are only about five stores in this burg."

"A hardware store," Annie answered. Frank didn't recall Bethel Ridge had one. "She ran off with a hardware store owner from the suburbs a long time ago." The answer snapped Frank's head back and his eyes down. How could she just say that! He could hardly tell her father his last name.

"Why?"

"She thought she'd like being a minister's wife, but she didn't. She thought she'd like being a mother, but she didn't." He stole a glance at her. Her face and eyes were sad, but not broken. He'd be drunk all the time if that was his story. Like he wasn't anyway. "That's why we live in little towns. There's a shortage of ministers, but the big towns don't like divorced ones even when the divorce isn't their fault."

He fled that subject, too. "How's Shmitty?" he tried.

"In jail. His girl friend told him she's pregnant, so he got drunk and beat her up so badly she lost the baby." It was the first time Frank saw anger invade Annie's countenance. "That's who Dad's counseling now. She's terrified and heartbroken."

"Damn him," Frank muttered, deflecting the thought that could be him. "I think I'd better call Betts."

"Sure. Dad asked the police to wait if they're planning to pick you up," Annie told him, her eyes full of light for the first message and sadness for the second. "He thinks you need help. He wants to try to convince you to get it. Before you follow Shmitty to prison."

The words broke Frank. Annie sat across the table with her hands atop one another. She said no words and made no move to comfort him, just watched him.

The screen door squeaked. "Dad's home," Annie said. "I'll get your clothes while you two talk. I'll be back before you're done. Hi, Dad," she said as he entered.

Her father touched her on the shoulder as she passed by on her way to the basement. He grabbed a glass from the counter and sat down across from Frank. "You look warm, but you do smell better," he said as he poured them both a tall glass of water.

Greg Schwarz

Greg Schwarz was enraged. The attack on Robert Baker and the attitudes of too many students about it had been like powerhouse punches to his gut. Then last night Pete Warrum had called to seek support for the school board's decision to overturn the suspensions of Jerry Jons and Ed Warrum. He'd heatedly declined. Now the local radio station was shouting the news of the Wednesday raid of a huge drinking party northeast of Blue Lake, a number of high schoolers among those arrested. The multiple disasters crumpled him into his kitchen chair where he sat head in hands. He'd spurned offers from suburban schools for this! Could anything be worse than the place he loved racing to hell in a hand basket?

He should call in sick, sick and tired of it all. He banged his fists on the table, bolted out of the chair, and nearly concaved the door as he slammed out of his apartment.

Janis James waited on the sidewalk for him as he stormed out of the building and steamed towards her. "You've been listening to the radio," she said.

"So have you. You're here to save me from myself."

"Well, I admit I could hear your bacon sizzling as soon as I turned on the morning news. Between that, Robert Baker, and this heat, I had visions of spontaneous combustion crisping you into a thousand little Greggies."

"You have not yet heard about the board's action concerning Warrum and Jons."

"They're desperate to prove you're right, and I'm wrong," Janis frowned after Greg growled the details. "Darn them anyway. But, Greg," she brightened, "right after the news, I began devising a plan to restore balance and pride in our school. I came up with a good one."

Her idea was to organize a voluntary Saturday cleanup of the party site. "It might be good if anyone signs on, which I doubt," Greg said. But by the time they neared the school, he'd agreed to help her present the proposal to Sam Strand.

The principal responded positively. "I'll support the idea if you cap the number of students allowed to go. If you recruit teachers for supervision to assure this doesn't become another disaster. If you contact the Sheriff's Department for clearance and security to take care of anyone who shows up to spoil things. If all that flies, I'll contact the city and county for supplies, the bus garage to set up transportation, and the cafeteria about preparing sack lunches. If it's all a go, I'll include your plan in the afternoon announcements." He allowed himself a smile. "Thanks. Lord knows I needed a jolt of hope today."

❖ ❖ ❖

Janis' plan had wings. Immediately after school, fifty students and ten teachers funneled into her room. The quota would easily be achieved Friday. More teachers would undoubtedly add their names.

Greg acknowledged that to Janis after track practice. "You were right and I'm glad," he told her. Then his grumble returned. "I just finished a shouting match with Pete Warrum in the center of the football field. It's like throwing up into a toilet and expecting it to sprout roses." Janis grimaced and sighed. "I could have said no minds were changed," Greg said, "but that's how it felt."

"I've obviously become unselective as my impending spinsterhood approaches," the business teacher said. "Or maybe I just like the idea of 'warts and all.'" She picked up the signup sheet. "I don't know all these kids, but they must be all right if they want to do this. However, we need to comb the list for reliable leaders. Otherwise this could end up being kids and woods, and 'can I name her after you, Miss James?' Oh, Ed Warrum came in and said he'd have to work at his dad's store in the morning, but he'd like to join us in the afternoon if that's okay."

The educators fussed over the list for hours. Janis' enthusiasm enabled the return of his. Huge cumulus thunderheads were rolling on the horizon by time they'd completed their tasks. "Can you watch a storm and eat pizza at the same time?" Janis inquired.

"If the pizza's Ronald's and the company's congenial," Greg answered.

Ronald's was nearly empty. The teachers slid into a window booth to await the storm. Sarah Zahn, a favorite of Greg's, approached. She smiled broadly, probably delighted with the gossip the two were furnishing.

"Eating pizza earlier in the day doesn't mean you're a pizza-holic, does it, Sarah?" Greg asked.

"Of course not, Mr. Schwarz. Not if it's Ronald's pizza. Not even if you eat it for breakfast. Hello, Miss James," the waitress chirped. "Menu?"

"Unnecessary. Your House Specials are always wonderful if that's okay with Mr. Schwarz.

"Absolutely. Personally, I never order anything else."

"I heard the announcement about the cleanup," Sarah said. "I had to work right after school, so I didn't sign up. Can you add my name to the list or is it too late?"

"We'll be pleased to," Janis said.

"Well, good. That makes me feel better." Sarah half turned and called, "Large House Special," then returned her attention to the teachers. "Have you heard anything about Mr. Baker? I feel terrible about what happened to him. At least it didn't happen in our class. But we were never very nice to him either."

"I don't know much. I feel bad, too," Greg admitted.

"Well, if you visit him, tell him a lot of us are really sorry. But I'm supposed to be working," she brightened, pushing her smile into place. "Anything to drink?"

As they ate, lightning flashed, thunder rolled and rain cascaded against the window. After the storm ended, the teachers walked to Janice's residence in the storm's after-mist. Janis shivered and slipped her arm through Greg's. She leaned her shoulder against his, rushing electricity along the entire length of his arm. He could not help but raise it and extend it around her shoulders to shield her from the windy wet. She wrapped her freed arm around his waist. They walked that way all the way to her house despite any eyes that might be watching their progress.

The thunderstorm chased the heat from the region, trailing cool, blue days in its wake. All who'd signed up showed up Saturday morning to fill two school buses. When they arrived at the barricaded entrance to the site, Sam Strand and Kyle Hunter awaited beside a school van packed with lunches, sodas, and the boxes of trash bags.

"A few of us spent most of last Saturday here," Billy Cloud told Greg as the volunteers disembarked. "But not causing this. Look at that crap," he scowled as they surveyed the riot of cans, bottles, broken glass, and trash visible from where they stood to as far as they could see.

"Sheriff says the entire area is one big garbage dump, but the worst is further in. You know that area?" Greg inquired. Billy nodded. "Good. I'm sending most of the teams with you. The rest will work their way in while you work your way out." The student nodded. "Miss James and I will be up to help after we get organized."

"Steep hill up that way, Coach. Moon Ribbon Ridge. A man your age ought to think twice about trying to climb the Moon. Maybe you better just send Miss James."

"Billy wasn't just blowing smoke," Greg puffed as he and Janis accomplished their ascent of the rutted, rain-slicked incline half an hour later. Bulging black garbage bags, tied and piled, greeted them on the ridge. Nevertheless, plentiful evidence of desecration remained. Huge black fire smudges defiled the ridge and meadow, more cans and bottles glinting in the sun. Trees exhibited the consequences of crude pruning and crass climbing. Some younger trees had been totally toppled.

"Depressing, isn't it," Billy said as he joined the teachers. "You should see the crap we've bagged. My folks and I thought this place was sacred," he finished before whirling down the muddied path to the meadow.

Greg Schwarz loved what this day was becoming. He loved the sense of community that he feared had disappeared from Blue Lake High School. Right now he loved teaching. What other profession could provoke the surge of exhilaration he felt at this moment?

He also loved observing the easy comfort with which his planning partner moved among the volunteers. He was a lucky man, he knew as he watched her. During one transfixed moment Billy Cloud sidled by. "Uh-huh," the boy said with a smile before sidling onward.

❖ ❖ ❖

It was a dirty, weary, self-satisfied group of students and teachers who boarded the buses shortly before six o'clock. Patty Light drifted over to the organizers. "Thank you for this. I was down about everything on Thursday, and then that announcement about the cleanup came over the loud speaker. It saved my day," she told them before continuing towards the bus.

"Quite a few juniors here," Shellie Chaine informed Kyle as she passed by with the last of the garbage bags in tow. "I hope this proves a little bit to you."

"A little bit," Kyle answered, showing her a barely separated thumb and forefinger. "Only about this far to go," he said, extending his arms full length.

"You'll see," she sang, prancing away with the bags.

Sam Strand focused his attention on Janis and Greg. "I needed this day desperately. Thanks for providing it."

"The thanks belong to Janis. The plan was hers."

As Janis followed the final bus riders, Kyle turned to Greg. "So Janis is responsible for creating this silk purse out of a sow's ear, Greg?"

"Absolutely."

"Seems to me like a good description of your relationship as well."

"Absolutely. Hey, I got to ride Bus One back. I'm supposed to be helping Barnes with supervision. Of course I could ride with you guys."

"Absolutely not," Sam Strand glowered, suppressing a grin quite successfully.

Billy Cloud

The Sunday afternoon meeting began with Patty Light introducing the two males she'd invited to Elaine Stafford's office. The four participants were seated in chairs arranged to simulate a circle. Patty addressed Billy and Mr. Hunter. "I asked if we could meet here so I can try to explain the reasons I am who I am. I need you to know, and you deserve to. I wish Mr. Baker was here too. I need Elaine because I need her to help me do this."

"I'm glad you accepted Patty's invitation," Elaine said. "'Help' isn't a word she uses easily or often. You can take great satisfaction that you were essential to her wanting it, seeking it, and accepting it."

Billy shifted his attention from the counselor to his friend. Her hands were clasped in her lap, her eyes anxious. Just like that night at her house. He fought an urge to tell her she didn't have to go through with this, but he knew suggesting that would be doing her no favor, or him either.

Mr. Baker became the first topic. Billy listened to Patty retell Wednesday's details. "You know that notion I wrote in my journal about the mark of Cain?" she asked Elaine. "It's been pounding in my head again. Look at what happened. I still wonder if I'm a curse to those I love. So many end up enduring so much pain."

Billy broke his silence. "I sure don't think so, Patty. I'm walking upright. Mr. Hunter is. Ed is."

"So far. Mr. Baker was all right four days ago, too."

"Do you have more to say about that, Billy?"

"Yes. If she lets herself believe something like that, she'll have to stay away from Mr. Baker and everyone else. That would be awful for her, Mr. Baker, and us."

"I agree. But by the end of the afternoon you'll better understand why that idea keeps popping into her head."

Mr. Hunter leaned forward in his chair. "I was going to save this until the end, but I think I should share it now, if that's all right with you, Miss Stafford."

"By all means."

"I stopped by the hospital this morning to check on Mr. Baker. They told me no one has succeeded in breaking his silence, so I could do no harm if I stopped by his room. So I did. When I got there, his door was open so I walked in. He was standing by his window staring out. I asked how he was. No response. Just kept staring out the window. I told him he'd be surprised how many students are asking about him. No response. Then I told him I'd be seeing you two today and asked if there was anything he wanted me to tell you. That's when he finally turned around. He said, 'You tell them that nothing tragic happened. I've still got my eye. Nobody died. I'll be all right. You tell them that.' That's almost all he said," Mr. Hunter cautioned. "He did add, 'Tell them I'm sorry I let them down.' I told him he hadn't let anyone down. What I hope you'll remember is that the first words he's spoken since Wednesday were spoken because of you."

Patty hands had flown to her cheeks as Mr. Hunter described the visit and still remained there.

"He let us down?" Billy mused. "Heck, he put us ahead of his own welfare."

"I think we're ready to refocus on Patty," Elaine said.

"Elaine believes sharing my story will reduce its power over me. I do, too. It won't be easy for me to tell or for you to hear, though."

"As you said, the devil is in the details," Billy said.

Patty dropped her hands and folded her fingers around the arms of her chair. "He's all over them. If you run for the door, I won't blame you. But I hope you won't."

"I won't. I'll be here until the last word is done."

Robert Baker

During the first days of hospitalization, Robert Baker inhabited an oasis. His brain and body had numbed into protective shock. He felt no pain when they stitched his wound. His brain refused to register questions. He was at peace – if peace is the absence of everything. He accepted proffered pills without thought. The combination of shock, exhaustion and drugs sank him into dream-free sleep. When he was awake, the world remained a distant dream. Voices entered his ears as though the speakers were in faraway rooms. There was no need to respond. Words were useless anyway.

He might have preferred to stay in that state forever. But it wore away. Perhaps they reduced the dosage of the pills. Unpleasant dreams of chaotic classrooms, students sneering his name, and teachers closing doors just as he approached resurfaced.

He refused a third round of the drugs with a wordless wave of his hands. He left his bed to shuffle the hospital halls because they made him do it. Out there, his throbbing wound was visual evidence of his failures. He tunneled his eyes, zipped his lips tight as a winter coat, and crawled beneath his covers when they returned him to his room.

By Sunday morning the shock had drained. He bolted out of bed to escape yet another dream of a classroom gone wrong. He pressed his head against the room's window wishing he had the courage to smash through it and disappear into the darkness. His next thought was that he wouldn't have dreams like this, thoughts like this, a life like this if he hadn't been so weak, if he had been smart enough to stop things the moment they began, tough enough to tough it out. He wouldn't be standing here like a child, his forehead against the window glass. He'd be standing in front of his classes at Blue Lake High School, his neon cheek a testament to the consequences of cruelty and indifference. He'd assign *The Red Badge of Courage*, using his wound as a mute metaphor. That would have cowed his classes! That would have vanquished the laughter, jeers, and sneers from the battlefield his classroom had become.

That notion was in play when Kyle Hunter's voice snapped the silence in two. Robert's nerves whipped like loose wires. What was Kyle doing in his room? Sent by the school to tell him to get on the stick and write lesson plans so someone could finish the job he couldn't handle?

He turned from the window and awaited the stupid reasons for this intrusion.

The reasons turned out to be Patty Light and Billy Cloud. Kyle's invocation of those names crumbled Robert's resolve. Kyle explained he would be joining them that afternoon at a counseling session and wondered if Robert had any messages to convey to them. He had to respond, especially since he'd undoubtedly caused their need for counseling. "You tell them," he managed, his voice distant in his own ears, "you tell them that nothing tragic happened. Nobody died. I've still got my eye. I'll be all right. You tell them that. Tell them I'm sorry I let them down." Then he shut down.

Odd, he realized later, until he'd heard himself say so, he had not thought he'd ever be all right. It was the names and their bearer that created the crease though which the words slipped and germinated a desire to halt his drift. There were people out there who mattered, people to whom he owed an effort. By Tuesday afternoon, he decided it was time to reward their caring. He walked to the nurses' station and requested an appointment with the hospital psychologist.

Two days later, the psychologist added Social Service counselor Elaine Stafford to the sessions. The session was good for him. Miss Stafford responded to his questions and notions with real empathy and understanding. The return route to his room took him past the small lunchroom shared by patients in the psychiatric and drug and alcohol wards, but never at the same time. The two groups were housed at opposite ends of the same hospital wing two sets of doors in between. The reason for separation was obvious. What might aid one group could kill the other. One of the groups was entering the lunchroom. Since Robert had yet to do that, he averted his eyes stared straight ahead and walked on.

He'd barely entered his room to continue to avoid opening the mail on the table beside his bed when he became aware someone was standing in his doorway.

"Mr. Baker?" a feminine voice addressed him. He turned and saw a young woman clad in a white blouse and jeans. "I'm sorry to bother you, Mr. Baker. I'm Lorraine Lumen. I work at the other end of the wing. I have a highly irregular request, which you are free to reject. There's a young man from the other ward who would like to talk to you. I told him we don't normally allow intermingling, but he says he's the one who's responsible for you being here."

The name Ed Warrum popped into his brain, and he angrily shook his head. He knew better. There was another obvious possibility. Maybe a visit from Frank Marin would end that obsession.

"I'll tell him," the lady said, turning to leave.

"No, no, not that. I need to talk to this young man. I need to see his face and hear what he has to say," Robert insisted. "His name's Frank, isn't it?"

"Yes, it is."

"Talking to Frank might help my recovery."

"Well, all right then," the woman said. She crooked her finger, and Frank Marin appeared. Robert motioned for him to enter. Miss Lumen stepped inside the room and watched intently from its wall.

Frank stood in front of the man he'd attacked eight days ago, his head bowed, his hands shoved deep into his hospital robe pockets. Seeing Frank shorn of much of his hair, his jacket, and his boots was like seeing him naked. Robert resisted an impulse to avert his eyes.

The teenager worked his jaw, unable to speak. "Frank?" Robert said quietly. The boy jerked up his head. "Miss Lumen said you wanted to talk to me."

"I . . . uh . . . I . . . uh . . . I needed . . . I wanted . . . " the boy tried, quit, began again. "I . . . want to tell you I'm . . . uh . . . sorry . . . about what happened."

"I hope," Robert said. He should be furious with Frank, but for some mysterious reason he couldn't be.

"It . . . it . . . it was nothin' personal." Frank's voice was flat as a winter prairie. Nevertheless Robert believed this boy for whom making words and connections seemed terrifically difficult. "It was just . . . it just worked out that way." The boy shifted nervously on his slippered feet.

"That's it?"

"No, sir," the other managed. "Your face. If you hadn't . . . I couldn't stop myself. The kids . . . I'd had . . . I couldn't stop myself," he trailed off.

"That's why you're here. In treatment?"

"Yeah. That . . . and because my choice was this or . . . or a jail cell," the boy admitted. "That helped me decide."

"You're lucky," Robert said. "I hope it works out."

"Frank, you need to get to the lunchroom," the women at the wall interrupted.

"Yeah. Well . . . thanks, Mr. Baker, for letting . . . letting me talk to you. Mrs. Lumen said you didn't have to."

He watched Frank shuffle toward the door. "Good luck," he said as the boy left.

Robert wandered to the window, turned the green institutional chair beneath it toward the day and sat down. He felt a little dance in his chest. He cared. He genuinely cared about Frank Marin. He cared about someone besides himself, other than Patty Light and Billy Cloud. He had, in fact, cared about the students in his classes for a long time, but had forgotten that was true. Even on The Day, he'd noted Jerry Jons' altered demeanor and had expressed concern to poor, desperate Alan Barberie. Other faces and names flitted through his mind. It was true even as he was being herded to the edge of the cliff. The joy of knowing that collided with a sense of all that had been lost and overwhelmed him. Tears burst from his eyes. He let them flow without wiping them away, even those that clung to and stung the stitched wound on his swollen cheek.

He cried so long he thought he would never quit. "God, I'm crazy as a loon," he sobbed.

That was when Elaine Stafford slid a chair she'd found somewhere next to his and sat down. Startled, Robert snapped his head back so fast it could have flown right off his neck and bounced on the floor right out the door. Bounced down the hall next to the wall, past the nurses' station with great elation. He exploded into raucous laughter. He could do nothing except cover his face until he coughed to a stop.

"Hope you brought the strait jacket," he half-chortled, half cried. "I've gone bazookas."

"No," she replied quietly. "Why?"

"I've lost every marble I had left," he whispered.

"I don't think so," she said.

"You just watched me laughing like a crazy man," he pointed out, rubbing the sweaty palms of his hands on his pants. "You shoulda seen what I was laughing at. Two minutes before that I was crying like a baby."

"I know. I've been observing you from the hall."

Her admission provoked a wild mix of emotions. He felt as exposed as if she had seen him naked and not turned her head, yet grateful that what he still suspected was a second breakdown hadn't gone unnoticed. He didn't know what to do with the mix, so he turned it into aggression. "You find breakdowns entertaining?"

"No. But I'd describe what you've been doing as a breakthrough, not a breakdown."

He peered into her green eyes. "You're serious aren't you," he said, quiet as a prayer.

"I'm serious."

"How can that be true? I totally lost control."

"That must have been a terrific release. To let go."

"It felt insane."

"I think it's the beginning of healing."

"Oh, God," he breathed.

"When you walked into the counseling office today, you were crouched like a boxer coming out for the tenth round after being hammered for nine. Now you're sitting with your back almost against your chair even though I'm here without your permission. You're looking at me instead of the floor. I think your healing has begun."

"So," Robert Baker asked because he did not want Elaine Stafford to leave and had to slow the speed of this experience, "Why are you still here? Do you work here?"

"No," she answered. She studied his face. "Because I work with kids referred by the high school. I'm working with several who care a great deal about you. Two of them pleaded that I find some way to tell you I've been working with them. Patty Light and Ed Warrum."

"Oh. Oh," he said and panicked. "It's because of me. That's why they're seeing you. Because of me."

"No, it isn't. Your name comes up often because they care about you. But, no. Patty has issues from years ago that need attention now." She leaned over and lifted her purse from the floor. She opened it and extracted three envelopes. "She sent two of these with me. She wants you to read them when you're ready." Elaine retrieved a third envelope. "This is from Ed. He said to tell you it's an apology and an explanation. I had a meeting with Patty as well as Billy Cloud and Kyle Hunter, who also expressed their hopes for you Sunday. Patty wishes you could have been there too, perhaps most of all."

"I don't think I'd have been too helpful last Sunday."

"Oh, but you were, Robert, you were! You should have seen Patty's face when Kyle relayed your message!"

"I might start crying again," Robert cautioned.

"That would be fine," Elaine said. "But before you dissolve and we can't talk for awhile, I want you to know that Patty told me one of her letters tells you everything she's talked about in our sessions because she wants you to know everything there is to know. I hope you'll read it while I'm here in case it creates questions that need answers." She glanced at the stack of envelopes leaning against one another on his bedside table. "I hope you'll read those, too. I think you need to find out that Patty, Billy, Kyle, and Ed aren't the only ones who care about you. I think you're ready to know that now."

Patty Light

Dear Mr. Baker

Now that you've read my first letter, I want to tell you again that I wish with all my heart you could have been sitting with Billy, Mr. Hunter, Miss Stafford and me Sunday because no one matters more to me than you do.

For a moment, I thought about not writing, not talking, not burdening anyone, letting my story remain a secret between my mother and me. Leaving Miss Stafford out. Leaving Mr. Hunter to wonder forever if his insights were accurate. Letting Billy ride the roller coaster of my inexplicable moods until he jumped off and ran. Crumpling the letter I wrote telling you everything I could and letting you think of me only as a student with an insatiable thirst for knowledge.

The decision to press on wasn't hard. I was afraid when I started my letter to you and afraid when I thought about the other two men I have chosen to share "Patty's Story" with since it is another man who is an important, awful character in that story. So I reminded myself that you are not just men. Mr. Hunter encouraged my words and had already read much of what I was about to say in another way. Billy Cloud has seen my anger, fear, and tears, but also my laughter and joy. And you, Mr. Robert Baker, have inspired my mind and touched my heart more deeply than anyone I have ever known.

Since you are reading this, you have already read the once-upon-a-time secrets of my life. You have accepted me as who I am. Now I am overflowing with hope. Because you have let me grow to know you, I am overflowing with hope for you, too.

You have read my entire story and this letter. That means you are healing, too, and my heart is singing because that is so.

With Hope and Caring,
Patty

Ed Warrum

Ed Warrum knew he and Jerry Jons shouldn't be at the regional track meet, but they were. It wasn't all bad being here, of course. It was fun to cheer on Hannah Blakely, Sally Long Arrow and Billy Cloud and the relay team, all of whom qualified for the state meet.

He had less enthusiasm for his own events. Jerry, apparently unfettered by conscience, contended in the shot put until the final round. He simply wasn't good enough to place. Ed whirled and hurled the discus with technique, but not passion. His native ability enabled him to finish one place short of a trip to State, too. He knew that would drive Pete Warrum crazy. Ed heard the bellow of disappointment after his last toss.

He joined Billy as they headed for the school van after the meet. "Nice work," he said, extending a hand. "There aren't many qualifying for State in three events."

"Thanks. You came close. Maybe next year."

"Maybe."

Pete Warrum stormed to the van and vice-gripped Ed's shoulder just as he placed his foot on the first step. "Spite," he heard his father hiss.

"That's crap," Billy said from the step above.

Ed refused response. He wrenched his shoulder free and ascended into the van. He slumped into the back seat without looking up or out, even when he heard Mr. Schwarz and his father shouting outside the vehicle.

Instead he leaned down, unzipped his duffle bag, and reached in. His fingers found the ragged edges of the paperback Elaine Stafford had given him at their last counseling session. She'd suggested "Death of a Salesman" might offer insights into his father's behavior. That would be a miracle. He opened the book to the page he'd bookmarked. Willy and Biff Loman were going at it again. He could relate to that. The Warrums weren't the only family in the world tearing each other apart.

Billy sat to his left and Sally Long Arrow to his right. "Relentless isn't he," Billy said.

"At least you've got your defenders," Sally pointed out as Coach Schwarz thumped red-faced into the driver's seat and jammed the engine to life.

"Easy there, Coach," Head Coach Hank Vetter cautioned. "You could blow two gaskets. Yours and this old buggy's."

"That guy drives me nuts. I'd like to shot put him a hundred yards."

"He's not worth it."

"Hey, son on board," Billy called from the back seat.

"Sorry," Mr. Schwarz tossed over his shoulder. "I got a big mouth."

"Haven't heard a thing I disagree with yet," Ed muttered into his book. The entire group whooped.

"What!" Ed growled.

"Mist . . . Mister . . . Mister Schwarz," Sally managed between bubbles of laughter. "He said . . . he said . . . he's got a big mouth, and you . . . you said . . . he hadn't said a thing . . . " then collapsed against the back of the seat, the bubbles coalescing into streams of levity.

"Timing, my friend, is everything," Billy said. "All great comedians know that."

The van's inhabitants rocked with laughter. Even Ed.

Greg Schwarz

Greg Schwarz loved days like this. He loved the contingent representing Blue Lake High School at the State Track Meet, quality, hardworking kids who achieved because of maximum efforts and excellent attitudes. He loved the grace and fire of all the athletes he was watching. He loved that Janis James was in the stands waiting for him as he trotted up the steps.

Janis smiled as he plopped down beside her. "You and Hank are as wired as the kids."

"Yup. Look at the guy," he chuckled, pointing at the coach sprinting on the infield grass.

"I'm glad Kitty couldn't come," he told Janis, not noticing her smile disappear from her face. Girls' track coach Kitty Kittelson had quit coaching last summer. She'd declined Vetter's invitation to chaperone. Janis had taken her place.

The starter gun popped and puffed, and the relay runners leapt out of the starting blocks. The Blue Lake boys ran with the long, smooth strides that had carried Billy Cloud to a second place finish in last night's 880 and first in this morning's 440-yard dash. After receiving the baton for the final lap of the relay, Billy lengthened the lead his predecessors provided. "Yes, yes, yes!" the coach exploded as the boy flew across the finish line.

It was a great day all day. Hannah Blakely's courageous kick on the final curve of the girls' 880 propelled her past two competitors into a second place. That was followed by the pure pleasure of watching Sally Long Arrow's gorgeous romp around the track as she sailed to victory in the mile run, the final event of the meet. Her win elevated the team to second place.

"That was beautiful!" Janis exclaimed. "Kitty should have been here to watch those girls of hers." As the teammates rushed towards one another to celebrate,

Greg rose to join them. Janis didn't. "No you go ahead," she said. "This is for competitors and coaches." Greg grinned and rambled down to the field.

"Hank's determined to fulfill his promise that if I convinced you to chaperone the girls, he'd take the kids on a tour of the U after the meet and treat them to dinner and a movie," Greg told Janis as he stood in the doorway of her hotel room. "Hank's that kind of guy."

"Do the girls know?" Janis asked, hands on hips. Greg nodded. "So I'm the only one who doesn't?"

Greg had expected enthusiasm, not irritation. "Well, I didn't want to make it seem like I was asking you to chaperone just so I could get you alone in the Cities." He was mystified.

"Can you at least give me time to talk to the girls and shower?"

"Well, sure," he answered as she shut the door none too gently. "Geez," he muttered, staring at the closed door. "Geez," he repeated, shoving his hands into his pockets and slumping down the hall to the room he and Hank shared. Something was wrong, and it was pretty obvious that something was him.

"We eat here whenever we get to the Cities. Their steak is terrific," Greg told Janis James. She ordered the house salad. She stared hard at him like she had a few hours earlier. This was bad. "You aren't trying to lose weight, are you? You don't need to," he fumbled.

"The only weight I'm trying to lose is in my head," Janis snapped. "I'm not hungry right now. Okay?"

He'd never seen Janis James like this. His emotions tumbled into free fall, and his mind followed. It was too clear she'd reached the conclusion he'd expected from the moment she'd shown interest in him.

"Oh, Greg," she said. She paused as the waiter slipped her salad on the table. She picked at it with her fork, speared a leaf of lettuce and twirled it on the tines. "It's me, Greg. I'm so stupid and fake." She might as well have driven a spike right between his eyes.

"What?" he rasped.

"Greg, I'm talking about me, not you."

"What?"

"Steak." The waiter, who had returned unnoticed, said. "I forgot to ask how you wanted your steak, sir."

"No, I . . . I mean yes, I ordered . . . . I mean no, I wasn't . . . I mean, yes, I ordered the steak, I mean medium. No, rare." That's when he heard Janis laugh.

"Greggie, Greggie, Greggie," she chimed. "I just love you, Greg Schwarz."

"What?" he gasped.

The waiter remained at the table. "Sir," he said in a voice brimming with compassion, "if you'd like, sir, we could reserve a table for you for later in the evening. And, ma'am, the help staff can consume your salad during their break." All Greg could do was stare at the waiter. "Frankly, ma'am, it doesn't look like either one of you would be able to swallow right now," the waiter told her.

"I think that's an accurate observation," Janis replied. "Yes, that would be very nice of you. We need to go for a walk and see if we can find out where we left our saliva."

"Very fine, ma'am," the waiter smiled as he retrieved the salad. "Good luck in your search, ma'am. Sir. Take your time. We're open until midnight," he concluded before turning smartly on his heel and heading toward the kitchen balancing Janis' salad on his fingertips.

"I feel like I'm riding one of those tilt-a-whirl cars at the fair," Greg admitted after the two had walked several blocks, "the ones that whirl just slow enough to make you feel like you're going to toss your cookies."

"Poor Greg," Janis sympathized. "It's my fault. I should have told you right away."

"Oh, geez," Greg moaned. "Here we go again."

They were near the river. "Can we sit here for awhile?" Janis suggested, pointing at the wooden benches. "I do need to talk to you. But it's not about us. I should have told you that right away because you keep thinking it is."

"You read my mind?"

"Your face. It's like reading a *Dick and Jane* book."

They sat on the bench. She gazed at the water's reflection of the lights. He took a deep breath, exhaled, watched her and waited warily.

"I called Kitty this afternoon," Janis started. "I told her I would. That's why I was so distressed when you came to the room. She should have been in that room, not me. I called to let her know how her girls, did. Right away she started crying with happiness for those girls, but sadness, too, at not being here to cheer them on. I told her I'd get the girls from next door so she could congratulate them. So Hannah and Sally came over and sat on my bed telling Kitty all about the races, and pretty soon they were crying, and she was crying, and I was staring out the window crying. She loves those girls, Greg, and cares so much about them. They love her. She should have been here."

"That isn't your fault."

"I know that. But I feel very guilty. Kitty and her daughter Kitten should have been here," she persisted. "I need to tell you why they aren't. I don't want to because what I say will reignite fires I'd hoped were doused. But if I don't, I'll drive us both crazy."

Greg thought he knew the story. Kitty Kittelson had coached girls track with devotion and skill for five years. Kitten, her seven-year-old daughter, had been at almost every practice and meet since she was two and had become the team mascot. Kitty had dropped that duty last summer. The board combined the boys and girls teams and assigned he and Vetter to be the track coaches. He figured Kitty had decided to devote more time to Kitten than coaching allowed and that was that.

"Kitty revealed her reason for quitting to me last Tuesday night after adult swimming. We were changing in the coaches' office.

"As we were chatting, we caught glimpses of women heading to or from the showers. Kitty said, 'That's how they got me to quit." She told me how the school board had pressured her near the end of last season to quit coaching," Janis said. "They began by insinuating that sending a couple of girls to State every few years wasn't good enough. That didn't work, but it planted seeds of doubt. She told them she'd try to do better."

"She was great," Greg said. "Five girls qualified three years ago. The talent wasn't ready the last few years."

"The board wanted her out. Period. When she didn't quit, they began visiting her house. Each visit was worse than the one before. Listen to this," Janet hissed, her eyes narrowing, "She wouldn't say who it was, but the last one showed up at her house one night in June. The guy plopped down on her sofa. Kitten was sitting at the dining room table reading a book. This guy told Kitty that her track girls' parents were very upset because their girls were complaining about Kitten sitting in the coaches' office staring at them with way too much interest after they showered. He said a lot of the girls thought both she and her daughter were pretty weird."

"That's sick. The whole track team loves them both."

"It gets worse, Greg. Kitty tells this board member there is nothing weird about either of them. He responds by saying right out loud in Kitty's living room with her daughter in the next room that Kitty's husband must have had some reason for leaving her and the kid. She tells him, 'Yeah, that nineteen-year-old chick with the short skirt at the convenience store.' That was when Kitty realized she was dealing with a nasty nut case. She tried to stay calm. She told him she'd contact the girls and their parents to find out if there was a problem."

"There wasn't."

"It gets worse, Greg! Kitty looks into the other room, and her daughter is sitting at the dining room table with her head sunk down on her book, big tears raining on the pages. Kitty rises to comfort her daughter. This jerk stops her dead in her tracks when he says, 'There's one more thing, Miss Kittelson. We're told that you and the girl have been seen going into the boys locker room. One can assume the reasons for that.' Kitty goes ballistic. 'Yes,' she tells him, I've been there. Sometimes Vetter or Schwarz calls when all the boys are gone. We meet in their office to talk, or they come to my office in the girls' locker room under the same conditions for the same reason. Have you talked to them?' 'Some boys say you and your daughter have sat in the office watching them with big smiles on your faces,' the jerk tells her. Kitty's daughter totally loses it then. She is sobbing and screaming, 'I didn't do that, Momma. I didn't do that.' This guy hasn't moved an inch on that sofa. Finally Kitty screams, 'All right! All right! You get what you want! I quit! I quit! Now get the hell out of my house!'"

"Good Lord!"

"I selfishly didn't want to tell you this. I didn't want to fuel your desire to leave Blue Lake. You'll be darn disappointed to learn another reason I hated to tell you is that it proves you're too right, and I'm too wrong."

"So what do we do? Go to the hotel and call and tell those administrators I've changed my mind? Ask if they have an opening for a business teacher?"

"You can if you want to, except for the part about the business teacher. I still don't want to leave Blue Lake."

"Got a better idea?"

"Don't we have a union?"

"We do. There didn't used to be much need for it though. Great administrators. Great faculty. College town. It got bored and went to sleep."

"Can't we wake it up? Can't we stay and fight?"

"We can. But it might get nasty."

"It already has," Janis said. "Kitty talked to Ted Gerney when he was here. His story is remarkably similar to hers. She was relieved because she thought she was the only one. Don't you wonder how many more there might be keeping quiet because think they're the only ones and there's nowhere to turn?"

JUNE

Gail Hunter

As had recently become her habit, Gail Hunter extracted the Trib's sports section first. An article on the State Track Meet dominated its front page. She searched for Blue Lake High School names. Doing so offered her a connection to the school she'd all but severed. She was pleased to see the Lakers had taken second place in their division. She searched the article for Ed Warrum's name, but it wasn't there. Billy Cloud's was, twice. Hannah Blakely. Sally Long Arrow. The boy's relay team.

The dominant photo on the page pictured Sally Long Arrow flying across the finish line, both feet off the ground, a radiant smile on her face. Gail felt a rush of admiration for this girl captured at her zenith.

There was a time Gail attended track meets with Kyle. Well, not with him. He'd inherited the public address duties for many track meets. So she'd actually attended track events alone too. So she stopped going. But he didn't.

She lost her babies. He didn't change a thing. He was overflowing with escapes. So she crossed sports off the list of things she'd do. She dropped sports from the topics she shared with Kyle to punish him for his obtuseness. He played into that by dropping that topic into that hidden bin where everything having to do with his work disappeared. She'd countered by taking a part time job at Pete Warrum's store. But being around that man was like taking a hammer and beating rusty nails into her ears.

"Is everything all right, Ma'am?"

Startled, Gail stared at the middle-aged waitress hovering by her table. The lady had wound her apron into a ball around her hands. Her flushed face was apprehensive. My gosh, Gail realized, I must look like all seven furies rolled into one. "It's fine," she answered, forcing a smile through her rigid face. "Bad day."

"Well, I can understand that," the waitress replied. "I know about that. You're sure the food's okay then?"

Gail had no idea whether the egg, toast, sausage, and coffee were any good or not. She'd hardly touched them. But she replied, "Fine," and the waitress hurried straight to the kitchen. 'My Lord,' Gail could imagine her saying, 'that woman out there scared me half to death. I was afraid she was going to throw the plate at me.' She extracted a five-dollar bill from her purse and slid it under her cup as compensation. She sighed heavily in an attempt to exhale her intimidation factor and walked to the register to pay her bill.

She wandered out of the restaurant and down the hall toward the bar. It was the first time she'd stopped at this Holiday Inn since March. She reminded herself she'd stopped today to once and forever put a crimp in the Elvis factor that characterized her relationship with Wayne Mars.

The bar's odor of stale beer and cigarettes wafted down the hall. She continued into the area anyway. One man was sitting at the bar, a beer in front of him, his head tilted toward the brew. He's in trouble, she thought. She eyed the chairs stacked upside down on the tables, and the dance floor that half mooned a small stage. Hard to believe this place had been glittering and full of heat the night of the storm.

Good thing the stage was all that had been mounted then or since. That kept the Elvis factor in place. Tantalizing possibilities, avoided realities. Booze and surprise had threatened a different result that night and prevented it as well. His flatulence may have saved her. She had to smile. Timing is everything.

To be thinking of that and him interfered with her self-assurance that she was doing terrific work for her company, a fact borne out in numbers and letters of praise sent to headquarters by clients. But because Wayne Mars was involved, she wondered if she maintained employment because she was the best piece of possibility in the place, thus reducing her accomplishments to nothing special at all. Sometimes that drove her half nuts. That was definitely the down side.

She wheeled on her heel, left the bar and hurried out the Inn door into the bursting fragrance of the June morning. She inhaled the cleansed air and wondered why she'd spent so many minutes inside.

It was hot inside the Volvo, so she rolled down its windows to let in the air. She started the car and shifted into reverse taking pleasure in the smooth feel of the shift knob under her palm, and left the motel. She merged into the highway traffic and continued driving north.

"Ah," she sighed. This day was too blue and green and lovely to lose. The beauty of the forested north moved her heart, and its piney scent dominated the air whirling through the car. She wanted to whoop with joy.

Poor Kyle, she thought, a few miles up the road. How much of everything was his fault? Did he deserve all those layers of blame she kept chanting in her mind? Was he the only distant and silent one? Shouldn't she be bursting with admiration for him doing the best he could for his clients, just as she was for hers now? Were they more alike than different?

For Kyle, it was the bike, the pickup, and papers to correct. He'd developed that pattern early on and it rarely varied. That was part of the problem. Everything new in his life occurred in the classroom. He wanted the world outside it to remain forever the same.

She wondered if he'd ever experienced the Elvis factor. Or had experienced it over and over. Legions of lovely or talented or sensitive or interesting or needy young ladies paraded through his room year after year, some of whom must be sharing their deepest selves within those journals and reveling in his interest, understanding, and compassion. Was he oblivious to that? How would you know? Maybe she should ask him.

Somehow she was aware this hadn't been a good year for Blue Lake High School. Kyle must have hinted at a few things. Gerney was gone. Pete Warrum's school board had crapped all over Red Howard and Sam Strand. A teacher named Robert Baker was having problems. She was aware all of this bothered her husband even if he hadn't directly told her so. Or maybe he couldn't find an opening through the fortresses of her old hurts and new interests.

Well. She'd been thinking solely and seriously about Kyle for many miles. That was progress. It occurred to her as she drove the tree-lined road that she hadn't once questioned her link in the chain of circumstances that made The Impending Decision such a huge factor in the first place. She'd never asked herself why she'd squirreled Kyle's columns into her suitcase and presented them to the company. She'd never asked herself why The Decision had become a question with only one right answer. She wondered why it was necessary to pressure Kyle about it every chance she got. She wanted to believe it was because she wanted change to open up his life the way it had opened hers. Or to make it possible for him to receive the economic rewards teaching would never provide. But for the first time she was confused about the whole thing. For the first time she doubted the righteousness of her cause. Lousy timing! She whacked the steering wheel with her hand. She could cry with the frustration of it. Maybe she already was. Or maybe it was just the streaming wind that was washing moisture from her eyes and down her cheeks.

Kyle Hunter

Kyle Hunter awoke at six a.m. Sunday morning. Gail had not come home early. Graduation was history. She'd missed it for the first time in years.

He was wide awake. Dawn was dawning. He chomped down some raisin bran and watched the sun light and shadow the day. For the first time in ten months he had no journals, no papers, no tests to correct, no lessons to create. If he sat and waited, that would not be good. He'd render each minute five minutes long and be ready to ignite by the time she arrived.

He showered and decided church was an option. Though they'd never joined any since they married, they'd attended most of the churches wherever they'd lived. If they found a minister or congregation they particularly enjoyed, they unbalanced the rotation in that church's favor.

Such had been the case with Downtown Lutheran. That church felt full of light. The minister enhanced his Sunday services with passion and laughter. The word around school was that he worked well with kids. Kyle and Gail hadn't attended since early November, but he was aware that Pastor Barker had departed for Nigeria. Kyle had heard nothing about his replacement. Hopefully he or she was worthy. Church would be a good place to spend an hour.

❖   ❖   ❖

The atmosphere at Downtown Lutheran had completely changed. The college students had all but disappeared. The parishioners sat erect and joyless. If Kyle hadn't found Greg and Janis sitting in a back pew and joined them, he'd have fled during the frigid sermon. The world would definitely end in ice if this minister had his way. Maybe someone needed this. He sure didn't.

The three teachers bolted for the door as soon as the benediction was voiced. The sun outside seemed blindingly bright in contrast to the dimness within.

"That was fun," Greg declared.

"Sinners in the Hands of an Angry Clod," Kyle said. "I think I'm beginning to thaw. So what brought you two to this iceberg? Need to cool your ardor?"

"We're kind of looking for a church," Greg explained.

"Uh huh," Kyle smiled, "if I catch your drift."

"You could have inside," Janis said. "This church must be in the Siberian Synod."

"It was more like the Hawaiian Synod last time I visited. Their search committee must be the spiritual brothers of our school board."

"Speaking of which," Greg said, "after Janis was done dangling me by a thread off the highest Cities bridge . . . "

"Drama Queen!" Janis scowled. "What he's trying to say is I put my scissors away when he promised he wouldn't cut and run if I reeled him back up."

"Metaphor madness! Does this conversation have a point beyond illustrating your questionable ability to develop shared images?"

"It does," she assured him. "Greggie?"

"Greggie? I'll use that appellation from now on."

"In all seriousness, my friend, Janis gave me reasons to run, then challenged me to stay. Including the fact that she is. Not just to stay, but to fight the madness. Beginning with resuscitation of our moribund union."

"Resuscitation! Moribund! You make me proud, Greggie."

"Perhaps we should grab a cup of coffee before continuing this masterful discourse," Greg said. "Admiral Dead Bird back there looks distraught that anyone is smiling so close to the iceberg."

"Masterful discourse! A bit distraught! Janis, what you have done for this man! The face is familiar, but the brain in this thing works! Sure," he concluded. "You two are way more fun than watching grass grow."

❖   ❖   ❖

He was sitting on a lawn chair in the backyard. There was nowhere in the world that did a perfect June afternoon like this state. A fresh breeze to tease the hair and caress the skin and send early season mosquitoes sailing, fluffy white clouds to accent the deep blue sky . . . He heard the throb of the Volvo motor just before the car turned into the driveway. His mood dived into wariness, and his stomach tightened. He pulled on his tee shirt as though it was light armor, slipped on his tennis shoes, and walked to the front of the house to find out what kind of music was playing today.

Or more to the point, to find out how soon the Topic of the Day would dominate the rest of it.

Gail Hunter's greeting – "Can we take a walk in the woods?" – caught Kyle by surprise. Without taking her suitcase inside or awaiting reply, she disappeared around the end of the house. He suspected that she preferred that the trees witness this latest battle of wills. For the Hunters, the art of discussion had morphed into the artlessness of argument. The house had undoubtedly heard enough of that already.

He walked a short distance behind his wife expecting a purposeful power pace. Instead Gail slowed to a stroll and immersed in her surroundings. Kyle conjectured, that she was organizing her talking points so she could Zamboni right over his.

He diverted himself by observing the way the embroidered pockets of her jeans danced with the movement of her hips. It was true she had become even more enticing. Change had been as good for her as it had been lousy for him.

After hiking more than a mile, they arrived at the wildflower meadow that fronted a low ridge to the north. It had been a traditional pausing place for them. Gail bent to test the grass for dampness, then pointed to the rise. "Can we sit there awhile?" she asked. He nodded and followed her across the field.

She sat down on the spine of the ridge, drew up her knees and clasped her hands around them. He watched her do that, then sat a short distance away from her, stared into the meadow and awaited her words.

"When I was riding home, I had to open the windows because it was so hot in the car," she told him.

Well, that was a non-too-subtle introductory statement. "Sorry we couldn't afford to fix the air conditioning on my salary," he grumped. "Maybe now that you're . . . "

"I was glad," she interrupted. "The wind was so refreshing and the air was so fragrant. I'd forgotten that."

Caught off guard again, "Well. Good," was all he could muster.

"It made me . . . emotional. It made me think. That's why I wanted to walk right away." She was striving hard to communicate with him. If her train of thought left him standing at the station, maybe it was because he was unwilling to risk climbing aboard.

He turned toward her. "I'm glad you suggested it."

"How was graduation?" she shifted. "Were you sad to see the seniors go?"

Reluctant to drop his paranoia, his brain finished her thought with 'since it might be your last senior class at Blue Lake High School.' "Graduations are always beautiful and sad. Like sunsets. Or October."

"Did they cry?"

"The girls? Sure. They're smart enough to know their lives are about to change forever. Maybe the guys are, too, but they aren't about to show it."

She offered a sad smile. "You're lucky you teach seniors. Kids always look up their senior teachers."

"Some do. Especially guys. They're the most lost."

"You like that," she stated. "You'd miss it."

"Yes and yes." He stared at her blue eyes. "What's going on, Gail?"

"I stopped for breakfast and scared a very nice waitress half to death with the look on my face. Later I opened the car windows and my demons were whizzing around in my head before the wind caught hold of them," she answered obliquely, rocking slightly, her chin touching her knees. He was totally disarmed.

"I suppose we have to cut to the chase," he said.

"All right," she agreed, sounding reluctant. "Kerns Company needs to know your decision."

"What do you want to hear?"

"Your decision," she said unhelpfully. But her eyes lacked the flint he'd seen ever since September.

"It wasn't an easy one to make. Either way," he felt compelled to tell her.

"I realize that. But not until today. It seemed simple."

"I can't take the job, Gail. Maybe after the next school year. Not now." He'd lived this declaration a hundred times since January 1st. In his imagination it was voiced in the little house, the final words of a short, combustible conversation that began in smoke and finished in the immolation of their relationship. It hadn't been like this.

"Why?" she needed to ask, the question a question.

"There are students I can't leave behind. Things going on that I can't turn my back on without a fight."

"Won't that always be true, Kyle?"

"No doubt. Some days I can hardly stand it. But I can only try to do something about it if I stick around."

"You know that advertising job probably won't be a choice in a year. You know your loyalty will most likely be rewarded the same way Sam's and Red's was."

"I know. It doesn't make sense. But it hurts my heart every time I think of leaving."

"I won't quit my job either, Kyle," she said softly, but firmly. "I'm not going to. It's opened up my life." She peered into his face. "Does all this seem as risky to you as it does to me?"

"It does. It scares me to death. I haven't been any good at this so far. I was afraid we were going to have an either-or conversation. If I had to make that choice, I might land in the hospital next to Robert."

"Robert?" she asked, puzzled. "Robert Baker?"

"I didn't tell you about Robert?" he asked. "No, I suppose I didn't. I suppose I was afraid if I told you about Robert, it would confirm how bonkers my decision is." He pushed himself to his feet and reached for her hands.

"I'd like us to have dinner at the Duck Blind tonight," he implored as she grasped his hands and let him help her up. "They've missed you. I'll talk about Robert then."

He could remember no day in his life when he'd felt so many contrasting emotions. If he was Patty Light, he'd imagine himself soaring and diving and somersaulting through the clouds beneath the blue sky. Because he was Kyle Hunter, he followed the path back to the log house behind his wife, taking momentarily unfettered pleasure in watching those dancing pockets. Because he was who he was, he occasionally shifted his focus and peered into the woods. He should have been incredulous to discover that small patches of snow still survived deep beneath the boughs of pines trees, but he wasn't.

Billy Cloud

It was six a.m. when Billy Cloud finished breakfast and descended the front steps of the Cloud House. As had become his recent habit, he stopped and faced the four directions before trotting to the road. He waved just in case the Warrum's were looking out their windows and broke into an easy jog.

His destination was Patty Light's house. Their friendship had ascended since the session in Elaine Stafford's office. What he'd heard had and hadn't shocked him. His parents had never hidden from him the ways people find to make each others' lives – and their own – more difficult. It had elevated his admiration for and understanding of Patty Light several more notches. His purpose today was to accompany her to the first day of her summer employment at Blue Lake High School.

He was vaguely disappointed when Ed Warrum eased his mother's car alongside him just before he reached the city limits.

"Darn. I thought you'd somersault into the ditch when you heard a Warrum car coming," Ed shouted through the open window over the pinging motor.

Billy retained his pace and the car matched it. "Incredibly, I didn't hear it."

"You want a ride?"

"I don't. But your exhaust is making me faint, and I have a hunch you're going to pace me until I give in."

"Actually, 'no' is unacceptable," Ed acknowledged. He pushed open the passenger door.

"Ah, is dooring the latest craze?"

"Yup. Darn it, missed. Well, it's open. Might as well get in. Where you headed?"

"Patty's place," Billy said, settling into the seat.

Ed shifted the car and conversation into gear. "I got a letter from Mr. Baker," he announced. That fact touched Billy, and he clamped his lips so no clever rejoinders could escape. "I wrote him to apologize and explain. What I want to tell you is his letter said he's the one who needed to apologize.

Said he'd been wrong about me the whole year and thanked me for what I did after the way he'd treated me. Heck, he never did anything to me."

"I'm glad to hear all that. Say, aren't you going to work?" Billy reached for the door handle. "You can let me out here. Indian boy knows walking."

"No. I mean yes. But, no, I don't want to let you out. I mean, I will eventually. I'm not kidnapping you."

"Whew," Billy whistled. "What a relief. My folks might not pay the ransom."

"I'm not anxious to get to work. Mother filed for divorce. Dad got served the papers yesterday. I reckon he'll be more of an ass than ever today."

"Definitely deserves another whew. You okay?"

"Ridiculously enough, part of me is sad. Even Jenny shed a few tears when Mother told us despite the fact Dad hasn't changed a bit since we left. Overall, I'm okay. Think Patty might like a ride? I like her company, too."

"I know. She might. She prefers to walk, but she's pretty excited about starting her job."

"You could've worked there, too?"

"I could have. But Dad and Mom are teaching classes up on the Reservation. I'm going to take both classes and tutor some younger kids. I figure it's time I spent more time there. There's the house."

Ed eased his mother's car to a stop. Patty appeared almost immediately, easing the loose-hinged door back in place after exiting. Billy watched her descend the steps. She was extra radiant. As he watched, a figure materialized behind the door, barely discernible in the morning light. Her mother knows I see her, and she's staying there, Billy mused. That's something.

He shifted focus to his friend. "This guy here has started a taxi service and needs all the fares he can force into his vehicle. Besides he thinks you're swell. I'm his shill, so I'm supposed to convince you to accept a ride to school despite his lousy driving skills. I'd accept if I were you because I'll be in the car, too."

"Well, sure," she said as Billy opened the back door for her, "despite the company he keeps." Before getting into the car, she turned. His eyes followed hers. Her mother remained behind the door. Patty gave her a small wave and got in the car.

Billy considered sliding in beside her, but shut the door and resumed the passenger's seat. "She's proud of you," he said over his shoulder.

"Yes."

"You're going to talk to Mr. S. today?"

"Yes. Good morning, Ed."

"Ed has a tale of two letters to tell you," Billy informed her. "You'll like it."

Sam Strand

Sam Strand had worked from eight a.m. to ten p.m. for three days straight. He wanted to get all the reports finished. He wanted to walk out tomorrow with nothing but memories trailing him out of the building.

Ordinarily he'd be leaning against the counter in the main office on this last teachers' day of the school year, joking with them as they signed out, supposedly for the summer. Doing that this year would be too emotional. Those who wanted would find their way to his office, and nearly all did. They thanked him and assured him he'd be sorely missed. Many apologized that they had somehow contributed to making this a difficult year. He told them they'd performed heroically and that there was no way the past ten months had been easy for anyone.

He was heaving the last in a series of sighs out his office window when Red Howard and Greg Schwarz entered. "You're looking a little haggard," Red noted. "I suspect retirement may finally seem inviting to you."

"I'm getting there. Knowing you'll be available for a cup of coffee helps."

"Likewise. I hate to leave the mess this school board, state, and country have created for others to clean up, though," Red said, his smile fading.

"You think?" Sam grimaced. "The latest scuttlebutt from Anderson is that the board's decided they can save a lot of money for their favorite things by never hiring a vice principal. The usual six to one vote. Anderson fought it. He's looking into laws and precedence. But he's spitting in the wind as far as they're concerned."

"Makes this guy mad he has anything to do with the only thing they care about," Greg groused. "I'm glad you guys won't have to put up with it any longer."

"Wish it was that easy, Greg. Red and I have loved this place and our jobs for too long. The pain of watching it crumble won't end when we walk out the door. Sam forced a wrinkled smile. "But an optimist would point out that in a year, two of those yahoos' seats will come up for a vote. If we work at it, we may find folks with working brains who are willing to take up the challenge. And, my friend," he added, tapping a large index finger on Greg's chest, "the tundra wireless has informed me that you and Janis are dedicated to getting the union up and huffing.

"Well, boys, I have to sign off on these reports. But before you go," he said as he extended his hand, "I thank you for working with me. I'm going to miss being around you on a daily basis as much as I'll miss this job."

"And that," Red told Greg, "is as huge a compliment as you'll receive in your entire life. Treasure it."

❖　❖　❖

Sam settled into the leather chair he'd been provided at the beginning of the year as a pre-retirement gift. He'd been around a long time, maybe one year too long. This year had been like running rapids in a leaky canoe. He signed off on the paper work after rereading his personal message to the Board of Education. He was a good soldier. He'd fought most of his battles in private. When he'd had to go public, he did. But this year had been something else. You couldn't blame the board for all of that, of course. A complacent public had elected the single agenda majority.

He sat for a long time staring at the chair always at the ready on the other side of the desk. A parade of students had occupied it over the years. He was convinced he'd had more hits than misses in dealing with them. When he struck out, it wasn't from lack of effort. He lodged that conviction in the center of his brain.

He heard footsteps and broke his ruminations. Patty Light walked through the open office door. "Well, young lady," he said, "how's your first day?" She was one of the good things he'd accomplished. Seeing her reminded him of how much he was going to miss the rewarding side of working with kids.

"It's great, Mr. Strand," she said, eyes shining. Those expressive eyes touched his heart. "I love it. Everyone in the office is so helpful. Thank you for making it possible."

He was sure his own eyes were shiny. "It was my pleasure, Patty. You earned it."

"Mr. Strand," the girl asked, "do you have a few minutes?"

"Always. Have a seat. It will be nice to have someone sitting in that chair who wants to be there."

"I'm sorry to bother you about this."

"It's no bother."

She sat quiet for a moment, studying his face.

"Mr. Hunter suggested . . . " she started, then stopped. "Mr. Strand, I'd like to talk to you about my mother."

Robert Baker

For the first time since September Robert Baker approached Blue Lake High School in his car. The building's morning shadow encased the western grounds, the houses across the street, and his packed car paused at the stop sign. He fought an impulse to turn right toward the stoplight and slide unnoticed out of town. He shook his head in dismay. He hadn't worked through weeks of therapy to skulk away like that.

He'd waited until Wednesday to return to the school, however. After Kyle picked him up at the hospital late Monday afternoon and dropped him at his apartment, he'd spent the remainder of that day and all of Tuesday packing. When today's sun was still a promise on the horizon, he'd backed his car out of the garage behind the apartment building. Almost all he owned was loaded. All that was left to do was pick up the books and materials he'd brought to school, check final grades given to his students, return his keys, leave the letters, and sign out.

He could have gone to the school in the semi-dark, parked behind it, and entered the school with the early arriving custodians, but that would have been old behavior. He and Elaine Stafford, who had given him eight of her evenings over the past two weeks, had agreed that repeating old behaviors was a bad idea. He could have asked Kyle to retrieve the books, copy the grades, and return his keys, but avoidance was a worse idea. Reentering the school and being in his room were necessary steps in his recovery. Besides there wouldn't be battalions of students trailing him around. He turned left and then right into the parking lot behind the school. It was eight o'clock. He exhaled with a whistling sound, grabbed the empty cardboard box from the passenger's seat, flipped the letters into it, and entered the school. He wondered if Dan Crannan was here. He'd definitely mistaken the message of Dan's smirks. The man had written a complimentary note of support in the card he'd sent. Ed Warrum hadn't been Robert's only mistake in judgment.

The teachers' lounge door was open and empty. He walked to the stairwell and ascended the three flights without encountering anyone. He took his room key from his pants pocket as he approached. His hands shook slightly as he inserted the key.

He stepped into room 313. The drapes were open. Unlike his last day, the student desks were aligned in disciplined rows. He was relieved that the desks didn't immediately fill with images of indifferent, defiant, and angry faces.

He turned, opened the storage closet by the door, and retrieved his books. He carried the books to the teacher's desk, stared at its cleared surface and set them on it. Add stacks of papers, tests, and a couple open books and it would look normal. He'd worked hard at this job. He'd give himself an A for effort if not results.

He plopped down in the teacher's chair and opened the top desk drawer. Someone had made copies of his grade book pages for each class, a note paper-clipped atop them. He laid the note aside and scanned the grade sheets. Most students had improved since his exit. That should tell me something, he grimaced. Then he read the note. "These kids have learned from you. They knew a significant amount about the subject matter reviewed. The improvement in their grades is a result of them putting what they've learned to work. It's also their way of trying to make up for what happened." Anderson and Strand signed the note.

Well, that was something.

The other drawers contained pens, pencils, and the notebooks from his old college courses. He loaded the books and notebooks into the box, clipped two pens in his shirt pocket, and left the rest for the room's next occupant.

He sat down and stared at the student desks. Still no ghosts. Reliving this year's events in the safety of therapy must have worked. The cards he received must have had a positive effect. So, too, had Kyle's assurance about the attitudes at the assemblies. Maybe some good would derive from what he'd experienced. Be his legacy. Not Ted Gerney's, but something nevertheless.

He inserted the note and copied grades into a book and rose. He dug under the books for the letters, and placed them on top. Then suddenly he was wondering if things would have been different had he been facing the class that day instead of the blackboard, or even if he'd been sane enough to remove his suit coat in the blazing heat? What expressions had played on their faces? Malice? Amusement? Astonishment? Shock? Most likely all of the above, but he'd never know. He did know these thoughts signified that not all the ghosts were vanquished, and that it was time to leave the room.

He descended to the first floor. He entered the main office and there was Patty Light busily placing folders in the files behind the counter. Kyle had told him she'd be working at the school during the summer, but hadn't said where. Seeing her now, he could feel the strong resolve expressed in his letters begin to dissolve. This girl's spirit could melt a concrete statue.

She heard the door shush to a close and glanced over her shoulder. "Mr. Baker!" she breathed, setting the folders atop a filing cabinet, and then, "Oh." She half-danced to the counter, her eyes brimming. "Mr. Baker," she said again, a flickering smile contradicting and reinforcing the threat of tears, hers and his both.

"Hello, Patty," he said, his voice catching as he placed the box on the counter. "If there's one person I hoped to see today, it's you. And here you are." He retrieved his room keys, and placed them on the counter. "Are you taking care of these?"

"Yes, I am," she said with only a hint of pride. "The secretaries are having a year-end luncheon," she explained. "I'm working at the school all summer and taking a writing class at the college three afternoons a week. Mr. Baker," she said, her voice a quiet song of excitement, "it's because of you and Mr. Strand and Mr. Hunter . . . I'm so glad to see you," she interrupted herself. "You look so good. You are all right, aren't you."

"Yes, I am. Mr. Hunter must have relayed my promise. I'm all right." He paused, then continued, "Hearing your name and Billy's changed the direction I was going. It gave me hope and purpose. Your letters, too. I will be eternally grateful for the many ways you've saved me."

He watched her face fall toward another sadness he hadn't wished to provoke. "Mr. Baker," she said, "you're leaving, aren't you."

"I am," he answered because she deserved honesty. "I need to," he told her, "I don't know if next year would be like this year, but I really don't want to find out either. If it was different, I wouldn't know if it was because I was any good or they were afraid I'd fall apart at the seams. If it wasn't . . ." He saw her tears well again. "I hope you'll want to keep in contact with me," he said. "You're very important to me. You will always be. You'll help me remember that what's good makes what's not good worth it."

"That would be wonderful." She reached under the counter and retrieved two small pieces of paper and a pen. She slid one across the counter. "Since you must. Your address please," she said.

He wrote his parents' address. "I'm running home to Momma," he joked. "Hopefully this won't still be my address when I'm fifty."

"Here's mine," she said, exchanging her piece of paper for his. "Hopefully I won't be at this one forever either." They laughed lightly. Then she said, "Mr. Baker. I almost forgot to tell you we're going to try an intervention with my mother."

"That's terrific," he said. "I'll be praying it works."

Then he remembered the list of the names of his freshmen that he'd written down yesterday and put in an envelope. He took it out from underneath the letters and handed it to Patty. "These are my first period freshmen study hall heroes," her told her. "Would you do me a favor and find out who they are and check on how they're doing next year when you have time? I know it's a lot to ask. I was going to leave it with Greg . . ."

"I'd love to. Jenny Warrum told us about them. She already knows some of them. I'll know she'll help me do that."

They stood with their hands atop either side of the box of books he'd placed on the counter. "I'd better get going," he said. "It's a long drive." He lifted the letters from the box and handed them to her. "Put these in Anderson, Hunter, and Strand's P.O. boxes will you? And please thank Billy for me. And Ed. Tell Ed thanks, too. And thank yourself for sharing Elaine Stafford with me."

"Wait. Wait. I almost forgot." She disappeared behind the counter and reappeared with a wrapped package in her hands. "Mr. Strand took Mr. Hunter and myself to the Cloud House two weeks ago, and we asked Mr. Cloud if he could paint a picture for us. Mr. Cloud painted it. It's perfect. We brought it to the hospital, but they don't allow outside art to be placed in rooms." She placed the gift in his hands. "I think you should wait until you get home so it's protected on the trip. And open it then because I want you to know that kindred spirits dwell with one another no matter what."

"The wrapping is beautiful," he told her. It was of Indian design with words scripted on both sides. "What does it say," he asked.

"Billy and I chose it. It says 'May all be beautiful as you wander,'" she said, her gaze directly on his face, her soul in her eyes. "Oh, I hope it is. I believe it will be."

"Well, then, 'In beauty it is finished,'" he quoted from the Navaho chant, his heart overflowing. He placed the painting in the box. "In beauty, in beauty, in beauty," he read aloud. He reached across the box to touch her hand briefly, then lifted the box off the counter and backed out the door looking at her. "Thank you for that, too."

Sam Strand

Sam Strand had promised himself he would not be seated in his office at Blue Lake High School on Wednesday afternoon but he was. His memory of the ending of his career in education could not be only of plowing through stacks of forms and reports and leaving this office exhausted. Both he and the school deserved better.

He was glad he'd chosen to be here. He was sure Kyle Hunter would show up, too. Both could no more stay away than they could fly. Both had managed to miss the morning, but afternoon would be a different story.

He stopped by the main office shortly after one o'clock to smile at Patty Light and ask how she was doing. "Just great," she'd tried, and then amended, "Happy. Sad. Mr. Baker was in this morning. I gave him the painting. He left letters for you, Mr. Hunter and Mr. Anderson. Shall I get yours?"

"Please. I can tell by the look on your face that his message is not what we'd prefer."

She'd retrieved the letter and returned to the counter. "I hope for what's best for him. But I feel very sad."

"Me, too," Sam said. "But let's cheer up a bit, Patty, by reminding ourselves that tomorrow we will be visiting with your mother."

"I think that's a good idea," she'd answered. "Now I'm happy-sad-nervous-excited-terrified."

"Take care. Have as good a day as possible," Sam said as he left.

"You have a good day, too," she called and meant it. That was one of her endearing characteristics, he mused as he climbed the stairs to his office, the letter clutched between the thumb and forefinger of his left hand.

He was reading Robert's resignation letter when Kyle wandered in. He continued reading as Kyle glanced at the envelope, then crossed the room to the window. He stared down at the green front lawn until Sam's heavy sigh signaled he'd finished reading. Kyle re-crossed and sat across the desk from the principal.

"It's from Robert. His resignation. It makes me sad. It's full of gratitude for my feeble efforts to help him."

"Weren't feeble," Kyle corrected. "You did everything you could. The cards Robert was dealt were stacked against him and you, too. And there were way too many jokers in the deck."

"For sure. Still, it makes me angry. The young man could become an excellent teacher. He's smart and knowledgeable, he tries hard, and he's sensitive. I don't think education can afford to spit out young people with potential like that. I'll suggest to Anderson that he write a letter to him encouraging him to take a leave instead. But I doubt that Robert will stay in teaching." He tossed his hands in the air and dropped them on the desk. "Would I tell him to? I don't know. Could I assure him that things would get better as time passes? You know, of course, that Barnes is resigning. Sheer exhaustion. Kitty's checking out other options. So are others. Anderson and I have stacks of letters inquiring about Greg. He's still here out of loyalty and disappointment that elsewhere doesn't look so good either. Mostly because of Janis. God bless her. But how long before he finds a school that believes in balance?"

Sam pointed at his friend. "Even you. You've been wrestling the bear since Christmas. If someone who loves teaching and kids as much as you considers changing professions . . ."

"Never thought I'd ever think about not teaching," Kyle admitted. "It broke my heart every time I did. I never expected or wanted to do anything else. But this year made me doubt myself."

"Yes." Sam changed the subject. "I want to take a walk around the school," he said, rising. "I want to walk every foot of every floor. I'd like you to come with me. You've already heard all my stories, so you'll know who and what I'm thinking and feeling about, and I won't have to say a word unless I want to. I thought I wanted to do this alone, but I don't. I want to walk these empty halls with a friend."

"It will be my privilege."

The principal paused at the door of his office, turned and stared into it. "I'm going to miss it," he told Kyle. "I can remember the names of over a thousand students, and not just the ones who've sat in that chair. Used to know almost all the students in the school by name halfway through the year." He paused again at the outer door before commencing into the hall. "Every year at this time I think of an essay a friend of mine named Mike wrote back in my college days. It was published in the literary magazine. Had to do with the day after school ended, rooms empty, students and teachers gone, only your own footsteps echoing down the halls. The last line was, 'The loneliness of the last to leave hangs heavily upon the heart.' That's been true every year. But this is the last time I'll be doing this in the same way I've done it all these years, and my heart feels particularly weighted. To tell you the truth, I don't want to feel that much loneliness right now."

Sam Strand gazed at his friend for a moment, lifted his hands, palms up, and shrugged his shoulders. He dropped his hands into his pockets and proceeded down the hall, Kyle beside him, their passage echoing off the lockers and walls in the silence.

Robert Baker

Robert Baker surprised himself at the corner stoplight. He'd expected to turn right on the road that would take him out of town. Instead he went straight ahead toward the lake and the college. He'd been imprisoned by his situation. Whether he had no choice or had made the choice to put himself under house arrest, the consequence was he had little knowledge of the town he'd lived in for more than nine months.

He was approaching the college for the first time since he'd fled Ted Gerney's brilliant return last winter. A trickle of students plied the sidewalks. Propelled by impulse, he turned onto the road into Lake Park. Blue Lake and its beach lay at the south end of the park where his attention was drawn to a tall boy and blonde girl standing on the beach. The boy looked like Frank Marin.

Robert spotted an empty parking space around the curve of the road and eased into it. Then he focused his attention on the couple and removed any doubt that the boy was, indeed, Frank Marin. The girl, a woman actually, was clad in a red bikini. She was dancing back and forth in front of Frank, who seemed to be trying to get past her. She was pointing with one hand at something on the sand. The other held a can poised halfway between her hip and her lips. Frank was pointing at the can and she at herself as she continued to impede the boy's progress. Finally Frank placed his hands on her upper arms and held her still as he pivoted around her. Robert couldn't decipher the words she hurled after Frank, only the desperate quality in her voice. At the edge of his vision, he saw the boy had stopped walking and turned toward the blonde. She leaned down, opened a cooler and extracted a six-pack of beer from it, minus two, and dangled the cans by their plastic holder. Keep walking, Frank, Robert's mind encouraged. Frank remained stationary staring at the female, temptation swinging loosely beneath her left hand as she raised the can in her right and inhaled its contents, her hips swaying slightly, the dangling cans swinging like bloated wind chimes with her movement. Frank took several uncertain steps towards her and raised his hands in confusion.

Robert opened the door of his car. He slid out and shut the door softly so as not to attract the attention of the woman, whose hips were now moving in rounder motion, their thrust aimed in Frank's direction. The boy was standing, hands in pockets, eyeing the woman intently. Robert could sense the twin thirsts building in Frank's brain and body.

He paused as if to inspect the contents of the car's packed back seat. Then he continued across the road until he was within Frank's line of vision and several yards behind the gesticulating woman.

Frank had begun to return down the path when he spied Robert standing in the road staring at him. He halted dead in his tracks. Walk the other way, Frank, Robert's mind chanted, though he said nothing. The woman extended the can in the boy's direction. Frank shook his head, spun around and walked up the path.

The woman ground to a halt, the can descending before she jerked it upward, took a long drink, and hurled it toward the lake, losing her grip on the four pack, which twirled once in the air on its way to the sand.

Her awkward follow-through brought Robert into view. She turned fully towards him and stared. He waited for a string of invectives to fly in his direction.

Instead she pointed at the downed cans and said, her words thickened, "Hey, you're kinda cute. You wanna beer? Got twelve more in the cooler." There was plea and pain in her voice that belied the leer on her face.

"No thanks," he answered. He pointed at his car. "Got a long drive ahead of me." He crossed the road and stopped by the trunk. He glanced at the woman, crouched on the sand, plying another beer from the plastic, her eyes fixed on him with bleary wonder. "Take it easy. Get some help," he called.

"Easy is my middle name," she called back.

He slid behind the steering wheel of his car. He turned left at the park's exit. He proceeded downtown and was paused by a stoplight. Two boys and a girl crossed the street right in front of him, all three staring through his windshield. The shorter boy pivoted halfway across and pointed at him, his face screwed into an ugly scowl, his hands making circular motions at his temples. The girl grabbed his arms and yanked them down, her face thrust angrily at his. The taller boy stepped behind the other and propelled him across the street with a shove. He looked at Robert and continued to the curb.

That's the way it would most likely be if he made a different choice. Exactly like that.

He glanced at the light and wondered how long it had been green. He proceeded through the intersection, and turned right at the next stoplight onto the highway, the road that would take him around, then away from Blue Lake. Relief, regrets, sorrows, rewards; relief, regrets, sorrows, rewards washed through him one after another like the waves washing in the wind across the surface of Blue Lake.